DAVID ADAMS CLEVELAND

LOVE'S ATTRACTION

For Maryse with best wishes—
Enjoy.!

David A. Cleveland

7/31/14

W | **Winsted Press**

NEW YORK . 2013

JACKET DESIGN BY JASON BOOHER

FIRST EDITION

PUBLISHED BY WINSTED PRESS
1995 BROADWAY, NEW YORK, NY 10023

MANUFACTURED IN THE UNITED STATES OF AMERICA
ISBN 978-0-9889022-0-6

0 9 8 7 6 5 4 3 2 1

Publisher's Cataloging-in-Publication Data

Cleveland, David Adams.
  Love's attraction / David Adams Cleveland.
    p. cm.
  ISBN: 978-0-9889022-0-6 (hardcover)
  ISBN: 978-0-9889022-1-3 (e-book)
  1. Man-woman relationships—Fiction. 2. Loss (Psychology)—
Fiction. 3. Concord (Mass.)—Fiction. 4. Venice (Italy)—
Fiction.   I. Title.
PS3603.L48 L68 2013
813—dc23
                                                    2013931855

As always, for Patricia, who lighted the long road with love
and enduring faith in the writing life. And our book-loving boys,
Carter and Christopher, who never let their dad
forget the enchantments of youth.

Nam quod fuit ante, relictum est, fitque, quod haut fuerat,
momentaque cuncta novantur.

For that which once existed is no more, and that which was not has
come to be; and so the whole round of motion is gone through again.

—OVID, THE METAMORPHOSES

Time is but the stream I go a-fishing in. I drink at it; but while
I drink I see the sandy bottom and detect how shallow it is. Its thin
current slides away, but eternity remains. I would drink deeper;
fish in the sky, whose bottom is pebbly with stars.

—HENRY DAVID THOREAU

PART ONE

CHAPTER 1

Michael slipped the rusty kitchen knife under the envelope flap. The postino must have put the letter on the table after he'd left for work. He smiled at Joe Palmer's forthright blue longhand on the back of an old invoice—how typical—the words voicing a Boston Brahmin if slightly nasal tone, conjuring Joe's splendid farm stand and his bowed apple trees at dusk like flat brush marks of olive green against the lavender mist of the Concord River.... *done a terrible thing … HIV positive … her bloodwork also showed traces of artemisinin, an antimalarial drug … a hysterectomy at some point—poor dear.* As Michael read the words again in the light of the hanging bulb they seemed to lose all familiarity and a pensive sense of loss filled him. The words were like a dissolvent to the very memories they invoked—some faltering in the moments of recall, others transforming as if a sharp wind had swept into a neatly arranged room and left it in disarray. His large callused hands, dried plaster under the broken nails, shook as he folded the page with a glance at the letterhead on the verso: *Palmer Farms: Fresh Today – Gone Tomorrow*. Then he pocketed the letter.

For a moment he simply marveled: how was it that his life could become so prey to mere words?

"HIV positive … artemisinin … " he murmured, as if sounding the syllables might shear the thing of its fictile power, at least declare it friend or foe. "Malaria?"

His pulse quickened. He glanced to the kitchen alcove where once she'd prepared their meals, at the claw-footed bathtub in the corner, seeing the slick articulated whiteness of her shoulders as she poured water from a can over her blond hair. It was almost as if he'd been caught in a lie … or had the world been caught in a lie? He moved outside, retreating into the cool moonlit night. The spring air was a relief, softly humid and sweet with rosemary and marjoram from the overgrown garden plot planted the year before she'd left him. The dazzling moonlight, strangely, seemed to cauterize the seepage of memory, holding fast her lingering presence—there in the silence of the crickets' chirp. Then she seemed to be slipping away, mocking him, even if her name was on the deed to the tiny stucco cottage they had shared, if the milky clutter of the untended trellises still waited her hand. Even the terracotta dovecote by the myrtle hedge, abandoned by all except two stalwart barn swallows, seemed a fugitive hope. Along with the scattered marble artifacts scavenged over the centuries from the excavations on Torcello. The fragments of white marble were sunk in the dark earth, fiery and aglow as if bits of the moon had been flung down in sudden fury.

Michael Collins, or Giovanni Maronetti as he was known to his fellow workers restoring the roof of the nearby baptistery, had been a fugitive for nearly two years and some measure of the panic that gripped him now he well understood. But this was less about fears of discovery: his world was being turned upside down. He drifted towards the gate in the myrtle hedge, the leaves reflecting silver splinters of moonlight, where an upright fragment of a narrow fluted column served as a gatepost. He touched its worn flank. The lingering heat of the spring sunshine reminded him of the curve of her thigh. "Sandra?" But even such a stone-imbedded memory failed to arrest the tidal currents of metamorphosis that had now, once more, been set in motion. Yet how could he complain: hadn't they exulted in their mastery of such ambiguities. "Artemisinin." He lifted his eyes to an answering rustle where a breeze swayed the lithe tops of the poplars along the path. The trees were starkly silhouetted against the brilliantly lit façade of the campanile of Santa Maria Assunta.

The eerie sight, the electric brightness of the eighth-century brick-work, caused him to catch his breath. Then, summoning the hardened nerve of the consummate time-traveler, he gripped the ancient terminus to steady himself and strengthen his resolve. Under his gaze, the poplars became still and resumed their silent vigil. He had labored in the tower's welcoming shadow for over a year and yet its fretted brickwork and four elegant windows seemed only another sorry reminder of man's ridiculous aspiration to defy gravity's sway by reaching heavenward. An aspiration that had less to do with escaping earthly snares than spying out mortal threats from afar … or ringing blessings out of an indifferent sky. With barely a backward glance, he pushed off and headed down the path.

Stepping into his moored sandolo, it was as if a weight had been lifted. With three or four passes of the oar he was out of the tiny side canal and scudding over the stillness of the lagoon. Once beyond the shoreline the crystalline glare of the moon enveloped creation like some cosmic wildfire. He headed south by southeast, following the wake of the moon where it led to the lido channel and the sea beyond, the smell of brine mixing with the breezes from the snowcapped shoulders of the distant Alpine altars. At each stroke the alabaster shimmer of sky and water only intensified, muting both glittering stars and mainland lights, until the rhythm of the oar and his graceful two-step buoyed on silence seemed the sole remnant of his life's worth, of one waylaid and then cheated by names. That and the twin orbs embracing lagoon and sky.

Breaking one spell and casting another, staccato flashes sped like tracer-rounds across the prow of the sandolo. He froze in mid stroke. There in the distance a ghostly airliner began its descent into Venice's Marco Polo airport. The sight of the aircraft awoke him to another beginning—another terminus point. This at the confluence of the Concord and Merrimack rivers, glimpsed at ten thousand feet from the Washington/Boston shuttle two years before, and the unpleasant task of wrapping up his brother Jimmy's affairs—and the funeral in Lowell on the morrow. Stacked up over Logan Airport, he'd been drawn to the mesmerizing scrawl of those two rivers northwest of Boston, the Concord's silver capillary merging with the swollen artery of the Merrimack at Lowell, where it turned east to Newburyport and the sea. His home ground turned into a landscape of political expediency… and illegitimate gain for more than a few. Something he had seen from that towering height had unnerved him.

By the time the plane finally landed, with four Johnny Walker miniatures under his belt, he was a mess. He gripped the wheel of the Hertz rental like a drowning man, only to have his hands freeze at the turnoff from I-95 for Lowell. The Ford Taurus had surged ahead as if it had a mind of its own. Worry, stress, the grand jury probes into the construction contracts on the rebuilding of Lowell in the eighties and nineties?—none of that had really bothered him. Not Michael Collins, the respected Washington operator, deal maker, chief aide to one of the most powerful congressmen in Washington. He'd been too canny for such idiocy, the kind of kickbacks and bribes uncovered by the Boston Globe. He found such shenanigans beneath contempt. And just to demonstrate his point, he'd brought along a FedEx pack crammed with $400,000 in cash, the bribe—date stamped by his secretary—he was returning to its ostensible owner by way of the Worcester chief of police.

In a hazy stupor, he had cruised on past the exit for Lowell, waiting, waiting for something … some clarity of conscience to gain traction in the onrush of headlights. Something about those horizon-wide rivers glimpsed from miles up reminded him of the names that had encompassed the lives of his family and hers and all the stories of their people—all in peril of disappearing without a trace due to his betrayal. And another reminder of the stranger he'd become to himself. If not the searing echo of his brother Jimmy's disgusted riposte: "You, Michael, and just who do you think you are, boy-o? But of course, the rootless wonder of the world and world's expert at forgetting where the hell you came from." With inchoate panic short-circuiting every nerve in his body, he'd cruised past the next exit for Lowell, Route 225 by way of Carlisle and Chelmsford. His hands had remained in a death grip on the steering wheel of that new-car-smelling Ford … the white-knuckle grip of a legal gunslinger whose glory days might just end in shambles before a grand jury. What he'd wanted on that hot September evening two years before was to *feel* again, something of the joy the names of those rivers had once invoked, the Concord and Merrimack of his youth on River Street, as if those names out of his childhood might yet return to him the past he'd first scorned and then neglected, and with it the names and places that were his to now embrace, to love if he could, or fail to love at his soul's peril.

When the exit off I-95 onto Route 2A, the old Lexington-Concord Road, had appeared in his headlights, his hands, inexplicably, had relaxed on the wheel and he had made the turn.

Now the gentle buoying of the lagoon recalled the welcoming rise and fall of shallow hills and the looming silhouettes of ancient oaks among fieldstone walls, the shadowy sprays of Queen Anne's lace and traces of orange from summer-tattered tiger lilies bowing him onwards. He'd been punching the SEEK button on the FM dial, finally tuning in his favorite golden oldies station. The lyrics had swept him back to his days as a scholarship kid at prestigious Emerson Academy in Concord.

"Sandra Palmer," he said, recalling the moment of recognition.

Keeping the oar poised in the silence, he watched intently as the drops from the blade patterned the rim of brilliant darkness.

Her name had been exiled to near obscurity until his first glimpse of the Concord Inn on Monument Square, where his mother had waitressed after her breakup with his deadbeat father and escape from Lowell. Or perhaps it had been the song on the radio, 'Slow Dancin'… the old Johnny Rivers ballad: the song that had let Sandra Palmer get her clutches on that idiotically naïve scholarship kid who should have known better. Her name had been enough to head him toward the faculty parking lot where he shed his jacket and tie and began a quick survey of disasters past and present.

Only to find that nothing had changed. The gothic chapel presided in dreary silence over the semi-circle of Georgian-revival school buildings. The stately oaks and maples were perhaps a tad more stately. It was a week or so before the kids would return from summer vacation. Twenty five years since he'd been kicked out, the winter of his senior year, and with it a Harvard rowing scholarship … and a tour of Vietnam that ended in another horror story. All thanks to Sandra Palmer.

Again he dug in with his oar, this time with the added conviction that speed and determination might yet put him beyond caring about names and places and the infidelities in their wake. He stared back a moment at the distant campanile of Torcello, a white flicker on the near horizon, only to recall a perplexed version of Michael Collins waiting in the shadow of another tower on that hot summer night, perspiring in his shirt sleeves, lost in memories of a younger Michael Collins on an Indian summer evening in 1969... and of those fine blue eyes that had singled him out from among all those fine young men.

In the distance now the soothing sound of waves. A spark of recognition went through him.

He leaned into the oar with sudden urgency, clutching it against his chest to get his full weight into the stroke, grunting as he made for the obliterating void of teaming white and the sloughing of memory's bonds. And yet as he knew only too well, his was a lesson in endurance—outlasting love's attraction, and a lesson he had failed to heed more than once. Beginning on that hot summer night when he first embarked upon the path of metamorphosis—on the brink, then as now, not only of reinventing himself but of raising Sandra Palmer from her grave in Sleepy Hollow.

CHAPTER 2

———

1 9 6 9

"Hey, Collins." The hand on his shoulder nearly ripped him a clean 180 with its sudden forcefulness. "Where the hell you going, suited up like that?"

Michael grimaced into the stoned face of his classmate, whose blond hair dangled over the open collar of an untucked paisley shirt. His bell-bottom jeans were inscribed with peace signs, and he wore three-hundred-dollar snakeskin boots.

"Alcott dance, or have I been misinformed?"

His feeble stab at levity, his ever-failing attempt at savoir faire seemed to have the usual effect.

"Hey man, where've you been, Collins?" The tall youth shook his mop of ringlets and blew out a lung-deep cloud of smoke. He indulged in a spacey examination of the face before him: the neatly clipped wavy dark hair, aquiline nose, the intersection of the jawline corralling a swirl of half dimple, heavy eyebrows clenched above apprehensive mocha eyes. "I mean, man, they threw out the dress code for mixers almost a year ago. And you" —he poked a finger in Michael's chest— "you are looking totally doubtful in that coat and tie. Whadya think this is, man, *American Bandstand*? You think you can charm these chicks in that getup—forget it. They'll freak."

Michael's tie was yanked down and flipped over his shoulder. A bleary laugh. Another classmate careened past with a snide comment.

"Hey, Lowell boy, off to the high school prom. Maybe you'll find your-self a cheerleader. But with those gorgeous Frankie Avalon peepers—who knows … maybe you'll find yourself a big-tits Annette Funicello."

A departing hoot of laughter and Michael Collins was alone again on the path. He frowned and turned toward the distant tree line and the river, as if for sympathy or help, while he struggled to unknot his tie and retie it. He was soaked in nervous sweat. October, Indian summer like nothing in living memory. The heat rose from the distant playing fields in hazy updrafts, the brassy glint of the river just visible through the thinning branches. His eye was distracted by animated figures headed for the dining hall and ground zero. Alerted by the squeal of air brakes and the clatter of bus doors opening as the Alcott Academy girls arrived in the parking lot, he pushed a hand through his Brylcreem'd hair. The smell of dope wafted over the green, only to be drowned by the liberal doses of English Leather cologne he'd applied in the gym.

He had to be out of his mind.

The foyer of the dining hall was nose-to-nose adolescent angst and swagger, boys and girls lined up opposite one another, waiting for the pairings to be made. Michael merged himself with his sometime chums, facing the preening self-conscious females who stared back with shiny faces—those who already had dates. The others, who were up for grabs, tended toward an inspection of the patterns in the parquet floor. The young men were, with one glaring exception, thoroughly dressed down; the young women ran the gamut from tight miniskirted daring to flowering hippie chic. But even the worst-dressed girls had little luck in disguising their pedigree, the long athletic bodies and broad shoulders and curving calves shaped by childhoods of ballet and riding and competitive swimming. The tall slumped a little to reduce an imperious carriage, while the short stood straight and thrust forward an appealing bust or bright smile. The place reeked of Chanel No. 5 and Right Guard. In the faculty lounge, the chaperones mingled, exchanging brave faces and exasperated sighs.

Of course he was well acquainted by now with these Alcott Academy Yankee blue bloods. He had glimpsed them in the Baskin-Robbins on Main Street with fudge-stained lips, parading back from lacrosse and field hockey, sticks thrown across their shoulders, muddy-kneed, cheeks blazing. Many wore glinting braces, or they had already-perfect white teeth. Their fair hair was frizzy and beribboned—and they were utterly aloof from the likes of him. His mother waited on their parents at Sunday lunch at the inn. For three years, they had lingered in his thoughts like emanations of the town itself and its literary lights, part of that white clapboard Colonial loveliness amid rolling pastures and vestigial orchards. The Alcott girls, with their display of good breeding, had always seemed impossibly fine and free. A race apart.

"You're here," she said, tapping his shoulder.

He had missed Sandra Palmer's intrepid dash across the room. They had met six weeks before when he'd come upon her as he jogged along a path by the Concord River. She had been standing before her canvas, brushes splayed in her left hand, so preoccupied with her work as not to notice him until he spoke admiringly of her landscape painting. There had been something familiar about her face, something that had haunted him for days. Their awkward chat had led to more meetings. A frappe at Baskin-Robbins. He'd posed for portrait sketches. She had given him one of her landscapes in return. Unbelievably, she seemed to like him. Maybe she was only intrigued: a scholarship kid from Lowell who played Chopin and spouted Thoreau. They had agreed, a last-minute thing, to meet at the annual fall dance of their sister-brother schools.

Now Sandra Palmer hovered all breathless before him, blond hair pulled tight off a luxurious forehead, cobalt blue eyes brimming with her daring, and barely a hint of makeup.

He said, "I made a frame for your painting—my painting."

"Painting?"

"The canvas you gave me."

"Forget that—did you put me down as your date?"

"Date?"

Her voice was a little panicked. "I was only just able to get myself on the list for the dance. Not only that—if you don't specifically request someone, they just match you up according to height."

A little crestfallen, he stared into the desperate blue of her eyes. A quick calculation of their relative height. Someone from behind shoved him in the back and laughed.

"Go tell your chairman," she said, bringing her face close to emphasize her command. Her eyes flashed a warning in the direction of the giggling perpetrator of the shove. The scent of her wafted over him and his head pulsed with giddy joy. She squeezed his hand and scampered back across the room to the hoots of nearby boys.

"You want whom?" The Emerson Academy dance committee chairman leaned into him with a smirk.

"Sandra Palmer."

"Sandra Palmer," the chairman echoed to his counterpart, a tall girl with frizzy black hair and a shapely nose, who was wearing a flowered peasant dress.

"Sandra …" she managed to say with a surprised jut of her jaw. "Sandra Palmer?" Her pencil careened down her list. "Don't you mean—" She squinted at the typed list and a blacked-out name where another had been added in red ink to the side. "No, you're okay—right here, Sandra Palmer." She put a check mark by the name. She shrugged, giving her handsome counterpart a puzzled look. "Well, you never know."

"You *know her*, Collins?" asked the Emerson chairman.

"Sure," Michael replied in an armor-plated deadpan.

"Keep it under control there, boy," the chairman said in a stage whisper, flashing a knowing glance in the direction of the tall girl at his elbow. Marking a furious check on his own list, the chairman bawled out, "Collins," as if to the farthest reaches of the dining hall.

"Sandra Palmer, please," the Alcott chairman chimed softly in turn, surveying the crowd, as if quite certain the name would fail to produce a living specimen.

She appeared from the melee of chattering nervousness with head held high—the picture of aplomb. Her pearls accentuated the discreet neckline of her cream-colored silk blouse. The pleats of her knee-length pastel blue skirt barely moved as she walked. Her hair, pulled up into a chignon, displayed her classic beauty from every angle. He was so used to seeing her outdoors, where she dressed in jeans and sneakers, her hair loose, that she seemed another person now, especially in such charged surroundings. There was something naturally guileless in her demeanor, a repose verging on sadness, which made him feel he was seeing her for the first time.

The Alcott chairman pulled Sandra aside for a moment in a hurried exchange of girl talk, something about the list.

Then with an official handshake, Michael and Sandra headed up the spiral staircase to the dining room while less problematic pairings were called out in quick succession behind them.

"I was late signing up; they'd closed the list," she said, as if irritated at herself. "Luckily, one of the other girls dropped out."

She walked swiftly and purposely ahead of him, as if she knew exactly where she was going, where she wanted to be seated. He followed in her wake. Then she stopped. Turning toward him, the pale ridge of her long nose lifting like a bowsprit in calm seas, she began a survey of the oak-paneled walls, hung with distinguished portraits of past headmasters and esteemed alumni.

"There he is," she said, stopping before a large portrait in a heavy gilded frame. "My grandfather. It's a self-portrait—see. He was a famous painter in his day, but nobody remembers him now." She indicated another portrait of the founder of the school. "That's by John Singer Sargent. He and my grandfather were pals."

They moved to one of the dining tables, where he pulled out her chair and she dropped into it with an excited "Thank you." He paused, gazing up at the painting he'd passed almost every day for years but had barely noticed. The figure was tall and debonair in a morning coat and wide silk tie. But for the paintbrush and loaded palette in hand, he might have passed for a typical turn-of-the-century financier. There was something, too, in the intensely focused eyes, which shone with a pale, distant light, as if making a critical appraisal of the viewer's space. Looking at the shadowy background, he could just make out hints of an easel, studio props, blue-and-white Chinese ginger jars, sketches of a bridge in Venice tacked to a wall.

He thought, *A life devoted to beauty.*

"Sit down, Michael."

"Huh …"

He couldn't take his eyes off the painting of her grandfather—something about the forceful line of the jaw, the crease of reddish blond hair, the aura of refinement. Or perhaps it had more to do with the vague atmosphere around the figure, an ambience that hinted at the enduring and unspoiled, the love of fine things.

Here was the clue that his young mind would fail to grasp, which twenty-odd years later would change his life. Joseph Palmer, Sandra's grandfather, scandal-ridden scion from an old Lowell mill-owning family, had, in effect, created the world as Michael Collins knew it.

She tapped his elbow. "Come on, it's no big deal."

"You don't look at all like him," he said, segueing from dreamy wonder to this mundane observation as he sat down beside her.

Sandra Palmer rolled her eyes.

"You should see the paintings of his model, his wife … his *nudes*." She whispered the last word close to his ear and laughed on a wicked little singsongy note, nervously touching her face. "My paternal grandmother, Sandra Chillingworth Palmer. Oh, you'd blush all right."

She pressed her hand over his where it rested on the linen tabletop, as if fearful her teasing might frighten him off.

"Sandra Chillingworth Palmer," he repeated in a half whisper, unable to resist pronouncing the name.

He glanced to her eager face (the familiarity of first meeting now replaced with the familiarity of the previous weeks), her flashing eyes intent on the comings and goings around them, and then back to the painting, and again to her clinging hand covering his. He saw in the flecks of dried paint on her hands and her broken, dirty nails the miraculous evidence of continuity between generations … and his timid graft into the splendid world of her progenitors.

The first few times they had met, when he'd run into her while she was painting on the path by the river, she'd been a diligent and somewhat distant perfectionist. Now, released from toil, she was radiant and relaxed. Intent on enjoying herself, drawing him out.

He said, as if to force his advantage, "The Palmer Library—I guess that was the general, your great-grandfather, you said, the friend of Thoreau?"

Her mind was elsewhere. She eyed the other girls sashaying their way to the tables.

"You won't believe the kind of stuff I heard on the bus coming over here."

"So, being an artist runs in the family."

"Artist? Oh, don't tell that to my mother. I always wanted Paris and the Beaux-Arts, but Mom says, not over her dead body: She says it's Radcliffe or I'm fried rice." She squeezed his hand and then jerked hers back in a comic show of propriety. "You are lucky you've got me. With the others, you'd be catnip under the sofa."

He turned to her blazing eyes—charged particles of blue and gray-green in the irises taking in every movement in the vicinity.

"You say the weirdest things."

"But I'll protect you." She laughed. "Really I will—promise."

"Miss Palmer Mill."

She slapped his hand, playful but decisive.

"Don't start that again. For Christ's sake, I've never even been to *your* Palmer Mill."

He was captivated by her family connections, and she cared not a jot. The Palmer Mill on the Pawtucket Canal in his hometown of Lowell still loomed as a fixture from his childhood landscape, as compelling a name and imposing a building as anything he could remember. And here he was sitting next to a Palmer beneath a portrait of another Palmer, as if something of the mythic grandeur of the past had singled him out.

"'Catnip under the sofa?'" he said slowly, pondering her expression, as if it might be the key to the world that hovered tantalizingly at his elbow.

She meowed softly. "The others scratch, but I promise I'll be a very good little girl."

Smiling gamely, he glanced once more to the portrait of her grandfather, feeling an overwhelming rush of gladness, some inexplicable desire to shout out her name. Imagine: a great-grandfather who knew Thoreau!

He handed her a Coke. She sat on the stone balustrade of the veranda outside the dining hall, fingering a leaf that had fallen from one of the miniature dogwoods.

"I wasn't impressed, okay." She put a hand on his shoulder and continued her reassurance. "Listen, I don't care where they buy their dope, who was dropping acid on the beach at Gay Head, and who the hell cares about not getting carded at Club Forty-seven?"

The moan of an electric guitar and the desultory rattle of drums echoed behind them as the band finished warming up.

"You never feel, like you're missing out?"

"Smoking dope on Boston Common, breaking into offices—people getting messed up? That won't change anything."

He was taken aback by her charged tone, the vehemence and hurt so close to the surface.

"Come the revolution."

"I don't want things to change. I want things to stay as they are." She gestured at the circling dusk, her expressive hands conjuring pale lawns and trees of fall-dry leaves and silvery splashes of light in the woods near the river, just a hint of the birthing curve of the moon. "Like us."

She threw back her head and looked at him straight on. "Isn't that what you want?"

He had an uneasy sense that she had co-opted him for her club, perhaps some hidebound secret society of one: hard on herself and harder on others. He found himself distracted by a couple making out in the grass below them.

He finally replied. "Well, we know what they want."

"Getting laid, you mean. Guys," she said with a dismissive wave. And then, as if she recognized the girl in the grass, she repeated more softly, "Guys."

"And the girls?"

"Sure, but we want love. We want to be better than the boys. We want love that will fill our sails and blow us far far away."

"And me in my coat and tie."

"Your hero Thoreau would understand ... I guess."

"He could be a little strange."

"Not change, but changelessness. What's underneath, to get your teeth into, to love ... well, forever." Her eyes widened for emphasis. "That's what I felt when you played that Chopin for me."

He winced at the thought. When he'd helped her carry her painting stuff back to school, she had talked him into going by the auditorium and playing the concert grand. "I screwed it up," he said. Actually, he'd loved the sound of the Steinway and the acoustics of the hall.

"What's your problem—you want to be *more* like those spoiled idiots in your class? Well ..."

She stood, grabbed the collar of his jacket, and stripped it from him, then his tie, pulling open the top buttons of his shirt. Then she began her own transformation: extracting the bobby pins from her hair until it hung down her back, removing her pearls and stuffing them into the pocket of his corduroys.

"Now you're *the* groovy dude," she said, standing back to observe her handiwork. "And we—we'll blend right in. But underneath we'll stay just the same."

He blushed and laughed, and she laughed. She came closer and raised her eyebrows and slowly undid the top button of her blouse, a dubious glance down at what she had to show and another laugh, this more brittle and high-pitched than the first. It seemed to break something in him.

"You're …" He pulled a nervous hand through his dark hair and got the words out. "You're really beautiful."

She bent forward and kissed him on the lips chastely, but lingering with the pleasure of the moment.

"I can't believe I did that," she said.

He stood trembling, licking at his lips as if to keep the thing from fading. His mind went blank, as if his head had suddenly filled with nervous static.

"I checked out that story in the library, about your great-grandfather," he said, grasping at the first thing that came to mind, the thing that burned in his imagination. "You know, about Thoreau accompanying Captain Palmer to the train after the fall of Fort Sumter, before he went off to war."

She looked at him with fond incredulity and wiped a tear from her eye, her shoulders going lax.

"That's what's so nice about you; you'll never let things get out of control."

"I'm such an idiot."

"No you're not. You're better than any one of them." She took his hand and sucked in her lower lip, as if a little surprised at herself. "I'm just giving you a hard time. Actually, some of my nicest memories are walking with my dad when I was a kid, off the beaten track. Places where Thoreau had gone and written about, where my great-grandfather had tagged along as a boy on Thoreau's surveying jobs. I was just too young to appreciate it the way my dad was into it."

"Thoreau was such a fervid abolitionist, but I can't imagine him ever marching off to war, or giving a soldier a hearty send-off."

"My great-grandfather, to hear my father tell it, went through hell." She paused, as if hearing the echo of another voice. "Came back from the Civil War a broken and disillusioned man."

He watched her face intently where it was enveloped in a radiance of pale blue light filtering out from the French doors. There was something in her voice and her sad, reflective eyes that seemed to move him beyond himself, over the fields and woods with their sounds, the last crickets chirping, as if the very cadences in her voice invoked other voices, places and names from which something of her had sprung, sounding in him memories, which he, as yet, could not fathom.

She said with a wistful half sigh, "My dad used to take me to Thoreau's grave in Sleepy Hollow after we'd visit the grave of General Palmer, and my grandmother's. Now *she* was something else, a Chillingworth, Sandra Chillingworth Palmer. She was a child prodigy—like you, on the piano. You should go see her monument; it's the most beautiful thing in Sleepy Hollow. Of course, my mother disapproved...." Her voice seemed to lose momentum and she laughed quietly. "Old Concord, her family, North Bridge and then some. Nobody can live up to that."

He was entranced, his thoughts drifting again to the self-portrait of the artist in the dining room.

"So, you were named after your grandmother."

A flicker of a smile passed across her lips. "I guess so."

"Did you know your grandfather, the painter?"

"Oh, no, Joseph Palmer died long before I was born. But he *haunts* us." She laughed, as if making light of the word *haunts*. "I mean his paintings, his women. My grandfather moved his studio from Concord to the Berkshires toward the end of his life. A lot of his stuff is still there. My father used to take me to the old place as a kid … kind of like an old farm. My mother hated it: 'And thank God for small mercies, just as long as those hideous things are kept under lock and key,' she'd say."

He had to smile at what he took to be her imitation of her mother's tone, right down to the fluttering nervous fingers patting at her hair, the ramrod posture.

"Your mother doesn't like his paintings?"

"Let's just say Joseph Palmer had a thing about women. Perhaps he loved them a little *too* much." She smiled self-consciously. "But he was a great artist, even if nobody remembers him now."

"Do you know what Thoreau said about love? You have to 'discipline yourself only to yield to love,' to suffer the attraction."

"To suffer love's attraction," she said slowly, dreamily, as if needing to fathom the notion in her own voice.

The band inside the dining hall began to play, the rising scream of an electric guitar searing the silences of the past, which had been creeping into their conversation. She listened and a smile of relief came to her lips, a shake of her head transforming her long hair into a stream of liquid highlights.

"Tell me something," she asked. "The Thoreau thing—I mean you, a guy from Lowell and everything—why Thoreau? What's the big deal?"

He shook his head self-consciously. "Stupid, isn't it? Somebody gave me a copy of *Walden* as a little kid. And Lowell, well, it's the pits. And the thing that got to me about Thoreau was … if you can just step back, shift your gaze from the world the way you *think* it is, you'll find that everything can be different, that things have a purpose. Kind of like what Thoreau wrote about in *Walden*, about being in touch with all times and places, like being reborn."

She laughed at his infatuated tone and raised her eyebrows in mock horror.

"I like that … being reborn—with a purpose?"

"Like the hidden structures of the mind, that it's not just random chance."

She continued to examine his face, as if she had suddenly recognized something in his prominent nose, the heavy mobile brows shadowing his rapt eyes.

"Are we nuts?" She held out her palms, as if the issue were still in balance. "You a poet and teacher—or was it a pianist? Me a second-rate artist. What do you think, Harvard scholarship and Radcliffe legacy, two antediluvians on a road to nowhere. And where will we be twenty years from now, Michael Collins—what will the world possibly want with the likes of us?"

There it was again, her penchant to slot them into some boring, if unpredictable, future together. If that was her assumption, he found it comforting and disconcerting in equal measure.

The band began churning the decibels. Disheveled, spacey-eyed boys and girls straggled inside from the lawn, pulling down skirts, adjusting grass-stained jeans, checking lipstick: weary but eager sinners merging into the tortured sound.

"So," he said.

"Maybe," she countered with a shrug and a girlish curtsy. "Time enough to get on the bandwagon."

They stood on edge of the dance floor a moment, before a wall of imploding, ricocheting light. He shook his head as she took his hand.

"Don't worry, it's not dancing. I've had ten years of ballet—believe me, it's not dancing."

She guided him into the melee of bodies and then, just like that, left him, drifted off into her own sphere of motion, merging with the jarring rhythms, the white shock of the strobes, the swirl of turquoise blue. Yet all the while she retained an inner serenity, unlike the self-conscious ecstasy of the others. He felt abandoned and exposed, a klutz, a fraud. He tried to draw nearer to her on the dance floor, but he felt so outside the music, music that was like liquid oxygen to the inflamed passions all around him. He watched her long legs, the rhythmic grace of her arms, her face flushed with perspiration, eyes a rapturous deep blue. How could she ignore him so? A moment later, what he took as a wince of pain in her eyes turned into the flash of a pirouette. The extraordinary maneuver left him feeling like a bit of flotsam bobbing in her wake. The other dancers began to notice her. Envious glances came her way, the girls in particular: curious, surprised, a hint of wonderment at an uncharacteristic display. He fell back farther.

Then it was as though he were passing into the eye of the storm. The sea of sound poured away and the band segued into a lilting ballad, 'Slow Dancin',' by Johnny Rivers, sung in an appealing nasal twang by the lead guitarist. She hovered before him, smiling, holding her hair off her neck to cool down, and an instant later she held his hand and was guiding him into a safe and dignified two-step, intimations of bygone propriety and society tea dances.

The scent of her perfume or shampoo smoldered in his nostrils, further putting him under the spell of the music. His every pore seemed suddenly filled with longing: the softness of her hair against his cheek, warm breath on his neck, the curve of her backbone and the catch of her bra beneath her silk blouse, her fingers intertwined with his, responding squeeze for squeeze. His heart lurched. He felt her shudder, another seismic shift, and her arm circled his neck, her face finding refuge against his protective chest. Her breasts pressed into him. He feared he would faint with gladness. He closed his eyes and found his thoughts drifting off to the warm ache of that long Indian summer, seeing the purple meadow grasses where he'd found her painting along the path by the river, feeling the lift of the tall white pine that shadowed the course of the Concord, where he loved to row.

"Come on, Collins."

A hard slap on the shoulder pulled him reeling back. The faculty chaperone gave a perfunctory scowl.

"You, boy—yes, you—should know better. Why don't you two go get a drink and cool down."

Sandra turned without a word and simply walked away, as if refusing to dignify the rudeness and injustice of being singled out, what with the make-out scene all over the dance floor. Following, he caught sight of the Emerson Academy dance chairman near the faculty lounge, arm draped around his Alcott Academy counterpart, a barely disguised smirk of triumph on his face. His date, the tall, angular girl with frizzy black hair, looked uneasy, her fingers twisted into her Indian bead belt. She gave a guilty downward glance as he passed by.

"The hell with them," Sandra fumed, tears in her eyes as she blinked up at the pale sky from the farthest corner of the veranda.

"It's just me—so screw it."

"Notice how anything genuine gets stomped on these days."

He sighed, resigned. "Some get cut more slack around here than others."

"Stop feeling so goddamn sorry for yourself. You think because you're from Lowell, because you're a scholarship kid, that you're not as good? Stand up to the bastards."

He saluted with a swagger of his shoulders. "Yes, ma'am."

"Let's get out of here."

"We're not supposed to leave the dance."

"Just a minute ago, you wanted to *be* like them." She waved at the lawns.

"No I didn't."

"Then ... be better, be braver."

"Yeah, well, people have gotten kicked out for less."

"The hell with it."

"Easy for you to say; I don't have a trust fund to fall back on."

She shook her head with disappointment. "What the hell do you know about anything? See you round, *Thoreau*."

With that, she hopped the wall down to the lawn, struggled for a moment to get her shoes off and tossed them under some box shrubs, and was off across the lawn in the direction of the path to the river.

She didn't even bother to glance back. He sat for a few minutes, determined not to feel sorry for himself. His hand enveloped her string of pearls.

He followed along the path she'd taken toward the river. The moon rode high atop the battered branches, a great silver eye awatch over the white woods. He loved how everything was bathed in milky iridescence, the birch trunks appearing against the surrounding woods like swelling seams of molten cream. Walking got the heat back up in him and the smell of dry leaves underfoot was like an infusion of incense from night's high altar. Alone, he became light-headed, as if striding above himself, deliciously beyond caring in a land of liquid white. He spread his arms, a lunatic worshiper. A crazed rendition of the *Moonlight Sonata* beneath his mobile fingertips. Humming the notes like some crazed Glenn Gould (his mother idolized Glenn Gould), he luxuriated in the moonlight beating down on his bare skin.

And then, another apparition, a deeper enchantment still, appearing over a shallow rise in the path—the river, brimming and swollen, an albino flood of light that threatened to drown out the silhouetted trees bowed to its shallow banks. And then farther on, the sloping boathouse roof, a deep pearl gray indigo.

He sat quietly on the wooden dock of the boathouse, letting the dance of white on the river weave its hypnotic spell. He was happiest being alone. In some ways, it was almost better thinking about Sandra Palmer than having to deal with a flesh-and-blood presence that enforced demands he would never be able to fulfill. His years at Emerson Academy had made him quite the expert at keeping his head low, remaining a genial presence while letting the accumulated slights and not so subtle putdowns roll off his back. He'd learned to hide in his studies, curl up with his favorite books in the library, lose himself in hours of piano practice, in rowing on the river. He would graduate top in his class. He was the best rower in the school and should have been elected captain of crew—but he hadn't let it bother him. There was always the retreat into himself. Even now, he longed for the library and his favorite study carrel, where he would prepare for the upcoming AP American literature exam.

"Coward and toady," he muttered to himself, imitating Sandra's intonation.

Then a discordant note, a sound like sobbing from somewhere nearby. At first, he thought it was only the rush of water sluicing past the dock, that most comforting of sounds, but then realized it was coming from the boathouse. He turned, to see bats dropping into the night from under the eaves. He got up, still inside the dream of his exclusion and his lonely communion with the voices stored on library shelves. The sliding door of the boathouse was ajar. He pushed it open, the rusty squeak of the rollers waking something in him. Shafts of moonlight fretted the many tall windows, illuminating the racks of sleek shells. Inside, the heat of the day had brewed a potent aroma of varnish and seasoned wood. Some instinct for danger caused him to look up at the viewing gallery, a second-floor spectator area for watching races. It had been closed for years because the hand-carved railings were in need of repair. The stairway had been roped off. But he was sure he heard footsteps above.

"Be careful," he cried out into the shadowy upper reaches, squinting toward the gallery railing that ran along one side of the building. His voice—*careful … careful*—echoed, as if mocking his innate timidity.

"It's okay," she called back, coming into view like a phantom of herself, a hand on the railing. "I came up here dozens of times with my father when I was a kid."

"It's closed; it's not safe."

She made a face, as if her accustomed prowess or good sense were being called into question, and headed for the stairs.

A sickening crack exploded in the heated air, and at the same instant she seemed to pitch violently forward as a stair and part of the banister gave way. It was almost as if he'd seen it happen before it happened, the speed of three or four steps, the calm concentration as he managed to break her fall, her arm and shoulder slamming into his chest and tumbling them both to the floor. They lay stunned, he more than she, the breath knocked out of him.

"You okay?" She was the first up, rubbing a scraped elbow.

"I don't know." He was trying to register the throb in his head.

"Shit, I'm sorry. What a jerk."

"You scared me, that's all."

"You saved me." She examined her elbow. "Why the hell did I come *here—of all places*?"

He found a wadded napkin in his pocket and gave it to her.

"You okay?" he asked, getting to his feet and surveying the debris.

"A scratch."

He shook his head anxiously. "Jeest, what do we say about this?"

"We weren't here," she said, holding the napkin to her elbow.

He shot a dark look toward her—the white napkin blotting blood recalling another moment of terror from years before. The color was coming back into her pale face. *We weren't here.* The ease of that retort, instead of striking him as devious, confirmed for him her capacity to put bad things behind and move on.

"Right." He kicked at a bit of broken banister.

She raised an eyebrow and went over to a carved wooden dedication plaque by the staircase and tapped it. He peered at the gold lettering, squinting to read the inscription.

"Joseph Palmer Memorial Viewing Gallery," he said. "Your grandfather, the artist—they dedicated a viewing gallery to him?"

"We are," she said, her voice rising imperiously, "practically enshrined here. My grandfather loved Eakin's rowing pictures. When he worked in Venice before the First World War, he had a one-man shell shipped from Henley so he could row the canals." She walked down the lines of plaques set into the tongue-and-groove paneling and pointed out more Palmers. "My dad's crew of 1932, when they won the New England schoolboy championships. Three years later, he captained the Harvard crew that won the nationals. Year after that, his boat got a gold in the '36 Berlin Olympics."

"Wow." He blew out his cheeks, genuinely impressed.

She stood for a moment imprisoned in a shadow grid of sashes, then moved to his side, looking chagrined, perhaps concerned she had only managed to feed his idolatry. She took one palm and then the other, touching his many calluses as if to count them.

"Flesh-and-blood souvenir," she said, placing the wadded and bloody napkin in his palm and closing his fingers around it with her hands. "Know what? Rowing doesn't fit your poor-boy image."

This only half-kidding accusation perplexed him, and he hung his head for an instant, as if anticipating worse.

"Hey, it was crew or *baseball*," he said with unconcealed loathing.

"My father would love you, big, strapping, literal-minded son he never had ... *another rower*."

She turned with a hint of disgust and walked away through the varnished half-light and out into the brilliant night. He turned for a parting look at the mess and then followed. She was sitting on the edge of the dock, dipping her toes in the water.

"He used to drag me here for races to watch the guys row their hearts out. He was so into it. 'They think they'll last forever' was what he used to tell me. 'That's what it feels like, Sandy, when you've got a head of steam up ... as if it's the world going by and not you.'"

He sat down, intent on her expression, intrigued at the voice behind the voice.

"Sandy?" he murmured, as if testing the sound.

"Sandra ... Sandra, just call me Sandra."

Then he added his two bits. "Until the end of the race—win or lose—when you're just coughing up your lungs."

"Parents tell you what they think you should hear." Then, with a forced cheerfulness, singing: "'With a hip and a hop and blow the old captain down.'"

A snatched moment from her childhood? Another quirky family expression? He thought of the crap his father used to toss around.

He put a hand on her shoulder. "If I didn't know better, I'd think you actually missed your father."

"My mother pretends like the divorce never happened. Know what her favorite saying is?" She lifted her chin. "'With all the interesting things in the world, no one has a right to be sad.'"

She shivered, as if she'd gotten her mother's matronly Brahman drawl a little too perfect.

He piped up then, prompted to offer his stab at consolation: "It was the happiest day of my life ... when my dad walked out."

She closed her eyes and shook her head. "It changed everything."

He added. "For the best."

"I think divorce is different, though," she said. "It's so, so ... premeditated and official."

"My greatest fear is that he'll just turn up again on the doorstep."

She flipped a toe and sent a fountain of water into the air.

"Don't you think maybe you're the one who's being a little hard?" she asked. "I mean, your father *is* your father."

"You don't want to know."

"You don't have a corner on shit, you know. Our little lives aren't so perfect."

"You don't want to know."

"Try me. I'm not going to ... *like* you any less."

"He was a drunk and a brawler, always playing at being more Irish than the Irish. He … beat up my mother."

"Jesus."

"He used to drag me and my brother to Red Sox games at Fenway Park. We'd sit in the bleachers with his pals. They'd yell insults at the black players on the other teams. Once, he took an empty beer cup and he just—right there in front of everyone—pissed into it, and threw the whole thing at this right fielder on the Washington Senators, Fred Valentine. Hit him in the back. The Fenway cops arrested him. My brother and I sat in the police station for ten hours until my mother came to get us."

She turned with a sympathetic expression, watching the reflections on his face, reaching to trace the half dimple on his chin.

"Well, my mother goes three days a week to see her therapist in Cambridge," Sandra said. "If it wasn't for her DAR stuff, I think she'd go nuts."

"Maybe we'd better get back to the dance." He glanced apprehensively over his shoulder at the boathouse and then again to the ripples careening outward from where her foot played in the water.

"I shouldn't tell you this," she said, "but I went to the inn last week. I couldn't help it—I was curious to see your mother." She touched his hand. "Don't worry, I didn't say anything. But at least I know where your nose came from." She laughed and nuzzled at his neck. "You'll let me do a few more portrait drawings, won't you?"

"We'd better go."

"Your mom is very pretty, although the Roman nose looks better on you."

"You should hear her play the piano."

"As good as you?"

"She could have been a concert pianist." He looked down at his hands. "Now she's taking an accounting course at UMass. They've promised her a job at reception. Then she wants to travel. Mom promised to take me to Venice, where my grandfather came from."

Sandra held one foot out straight, watching drops of water drip from her heel, as if perplexed by something he'd said.

"You'd like Venice."

"You've been there?"

"Sort of."

"How, sort of?"

"With my mother."

"Okay."

"Ah, I know," she declared, "let's get away from the world. We'll take the race dingy." She scrambled up. "You row."

"We can't do that."

"We'll row our hearts out. We'll row all the way to Venice, or San Francisco if you like. We'll wear flowers in our hair. We'll disappear where no one will ever find us."

"Let's get back, okay?"

"Haven't you ever dreamed of just disappearing?"

"It's late."

"C'mon, help me get it in the water."

"Sandra, I wasn't even supposed to leave the dance with you; the mess in the boathouse is enough to get us in big trouble."

It was as if he had ceased to exist. She went to the side of the boathouse, where the aluminum dingy leaned up against the wall, wrestled it around onto the sloping dock, pulled it down to the edge, and shoved it into the water. She tied the painter to a ringbolt and went back for the oars. He stubbornly remained seated, although not unimpressed. She got in the boat, put the oars in the locks, and untied the painter. Hiking her skirt, she sat, gave a comic spit into her palms, grabbed the oars and spun the small boat in a flashy half turn, and then backed it into the dock, eyeing him precisely, a hint of sweat at the underarms of her blouse.

"You coming?"

"Hey," he said, "chip off the old block."

She made a face and then a mocking swagger. "No balls, no blue chip." She spun the boat a 360.

He glanced at his watch.

"Just a few minutes," she said. "For something … memorable."

"Okay, but I'm rowing."

"Aye, aye, Captain—*my captain.*"

He stepped into the back and they switched places, facing each other while he rowed. He put his back into it. Beyond the overhang of the trees, the moonlight was almost blinding, while ahead stretched a frosted highway, a smooth surface like fine polished alabaster.

"This is such a romantic thing, don't you think?" she said.

"A fool's errand."

She was trailing her fingers in the water. Above them, the white pine reached into the moonlit sky.

"How come you never talk about your brother, Jimmy?"

He fixed her with a "You don't want to know" expression, seeing her blouse saturated with highlights, seams like inlaid bands of ivory, hinted outline of her bra a reticent but pleasing presence.

She prompted him. "You don't get along."

He pulled hard, once, twice, three times, letting the glide come and fill out the nests of water where the oar had dipped.

"We're just different."

"How different?"

"I don't ask you all this stuff."

"Go ahead."

"It's just …" The oar hovered, dripping, the slow current easing them on. "Even after we moved to Carlisle, when Mom got the job at the inn, Jimmy insisted on taking the bus back to Lowell every day. Now he's captain of football and baseball at Lowell High. Let me tell you, the place has gone to the dogs."

"Not a smart kid like you—getting out, huh?"

"He thinks I'm uppity, a snob, that I talked Mom into leaving Lowell, that I think I'm too good for Lowell."

She stared into his eyes. "Sometimes I think we are born happy. But then things accumulate." She turned and squinted at the far bank, as if trying to visualize some thought. "Maybe if we could just jettison the bad things, simplify."

"Thoreau would be all for that." He dug in the oars and the dingy shot forward.

"I'll bet your Thoreau *deal* goes over like a lead balloon with your classmates."

"I'd never talk about stuff like that … just to you."

She seemed amused. "Well, maybe we should do a Thoreau—you and me." Her eyes lighted up. "We'll jettison the ugly baggage of our young lives—simplify, right? Hide ourselves from the world."

He began pulling harder on the oars, as if to get up to speed.

"Get down to the essentials," he puffed.

"Lies," she intoned, and made a motion of tossing something overboard.

"Lies," he echoed.

"Jealousy." She made a pantomime of lifting something heavy and shoving it over the side.

"Jealousy."

"Hatred and resentment," she said.

"Hate," he affirmed, pulling harder still, as if to do his bit.

"*Infanticide,*" she said in an even precise voice, again looking him straight in the eye.

He paused in mid-stroke, about to mimic back the words, and then, seeing the sharp arch of her brows pressed to an uncertain crease between her eyes, thought better of it.

"I'm not into this stuff, ritzy little mind games."

"Then how about I killed my baby brother?"

"Okay," he snapped, turning the boat. "That's it, time to get back."

"No, damn it," she shouted, and smacked his knee. "Keep going. I'm not finished."

"I'm not into this, Sandra."

She gripped his knees, gritting her teeth as if to force the words. "I'm not playing a goddamn game with you." She bowed her head. "Keep going."

He turned the boat slowly, as if the strength had drained from him.

"This is crazy," he said. Then, lowering his voice and staring at her: "You're not serious—right?"

"It was a few years ago. My parents finally got the boy they'd wanted. He was about a year old. For the longest time, Mom would never leave him, like baby Joey—the third—was the only thing holding the family together. Then Dad insisted they start having a normal life again, going out and stuff. I was babysitting. I was downstairs doing my homework and I heard Joey crying. I went up and got him out of his crib and put him on the changing table. His diaper was soaked. There weren't any more diapers under the changing table, so I went out to the hall closet to get a new pack. There was this terrible thump, and I ran back and found the baby on the floor. He was facedown, not crying, not moving. I was terrified. I picked him up and put him back on the table. His eyes were closed. I was freaked. I felt for his heart but couldn't feel anything. I shook him. I was crying. I was scared. I was about to go run to the phone and call the hospital or something, when, just like that, Joey opened his eyes and began to whimper.

"I was so relieved, I almost fainted. I picked him up again, held him; he seemed fine. I put on a diaper and got a bottle, and in no time he was fast asleep. I put him back in the crib. I went downstairs. And I was so terrified of what had happened—maybe a minute when he was unconscious—that I had to block it out, kind of pretend it never happened. I even got a bottle of wine from the icebox and started drinking it, and I don't even really like wine. Then I got so tired, like I was going to faint. I went upstairs and listened at the door of the nursery. But I was too scared to actually go in. Can you believe it? So I went to bed, wanting sleep, oblivion. I was just so scared."

For a second, she found his eyes, then quickly returned her gaze to her lap, where her hands remained entwined.

"I was awakened in the morning by the siren, an ambulance. I rushed to the window. My parents were downstairs on the drive with the baby, rushing for the back of the ambulance. And then they were gone and I was alone. I panicked. I was sick. I threw up. I wanted to make it go away, that sound, that awful thump when he hit the floor. I cowered under the covers, crying. Eventually, my father came back. He found me and told me that my baby brother had died in the night. He didn't know why. He could barely speak. He asked me if everything had been okay. I said sure. They did an autopsy; they called it 'sudden crib death.' No way of explaining it—it just happens. I wanted to tell them about him falling from the changing table, but I just couldn't. Anyway, it seemed Mom had checked him when she'd come home and he'd been okay."

"So it was an accident."

"Nothing is an accident."

"It's not your fault."

"I should have called the doctor." She wiped her tears.

"But he was okay."

"Well, he *wasn't* okay," she snapped.

"It was an accident."

"I was so jealous."

"No, no, don't do that." He grabbed her shoulders and drew her to him. She remained hard in his embrace, petrified. He struggled to offer comfort. "Like ... like what my grandfather used to call 'a flaw in the stone,'" he said. "It happens. He'd be working on a beautiful piece of marble, and when he was halfway finished, there'd be a fissure, a weakness that couldn't be worked around. When that happens, you just have to let it go and begin again."

He felt her shudder.

"But we're not works of art, are we?"

He took her face in his hands and kissed her wet cheek, kneeling in the space between them to embrace her fully, the wild beating of her heart like a caged and desperate thing. She kissed him and bent her head back and took his hands in hers.

"I never told you, but I fell in love with your hands on first sight— really," she said. She kissed his palms and he closed his eyes.

For a long moment, as if their glide in the current might never cease, he felt suspended in air, buoyed by the sky and trees, the mist rising and beginning to envelope them. Then he realized she was shivering and he reached to rub her back. The touch of her seemed to become words spilling from his lips.

"You should have seen my grandfather work, knocking off fist-size chunks of marble, and then he'd go at it with needle-size chisels, doing the most amazing detailed work, as if all the time it was in his mind, there in the stone, before he was even halfway done, like the stone was coming to life under his hands."

"I didn't know your grandfather was an artist."

"He was a stonecutter from Venice. He carved funeral monuments for a living. But yes, he was an artist."

"See, something we have in common," she said with an encouraging smile.

He took a deep breath, now the scents of her body mixing with the smells of the river and the dry leaves along the riverbank.

"Do you think?"

She said, "Like what you said about Thoreau. What an artist does, finding a viewpoint, a perspective that is different from that of the crowd, that reveals the secret links in our lives, the truth hidden to others. Aren't I different now, now that you know the truth about me?"

A fillip of panic rippled in his chest, seeing her eyes so concentrated, as if she were intent on getting to the bottom of him. She raised her lips and her tongue found his. He pulled away, genuinely shocked at the instinct for sensual gratification coming so soon after her admission of guilt and loss. The boat rocked, and he grabbed the gunwales and got himself in his seat.

"We'd better get back."

She drew herself up, wiping quickly at her eyes, composing herself.

"No," she cried out, "keep going."

"No, I won't."

"Then tell me your secret. I told you mine. See if it makes a difference."

"I don't have any."

"Yes you do, the thing you'd never admit to anyone else but me."

He collapsed on the oars, breathing hard. He nodded to himself, getting it out slowly, barely a whisper.

"Not a day goes by, not one, that I don't hope—pray—my father's dead."

The silence. The drip of sweat from his chin. She reached to the line of his jaw to catch a drop. He couldn't look at her.

The admission opened a terrifying chasm in him, as if his family's escape from the run-down house on River Street, from the wreckage of Lowell, and his privileged years at Emerson Academy were all a blundering attempt to paper over that abyss of shame and hatred. Held in her sympathetic gaze, he felt utterly vulnerable, trapped, as if all she was about was a ploy to put him at her mercy.

"My father had a temper like lightning out of a clear sky. I was there when he broke my mother's nose. I thought he'd killed her. This was only a few months after my grandfather drowned in an accident."

"An accident?" she said, her voice just above a hush.

He told her about the violent windstorm that had hit Lowell in July of that year, a storm that had blown down trees and telephone lines for miles around. His grandfather Giovanni walked home from his workshop near the city cemetery every day, following the path along the Pawtucket Canal, which had once provided waterpower for the mills in Lowell. The day of the storm, Giovanni didn't show up for dinner. They assumed he'd been held up and was seeking shelter until the storm blew over. The next morning, they found his body in the canal, near the lock where the Pawtucket Canal emptied into the Merrimack River.

"Giovanni *was* our family. My father, who was Irish, hated him for being Italian. He hated him for having a job, for being an artist. I blame my father, too, I don't know, for being happy that Giovanni drowned, I guess."

She touched his face. There was relief in her voice.

"There, that wasn't so bad. Do you feel it … the difference?"

She smiled, reaching a curious hand to his face, exploring his cheekbones, his nose, as if glad to have her chance to soothe his hurt and merge his vulnerability with hers. Then, as if by sudden impulse, she seized his right hand where it grasped the oar and brought it to her cheek and then her mouth, maneuvering his ring finger into her teeth and biting down with slow, concerted pressure. She looked into his troubled eyes as she bit, fixing his gaze in hers, as if searching for signs of pain or surrender, biting harder still, until his eyes fluttered with what, under different circumstances, might have been interpreted as joy or release. Then she let the finger slip from her teeth, kissing the red indents above the joint.

"So," she declared, "let it be your grandfather's hands … who you really are."

This incantation was another shock to his system, this near-ritual act of exorcism. It was as if she knew the truth: that he lived in terror of his father's temper in himself—the troll under the bridge—and so maintained, at almost any cost, a pose of equanimity to the world.

Unable to say as much, he gave in to the instinct to flee. He began hauling mightily on the oars and turned the dinghy in a smooth, powerful arc.

"Wait," she said, and grabbed an oar. "Let's keep going. My old house is just a bit farther down the river."

"It's late."

"We had an apple orchard. You'd like it there. I'll make you happy there."

Something in her look—the moonlit sharpness of her eyes, her lower lip drawn tight—scared him.

"No." And he continued rowing, harder than before.

The sylvan moonscape swirled about them, the night dizzy with release. The bow plunged ahead. The current had taken them a fair way downstream, and soon he was sweating with his exertions. Strangely, his body had never felt so alive, reveling with renewed confidence, as if released from a purgatory of self-doubt.

"Well, I just wanted to see the old place." She turned back with a wistful glance. "We had to give it up when my parents got divorced. It was a nice old house, expensive to maintain—too much for Mom to keep. My dad's family had it for almost a hundred and fifty years. It had this funny brick tower, kind of like a crow's nest. You'd like that—Thoreau visited there. You could see everything from up there: our meadows and the orchard and the stone walls. You would have loved the apple orchard. And the old stone walls, it was almost like you could feel—when I'd draw them—the hope and love that had gone into their building."

He could picture her beautiful home in his mind, so unlike his own family's ramshackle house on River Street in Lowell of years before. Soon he was caught up in the speed and the glide and his body's delight in the rhythm of the stroke. He was eager to get back to the safety of his life in the library and music practice rooms, the danger zone confined to memory again. He was thinking, too, of Thoreau and his brother returning home from their trip on the Concord and Merrimack rivers. The brothers had set a sail. A following wind, a beautiful day ... it was the happiest day of Thoreau's life.

Michael was quick to get the boat out and pull it up the sloping dock and back into position against the wall of the boathouse. He placed the oars in the pegs against the wall exactly as they had been. He surveyed the result, as if needing to confirm that nothing had really happened. When he turned to find her, he saw her standing in a copse off to the side of the river, in the shadow of an enormous white pine.

"You must think I'm pretty weird," she said as he came to her. She turned her face upward into the moonlight, as if momentarily flustered by the spotlight shining between the branches. Her cheeks were flushed. She was breathing hard, as if it were she who had rowed them back.

"I think you're really nice."

She reached for his hand.

"Nice, but not pretty."

Her face glowed a luminous white.

"You are beautiful."

"Not like Sandra Chillingworth Palmer. She inspired Joseph Palmer—I mean really inspired." She raised herself to full height and threw her head back as if to assume a characteristic pose. "Now, *she* was something, one of the great society beauties of her day. Wait till you see his paintings of her." She giggled. "You'll forget all about me."

He glanced at his watch but couldn't make out the time without being obvious.

"Shall we get going?"

"Beautiful enough that you want to make love to me?"

"Jesus."

She squeezed his hand.

"I mean, I wouldn't mind," she said.

"Just like that, just like the others," he replied.

She stared at him, her lips aquiver, as if she'd been taken down a notch or two.

"Don't you think we're ridiculous? I mean, you—you and all your Thoreau. Thoreau is for old guys like my father. And me—look at me, eighteen—eighteen: never been touched by a guy. How sad, how ridiculous is that."

"So," he said, as if compelled to defend her honor. "We are different."

"No, we *are* different ... *now.*"

"Because we don't have any dope stashed somewhere, a six-pack waiting," he said.

"They're all playacting." She thought a moment. "Because" —she breathed deeply, as if of the moonlight itself— "we've told the truth, who we really are." She reached searching fingers to his cheek. "You see, I've discovered who you really are." She slipped her hand behind his neck and drew him to within inches of her face, as if locking in his new identity.

"I thought it was supposed to be, you know ..."

"Out of control?" she asked. "How about ... getting down to essentials?"

She shrugged and began with the buttons of her blouse and quickly had it in a heap at her ankles. She was almost perfunctory. Her bra followed. Her breasts were larger than he'd imagined, firm and white, with tiny pointed nipples. She pulled off her skirt and panties with one motion and stood naked before him. Her tall, gangly adolescent figure was well formed, her sleek muscled legs showing the result of years of ballet classes. Her hips were a little bony, and she had almost boyish buttocks to go along with her wispy blond pubic triangle, not an extra pound anywhere.

"So," she demanded, biting her lip, "what do you think?"

"You're incredible," he said, reaching to her shoulder, his hand trembling.

"I have never done this before, in case you're interested," she said.

"You're beautiful and so brave."

"Enough to lose control?"

He caressed her breasts, wanting to know the soft contours, the roughness of the nipples, those pointed centers touching off a blood rush from his shoulders downward, the like of which he'd never known. She pulled his head down to kiss him, slow and certain now. All he wanted were days and weeks to explore her kisses, for his hands to rummage every surface and angle and sheltered declivity, to worship before her downy flesh.

"Get out of your things." Her voice was commanding.

What might have remained to him in the way of prudence or skepticism, much less self-control, had already been discarded in the course of their conversation on the river.

He turned reluctantly, more afraid of losing the vision of her than of revealing himself, fumbling with the last shreds of an impossible dignity as he undressed, especially when confronted with the obscene bulge in his briefs.

"No fair, I want to see." She came around and carefully eyed him up and down, the artist her model. "Nice," she purred, kissing him. "And the rest?" Her lips hovered close to his while he managed to get his briefs down and off. She kissed him again and reached down at the same time to touch him, squeezing gently, eyes shining as she eased back to see him. "Wow," she whispered, "does that hurt?"

"No." He was torn between looking at her breasts and at where she was holding him.

"It's incredible." Her curious fingers seemed to have a mind of their own. "Does that mean you're out of control?"

"I don't think you're supposed to talk about it so much." He bent forward, daring himself to do the thing he wanted most, kissing her nipples, taking them one at a time in his mouth.

They knelt in the pine needles, and she seemed very happy for him to keep tonguing and kissing her breasts, she stroking his hair and cheeks, touching his erection. Above, the airy boughs of white pine were sprays of palest amber on pewter cream.

And then he became aware of her voice, as if something in her breathy flesh had connected in her to form a new resolve.

"Michael, I think I'm ready now."

She drew his face to her lips and then pulled him forward onto her.

"Maybe we should wait."

"No, no, not now ... come on."

He knelt back on his knees between her thighs, her white body stretched upon the dark earth, the look of her like that—thrilling.

"Are you okay? Know what I mean? Shouldn't I be using something?"

"I'm fine, I'm fine." The eagerness in her face, the incredible desire in the electric whites of her eyes, was something unimagined in his young life. "I'm a big girl, Michael."

She reached and touched him, and he was hard again.

He brought himself over her. She tried adjusting her pelvis, angling higher.

"Sorry," he whispered, "I'm not very good at this."

She grimaced at his awkward thrusts and kissed the side of his face.

"Okay, okay ..." She was reaching down, guiding him. "There, now, there ... push, ugh."

She was a little dry, initially, and tense despite all her ardor, and the mechanics were beginning to inhibit the flow of things. For a moment, she became very quiet, as if drawing strength in memory, or drawing resolve from her own bloodline, something of the practical genius of her race coming to her rescue. She pushed him up very gently to his knees, lifted herself, and daintily spit into her fingertips, then reached to wet the tip of him and bring him back with two strong strokes.

Her hand at his neck poured him down once again.

"Here, darling." The expression, or her husky voice, as if prompted out of some ever-present past, woke him fully to reassuring instinct. "Yes, yes, there—there you are. Oh, do you feel it, Michael?" At this, he paused a moment, pulling himself up to stare into the sharded star points of her eyes. "Yes, stay with me, stay with me, just like that. Ugh—so much of you. You are good, you're so good. Slowly, slowly … can you feel me? Can you? Oh my God. Keep kissing me. Darling, Michael, you're mine, you're really mine."

CHAPTER 3

He stood a while longer now, thirty years later, on the riverbank, strangely immune to the scene of their lovemaking, feeling almost nothing as he dissected his remembered lust. What an idiot he'd been to swallow her story about the accident with the baby, and he little better with his self-indulgent spouting of Thoreau. And he'd probably been a terrible lover in the bargain. He'd had no idea—back then, technically—about woman's satisfactions. But she hadn't seemed unhappy about his performance. In fact, she'd clung on and on, not wanting to get dressed, not wanting to leave this place. Their good-byes had been tender and caring, filled with every expectation of seeing one another again. He'd been so in love that the subsequent disaster of being collared on the way back to his dorm by a team of faculty members on the lookout for the missing couple had hardly fazed him.

In his disciplinary interview with the headmaster the following day, he'd been forthright in his explanation for the broken banister in the boathouse—as if galvanized by her pluck and nonchalance. He was certainly not his usual sycophantic, cringing self. The headmaster had stormed around his office, repeating the name Palmer, as if incredulous that he, Michael Collins, sitting with ramrod-straight equanimity, a scholarship kid from Lowell, had dared to tamper with such a girl, daughter of an alumnus and granddaughter of another. Michael was put on disciplinary probation, restricted to campus, and warned against further contact with Sandra Palmer.

He went through those agonizing months of probation in his mind as if compiling a brief, tiptoeing toward his final disastrous confrontation with Sandra Palmer on a freezing February afternoon near Monument Square in Concord.

"Sandra."

He'd shouted her name, surprising himself. She stopped, a figure in a long loden coat of hunter green, her chin bent to a fur-lined collar, breath snatched in bursts by the bitter wind. Then she turned as he ran up to her.

"You've, you've ... cut your hair," he stammered, steadying himself on the icy sidewalk.

"What?" Her blue eyes blazed, distracted.

"I've been trying to reach you. You got my letters, didn't you?"

She bridled, wind flicking her blond bangs, as she pulled herself to full height.

"I don't know what the hell you're talking about."

"I tried phoning over Christmas, but I couldn't find your new number. I even went to your old house."

"Jesus—gotta go." She scowled and turned to continue on, preoccupied.

"Sandra, wait, listen. I really wanted to see you, but I've been on probation, restricted to campus. Hell, I almost got kicked out." He made a grab at her arm and she turned at his touch.

"I'm late, see, and I don't know what the fuck you want, but I really don't want any—okay?"

"Sandra?"

The hard edges of her mouth softened a moment at the hint of panic in his voice. For a few seconds, her face registered concern, a vague simmering realization; then there was a fierce dismissive tightening of her eyes.

"I really do have to go."

The flashing note of sympathy only encouraged him.

"You promised to write."

"Write? God, who has time to write anymore."

He scanned the plowed street. "I'm not supposed to see you, talk to you."

"Well," she snorted, "you got that much right."

He gripped her arm forcefully, resisting her effort to pull free as he fumbled for words.

She screamed. "Hey."

"Didn't any of it matter to you—mean anything?"

"You gotta be joking. Asshole. Let the fuck go."

She snatched her arm free and backed away, cautioning him with raised and flattened palms, her high black boots crunching on the salted sidewalk.

"Is that it? Is that all it meant?" He was wiping at tears of horrified frustration.

The wind howled, staggering them. Then seconds of raw silence as a powder of snow spewed up in a blinding onslaught. She rubbed at her reddened face, her lips relaxing at the edges and her chin rising, poised in unaccustomed sympathy toward the handsome young man shivering in a blue parka.

"Ah, listen, okay ..." She looked around, as if chastened by some force of nature, something akin to guilt. "Maybe we could go get a hot chocolate or something." Her voice faltered, as if she were trespassing on some inner resolve or interrupted by some latent kindness in her nature. "The inn is right here—okay?"

She turned suddenly, as if needing to embrace her better self, get it done before she could change her mind.

"No, I can't do that—*you know*, my mother."

He saw her bridle, as if his admitted embarrassment had shattered her crystallizing resolution. A note of panic snapped in her voice.

"Your mother?"

"You know."

"Yeah, right—bad idea, *terrible idea*. I really got to go."

She walked away. He ran and grabbed her.

"Let go, you pathetic jerk."

"Please."

"Who the *hell* do you think *you* are?"

"So it was a joke—everything we talked about?"

"Get lost, okay. Get the fuck away from me."

The immediacy of recollected pain was so electric that he staggered, terrified as he almost tumbled into the river from the sloping bank. He stood, panting over the dark water, as if some part of him had actually fallen in and he was peering after the disappearing body.

"Sandra …"

Her devastating words had sparked such anger in the young man he'd once been that he had returned to school, gone down to the river, and systematically broken every window in the boathouse. She had released his father's temper in him, and his horror at the result had led him to a life of subterfuge and meticulous calculation. No one had ever gotten to him like that again: He'd lived a life in which he would never be rendered so vulnerable.

And yet, holding his ground on the riverbank, the pain of that final exchange dulling, he found himself intensely curious. The odd disconnects in their conversation were now so apparent. It was as if the space of years brought the night of the dance and their last meeting four months later on Monument Square into such tantalizing proximity that he could not quite believe she, the girl at the dance, was the same one he'd met later; or that human nature could so readily be transformed into a thing of ugliness and reproach. He rolled his eyes. Happens all the time, Michael. But his cynicism was tempered by the certainty that if such an exchange had occurred in a trial, he would have known that Sandra Palmer was lying through her teeth. She'd known all about his mother being at the inn, how shy and embarrassed he'd been to admit she worked as a waitress, never mind taking a friend there.

Worse, his cold analysis left him with a gnawing sense that he had made a profound and stupid mistake, the full cost for which was only now becoming apparent.

A flashlight beam exploded across his face.

"Hey," he cried in surprise, shielding his eyes.

"Sorry, mister, but I think it's probably time you got going."

The night watchman lowered the beam to his chest, then lower, to where his left hand was stuck in a pocket, the right holding a dangling tie.

"Christ, you scared the hell out of me. How about turning that thing off."

"What are you doing here?"

"I went to school here. I rowed on the river."

"Old kid, huh?" The watchman lowered the beam to the wooden dock and flicked it off. In the dull moonlight, his quarry was easily visible in his pinstripe trousers and white oxford shirt, unbuttoned at the collar, sleeves rolled up. "Saw you pull into the faculty parking lot and followed you down here. Can't have people showing up at all hours."

"Ridiculous." Michael stuck the tie in his shirt pocket. "I was just driving nearby, heard this oldie from my senior year, and just had this need to see the place."

He turned from the leaden surface of the river to look at the older man, whose gray hair stuck out from beneath a Red Sox baseball cap. His leather utility belt was hung with keys, cuffs, time box, mace, and God knows what else. The watchman holstered the long-barreled flashlight.

"You might be comforted to know how often it happens."

"Happens?"

"Old kids like you dropping by at all hours."

"No kidding."

They turned, as if at a wordless signal, and began walking up the path through the trees. The expression the watchman used kept bobbing up in his mind … *old kids.* Such a poignant oxymoron, as if something of youth never fades, the something never entirely obscured by the adult mask. He stopped as they passed the boathouse.

"I don't suppose you've got a key … to the boathouse?"

The watchman eyed him uneasily. "I do, but I can't let you in—insurance regulations, among other things. You okay?"

"Thought I'd take a peek—old times' sake."

They continued walking, the illumination from above enough to see the path but little of the surrounding woods. The watchman pulled off his Red Sox cap and scratched his head.

"I didn't mean to startle you back there, but you can't be too careful these days. About a year ago, guy about your age showed up here one night. Now, I didn't see him, you understand. But this guy had walked all the way from Brookline, walked most of the day. People had seen him on the road. Must have gotten here about two in the morning. That's what the police figure anyway. Goes into the chapel, sits and reads a prayer book—they found the book open in the first pew—and then goes up to the top of the bell tower and jumps. Now, the amazing thing, I must have seen the body half a dozen times that night, passed within twenty feet of where it lay next to some leaf bags at the base of the tower. But, see, I think it's just another bag. Like I said, it was dark, moonless. Imagine my surprise at first dawn. I'm making my last round and there is this guy I've been seeing all night, with his face in the grass, crumpled like a pretzel. And he's a stiff. I felt like I'd really messed up."

"How'd they know it wasn't just an accident?"

"Legs were all broken up. Accident, they go headfirst."

"Huh."

"They say he'd been depressed. A banker, worth millions, too. Guess he'd been divorced. A religious man. I went to the memorial service in the chapel. Figured maybe I owed it to the guy, it being me who found him. Quite a fellow, to hear people tell it. Tears all around. Lovely kids, too."

"Married guy?"

"Yeah, with kids. Can you believe it?"

"No, I can't, I can't."

"But you want to know the really strange part? The chapel is often left unlocked, but the bell tower is always locked, very strict about that, what with the big bells up there and everything. But this guy, he had a key, had a key from the days when he was a bell ringer, when he was a kid twenty-five years ago. Kept the key all that time and nobody had ever changed the lock. He left the key on a table up there, as if he'd just forgot to return it."

"Or … he'd been keeping it all that time—just for that purpose."

They stopped a moment where the path to the river emerged from the woods and stared up at the vague contours of the chapel tower. Michael found himself oddly taken with the old watchman. His accent, and his demeanor reminded him of his father, or the man his father might have become if he hadn't run off to the Alaskan oil boom of the late sixties. This was how his father might have been if he'd stayed and moved to the suburbs like everybody else, maybe to work construction in the suburban housing boom, or even as a night watchman. And the watchman's story, his bafflement about the suicide, registered as a kind of omen to Michael of what lay in store for his own empty life, as if his out-of-character behavior and scruffy, unshaven face, had raised concerns along those lines in the mind of the old man at his elbow.

Feeling as if his life, or maybe all life, had taken on the liquid quality of passing time, he thought back again to Sandra's words about Thoreau, echoing his own on the veranda of the dining hall: When you stepped away from the habitual path—even an inch, how it all might be different, how a deeper truth might be staring you in the face. And a different life.

The watchman shook his head. "Funny, I can't quite come up with his name."

"Huh?"

"The name of the jumper."

"I don't want to know. Just in case I remember him as a kid … someone from my class."

"And what class was that?"

Michael's reticence seemed to melt from him and he was more forthcoming than might have been wise under the circumstances.

"Nineteen seventy."

"A few years before I started working here. Vietnam times. Hope you weren't one of those protest hippie types. Had my fill of them back then."

"Me, hell, I was a straight arrow. Had to be—I was a scholarship kid. February 1970, they kicked me out of this place. Lost my college deferment and got drafted. Ended up in Vietnam."

"Kicked out. What did you do, lad?"

"Oh, I broke a few windows."

"A few windows, was it?"

"Just a few."

"Well, and a veteran. You are a rare bird for these parts."

They continued walking past the soccer fields.

"Not much has changed," Michael said.

"People your age coming back, they say it's a country club now, what with the girls and all."

"I'd forgotten it had gone coed."

"Hey, you don't want to know. Me on night shift …" The man raised his eyebrows in a devil-may-care expression. "Like bunnies, they are, and it would tax your wildest dreams the places they find to have it off with one another."

"A lot of sex, huh?"

"Can you blame them, shacked up cheek by jowl. Christ, the infirmary hands the stuff out—condoms, pills, you name it. AIDS awareness. Course, none of my business. Powers that be don't want to know what goes on. So I keep my mouth shut and just tell the kids to move on."

They were walking toward the parking lot near the dining hall. Michael contemplated asking the watchman if he might let him in to see the portrait of Joseph Palmer, then thought better of it.

Instead, he offered a jovial reply. "Bet you're a popular guy."

"The late shift is a breeze. My brother Frank does the six to midnight—that's trouble. After twelve, even the kids got to get some shut-eye."

"You two work the same job, huh?"

"Hell, we served in the Pacific together. Best time of our lives. It's always with us—know what I mean?"

"Hot, though. Hard to believe it's September."

"Hey, beats winter, mister. Freeze your nuts off in a job like this."

"I'll bet."

"I'll tell you, when it's hot like this, stars out, takes me right back to Gugan, little island in the Marianas where me and Frank spent two years in the Army Air Corps. Just an island and a runway—about it. A stepping-stone for long-range bombers, emergency strip if somebody got into trouble. At night, me and Frank set up our hammocks between palm trees near the runway. Buck naked beneath the stars, the sound of the sea, breeze in your hair, suspended beneath more stars than you can imagine. No mosquitoes, neither. Never saw a Jap. And those nights, like you was staring into the eye of heaven. Still dream about it, dream about dreams—know what I mean? And when Frank comes and relieves me round midnight, puts his hand on my shoulder and points up to the stars—doesn't have to say a word. It's like we was back there all those years before, back on Gugan. I tell you, like a dream."

"A dream, huh … like a dream I had this afternoon ten thousand feet over Logan."

"A sky high dream was it?"

"Back when my brother and I—when we were kids—played along the banks of the Concord. We always wore identical Red Sox caps … as if it could have changed anything."

The old man nodded knowingly.

"And in the morning, me and Frank would be wakened by this sound: smack, smack, smack. Know what—seagulls dropping clams onto the runway. Me and Frank could never figure it, what the hell those gulls did before we built that runway."

"They say the Sox are having a great year."

"You sure you're okay?"

"I just flew into Boston; I'm on my way to my brother's funeral."

"Sorry to hear that."

"It's okay. We weren't exactly close."

"Somewhere around here, the funeral?"

"No, up river a bit ... Lowell."

"Lowell. No kidding. Frank and me were born and raised in Lowell, but we got our butts out after the war, before it went to hell in a handbasket. Not that the Depression was a bed of roses."

"Yeah, me and Jimmy, too. Born and raised."

"Funny," said the night watchman, turning to the younger man in his white shirt and dress pants and black wing tips, scrutinizing the angular face, the slanted ridge of the nose, the dark wavy hair with a businesslike cut showing streaks of gray above the ears. "To hear you ... well, I'd never know you was from Lowell."

"Been living in Washington for nearly twenty years."

"Ah, guess that explains it."

"Too long in fact."

"I guess with the impeachment stuff last year, the scandals."

"You got it, a lifetime trying to stay out of trouble."

They reached the parking lot and walked to his Ford Taurus.

"Sorry about your brother. Hope it wasn't a nasty case of the big C or anything."

"He was an alcoholic. He fell off a telephone pole at two in the morning trying to wire into his neighbor's cable connection."

"Jesus, Mary, and Joseph ... for a cable connection?"

"Jimmy, what can I say. He was a chip off the old block. Always looking to squeeze one by."

"What did you say your name was?"

"Collins, Michael Collins."

The night watchman removed his cap and wiped at his brow with his sleeve, pondering the younger man as he opened the door to his rental car.

"Collins, familiar name."

"There're millions."

"Jimbo, Jimbo Collins—was it minor-league ball? Maybe American Legion ball in the early fifties."

Michael ignored the reference, choosing not to remember.

"Our father … lots of aspirations," he said. He slid into his seat and reached up a hand. "It's nice meeting you."

"Sure you're okay driving?"

"It's just up the river."

"Right—same river, but night and day in my book."

"Hey, haven't you heard? Lowell's made a big comeback in the last two decades."

"That's what they tell me, but wild horses couldn't drag me back."

"Check it out, man, you'll hardly recognize parts of the downtown along the Pawtucket Canal. Take it from me."

Michael held out his hand.

"A scholarship kid from Lowell—huh. Well, good for you, boy. Hey, and remember what my brother Frank always tells me: 'Get a grip, man—we're all stardust.'"

"Stardust, huh. Well …"

The kind words of the night watchman distracted him for a few minutes more before he remembered the FedEx pack containing $400,000 in fifty-dollar bills in the trunk.

CHAPTER 4

A s he turned the car on to River Street in Lowell, he half-expected to find the streets of Victorian gingerbread double-deckers—turn-of-the-century ticky-tack affairs right out of a Sears catalog—bulldozed for pricey new condos or the near ruins he recalled from childhood. And yet, it was almost how he'd remembered, except…. He slowed the car to a crawl. The neighborhood seemed spruced up, with lots of bright colors and white picket fences, Japanese miniature maples, immaculate gardens and porch swings. He pulled up in front of their old house and squinted in the glow of the modern streetlights that had replaced the broken and missing lamps of memory. The clapboard house—which had become Jimmy's house—had been painted kelly green with tan shutters and Anderson double-glazed windows, by the look of them. There was a new front porch, a brass eagle knocker, and a brick walkway to boot. Gone were the rusted chain-link fence and trashed front yard.

Well, maybe Jimmy had made an effort at respectability after all.

As he got out of the car and fumbled for the key sent to him by Father Murphy, he began to hear Spanish voices rich with laughter and Latino music from a boom box. A guy was washing his car down the street. The curbs were lined with late-model compacts and high-riding heaps painted with bright, wild designs.

How about that—his childhood vision transformed into a vibrant Hispanic neighborhood with touches right out of Martha Stewart. He didn't know whether to laugh or cry: his melting-pot hometown cease-lessly reshuffling the deck so that jokers like Michael Collins could float free.

Jimmy had stuck, kept up appearances like good ole lace-curtain Irish. Good for you, boy-o. Some fifteen or twenty years before, Jimmy had bought back the family home for a song, in the days before the Lowell Plan, when the city was still a disaster zone after all the mills had closed. Later, Jimmy had trouble with the tax bill, once housing prices were on the rise with the city's new prosperity. So Jimmy called his big-shot brother in D.C. for a loan. That's when Michael had gotten his brother a job driving for the congressman's reelection campaign. Jimmy had never invited him by the old house. The few times they'd met over the previous years, when Michael had flown in from Washington for a ribbon-cutting ceremony or some such event, it had always been on neutral ground at a local pub or bar. According to Father Murphy, there were still a few tax bills outstanding.

As Michael mated the key with the lock on the front door, Jimmy's romantic riffs sprang to mind, all his inebriated nostalgia passed down father to son like a badge of misbegotten honor, and all their dead-end arguments over building projects to get the city moving ahead.

"It's all the Irish really had in this country, Michael, these old neighborhoods, all we'll ever have of a real community. Knock them down for Yuppie condos and there'll be nothing left."

"Know what makes America great, Jimmy? Nobody gives a fuck where you're from or what your father did, only what you've got to offer."

"Michael, you are truly a rare creature—or maybe you are the future: a man without a past."

With his brother's words ringing in his ears, he took a deep breath and turned the key in the lock and entered.

The smells stopped him dead. He felt for the light switch in the narrow hall. The place was a mess, seething with old newspapers and magazine stacked in the corners, clear plastic bags full of returnables. And worse: the stink of booze, beer stains on the linoleum flooring, the damp plaster. It was worse even than when the family had lived in the house, when his grandfather Giovanni would attempt repairs as best he could. Michael moved on to the tiny living room-dining room, and was shocked to find that Jimmy had filled the house with old furniture, even an old upright piano with shattered keyboard to approximate the look and feel of the place when they'd lived there as a family. Scattered about were furnishings from their mother's apartment in Carlisle, the few things she'd brought with her, right down to the piano music stacked on the upright.

"Un-fucking-believable." He shook his head. "Jimmy ... Jimmy ...
Jimmy."

He stepped back from the piano.

He pictured his father's flushed face and bloodshot eyes as he took his
swing, a right uppercut, and flattened his mother's nose. He'd knocked
her to the floor, where she'd lain screaming, thrashing about, spitting
blood, the flesh and cartilage that had been her nose flapping against
her cheek. Twelve years old and he'd led his mother by the hand to a
neighbor's car and then the emergency room, a kitchen towel wadded
against her face. His father had left for good the next morning when he
woke from his stupor and remembered what he'd done ... or when he'd
seen the blood on the floor.

As if to expunge the scene, Michael began leafing through the piano
music, much of it from the thirties, when his mother had been growing
up. She'd passed the music on to him when he began lessons with her.
He found the well-worn edition of Chopin Etudes and paged through the
score, smiling at his mother's fingerings and annotations: *Michael, let the
music sing in the adagio and then let your playing sing along; Michael,
listen to what you're playing and* stop *reading the notes.*

"Oh God ..."

How his mother knew him, his strengths and weaknesses. She knew
him before he even knew himself.

He took a deep breath and walked into the kitchen, where he was
immediately confronted with the ancient porcelain sink and brass tap and
the memories of his mother bent over it as the blood spewed from her
smashed nose. Not a thing changed or renovated. He touched the worn
handle of the near-antique Frigidaire. At the very least, Jimmy would've
had to replace the compressor. Jimmy could fix anything, just like his old
man. The exterior renovations had been pure facade, so the neighbors
wouldn't complain or get nosy. No wonder Jimmy hadn't offered to have
him come round to visit.

His chest heaved with incipient anger, that Jimmy should try to
hold on to the physical proof of memory like this—what others slip
into photo albums, what until just moments before had been his and
his alone tucked safely away in the depths of his mind. Except now
Jimmy was gone and such a history as existed in this place was truly
his, exclusively his ... and when the house was sold off to pay back taxes

and got scraped or renovated, those memories, too, could be properly consigned to the dustbin.

He smiled icily at the thought.

He turned to the narrow staircase, mounted the stairs, and at the top he went into what had been their boyhood bedroom. A tiny fridge, seemingly on its last legs, made a spooky knocking noise; he found an open carton of milk inside, two Burger king bags, doughnuts, a six-pack of Miller. In the corners and in the back of the closet, he discovered empty vodka bottles. There was a mattress on the floor with disheveled and dirty sheets. Red Sox and Bruins posters were duct-taped to the peeling walls. The ancient Zenith television by the single window had cable lines hanging lose. The stink was somewhere between a boys' locker room and a blue-collar bar.

A well-aimed kick with the sole of his shoe sent the television crashing to the floor. For a moment, he stood stunned by the flash of violence in himself that had seemingly come out of nowhere … as if he'd ever been able to save Jimmy from himself.

Then, regaining his composure, he began a careful examination, perhaps a forensic evaluation of family pathologies. A photo of their dad, Jimbo Collins, in an American Legion baseball uniform, posed with his team; the coach, a smiling Father Murphy—younger than Michael remembered from childhood—stood front and center with a bat on his shoulder. He examined the large fistlike face of his father for a moment, the compact nose, a cocky slant to the eyebrows, blond hair slicked back in typical early sixties fashion. Michael smiled to himself, as if in imitation, at the anger compressed behind that troubled grin.

He turned to another photo, a black-and-white publicity shot of their mother in profile at the piano, with her name, Moira Maronetti, in large black letters along the bottom. He figured it must be from the last years of the Depression, when she had played local college recital halls in hopes of a piano scholarship at the New England Conservatory. He picked up the photograph and angled it toward the light from the window. She was pretty all right, even with that Maronetti nose, lovely deep-set eyes intent on the keyboard, large hands for a woman … perhaps more handsome than beautiful.

How could she have married that creep?

He extracted the photo from the frame, nudged by a hint of jealousy (or was it triumph?) and with the realization that he'd never had any family photos around his place and almost nothing on the walls except posters and architectural renderings of the old mills to be renovated. Something his onetime fiancée, Catherine, had commented on with that ditzy wringing of her hands: *Michael, surely you've got some family ... somewhere?*

On the bureau were shoe boxes of baseballs signed by Red Sox teams from the eighties and nineties, but strangely nothing going back to their childhood in the sixties, when their dad had enlisted his boys in his Fenway Park "bleacher-preachers," so they'd called themselves, when each time at bat lefty Carl Yastrzemski had put a buzz through Jimbo's crowd like a Baptist choir on cocaine highs. Michael shivered at the memories of being dragged to Fenway Park.

As he pivoted from the bureau, his shoe hit something. He bent down. Sticking out from under the bureau were the remnants of a Lionel train set, bits of track mostly, old, too, at least from his father's time, maybe even something Jimbo Collins had had as a kid. Always his father's proud boast: how his great-grandfather—or maybe it had been his great-great-grandfather—Michael was never sure—had built the Boston and Fitchburg railroad. As tiny kids, living in their grandmother's home in the Acre, Lowell's original Irish enclave, they had played with electric trains. Jimbo Collins had set up the tracks in their bedroom and later around the Christmas tree, Michael and Jimmy sitting there in the middle, watching the train go around while Jimbo, hand on the throttle, slugged back cans of Budweiser.

He picked up a curved bit of the miniature track, the connectors bent, dusty ... and yet the object intrigued him, stirred some vague allegiance. He casually stuck the thing in his coat pocket along with the photograph of his mother.

He took a last survey; clearly, Jimmy had *lived* in his bedroom.

Bachelor pad: something he and Jimmy had in common.

Strangely, his grandfather Giovanni's bedroom across the hall from the single bathroom was empty, as if Jimmy had been unable to conjure any means of populating it with artifacts, much less using it for storage. Even when Giovanni had been using the bedroom, he kept no more than the bare essentials: a bed and dresser and coatrack, as if his real life was up in his workshop at the graveyard. Or as if the real one was his earlier life with his wife, Moira Shannon, at the old house in the Acre, before Moira died and her daughter hooked up with a no-good racist brawler.

Giovanni had never really felt at home in the house on River Street; he was always late for dinner, always taking his good time by way of the long detour of the Pawtucket Canal, always leaving his son-in-law, Jimbo Collins, spitting mad and cursing out the old man as dinner waited. How many times had Michael's mother sent him off to Giovanni's workshop, cheek by jowl with the municipal cemetery, or out along the path by the Pawtucket Canal to hurry his grandfather along before mean-tempered Jimbo did something awful? How they'd lived in fear of Jimbo's temper.

He shook his head and moved on. Giovanni's empty bedroom lingered in his mind, epitomizing the lost world of his grandfather, which had remained concealed from him by chance or design.

His mother's old bedroom turned out to have quite the opposite effect. Standing in the doorway, he couldn't believe his eyes. Jimmy had obviously rescued most of her stuff from the apartment in Carlisle, things she'd originally brought from River Street. He had then carefully re-created her room, right down to the bed with the brass railings, her brushes and combs on the oak dresser, the cherry-wood mirror, Giovanni's rolltop desk, come from his shop after he drowned, and an etching of Venice on the wall next to the mirror. What's more, the room was immaculate, clean, dusted, smelling of lemon Pledge, the smell their mother loved.

The sensations of his mother's life, as if he had popped the cork on a vintage wine, streamed in upon him, so much so that he reached out for the brass bedstead to steady himself. The place was like a shrine; as if Jimmy had tried to steal the life of their mother the way he tried to steal cable transmissions.

Despite what he had considered exclusively his own in memory, he had to admit Jimmy had done him one better.

"Jesus, Mary, and Joseph, Jimmy, get a fucking life, will ya."

And yet he had to smile through his tears at what he'd always thought of as Jimmy's pathological nostalgia, that streak of romantic Irishness.

Surveying the room from his mother's bed, he found himself taken back to a night long before. Early evening, it had been, when he'd been picked up by the police under the Andover Street bridge. He had been reading and had lost track of the time, a habit that pissed off his father and placed him firmly in Giovanni's camp. "Just like your brainless Wop grandpa," Jimbo would say.

Later, lying on his mother's bed in his pajamas, an old library copy of *Walden* in hand, he had been going on and on about Thoreau and Concord, asking a million questions. His mother had been standing before her mirror, listening patiently, combing her long raven-colored hair. Next to the mirror on the wall was the etching of Venice that had once hung in Giovanni's shop. From where Michael had lain on the bed, he could see her face reflected in the glass of the etching, her familiar brown eyes and prominent nose transposed to a faraway scene of a bridge over a canal, where two women with parasols stood watching their reflections in the water below. Giovanni had been dead over a year by then, drowned on the night of that terrible summer windstorm that had brought down trees and power lines all over the city—a week's cleanup. His father had disappeared six months later, after Giovanni's accident. That evening, his brother, Jimmy, was off to a Red Sox game with Father Murphy. Father Murphy had taken Jimmy under his wing, giving up on Michael, the "bookworm brother."

He'd had his mother to himself.

"Did you know he built this little house by the side of Walden Pond, just big enough for himself?"

"Is that right, Michael."

"And his bed and a writing table and his books, of course."

"Books, huh, of course. But not a piano?"

"Oh, Mom … And do you know that the Concord River, our river, goes all the way to the town of Concord?"

"Is that how it got its name, do you think, from the town? Or was it the river that gave the name to the town?"

"It had another name in the beginning, an Indian name, the Musketa-quid. That what the Indians called it; it means 'grass-ground river.'"

Moira turned from her vigil in the mirror to her precocious child and smiled at his enthusiasm. Then she went to the drawer of Giovanni's rolltop desk and pulled out—as if by sleight of hand—the very same book, except this *Walden* was bound in green morocco leather with gold lettering and smelled of beeswax and old bindings, and just a hint of the powdered marble that had pervaded everything in Giovanni's shop.

She handed the book to her son.

"Strange thing," she said, "Giovanni had no real interest in books. He had a hard time making it through the newspaper."

They had compared the volumes, his a beat-up omnibus edition from a library sale, Giovanni's a rare numbered and limited edition, exquisitely bound, expensive, the fine morocco leather talismanic when held in the hands. This coincidence—although he had seen it as *no* coincidence—was the first intimation in his young mind of a new faith: a belief in the existence of a better world than the run-down streets of Lowell. What his mother called, "higher things."

"It's like the genius of Chopin, Michael. Can't you feel it? All those years ago, Michael—think of it, finding its way to your fingertips."

The book had been the thing, providing the imaginative leap for their escape from Lowell.

For Moira Maronetti Collins had taken to reading the green morocco *Walden*; and in the days to follow, it had become a kind of genial code between mother and son, a bedrock of renewed hope after the terrible events of the previous year. The book buoyed their days. One thing led to another, and within the year Moira had sold the house on River Street for next to nothing, gotten herself a rental apartment in Carlisle, a waitressing job at the Concord Inn, and later had marched right on into the flossy admissions office of nearby Emerson Academy (the walls hung with original Audubon prints) and found out about the scholarship possibilities for her bookish son. While Jimmy, obdurate, faithful Jimmy, had insisted on taking the bus every day from Carlisle back to high school in Lowell.

Michael sat dazed, as if the short-circuited emotions of a previous existence were beginning to come through to him again.

His trepidation mounting, he went to the rolltop desk and opened the top drawer. He blinked. The green morocco *Walden* was right where his mother had always kept it. He picked it up, smelled again the beeswax and leather and marble dust and old binding. He leafed through the underlined and annotated pages. There was a folded letter from the manager of the Concord Inn confirming his mother's waitressing job. Then, as he replaced the letter under the front cover, he noticed the striking bookplate in black and crimson, a depiction of palette and brushes and the inscription: *Joseph Palmer – Ars Longa, Vita Brevis.*

He was dumbstruck. Had he missed this as a kid? Had his mother noticed? Had he forgotten all about it? He stared at the bookplate as if he'd been handed an indictment for criminal negligence. Had his grandfather known Sandra's grandfather, the artist?

It was a sign; he was sure of it. He was not a superstitious man, nor a religious one; he was a lawyer, for Christ sake. Here in this black-and-crimson bookplate was the clearest evidence of his obtuseness: But for his blindness, there might have been a better life than one of legal contracts, of laws and legislation interpreted and drawn up to further the advantage of some, while keeping others out of trouble.

In the backwash of this leap of illogic, he drifted over to the single window and looked out over River Street: no longer the slum of memory, but part of a charming and vibrant ethnic community. Across the street, beyond the rooftops, was just a glinting hint of the Concord River, only three hundred yards before it entered the Merrimack, along the shore where he and Jimmy had played….

And like that, the vision he'd been grasping at—that daydream at ten thousand feet—since the airport came back to him. It was an image of two brothers standing on a large flat rock in the middle of the Concord River. The rock was connected to the shore by way of a painstakingly constructed causeway of stepping-stones. Days and days of labor it had taken them to create their tiny island retreat from the world of adult rancor—a place where they could collect treasures floating downstream. He saw his and Jimmy's faces reflected in the river, partially shadowed by Red Sox caps, their high-top Keds soaked, a spring freshet bubbling in patterns of filigreed gold passed their small vantage point. And contained within that picture of two brothers with arms around each other's shoulders, an unprecedented surge of good feeling—happiness of a kind that tingled the hairs at the back of his neck.

What was invoked was something of the first year the family had moved from the old Irish enclave in the Acre to their new home on River Street. His grandfather Giovanni's funerary-monument business had been thriving. This was just before his father got injured on the construction of the Route 495 flyover, before his mother had to give up her piano teaching for a better-paying job at the storage warehouse, when she still practiced the piano half the night. It had to be sometime before his father's drinking began in earnest and with it the quarrelsome hatred that would turn the family into enemy camps.

Before Giovanni's accidental drowning … and before the family disintegrated.

When he and Jimmy, best pals, had stood against the world.

For that rarest of moments, he tried to hold on to the fleeting sense of well-being that presupposed a place of repose, of a wholeness within that envelope of space where two boys gazed into the flowing river, which brought them the most fabulous treasures of waning childhood: inner tubes, splintered paddles and knotted ropes, yellow life jackets swept down from an upstream world as yet unnavigated and barely imagined: Thoreau's Concord.

He lifted his gaze now to the distant flanks of the Pawtucket Canal and the silhouetted roofline of the Palmer Mill (built by Sandra Palmer's great-great-grandfather) and now under threat by construction magnate Jack Mahoney, who wanted to turn it into an upscale mall.

"Palmer Mill Mall," he muttered dismissively, remembering that FedEx pack, the bribe sent to him by Jack Mahoney, sitting in the trunk of his car.

He grimaced and closed his eyes as if to dismiss this sad coda to an otherwise-unblemished career.

When he opened his eyes again, he found himself staring at the telephone pole on the near curb, which carried the electric and cable lines, the pole from which his brother had fallen, crashing through the windshield of a late-model Chevy Impala. The coroner reported Jimmy's death as due to loss of blood from a four-inch cut on the side of his neck. The owner of the Impala was looking for compensation. He thought of the night watchman's story about the old kid jumping from the tower. He shuddered, feeling the fall in himself, hearing voices from the past conjuring premonitions about his dismal prospects.

He went back to the desk and the green morocco *Walden*, and as he did, his gaze settled on the etching of Venice hanging by the mirror.

It was as if he knew, as if he'd known all along.

He took down the etching and began to examine the scene of the two women on a bridge over the canal. They wore old-fashioned gowns and carried parasols angled across their bent shoulders. They contemplated their reflections in the canal below. Even though their faces were in shadow, enough of their features were visible to hint at a pedigreed and aloof beauty. Something familiar … and yet not.

He turned the frame over to the crinkled and loose cardboard backing and rusty brads. The thing was old. It had hung in Giovanni's shop by his desk for as long as Michael could remember. Turning it to the front, he noticed that the etching had slipped in the matting, covering the plate mark and anything in the way of a title or signature. A moment later, he was stripping off the brittle brown paper backing and finally maneuvering out the warped cardboard. A folded bit of yellowed newspaper fell out, and as it did, the matting opened and the etching slipped free from its torn mounts. He held up the bit of antique laid paper to the light, seeing the half-crown watermark like a ghost behind the veil of ink; and then held it out to read the neat inscription that had been covered by the matting.

The etching had been titled on the bottom left corner: *Sisters*.

And to the right of this read:

To my friend and fellow artist, Giovanni Maronetti, for all his enduring gifts to me and my loved ones during these difficult days, Joseph Palmer. Artist's proof number one, Venice, 1914.

He carried this most delicate of time's offerings over to the desk and propped it against the green morocco *Walden*.

"*Joseph Palmer*," he intoned, and again, as if hearing the name in his own voice set the seal on the new reality. "*Joseph Palmer and Giovanni Maronetti*."

The name returned him to the large portrait in the school dining hall of Sandra's artist grandfather: the compact staring face and glinting eyes and the lush blue atmosphere of the artist's studio … the sketches of Venice and the figure studies.

Just saying the names seemed to release him from the purgatory of the previous hours and days, as if he'd turned the key to a lost faith in a world of correspondences, where the finest things outlast time.

"*Sisters* …" He squinted again to read the inscription. "Sandra … Sandra … Palmer."

In the dim light of the single overhead bulb in his mother's old bedroom, he bent to the etching of the bridge and the two women, in search of what precisely he had gotten wrong. Here was another proof of his hidebound and hermetic existence: yes, a total failure of imagination.

In the minutes that followed, he found himself enthralled by the tiniest details of the etching, the way the filigree of hatched lines and inky blottings implied things not quite there, things to stir the admiration of a true connoisseur. How the halftones seemed to vibrate mysteriously under his gaze. Even the swirl of the artist's fingerprint in the watery passages of retroussage mirrored some vagrant sensation in himself: that genuineness of purpose—and escape—once glimpsed in the pages of Thoreau.

To live wild and free.

And everything he had lost sight of.

He reached a fingertip to the artist's inky thumbprint, sensing in that vague nimbus the consubstantial crossing point between art and life.

CHAPTER 5

From the air-conditioned safety of his factory-fresh Ford Taurus, Michael reviewed his handiwork. Downtown Lowell seemed even more well scrubbed, trendy, and upscale than he remembered from past years' attendance at ribbon-cutting ceremonies. The converted mill buildings housing an array of small to medium-size high-tech firms fairly gushed prosperity: parking lots glittering with Grand Cherokees and Mercedes, nearby Starbucks vying with Coffee Express, sushi bars elbowing modern Milanese restaurants—northern Italian cuisine as opposed to southern, all sheltering under candy-stripped Victorian awnings. Every detail—he'd written the statutes—had to be scrupulously vetted by the historical preservation commission. Tourists wandered the reinstalled cobblestone streets, soaking up the historical atmosphere. The National Parks Mill Museum in the old Appleton Mill—centerpiece and keystone to the entire Lowell Plan—was positively effusive with colorful banners draped from its brick walls, proclaiming various upcoming ethnic festivals and craft fairs. Yellow school buses (the education angle had always been front and center in the enabling legislation) bunkered entire side streets.

Michael drove slowly, savoring the prospect of the Pawtucket Canal: Grand Canal, the dynamo that had fed the nineteenth-century city, once delivering waterpower from the Merrimack to run thousands of clattering, dust-spewing looms, now the scene for many a power lunch as the business-suited patrons of the Lowell Hilton and convention center took a stroll past the preserved sites of what had been one of the wonders of the first industrial age. He craned his neck to spot the telltale brickwork of the old Palmer Mill, grandest of the grand and the only mill left unrenovated—and therefore prey to the ravenous ambition of Jack Mahoney, his boss's biggest campaign contributor and source of the FedEx pack containing $400,000.

And thus his three o'clock appointment with the police chief in Worcester.

The likes of Jack Mahoney were partly the reason he felt no pride or satisfaction in his accomplishments: the tawdry downtown disaster area of his youth now smothered in gentrification. If anything, he felt a mild glow of professionalism at the brokering of public and private interests, the leveraging of federal and state and local funding—innovative at the time and, for the most part, managed from afar in relative anonymity. Or had it more to do with the way Jimmy saw things: Michael's revenge on an embarrassing childhood, in the diversion of tens of millions of federal and state dollars to sweep away the world of the past. But they had preserved the past; they made it useful again.

The new high-tech Lowell had made Michael a rising star in the district for a few years in the late eighties. The congressman had let it be known for almost a decade that Michael Collins was his anointed successor. It had got to the point where they hired media advisers to plan the campaign, to package him properly—get the product placed early to appeal to the widest number of voters. Whereas his boss had gotten his start in the old machine politics based on the ethnic Irish enclaves in Lowell and Lawrence, the marketing guys saw Michael Collins as the perfect software upgrade to appeal to the suburban upwardly mobile professionals and soccer moms who wanted to protect their daughters' rights to an abortion. They refined his take-away message on jobs, education, health care, and the environment.

But what was going to be his distinctive touch: Who was he going to be? Poor guy from Lowell who made it big? Big deal. Vietnam hero? That had been such a total fuckup that it pained him to think of it. And then there was his alcoholic brother, who'd prove an embarrassment every time he opened his mouth. And dig a little deeper: his father—not just a no-good unemployed construction worker and big-time boozer but also a wife beater, not to mention a racist and a family deserter in the bargain. Hey, a big IRA supporter, too; thus his son's catchy name. All the baggage he didn't even want to think about.

And then there was the wife thing, the dutiful spouse ever at his side, the perfect marketing team to sell family values. God forbid there should be any misperceptions by the working-class voters, even if Massachusetts already had one celebrity gay congressman—and one was enough. And let's face it, that's how Catherine, his ex-fiancée and Mid-Atlantic sales rep for a high-end Italian textile firm, got interested in him in the first place: good career move for her, too. Catherine's eyes had glittered at the prospect: the Washington political scene, along with the possibility to represent some of Boston's toniest suburbs.

As he turned north a few blocks, thirty years seemed to fall away. He was back in Lowell's oldest ethnic neighborhood, the Acre, home to generations of Irish, and still an eyesore of run-down tenements and abandoned housing projects from the heyday of urban renewal in the sixties. At the church of St. Agnes, he ran the car up on the curb and slammed on the brakes—inches from smashing into the parked car in front. Then he rested his forehead on the steering wheel until his breathing calmed. He examined his face in the rearview mirror. He'd fallen asleep at some point on his mother's old bed and awakened late, disoriented, unwashed and unshaven, looking like roadkill and feeling worse. But perhaps this was the way a man should look after the devastating loss of a brother.

"Okay, Michael. Just do it. Just get to the funeral Mass and play your part, boy."

He got out and surveyed St. Agnes, dismal parish church for the Acre, a squat pseudo-Romanesque relic that looked like some miraculous survivor in the bombed Ruhr. The place still gave him the willies. A few times he'd been dragged here to Mass by his father, who was ever dutiful to the faith of his Irish ancestors—for all of the split second it took him to cross himself, that is.

Michael walked across the street to the entrance steps and stopped to listen. The organ was playing. The service had started. He took a seat in the very back of the nave, surprised at the large turnout of mourners, pressed into the seats at the front, nearest the coffin. The candlelit altar looked spectacular with sprays of yellow flowers—the florist actually had done what he had been paid to do. Michael had insisted on a closed coffin, a compromise with Father Murphy, who had entreated him not to have the body cremated. The old priest, ninety if he was a day, was conducting the service in a deep, rich voice, the old voice of the Acre, of his father and all his drunken baseball pals. Father Murphy had scared the bejesus out of him as a kid, what with that terrible ragged scar down his right cheek—badge of honor he'd acquired in defense of the Acre at age fourteen.

Breathing deeply of the incense-laden air to calm his nerves, he inventoried the thousands of inscribed names on the walls—many carved by his grandfather Giovanni Maronetti, generations of mill workers reduced at last to lists and dry statistics in the history books. Who would light candles to them? Hell, he could still bump into people—like that night watchman at Emerson Academy—who wouldn't admit to having been born in Lowell unless pressed.

Finally, he bowed his head and tried to pray, listening to Father Murphy's droning Latin verses and the inaudible responses, wondering why he'd never felt a connection to that ancient community of believers. The close flickering darkness of St. Agnes produced nothing good in the way of memory, much less hope, only a desire to be away from the place as soon as possible. After all, Giovanni had been an Italian socialist of the old school, with an inbred hatred of clergy. His mother had never darkened the door of a church in her life, except to play the piano at an occasional service.

He withdrew his left hand from where he habitually kept it in his pocket and stared at the scarred and missing fingers, third and fourth digits torn off above the knuckle. Giovanni's hands, his mother had said—perfect for piano, artist's hands, according to Sandra Palmer. The bizarre wound (the circumstances he'd never admitted to anyone) had meant an end to both piano and competitive rowing. He held up his right hand and squinted in the dim light at the knuckle Sandra had taken in her teeth, as if something of the bite mark might still be there.

After the service, he stood on the steps outside St. Agnes with Father Murphy, left hand returned to his pocket, and thanked the mourners. The grieving faces galled him, the sentiments even more:

"Last of his kind was Jimmy, a truly fun-loving man."

"Finbar's won't be the same without him."

"I'll think of him every time I see the green of Fenway."

"My goodness you look nothing like Jimmy. Who'd have known you was brothers."

Then he and Father Murphy chatted amiably for a few minutes, going over the details for the burial service to follow and the party to celebrate

Jimmy's life that evening. Father Murphy leaned on his aluminum cane and shook the hand of the younger man with a lingering bony handshake.

"Michael, it's good to see you, even if it is under such unfortunate circumstances."

"Sorry again, Father, for being late."

He yearned to don his sunglasses again in the glare of the sunshine, reassume his anonymity and get it the hell over with. Under the gaze of the wizened priest, the white hair setting off the unflinching gray eyes, he felt transformed back into the sniveling child who had refused to play on the Little League team or attend Sunday school.

"I can't tell you, my boy, how much you remind me of your grandfather Giovanni—that Michelangelo face of yours. My goodness, it takes me back to the old days. He was such a handsome man was young Giovanni."

"My *wop* grandfather—that's how dad put it."

"Ah, no need to get into all that sad business now. I prefer to remember the boy who was a demon reader, the boy we all knew would make something of himself." Father Murphy gave his arm an affectionate squeeze.

They paused to shake hands with two old men who had taken their time leaving the service.

"I would never have thought Jimmy had so many friends," Michael said, watching the two men amble off.

Father Murphy held up a shaking hand. "Too many drinking friends, I fear."

"Chip off the old block, huh?"

"Your dad was a bad luck case if ever there was one, Michael. But your Jimmy, now, say what you like, he was a man alive to how he lived."

"Stealing cable transmissions?"

"Always on the lookout for a bargain." Father Murphy straightened up suddenly, an expression of delight on his face as his tufted eyebrows sprang to attention. "Do you remember the time you helped Pearl Ellis home with her books from the annual library sale? And old Pearl—a mender at the Appleton Mill in the old days—mouth like a sailor but soul of an angel—had a whole shopping bag full of books she'd bought. Big reader was old Pearly. I asked you to leave the cash box and help her take her books home. Off you went, Pearl yacking a mile a minute. And I expected you back in no time, but an hour passes and no Michael. Another hour passes. I call your ma at work and she hasn't seen you. I get someone to go over to Pearl's; she's tucked up reading and hasn't seen hide nor hair of young Michael since he dropped off her books. So I get Connor McClury, wave down his squad car and ask him to keep an eye out. We get half the force out looking for you by evening. And lo and behold, Connor, fearing the worst, checks the towpath of the Pawtucket Canal and he spots the young man huddled under the abutment of the Andover Street Bridge, reading a damn book. I remember Connor laughing about it later: 'Kid couldn't even tell me what day of the week it was.' Seems Pearl had given you one of her books for helping her home."

Michael felt a slow smile easing up the corners of his mouth. He reached inside his suit pocket for his dark glasses.

"It was a Thoreau omnibus: *Walden* and *A Week on the Concord and Merrimack Rivers*. The inside cover had a map of the rivers, with names of all the places visited, and an illustration of the rowboat and the two brothers. There was an ex libris plate from the Lowell Institute. Publisher was Ticknor and Fields, the 1938 edition, a cheaper version of the 1924 limited edition in leather covers. Hey, you know what? I still have that book … somewhere."

Father Murphy chuckled. "Some things we never forget."

"Or do you suppose we forget to remember, Father?"

"At my age, well … Did you find anything at Jimmy's?"

"A few odds and ends."

"Good, good. The house will bring something in that neighborhood. Those Hispanic families stick together; they all have cousins or siblings who would love to get their hands on Jimmy's place."

"Is that right? I didn't notice too many Hispanics at the service."

"They keep to themselves, have their own Catholic church across town, and many are Pentecostals. But Jimmy hung on up there on River Street … 'last of the wine,' he'd always joke."

"Loyal to his lights, I guess."

"That he was, and far as I know, he didn't have a will. Perhaps we can go over that later."

"And … the taxes?"

"That, too."

"Hot day to stand around a grave, Father."

"I'll make it fast, if it's all right by you."

"Fine by me, Father. You lead the way."

Father Murphy was as good as his word. At the end of the burial service, Michael put on his best official face and quickly shook every hand he could find among the mourners, then made a hasty retreat to a nearby bench in the shade of a massive oak. With little sleep the night before, he feared he was going to faint in the heat, and he gripped the edge of the bench and bent forward toward his knees. Sweat dripped off his nose. Then he was aware of the quick, jarring chatter of the cicadas, the sound and humidity like one enormous fever-addled lung swaddling the earth. A hundred feet off, the mourners still circulated at the grave site, shaking hands with Father Murphy and casting handfuls of dirt onto the coffin. He felt bad to have rushed off, but perhaps they would think him overwhelmed with grief.

As the gathering wound down, his mind drifted back to the previous night and to his renewed determination to get to the bottom of a failed life.

Those around the grave seemed two ends of the spectrum: the kids Jimmy had coached in Little League, with whom he'd shot hoops; and older folks who'd known him as a kid, whose roofs he'd fixed, with whom he'd shared gripes about all the changes in Lowell.

Friends.

The teenage boys in their team jerseys and over-the-knee shorts, with hangdog expressions every one, looked ripped up and out of place. The men and women in their seventies and eighties were taking it more in stride: They knew the drill. Some of the gray-haired women held umbrellas to shield themselves from the sun; the men wore wrinkled suits and fedoras fashionable in the fifties. Father Murphy was encouraging everyone to move on and get out of the heat.

The older mourners began disappearing with slow-motion steps along the paths, wandering over to familiar stones, perhaps to have a last visit with a memory-dimmed name. The teens headed out in brazen, swaggering groups, leaping gravestones in blithe contempt for death. Michael's gaze returned to the low mound of dirt to the side of his brother's grave, then to the impressive monument just beyond, his grandmother Moira Shannon Maronetti's monument, which faced west toward the river. In the noonday sun, the carved face of the seated female figure was still in shadow beneath the exaggerated hood of a robe. He squinted. The firm brow, tapering nose, and expressive lips spoke to him of his grandmother's long-suffering dignity, the gaze of the figure one more of glad remembrance than contemplation of a miserable fate.

He surveyed the surrounding monuments. Giovanni's feminine personages were everywhere, some with bowed heads, or faces hooded in mourning; here and there, neoclassical angels trailed long robes. A few bared their fine girlish breasts to the noonday sun (evocations of perished youth and beauty), while others, with a backward glance of grief, spoke of a lifetime of exhausting labor in Lowell's mills. All portrayed characteristic nobility, the eyes heavy-lidded, evoking both resignation and stoic resolve, along with a suggestion of ecstatic release. How many of these had he watched being carved as a young boy? He remembered seeing his grandfather's massive hands fingering the marble, feeling for the detailing along the tendons of the neck, the nose, the lips, those often androgynous lips, which to him, even as a child, seemed poised in mid-sigh, perhaps desiring to pass on some secret, if only the living cared to hear.

Now they spoke to him of their creator's love and—in the same moment … all his grandson's losses.

Wiping at his eyes, he turned back to the family graves and his mother's bland and ugly gravestone—another one of Jimmy's screwups. She had died of breast cancer—and fast, less than three months after the diagnosis, in the fall of 1972. He'd never forgiven Jimmy for not telling him, not getting him back in time from Vietnam to see her before she died. At her funeral, barely a word had been exchanged.

He blotted tears on his shirtsleeves, his eyes going again to the magnificent monument for Moira Shannon Maronetti, who had died when he was six of esophageal cancer. Giovanni had spent a year, off and on, agonizing over the monument to his wife; he blamed the mill owners and the doctors for covering up the cause of the cancer—the cotton dust she had breathed for decades.

Michael felt as if he recognized something more in the face.

Looking around as if suddenly attuned to the presence of others, he inventoried the dozens of carved women's faces. Some had expressions of near orgasmic ecstasy … and again he was with Sandra Palmer on that moonlit bank by the Concord River.

"Palmer and Maronetti," he said aloud.

Then he shook his head. "For God's sake, get a hold of yourself, Michael."

His father's scolding voice echoing in his own only added to his consternation. The resemblance to Sandra Palmer in his grandfather's carved faces was so readily apparent that he couldn't believe he hadn't noticed it in the past. He bent forward, squinting. The angle between the large brow and the tapering nose, the inward, pensive stare ... aloof, aristocratic, high-minded. He began to tremble, his lawyerly cool crumbling.

And also, something in the rapturous expressions of the marble faces spoke to him of the hidden desires of women, to which his life had been closed.

His reverie was disturbed by a vivid movement of lemon yellow moving across his field of vision. A little girl with blond hair stood on tiptoe to look into the face of Giovanni's marble figure. She couldn't have been more than three or four. She was struggling to reach up, as if to kiss the stony lips, when she was grabbed by a tall middle-aged woman, her mother, presumably—who had been in deep conversation with Father Murphy. The woman wore a battered straw hat over her auburn hair, and tears shone in her eyes. She was one of the few mourners anywhere near his or Jimmy's age. The little girl with sunlit ringlets let out a screech and pulled on her mother's arm, a pendulum arc back and forth, while the mother got in some last words. Father Murphy knelt, spoke to the child, and held out a hand, pulling the girl into a brief hug and giving her a parting kiss on her head. The girl flew off down the path and the tall mother followed wearily, regretfully, steps dragging, Ace bandage on an injured ankle. Father Murphy stood leaning on his cane and watched her go, speaking words after her, waving. The little girl stopped on the path, turned, saw her mother coming, and flitted off again like a windblown scarf among the stones.

"Never thought I'd live to see this day." Father Murphy sat stiffly beside him, tucking his cane between his knees, his tawny, clean-shaven jaw directed at the grave site.

Michael wiped at the tears in his eyes. "Thank you, Father, for the fine words you spoke for Jimmy."

"Futile things when put in the place of a life."

"I can't thank you enough." Michael dabbed his cheek with a shirt-sleeve. "I had no idea ... all these people."

"The little girl was his, you know."

"The little blonde?"

"Mother is a social worker. Refused to marry him until he gave up the drink."

"His daughter ..." He stared off in the direction of the parking lot. "What's her name?"

"Forgive me, I shouldn't be telling you this. It's not common knowledge."

"And there's no will, you said."

"That's right."

"Well, I can take care of that, Father, see that she and the girl are beneficiaries of the sale of the house."

"That would be fine, Michael. Very fine."

"Jimmy was always telling me how he was almost off the stuff."

"Jimmy was a romantic. It was the weakness from which all his strength flowed. People loved him because he lived the life he believed in and never sought advantage. What you saw in Jimmy was what you got. Loyal to a fault."

"Chip off the old block."

"Forgive me for saying it—and I loved your father—but Jimmy was a better man than he was. In your father, it was all weakness."

Michael turned to look at the old man, clerical collar stained yellow, his black shirt soaked through under the arms, the nearly transparent scar from temple to jaw holding and sliding droplets of sweat.

"To hear Dad tell it, his people built every inch of the railroad from Boston to San Francisco."

"Nothing was ever enough with your dad that it didn't turn to a bad taste in his mouth. The accident with Giovanni—everything."

The word *accident* sent an unexpected shiver through him.

"The accident?"

"Ah, now there's a sight for sore eyes." Father Murphy smiled in the direction of the grave, where a young man in jeans and a Bruins T-shirt had arrived with a shovel over his shoulder. "Don't see it done by hand anymore. But they couldn't get the backhoe into this part of the old burying ground."

"You were saying, Father, about Giovanni and the accident."

"Oh, Jimmy would come every six months or so to confession to run that by me again."

"When Giovanni drowned?"

Father Murphy eyed the younger man a moment. "You and Jimmy talked about it—surely?"

"The accident?"

The old man examined Michael's face, hoping to find what he was looking for, and when he didn't, he shook his head, an expression of chagrin on his face.

"My goodness." Father Murphy looked skyward and nodded. "Surely you remember it, a day like this, hotter than blazes, and then the terrible storm that came out of it, knocking down half the trees in the city. I was coaching your dad at third base, American Legion ball against a team from Lawrence. And old Jimbo had the game of his life, four hits and an eleventh-inning homer with two men on to win it for us. I remember his shot rising into the heat of that yellow sky and the smile on your dad's face as he rounded the bases, like he was sixteen again. And young Jimmy in the stands, giving him the thumbs-up, the boy shouting himself hoarse.

"We drank till we were feeling no pain at the Blue Skip Bar, and all the fellas were slapping your dad on the back and offering congratulations. Ah, after all his troubles, to see the light of pride in that man's eyes. And I remember thinking, Jimbo boy, nobody can take this away from you. I hoped it might be a blessing, change his luck for the better. But that was the thing about your dad: When a bit of goodness came his way, it turned soon into bitterness for all he'd lacked before. And then he had to go and take that bat home with him, the bat he'd won the game with. I'll never forget him walking away down the street, demonstrating the cut he'd taken—over and over, for little Jimmy, as if the doing hadn't been enough."

Father Murphy winced and shifted his gaze to where the workman was beginning to shovel spates of brown earth into the grave. Then he fumbled in his shirt pocket for a battered pack of Camels.

"Every time Jimmy came to confession, he'd speculate on the probabilities of the thing—if only they'd taken the turn on Andover street, hadn't missed the bus by thirty seconds, and those thunderheads rolling in like Armageddon itself from the west. You see, at the last moment they decided to take the shortcut along the Pawtucket Canal. And there was Giovanni, sitting all alone, smoking his pipe across from the old Palmer Mill. I guess it was something of a family joke, Giovanni taking his time getting home from his workshop, always late for dinner. And that was the thing, I suppose, that young Jimmy blamed himself for—for saying purely spontaneous, what must have been in his dad's heart, you see. 'Grandpa should have seen it, Dad; he should have seen the home run.' That was all it took to set Jimbo off.

"Next minute, he was down on the towpath, haranguing poor old Giovanni, the way he did when the drink and anger were up in him. And all the while the sky was darkening, thunder crashing like doom. Giovanni had heard it all before and just calmly went on with his smoking, sitting on a post, silent as stone, not even bothering with a glance at his son-in-law. So Jimbo started picking up these pebbles, tossing them up and smacking them with the bat in Giovanni's direction. The old man doesn't budge. By this time, the rain is beginning to spit, the air heavy like lead. Little Jimmy is so upset, he's pulling and pleading with his dad to give it up and come on home. Then Giovanni finally stands and turns to face his antagonist; he waves a large hand in a dismissive gesture, perhaps a curse in Italian at the maniac with the bat, motioning his grandson to come along home with him. That's when Jimbo did it, screamed some obscenity and picked up this plum-size rock. Whack."

Father Murphy fumbled to light his cigarette, pausing as if to listen to the clatter of dirt on the coffin.

"Like a bullet. That's what your brother used to say, a bullet. Didn't even see it hit, just the cry of his grandfather, his head snapped back, a surprised hand to his face, as if maybe trying to catch the pipe falling from his lips, reeling backward—and like that he was gone. Little Jimmy was the first to reach the edge of the canal. He saw the old man floating away, facedown and headed south with the current. He screamed for his father, pleading with him to get his grandpa out. Jimbo stood there unbelieving, sullen and silent. Jimmy kept screaming for his dad to do something.

"Then a hand clamped over his mouth and he heard his father whispering into his ear to shut up, saying that the old man was faking it, that he was really swimming off. 'See, see,'—he pointed with the bat—'he's swimming.' Jimmy would always repeat that to me—'swimming … swimming'—as if maybe it might have been true, that he'd just fallen in and gone swimming and maybe later hadn't been able to swim anymore. The truth was, Jimbo didn't know how to swim, and he'd always been terrified of water for that reason. Probably why he dragged Jimmy away from the edge, but not before he'd kicked the smoking pipe into the water and then tossed his bat in after. And the skies opened up on them, a flood of rain, a wall of rain, so much that they huddled in the shelter of the embankment—God only knew what must have been going through Jimmy's mind—the whole world disappearing in sheets of rain."

Michael rocked forward and back where he sat. "Oh my God … oh my God."

Father Murphy took a deep drag on his cigarette and let out the smoke slowly, placing a hand on the shoulder of the younger man, who had bowed his face into his hands.

"So—Jimmy never told you about it?"

He shook his head.

Father Murphy gripped Michael's arm. "Jimbo swore the boy to silence—a point of loyalty. You see, it was to be an accident not worth the telling."

"*Accident?*" Michael let out a compressed sigh and looked up, blinking into the haze and heat. From the abrupt clarity about Jimmy's hidden trauma, he found himself instantly recalling Sandra Palmer telling him in the dingy about the accident on the changing table, when her baby brother had fallen. So long dismissed as a stunt, but he now realized she'd been telling him the truth. She, like Jimmy, might well have wanted to conceal such a thing from her family, as well as from a young man she'd known for only a couple of months. To spill the beans like that had either been an act of folly or desperate trust, a need to share and unburden herself. The implications ran riot in his mind and left him fumbling to square his conflicting emotions … that she might have trusted him, and yet Jimmy, his own brother, had never trusted him enough.

Michael finally got it out. "They … they arrived late for dinner, soaked to the skin. Jimmy threw up all over the dinner table."

Father Murphy popped his lower lip. "And you know, years later I'd see Jimmy at a Fourth of July picnic in the park, off to the side of the softball game, picking up stones, taking his cuts, still figuring the probabilities of the thing."

"Even when Dad up and left, Jimmy stuck by him. Can you believe it—loyalty to that."

"It's the leaving that does it and the silence that follows—cruel a sport as they come."

"And yet, it's as if Mom and I knew and yet we didn't want to know."

"It's the silence that as good as kills—in the end."

Michael looked up, seeing the glazed, distant stare of the old man, the nicotine-stained fingers pressed against withered lips. The sound of the flung dirt had softened, just audible over the chorus of the cicadas.

He swiped at his sweating brow with his shirtsleeve. *Poor guy's going to keel over in this heat.*

Father Murphy twisted his cane into the dirt at their feet. "It's been a long while since I've been in the old part of the cemetery, since I've seen so much of Giovanni's work."

"Thank you, Father. You know, I'm almost relieved. When you first mentioned the baseball bat, I was thinking the worst." He loosened his tie. "You never heard from Dad again, did you?"

"No. He used to talk about all the opportunities for a young man in Alaska. During the oil-boom years, when a fella could get rich. I always figured he headed up there."

"Railroads, pipelines. Father, you know the thing that haunted me, when we left Lowell and I went away to school? I wanted him dead. I wanted it finished."

"But Michael, he'd still have been your father."

"So Mother and I could get on with our new lives, Jimmy, too."

"Jimbo, I remember from the old days, was a young and gifted ballplayer with a rifle for a right arm, a romancer, a lovely kid with all the future ahead of him. Injuries, disappointments. As a young man, he made your ma laugh. He'd come to visit her when she practiced in the church hall. He'd bring her wildflowers from some construction site north of Lawrence. A lovely couple, they were. I can still hear Moira's laugh."

"Except for the disappointments, huh?"

"You know, Michael, I was just thinking, looking at your grandma's monument there, how it was when Giovanni first came to town—a small suitcase, one room on Warren Street. First doing inscriptions at St. Agnes and then later, when his memorials, his lovely sad lasses, began to catch on so, building his workshop up here."

"I loved coming up here to watch him work."

"And let me tell you, he never compromised his work, never gouged on prices, best marble the family could afford, never cut corners. How many people can say that about their work today?"

"I hear you, Father."

Father Murphy lifted his hand, gesturing toward the brow of the hill, where it fell off to the Concord River below.

"You know, just now, looking at your grandma's monument, I was thinking that even though the face is so different, there is something of the woman in that stone, something of how I remember Moira sitting on the front stoop in the twilight, come home from the mill bone-weary and pausing a moment to watch the world go by. And how many others, or is it just me imagining things, all the names? I wasn't always crazy about Giovanni's strange undressed women—not exactly standard fare, if you take my meaning—but I see how people came around to his creations. Even the most modest Irish. They always respected a man who worked with his hands, who could make something so fine to last the ages. Your grandma's people came around to him, and all his sad lasses—finally, his being Italian and all."

Father Murphy smiled at the younger man.

"Father, did you ever hear of an artist name of Palmer, Joseph Palmer? Did Grandpa ever mention such a name to you?"

"Palmer, as in the Palmer Mill?"

"Yes, same family."

"No, not that I can remember. But Giovanni loved that old mill building; something about the brickwork took his fancy. I recall him telling me that once."

"The brickwork, huh?"

Michael glanced off toward the distant Pawtucket Canal, where the sky pulsed with lemony heat.

"I look at you, Michael, and I see him again, those large eyebrows caked in white dust and his red bandanna."

"Thank you again, Father, for everything."

"You've done great things, Michael, great things."

Great things! The words rattled and protested in his brain. And worse, he was immediately put in mind of a conversation he'd had the week before with another old man with a vague Irish lilt. Another lover of the Palmer Mill.

The congressman had been sitting back in his chair, shouting into the phone. His vast mahogany desktop was bunkered with inboxes, unread newspapers, a television, and scattered memorabilia of forty-plus years of string pulling for his district.

"Fuck you, and tell Mahoney to shoehorn his dick back into his pants." The congressman dropped the receiver into its chrome cradle, adjusted his dark glasses, and pushed the lank folds of silver gray hair off his forehead. "Mahoney, the stupid son of a bitch, is so fixated on the Palmer Mill project that even a Heimlich maneuver won't get him to choke it up."

"I thought everyone agreed, under present circumstances, to let it drop," Michael replied.

"You tell Mahoney."

"I already told him, and it's your decision."

The old man nodded at his onetime protégé and bent to tweak the control on the venetian blinds and let in a tad more light. The shadow streaks on the wall thinned, revealing more of the black-framed photos of restored mill buildings and architects' drawings for the pedestrian bridge over the Pawtucket Canal.

"Know what you realize as you get on, Michael? It gets to be less and less your decision. Besides, I'm a dead duck, right?"

"Lame duck, please. And we've got enough trouble as it is with the grand jury."

"Hey, where's the old fire in the belly?"

"And you were going to bow out gracefully, remember?"

"Hey." The congressman held up a liver-spotted hand. "I got a new pair of laser-enhanced eyes. I'm going to see the world again like a young man, actually *see* my three woods land in the rough."

"Just stay away from Mahoney and maybe you'll be home free," said Michael.

"While the going's good."

"You don't have any … well, arrangements with him, once you're out of office?"

"You wouldn't let me do that, Michael."

"That's what you pay me for."

"Covering my ass all these years on the Lowell Plan."

"The Lowell Plan is completed."

"Michael, Michael … where have you been?" The old man pulled down his dark glasses and peered over the tops, inspecting the younger man, as if needful of reading something in the contours of the face before him. Nodding, he said, "These trains leave the station longer ago than you ever imagine."

"Just say no."

"Capstone to the whole Lowell Plan. The Palmer Mill Mall will be the—"

"Jewel in the crown."

"You always did have a way with words."

"How about this: grand jury, heat from the statehouse, indictments from the state's attorney? Why the hell is Mahoney pushing his dumb luck?"

"He thinks if he backs off, they'll take it as a sign of weakness."

"Then don't back him. Wash your hands of it."

"You think they've got something?"

"There are always … irregularities."

"Ah, irregularities is it now, but nothing more."

"Anytime they convene a grand jury, people talk. Any determined asshole prosecutor can indict a ham sandwich."

"You think it's just politics, or have they've really got something?"

"It's always politics, payback time, smear campaign, take your pick."

"I still wish it was *you*, Michael, sitting in this seat come January."

"Perish the thought."

"Sometimes I feel like a last hurrah. What do you guys—the Woodstock generation—call it?"

"A last rush."

"I always liked that."

"And I was washing dishes at the Concord Inn, summer of '68."

"And the Palmer Mill Mall has a nice ring to it."

"You'd be out of your fucking mind."

"Michael, Michael me boy." The congressman always laid on the Irish brogue when matters got dicey. "The fellows in the building trades" —he held up a fist—"they are a brotherhood. They've been greasing the skids for one another since they were in diapers."

"One blabs and all the others run to cover their asses."

"You know, Michael, ever since you turned down the district, Mahoney's had it in for you. You worry the man."

"Fuck him."

"I mean, Michael, a man who doesn't take what's offered—well, they can't figure where you come out on anything. You just don't add up."

Michael turned now from the inland sea of marble monuments and sighed. "Father, here's a little story for you; I'd be interested in your thoughts. About a week ago, before I heard about Jimmy, a FedEx pack finds its way onto my desk. Just sitting there and not a word from anybody. There's a typed shipping label showing a FedEx drop-off point in Worcester and my name with my Rayburn Building address in Washington. It's marked personal and confidential. And get this: It's dated September 1992. Seven years ago. I was about to throw it out, figuring it was a bunch of out-of-date documents that had gotten waylaid. Then curiosity got the better of me. I opened the thing. Neatly arranged inside were stacks of fifty-dollar bills. The currency had been circulated, the serial numbers were random, and, most crucially for the intended purpose, the dates were before 1992. I figured it was close to four hundred thousand dollars."

"A bribe was it?" asked Father Murphy, seeming to relish the tale.

"A payoff, or more like hush money … and, given the seven years that had passed when I might theoretically have received it, beyond the statue of limitations. It would be hard to prosecute me for keeping the money under almost any circumstances."

"A tidy sum," said Father Murphy.

"The FedEx pack is in the trunk of my car over in the parking lot."

"I see."

"Have you heard about the investigation into corruption on the Lowell Plan out of the statehouse, the convening of a grand jury to gather evidence?"

"Yes, I believe I have."

"Well, that FedEx pack sits there like a little time bomb."

"Whether you take it or not."

"If I do nothing and I'm called by the grand jury and admit to nothing, I'm in, hook, line, and sinker."

"Did you do anything illegal?"

"I'm paid to be scrupulous and make sure the *i*'s are dotted and the *t*'s crossed. I knew or suspected when things weren't done totally on the up-and-up; I knew enough not to ask awkward questions or ask for precise figures. I never took a red cent."

"So, there's nothing on your conscience?"

"On my conscience … plenty. But I never did anything for personal gain."

"You helped rebuild Lowell."

"That has a nice ring."

"And the money?"

"Before I left Washington, I showed the cash to my secretary; in her presence, I resealed the FedEx pack and had it time-stamped, and had her make an appointment for three o'clock this afternoon for me to meet with the chief of police in Worcester to turn over the money."

"Then, Michael, you're doing the right thing."

"Let's hope so, Father. But all hell will break loose. The gentleman who sent me the money—and that FedEx pack required prodigious forethought and planning—is a powerful man, even a respected one, and believe me, his name is known far and wide: He will know that I'm not playing ball."

"Will it put you in danger?"

"Physical danger? I don't imagine so, no, but it might severely complicate my life." Michael slipped on his dark glasses and turned to the old priest and smiled as if with a characteristic brightness.

"Bless you, Michael."

"You said, Father, about Jimmy … he was loved."

"Good things. And a woman, too, and a daughter who loved him."

"Does the little girl know that Jimmy was her dad?"

"I think the deal was, when they married—if they married, Deloris was going to tell her. If, Uncle Jimmy quit for good."

"And yet it wasn't enough?"

"Deloris is an educated woman, mind of her own. A professional woman. She knows the score."

"Ah, and the little girl: She seemed mindless of what had happened."

"Doesn't it give you hope, how children can be so careless of life's defeats?"

"Perhaps they lack the memory to know better."

"How about you, Michael? You'd be a catch."

"Father, I've come close—very. It's just … it always seemed something else they wanted."

"Something else?"

"Sometimes I feel as if I lost sight of that something, a long time ago, and, well, thanks to you, Father, perhaps I'm back on the trail."

Father Murphy held up his cane, elbows bent, as if he'd take a little cut. "It doesn't take much."

"To *lose* your soul."

"The silence." Father Murphy touched the side of his face, the scar… the eye. "I was three days in the hospital with the stitches and loss of blood. Second night, I could barely walk, but I slipped out of the ward at four in the morning and went round to the house of the lad who did it. I climbed in a kitchen window and found my way to his room. Asleep, he was, like a lamb. I took his pillow and, easy as you please, smothered the nasty little bugger. By four-foty-five, I was back in the ward. No one ever knew a thing. But the way I figue it, if I hadn't gone into the priesthod, I would've turnd out a killer."

CHAPTER 6

H
e stood in the tarry heat of the cemetery parking lot, staring into the open trunk of the Ford Taurus, feeling enervated, marooned. The FedEx pack containing Mahoney's money lay on top of his unzipped bag. He put it aside for a moment and picked up the etching of Venice and the green morocco *Walden*. He brought the book to his face and breathed deeply, as if its words might yet find release within himself. He then placed it and the etching on the top of his bag. Next to them he arranged the bit of toy railroad track and the publicity photo of his mother. For a moment more, he pondered these scavenged objects from a defunct life, all that was left of his family in this place … except the marble figures. Giovanni's "sad lasses" would endure. He stowed the objects carefully in his overnight bag and looked at his watch. A few hours before he needed to be in Worcester.

Mahoney would have his question answered and Michael would either be drawing a line under a misspent career or drawing a line in the sand…perhaps both.

At the very least, the Palmer Mill Mall project would be put on hold and Mahoney would have a fit. Michael could just see his jowls tighten and flush with indignant anger, every other word punctuated with the usual expletives. Michael remembered something his boss the congressman had told him once about Mahoney, an admonitory tale to clue in his young aide about the kind of man he'd be dealing with.

"You want to know something about Jack Mahoney—let me tell you a little story the man once told me with relish. His dad's in a retirement home, a real nice place, according to Mahoney; dutiful son is paying all the bills. Dad's over eighty—now this was ten, fifteen years back, Mahoney is telling me this—and the old man worked most of his life in the Boot Mill. At that time, Mahoney had his offices in the Boot Mill, for which his firm had done most of the restoration work. Oh, beautiful offices, they were, with old pine flooring and potted plants and fine Italian furniture, and all the old beams and brickwork showing, period white-sashed windows looking out over the Pawtucket Canal. So one sunny day, Mahoney has this idea. See, he has a stretch limo go over to the retirement home and pick up his dad to bring him by his office for lunch. Hasn't seen his dad for a year, but he figures this will be a nice gesture, show his dad what his son has amounted to in the world. So the old man is chauffeured over and Mahoney has his secretary show him up to the office. Dear old dad is near speechless, wide-eyed—'could have blown him over with a feather,' was how Mahoney put it. He shows his dad all around the place, all the other wonderfully appointed offices of the high-tech firms, explaining how they painstakingly preserved the character of the building—the mill where his dad had worked, see. And then the proud son has a spectacular catered lunch brought into his private office, oysters on the half shell and lobster tails. After lunch, Mahoney walks his dad down to the waiting limo for the ride back to the retirement home. The old fella was pretty shaky to start, but as they're heading for the door, he freezes up. There are tears streaming down his face; Mahoney doesn't think he's going to make it. But he gets the old guy in the limo and as he's sayin' good-bye, he asks him what the trouble is. His father turns his tearful eyes to his son and shakes his head: 'They'll never know,' he finally gets out; 'nobody will ever know how terrible the work was, what a hell we endured.' As Mahoney told me this, he proudly reproduced the parting smile he gave his dad—beatific it was, too—as he closed the door of the limo on his old man: 'A good thing, too, Da, a good thing, too,' he tells him."

The way Michael figured it, Mahoney's crew would head for the hills to lie low until after the election. But then, two of his lieutenants—and they weren't exactly on a short leash—had already been subpoenaed by the grand jury; they might come after Michael. But like his father had always said, "If there's going to be a fight, Mikey, you get in the first punch, boy, and make sure it counts." He had to smile at that: If there was any fight in him, maybe it did come from the bastard. But now the business in Worcester didn't feel as much like a fight to protect his ass as a determined act to move his life in a new direction. He wasn't going to go to the police chief, cast aspersions or speculate; he was going to tell the truth: "Somebody sent me a fat envelope of cash and I don't want it. Here."

There would be no going back. He and the boss were done; the congressman had told him to go on vacation after the funeral, use up his comp time and make himself scarce. Hell, they were all in Mahoney's pocket, including the boss; they were all running scared.

Make himself scarce, just disappear. How appealing that thought.

He shook his head in wonder, feeling light-headed at finding himself standing in the cemetery parking lot and his brother gone, and the world of his childhood flickering out. He couldn't even recognize the place where Giovanni's workshop had been, torn down after his death to make way for an expansion of the cemetery. Father Murphy, the last of a breed, whose fine words would fail, too.

And all those years his brother, Jimmy, had covered up *Giovanni's accident*, in some misbegotten loyalty to good ole Jimbo Collins.

Leaving him and Jimmy strangers at the last.

"The awful silence," as Father Murphy had called it.

Again, the thought put him in mind of Thoreau, as if something of his adolescent infatuations had reclaimed him. How Thoreau had known all about silence, but a silence teeming with life; he had cultivated silence as a way of losing himself and repeopling the world from within. A past as alive as the mind attuned to know it.

This teasing flow of notions caused him to gaze downstream to where a line of dusky orange-hued maples obscured the far bank of the Concord River. Just beyond appeared the faintest smudge of smoky brick tracing the flanks of the Pawtucket Canal, and the Palmer Mill, casus belli for him and Mahoney.

His head throbbed. Coffee, he hadn't even had a cup of coffee that morning; no wonder he felt so faint, so out of it.

Discovering the FedEx pack in his hands, he threw it back in the trunk and slammed the lid shut.

"Brickwork," he mumbled to himself.

Giovanni's gift, like Thoreau's, he reflected, was to see what other mortals missed. Perhaps that was what had prompted Giovanni to walk all those miles every day, waking in the morning to take the path along the Concord River to his workshop in the cemetery, returning in the evening by way of the Pawtucket Canal—an enormous detour—and past the Palmer Mill, to keep the feel of the world at his fingertips … and the face of a woman.

Memories of those walks sealed Michael's resolution: He would travel the whole circuit from the graveyard along the river to the Pawtucket Canal and back around to River Street and then return to the graveyard along the river path. He would see with his grandfather's eyes, or purge himself of the memory. He would complete the habitual circuit that had been his grandfather's daily existence … and the place where he had lingered … and been killed, *the accident*. And maybe in doing so, widening his orbit and gaining momentum for the outward journey, he would find the necessary escape velocity, enough to go on, enough to be his own man again, free of inertia's chokehold.

With these encouragements to himself, he followed the overgrown path down to the river, a route he'd walked hundreds of times in childhood—sent by his mother to make sure Giovanni got home on time—trying to match his footsteps with those gone before. To complete something left incomplete. To rediscover the impulse to joy, which in boyhood had glittered along the river's banks. He held out his good hand to the spiky tufts of purple grass, the white sprays of Queen Anne's lace, breathing the scent of sweet fern. At the foot of the path, where it turned to follow the river, he stood a moment to watch the smooth, lazy glide of the water between green and leafy banks: Gravity translated into liquid crystal, sparking an urge to flee one life for another.

Farther on, an upturned rowboat lay across the familiar path. What a joyous sight! It was old, verging on the antique, a thing of solid oak planking with cast-iron oarlocks. The ribbed keel was thick with chipped white paint, a lovely blue trim along the gunwales. Two carved oars, sheathed in spiderwebs, lay sheltered in the grass beneath. He touched the planking, beguiled by the fine workmanship—how the abandoned skiff seemed to fit itself into some preexisting life. Something about Thoreau and his brother and their journey up the Concord and Merrimack. What had happened to Thoreau's beloved brother, John? Hadn't he died, and young, too, of some awful blood disease, or was it an infection?

It rankled that he could no longer summon the details.

He shifted his vantage point slightly along the bank.

Strange, the boat, with no houses nearby or access route in sight.

He made the long detour at the Newbury Street bridge, just the way Giovanni always had, past the backwater of auto-repair shops, gas stations, and minimarts for the commuting traffic heading west, and gained the upper reaches of the Pawtucket Canal. He walked slowly along the canal path, trying to match his pace to his grandfather's, letting the magnificent facades of the old mills—all renovated now and home to high-tech firms—pass in slow procession. He wanted to feel the old man's infatuation as his own, the gravity of his steps and the near-ritual indulgence of his eye, as if Giovanni's memory might merge into his own and thus help him understand all those lovely marble figures in the cemetery ... and Giovanni's connections with the artist Joseph Palmer.

Ahead of him, the Palmer Mill slowly came into view around the bend of the canal, a great arc of brick and white-sashed windows, that ungainly amalgam of domestic and industrial detail, like a line of titanic boxcars rounding a broad bend of track. In the crunch of gravel, the tug of his grandfather's hand.

He halted. A large yellow banner hung from the roofline of the abandoned mill: Mahoney Construction, Inc. Site of the Palmer Mill Mall.

The gall of the pig. He couldn't even wait to get the zoning variances resolved before having his name emblazoned on the building, as if by sticking his name up there, he could claim the future as his own. Who the fuck had he bribed to get that sign hung?

Michael shook his head and swallowed the anger that threatened to short-circuit the better sensibilities leading him elsewhere.

Right across from the mill, where granite steps descended to the path from Andover Street, he surveyed the area where the accident must have happened, the stone stanchion where Giovanni had been sitting smoking his pipe.

He walked to the granite stanchion, his palm grazing the worn stone, Father Murphy's voice repeating like an incantation in his mind.

Across the canal, the Palmer Mill was a drunken derelict compared to the renovated mills, but still a proud and handsome building. He looked at the white-sashed windows fanning out before him and then linking up with their mirrored twins in the canal below, where the reflected brickwork was intensified to a rich russet-ocher. The windowpanes, some broken, many with the swirls and deformities of handmade glass, began to gleam like lozenges of jade enamel in a Byzantine rood screen. A last great artifact of the first industrial age, and, too, the embodiment of an imperial name … at least in the eyes of a small boy led by his grandfather.

How odd it had seemed over the weeks he'd known Sandra Palmer, first infatuated and then in love, that she had denied or dismissed the connection with this building. She had never even been to Lowell!

Palmer and Maronetti.

So Giovanni had known Joseph Palmer in Venice and perhaps later when he had immigrated to the States after World War I. Sandra had mentioned something about Sleepy Hollow, but he couldn't quite see it in his mind. Why would Giovanni have made himself late for dinner almost every night, to walk along the Pawtucket Canal and past the Palmer Mill? Michael continued staring at the waterborne reflection of the mill, the patterns of brick and mortar shifting and breaking apart and re-forming, as if intent on tantalizing him further. The brickwork, yes, different from the other mills, showing variations and odd herringbone patterns—decorative patterns with no discernible utilitarian function.

Was the canal a reminder of the Venice of his youth, of all that he'd left behind? Or was Giovanni, like Thoreau, always guided by some inner compass, so that every passing hour, every quotidian detail yielded a new face? Again, such thoughts were like fire in his veins. Wasn't that how he had discovered Sandra Palmer in the first place, jogging along the river path and running into her while she painted outdoors? He hadn't been able to take his eyes off her face, nor she his.

He remembered how as a boy he'd watched his grandfather carve some of his very last figures, all with the same nobility and proud beauty, as if impelled to people the countryside with emanations from his long walks, his dreams, his past. For a child, the making of those figures was a thing of purest magic. And yet, Michael now saw in those marble faces a lament for a lost love, something unfinished, perhaps abandoned; and in that love transmuted to stone, a terrible disappointment.

And in this train of speculation, he felt a crystallizing certainty that his meeting Sandra Palmer along the banks of the Concord River all those years before had not been pure chance, but a reflection, even a reincarnation of a love lain dormant, a love only waiting to be rekindled. What he had found in her face, and she in his, partook of this same love: the love that had inspired the work of their grandfathers.

He brought his hands to his throbbing temples. "Get a hold of yourself, Michael, for fuck sake."

He shook his head at what his practical mother had dismissed as his romantic Irish streak, reasoning that the accumulated tensions and stress of the last few days were distorting his judgment. But he found himself almost beyond caring, preferring fantasy to fact.

"Sandra, Sandra Palmer."

Even repeating her name sent his heart racing into overdrive.

Darling, Michael, you're mine, you're really mine.

He turned—surprised—from the edge of the canal and the specter of the derelict mill to the gray stonework of the embankment; and as he did, he was seized by a blip of sensation, a shock, a jolt, less than an instant, about the time it takes for a plum-size stone to crush a fleshy temple.

He turned back, as if seeing himself falling.

If Sandra Palmer was a lie, then everything was a lie … and there was no hope.

The thought of such an arbitrary and cruel universe was untenable.

He reached down and picked up a pebble from the path and gamely tossed it in the canal, watching the ranks of white-sashed windows shatter, then once again link themselves up, as if to confirm the solid armature of a world faithfully conceived and rightly seen.

And in this consoling vision, a belief in second chances.

He lingered a moment more, as if trying to decipher the patterns in the acres of handmade brick and glass on the far side of the canal, how the herringbone diagonals threaded the horizontals, like the warp and woof of a monumental tapestry. The creator's signature, he thought, not unlike the poised sensuous lips of Giovanni's sad lasses, or even an artist's inky thumbprint.

He had to know … even if Sandra Palmer had turned into a cruel and spoiled middle-aged bitch.

He staggered a little as he left the restaurant; a whole bottle of wine with only a pasta salad was more than he was used to. Too many drinks and he began to feel sorry for himself or angry at the world—chip off the old block. Funny thing, the sultry afternoon seemed to have emptied the city. Ahead, heated thermals shimmered off the ribbon of concrete suspended between the rusty guardrails of the dilapidated Andover Street bridge. The sidewalk of the bridge was showing wear and was full of potholes.

"The thing that really pisses me off," he said to himself, "is that Mahoney never bid for the bridge work, nor road maintenance, anything smacking of infrastructure. Not enough visibility. Just the glamour projects, the money tills, where he could plaster his slimeball name for all the world to see."

From behind, as if in reply to his harangue, the pawing impatient rev of a supercharged V-8, the quick acceleration of a large hunk of galvanized steel and rubber. It was a solitary sound, encompassing, but not necessarily threatening, not to one slightly tipsy and still intent on time travel.

He halted near mid-span and, lowering his sunglasses, glanced up the Pawtucket Canal toward the lock that released the diverted water back into the Merrimack. If his grandfather's body had not got caught up in the weir next to the lock and had instead been swept into the Merrimack on the night of that terrible storm, Giovanni might never have been found. The Merrimack had been in full flood the following day all the way to Newburyport.

Then he heard the slight hiccup of a powerful engine transitioning into a higher gear. That woke something in him, a visceral distaste for badly handled machinery or teenage road tricks. He turned and saw a battered red pickup jerk forward as it picked up more speed. Coming right at him. Massive tires rising onto the sidewalk, a wobbly missile locked on target. A glaze of dazzling sunlight in the tinted windshield. He grabbed the heated guardrail. "Ouch." His addled brain dwelled for an instant on the hot railing. And in spite of himself, he smiled.

The thing had all the hallmarks of Mahoney: calculation and ambition and careless risk. The truck was a red blur, an ugly workhorse ready to finish another dirty job. He faced the oncoming pickup head-on, its front end jarring, so that even if it had a license plate, it would be hard to read. No plate, huh? Mahoney always liked to scare the competition, go for the stick before the carrot had even been properly rejected. Had his secretary in Washington blabbed? The police chief in Worcester, in Mahoney's pocket, too?

And Mahoney: Well then, we fucking better put the fear of God into the son of a bitch.

Kathunka, kathunka, kathunka.

The sound of tires on the sidewalk, a trajectory that had not veered an inch, was just enough to engage his instinct for survival. He grabbed the burning guardrail and braced himself, as if all he had to worry about might be the windsheer. A part of him was still prepared to let it happen, just to prove to himself that he would never let Mahoney get away with threatening him. But this fleeting stab of anger to preserve his dignity splintered as the left fender popped a support on the guardrail, a sickening crump, a geyser of sparks—which was well behind him or above him as he felt the rush of cooling air and the even more luxurious swelling green of the water.

His jump, forty, maybe fifty feet into the canal, as good as another life.

The notion was as good as born in the moment he broke the surface.

It might have had something to do with the impact that slapped the back of his head and left him woozy for seconds as he bobbed to the surface. He felt his face for a cut to explain the throb in his head and the ringing in his ears. But concern for his survival was soon replaced by the realization that there was nobody around, no faces on the bridge or along the embankment to witness his undignified exit. No help anywhere! Above him, the rusted underbelly of the bridge began a steady retreat. The canal seemed narrower than he might have expected. Where the hell was everyone? Then the putrid stink of the water registered, the oily green surface. That got him swimming hard, the sense that he was really in one great sewer, headed for oblivion, that and a vague wonderment at his shared fate with his grandfather Giovanni. This formed itself into a question: Would the world he had just left really be a safer place for the likes of Mahoney and company without him in it?

About five hundred feet down the canal, he found a break in the high embankment—a construction project to run a pipe under the canal—where he was able to catch hold of some rusty rebars sticking out above the waterline. Pulling himself up and standing on the lowest of the rebars allowed him to get his torso over the embankment and onto dry ground. He sat, stunned, his heart pumping conflicting instincts through his brain. Then, noticing the sludge clinging all over, he began to wipe at himself with the disconcerted awkwardness of a child who had soiled itself. The back of his neck was sore, as if he'd taken a rabbit punch. There was a constant ringing in his ears.

He stood, shaking, squinting in the hazy sunlight. Sunglasses lost. But where were the people to help him? He panicked, terrified that maybe the pickup truck and its crew might return to finish the job. He ran through the surrounding construction area, hurtled over a temporary chain-link fence into a kind of no-man's-land, a narrow isthmus between the Pawtucket Canal and the Concord River, overgrown with dry grass and mullions, littered with old boards, cinder block, broken bottles. He knew it like a second self from childhood when he and Jimmy had combed it weekly for good junk to sell. He moved faster, running, crouching, running again until he got to the shallows of the Concord River, where he negotiated an obstacle course of worn tires and rusted barrels, pausing a moment to wash off the most offensive of the goo, then wading in deeper and swimming across the river to the sanctuary of the far bank.

From here on, it was a cinch, as if he'd had it all planned.

He felt refreshed and clean again. In a matter of minutes, his skin had dried in the soft heat and he was walking with renewed vigor. Once past the first set of shallow falls, just two hundred yards from where they had lived on River Street, he turned to an unused trail that wound inland and came in behind the cemetery, conveniently ending in the copse of maples bordering the parking lot. Twenty minutes at a fast pace and he had the Ford Taurus in sight from behind the concealing trees. There was a blue Nissan pickup truck in the parking lot with lawn mowers and gardening equipment in the back, probably belonging to the guy who was tidying up Jimmy's grave site. He waited a few minutes to see if anyone else might show up and then decided he could wait no longer.

He removed his car keys from a still-soggy pocket and opened the trunk. Reaching into the small suitcase, he carefully removed a change of clothes: a pair of jeans, green generic sports shirt, socks, underwear, running shoes. Then he tucked the photo of his mother into the green morocco *Walden* and stashed it, along with the etching and the bit of railroad track, into a canvas backpack. He eyed the FedEx pack for a few seconds before including it, too. With the backpack over his shoulder, he closed the trunk and headed back into the copse of maples.

He changed quickly and then carefully stuck his wet clothes and shoes into a hollow beneath the roots of a maple, pushing them in as deep as they would go, about up to his elbow, then added his wallet and keys, everything in his pockets. For good measure, he collected some mud and moss, pushing this gamey mucilage, along with handfuls of old leaves, into the opening until the hollow was sealed. Then checking the immediate area to make sure he hadn't disturbed anything or left footprints, he wound his way down the bluff to the old rowboat along the river path.

He flipped it, got the oars set, and pushed it into the shallows; just the bow rested in the grass and mud of the shoreline. For a moment, he stood on the bank, staring down at his shadowy reflection next to that of his small craft. "It was *blood poisoning*," he announced to himself. "Thoreau's brother cut his finger shaving and died of lockjaw ten days later. Terrible ... my God, how terrible." He rubbed his aching neck, massaged his ears as if to relieve the buzzing, or perhaps ascertain the reality of his voice. Of the loss of a brother. Then, combing his hair as best he could, he bent to wash his hands in the clear water.

It was almost as if he'd planned the whole thing.

CHAPTER 7

———

Once he was rowing upstream, even the shadow of doubt faded and a huge calm enveloped him, his muscle memory engaging completely in the draw of the oars, the glide, the blithe blue of the sky reflecting in the river behind. The ringing in his ears began to fade.

Amazing how quickly any signs of the city evaporated in grassy banks and leafy trees, with only a few modest homes in the distance. And in a few minutes more, meadows and rural vistas and the occasional farm surrounded him. The banks on either side were a state-protected refuge; he'd even had a hand in passing the environmental legislation to preserve the land along the Concord and prevent further building along its banks. With each stroke, it was like being drawn into the heart of a bucolic past.

He rowed with a strength he had no idea he possessed, a dead man awakening to a new life.

The truth of his fall from the bridge and survival began to clarify. The attempt on his life—maybe just a warning that had come too close for comfort—confirmed for him the sham of a previous existence he was well rid of. He had been tempting fate, and fate just bit him back. Whether he was experiencing shock, panic, or exhilaration at his escape, it didn't matter; he felt so alive that what had come before just mystified him.

He rowed harder, as if addicted to the good feeling pumped to his brain. It was upriver all the way ... the possibility of reinvention.

The worn handles of the heavy oars fitted him as well as could be expected, even without the special left-hand prosthesis he used for rowing a single shell on the Potomac. But he barely thought of himself as *rowing*—it was more an exploration of himself as he had once been on that night navigating Sandra Palmer toward her childhood home—the home they never reached—relieving that earnest young man with an older but wiser captain, so allowing the past and present to unfold in tandem.

"Yes, yes, yes, yes ..." Wasn't that it—what Thoreau would have called his "doubleness"?

To port, he found the dejected tresses of an autumn willow bowed to the river; to starboard, a massive creeper-cloaked oak; ahead, an abandoned barn weathered to russet-green; while the banks to east and west, fading in his wake, showed overgrown pastures repopulated with pigweed and cattails, where sprays of golden chrysanthemums—escapees, too—from distant gardens waved in the breeze.

He had enough presence of mind to wonder if his enthusiasm was due to traumatic shock, but he reasoned that such profound joy could not result from physical injury or even relief at surviving a hit-and-run accident staged by Maloney's people.

Something of an immemorial love had been rekindled in him: He would find and forgive Sandra Palmer—neither judge her nor hate her: a state of grace presaged in the lavender-tinged grasses corralled within stonewall ramparts, and the picket lines of yellow mullion, behind which, epaulets of crimson sarsaparilla faded in and out of shadow.

While above, further assuring the success of his quest, a solitary marsh hawk, wings wide to the thermals, scouted the rower's exposed flanks.

Only by late afternoon did his flesh-and-blood self signal its flagging enthusiasm for this sport. His palms were raw, his left-hand grip failing, neck sunburned, back a protesting knot of pain. He turned, close to exhaustion, and saw it: just beyond a single white pine flagging a spot on the near shoreline, the brick tower topped by an onion-shaped gold cupola. Once before, on a cold winter day, he had seen that gold cupola when he'd come to this place looking for Sandra. It had been Christmas vacation of his senior year.

He shipped his oars, letting the glide bring him closer. It was just as she'd described it: the old apple orchard, a stone wall dipping into the flooded shallows, and next door a meadow lifting from the river's edge in tussocks of wild grasses, merging into a slope of sweet fern and wildflowers, bordered by a picket fence and formal garden—all of this splendor capped by a sprawling white clapboard colonial home with an anomalous lookout tower.

The bow nudged the shore. He shouldered his backpack and managed to get to dry land without muddying his shoes. He was very stiff and his arms and shoulders suddenly ached like the devil; his left hand had taken on a palsied shaking. For a moment, he stood stock-still, wondering if his journey had really happened. It was as if he'd dreamed it. But no, there was the antique craft, a small skiff to serve a larger ship. He touched the bow tip, fingering the splintered white paint while trying to fathom the thing; then a feeling of resignation or resolve surged through him, and he simply shoved the boat off and watched for a minute as it drifted away downstream … the evidence.

He massaged his temples and the ringing in his ears calmed … and he knew he was safe. And the sense of safety merged into something akin to happiness and this into an intense curiosity as to the nature of this happiness.

He began walking toward the house. The hum of crickets directed his gaze again to the orchard beyond the wall, where the appealing stooped forms of the apple trees shouldered the mottled red of first fruit. *I'll make you happy there.* His heart leapt with terror at the memory of her voice in the dinghy, as if again urging him on to danger. Under his continued scrutiny, the bowed trees gained a mysterious presence he couldn't shake. He breathed deeply of the aroma of scythed hay and sweet fern and reached down to the comforting strands of pearly everlasting growing amid the hummocks of wild grass. And in the touch, another voice rose to memory, the words of a poet coming to terms with the death of a brother: *When we look over the fields we are not saddened because the particular flowers or grasses will wither—for the law of their death is the law of new life.*

Buoyed in this confluence of voices, he moved on, lifting his face to the cooling breeze off the river.

Drawing closer to the house, he inspected the strange brick tower, which jutted like an elongated chimney above the roofline. The gold onion-shaped cupola had the look of an exotic hybrid, a hint of Byzantium translated to a Colonial setting. On closer inspection, as he went through the gate and into the formal gardens, he could make out an observation area beneath the cupola, which was capped by a traditional New England weather vane. He squinted. A leaping fish, maybe a dolphin or whale, rising from the crossed compass points. And in the brickwork of the tower—he cupped a hand over his eyes—the same herringbone patterns as in the facade of the Palmer Mill.

The garden looked to be of Victorian vintage and suffering from lack of upkeep. A small pond in the center was choked with leaves from an ailing willow, and the brick paths were uneven and rutted with roots. The flower beds looked in need of a good weeding and pruning and probably a thorough mulching. Only the large rose garden that extended along the south-facing side of the house seemed to be thriving, glutted with bouquets of damask and yellow and salmon pink. The scent of these roses carried everywhere, as if boosted by the saturating warmth of the late-afternoon sun. He lingered among the roses, eyeing the dormer windows above with their views over the back garden and the river beyond. Wisteria, weaving gnarled and complex tapestries, spilled from the third-story windows to the ground, providing ready handholds to dare the intrepid climber to an assault.

Heedless of trespassing, he continued poking around, peeking in lower-story windows, only to find disappointing glimpses of rooms and furniture that struck him as European in style. The large front door, a dark green rectangle enshrined in a white portico, retained the brass eagle door knocker he recalled from Christmas vacation all those years before. There had been snowdrifts in the unplowed driveway. He gave the brass knocker a vigorous few raps, as he had on that winter day of long ago, but then immediately turned away from the hollow echo, a foreboding of the phantom voices that had urged him on to this place.

Not a car in the driveway.

Then, as he walked back and forth across the ankle-high grass of the lawn, surveying the house from various angles, he was startled by a very real voice from the neighboring garden.

"Can I help you, young man?"

In the yard next door, an older woman was standing by a yew hedge, clippers in one hand, her free hand shading her eyes: Her stooped yet alert posture indicated something akin to bemused annoyance. He looked at her and then to the enormous faux-Tudor house behind.

He was instantly overcome with the strangest sensation: a place and a person existing in perfect stasis … just as he.

"Funny-looking tower," he finally managed to say, giving voice to his thought of a minute before.

"You're not another art historian come to pick over the place, are you?"

He walked the short distance to where she stood in her rather frumpy and matronly blue denim dress, her face delicately, exquisitely lined, with the orchid white complexion of someone who had assiduously forgone a lifetime of exposure to the sun.

"How did you know?" he replied with genuine curiosity.

She cocked an eyebrow. "Seems like the place has been crawling with academics recently, especially since the big Palmer retrospective at the Museum of Fine Arts two years ago."

"Well, you know how *they* can be." He forced a smile, sensing the tightness of his sunburned cheeks as he glanced back over his shoulder. "Have to admit, the house is pretty unusual."

"More a mongrel breed when you examine the bones. And the watch-tower has a quirky anachronistic charm, according to some." She said this with a half gesture toward her own place, which was all of a kind. "Began as a simple farmhouse and got built onto, but it's normally the rose garden and the back orchard—*my orchard*—where Palmer did his early landscapes, where he posed Sandra Chillingworth: That's what most of the people seem to find interesting. A landscape of his went for three hundred thousand dollars last spring at Skinner's."

He feigned surprise, inwardly exulting at the ease with which she seemed to be handing him his longed-for new life. "No kidding. Funny, I must have missed it."

She dropped her clippers, pulled off a gardening glove, and reached for her glasses, which dangled from a purple lanyard on her ample bosom.

"Gardens have gone to pot—except the roses, which seem indestructible. A French family owns the place now. They go back to Provence for months at a time, and the garden service they use employs mostly high school kids, who do more damage than good. Takes intelligence, love, a historic garden like that. Now his orchard—my orchard, our orchard—is pretty much as the artist knew it. I've been careful not to fool with it, even though the trees could probably use more pruning than they get. My late husband used to give them a pretty good going-over every fall."

He became acutely aware of her magnified fish-bowl stare behind the glasses.

"Well," he said, pausing a moment as if to get his arms around her words. "You see, I actually knew his granddaughter, Sandra Palmer, when I was at Emerson Academy and she was at Alcott Academy."

The large eyes blinked. She let out a deep breath.

"My late husband went to Emerson with her dad, Joe Palmer." She stepped back from the hedge and glanced obliquely at the house next door. "Poor Abby." She sighed and shook her head. "We were close, Sandra's mother and I ... and the girls. You know, that house had been in the Palmer family for almost a hundred and fifty years. Then, like that, it seems, money problems and divorce. Abby moved up the road to Carlisle. Gave up the DAR. We exchanged Christmas cards for a few years, but then we lost touch."

"Girls? Sandra had a sister?"

"Yes, they were twins. Sandra had a twin sister, Angela."

"Of course, of course. I'd forgotten that."

"Abby was no slouch herself, of course. Her family were Hosmers ... old, old Concord. Her people fought at North Bridge. She collected antique furniture, you know, like a demon."

She turned at the sound of a passing car, a minivan with children in the back. A honk. She waved.

"Funny thing," he said. "I've been meaning to do more research on Joseph Palmer. There was a self-portrait in the dining room at school. I know his etchings quite well. And Sandra always seemed ... well, quite in awe of his work."

"As well she might. The twins were the spitting image of his wife and model, Sandra Chillingworth Palmer. Thrill you to the bone to see that lovely Gibson-girl face come back to life as they grew up." Her squinting eyes swept slowly from side to side as if trying to catch some elusive movement among the hedges. "Sandra and Angela, looking so much like the famous Chillingworth twins, well, it drove Abby wild. She was Hosmer-proud, among other things." She turned again toward the house, her face brightening. "It was almost like Sandra Chillingworth Palmer, that gorgeous, ill-fated woman, had been reborn, twice over, as if to make sure of it."

"To make sure?"

"Nature, don't you know, abhors extinction, always puts up a gallant fight."

"The Chillingworth twins, of course."

"Nature's way of hedging her bets."

She made a fist and then opened her empty palm, as if a little surprised at herself. The look in her milky gray eyes went right through him: the presence of enduring affection, a personal association with such names and places, of the family that had flourished here and was no more. He felt suddenly drained, overcome by thirst.

"Could I ask you a great favor? I've just walked quite a way and I was wondering if I might be able to get a glass of water."

"By all means." She picked up the clippers where she had left them in the grass. "I've got a Joseph Palmer myself you should see."

"Yes?"

"And poor you, walked all the way from town on a hot day like this?"

He thought a moment and it felt almost true. "Yes ... I didn't realize it was quite so far."

She waved him forward as she headed for her front door of rusticated oak on heavy iron hinges.

"Staying at the inn?"

"The inn ... yes, yes."

"I'm Marge Hathaway. Forgive me, I didn't get your name."

"Channing ..." It was the first thing that popped into his mind. "William Channing."

"Boston Channings?"

"No, Midwest."

"Friend of Thoreau, if I'm not mistaken," she said with a teasing smile. "William Channing, second-rate poet."

"I always thought he managed a few good things."

He slipped into the bathroom while she prepared the iced tea. He was shocked by the sunburned face in the mirror, the bloodshot eyes and matted, oily hair. If she could see worth a damn, the poor lady would have died of fright. Fortunately, there was a comb in the medicine cabinet and a bottle of Tylenol. He swallowed three capsules, put a few more in his pocket, and splashed cold water on his face. Then he sat for a couple of minutes on the toilet with eyes closed, trying to settle his agitated mind.

He found her sitting on the sofa with a photo album open in her lap, totally absorbed.

"Help yourself to the iced tea," she said.

He poured himself a glass from the pitcher on the side table, spiked it with two teaspoons of sugar, and drained it. He poured another and then sat down next to her.

"Here they are again," she said in a ruminative voice, as if she'd been trying to settle some internal argument with herself. Her finger went to the square snapshots, the color badly faded.

Two identical blond girls in matching blue-and-white smocks playing along the brick paths by the rosebushes; rolling in the grass by the topiary hedges while holding hands; in bathing suits, sitting patiently on the tailgate of a Ford station wagon by the beach, sandy arms around each other's shoulders.

"Abigail couldn't resist dressing them in identical outfits until they were almost teenagers, even though she knew better. They were over here all the time playing hide-and-seek in the hedges, or down gathering apples in the orchard. Now, there's one of *your* Sandra."

He bent forward toward her pointing finger and a photo of a teenager in blue jeans and a white blouse, seated on a fieldstone wall with sketch pad and pencil poised.

"Her grandfather's talent. Determined like the devil. Sometimes I'd see her out drawing for hours. Funny thing, adolescence—for ten, twelve years, those twins were inseparable pals; then suddenly they're different as night and day. Sandra was a shy loner, self-motivated. Angela, well, her father, Joe, always said, 'Like my mother, beauty and talent to twist men into knots.' It happens, you know; genes skip a generation and ghosts reappear."

The crisp contours of Sandra's young face, the set jaw, the critical focus of the eyes on something outside the frame of the photo, the wisps of hair off the long neck: It was all there with him again.

"That's Joe junior, the twins' father." A tall angular man getting out of a one-man scull, twin daughters on the dock clapping admiringly, welcoming the athlete's return. "Handsome as they come. Olympic rower. Navy officer in the war, ran the place like a ship. Poor Abby, tough for any wife… ."

She continued flipping the pages. Mostly, they were family photos: a younger Marge Hathaway with a short, balding man at a Harvard reunion; a middle-aged couple in foul-weather gear on a sailboat off Mount Desert Island; their son sporting a crew cut as he played football for Harvard, then sitting in the cockpit of a helicopter in his army uniform, then on home leave in dress khaki, standing in the orchard, then at a Harvard-Yale game in uniform, arm around a young, laughing, blond-haired girl wearing a Harvard football jersey and torn jeans, a red bandanna tied around her forehead. She had sneaked a hand behind his head and was holding up two fingers in a peace sign.

"Who's that?" he asked.

"Angela, remember, Sandra's twin," she said, keeping the pages turning. "Just as well—she was as wild as they come. Now, there's Abigail and me at the DAR lecture at Symphony Hall on Patriots' Day. McGeorge Bundy was the speaker. The police had to rid the place of hecklers. I remember telling Abby how lucky she was to have girls."

He looked up from the album as if touched by an invisible hand and saw a slant of sunlight through the leaded-glass bay windows reflected in a patch of amber on the oak-paneled walls, and gleams of silver from the framed photos on the baby grand piano. He followed the light back to the window and beyond to the sensuous shapes of the topiary, and then past the oaks to the upper-story gabled windows of the Palmer place, where glittering sheets of reflected glare hollowed the white clapboard. He started, an involuntary contraction in his shoulders, causing his gaze to retreat. And there, just to the right of the bay window, was a small painting in an ornately carved gold frame.

The ice in his empty glass rattled as he put it on the silver serving tray and went to the painting. The resemblance to Sandra astonished him. A begowned young woman stood in the high meadow grass, a froth of white blossoms in the apple trees behind, blottings of pastel creams against a cerulean sky. Her turquoise gown was a diaphanous sheet of flame in the waning light of afternoon, while the tall, slender figure beneath was revealed in daring décolletage, in turn setting off the sumptuous line of the shoulders and the narrow meditative face. A tiny plaque at the bottom of the frame gave the title: *Spring*.

"Abby sold me that the day she moved out. I paid her a thousand dollars and thought I was doing her a favor. The appraiser put it at a hundred thousand last year for insurance purposes."

"It's a lovely example," he said.

"Sandra Chillingworth Palmer. It was Joe's idea to name the girls after their grandmother and her sister, the Chillingworth twins. Abby wanted nothing to do with the Chillingworth crowd and Manchester-by-the-Sea; she despised them."

He lightly touched the supple canvas, feeling it breathe under his fingertips.

"What was it about the Chillingworths?"

"Sandra Chillingworth was the great society beauty of her day. A child piano prodigy. At sixteen, she played Mozart in Symphony Hall. Then she began posing for Joseph Palmer. The artist made her famous, or she him. They were like movie stars in their day. Her photo could sell out an evening edition, a million bars of Ivory soap, so it was said. Her sister was something of a minor poet, but Abby found her, batty old Aunt Angela, a little hard to take."

He brought his face closer to the canvas, the smooth, muted tonalities of the paint blending to a lacquerlike surface, absorbing and giving off light with a vibrant glow. For a moment, he became absorbed in the deep-lidded eyes, a catch of breath, the dipping flight of a swallow, a wisteria bloom dangling in her fingers ... so like Giovanni's sad lasses.

"It looks just like Sandra."

"Like I said, old families, good genes like that, they persevere over time. It gives one hope, don't you think?"

It was as if she were prompting him to acknowledge his most hidden fantasies.

"I lost touch with Sandra after school."

"Sandra went to Europe sometime in her senior year. She was with-drawn suddenly, I think, and went to Switzerland to study art. Angela went to the West Coast—and good riddance—Berkeley, I think it was. Abby was disappointed; they were set on Radcliffe. But I'm not sure she could've even afforded it by then."

"Switzerland? Her senior year?"

"Abby and I lost touch after she moved out of the old house. But I remember something from somebody about Sandra leaving suddenly."

"Have you heard anything since?"

He turned abruptly from the painting and moved to the grand piano and the silver-framed photos. Marge Hathaway rose from the sofa and went over to adjust the curtains, pulling a blind in a bay window, something catching her eye outside.

"Yes, now that you ask. Oh, about a year ago this time, there was a hot spell, a dose of Indian summer. I was down in the lower garden and I saw a woman in the orchard. She was just standing there, staring off, like her mind was a million miles away. When I came closer, I recognized her immediately. It was Sandra. I called to her. She turned and smiled and walked toward me. She'd cut her hair and she looked a little worse for wear, as if she hadn't had any sleep. Her jeans were dirty with grass stains, like when she was a kid. She kissed me and we chatted. She was just visiting, she told me, just passing through. She was still lovely to behold, still the Chillingworth good looks—the chiseled features, Joe's blue eyes. I did find her a little distant and preoccupied and not willing to offer much. I asked if she had gone on to be an artist; as a little girl, she always told me she was going to be an artist like her grandfather. Her face lit up a moment and she nodded. 'Yes, I suppose … I suppose you could say that.' I asked her up to the house for some iced tea, but she seemed a little agitated and told me she had to run. She had tears in her eyes when she turned away. I was quite touched."

He stood listening, mesmerized.

"Do you hear much about her or her sister, or the rest of her family?"

"Since my husband died a few years back, I've been very bad about newspapers. I can't even be bothered to watch the news much. I barely see anyone. One stops caring. I reproach myself for this, but there it is." She glanced into her palm. "I would rather be gardening."

Among the silver-framed photos was an official portrait of a handsome army officer in dress uniform. Another was of a graveside ceremony, an American flag folded in a tight triangle as it was being handed to grieving parents. Next to this, a rosewood-framed Purple Heart on black velvet.

"You won't mention the painting to anyone, will you, Mr. Channing?" She glanced at him a moment and then returned her gaze to the window and the tired oaks and the blaze of white clapboard and glass beyond. "The man from Skinner's, a very nice man, said I really should be discreet."

"No, not a word. But thank you for showing it to me."

She handed him a thick art catalog emblazoned with a reproduction of a painting showing two women standing on a bridge in Venice. *Joseph Palmer: Sunlight and Scandal — The Life and Art of an American Master.*

"That's the retrospective catalog from the MFA show I was telling you about."

"Wonderful reproductions," he said as he began leafing through with trembling hands.

"Joe, Sandra's dad, is still around, I think. Somebody said he took up farming."

"Farming?"

"You know, this was all one farm originally. There is a great story—you've probably already come across it in your research—about the first Palmer in Concord, the sea captain who rowed his way up the river from his mill in Lowell and bought the Hosmer farm. It's in all the local histories." The sunlight sparked in her gray eyes and she angled her head into the shade of the blind. "Quite a family: captains, generals, artists—well, you never know."

"Rowed ... from Lowell?"

"Famous story."

"I'd forgotten about the connection with the Palmer Mill in Lowell." He looked up from the color reproductions as if not quite sure where he was.

"Yes, Lowell—that's right. But I think the original money was made in shipping."

"They knew Thoreau."

She smiled with the sure grace of the consummate insider. "Around here, somebody always had someone who knew Thoreau. And what did you say your book was on, Mr. Channing?"

He finally set the catalog aside and then joined her by the window.

"On Thoreau ... I'm writing a book about Thoreau and American landscape painting."

"Ah, so that's your connection, then; I knew it the moment I laid eyes on you."

"Thank you for the iced tea. Perhaps I'll have one more glass for the road ... and a quick look at your orchard."

She gave a shy girlish giggle and passed a shaking hand through her nearly white hair.

"Would you like me to call you a taxi for the trip back to town?"

"No thanks, I'm happy to walk."

"You know, you can find it—the Chillingworth memorial, not far from Thoreau's grave in Sleepy Hollow."

He finished pouring the iced tea.

"Yes."

"Sandra Chillingworth Palmer. Your Sandra's grandmother. She died in Venice giving birth to Joe. A tragic tale. Oh, but the memorial is a fine thing, the most poignant and beautiful thing in the whole place."

CHAPTER 8

E xhausted and giddy as he was, her words kept him going: "Your
Sandra's grandmother."

It was all clear to him, as clear as the new life he hankered
after: Sandra had been taken out of school; perhaps she hadn't
even gotten his letters. They hadn't had a chance to say good-bye. And
so it must have been Angela who had blown him off on that freezing
February day on Monument Square; Marge Hathaway's intonation rang
in his ears: "And good riddance."

When he finally reached Sleepy Hollow, he was dumbfounded by how
quickly he was able to find the memorial, which was two hundred feet
south of Thoreau's grave, just where Marge Hathaway had said it was.
With all his schoolboy visits to Thoreau's simple headstone, he'd obviously failed to notice the prominent monument set amid the long line of
Palmer graves. A matter of a few yards, a stray glance, and he would have
recognized it immediately: not an exact replica of the seated figure over
Moira Shannon's—*his grandmother's*—grave, but close enough.

Giovanni's masterpiece. One look was all it took: the evidence sealing
his belief in the intermingled fate of their families, of his ineluctable tie
to Sandra Palmer.

The eyes of the Sandra Chillingworth Palmer figure were different
from those in Moira Shannon Maronetti's monument, less meditative
and more alive, as if consumed with a desire forgone, a life abruptly
extinguished—head held high in a disturbing scrutiny of the eastern
horizon. A young woman who had died in her prime. In the mauve-
gray light of dusk, the cream-colored marble radiated an eerie nacreous
glow. Unlike the Lowell version, the hood was folded back on bare

shoulders, displaying her elegant oval head and long hair pulled up tight behind—a chignon, uncannily echoed by Sandra's at the dance. The open folds of the robe fully revealed the torso and the figure's small but fully rounded breasts. A seated model taking her pose. There was no denying the bold and sensuous intent of the carving. His fingers moved from the delicate lines of the face to the tendons of the neck to the supple breasts and rough points of the nipples, the goose-bumped ridge of the aureoles and slight indent at the very tips. This tactile realization took him over. This was the white heat of first incarnation, of all that would follow: the many stylized variations—Giovanni's sad lasses, strikingly good and some supremely beautiful, but lacking the raw emotive power of the original. He went again and again to the ridge of the cheekbones, the corded tendons at the throat, the mobile lips of a mystic goddess parted as if to whisper a prophecy into the supplicant's ear.

He was dizzy, aroused, past and present alive at his fingertips. He sank to his knees in the waning light so that he could better make out the intaglio inscription.

Sandra Chillingworth Palmer
Born 1893 – Died in Venice, 1914
In Memoriam
To my darling wife, who died as she lived,
giving life and light to the world.

Something in the stark inscription caused him to rise quickly and stand back, to take in the sweep of the Palmer graves. Each stone embraced a shadow, and these in turn were crossed by longer, column-shaped shadows spreading from the temple confines of a nearby grove of white pine. An indefinable jolt of terror or joy—the thing he'd been moving toward all day—swam up in his constricted veins. He moved to the last monument in the line; in the deepening dusk, it seemed like some keystone in a Paleolithic solar calendar. The granite marker was of recent vintage, a clean powder gray, unweathered, free of lichen and damp. The inscription was terse, chiseled deep, and easy to read. When he saw her name, his churning stomach gave way and he was violently sick.

Sandra Hosmer Palmer
October 15, 1950 – October 15, 1998
Beloved daughter and artist.
May your wandering spirit find its way home.

He knew it wasn't so. Marge Hathaway had seen her within the year; she would have known if Sandra had died. It wasn't possible. He saw Sandra as Marge had described her in the orchard: hair shorter, still beautiful ... "a little worse for wear."

When he finally managed to pull himself together, he sat staring at the cold stone, now a little less than a year old and the ground still soft. He crawled back from the grave, and as he did so, his hand struck another stone, a tiny slab of marble almost hidden in the grass. He wiped off the pine needles and squinted to read the inscription in the failing light.

Baby Joey
1966

The child's grave, her baby brother ... who'd fallen off the changing table. The accident. His rush of grief and doubt was staunched for a moment with the balm of certitude: She hadn't been lying to him after all. Everything she had told him that night on the river, how she'd reached to him for help, *had* been true.

Unlike Jimmy, she had told the truth about the accident. The word *accident*, passing through his mind, sealed a sense of correspondence between those events, Giovanni's drowning and the death of the Palmer baby. From the silence surrounding both had come disaster, and this moment only the last in a line. He turned in agony toward the star-crowded sky. Like a medieval theologian, he craved a comforting pattern, a hierarchy of linked spheres with the godhead of self as prime mover, where things had their allotted place.

As he trudged the last blocks to town, he began groping for the links to bind this newly emergent past to his present plight. Another victim of life's crapshoot? How he—once the ultimate control-freak lawyer—bridled at the possibility. At the stupidity.

And Jimmy ... the truth? If it had really been an accident, Jimmy would have said something to him, defended their dad with an elaborate plea as to the probabilities of hitting someone with a batted stone. Jimbo, drunk and full of himself, had probably hauled off and slammed Giovanni with the bat and shoved him in the canal.

He groaned inwardly at the awful thought of his brother's complicity in such a dreadful cover-up.

And what about Sandra? She hadn't said a word about her twin sister, Angela. A sin of omission? Another thing, given his career of turning a blind eye, they had in common.

He saw Monument Square ahead. At the top of the expansive green sward was the welcoming gray clapboard facade of the Concord Inn, while straight ahead lay the turn onto Main Street where he'd confronted Sandra on that bitterly cold February afternoon.

Except it hadn't been Sandra.

William Channing, aka Michael Collins, seized the moment to dissect the disastrous conversation of years before: his coming off a bigger fool than ever.

You've, you've … cut your hair….
Write? God, who has time to write anymore….
Didn't any of it matter to you—mean anything?
You gotta be joking. Asshole. Let the fuck go… .
Maybe we could go get a hot chocolate or something. The Inn is right here—okay?
No, I can't do that … you know, my mother."
Your mother?
You know.
Yeah, right—bad idea, terrible idea. *I really got to go.*

He stood mortified on the curb in the spotlight glare of a streetlight as he replayed those moments over and over in his mind. It had been Sandra's twin sister, Angela: "wild as they come," according to Marge Hathaway. Angela, who had brushed him off with such gut-wrenching disdain.

To William Channing—*how the devil had he come up with William Channing?*—this was only too obvious: She hadn't even known about his mother working at the inn.

And following on from his clueless myopia and Angela's booted heel turned in the gritty slush, everything had gone wrong with his fucked-up life.

Those bare winter-starved trees along the path to the river; the steady serial echoing smash as the wielded oar blade took out every window in the boathouse, 122 according to the headmaster's letter. And that very evening, the look of stricken horror on his mother's face behind the reception counter at the inn when he'd been dropped off by cab with one duffel bag and a cardboard box full of his precious books—"Oh my God, a temper like your father." And this leading to the smell of cordite and the exploded flesh of his mangled hand in Vietnam ... and the smoking candles and incense in St. Agnes and his mother's face lying in waxen emptiness ... and all the rest of the sorry mess.

A bogus life had come out of Angela's cruelty and his gullibility.

William Channing, poet and stalwart friend of Thoreau, could be a little more circumspect.

There had been the broken banister in the boathouse, Sandra had missed the bus and check-in, and he was a rough diamond from the wrong side of the tracks—that's why no one would give him a straight answer about Sandra when he'd tried to contact her. They had been warned. Angela, too.

The way William Channing saw it, Sandra had been the best thing to happen to him; but for his lack of faith or witless naïveté, she would still be alive.

He blinked up at the streetlight and then looked to the enormous obelisk in the center of the square, carved with the names of Concord's Civil War dead. Cold comfort in the litany of human disaster there.

Where had he been a year ago on October 15? Arguing with his soon-to-be ex-fiancée, Catherine, about whether or not to sell his Capitol Hill town house and move to more fashionable Georgetown—in a down market? Recriminations from Catherine that he'd refused to run for Congressman Neeley's seat.

October 15? She had died on her birthday. How could that happen, unless...

"Oh Christ, not that!"

The Emerson-Alcott dance had been on October 15. If she had been born in 1950, it had been Sandra's nineteenth birthday. *Eighteen—eighteen: never been touched by a guy.* Why had she lied about her birthday?

And how could she be dead? Marge Hathaway had seen her alive less than a year ago, "a hot spell." He could still feel her life, her joy, her laughter.

"Michael, for Christ's sake, man." He grabbed at his pounding head, terrified he might be going crazy.

The mistaken identity, the misapprehension … to have it twisted free of his soul so abruptly—one thing become another—left such a terrifying gap that the thought of a new identity gave immediate comfort.

He shifted his backpack, longing for rest, and turned again to the softly lit gray clapboard sprawl of the Concord Inn—a stage set for a new and better life. William Channing smiled. He walked slowly, as if needing to absorb the scene piecemeal: the broken wagon wheel sunk in the grass, the hand-painted sign of the inn, the wooden plow and rusted sleigh and white flagpole—artifacts to ground the illusion of an authentic Colonial sanctuary.

A place where William Channing might feel right at home.

Had not Thoreau's family once owned part of the inn? Hadn't his mother's years at the inn been her happiest? The inn *was* the town and its people, a welcoming symbol that a community transcends the calamities of its members.

As he came nearer, he remembered the period rooms and antiques, the scent of pine floors and beeswax and oak fires, roast beef and Yorkshire pudding on Sunday. And the summer he had washed dishes. Sitting with his mother on her break in the abandoned dining room after Sunday's formal luncheon. Listening to her play the piano in the cocktail lounge and later sitting with a silver pot of hot chocolate giving up a trickle of steam. Her proud smile for the scholarship kid from Lowell who was well on the way to a higher life—Harvard, as she saw it. And the gentle touch of her hand and love's reflected light in her chestnut-colored eyes.

William Channing, literary man and chronicler—new script in hand— eased up a confident smile. All were in his power now, to return with him from the shadows for a second chance … in light of new evidence.

His mother would certainly approve.

"You don't have a reservation?"

The receptionist eyed him skeptically from under mousy bangs.

"I'm a day early, an academic conference in Cambridge that bored me to oblivion. I hiked the battle road all the way out here—heat almost got to me. I had a room at the Holiday Inn, but I thought I'd give you a try."

She tapped at her computer terminal—the only noticeable change in over twenty-five years—her face bathed in a bluish glare.

"There's a cancellation, a regular client, professor at Wayne State, comes every October for a month to do research. Problems at home. But I'm afraid it's one of the original period rooms, the Thoreau Room, upstairs, a small suite with bathroom, expensive."

"Thoreau Room?"

"Yeah, you know, we've got 'em all: Emerson Room, Louisa May Alcott Room, Hawthorne...."

"But this is *the* Thoreau Room?"

"One and only."

"That's fine."

She squinted. "Two hundred and eighty-five a night."

"Fine."

Eyebrows narrowing, she snapped a finger at the keyboard and an ink-jet printer shimmied to life at her elbow.

"We take MasterCard, Visa, AmEx."

"Why don't I pay cash, right now." He fished in the backpack at his feet. "Say for the first week." He awkwardly began to count out the bills on the reception counter, keeping his left hand out of sight, barely able to concentrate on the task as things caught his eye. "My bags are at the Holiday Inn in Cambridge; I'll have them sent out by taxi first thing tomorrow."

She took the money and handed him a registration form and key.

"That's fine, Mr...."

"William Channing," he said as he signed the form.

"Mr. Channing, welcome to the Concord Inn. You'll find your room at the top of the stairs right around the corner, on the way to the dining room. I hope you enjoy your stay."

He slept for the better part of two days, much of the time with a raging fever. He got up only to drink, to take Tylenol, to use the bathroom, and to stare out the bay window over Monument Square. He was aware there had been a change in the weather, a cold snap. The room at night became very cold, but the location of the thermostat escaped him. He huddled under his blue comforter to conserve warmth, balling himself into a fetal position to better concentrate himself, to recharge his powers so that he might emerge from his battered chrysalis and fully assume his new role.

After his fever broke, he spent another day lying in bed, girding himself for what was to come and analyzing the detailed map of time's accretion in the decor of his room. A brass warming pan hung at a quirky angle on the tongue-and-groove paneling under the eaves, and good Colonial Revival furnishings were scattered tastefully about. Presiding above the rolltop desk was a curly maple-framed daguerreotype of the bearded middle-aged Henry David Thoreau. Mentor and friend to one William Channing. And below this, a framed excerpt from Thoreau.

My dwelling was small, and I could hardly entertain an echo in it; but it seemed larger for being a single apartment and remote from neighbors. All the attractions of a house were concentrated in one room.

Taking this cue, he contemplated how he might merge his life with that of the inn … safe and sound within plain sight.

And in so doing, he found himself becoming entranced with the refracted sunlight playing over the bay windows: a transparent triptych on the massive altar of the sky. Windows entered his dreams and daydreams, drawing him back to memories of the Pawtucket Canal and those reflected ranks of white-sashed windows in the Palmer Mill. Or as he had been as a boy, watching Giovanni though the single window in his shop—his grandfather's large sweaty hands caked with marble dust, going after the last details in his sculpture with the tiniest chisels, as if one more tap, one last nudge of a grain might waken the sleeper from her stone.

And those 122 panes he had systematically smashed in the boathouse.

Sometimes he'd sit up against the brass railing of his bed and just stare at the bay windows with the fervor of a cabalist, intent on fathoming the flaws and whorls and arabesques in the antique panes. There, a reflecting pool, where night metamorphosed into the wisteria purple of dawn, and the ruddy dusk faded to silver moonlight, and night again, prey to the beams of searching headlights that fell on his watching eyes with painful suddenness.

In the transition from past to some new state of being, he felt a terrific power—poised to leap, though his aim was still unsure.

And there were sounds. He'd press his ear against the massive old beams under the flowered wallpaper, listening to the heart of the inn and the routine thrum of voices: greetings and farewells in the reception area, laughter as tables were set in the dining room, the piano in the cocktail lounge. And memories flooded in of a long-ago summer dishwashing job, when he was on the cusp of fulfilling his mother's dreams for him. Toward evening came a tide of inebriated cheer as the television was tuned to the Red Sox game in the pub directly below his room, punctuated by shouts of encouragement from the regulars. All the murmuring community of voices seemed intent on sharing their secret lives with him.

Only hunger and concern that a reputation for undue eccentricity might hinder future plans galvanized him into action.

He managed to sneak down the back stairs and get to a pharmacy and clothing store and back to his room without being spotted by the inn staff. Then he showered. After contemplating his week's growth of beard in the bathroom mirror, he took the daguerreotype of Thoreau from its place over the desk and placed it on the counter in front of the mirror. He stared at his transparent reflection in the glass, which neatly overlaid the craggy, weathered face of the poet, moving forward and back to get the line of the chin whiskers in vague congruence.

And as he did so, the passage of the years from his first adolescent infatuation to the present moment crystallized in him. Where once Thoreau's stoic gaze had suggested an august seer and mentor, Michael now saw Thoreau as a man of thirty-nine with unruly dark hair and stringy Galway beard, younger than Michael's present self but prematurely aged by the incipient tuberculosis that would kill him within six years, at only forty-five. A man who had sustained loss after loss, rejected by the two women he'd loved, devastated by his brother John's early death, then his sister's, surrounded by a family of spinster aunts. These were losses and disappointments, which had turned Thoreau into a confirmed bachelor, facetious and skeptical of women; a man who had succeeded at many practical things but remained tortured by feelings of failure in his chosen field as writer and naturalist. He had been frustrated, too, in a life of inquiry running out of time, by his inability to discern the underlying principals—the theory of evolution and genetic inheritance nearly within his grasp—that explained the connections between all living things, notwithstanding the power of love, the attraction.

Gazing into the daguerreotype—*if their Roman noses didn't almost match!*—Michael finally picked up his razor and trimmed his beard to as close an approximation of Thoreau's chin whiskers as he could manage.

He rolled his eyes at the result, his little inside joke. "What the hell."

William Channing replaced the portrait of his confidant on the wall above the desk.

So transformed and casually reattired, he had himself an enormous breakfast in the dining room and began to go through as many newspapers as he could to see if his disappearance had been noticed. Nothing. He chatted amiably with the staff, introducing himself with pronounced bonhomie, making sure he got his story around with sufficient and compelling detail: an enthusiastic Thoreau scholar in town to flesh out arcane aspects of his subject's life. Fortunately, though sadly, he found no familiar faces—probably just as well—among the inn staff, no one, as far as he could make out, from his mother's time, from his summer washing dishes.

Back in his room, he checked the morning news on television. Again nothing. Maybe Mahoney's henchmen didn't know quite what to make of what had happened. The sense of freedom and possibility derived from such ambiguities buoyed him further.

Sitting purposively at the rolltop desk, he unpacked his backpack. He leaned the etching of the bridge in Venice in its old matting against the rear of the desk, thinking he needed to do something to better protect the fragile paper. He put the green morocco *Walden* in a place of honor on the desktop. He removed the photo of his mother from between its pages and placed it off to the side of the desk—an antique silver frame would do nicely. The bit of toy railroad track he contemplated for a moment, then grudgingly found a spot for it, too, on the desk.

The FedEx pack he hid behind a phone book in the bottom drawer of the desk.

With his room so repopulated, he nodded to the votary figure above the desk and sauntered out into the cool sunlight of early fall.

The campus of Alcott Academy—out of bounds in his school days except for glee club concerts and the like—was about as he remembered it from the entrance on Main Street. As he walked the circling pathways between the clapboard-style buildings, some original, some newer, post-modern additions, he found little to distinguish the young women he saw from those he recalled from decades before. Their hair seemed shorter and their clothes darker, a bit baggier, lots of pockets, designer backpacks and serious trail boots. He found his way to the school library and was relieved to find his presence went unregarded. Once in the reading room, he was quickly able to lay his hands on the yearbook he was looking for. Among the senior-class photos were the Palmer twins on facing pages. Angela's was a typical three-quarter studio shot like the other senior photos. Her hair was cut short in a line of bangs and the expression on her face was one, it struck him, of cool—yes, cruel—ferocity, a smile of self-satisfied triumph. There was a kind of preening strength and self-worth in her flinty beauty. The lines beneath the photo read, "Angie baby, off to Berkeley to become a West Coast rocker, but you still light my fire. Voted most likely to give Gracie Slick a run for her money."

Sandra's photograph was not a studio portrait, but seemingly an informal substitute, perhaps a family snapshot. Her profiled face was relaxed, with a dreamy, distant look in the large eyes. She looked younger than her sister, perhaps because of the long hair to her shoulders or because the photo might have been a year or two out of date.

"Art school in Europe. Our class artist and class act, who faded too soon from our rogues' gallery. Voted the next Mary Cassatt," her caption read.

He continued leafing slowly through the yearbook, seeking their names, more photographs. There were shots of Angela in a production of Arthur Miller's *The Crucible*, and in senior ballet class, showing a tall, sinewy figure with sleek legs and exquisitely arched feet. He caught glimpses of that rebellious senior year: bell-bottom jeans, peace marches, and bleary-eyed faces with fists upraised in protest. A whole section was devoted to the Emerson dance—high point of senior year. Pages of snapshot pastiches: couples in heated clinches on the dance floor, kissing on a sofa; six girls in various states of dishevelment standing in triumph by the exit door of the bus, arms around one another, each holding up an article of clothing—a tie, a shoelace, a belt, a pair of boy's briefs—a war party returning with scalps.

The old anger swelled up in him over the fact that he and Sandra had been singled out for disciplinary action, what with the excesses going on all around. He shook it off, that old poison, and went to find the back issues of the Alcott Academy alumnae magazine. In the class notes from the previous winter's issue there was a remembrance written by the 1970 class secretary.

I'm sure it came as much of a shock to most of you as it did to me last fall when I found out about the suicide of our classmate Sandra Palmer in her Cambridge apartment. I have spoken to many of you about this tragedy and we are all at a loss to explain it, much less to come to terms with our memories of Sandra. One grieves, of course, for what must have been her unhappiness, but also for the fact that we let her get away from us, that we could have so completely lost touch. I, for one, did not even know she had returned to the States and lived only forty minutes away, doing graduate work at Harvard. I am haunted by her memory.

As you all know, Angela was my best friend. And yet when my thoughts drift back to those "wild and crazy" days of our youth, memories of Sandra surprise me: poetic images, quiet islands of normalcy in the maelstrom of our rebelliousness. Through it all, good old Sandra—dedicated, motivated, loyal to her lights—was painting, always painting or drawing. I remember her searching expressions, always on the lookout, angling her head to catch a stray ray of light or color shaping a cloud or tree. In case any of you have forgotten, she won the Ralph Bradley art prize for New England independent schools three years running, a record never equaled. How many times did one come upon her silently working in the studio late at night, maybe with Tom Rush or Judy Collins playing on WCRB, or sketching outside in all manner of weather? She was a perfectionist when most of us didn't give a damn about anything except ourselves. She seemed immune from all the cynicism. We hinted scorn for her predictable, boring, comfortable clothes, neither rad-chic nor flattering. Was she ahead of her time?

Perhaps my sadness and consternation have something to do with her paintings. I recently discovered a cache of her work in an old locker in the basement of the studio, which she must have abandoned when she left us so suddenly before Christmas of senior year. I have mounted an exhibit of these paintings in the dining hall and in my dormitory. They are very good. One feels she lived a different life, somehow better. Come back and have a look at Sandra's paintings, see what you missed. You will be astonished.

She was a stranger in our midst. Sometimes I wonder if it is because I was so close to Angela—oh, Angie baby, where have you been, girl?—that I failed to appreciate Sandra. Of course, Angela was everything Sandra was not—yet in my memory, they begin to merge, and not simply because they were twins. Angela was, underneath, the most determined and creative soul I have ever known. Were they the reverse image of the same smoldering spirit? And so in almost equal measure, it saddens me that I have lost touch with Angela since her first years at Berkeley. If tragedy was to strike, one imagines it might have been Angela—Angie burning herself out à la Janis Joplin, but not before, like an Atlas rocket self-destructing on the pad, lighting up the world. But Sandra—no. How often I find myself lingering with her paintings and believing that, in the end, she may have been the best of us. Perhaps it is just an age thing—and I, a teacher! I like to think she embodied the finer virtues, things I try to pass on to my girls: selflessness, loyalty to a vision, integrity, and a focus on what you have to give as a woman. At least the paintings remind me each day how little I knew her, how hard it is to love, to see, to feel … of a friendship neglected.

If anyone has heard anything about Angela Palmer—or if by some miracle, Angie, you should see this—please let me know. Why don't we all make more of an effort to keep in touch. Love to you all, Ruthie Horowitz Cunningham.

He slumped into a chair, a wave of despair bearing down on him, and tried to hold back his tears.

Anything but suicide.

Suicide? The word grated against every fiber of his being, feeding the awful premonition that had suffused his mind at the night watchman's description of the jumper from the bell tower … the terrible sense of premeditation in the act. As if Sandra's tragedy had, unbeknownst to him, hung over him for the last year, directing him to confront his own demons before it was too late.

Carefully drying off his face with his sleeve, he went back to the yearbook and found Ruth Horowitz, author of the remembrance. The face with its prominent nose was familiar: frizzy dark hair, striking heavy eyebrows, fixed, fully shaped lips, a lean athletic eagerness in the thrust of the narrow chin. He read the lines below the photo: "Captain of tennis, dance committee chairman, Princeton-bound. Baby Ruth off to Tigertown to sharpen her claws on the coolest guys around. Voted most likely to kick Chrissie Evert's butt."

He remembered her all right, standing by the door of the faculty lounge in the clutches of his nemesis, the Emerson Academy social chairman, after he and Sandra had been given the heave-ho from the dance floor.

Sandra's paintings hung in the common rooms of the dining hall. There were about twenty, small landscape studies on canvas board with cheap strip frames. He saw, even in the sketches and studies, the precocity of her hand, the already-refined sensibility for delicate tonal transitions and atmospheric forms that he'd noticed in Marge Hathaway's painting by her grandfather. Studying a larger, more finished canvas, he was drawn to a meandering lichen-stained fieldstone wall fretted with olive green meadow grasses and purple creepers, an orchard beyond ... familiar from his walk in the meadow up from the bank of the Concord River to the Palmer house—and yet not. The same wall where she'd been photographed sketching, he realized, remembering the picture in Marge Hathaway's album. The orchard behind, where her grandmother had posed for Joseph Palmer's paintings. Where Marge had found Sandra standing, lost in thought. Her home ground now known to him as if for a lifetime, only here translated into a scene of loneliness and loss, as if she'd purposively adjusted the off-kilter perspective and removed herself from her own creation.

Immersed in the scene, he recalled her intrigued response to him on the night of the dance: *"With a purpose?"*

And there it was again, the echo of a better self nipping at his heels: Thoreau's faith that the true purpose of life is only discovered in the silence off the beaten path, where past and future collude to form the eternal now.

What had she said to him about the challenge of change ... to hold on to changelessness? And in this, as implied by the remembrance in the alumnae news, her life and death—even her art—were further reminders of their generation's failure to hold on to things of value.

He found his way to the tennis courts and took a seat in a thin rank of bleachers to watch an ongoing practice. The coach was a tall, dark-haired woman in her mid-forties, wearing a white cap and white Nike warm-up suit. He recognized Ruth Horowitz from her yearbook photo. She was putting the girls through a drill of alternating backhand and forehand cross-court drives. The girls, seventeen and eighteen, he thought, dashed from corner to corner with determined grunts punctuated a millisecond later by the thwack of the ball. They were sweating hard in the cool afternoon. Their coach was encouraging them, shouting, cajoling. Then she took the place of one of the girls to demonstrate; still fast and graceful, she hit the ball with precision. The spectacle of movement tapped something in him: the flight of the ball, the fitness and energy of the young women—the team effort. Tears came to his eyes. He could not believe they would ever grow old, that life could break them—how any one of them could ever take her own life.

"Hi, can I help you with something?"

He stood and climbed down to where the girls' tennis coach had stopped at the gate of the court.

"You're good with them," he said, seeing the defensive tightening in her lips, her brown eyes intent beneath her cap, the tiniest lines radiating at the corners, more time in the sun than she probably cared to think about.

"Thank you. They're great girls." She cocked her head, examining his face. "Do I know you?"

"I was very moved by your tribute to Sandra Palmer in the alumnae magazine."

He saw a near paralysis come over her face and then give way under pressure of a deep intake of breath and sigh of release.

"My God, I thought it was you. I remember your face."

"Ruth Horowitz?"

"Cunningham, Ruthie." She said it like a new recruit to an officer, shaking her head and pulling off her cap. "Somehow, I figured it had to be only a matter of time before *you* showed up."

"I didn't know until the other day."

He could detect in the stiffening of her back and shoulders that his reply had floored her, returning her to her own first knowledge of the tragedy, and from there a straight drop into scenes of their youth.

"Oh ... you poor thing." She touched his elbow, an instinct to reach across the vast divide and make sure he was really there. "You remember me, right, from the dance?"

"Dance chairman."

"Chairwoman—whatever." She smiled, then shrugged, nervously fingering the Prince racket in her hand, pressing a string into place. "When you weren't at the funeral... ." She shrugged.

"I never spoke a word to her after that night at the dance."

She bit her lip. "And you know, she wasn't supposed to be at the dance. That's what really threw me. Angela, her sister, was supposed to be there; it was the biggest deal of the year. And their birthday. The list had been closed for weeks. And somehow Sandra talked Angie into letting her go in her place. Sandra never went to dances—never.... She was clueless about guys."

"She traded places?"

"Beats me how it happened."

"I'd never been to a dance, either. We thought it would be fun to give it a try."

"A try!" Her face became distorted. "Angela was so pissed that she'd missed the whole thing—boy, that Goody-Two-shoes had stolen her limelight, and gotten laid to boot."

She put a hand to her lips.

"Is that what it was about?"

Ruthie Cunningham pulled a towel around her neck, drawing herself up as if to regain a faltering dignity.

"You," she said with a curious smile, "haven't changed all that much from her drawings."

"Drawings?"

"I found a whole mess of her drawings." She winced. "Well, I mean, you guys really screwed up big-time."

"You mean ... we got caught?"

"Caught! You got the prize for stupidity." Her voice rose with alarm. "Not to show up for the bus, an hour late, so that they actually had to go out and *search* for you—what did you expect?"

"Sandra said she would just make her own way back and that it wouldn't be a big deal."

"Shit—excuse my French—she didn't know the drill; she'd never been to a dance. You could get away with almost anything as long as you showed up at the goddamn bus and checked in with the faculty chaperone. Then at least *they* were off the hook. Believe me, I know about these things ... *now*."

"She got into trouble, huh?"

"We refer to it in this newly enlightened age as a 'nightmare of deep do-do.'"

"Well hell, I almost got kicked out right then and there. I was put on probation and restricted to campus until Christmas."

"You were a bad boy." She looked at him, pained, then turned her gaze away. "There was stuff going around—you know how it is…. She'd been seduced, and worse."

"Worse?"

"That she'd been raped, that you'd taken advantage of her, that you were a scholarship kid with an ax to grind, something to prove."

"It wasn't that way at all."

She slumped and put a hand to the chain-link fence to steady herself.

"I know."

He stared at her averted face, the creep of sympathy in her eyes.

"Like you said, we were stupid."

She threw up a hand in frustration.

"You gotta understand, she was this … perfect girl, not a troublemaker like Angela. She was like an anachronism of the fifties or something. Then like that, out of the blue, she goes off the deep end and gets herself pregnant."

"Pregnant?"

"Let me tell you, it even shook up Angie, her sister. Totally weirded her out. Angie cut her hair, dressed like some fashion puss. Threw the gang for a loop."

Something was pressing on his diaphragm, a weight, almost to the point of choking. He forced his dry lips to form each syllable. "She … was … pregnant?"

Ruthie Cunningham took a step back, taking all of him in.

"You … didn't know?"

"I wrote letters. I tried… ."

"Listen, I got to go. I've got an AP section in English in a few minutes."

"Can we—"

"Are you in town?"

"Yeah, I'm staying at the inn."

"Okay. Let me see—let me see." She made a mental checklist. "After dinner, there's my dorm and then a faculty meeting. How about we meet for a drink in the pub, say ten o'clock?"

"That would be fine."

She held out her hand, wiped it on her towel, and held it out again.

"Sorry, I've forgotten your name," she said.

He looked into her face, seeing again, for an instant, the young girl she'd been at the dance. As he gave his name, he thought he detected a flicker of uncertainty in the corners of her eyes.

"Channing, Bill Channing."

CHAPTER 9

In the computer room of the Concord Free Library, he turned to the task he had been dreading.

HARVARD GRAD STUDENT
SUICIDE IN BOYLSTON STREET APARTMENT
CAUSES LANDLADY HEART ATTACK

The *Boston Globe* Internet archive produced six related stories in the space of a little over two weeks, from October into November of the previous year, a tight little bell curve of interest that fell off almost as quickly as it appeared. The story had made it to page three and then quietly disappeared to the back pages. That he'd missed it only figured, since he'd given up bothering with the local papers years before. Last October, he and Catherine had begun fighting like cats and dogs. The first story was purely factual, then more details, followed by interpretative and increasingly speculative stuff. He scanned the articles with a veteran eye for press hype. How many media life cycles had he tracked in his day?

Sandra Palmer, a suicide, was found by her stricken landlady. A self-inflicted knife wound. Dead three to four days before being discovered. No signs of forced entry or foul play. Harvard University spokesman expressed shock and dismay. The deceased had lived and worked for many years in Europe before returning to Harvard for graduate work in art history.

The follow-up stories promoted the usual suppositions: fascination and gloating that another member of the success-obsessed Harvard elite had bitten the dust. Then even juicer speculations: another neurotic, highly strung product of an old and distinguished but fatally dysfunctional family having succumbed to drugs and depression in the competitive academic rat race. Except there had been no drugs, no drinking, no signs of depression, no dramatic mood swings, no broken hearts or stormy relationships, no academic or career pressures. And she'd been away from her family for years. Just widespread incomprehension from teachers, students, and friends. By every account, she had been a mature woman with a successful and gratifying career in art restoration. Her professors were unreservedly enthusiastic about her work and the hands-on experience she brought to her studies. The undergraduates in the seminar she taught were infatuated with her and with the nitty-gritty insights she brought to her teaching. The same words kept appearing: *serious, absorbed, dedicated, brilliant, European sophistication, stylish, earnest, friendly, down-to-earth, no hidden agendas*. As far as anyone knew, she had never married, but she seemed to have had an ample number of friends, although few—when specifically questioned—had felt particularly close or had known her *that* well. Most assumed she'd had a *life* or a *past*, at least a circle of friends, probably back in Europe.

The only indiscretion turned up by the *Globe* reporter was that she had been dating a Harvard undergraduate, a student of hers in an introductory course on Renaissance art; both had kept it quiet, for obvious reasons. Bottom line: Everybody who had known her was appalled and incredulous about what had happened. As he read the final stories, he could feel the reporter's frustration as line after line of inquiry dried up. The aloof father, now an organic farmer in Concord, had been reticent to talk but had told of meeting with his daughter a few times since her return the previous year, finding her to be in top form, happy to be back in the States—no hint of a problem. Mother an Alzheimer's case in a semiprivate assisted-living home in Worcester. Sandra Palmer had everything going for her.

Except she was dead ... a woman who had carried his child. And by stabbing herself.

"Christ."

He stared at the blinking cursor and her name in the tiny window of the search bar: Sandra Palmer. He felt sick to his stomach.

It just didn't add up. He sensed inconsistencies everywhere. Even a weird echo of his earlier missteps: He'd been fooled once or had made a terrible mistake and he wouldn't—ever—do so again. And what about her pregnancy? Had she had their child?

In vague desperation, casting around for his next step, he idly typed in his own name over hers and clicked the NEW SEARCH icon. A Reuters article, reprinted in the late edition of the *Lowell Sun* of September 20, popped up.

TOP AIDE TO CONGRESSMAN MISSING IN LOWELL

Lowell police reported yesterday identifying the abandoned rental car of Capitol Hill aide Michael Collins in the parking lot of the municipal cemetery. Collins had attended his brother's funeral a few days previously but had failed to show up at a family gathering following the burial. The police report that Mr. Collins also missed a meeting in Worcester scheduled for that same day. A spokesman in the congressman's office in Washington says that Mr. Collins was on an extended leave of absence after the sudden death of his brother and had not been expected to return to the office for a few weeks. He left no itinerary with his secretary. Michael Collins was last seen at a restaurant on Andover Street.

In a related incident, police are checking into what they are describing as a possible hit-and-run accident that same day on the Andover Street bridge, in which an unidentified red pickup truck struck the guardrail, possibly hitting a pedestrian. There were no immediate eyewitnesses to the incident, but two nearby residents who heard the collision and saw the vehicle speeding from the scene gave conflicting accounts that a pedestrian might have been thrown into the Pawtucket Canal and subsequently swept downstream. Detectives refused comment as to whether they suspect a connection between the disappearance of Mr. Collins and the accident on the Andover Street bridge. An ongoing police investigation is under way.

As he read the words, the sensation of falling came back to him again, absent the impact of the water. It was more a comforting sense of surcease, of drawing a warm cloak of anonymity around his shoulders. He clicked on the next article, a piece from the *Boston Globe*, also dated September 20.

Prosecutors in the state attorney general's office released a list of indictments yesterday coming out of the ongoing grand jury investigation into campaign finance irregularities and related construction contracts related to the Lowell Plan in the early 1990s. The indictments included Congressman Neeley's top aide, Michael Collins, and other members of the congressman's staff both in Washington and Worcester, along with a number of prominent local builders and politicians.

As he read the rest, he couldn't resist a knowing smile—confirming his better instincts: Timing was everything. He was delighted to be rid of that stupid name he'd been saddled with by his father in some misbegotten romantic allegiance to Irish nationalism. Now it was just another name in cyberspace, surrounded by half-truths and lies, just as her story was full of inaccuracies.

Although, even from the perspective of cyberspace, he had to give it to Mahoney: Every angle worked to perfection. Mahoney had obviously had his lieutenants drag Michael's name through the mud for the delectation of the grand jury. They'd make him, dead or alive, the centerpiece of a political show trial. Now missing and trapped with the cash: the perfect fall guy. He saw precisely what was to come.

But none of this unduly perturbed him, because he felt safe, especially with his true identity tucked away out there in the ether, or even in the newspapers ... a mere name on a page. Let Mahoney take his best shots, heap what dirt he liked: There would be time. In the meanwhile, he felt an odd sense of creeping joy, of vital possibilities, as if he were in search of the truth about what he might have been, had he not given up on the young man that maybe—just maybe, Sandra Palmer had loved.

He tapped the SEARCH icon for the permanent holdings of the Concord Free Library and typed in the name Palmer. The titles of books appeared as if at the wave of a necromancer's wand—old friends just waiting for his call. After all, they were family, *his* Sandra's blood, *his* grandfather's friend and colleague. *His* and Sandra's child would have carried their blood.

The Memoirs of Captain Samuel Hoar Palmer: Reflections on the Seafaring Life During the Era of Napoléon and the Beginnings of Water-powered Indus-try in Lowell. Privately published, 1844.

The War Diary and Letters of General Joseph Manning Palmer. Ticknor and Fields, 1869.

Joseph Palmer: Sunlight and Scandal — The Life and Art of an American Master. Laura Ryder, exhibition catalog. Boston Museum of Fine Arts, 1997.

A builder, a warrior, an artist … a bloodline not easily dismissed.

"Here you go, Bill," said the bartender, getting him his second Heineken. "How's the book coming?"

Two minutes and he was already on a first-name basis with Jack. Or maybe Jack had him mixed up with somebody else.

"Fine, Jack," he said. "Slowly but surely."

He smiled at the ginger-haired bartender as Jack gave the rosewood countertop another swipe with his bar rag. Over Jack's shoulder, hanging against the pine-paneled wall, was a constellation of rusted horseshoes, branding irons, a washboard, and various bits of antique farm equipment from a vanished bucolic age.

There had been a few moments on the way back to the inn from the library when he'd had doubts, when he'd seriously wondered if he wasn't out of his mind. But then arriving back in his room, he had picked up the green morocco *Walden*, which had once belonged to Joseph Palmer (the retrospective catalog called the artist "a self-described disciple of Henry David Thoreau"), and opened to a page that contained marginal annotations in the same precise hand as had signed, titled, and dedicated the etching to his grandfather Giovanni.

I am time and the world, summer and winter, village life and routine, pesti-lence and famine, refreshing breezes—joy and sadness, life and death. Time is a delusion.

Paraphrases from Thoreau's journals ... an artist's dialogue with a fellow artist.

William Channing had smiled as he closed the book, glancing at the etching of Venice. Dimly, he'd discerned the crooked path he must follow.

His life was filling with voices ... ancient and modern.

"Ah, I know how it is. You're in good company." The barman indicated the half-filled room of oak tabletops and Windsor chairs. "Over there, the fella in jeans and sweatshirt, Tom Jandos. Good old Tommy, been writing his book about Thoreau for twenty-three years. Works as a park ranger over at Walden Pond. Saved Walden from the developers, you know. Tommy-Tom knows more about Thoreau than any living man, woman, or child—more than Thoreau knew about himself, more than he can ever get between the covers of a book."

"Is that right?" He glanced over his shoulder at a tall, lanky man—a scholarly rival?—bent to the tabletop, where he cradled a drink in his hands.

"And right over there, Annie Torcelli, works at Emerson's house doing interpretive tours. Bewitching is our Annie, and she'll have your mind twisted into more transcendental knots than a Virginia creeper."

"Umm, good man, Ralph Waldo."

"Dave Parker yonder, another park ranger, hangs out at North Bridge and Miriam's Corner for interpretive tours. Our Davey boy, why, he lives and breathes a single bloody Wednesday in 1775 like it's nobody's business—know what I mean? Little before your time."

"And some."

All these and other dreamers would soon become his regular company.

The bartender swiveled as the door banged.

"Ah, my boy, now if it's your tennis game needs improving and you're looking for a hot date Saturday night, this not so young lady is the answer to your prayers."

"Hey, Jack." They exchanged high fives. Ruthie Cunningham was wearing a pastel yellow Nike warm-up suit; her hair was damp and swept back from her tanned forehead, as if she'd just stepped out of a shower. "I'll have what he's having."

He stood to shake her hand. She shifted a manila envelope to her left hand and glanced up at the television.

"Red Sox fan, huh? What's the score?"

"No idea," he replied.

"Four-one, Sox, top of the fifth," said the bartender as he got her Heineken.

"I don't see many games in my neck of the woods," he said.

"And where might that be?" She tapped the bar impatiently.

"The Midwest. I'm an English professor at Wayne State University."

"And you're staying, here?" She gestured with outspread fingers.

"I'm actually here to do some work on Thoreau."

"No kidding." She cast a knowing eye toward the bartender. "Rooms are expensive."

"Hear you got the zoning passed on the tennis club," said Jack with a wink at Ruthie.

Michael looked at Jack and then back at Ruthie. "I have a neat little stipend for my sabbatical research project."

"Some people have all the luck." She picked up the bottle of Heineken, not bothering with the glass, and gave the wet circle on the counter a rub with her elbow, as if to save Jack the trouble. "Well, that makes us both overworked and underpaid academics, I guess." She took a long swig of the Heineken. "What did you say your name was again?"

"William—Bill—Channing."

She pushed off from the bar. "Bill, you know what really—thanks, Jack—pisses me off is how many of our contemporaries out to change the world ended up on Wall Street making a gazillion bucks."

"I guess it happens."

"Yeah, well, now I've got their goddamn children to teach, their daughters no less, and they want it even worse … among other things."

"Your girls at practice, you looked really good with them."

"Hey, compared to their mothers, I'm a bargain." She motioned toward the corner. "Let's get a table … *Bill*."

She was stopped by a waitress, who gave her a hug and kiss.

"Ruthie baby, long time no see."

"It's the start of term, Helen, know how it is."

The waitress gave him the once-over and passed by.

"Nice beard," Ruthie said as they sat.

He stroked his chin.

"I thought I'd give it a shot."

"The Thoreau look."

He shrugged.

"You seem to know everybody," he said.

"Aha," she said with a dismissive wave. "Summers, I run the Nike tennis camp—to make ends meet. This was the hottest summer I can remember. And this ... for all of us two-time losers in love and politics." She tipped her bottle to the rustic raw-beamed ceiling. "This is where we plot to get our piece of the action." She tapped the manila envelope on the table. "Anyway, I thought you should see some of this stuff."

She pulled out drawings, small pencil and charcoal sketches, and spread them on the table. None was particularly finished; they were more in the way of studies, the face at different angles, concentrating on the chin and half dimple, the dark eyebrows, the rugged line of the nose, a lank shock of hair.

A shivering numbness went up and down his spine when he saw these adolescent renditions of himself—another self—spread across the tabletop like a game of solitaire. "Jesus." He blew out his lips, pulling some of the drawings closer. "I forgot about these."

"She knew how to draw a face—Michael?"

He met her accusatory stare without hesitation.

"Short story is, I hated the name my dad stuck me with. First it was: Was I an IRA fanatic or something? And later: Was I the famous astronaut who didn't get to walk on the moon?"

She smiled, relieved.

"Hell, my father changed the name from Abromowitz to Horowitz because he liked the way the guy played Chopin. And then I kept my married name."

"*Hell*, what's in a name?"

"I gotta tell you, it was a little spooky seeing you there in the stands this morning. Then I've been a little spooked since it happened last fall."

"I'll bet."

"Angela, her sister, and I were real pals."

"Who should have been at the dance but wasn't."

"Listen, I was going to just leave you with the rest of this. But maybe you should look at it first." She pulled some papers out of the envelope. "I actually found the letters in the school files months ago when I was writing my remembrance; these are copies. As they say, you never met me and I never gave you these. Frankly, I'm aghast."

She handed him a letter written in an even, flowing script.

November 14, 1969

Dear, dear, my dearest Michael,

I'm desperately trying to get my head straight. How crazy, how absurd what happened. I can't believe it was me there saying and doing those things—what was I thinking? Please forgive me for having gotten you into so much trouble. I had no right to do that. I told them that I was to blame. I feel rotten that I may have screwed things up for you—amazed I could have been so wild—me, the paragon of good behavior, Mommy's "sensible girl."

Over the last days, the thing that has worried me the most was if I had simply given into the whole scene, gone with the flow, behaved like the other girls—everything would have been okay. But I had to be different. On the way to the dance in the bus, the other girls were going on so—I'd never heard such expectations about boys. It frightened me that I didn't feel like they did, that maybe there was something wrong with me. But then when I was actually with you, holding your hand, I began to understand what it meant to want someone. Even so, just because everybody else was doing it doesn't make it right.

But Michael, I can't help admitting that a big part of me feels that we didn't do anything wrong, that it was right and meant to be. I feel deeply, and I have always believed this, that in the end one must be true to oneself. In my life, at least in my painting, I've tried to be guided by an inner truth. Does that seem weird or phony? It is why I've always loved painting; because when you work hard enough to really see something clear, it registers so deeply, as if poured into the very crucible of your soul. Something becomes complete in you and you in it. You're such a fan of Thoreau, I'm sure you must know what I mean. All you have to do is open your eyes, it's everywhere. I mean the truth. A moral universe. Wasn't it Emerson who said that the whole of nature is a metaphor of the human mind? You see, I'm not quite as much a slouch on these things as you probably thought. But letting on, is another thing. People think I'm weird enough as it is.

Perhaps you felt a stranger to our woods, but weren't we all strangers once? I feel, as I remember your face, your eyes, when I try to draw from memory, that maybe you brought a renewed power, a fresh vision. I even went back to Thoreau, thinking I'd better bone up. Now I really understand what you were saying at the dance, about how Thoreau was trying to encourage his readers find a place where we can <u>be</u> ourselves, and find truth and purpose in our lives. So it's okay <u>not</u> to be like everyone else. To go your own way.

And this is why I refuse to deny my feelings. I love you, Michael. I am proud to say it. I am proud that we made love. Proud to have "let go" when it mattered and when it was right. My happiness is real and true and seems to glow in my breast like some glorious rose-madder fruit. It's as if my heart will burst with its ripeness.

Don't think me an idiot. Did I seem like a spoiled idiot to you, yakking away in the dinghy?

What I hate is all the cynicism and joyless laughter that goes on around me. People look at me like I was a numskull who got in over her head. The others endlessly dissect the night of the dance, going into lurid detail about their conquests, their narrow escapes, all in the game of one-upmanship. It was all a lark, a competition to show off their stuff. What a waste to make so light of the things that make us most human and put us in touch with the best part of ourselves.

But I feel free—for the first time in a long time. My love has made me free. I cringe that you will read this. You'll probably laugh. It's just I've been caged so long, living in the shadow of others, and I've finally come up for air. I'm not blaming my family. No excuses. You really helped me. You listened. I blink in the light after years in solitary. I hear the lost language of things. I see you.

When I close my eyes, I see your earnest, questioning face, the hint of fear in your eyes, the crease of a troubled brow. But there is your touch. I remember being with you by the river, in your arms with the moon's glow all around, that purest forgiving light and only the distant stars to share our lovemaking. For the first time in my life, I really felt like I belonged, in your arms, somewhere beyond the moon and stars. It was almost as if you had always been there, if only I'd known where to look. Beyond the moon and stars. If there is truth, it is in your loving arms.

I read back what I've written and I shudder. The ranting of a spoiled eigh-teen-year-old. I got you into trouble. I can't forgive myself for that. Please don't hate me. What else can I believe? If not in love and beauty and our bet-ter selves, then what? Otherwise, all that's left is hate and resentment. And I do know a little bit about that. But I'm running out of words. You must help me find them. You are the one who wants to be—a teacher, wasn't it? Help me. Write to me. Tell me I'm not crazy.

All I ask is that you won't hate me. That, I couldn't bear. And try to believe, if just a little, in what we were, what we are, what we found that night by the river. I'm dying to see you again once the fuss has blown over. I'm grounded; I'm stuck until at least Christmas. Keep the faith. Write me—even it's just about Thoreau. Take care of yourself. I do love you, as crazy and irresponsible and naïve as it is. Don't hate me, don't forget me. Love, Sandra

He stared at her signature, afraid if he raised his head, he might totally lose it. For a few moments, he caught a glimpse of the kid he'd once been, when her every word would have registered with unfailing joy.

Finally, Ruthie touched him gently on the arm. She had tears in her eyes.

"I know, I know … that letter floored me; it has haunted me for the last six months. It prompted what I wrote in the alumnae news." She blew at a stray strand of hair, her long nostrils flaring. "I envy her … to have felt like that at eighteen. It was as if her genuineness made everything we did seem that much more disingenuous." She smacked the table. "I mean, obviously, they confiscated the letter, intercepted it. It was in a stamped and addressed envelope that hadn't even been opened. I can't tell you how bad I feel."

"It's okay," he said, blinking. He was stupefied: it was precisely as he had imagined it only days before.

"No, it's not—it's rotten." She squeezed his arm.

"Sandra was nineteen; she lied about her age."

"Nineteen?"

"She was born in 1950."

Ruthie shrugged. "Here's the other thing I have. It's a letter from her mother to the headmistress."

December 20, 1969

Dear Jill:

Thank you for your thoughts on the phone the other day. As you know, the report from the doctor on Sandra's pregnancy absolutely devastated me. Sandra never showed an interest in boys, just the opposite. I am at a loss. She has always been such a studied, careful child. And she has been so consumed with her art studies and schoolwork that she seemed immune to the blandishments of others, especially Angela's crowd. Don't get me wrong. I'm not blaming the school. I blame myself. The divorce and the move have been very hard on the girls; I handled it badly. Also, as you well know, I have been so preoccupied with Angela over the last few years that poor Sandra has gotten short shrift. She was the easy one—painfully sentimental: Her attachments always ran so deep and strong. Did I miss something?

Although they both deny it, I have a sneaking suspicion that Angela may have had something to do with the circumstances. For years, growing up, they were inseparable. Then when Angela hit puberty and discovered boys, along with her rebellious streak, they seemed to go their separate ways—happily for Sandra, I think. But as you well know, in this crazy climate today where anything goes, Angela has become such an idol to the other girls. The "ringleader," as you put it. Sandra must have felt some pressure to live up to her other half. Angela can be so seductive. I have no doubt she would like to recruit Sandra to her camp and pull her down. Just between us, I think Angela has got a bit too much Palmer—Chillingworth—blood in her. Yet I've never mentioned a thing about the outrage and scandal surrounding their grandfather! I suppose it was another mistake on my part to put the two girls in the same school. At the very least, I should have had them both on the Pill.

Sandra sticks to her story: It was all her doing. She defends the boy and takes all the responsibility. She has always been a loyal soul—never said a bad word against Angela in her life. She says she really cares for this Collins character, but I agree with you that he must be kept out of the picture, for both their sakes. My lovely daughter's taste only extends so far. I have spoken to Joe, the girls' father, and he has promised to try and come up with the money to send her to the school in Geneva. The necessary options are available in Switzerland. A fresh start may be just what the doctor ordered. And, too, it will be a chance for Sandra to get away from Angela for a while and reestablish herself.

On the subject of Angela, maybe you can keep a sharp eye on her for the remainder of the year. Her grades seem to be holding up, but the attitude problem only worsens. It would be nice to have at least one of them go to Radcliffe, before it's totally swallowed by Harvard. But Angela is still intent on Berkeley. Perhaps with Sandra gone, she won't feel the need to play the rebel so much. Thanks for all your kind help on this. I'll be in touch soon, when plans for Switzerland are finalized. Best, Abigail Palmer

He slumped back in his chair and closed his eyes.

"Bitch," he spat.

"Listen," she said, fingering the bottle, "you got her daughter pregnant."

"It was my child, too."

"The way we heard it, you were bragging about your conquest, like it was a big joke."

"Is that what you think?"

He looked hard into her shiny face, the prominent nose, highlights of satiny yellow beneath her olive brown eyes. She licked at a tiny dark birthmark that extended the line of her lips at one corner of her mouth. She lowered her eyes.

"No, not after Sandra's letter. I could never have written a letter like that, not back then—a child struggling for adult feelings. It made me ashamed. I cried like a baby when I read it."

"Why would Sandra have lied about her age?"

"Well, it explains Angela—sort of, being precocious, I mean."

"Funny," he said. "It brings it back. So young, so stupid … and yet, maybe *they* were our better selves."

"*They* …" she muttered, a troubled look flooding into her eyes. "When we thought we could remake the world. When anything was possible."

He pulled himself up in his chair as if he'd been caught in a compromising position. "Do you know what happened to the baby?"

"No idea."

"So you don't know if she had an abortion or if she gave birth?"

"Who knows, she might have given it up for adoption."

"You went to the funeral?"

"If you can call it that." She rubbed her calloused palm. "Sad. Weird. Me, a couple of others girls from the class who lived nearby. Her father. The minister. Count 'em on two hands—that was it. If I hadn't called around, I wouldn't even have known there was a funeral to go to. Ten minutes—and such a beautiful place under those tall pines—a few words, pathetic."

"What about her father?"

"Totally out of it. Tall and gaunt, with a face like worn leather, in a wrinkled jacket and muddy boots. Not a tear, not a word. He couldn't even bring himself to look around to see who was there. I went to him by the grave to offer my condolences and he only nodded. Poor guy. I think her mother's in a nursing home someplace."

"And no mention of a child?"

"Nothing."

"And Angela?"

"Who knows. Nobody's seen her in over twenty years. I even asked him at the funeral about Angela. You'd think I'd asked about a stranger. He grunted, shook his head."

Michael took a last swallow from his bottle and picked up Sandra's letter again.

"It's so unfair," she said. "She was really in love and gets pregnant. While we just wanted to have fun."

"And not get pregnant."

"Not in the good old days."

"Good old days? You mean the Pill."

"And before AIDS."

"Except she wasn't on the Pill."

"She was in love—and you?"

The accusatory look from Ruthie pressed at his breastbone.

"Me ... what?"

"Were you in love with her?"

He motioned to Sandra's letter. "Like that ... oh my God." He shut his eyes and closed his fist tight round the empty bottle. He shook his head. "I wrote her, you know. I wrote her letters."

"Well, now we know *why* she didn't get them."

He tipped his empty bottle to the side and spun it on the tabletop, watching as it slowed.

"So why did Angela let her take her place at the dance?"

"Search me. She could get terrible cramps and be depressed before her period. Flying high one second, down in the dumps the next. Why she was so enamored of the Pill, among other things—it kind of evened things out. And then, later, after the dance, Angela was so fucking pissed."

"Because ... she missed out?"

"Hey, her sister scored." She shrugged. "Your guess is as good as mine."

"Like her mother said, a competitive thing?"

"No, no, I don't think so. More like—it's weird with twins. And I've taught a few over the years. They have a secret language; they intuit each other. Nothing is hidden. It's like Angela wasn't there with you, but she was—*she was*, and to have felt Sandra's ..."

He reached and spun the bottle again. "Genuineness, you said." He prompted: "While Angela was ..."

She stopped the bottle, neck pointed at him. "Helter-skelter."

He winced and looked up from where her hand covered the label.

"Sandra wanted ... I mean, I thought, looking back on it now, knowing...."

"She wanted to get pregnant."

He flung himself back in his chair and signaled to the waitress for another round and slowly took a breath.

"It wasn't as if we got carried away, you know."

The note of indignation in his voice brought a troubled grin to her face. "But you *did*." She leaned toward him, again exploring the tiny birthmark with her tongue. "You *really* did."

She placed her palm on the letter between them.

He said, "So, Angela was upset."

"She was a fucking sexual predator."

He eyed her sharply. "I can't believe you run a girls' dorm."

"I'm off duty and I'm feeling sorry for myself and, yes, I run a dorm, a good dorm, better than anybody, because I *know* ... better than anybody." She made a fist. "I was crazy about Angela, but if I had a girl in my dorm like her, well, I'd run her out of town."

He smiled acidly.

"I only had the pleasure of meeting her once," he said. "Just down the street, that winter. And she blew me off like a piece of shit."

"Ah, your reputation had preceded you."

"What Sandra wrote in her letter, about hate, resentment—could that have been about Angela?"

"There was a coolness in Angela, under the surface. But there was loyalty, too, between twins—especially those two. They would never wash their dirty laundry in public."

"So, Angela was a bitch?"

The beers arrived and she began downing hers.

"Listen, Angela was …" She sat back as if suddenly taken unawares by an oldie on the sound system. "She had antenna a mile wide—heard those whispers from deepest space. She was always the first to know: to drop LSD, to spin a disk that even the Boston DJs didn't have. At sixteen—or whatever, she took off by herself and hitchhiked to Woodstock. I've got the photo from *Life* magazine of her standing there in the mud with her tits hanging out. And she had tits, real tits. She was the toughest muffin on the block. She knew about sex—I mean *really* knew about sex. She lived in her skin. She was an exhibitionist. She jangled and jived and purred. And she was a lover like no other."

He brought his face close to hers, smelling the floral-scented lotion on her skin.

"Except she left you in the dust—*honey*."

"Hey—*honey-bun*, she was Madonna before Madonna. She was so far ahead of the curve, she was often out-a sight. After Sandra got shipped off to Geneva by mommy dearest, Angela cut her hair and retooled at Saks and started taking drama classes in Boston—strutting her stuff."

"Christ, you go on."

"If that had been Angela at that dance, *you* would have been sushi on a stick—a real mind-bender." She compressed her lips and blew a warning toot on the business end of her bottle. "You'd have found your little universe rearranged for you—big-time."

CHAPTER 10

He and Ruthie closed down the pub after one o'clock. They were a little drunk, she more than he. He walked her to her dorm at Alcott Academy and then headed back to the inn. Sandra's letter was in his pocket, her words already grafted to his life, along with the voices of her family found in the library that afternoon. A full moon, heavy like burnished bronze, hung in the milky sky. He found himself reaching out to the pale veneer of light as if needing to better shape the drifting veils of sensation. He breathed deeply, the downdrafts of cooler air releasing scents of pine and wood smoke.

Unused to excess alcohol, he nevertheless found himself full of nervous energy. He wondered if he might yet develop the taste, travel the road to hell and damnation in his father's footsteps. The netherworld through which he passed only confirmed his certainty: The voice in that letter, full of such determination and love—she could not have died by her own hand. Every instinct in his body cried out against such a fate. And needing confirmation of this, he found himself passing the inn and heading for her grave in Sleepy Hollow.

"Sleepy Hollow," he murmured, as if hearing the words in his own voice might clarify the oddity—that strange evocation of communal faith: that death of the beloved is only a sleep, an interregnum of the saved, while waiting for reunion with loved ones. But absent surviving memories or love, what a *hollow* then.

It perplexed him that he could barely remember what he'd written in his intercepted letters to Sandra. Had his expression of love come anything close to hers—had he had it in him? Or had he parroted more Thoreau to her—awkward Thoreau, who couldn't figure out women to save his life. Had his letters of mawkish endearments been laughed at by others, or confirmed suspicions about his intentions: a blue-collar scholarship kid making a play for a girl out of his league?

He lingered at the gates of the burying ground, the stone markers shadowed by moonlit white pines. The prospect of a cemetery at night calmed his agitated mind. A childhood spent fetching Giovanni home for dinner from his studio by the Lowell cemetery had left him with a workaday respect for such places, haunted not by the dead but by his grandfather's conviction that love memorialized outlasts death.

He paused at Thoreau's grave, now wondering if he was taking this Thoreau thing too far for his own good. A small cairn of pebbles had been piled at the base of the simple granite marker. Friends Henry never knew he had.

Suddenly, it came to Michael, what as a kid he couldn't understand: Thoreau had been haunted—not by graves, not so much by his dead brother and sister, but by missing lives—often lingering by abandoned cellar holes marked by purple lilacs to meditate on the fate of Concord's early inhabitants, defunct families with sons gone west with their dreams of gold and free land, and the daughters to a cotton mill in Lowell or Lawrence … families that had flourished and were no more. When Thoreau had bought the shanty (planks for his Walden home) from railroad worker James Collins, prototype of all Thoreau's sleepers, he'd contemplated the sad fate of the displaced man and his family, one of hundreds of Irish immigrants brought in to build the Boston and Fitchburg railway. Without Thoreau, the name of James Collins and the others would have been lost to history. The thought sent a chill through him.

"James Collins," he said, repeating the name out loud. As a boy, he'd wondered about that James Collins in the pages of *Walden*, intrigued and embarrassed in equal measure.

Such thoughts brought to mind Jimbo Collins's drunken boasts in half the bars between Lowell and Lawrence about his track-laying progenitor. Michael couldn't help a smile now at his father's antics, feeling some vague comfort that the extinction of his own family—he, last of the Mohicans—seemed of less moment considering the disaster of human life visible on every terrace and copse in the cemetery, much less the demise of the Palmer clan.

With a nod, he found a pebble and added it to the others on Thoreau's grave.

He walked down to the road on the way to the Palmer graves. The headlights of a parked car suddenly illuminated the road. He stopped, shielding his eyes. A short squawk of a siren and the police car moved slowly toward him. He moved aside as the officer rolled down his window.

"Sir, what are you doing here?"

"I was just up at Thoreau's grave, paying my respects."

"Sir, it's a little late for sight-seeing. May I see some identification, please."

"I'm a Thoreau scholar. I'm staying at the inn. I left my wallet in my room. I'm just out for some fresh air—one too many drinks at the pub. Jennifer at the front desk will vouch for me."

"Sir, what is your name?"

"William Channing—Bill."

"Jennifer is a fine lady. The guy who divorced her had to be out of his mind."

"He had to be an idiot; she's such an attractive redhead."

"Now you see, Bill, kids come here at night for parties. They get drunk and vandalize the graves."

"That's got to be a pain in the ass for you."

"Good night, Bill." The officer tipped his broad-brimmed hat. "You keep an eye out, okay."

The squad car continued on and exited the cemetery.

His heart was beating wildly as he continued. He'd have to get some identification, and pronto.

He found the line of Palmer graves, vividly aglow in the moonlight. Seeing the dim, plainspoken geometry of these monuments somehow softened the blow of Sandra's death. Like the meadow flowers, the stones implied the perennial, at the very least a steadfast linkage of blood binding the generations, of love so invested in the world as to outlast present disaster. And what of his fidelity to those fleshly bonds?

He held up his mangled hand and the half stump of his ring finger. Had he loved her enough?

Then he bent to the first grave in the line, easily making out the inscription, which had the look of white phosphorus in the moonlight, intent to decipher, if he could, the fragile code of life's knotted cord.

SAMUEL HOAR PALMER 1773–1861
CAPTAIN OF ALL HE SURVEYED

He could smell again the dusty pages as he had turned them in the library.

The patriarch, the wanderer, founder of the family fortune. His diary was a thing of understatement and narrow escapes. Trained as an engineer, he'd made his first fortune as a merchantman, running contraband cargoes in and out of Napoléon's Europe. Within two years he was captain of his own small brig, and ten years later he'd lost four fortunes and made five. He'd seen Venice in the last days before Napoléon's hordes despoiled that glorious republic. He'd sailed to Tahiti and Hawaii before these idyllic paradises had been ravaged by Western diseases.

And then, as if his gambler's instinct had suddenly grown cold, he'd cashed out of the China trade and joined in with Boston's moneyed crowd to invest his capital in a revolutionary project at the Pawtucket Falls on the Merrimack: the city of Lowell, city of canals, soon-to-be wonder of the manufacturing arts. In a matter of years, the onetime merchant prince had transformed himself into a captain of industry and had reverted to his first love: a fascination with machinery and technology, how rivers could be diverted, channeled into canals, and harnessed to power huge turbines.

Samuel Palmer's mill along the Pawtucket Canal in Lowell was not just bigger than the others but better designed. He'd handpicked the bricks and had them laid in diamond patterns to emulate the brickwork in the Doge's Palace. A remarkable bow to aesthetic concerns for a man obsessed with engineering efficiency. Management bored him; he left it to others. The Palmer Mill at its height in the 1840s and 1850s employed six hundred women, mill girls recruited from the surrounding area, many from failing farms and broken families forced to move west. Of the lives of his workers, it was said, he knew little and cared less. His diary spoke only of "improvements," of reinforcing canals and refining turbine designs, anything to promote greater efficiency of power transference.

And then one morning in his early sixties, as he wrote in his memoirs, everything changed.

It was a hot day in the early fall of '44 and I had just arrived in my carriage at the Lowell mill to check on the performance of a new turbine in the runway of the Pawtucket Canal which had been the object of some concern over the previous weeks. Suddenly, my attention was distracted. A young woman was being led out screaming and moaning by two other women. One hand was wrapped in a bloody bandage. The front of her dress was dreadfully stained. I immediately took charge and demanded to see the injury. The bandage was removed and a most horrifying wound displayed by the poor hysterical girl. Her hand was a bloody tatter of skin and bone. I got the unfortunate girl into my carriage and to my own doctor in short order. There was little to be done for her except take off the remainder somewhat above the left wrist.

Assured of her care, I made a hasty return to the mill, vowing to get to the bottom of the accident and find what machinery was to blame. The second-floor foreman was still engaged in cleaning the machinery of the remnants of human flesh. I demanded an explanation, seeing around me now row upon row of these young women's stricken faces. The foreman assured me that there had been no malfunction but that the worker, a Lizzy Norton, had been notoriously careless. I could tell by the watching faces that this evaluation did not ring true with her fellow workers. We then made a thorough examination of the machinery, and assurances were given that more care would be taken. At which point, one of the women, eyes blazing, confronted me. "The speed, sir," she cried out, "the hurry of it makes for accidents, sir." The foreman was quick to contradict her, explaining that the speed was no more than could be easily handled by the conscientious worker. After a few more minutes of sharp discussion, I felt a sudden impulse to escape the place.

I went for a walk along the Pawtucket Canal in the direction of the Concord River with the intention of relieving my mind. A black mood settled upon me—a thing I was prone to but which, in the past, I had been able to alleviate with some technical problem or busy activity. As I walked, I turned back to the mill—now I saw only a monstrosity, an abstraction. What had begun for me as a lovingly drawn series of calculations on paper, of the intersection of nature's power and my ingenuity, a process to channel those forces into productive gain, was suddenly abhorrent. Like the artist, I had fallen in love with my drawings, my plans. And yet this thing seemed utterly separate from me—something from Dante's circles holding these daughters of New England in thrall to my machinations. I had cheated death a thousand times to bring about this feat of engineering—this engine of enslavement.

I determined to walk off my despair. Soon after, reaching the end of the Pawtucket Canal, I came upon an old fisherman along the banks of the Concord River with his tiny skiff drawn up onshore. On the spot, I offered him fifty dollars for the craft, and he accepted with alacrity. I took possession of my craft and headed out into the stream with two good oars at my disposal. My spirits lifted somewhat as I realized I was again in command of such a craft, and the notion came upon me of letting the current take me downstream to the Merrimack and thence to Newburryport and the outlet to the sea. I thought only of escape. Perhaps the darker part of me wished to offer itself in sacrifice to the elements I had for so long sought to tame. And yet I entertained this temptation only a short time. Some part of me resisted and instead I found myself eagerly rowing upstream, against the currents of despair, my body joyous with the exertion.

The countryside through which I passed quickly improved as I went on. A Garden of Eden, it seemed, filled with small farms and orchards, stately elms and oaks draping the sky with their plumage. Never had I been happier. It then came into my mind that perhaps I had missed some turning in my life, that a chapter still remained unwritten. I had spent so much of my early days in flight from the strictures of my father. And even when returning a rich man, I remained distracted by the ambitions to build and design machines to put more wealth into my pockets. And yet here, around me on every side, was the undiscovered land of my birth, the heart of our young nation.

I was an exile returning to his childhood home, the rural life of my ancestors. By late afternoon, my back was in pain, my palms done for. I spied a farm along the river where cows quietly grazed. I put ashore there in hopes of food and refreshment and, most of all, rest. Stepping into the waterside meadow, I was immediately overwhelmed by the smells of autumn, captivated by the purple grasses and the loveliness of the stone walls, and the apple orchard beyond, laden with red and russet fruits, like flaming votive lamps in the lowering sun. A rosy mist overspread the river. The peace I felt in that moment was indescribable. It was as if all things in nature presented themselves in their eternal verities. I realized in that moment how much of my life had been a preoccupation with the outward details, to the utter neglect of the indwelling spirit.

My knock upon the door of the humble but solidly built farmhouse brought me face-to-face with its owner, a Mr. Eziekiel Hosmer, farmer, blacksmith, and carpenter. He and his wife, Hannah, welcomed me as a lost stranger, fed me, and offered me a bed for the night. Eziekiel built a roaring fire to fend off the chill that came with nightfall and dispatched a young rider from a neighboring farm back to Lowell and my family to assure them of my safety. We talked long into the night. My hosts were old and worn-out from their many years of hard labor on the land. Just to gaze into their flinty eyes, one felt the old vital blood of our democracy. The Hosmer homestead had been in the family for almost two hundred years. As a boy, Eziekiel had seen the redcoats at North Bridge; his father had fought and been wounded at Miriam's Corner. He and Hannah had two children. Thomas, the eldest, had gone west many years before to make his mark in the world, but after a few letters from Ohio, all correspondence had ceased and they feared him lost. To my chagrin, the daughter, Muriel, worked in the Appleton Mill in Lowell. They had always hoped she might marry and, with her husband, take over the farm. Of that eventuality, they had despaired also. The farm was in debt. Eziekiel had broken a leg a year before and it had failed to heal as strong. Hannah did what she could, but it was a sad business. Their faces showed their cares. I found it heartbreaking that this noble property had become a burden upon these hardy souls in their declining years. After a good night's sleep on a couch by their fire, I offered the following morning to purchase their farm at double what the market would have it. After few minute's deliberation, they accepted my offer and we shook hands on it over breakfast. They thought to go live near their daughter. And so the Hosmer farm became my country retreat and within a year my permanent home, and soon after the favored abode of the Concord Palmers.

William Channing could not resist an amazed smile.

Samuel Palmer had rowed from Lowell to Concord. He felt the hairs at the back of his neck rise.

How impossible it seemed that such a tiny plot of earth could contain such a larger-than-life personality—a man of such towering ambition as to blow off the likes of Jack Mahoney. He fingered the mustard-colored lichen-veined lettering on the captain's grave. A woman with such blood in her veins—he thought of Sandra picking herself up from that fall from the gallery, her impetuous move to drag the racing dingy into the water, spinning it with the oars.

How could she have killed herself?

He continued down the line to an impressive tea-colored marble obelisk erected by subscription from the Twentieth Massachusetts Regiment.

GENERAL JOSEPH MANNING PALMER
1829 – 1873

General Palmer had led troops from the Second Battle of Bull Run right through the Wilderness, to the Battle of the Crater during the siege of Petersburg, where he was captured with Negro troops while leading a charge on his wooden leg. He'd been wounded in action three separate times. His leg had been shot off at Antietam. But it was the dysentery and lack of medical attention in the Confederate prisoner of war camp—an expeditious exchange had been refused because of the Negro soldiers—that left his health broken, his remaining years plagued by stomach and intestinal complaints and failing strength. The general's diary and letters contained harrowing firsthand accounts of battle, but even more impressive had been the unquestioned faith in the Union and willingness to sacrifice in the abolitionist cause.

Near the very bottom of the obelisk, along its plinthlike base, an inscription had been clearly added in recent times, a humble addendum to a martial life, barely showing above the grass that grew up thick around the stone.

IN HIS BOYHOOD, A FRIEND AND COMPANION
TO THE POET HENRY DAVID THOREAU.

This was the great-grandfather Sandra had mentioned to him, who had known Thoreau, her words like wildfire in him then … and now. Thoreau, the great abolitionist, perhaps infusing the young man with his vision and soldier's sacrifice. Hadn't Sandra, too, brimmed over with quiet faith—even Ruth Cunningham had seen it—a faith in their integrity as caring and conscientious souls.

As if to confirm his growing conviction, he went over to his grandfather's memorial for Sandra Chillingworth Palmer and looked at the inscription that had been added in the back of it.

JOSEPH PALMER II 1869 – 1933
HUSBAND AND ARTIST

That was it. The artist's ashes had been spread in the orchard behind the house. Simply a chiseled line or two on the back of his wife's monument, as if he'd only been an invisible interpreter of her earthly beauty.

Facing the seated figure in her open robe, he took a deep breath and held it. The correspondence between Sandra Chillingworth Palmer's sorry end and her granddaughter's suicide was harrowing. Sandra's grandmother had died in her early twenties, after giving birth to her only child, in Venice. That at least was a death that could be understood … or had it been another accident, another disaster? As he stared at her marble flesh aglow in the moonlight, he recognized what an odd thing the monument was in this old Yankee burying ground—a stark, sensual nude amid so many prosaic symbols of mortality; how even in 1922, when it was dedicated, it must have caused a stir in proper Concord. And yet, Michael realized the appropriateness of the memorial. Joseph Palmer's last work, the late nudes, daring and erotic and searingly modern, constituted a total departure from the early sentimental figures. This had resulted in terrific scandal in the late1920s, when the Chillingworths had sued him for defamation of their dead daughter, forcing or encouraging the move of his studio from Concord to Stockbridge. It was the memory of his wife's body that had galvanized his declining years and inspired his late style, what a new generation of critics and historians were calling his greatest paintings—on a par with Klimt and Schiele.

Confronting Giovanni's marble figure, he was suddenly aware of how his grandfather must have been unconsciously imitating the dreamy eroticism of his painter colleague—how his white-bearded grandfather had always circled a sculpture in progress, eyeing it critically, marking with chalk where it needed more work. Michael had found nothing about Giovanni's sculpture in the library, nothing about a friendship with Joseph Palmer—"a fellow artist"—as if the capricious currents of the decades had sheared the sculptor from the bosom of the Palmer clan. Cast off, Giovanni had seemingly washed up without visible past on the shores of Depression-era Lowell in his makeshift workshop.

Michael reached out with his hands, glancing around as if fearful of some impropriety. Then he moved to the marble breasts. Sadness or longing had prompted the impulse, but the feel and contour of the stone was electric to his fingertips. Even the cold, gritty texture, hardened points against his palms, returned the moment to him when he had first touched Sandra's body with his two strong hands. He was aghast and yet thrilled. And with the sudden onslaught of a painful erection came the memory of all the guilt-ridden lust that had broken his reticent yet determined adolescent pride. But the power! That a creative genius could give shape to such an erotic fixation, removed from the contingencies of flesh and blood, and that it, like a seed having lain dormant over many years, had found in him life again. The law of death subsumed in the law of life. Only habitual propriety prevented him from indulging the release he yearned for.

Finally, his heart still pounding, he moved on, passing Sandra's stark grave—an imposter, a cheat, a mistaken identity!—to the tiny flat marker sunk in the earth.

BABY JOEY
1966

For a moment, the inscription in the stone seemed to draw out all the remaining strength in his body. He heard again her words as she told him about the baby falling off the changing table, the attendant terror and guilt: *Nothing is an accident.*

Her voice jolted him out of himself.

He touched the tiny chiseled letters in the stone … as if to a memorial for his own lost child, the child he and Sandra had conceived on the moonlit bank of the Concord River.

He resisted the impulse to go immediately to Sandra's apartment on Bolyston Street. Instead, on the following day, he made himself walk the streets off Harvard Square, lingering at the Fogg Museum and the art history department where she'd spent a good part of her year back in the States. He wanted to discover the lost rhythms of her day-to-day life, the context of what had been, by all descriptions, a simple life.

And yet as he walked the leaf-dappled paths of Harvard Yard—trying to get a feel for her Cambridge year, he kept stumbling on familiar scenes that distracted him with memories of his own pitifully short but dazzling visits to Harvard: the eager staff of the admissions office showing him around, the scholarship committee offering him the brass ring, topped off by the crew coach and alumni rowing fraternity promising him the moon and then some. Only to have it scuttled with the headmaster's succinct report of systematic and vicious vandalism—122 panes of broken glass in the boathouse, to be exact—and his subsequent expulsion. If he'd burned a flag or trashed a dean's office or spray-painted antiwar slogans, all might have been forgiven. But a troublemaker from the streets of Lowell had no place at Harvard in 1970, which had enough on its hands with homegrown troublemakers: sons and daughters of esteemed alumni, no less.

The house on Boylston Street where Sandra had lived was a gray-green Victorian clapboard with massive dormer windows and extensive well-kept gardens dotted with the tattered and desiccated remains of pastel blue hydrangea. It was enormous and just plain charming, far from the depressing and run-down heap of student housing he'd half-expected—the kind of ugliness that might have burdened a life used to loveliness. He opened the gate and walked the brick path to the front door, took a couple of deep breaths, and knocked.

"So," he said, a few minutes later, settling back in a ratty but comfortable chair in Gloria Landsdowne's cluttered living room, "it wasn't as if you were taking in a complete stranger when Sandra Palmer came to live here?"

"You were childhood friends?" The old lady, pushing her late seventies, had been hard to convince.

"High school. I was at Emerson Academy and she was at Alcott Academy."

"Yes, forgive me, you did mention that."

"I wish I'd had as nice a place when I was in graduate school."

"Well, you see, it was my late husband's idea to take in a graduate student from the department each year. We were both getting on, if you know what I mean. An extra set of hands. And she was thoroughly vetted by the department, and then I had two interviews with her. She couldn't have been nicer. Very well put together, lovely clothes, but not showy or expensive. She was well-spoken, her accent having something of a European ring, and she had expressive Italian hands. But I liked that. My husband was a medievalist, you see, and so we spent many years in Europe. She loved his things ... our collections." She waved a liver-spotted hand toward walls filled with dark canvases of wounded saints and baleful sinners, the cabinets of carved ivories and enameled Psalters. "From the inside, if you take my meaning."

"Inside?"

"She handled everything. Touch was as important as the seeing. Though she did have awful hands, poor dear."

"Awful?"

"She had restorer's hands." She whispered this revelation as she bent toward him, her skin pale and powdered.

"So." He shifted in his chair so as to keep his left hand out of sight, staring at the tiny red capillaries in her cheeks. "She didn't seem—what?—unhappy?"

"Happiness, unhappiness ... what a fine line to draw as one gets older. You probably think I never asked myself that question. But let me tell you, Mr. Channing, the apartment remains *unlet*."

"It must have been a terrible shock."

"It was *my* house, our children's home. And I don't know if she was unhappy or not, but she had no right to do that, no right at all."

"She wasn't married?"

"I asked her that point-blank on her first interview. No, she told me. But she smiled when she said it, a happy smile even, her lovely face and swanlike neck raised to me with the most insouciant expression, as if to say, Oh yes, when I am well and ready. You know, her students were crazy in love with her."

"She had a boyfriend."

"Thank God. I had a lesbian in there a few years back who adopted a stray gamine and the two of them used to sunbathe nude in the garden, which only attracted the neighborhood boys like flies. What a mess." She patted her perfectly coifed milky-blue hair, her gaze inclining toward an elaborately carved marble mantelpiece and a crystal vase of zinnias and gladioli, a blush of pinks and apricots and lush yellow.

"No signs of depression?"

"Poor boy—her admirer—I still see him occasionally stop at the front gate and look in."

"People say depression can hit you suddenly."

"I can't imagine she'd have time for such nonsense. Sandra would take a walk if something got her down. She was a *great* walker." She said this with a sudden enthusiasm, as if she'd just discovered some long-overlooked fact, the whole while keeping her eyes riveted on the flowers on the mantelpiece, where a ray of sunlight had appeared. "She walked everywhere. Didn't own a car, and I never knew her to call for a cab. She liked walking by the river at night, although I warned her more than once it was a foolish thing for a lovely girl like herself. Tempting fate."

"You said, 'got her down'—'if something got her down'?"

Mrs. Landsdowne's face dipped suddenly, a shy smile fluttering on her lips.

"Oh, I suppose it's something an older woman might detect in a younger … the hours, the days … when children might no longer be possible."

"She wanted children?"

"Oh my Lord, Mr. Channing, how would I know? One doesn't really talk about such things. But one *knows* just the same." She shot him a pointed look.

He settled back in the chair and again took in the artwork around the room.

"When I knew her, she was planning to be a painter."

"Well, there you are. She did watercolors. Fine things, too. That's hers in the hall there; she gave it to me on her first Christmas here."

"May I see?" He stood and went to the hallway and found the watercolor. A breezy, simple study of tumbled stones in sunlight with a backdrop of hunched and laden tree forms, a wash of stippled blue in the distance.

"It's nice," he called out.

"Take it if you like; I've been meaning to get rid of it."

He was stunned at the vehement high squeak of her voice and the ease of dismissing such a thing—a gift. He stepped back into the living room. Her face was bowed where she sat amid the clutter.

"Well, okay—thanks." He went back out to the hall, lifted the water-color from the wall, and placed it by the door. "It must have been nice for her, living so close to home, to Concord," he said.

She reached an unsteady hand to her walker. "Dismal, parochial place."

"Can I see the apartment?"

"The keys are on a hook by the front door." She nodded to herself and looked up toward where he stood staring at the mantelpiece. "I'm assuming the cleaners did a proper job. I had to get specialists in. She'd been there more than four days. It was hotter than Hades."

"A hot spell," he replied softly to himself.

A separate wooden staircase in the backyard gave access to the rental unit. He figured that at some point a few rooms on the first floor must have been blocked off and a new entrance added. The key turned easily, with the barest click. The air in the foyer was close and very warm, even with the recent chilly nights, as if something of the summer heat had persisted. Two steps farther and he could smell it, not bad exactly—chemical astringents, industrial-strength cleansers, and possibly disinfectants. Rubbing at his nose, he found the main living area to be a rather large efficiency: living room, dining area, small kitchenette, separate bathroom—shower, no bathtub—and tiny bedroom with a double bed, dresser, side table. Originally, it had probably been a large drawing room or solarium overlooking the back garden through a bay window. No furniture remained in the living room area, nothing on the kitchen shelves or in the drawers. The refrigerator door was propped open with a red garbage pail. In a back corner, cardboard boxes had been stacked, along with a computer and monitor, and a clear plastic refuse bag.

The bag contained toilet articles; most were European products. At the bottom of the bag was an English handmade wooden hairbrush. A thick nap of snipped bits of blond hair was embedded in the bristles. He smelled the brush, the hair, and then shoved it in his coat pocket.

The boxes contained mostly books and papers: Renaissance art history texts, academic journals, research material and pages photocopied from magazines, and printouts from what looked like a thesis in progress. Aside from a used checkbook from Harvard Trust, no letters, no bills, no diary, no photographs of family or friends. Presumably, these, along with passport, driver's license, and wallet, had been retrieved by the coroner's office to establish identity and then returned in due course to the family—in this case, to her father. That was the procedure as he remembered it from law school. He touched the computer monitor, the glass thick with dust; an indistinct tingle of longing traveled up his spine … that something of her remained behind the matte gray sheen of the screen.

He turned to go, but something familiar about the bay windows overlooking the gardens made him pause. They were not unlike his bay windows—twelve by twelve by twelve—at the inn. He lowered his gaze to the uneven checkerboard flooring, which was ablaze with cross-hatching of silvery afternoon sunlight. Then he looked left and right through the windows into the garden. The thirty-six rectangular apertures had the effect of an unstable collage: the dry hydrangea blooms merging with the tattered roses, here and there interspersed with a bristle of chocolate red where the branches of oaks dipped into the garden, while in the distance, the glitter of the Charles River and a clear sea blue sky provided a soft, unifying hue.

He felt a little dizzy in the thick air and the entrancing flower-besotted garden beyond and again pondered the fragile gridlike membrane of the bay window. Now he realized that the crusty, rain-spotted panes were filthy dirty. The tantalizing scene of moments before had become a faded landscape under yellowed varnish.

"Don't get emotionally involved," he said out loud, echoing the admonition of a canny law professor. "It will distort the evidence."

Seeing his vague reflection in the dirty glass, he lowered his eyes. Before him, stretching from the toes of his shoes, a pale strawberry-tinted nimbus poured across the parquet flooring. This saturating, ineradicable stain was marred only by an odd constellation of four silver dollar-size rings, which formed a precise square.

He knelt down and touched one of the tiny pale moons in the pink void. An instant later, he rose and beat a hasty retreat.

"Find what you wanted?"

It was a friendly accusation. Gloria Landsdowne stood with a hand on her mantelpiece, balancing herself, walker by her side.

"Trouble is, I'm not sure I'd recognize it if I did."

"Don't worry, at least no one can blame you. It's only natural. By golly, my late husband spent his entire life seeking answers to the most esoteric questions. You'd laugh—the endless speculation to establish the tie between some saintly figure in a tenth-century manuscript in Aachen and an illuminated Merovingian Psalter in Reims. And yet, he had a thoroughly purposeful mind. Everything had its place. I'll see something that he planted in the garden thirty years ago." She picked a wilted brown petal out of the flower arrangement and laid it on the mantel. "Ninety-nine times I'd spot it and think, Norman must've had an off day. And then, the hundredth time—presto: High season, the blossoms are all out, the sun is pouring through the oaks, and the borders around it have filled in; and it's as if he's standing right next to me, patting my hand the way he did."

"You're a lucky lady, Mrs. Landsdowne."

She turned from the window. "Luck runs out." Her eyebrows pressed upward. "Did they do a good job?"

"As good as might be expected."

"It was the children's playroom." She smiled as if relieved.

"Ah." He nodded, distracted by the trembling of her hand as she fingered the marble scrolling on the mantelpiece.

"We even left a comfortable old Queen Anne armchair in there. A family piece. We called it 'the Garibaldi chair' because the great Italian patriot was said to have sat in it on a visit to Boston in the 1860s."

"Total write-off, huh?"

"It's not right, not for someone like that."

"She seemed to take pretty good care of herself."

"You find that things creep up on you." She moved her face close to the flowers and breathed in their scent. He watched her arthritic fingers work their way over a garland of acanthus leaves, the sunlight turning the marble almost translucent. "Things you know and love over time establish themselves in your mind, a happy presence."

He noticed now how her eyes were tinted green without her glasses.

"As you say, as long as your luck holds."

"Do you know what I liked most about her? Her pluck, her courage. The little girl next door lost her cat up a tree. Bawling her head off because the stupid creature had gotten itself stuck in the upper branches. I was about to call the fire department, when Sandra came out of her apartment, comforted the child, and took her into the garage to help haul out a long aluminum ladder. She set it up against the tree—the tall oak by the drive—extended it full length, and, without so much as a moment's hesitation, zipped up the ladder, stepped onto the branch, and grabbed that devilish thing in one hand and got it down. I almost had my heart attack right then and there. The fiendish creature scratched and bit her poor hand something awful. She was a strong girl, Mr. Channing, positively fearless."

"Captains and generals," he said dreamily, bringing his knuckle to his lips.

"She liked children, gentle as can be."

"She ever say anything about children of her own?"

The old woman had turned to the mirror.

"I always thought … well, we were a pretty tough breed."

She examined her reflection in the gilt mirror over the mantelpiece; then her stare shifted to the half-bearded face presiding from the shadowed doorway of the foyer as if from a nineteenth-century portrait.

A little thrown by her watchful eyes, he said, "Sad she never had children." Her eyes did not waver. "Did she ever say anything about why she came back?"

In the mirror, the age lines above the wisps of eyebrow tightened and released.

"Her mother!" she exclaimed, raising her head in imitation. "She even laughed when she said it: 'always wanted me to go to Radcliffe.' I believe she went to visit her mother, in a hospital somewhere."

His knees wobbled. She had perfectly captured the cadence of the voice. He felt for the sharp bristles of the brush in the pocket of his jacket and squeezed hard.

"Did she ever mention her twin sister?"

"Sister? I assumed she was an only child."

"I would have thought her father, at least, would've come and gotten her things, the computer and the books."

"Are her personals still in there? I must have called half a dozen times. I left boatloads of messages."

"Listen, I'm staying in Concord right now, if you'd like me to take it out to him."

"Oh yes, yes. You're so kind." She turned suddenly, as if relieved. "My husband once grew a beard in imitation of Richard the Second in the Wilton Diptych. He kept it for a whole summer while on fellowship at Oxford. Foxgloves like you wouldn't believe. We always called it: 'the summer of his majesty's beard.'"

CHAPTER 11

——————

William Channing promised to be back with a cab by evening for the computer and books and the watercolor. He walked down to the Charles River. The clean contours of the Boston skyline were traced against the pale sky. He turned back a moment to the house, its Victorian profile showing behind the blur of red oaks, the glint of windows in sunlight: a reverse angle on his overactive imagination. He began to walk along the river path toward the Harvard and MIT boathouses, the path she had liked to walk, according to Gloria Landsdowne. The smell of the river and the crisp breeze and the swirl of bright leaves along the path energized his steps. He got out his cell phone and tried again for Detective Murray, who had been the toughest so far to pin down: a busy man, constantly on the move. But this time, he got right through to his car phone. He was just five blocks away. They agreed to meet on the path by the Harvard boathouse.

Detective Murray, a well-built man in his late forties, wore a blue parka vest and a Bruins sports shirt, jeans and Nikes; an automatic pistol was strapped to his hip. He kept an eye on his watch as they talked.

"I'm not going to tell you any different from the papers."

"I know and I'm taking your time, but it was such a shock to come back and find out—dead a year."

"Bitch of a thing."

"When we were seniors in high school, she was the light of my life."

Detective Murray eyed the man at his elbow. "Ain't that the worst. You remember every detail, never forget."

They stood at the railing watching an eight-man crew get its shell in the water.

"You see a lot of suicides?"

"Not like this, man, nothing quite like this."

"That bad, huh?"

"First there was the old landlady, reeling around in her own vomit. I had to get her squared away in the ambulance and off to the emergency room. She had a heart attack on the way. Then I had these two doofus rookies who'd called in the report, faces white, like their favorite puppy had been run over. It was about ten in the evening and hot like a Turkish bath. These two wouldn't go back in there—they had nerves like spaghetti. The coroner's department got delayed, a busy night—a heat spell always makes for busy nights. So I marched in and the smell stacked me up like a hip check into the boards. Now, I've done a few female suicides in my time. Most of the time they fuck it up—they wanted to fuck it up is what the textbooks tell you. When they manage it, it's mostly pills, drugs, gas maybe, monoxide poisoning; very occasionally, a chick might pull off a hanging. Gunshot to the head—I've heard about 'em in rural areas, never seen one myself.

"So I figure it's the bedroom, the bath, the slow drift into unconsciousness. But that's not where I found her. There's this big old high-backed chair, see, right in the middle of the living room facing, the windows. I couldn't even see her when I came in. But there was a mess of blood on the floor around the chair like you wouldn't believe. And I'm thinking, *Oh fuck, the bitch has gone and done herself with a gut shot*. But I couldn't even get around the chair without having to step in the sticky muck. And there she was. Four days—at least—in that heat. The flies had gotten to her. Fucking Jesus, Mary, and Joseph—what a sight. Not a delicate job, either. She'd taken one of those fancy Kraut kitchen knives and shoved the damn thing into her lower gut and pulled it right up to her breastbone. Now that, you don't see—you just don't see that. Not a determined, deliberate evisceration. The scary thing was her eyes, the only human thing left—jeest, the purpose in those blue eyes. Her hands were still on the hilt, holding it there. I suppose those samurai guys know how to do that shit, but a woman—a woman doesn't have that kind of strength—too fucking sexual."

The Harvard crew pushed off from the sloping dock and waited for the drift to clear them before they put in the oars.

Detective Murray looked at his watch.

"Shit, I can't believe I just told you that, and she an old girlfriend of yours."

Michael was seeing it and just as quickly trying not to. He increased his grip on the railing. "It's okay; it's been a long time." He held the brush in his left pocket while he concentrated on the action, seeing the oars dip, the rhythm come together, the long, hard bodies move as one. "She did do it—no question about that?"

"No question. Got to give her that."

"Coroner's report?"

"Negative—straightforward. Except a few weeks later the assistant coroner, she quit her job."

"Quit?"

"Yeah, yeah, what was her name—Miranda. Nice lady, real pro. She did the body in the apartment. I guess it threw her."

"The mess?"

"No, they see much worse. The scene … her place, her stuff, it was like nothing out of the ordinary. Like Miranda said, it could have been you or me."

"Could I talk to her, Miranda?"

"Call the coroner's office, tell them I suggested it. They should have her telephone number. Think she went back to school or something." Detective Murray turned an attentive stare toward the shell as it gathered steam. "Got to hand it to those Harvards. When they move, they move. Never seen them quite this close."

"What about a passport, letters, documents, credit cards?"

"What about them?"

"Did she have a passport, family photos around?"

"I don't remember. Coroner's office would have turned that stuff over to her dad." Detective Murray turned a curious eye his way. "Why do you care?"

He just shrugged in reply. "Her dad was a rower once. She used to talk about him."

"Strange man. Runs a frigging produce stand. They'd had lunch—he and the daughter—a few times. The man had nothing to say for himself—a tight-ass blue-blood Yankee if there ever was one."

"He must have been devastated."

"Could have fooled me. If it had been my daughter …"

"She had the most beautiful long blond hair."

"She'd cut that, too, right before she did herself."

"Why would she do that?"

"Search me. Ask Miranda. She'll probably have a theory for you. Miranda always had theories." Detective Murray glanced again at his wrist and pushed off from the railing. "People do strange things. There's a case up in Lowell that's been running on the FBI computer this week. Guy outta Washington goes to his brother's funeral and disappears off the face of the earth. They find his abandoned car and his baggage. There are conflicting reports that he either tried to drown himself or was in some kind of accident. And last week—can you beat it—he was indicted by a grand jury. Nobody can figure it."

"Maybe it was foul play."

"Your guess's good as mine."

"The feds, huh?"

"FBI butts into everything these days."

"What was the guy's name?"

"Collins."

"Like you say, people do strange things."

"Look at 'em go. I'm more a powerboat man myself. We party weekends at Oak Bluffs. When you move that fast over water, it's like a whole new lease on life. You know, after that poor girl, I lost my taste for the hard stuff. Never touch a drop now. Lost weight. I crew for my pal on his boat—a real adrenaline rush, let me tell you. Maybe I should take up rowing, what do you think?"

"It's different. But when you get up a head of steam—like you say: a whole new lease."

After Detective Murray left, he gave himself a few minutes more to watch the crews practice. Their seemingly effortless exertions helped dissipate the brutal images that threatened to swamp his mind. He could have been one of those boys in crimson; one of those boys could have been his son … their son. Their son or daughter could be rowing out there. Was that why she had come back to Harvard? To re-create the student days she never had, to be around young men and women who would be the age of her child? Did she look out at the Charles River as the rowers went by and think of him, of her father, of all the rowers in her family? Did she long for that child? Instead of answers, what kept floating into his mind was a horrific picture, something along the lines of a botched abortion.

When he withdrew his mangled left hand from the pocket of his jacket, he found it imprinted with tiny red indents from the bristles of her brush, bits of hair mashed into his palm.

Again, he heard Marge Hathaway's voice: *She'd cut her hair.*

He managed to distract himself over the next hour before his appointment with the *Globe* reporter, going from bank to bank in Harvard Square and up and down Massachusetts Avenue, buying banker's checks made out to William Channing in various uneven amounts in a range of five hundred to fifteen hundred dollars, for which he paid cash—cash from the grubstake Mahoney had provided him for a new life. Then he took a cab to Northeastern University, which had some notoriety in student circles for producing the best fake IDs in the Boston area. Liberally spreading fifty-dollar bills around, he quickly located the "ID guy," a grad student in the applied arts department. Within an hour, William Channing had a near-perfect Michigan driver's license with a Wayne State University address and a handsome photo of the bearded professor.

The *Globe* reporter was a lot younger than he'd imagined from their conversation on the phone. In his late twenties, he was tall, rangy, with a tangle of sandy hair and still-boyish features. A kid in a rush with nowhere to go, he decided after the first five minutes.

The reporter banged out the last notes on his keyboard with a recitalist's flare and turned to his questioner, who occupied a chair to the side of his computer.

"As I was saying, the reason I jumped my editor for that story was it had all the smells of a compelling indictment of a generation."

"Give me a break."

"No, no, really." The reporter leaned forward, speaking over the din of the newsroom. "Here she is, middle-aged baby boomer, product of the radical sixties, with all those aspiration to change the world, but she's opted for the Henry James thing and abandoned the New World for the Old. Then she comes back and finds, to her horror, that she recognizes nothing, that all her *compadres* have sold out and your hippie-dippy

Weatherman types are all on Wall Street selling fucking hedge funds to the masses."

"Death of—what? An illusion, idealism, a generation?"

"Implosion, more like it."

"But the peg wasn't there."

"Hey, she was a happy camper, and the only circles she ran in were the art history crowd. They treated her like Miss Ivory Snow—*so very close to the art*—one of her professorial wonks told me; like she'd been there, seen it all, done it all. They were a little in awe of her."

"Her professional accomplishments."

"Listen, I burned up the international phone lines and all I found was useless stuff. She got a degree in architecture from the University of Geneva. But she never practiced as an architect. It seems she tried to make it as a painter, even had shows in Geneva, Bern, Lausanne, but couldn't make enough of a living at it. She did some modeling to make ends meet, then drifted into restoration, a very peripatetic field. She lived in a dozen tiny places you never heard of, working on various projects, mostly in Italy and Austria. The last job was in Venice. She was highly respected. So she comes back to good old Harvard to buff up the credentials with a doctorate, maybe put a little gloss on what a lot of people think of as blue-collar work."

"Restoration work?"

"Manual labor."

"Hey, so is brain surgery."

"Listen, man, I'm not dissing her. She was the cat's meow in the department."

"But you came up a duster."

"Dude, I tried everything, even the reverse angle, the monster child-abuser-daddy scenario. Get this, Dad is a fucking Eagle Scout, senior prefect in school, Olympic oarsman, summa Harvard, navy Bronze Star; then in the fifties and sixties, he'd hooked up with these small innovative companies developing untried technologies, pharmaceuticals and agricultural products, ecologically sound projects before anyone even thought about such things, trying to push them to profitability. But he was ahead of his time; the world wasn't ready for this shit yet. His Harvard buddies—they all liked him, a real regular, idealistic guy—tried to steer him toward better deals, a niche where he could wet his beak. He wouldn't do it. The last company he was with, a late sixties Route one twenty-eight small-cap wonder, looked to be a winner. They were grabbing market shares but Daddy wants nothing of it. He quit, went bankrupt. And then—I kid you not—he's outta here lock, stock, and barrel. And where does he go? To Australia, to live with some frigging aborigines in the bush. Talk about dropping out. Her old man did you guys one better."

"So he wasn't messing with his daughters?"

"Daughters?"

"She had a twin sister."

"Right, right, I couldn't track her down. Her mother is a basket case in a nursing home."

"I hear the father is a farmer."

"Yeah, gets back from Australia in the late seventies and manages to scrape enough money together for a down payment on a derelict farm. Runs a fucking organic produce stand. Wouldn't return my calls. I went out there twice to try to collar him but he wouldn't give me the time of day, not on the subject of his daughter. Said it was none of my business."

"Which was true."

"Hey, it's a job."

William Channing shifted his weight in the chair, trying to keep his cool.

"She was a very determined young lady when I knew her in school."

The reporter popped his lips. "Let me tell you, that was one determined suicide. No halfhearted botched job for her."

"What did you think of the police work?"

"Total screwup. Fucking detective got put on administrative leave."

"Yeah."

"He was a renowned alcoholic—drunk on the crime scene. Bawling his eyes out and then punched a senior detective."

"I guess it was a bad scene."

"The pathologist who processed the body in the coroner's office, she quit the day after."

"She quit?"

"Got to hand it to her. The chick stuck to her guns, did what she had to do."

"The pathologist?"

"Nah, the Palmer chick. She had a life, maybe a simple life, but close to her work; they all said she loved the work, and they all loved her enthusiasm."

"But she killed herself."

The reporter tapped an idle finger at his keyboard.

"You know what they say about suicide: Unless you've been there, you'll never know, and by the time you've gotten that far, you're not exactly thinking rationally anyway."

"There was a rumor in high school that she got pregnant in the middle of her senior year and was shipped off by her mother to Geneva, where she had the baby."

"First I've heard of it."

"You check into the background, the family? You know, her grandfather was a painter."

"Who cares. Most people today don't even want to tell you what their dad does for a living. No one remembers past the latest *Seinfeld* reruns."

"Jesus Christ, how'd you ever get in this business?"

"Nothing personal, man." He held up a palm as if in mock surrender. "Just talk to our marketing guys about what the public wants to read about. Anyway, it was you guys, your generation that wanted to wipe the slate clean." He made an ironing motion with his flat palm. "We just skate on surfaces around here and breathe conformity. We're living like this endlessly repeated retro fantasy."

William Channing smiled wanly and turned from the insouciant grin of the reporter to check out the busy hum of the newsroom and the endless ranks of monitors and television screens and fax machines. Information age ... info without insight, detail without context, provisional lives bereft of wisdom.

"Maybe," he said, with a pensive stroke of his beard, "you should try your hand at some political reporting."

"Boring."

"What, aren't political scandals all the rage?"

"Same old shit, same old names—connect the dots—on the money trail. After what's been going on in the White House over the last years, nobody cares anymore—been there, done that."

"Forget the sex bit. Why not examine the moral dimensions, so to speak, the fine line between, say, selfish corruption—call it pure greed, the mafia kind of thing that creates nothing and saps the human spirit—and the kind of ego-driven corruption—call it pride or power, the need to build, to leave something behind—hell, misbegotten nostalgia, idealism even."

"Ambition," said the reporter.

"There you go. The kind of ambition that drives men to create monuments to themselves, possibly even advancing the public good in the process … laudable goals but questionable means."

"Subtle moral distinctions, huh?"

"Yes, like that guy—what's his name?—Collins. You know, the congressional aide who recently disappeared in Lowell. The police think maybe he committed suicide—jumped from a bridge. And a few days later, he's indicted by the grand jury for irregularities in the financing of contracts for the Lowell Plan. Now there's an interesting story and a real moral dilemma. Maybe the guy was doing his best for his constituents, maybe he despaired of his reputation, maybe he wanted to protect his family, or avoid ratting on friends—or maybe, he's been set up as the fall guy. A good reporter could really get his teeth into a story like that."

The reporter eyed his interlocutor with a narrowed gaze.

"Maybe he was pushed?"

William Channing shrugged. "There you go. I hear politics is a blood sport in this neck of the woods."

"But like I said, political corruption—boring," the reporter replied. "What the public craves is a blue Gap dress with semen stains—any day. You've got to have a sex angle."

"That's the problem with you people. You never want to get close to your subject, get to know them, inhabit their skin for a while to see what makes them tick. You prefer to stand off three hundred miles and launch cruise missiles."

"What did you say you did?"

"I didn't."

A disgruntled William Channing abruptly excused himself and left the *Globe* reporter before his alter ego let his frustrations get the better of him.

Besides, there was more housekeeping to get done. He rented a post office box at a mail-forwarding service center near the bus terminal off

Copley Square, paying six months up front, then went to a large and impersonal Bank of America branch and opened a checking account with a direct-debit Visa card attached. He deposited the bank checks he'd accumulated in Cambridge, using his new name, Michigan license, and his brother's Social Security number and giving the post office box as an address. He figured the Social Security number wouldn't draw scrutiny until tax time in the spring. It was a little dismaying how easy it all was to accomplish—almost second nature. The Visa card would be ready in two days.

The next stop, what he'd been yearning to get at all day, was the Boston Museum of Fine Arts, site of the major Joseph Palmer retrospective of two years before. The catalog, *Sunlight and Scandal*, he'd devoured twice after checking it out from the Concord library. Buying a copy for himself in the museum bookstore, he went in search of paintings by Joseph Palmer. He was amazed to find half a dozen Palmers in the American galleries given an alcove space of their own next to the Homers, Sargents, and Whistlers, not stuck away in storage, as he'd feared. A hometown boy who had made good. Clearly, the retrospective had reestablished Palmer's reputation, which had been at its height between 1900 and 1920, only to fall into near-obscurity by mid-century. By all accounts, a hot property in auction and dealing circles.

As William Channing went back and forth among Palmer's paintings, his breathing became shallow and slow, his whole body concentrated upon the artworks. All were familiar from the catalog. He couldn't resist the feeling that the paintings had been hung for his delectation—to the point that he was aware again of the presence of that ginger-haired artist, those acute, all-seeing eyes staring out of his self-portrait on the evening of the dance.

A Walden Thrush, dated 1913, was a huge canvas in a gilded Sanford White frame. Joseph Palmer's wife, Sandra Chillingworth Palmer, so familiar to him now from the photos and reproductions in the catalog, posed in a vast meadow of blurred turquoise encompassing almost the entire canvas. She was tall and thin and remote, an elegant society woman in a diaphanous low-cut gown, staring off in contemplation of the vast gloaming spaces surrounding her ... more a spirit of the meadow, an emanation of spirit. The branch of an enormous white pine saturated what remained of the fading horizon. The standing figure's arms were akimbo, a profiled pose to show off the famous long nose. Her expression was one of rapt attention, as though she hoped to catch the song of the reclusive hermit thrush.

Less a flesh-and-blood woman, more a transcendental vision—yes, a spirit encouraging the viewer to join her there in the quiet of the dusk.

He was stunned to realize how little the reproduction of the painting in the catalog suggested the power of the thing face-to-face.

Florians—Venice, 1914 … a world and ocean away. A plush rococo café interior with the Chillingworth sisters—twins identically dressed—seated across from each other, heads turned toward the viewer as if attracted to the watching figure captured in the mirror behind them: in the blurred smoky blue glass, a masculine face nearly hidden under the broad brim of a felt hat. The artist, perhaps, or an anticipated lover? The composition was a tour de force of sly illusion, the languorous stares of the elegant women completing a circuit of voyeurism and hints of forbidden pleasures, the lurking figure in the mirror and the viewer become one and the same.

It was as if the biographical details in the catalog were being fleshed out before his eyes. Joseph Palmer and his Boston society model Sandra Chillingworth had eloped to Venice in the fall of 1913, where they were married. The Chillingworths, old Boston distinguished family of bankers and art patrons, were devastated and threatened to disinherit their daughter and sue her husband. The mother, Martha Chillingworth, blamed Palmer for distracting her daughter from her true calling as a pianist. Only word that their wayward daughter was expecting a baby softened their anger. Angela Chillingworth, Sandra's twin sister, was dispatched to Venice in the spring of 1914 by their parents to encourage their wayward daughter to return expeditiously to Boston, with the understanding that all might be forgiven. For some reason, they lingered, and then Sandra Chillingworth Palmer went into premature labor and died from the aftereffects of a botched delivery at the hands of an incompetent Venetian doctor. In the fall of 1914, Angela Chillingworth returned with her sister's baby boy, Sandra's father, while Joseph Palmer remained in Europe, spending two years with the French medical corps on the western front before returning to Concord in late 1916.

Although Michael's grandfather's name wasn't mentioned in the catalog, he figured that at some point in the years immediately following the war, Joseph Palmer had brought Giovanni Maronetti over from Venice to sculpt his wife's monument in Sleepy Hollow.

Pondering these few facts of family history, he moved on to the next painting, also of Venice: *Sisters*, 1914. The Chillingworth twins posed at the wrought-iron railing of a bridge above a canal. The scene was the same as in his etching, except in the painting the faces of the women were fully visible beneath the yellow parasols angled off their shoulders. In the reflected glare from the water, their expressions displayed a pensive, well-bred beauty, and a hint of troubling suspicion in the eyes.

He checked for the museum guards and brought his face close to the canvas, touching the thick creamy daubs of paint. The painting lacked the intimacy of the inked lines in his etching: blond hair pulled back in a French twist, delicate sloping noses and sensuous full lips ... something about their expression?

What did they see in the canal below?

He flipped through the exhibition catalog to the discussion of the painting and an excerpt from Palmer's Venetian diary.

Sandra tires (from her pregnancy) by late morning. At her prompting—no, bold-faced, bullying insistence—she has recruited Angela to spell her. And then, pure inspiration, while I was working on my bridge pictures, they would often stand together and chat—and voilà, the composition was perfect. The two posed together at the apogee of the arc create a mysterious resonance, the mirrored images an additional abstract element complimenting the reflected span in the canal below. Of course, posed on the bridge, they exchange endless confidences and giggles—surely at my expense—during the tedious business of waiting for the light. It is like a secret language they use to exclude me. I try to read their faces. What do they know? If only I can get the look onto paper and canvas. I have become their cat's-paw.

The artist's questions seemed to echo his own, as if he'd spoken those words aloud and not read them in the catalog.

What were the women concealing from him, from each other? There was no such thing as secrets between twins. They had their secret language, as Ruthie Cunningham had explained to him in the pub.

He found himself spellbound at the thought: the parallel universe hinted at in the painting ... of twin sisters, a problematic pregnancy, and tragedy.

For a moment, the room seemed to spin, and he closed his eyes to return from the realm of speculation to what could be verified.

But such secrets were the reality, even in his own experience. Hadn't he always known that Jimmy had been concealing something awful, a thing he didn't want to share, and so had kept his distance over all those years? And he and Jimmy weren't even twins. But they *had* shared an unacknowledged horror at their father's complicity in the disaster of Giovanni's drowning—accident or not, that sin of omission, keeping them strangers.

How many times had he wanted to wring Jimmy's neck for some insignificant thing? What had seemed to him irrational anger. He'd dreaded meetings with his brother, for fear that anger would surface. And again he saw the image of his brother's face when they had been young boys. What pals they had been.

He wiped tears from his eyes.

Finally, willing himself back on track, he halted in front of one of Palmer's daring late paintings done from memory, *Dreaming Sisters*, 1924. This was the bombshell, the cause of yet another scandal between the artist and the Chillingworth family, which condemned him for the loss of their beloved daughter. The Chillingworth lawsuit had forced the museum to remove the painting from public view and place it in storage; the resulting publicity sent the artist fleeing from Concord to an old farm in Stockbridge, in the Berkshires, where Palmer had spent the rest of his days.

The nude women lay together in the grassy meadow in a half embrace of tangled limbs and disheveled hair, on the verge of sleep or just waking. The half-lidded eyes and parted lips hinted at a swoon or a burgeoning awareness, of some raw sensual gratification, a palpable air of postcoital bliss. Even the meadow grasses and flowers seemed to respond by entwining themselves around the women's outstretched limbs. The erotic charge of the canvas simmered in the tactile application of the paint and the luscious broad areas of muted tones.

He brought his face close to the canvas to see, to feel the energy of the brush strokes and then stepped back again to mid-distance to get a sense of the whole. It was easy to see why in the twenties the Chillingworths would have been aghast. The eye of the artist was unsparing. No mythic associations, no classical niceties: two modern women, tall and shapely and small-breasted, in ambiguous embrace, right down to their downy pubic hair and swollen pudenda.

For nearly seventy-five years, the painting had been locked away in the museum's storeroom, only to emerge two years ago for the retrospective, galvanizing the critical reappraisal.

As he walked the circuit of paintings, he was struck by how the creative spark, embodied in a masterpiece like a molten pocket of magma, will, one day, force its way back to the surface, searing and transforming the soul of the impassioned observer.

Joseph Palmer's art imaged the dynamic interchange when love's attraction blurs identity—as lover and beloved merge, so dissolving the boundaries of past and present. Or was the creation of such beauty just another form of dexterous subterfuge?

CHAPTER 12

Closing time sent him on his way and back to Cambridge to seek out his last and most difficult quarry of the day.

"So, tell me, Steve, whose idea was it for you to go to the show of her grandfather's paintings?"

He took the catalog from where he'd had it in his lap and dropped it on the table for full effect. The kid was driving him nuts—so fucking clueless. What could she have seen in him?

Steve Ballard looked across the table at the catalog and then at his interlocutor with guarded openness. Steve had been hard to find. He was now a junior, a sensitive mama's boy from Houston with a soft drawl and a childhood obsession with southwestern Indian textile design. It turned out he practically lived in Widener Library, deep in the bowels of the art history stacks, down a dark corridor in the cluttered confines of the graduate art reference room.

"She wanted me to go. She wanted me to see the paintings."

"Guided tour, huh? Led you by the hand."

"She'd been a couple of times already."

"So she was proud, wanted you to see his stuff?"

"I mean, it was a little embarrassing."

"I should say so. Those nudes are pretty powerful."

"Listen, Mr. Channing ..."

"Just call me, William, Steve—Bill will do, in fact."

"I know you were close once and all, but I'd really rather not talk about her."

"Well, let's just talk about art, then. Of course, the resemblance to

Sandra in some of the paintings is pretty amazing. Frankly, it floored me."

The youth of her onetime lover brought all his latent anger and hurt to the surface. How impossibly young he was, the age their child would be—the thing incestuous!

Ballard, seemingly overwhelmed, squeezed his fingers together, then peeled his hands wide as if to read a prompt he'd scribbled on a palm.

"Well, it was pretty amazing," the young man continued. "There was a whole gallery of the late nudes. And this one of the two gals lying in the grass together, like something out of Klimt or, maybe a touch of Pearlstein."

"Hot, huh?"

"I'd have been blushing, even if she hadn't been there."

"So what did she tell you? Did she tell you about the artist, or family anecdotes about her grandmother—or her great-aunt, who posed for those things? Was she proud, happy? Was she" —he leaned over and tapped the catalog—"turned on?"

"Hell, William—sir," Steve Ballard said with some show of indignation. "She was an artist. She was dazzled. She could barely get a word out. The work was very strong, very beautiful."

William Channing sat back, momentarily touched, squinting to better see the handsome lad, soft black curls framing his forehead, a touch of acne on his cheek, piles of books and note cards at his elbow. Everywhere the eye could see in the room, shelves and more shelves.

"If I remember, she was a damn good painter herself."

"Oh, yes, she was." He seemed to perk up. "She'd take a sketch pad with her whenever we'd go for a hike. It was like the seminar never stopped with her. She missed nothing. When you were with her, it was like a kaleidoscope. Everything—one moment to the next—could look different."

"I'll bet." He tried to meet the younger man's grayish brown eyes, the sharply arched brows, the crooked nose—Indian blood? "So why you, Steve? I mean, she was your instructor, an older lady. What about all the women your own age?"

The younger man bristled, rose in his chair, and then seemed to think better of it. Then he said, sotto voce, "It wasn't like that; she was different."

"You were young. You were—"

"She liked my work. She was interested in Native American art."

"And you were—never mind." William Channing raised a hand.

Steve picked up his pen and tapped the pad before him.

"Mr. Channing, there are days when I come in here and I just wait, thinking maybe she'll come and sit where you're sitting, that she'll go to her bookshelf and find her books just like she left them."

William grabbed the armrests as if a trigger had been pulled, his fierce stare holding the younger man in thrall. Then slowly he got up and went to the shelf of books the young man had pointed to.

Glancing back at the table, he said with the merest hint of sympathy, "You were pretty broke up."

"It was ... like, so sudden."

"These are her books?" He checked the back of one cover and then the next. "You mean to tell me you've been rechecking her books for ... a whole goddamn year?"

"I like it, having them there where she left them."

William pulled down another volume, flipping the pages, making mental notes.

"She ... tried to make me feel okay, you know, about her being older. She said in Italy a lot of the older gals like to have young men around as protectors. Not that she looked all that old."

"She'd been living in Venice?"

"She worked there doing restoration. She could tell you stuff about art that would blow you away, stuff that's not in the textbooks."

"She liked living in Venice, huh?"

"Venice was another world, she liked to say, where the past lives on."

"Ah, the past." He turned to the table. "Still looking good, was she?"

"She was beautiful."

For an instant, less, he saw himself in that same chair as a Harvard undergraduate. He squashed the vision by revving himself up again ... his father's ever-simmering anger.

"But hey, Steve, you're pretty smart, a Harvard boy—bet you're even a scholarship kid. Pulled yourself up by the bootstraps? Why you, Steve? Older guys around, professors, doctors, museum trustees—why you?"

Steve, lips tightening as if anticipating worse, pushed the point of his pen into the pad where he'd been doodling.

"Sir, that's why I feel kind of bad about the whole thing. You see, the way I figure, if I'd been old enough, more experienced, maybe I'd have seen it coming. Maybe there'd have been something I could have done."

"You mean she didn't come to *you* for help."

"Something like that."

"Then what did she come to *you* for?"

"I loved her, sir."

"Oh."

"I felt like I could tell her things and she'd understand."

"Oh yes, she was always understanding ... even at eighteen, or nineteen."

"I'm not that much of an expert on such things."

He saw the quiver in the young man's eyes, the pulse of despair, the sinking and the need to grab at rage—something—to stay buoyant. He knew enough to back off.

He said in a very calm tone, "Did she talk about her family?"

"She used to visit her mother in a home or a hospital in Worcester."

"What about her dad?"

"I don't think they were close or anything. I remember her going to have lunch with him. But she didn't like to talk about things like that, family things. She was very private."

He felt like yelling. "So what did you do? What did you talk about?"

"Art and books and stuff like that."

William Channing groaned to himself and waved his palms as if dispersing a malignant intrusion. "What about her sister? She had a twin sister, Angela. Did she mention her?"

"I don't know—once maybe."

"Once? Angela? What did she say?"

"It was nothing."

"Come on, tell me." He leaned closer. "My friend, I loved her, too. I need to know."

Steve Ballard winced. "It was kind of like something in bed—you know."

"In bed?"

"We'd had some wine. And she was doing this incredible kind of thing. And I kind of joked about it and asked her who the guy was who had showed her how to do that. And she laughed, blushing, and made a funny face. Then she told me how she picked it up from her sister—'the expert,' she said."

"'The expert'?" William Channing returned to the shelves and pushed at the spine of a book, sliding it in. "Kinky, huh?"

"Like I said, she was very private."

"But she liked sex. And she was good at it. And you were just a little more than eighteen and I bet you could just last and last and last. Is that it, she couldn't get enough?"

The young man's face drooped, his gaze following the sharp, jagged doodles on the pad: Navajo ... Nez Percé.

Ballard smiled at his antagonist. "*I* couldn't get enough." He folded his palms over his face and then removed them as if to display a different face. "What you want me to say is yes, I wished I could've been older and better for her."

"More experienced."

"She was so tender, so considerate."

"You don't mean she was afraid of corrupting you?"

"She said she didn't want to hurt me, like I was a kid or something. But she never did things halfway. It always had to be right ... real."

"Listen, Steve, she was older than you. You couldn't have expected her to fall madly in love with you. Hell, you were bound to go off with someone your own age, at some point, and leave her high and dry. She knew that, man."

A searching look came into young man's eyes. "She never wanted to use anything."

"'Anything'?"

"You know."

"Oh, right, so you had to kind of wait around for safe days and all that."

Steve made a little face, a hint of puzzlement.

"I don't think so."

"Are you telling me she was trying to get pregnant?"

"Why would she want to do that?"

"Jesus," William Channing lowered his face to his hand, pressing at his temples to forestall the incipient headache. He'd just rephrase the question he really wanted to ask.

"Tell me, Steve, did she ever talk about having a baby?"

"A baby?"

"You know—did she want kids?"

"Kids?"

"Someone told me she once *had* a kid."

Steve shook his head. "I never heard that."

"I mean, if she did, you'd have known, right? I mean, women are, you know, a little different afterward. Don't-cha know?"

"What?"

"Christ." He turned his face to the ceiling.

Steve said softly, almost as if pleading his case, "I've never known anyone like her."

"I'm sorry … I'm sorry to bust in on you like this." William pulled at his chin, as if needful of reestablishing his rightful persona. "I'm sorry for your loss."

He turned away and faced the dark shelves toward the back of the room. His shoulders rose and fell. There was the flicker of a fluorescent bulb in the ceiling.

Steve Ballard got up from his seat and went around to stare at the cover of the catalog.

"What you were saying about the exhibition …" He reached down to touch the cover, where her face—or a face very much like that of the woman he loved—was emblazoned. "It was so strange, when we walked through the exhibition. People turned to her for a moment, to stare, to wonder, a look of recognition—and then not. And when we came out, I remember how she turned back and there was this banner over the entrance of the museum, the dates and her grandfather's name. And she smiled this most beautiful smile, like she was *really* happy. 'It's almost as if he's come back,' that's what she said. 'Like somebody you haven't seen for the longest time, and you hear their voice … and there they are.'"

He staggered through the door of the inn with Sandra's computer in his arms and leaned against the reception counter to pick up his key.

"Mr. Channing—well, there you are." The red-haired receptionist offered a quirky smile of amusement. "You okay?"

"Sure, Jennifer—and please call me Bill. The cabdriver is going to help me with the rest."

"Say, Bill, have you been getting on the wrong side of the law recently?" She made a comical face. "Slotnik, police guy, dropped in this afternoon asking after you."

"Oh, him, I was walking off a long evening at the pub the other night in Sleepy Hollow, and he seemed to take exception to me being there."

"He likes to bust kids, especially rich kids. He's an ex-marine."

"You know what they say: Once a marine, always a marine."

She reached for his key and a pink message slip.

"I told him you were a busy guy. And by the way, the bookstore delivered about four boxes of books this afternoon. Can I run up and open the door for you?"

"No, it's okay. Just stick the key and the message on top here and I'll be fine."

The message was from Ruthie Cunningham.

"Boy, you're really moving in."

"I've got to get this book done, Jennifer—publish or perish. Am I too late for dinner?"

"You can still get a sandwich in the pub."

"Perfect. Thanks."

The moment he paid off the taxi driver and closed the door to his room, he went to the bay window and looked out over Monument Square. A police cruiser was parked in the distance at the turn into Main Street.

"Slotnik," he said. "What kind of name is that for a town police officer?" But with his new license tucked into his wallet, he felt more secure than ever in his modest aerie overlooking Concord.

He began setting up Sandra's computer on the Victorian rolltop desk, angling the monitor away from the bay windows to avoid glare, and carefully finding new spots for the etching and the silver-framed photo of his mother, and now Sandra's watercolor. He was consumed with his task, fingers shaking as he connected the components, as if something of her could still inhabit the machine. When it was ready, he stepped back from the desk to observe his handiwork, and as he did, he caught sight of the portrait of Thoreau on the wall. The fixed gaze of the seer struck deep in his conscience. He shrugged sheepishly.

"Henry ... I know, I know. I scammed the old lady and took the computer under false pretenses. I treated that Harvard kid badly. But I'd think you'd agree that I can't leave a stone unturned."

His half-in-jest confession to his mentor got him off the hook for the moment, and he pushed the button to boot up the computer. It whirred to life, going through its electronic checklist. He watched with the fascination of a voyeur.

The screen saver behind the standard Windows configuration was a Renaissance painting of an austere and ordered scholar's study where a monk or scribe sat at his inlaid desk, sunlight flooding in to illuminate his collections of manuscripts and ancient art objects.

As if in unconscious imitation, he sat again in his Windsor chair and bent to examine the screen.

The scholar in the painting sat poised with pen in hand, face turned to a window not visible to the viewer, perhaps distracted by a movement or summoned to reverie by a stray memory. A small white spaniel sat patiently at his feet. The painting was vaguely familiar, though he had no idea of the artist's name. But as he studied this portrait of human rapture suspended in the monitor before him, the strangest sensation came over him: that one of the glass panes in his bay window had translated itself to his desktop, an animate eye set to reveal the parallel universe of her past.

The sensation was so strong, he felt compelled to reach into his coat pocket and pull out the brush he'd taken from her apartment, inspecting the bristles and the strands of blond hair caught in them.

Then he bent forward and began a slow, deliberate exploration of her files. Her documents contained mostly working drafts, footnotes, and bibliography from her thesis on the Lombardi, a family of seventeenth-century Venetian sculptors and architects. He spent an hour reading through the thesis, coming upon turns of phrases and cadences that reminded him of her voice, but this was more frustrating than not, since much of the writing was objective, technical and academic, with only a few subjective passages offering any real sense of the person behind the text.

And then it struck him: She'd been doing her thesis on a family of Venetian sculptors, as if, consciously or not, she'd set out on a path that might have included his grandfather, Giovanni Maronetti, a path that might have eventually led her back to him.

Okay … that was a bit of a stretch.

He tried her AOL icon and found that she had an automatic password. He got her modem and phone jack and connected it into the phone line of his room. Clicking SIGN ON, he listened to the scamper of dial tones, and seconds later her account appeared. Amazing, it was still active. Her NEW MAIL icon blinked, hastening him on. There were over a dozen new E-mail messages, most of them replies from research libraries and collections about requests for documents and books. She'd made inquiries for material only a few days before she died—give or take—since the precise time of death was an estimate. Some replies had trickled in months later.

He clicked on OLD MAIL. Again, the usual stuff from databases and libraries. But then … He leaned forward, the very thing he was praying to find:

Dear Sandy, arriving Boston Oct. 12. Will call as soon as I get in. Can't wait to finally see you for our birthday bash! Too—too long. Love, Angie.

The date would place Angela Palmer in Cambridge only a few days before her sister's death.

He thought his eyes would pop from his skull as the pressure of the headache, which had begun in Cambridge, came on full bore. He was beside himself with panicked hope. He noted Angela's E-mail address on a pad just in case the computer might lose it.

He clicked on SENT MAIL, and found a message from October 12.

Oh Angie—yes. I can't wait. Yes, yes—too long! Give me a call the moment you get in, Love, Sandy.

And then, two days later, another from Sandra:

How dare you blame me for everything—does your self-absorbed cruelty know no bounds? Come back to the apartment and I'll tell you the whole truth if you can stand it. Better still, I'll show you the truth—my truth. Are you there, are you checking your E-mail?

That was it: a day or two before her death, a cry for understanding … the thing that needed to be told, to be shared—the sin of omission that might have saved her life.

And one last sent message, but addressed to herself, mistakenly so, with a two instead of a three after the name and so delivered to someone else's AOL account:

It's better this way. I've left you everything, bank documents, account numbers, passport, drivers license—everything. So live—live for us both. Love, Angie—love.

He flew across the room in a spasm of manic release, standing before the bay window, staring into the fluid darkness, seeing Sandra at her computer in her tiny apartment, tapping out a last cry to her sister to live ... to love.

Or was it Sandra? *Love, Angie—love.* That could be Angela's signature and a despairing plea to her twin before taking her own life.

His mind went into a tailspin and he rushed into the bathroom to down some Tylenol.

"Get a hold of yourself, goddamn it." He stared at himself in the bathroom mirror, at his stupid, ridiculous beard. Who the fuck was he fooling?

He sat down again in front of the computer, trying to engage his lawyerly brain to review the facts as he had them.

So ... Angela *had* been there. A reunion after decades apart. A birthday reconciliation gone toxic. Her presence had triggered something. At the very least, she was responsible for what happened to Sandra ... or was it Sandra who was responsible for what happened to Angela?

Marge Hathaway had seen Sandra, in the orchard sometime during that October heat spell of last year. Sandra's hair was shorter; she had seemed to Marge a little disoriented.

The possibility of reversal, of another case of mistaken identity, had him by the throat.

He went to her AOL home page and clicked around in a frenzy. Then he went to FAVORITES. Again, the usual libraries, along with some booksellers, Amazon.com ... and, SandyBlue.com.

Something about that name ... Sandy, how Sandra had signed her E-mail.

He paused and then clicked.

She appeared to him (Sandra Chillingworth Palmer the first name to pop into his head) as if a pure manifestation of his will: a gorgeous bare-breasted blonde in a beguiling pose surrounded by text.

Welcome to Sandy Blue for the best in health and sensual products for the turned-on and turned-out woman.

He entered the site, where he found pages of books on martial arts for women, sex manuals, videos, erotic toys, vitamins, beauty aides, diet plans, and exercise clothes and equipment devoted to the needs of today's most demanding modern woman. Just reading the product entries made him feel a neophyte among sophisticates. A fierce pride in the female body and mind. A lifestyle devoted to fitness and a supercharged determination to take on the world with joy and energy. He was amazed, flabbergasted. It was as if he'd stumbled into an exotic microcosm of the new female psyche: a warning to clueless males that they were about to be left in the dust.

He clicked on one of the videos: *Sandy Blue's Greatest Couples' Tape.* The cover contained another provocative and copyrighted photo of Sandy Blue with a promise to women: *To get your man turned on to what turns you on.*

He stared at the face, as proud and haughty and aloof as Sandra Chillingworth Palmer's in one of Joseph Palmer's paintings, but with a swaggering confidence and freedom in the body. She wasn't young, maybe mid-thirties, something from a decade before. So this is what had become of the wild Angela.

But without a credit card, the video would have to wait.

He returned to the home page of SandyBlue.com. There again, the face, the body, the long blond hair, not nineteen, but so youthful. She was beautiful and alive, so ... California dreaming. The blue eyes seemed to stare back at him, the soft curve of her small breasts to call for his touch: the stark line and flaring vee of her black lace panties. His electronic hand caressed her flesh in anticipation of metamorphosis: Where are you? Where do you want to go? Who are you?

He could just make out his bearded face in the reflection of the screen: the voyeur's stare in the mirror in Joseph's Palmer's painting *Florians* in the museum that afternoon. He felt mocked by the gods of memory.

There was an 800 number for ordering by phone. He called and finally got through to a customer-service person. The woman was very matter-of-fact about his inquiries on a woman's site. "Oh, we hear from boyfriends who've been recommended—like sometimes they want suggestions for a product, or a gift certificate for a birthday present." But all she could tell him was that SandyBlue.com had been in business for almost ten years. And that Sandy Blue had been a famous porn star back in the eighties. And yes, she owned the business, which was located north of

San Francisco, near Sonoma, but no one had seen her for years. She was supposed to be a very private person. But she did have a fan club, if he was interested. "A lot of girls' boyfriends are members, too, if you know what I mean," she said. "We teach them to be better lovers."

He wasn't quite sure what she meant, but he did manage to get a number for the corporate headquarters. When he called, it was the end of the workday on the coast and so he got a polite runaround. But one thing was clear: Sandy Blue wasn't in the office and she didn't speak to anyone except on her own time and in her own way. "She's a *very* private person," was repeated to him more than once. And it was Sandy Blue, not Sandy, not Ms. Blue. If she had a real name, they sounded truly ignorant of it and even a little hurt that he should question such brand-name loyalty. They wouldn't even take a message or pass on his telephone number.

Frustrated, he stared at the SandyBlue.com home page, then clicked back to Sandra's AOL home page and into her OLD MAIL file. He clicked on Angela's E-mail and then on the REPLY icon.

Cookingwithfire@aol.com.

He stared at the blinking cursor, waiting to send his message.

Something wasn't right. If Sandra had really taken her life in that Cambridge apartment, then Angela was at least partly responsible. Her subsequent absence, her invisibility (a no-show at the funeral) spoke volumes, perhaps of denial or guilt, fleeing a crime.

A crime? Or what if it had been Angela dead and stabbed by her own hand in that chair by the bay window? If so, Sandra might well have been so devastated, shaken to her very soul, that, perhaps panicking, she'd run away, back to her childhood home in Concord (where Marge had seen her in the orchard), and then back to Europe and her previous life.

"Michael, you are out of your friggin' mind."

One way to find out. He began to type.

Sandra: I have returned to Concord. I have returned to the inn. I have not forgotten you. I have never stopped loving you. Your secret is safe. Come back. I am waiting.

He paused, his brow furrowed in trepidation, and added to the message.

All I want is the truth. A friend of Thoreau.

He clicked the SEND icon.

He looked up at the picture of Thoreau, into the intense eyes presiding over his folly.

"Henry, if it's Angela, she'll blow me off or not answer at all."

The following morning, there was a reply.

Send again. Please clarify.

He repeated his message of the night before and gently clicked the SEND icon. He grimaced and turned to the etching of the two women on the bridge, which was displayed just to the side of the monitor. For a while, he gazed into the smudge of inky shadow, at the identical downturned faces contemplating their watery reflections.

He felt a shiver run up his spine. "Cat's-paw," he muttered, recalling the excerpt from Joseph Palmer's Venetian diary.

With that, he grabbed the pink message slip given him by the receptionist the night before, went to the bay window, and inspected the parked vehicles on the street.

He looked at Ruthie Cunningham's name on the message slip and the message: "Thinking about you." Ruthie knew his real name, though he'd told her that he'd changed it many years before. But he'd have to be careful with her, just in case.

CHAPTER 13

————•

Mr. Channing, this is Philip Ratner in San Francisco. You called the agency about a missing person you wanted located?"

"Yeah, thanks for returning my call. Actually, I'm not sure exactly how missing this person is. It seems most of her friends and family have been out of touch and no one's quite sure what's she'd been up to over the last twenty years or so."

"What do you want, Mr. Channing? These searches are expensive."

"Her name is Angela Palmer. I knew her briefly in the late sixties. She was my high school sweetheart. She went to Berkeley and should have graduated with the class of '74."

"She dropped out, disappeared?"

"Something like that. Her sister died last year and she didn't even make it to the funeral."

"And what if we find her for you?"

"I just had a thing for her, that's all."

"All this time?"

"Actually, I was fooling around on the Internet and I hit this Web site, SandyBlue.com, and there was a photograph of a woman; it looked just like her."

"Sandy Blue?"

"Do you know it?"

"Yeah, kind of a cult figure out here, feminist porn star, early to mid-eighties, I think."

"Feminist?"

"Yeah, tapes for women, for couples, that kind of thing."

"There may be a connection."

"Whatever relationship you had with this woman, would it have anything to do with her subsequent behavior or disappearance?"

"No."

"So, she's not trying to get away from you or anybody you know about?"

"No."

"A lot of these women in the porn industry were sexually abused as kids, or thought they were."

"*Thought?*"

"Recovered memories, but that's a whole 'nother can a worms. Now, let's see ... criminal issues at all, illegality of any sort?"

"Not that I know of."

"You just had a thing for her?"

"I'd like to talk to her. Find out how she's doing."

"Sandy Blue?"

"I'm just curious."

"Curiosity can be expensive."

"I'll pay whatever it takes—within reason—cash up front."

"Okay. You said Berkeley, class of '74."

"That's right."

"Okay. Anything relevant in the background that might help?"

"Old East Coast family, some money. Went to private school, rebel of her class, did drugs, sex, and rock and roll—whole nine yards, I suppose."

"Okay. Maybe in over her head, troubled relationships, possible addiction problems, probably changed her name at some point."

"You mean Sandy Blue?"

"If it is, the chicks in the adult-entertainment industry have gone through a dozen names by the time they're washed up. Many are addicted and worse ... HIV, you know."

"I don't think that's an issue here—or I hope not. She had a strong personality, lot of guts and determination. A leader—charismatic even. Out to change the world."

"Okay. That makes it easier. People will remember her. I'll start with Berkeley and Sandy Blue."

"What are the chances you can turn her up?"

"The chances are good. But how much time it will take is hard to say. People can't hide the way they used to, Mr. Channing. There's too much information out there, too much technology. Invariably, they trip a wire, somewhere."

"What normally does it?"

"Bank account, credit card, Social Security number. Even the best of them slip up. People are hardwired creatures of habit. In the end, they always go back to who they really are. They may know all the tricks—destroy pictures of themselves, wipe fingerprints, change names and birth dates and mother's maiden names on their financials, rent addresses from mail drops and use remailing services—but in the end, they're creatures of deeply rooted habit."

"They want to go home."

"They think they're starting new, but what's bred in the bone remains."

"Surely one *can* change?"

"There was this guy I was trying to locate last year. Fifteen years, nobody knows what's happened to him. But I knew from a childhood friend that his greatest dream was to be a pilot. So I checked all the flying clubs in eighteen states, put out his description, a big reward, and sure enough, somebody spotted him. New name, new job, new life, but the man was flying Piper Cubs on the weekends."

"I'll FedEx you the cash by this afternoon."

"Okay. I'll need at least five thousand to start."

"Make it ten. I'd like a rush job."

"Yes, sir."

"By the way, just as a matter of interest: These disappearing acts, how do they get themselves a new driver's license, say, or even a passport?"

"Driver's license is a cinch—just ask your seventeen-year-old kid. Passport takes a bit more doing."

He woke to another lovely fall day, the shattered clouds in the uppermost panes of his bay window bellied in tints of mauve and pink against a blue sky, and her computer blinking as if to welcome the sleeper back into the morning world.

It was another reply from cookingwithfire@aol.com.

Who are you? What do you want?

Rubbing sleep from his eyes, he agonized over his response. What he wanted—besides yelling down the roof, was to come clean to the woman he had loved at eighteen. Yet he dared not reveal himself, given his precarious situation—a stolen computer, false identity, and on the lam. Especially if the FBI were now on the case. He typed his cryptic reply and smacked the SEND icon.

William Channing, friend of Thoreau, resident of the inn. Waiting for you, Sandra. Your secret is safe. Love you.

It all began to take shape in his mind. Angela dead by suicide. A played-out aging porn queen, depressed, debilitated by disease. Killing herself in some kind of crazed revenge for something in their childhood, but not before leaving Sandra everything—her financial assets, her accounts, her identity—as a cruel joke. Sandra had fled the scene and then, traumatized, found herself drawn to explore the circumstances of her sister's misbegotten life and an explanation for her suicide. How better than to assume Angela's persona?

In the evenings, especially when he felt his expectations getting too out of control, he'd take a break and go downstairs to the pub for a reality check. Jack would always be there. A baseball game would be on the television over the bar, with the regulars sitting around and grouching about one thing or another. He liked these people and their predictable lives of gripes and complaints, and the fact that they liked him for being a Thoreau scholar who was writing a book about the titular saint of their town. They were respectful, as if he filled some necessary niche in their social ecosystem.

And this when the newspapers were beginning a trickle of stories about what was coming out of the grand jury, tales of one Michael Collins, illustrated by a photograph of a younger, clean-shaven version of the subject at a ribbon-cutting ceremony in the heyday of the Lowell Plan. Michael Collins, or his odd disappearance, was beginning to intrigue Lowell police and generate speculation among reporters that there was a connection between his disappearance and his indictment by the grand jury. William Channing began to relish these stories, almost gleeful to see how they were elaborated on and distorted, how the truth could be so easily twisted, until he could barely recognize the portrait of the man he'd once been: Washington insider, political operative, fixer and dealmaker—a man increasingly portrayed as at the center of an enormous scandal. If the lies put around by Jack Mahoney and his creatures were to be believed, Michael Collins might have arranged for kickbacks in the form of campaign contributions, and garnished a few bucks along the way for himself. Recently, the police chief in Worcester had weighed in, suggesting that Michael Collins, in arranging the meeting at which he didn't show, had mentioned a large sum of money: "My impression was that Mr. Collins was planning a confession, possibly turning over his ill-gotten gains."

Such tales did not so much worry William Channing as give him hope, reinforcing his conviction that little was as it was supposed to be ... that Sandra might well be alive and on her way home.

"Don't you get it, Bill? You've got to be something of a metaphysician, being a professor and all. Sally here, and Don—our favorite lawman—have just managed to get each other thoroughly depressed, and all in a day's work. Ain't that right, you two?"

William took another bite out of his sandwich and glanced at his two bar mates as they continued their edgy conversation in the glare of green from lovely Anaheim stadium and a twilight doubleheader between the Sox and Angels. Jack, as always, refereeing on his turf.

"Bill," the barman continued, "you know Don, Don Slotnik? He sure knows you."

William waved a hand at the policeman and smiled. "Sure, I'm his midnight rambler." Don gave him a thumbs-up.

"Go on, Don, tell Bill about the kids you picked up."

"Smashing mailboxes," said Don Slotnik with a twist of his large jowly head to loosen a crick in his neck.

"With baseball bats," said Jack, taking a swing with a near empty bottle of Chardonnay. "Get in a car, lean out the back window, ride down the road, and take them out one by one. Bam, bam, bam—ride 'em cowboy."

"Spoiled little assholes," said brassy haired Sally.

Jack rested a hand on the padded shoulder of Sally's Prada pinstripe suit. "See, Bill, Sally just sold this dream house for a million-plus off the Carlisle Road to the nicest young couple you could ever meet. They had a ball with Sally. He's an Internet guru; she's a telecom lawyer. Thrilled, they were, right, Sally?"

Sally sighed. "Six bedrooms, traditional colonial, perfect for a growing family."

"See what I mean, Bill," said Jack. "What goes around comes around."

"Local kids," said Don.

"Spoiled assholes," said Sally.

He looked at the others and reached for his Heineken. "Who the fuck needs kids anyway."

Just before bed, another reply from cookingwithfire@aol.com.
Stay where you are. Will come to you.

He was beside himself. And then a note of caution: If there were truly secrets out there, best he know them ahead of time and arrive at the table fully armed. Twenty years of experience and Michael Collins had, at least, that much advice to pass on to William Channing.

Joe Palmer, Sandra's father, was going to be the hardest nut to crack, if the experience with the *Boston Globe* reporter was anything to go by. The others were relatively straightforward to contact. He'd already gotten a letter out to the head doctor at the Worcester nursing home in hopes of arranging a visit with Sandra's mother, Abigail Palmer; he'd written Laura Ryder, author and curator of the Joseph Palmer retrospective at the Boston Museum of Fine Arts, who was in charge of the artist's Berkshire home, Sangamore. This had recently been upgraded to include a new museum, archives, and storage for the many paintings still in the possession of the estate. William Channing had expressed a special interest in Palmer's Venetian diary, which he hoped might elucidate some points in his work on Thoreau and American landscape painting. The only dead end was the Chillingworth family, Sandra's grandmother's family. With the death of Angela Chillingworth, Sandra's great-aunt, years before, the family had died out without a trace, and even their splendid country home in Manchester-by-the-sea had been torn down in 1978 for beachfront condos.

Joe Palmer was key, and he was going to take special handling. People spoke of him with affection but noted his reticence ... a very private man.

The Palmer Farm was located on the Lexington Road, about a mile and a half outside of Concord. An easy jog. And the location fitted in well with the daily route William Channing had established for himself, a regular and visible circuitous movement about the town. Habit and consistency, he decided, were his best bet if he was to ease himself under the radar screen of Sandra's father.

The subterfuge bothered him only a little. Who better than William Ellery Channing, bosom buddy of Thoreau, who had often accompanied Henry on his saunters around Concord? It was Henry's ubiquitous and quiet presence that drew the townspeople to him.

Likewise, William Channing wanted to become someone people would be comfortable enough with to share their thoughts. For his company alone, without the *something in return* that had so marked the life of political operative Michael Collins. The place, as Thoreau had put it, where you are not in false relations with men.

So, like his mentor, William jogged the meandering roads, stopping daily at Joe Palmer's produce stand, on the lookout, too, for the woman who had replied to his e-mail, a woman he pictured as tall and elegant and perhaps dressed with a European flare. He ran along Main Street, past Alcott Academy, upriver to his old school, and then past the Palmer homestead, the Palmer graves in Sleepy Hollow, and on to Walden Pond, then followed the railroad tracks back into town. It wouldn't be enough for him to wait for Sandra at the inn. He must become integral to the community, so that when she touched any angle or curve of his domain, he would know and she would know.

She'd go to see her father ... or would she ... could she?

At a passing glance, Joe Palmer's farm did not look like much. There was a tiny white clapboard farmhouse off a dirt road bordering a muddy barnyard and dilapidated rust red barn: a backwater caricature of the original Palmer homestead, it occurred to him. But on closer inspection, he could see that the place was well maintained. New farm machinery glinted in the sun. Beyond the barn, stretching toward the river, were row upon row of greenhouses, low and angular. A dirt and gravel road lined with giant oak trees bisected the farm and made a leafy border for the fields, the ones closest to the road thick with ripened corn. In the distance, closest to the river, a long swath of ragged and heavy-laden fruit trees nudged the western sky.

Most impressive was the farm stand itself: spacious and well constructed, with hand-fitted beam work and a light green canvas covering. A series of carved and painted signs had been hung along the road to indicate the available produce. The many varieties of apples were placed in a horseshoe of bins at the center of the stand, painstakingly stacked to show off the color and configuration of the fruit to best advantage. Each bin included a description of the particular variety: its origins, characteristics, and suggested uses. Everywhere he looked, something pleased the eye.

"Gee, I don't know where to start," he said to the young man in the John Deere cap behind the cash register. "Are you responsible for this setup?"

The cashier waved in the direction of the farm and the distant orchard.

"Joe's your man; the guy's a marketing genius. People from the city come by and want to buy his stand. Best organic produce around."

Following the waved hand, William could make out a figure at work in the orchard: tall, wiry, gray hair and prominent chin, overalls and a plaid shirt, long arms reaching up to a branch.

"So what do you suggest for a light snack while I catch my breath?"

The young man pointed to a nearby stack of apples. "Joe's specialty, an oldie but goodie, Roxbury Russet. Come over in the seventeenth century. Lots of sugar and medium acid. It makes a cider that goes down nice and easy if you're moving fast."

William picked up one of the shapely apples, a nugget of fall splendor, and bit into it.

"I'm not moving so fast anymore, but hey, this is great. So what is the guy, Johnny Appleseed or something?"

"He's the professor; nobody knows more about the New World apple."

"Seriously?"

"World's authority."

"You guys make a living with these?" He took another eager bite.

"Only the big growers make a go of it. The core business is same-day fresh-picked organic produce to the Boston restaurant trade."

"Bet that's hard work."

"Man, you don't wanna know. There was a killing frost last May; we had to cover two acres of tender squash with dirt and then brush it all off again—by hand."

He saw the man in the orchard put down a cutting tool, wipe at his face, and began to make his way toward the produce stand.

"Not old man's work."

"Not young's, either."

The cashier turned to ring up the purchases of another customer.

He took another bite of the apple, watching the loping gait of the old man along the road, seeing better the bony hands and windblown features and tensile strength of the aging athlete. He studied the bent but sturdy shoulders seemingly endowed with the perseverance of generations: his tough Puritan forbears; his great-grandfather, the captain who defied storm and wind and mountainous seas and the entire British and French navies, only to abandon the sea to harness a river and build a palace of industry; his grandfather the general, who had taken bullets in three limbs and died an agonizing death in the cause of liberty and union—as a boy, friend to the poet Thoreau; and, of course, his father, Joseph Palmer, an artist of breathtaking sensibility, who had endured the loss of his beloved wife. And this old man, one-time Olympic rower, father of a daughter—no, twin daughters—of such rare beauty and intelligence … and what of his losses?

The old man approached.

William Channing stepped from the shadows of the produce stand and held up his half-eaten apple in greeting, or salute.

The eyes of the old man lingered upon the younger, as if he recognized something in the face, or maybe the crew-necked sweatshirt emblazoned with the old school name and colors.

The old man seemed hesitant, but then he raised his hand in reply.

As he did, the deep past dropped away and William thought, *The guy's been to war in the South Pacific, lost a baby, gone through a divorce, seen his family scatter, one daughter to the West Coast, another to Europe. He went bankrupt, left to live with aborigines in Australia, then returned to scratch together a new life as a farmer on his native ground. Only to have one daughter return and kill herself practically on his doorstep.*

"Jesus Christ," he exclaimed under his breath.

The old man halted a moment on the path as if he'd heard the hissed cry from the lips of the younger, but then he turned again toward the door of his home.

Joe Palmer, tough as nails—no, tougher.

A few days after that, he spotted the roses.

On his regular afternoon jog, which took him past the Palmer graves, he found roses on Baby Joey's grave and Sandra's. To be precise, five on the child's grave and one on Sandra's—an allocation of grief that gave him pause.

The roses were fresh and must have been laid there that morning or afternoon.

Joe Palmer's young assistant at the farm stand had mentioned that Joe had been in Boston all day delivering produce to Boston restaurants.

She had returned.

William Channing was still pondering the appearance of the roses as he sat cooling his heels in Ruthie's suite of rooms with a cup of Starbucks best brew and Judy Collins playing in the background. The Judy Collins songs eased him out of his present impatience and back to a different time and place, but it wasn't exactly the kind of nostalgia trip he'd had in mind. Yet he took the opportunity to check out her digs, sipping his coffee, vaguely listening.

There wasn't a newspaper in sight, or even a weekly newsmagazine, only novels and classroom texts with dog-eared pages. Ruthie complained how she didn't even have time to read the newspaper anymore. But might something of the Michael Collins story have caught her eye? And she was very curious about him. Looking around her place, he couldn't believe how much space was devoted to her tennis business. The living room had the smell and feel of a small pro shop: stringing machine taking up an entire corner, a good dozen rackets with strings cut, a bunch of brand-new rackets still in shipping cartons, stacks of tennis shoes in boxes, a desk-top workstation littered with invoices. What did she do when she was stringing rackets: Watch the news on TV! By the window overlooking the back of the campus were photos of Ruthie playing the Virginia Slims tour in the late seventies: two photos of Ruthie with check and trophy, standing with a tournament referee, an inscribed photo from Chrissie Evert showing the two women shaking hands over the net.

When Ruthie returned, he'd gone back to the tennis photos.

"What did you say about roses?" she asked, still distracted, an ear bent in the direction of the dorm.

"I found a rose on Sandra's grave this afternoon."

"Yeah."

"You didn't—"

"Are you kidding. I wouldn't go near the place." She shivered.

"What about the other women in your year who went to Sandra's funeral—it's almost a year, would they be likely to pay their respects, so to speak?"

There were voices in the dorm. She bent her ear again, considering, and then shook her head.

"No, not their style."

"And her dad—I can't see it somehow."

The phone rang and Ruthie answered it and then went to the door of the dorm and called down the hall. A tall painfully thin blond girl appeared and Ruthie directed her to the kitchenette to take the call, arm around her shoulder, encouraging her in soft, persuasive tones.

"That young woman has been depressed for an entire month," she said quietly, returning to his side by the photos on the wall. "Mom's divorced. Doesn't even speak to Dad. They all communicate by E-mail. Anyway, Mom's off to Frankfurt to nail down a long-simmering M and A deal for a telecom giant, so she won't be around for Christmas. Mom's got a British boyfriend, so I'm told. Dad's remarried and living in Seattle with a new family she can't stand. And it always rains in Seattle. So Thanksgiving and Christmas are problematic."

"Did you kick her butt?" he asked, pointing to the photo of Ruthie and Chrissie Evert.

"I took the second set in the final of Boca Raton in 1975. I was serving for the match in the third set and her return clipped the net and dribbled over for a winner." She kissed her fingertips and pressed them to the younger face in the photo. "Been downhill from there." She eyed him in his running gear. "I can get you some better running shoes—cheap."

"Hey, you did what was in you, your talent. I wouldn't mind teaching English in a school like this with such good students."

"Right. You know what really pisses me off?" She indicated the phone conversation going on behind them. "That girl's mom was two years ahead of me in school. She's with Credit Suisse First Boston, making ten million dollars a year, as if the sixties didn't happen. And it's like she's asking me, Why can't you handle my daughter? Aren't I paying you enough?" Ruthie made a face as she squinted across the room, listening. "Have a seat while I nuke my coffee."

He could hear the girl talking in the kitchen, the hum of the microwave.

"And this town," Ruthie said, blowing at her steaming cup as she came back into the room. "The selectmen are giving me a hard time for failing to officially file a notification with the town of my interest in this new tennis club on Carlisle Road. I mean, shit, I invested everything from my half of the divorce settlement."

"You read about the indictments handed down by the grand jury in Boston for kickbacks in the construction industry—that mess up in Lowell?"

"What about Lowell?"

"Kickbacks in the construction industry to local politicians."

"Huh, oh, I never get to the papers."

"Will the girl be okay?"

"Of course she will. That's why" —she rubbed her thumb and forefinger together— "they pay me so well. You know something …" She flung herself down on the sofa like a moody adolescent. "These kids are obsessed with their bodies and so self-critical. They pride themselves on their sophistication; they talk endlessly—shamelessly—about technique. I blush. They play at lesbianism. They know all about multiple orgasms. They don't worry about pregnancy, but they're scared shitless about AIDS. And what, you ask, am I supposed to advise them? Officially, I'm supposed to encourage abstinence while making damn sure they use birth control, preferably condoms."

"Brave new world."

"No, not so brave. These kids are followers. All they want to do is fit in and be part of their peer group. They're terrified of standing out."

"Nothing like Angela, huh?"

She bared her teeth. "Angie—not a chance."

They heard the click as the girl hung up in the kitchen. Ruthie went to accompany her back to the dorm, grabbing a box of chocolate chip cookies from the counter as she went. He sat on the sofa, listening to Judy Collins.

Ruthie returned and carefully shut and locked the door to the dorm behind her.

"I guess," she said, nodding toward the dorm, "we had the luxury of breaking free of our mothers; these kids are all competing to take over … in lockstep. Or day trading." She picked up his coffee cup. "Want me to warm this up?" She walked over to the kitchenette. "You won't believe the stuff they find on the Internet."

He nodded and grimaced to himself. "Did the girl get it straightened out?"

"Neutral territory. Aspen for skiing over New Year's."

"What about the depression?"

"Well, I'll see if the chocolate chip cookies have been finished off by morning. She went to the doctor last week for an anorexia check and found she had a urinary infection. Turns out she had a labia ring put in and then got an infection."

"Jesus."

She yelled from the kitchenette. "Body piercing, let me tell you."

"Did Angela ever get depressed?"

"She never had time." She sat down next to him on the sofa and handed him his coffee. "And no, Angela and I weren't lovers."

"Did I say that?"

"I was married for five years; I know how men think."

"But she taught you everything you know."

"No." She frowned, then gave him an uneasy smile. "I never had the guts, not like Angie. You know what the difference is? For us, it was freedom, good-time sex, and, yes, romance; for them, it's like part of the corporate plan, conquest and self-realization to be tucked into the résumé. My little chicklets are going take over the world. "

"But you still idealize Angela?"

Ruthie's nut-brown eyes deepened.

"You know what I was called when I was here in school? A JAP. And I let it go because I was happy to be thought of that way, because the truth is, we were dirt-poor and I was on scholarship."

"You, too."

"That's what I loved about Angie. She could've cared less. It was like, Hey Ruthie, let's go hear Tim Hardin at Club Forty-seven tonight. We'd sign out for dinner with her great-aunt, Angela Chillingworth. Angie was crazy about her great-aunt—her namesake—and her neat place on the beach in Manchester. Except—one problem—the old lady was in a nursing home, or dead. With Angie, it was hard to get the right story. But—presto—there'd be a taxi waiting to take us into Cambridge. And Angie was so foxy, miniskirt up to her ass. By the time we got to Club Forty-seven, we were stoned. Bouncer waved us in past the line. Best table, drinks on the house. And there was Hardin onstage and he was singing to Angie. And I was looking at Angie and she was grinning at me. 'I fucked him at Woodstock,' she whispered. 'We shot heroin.' I was blown away.

"So after the gig, we went back into his dressing room. And just like that, Angie plonked herself on his lap and began French-kissing him. He had his hand on her ass and was going, 'Baby, oh baby, you feel so great, baby.' She was giving him a blow job. I was so high, I thought it was hysterical. And I could see how Angie was into it, like she had his whole fucking soul in her hand and was taking all she could get. Then suddenly, he was looking at me, Tim Hardin was looking at me like I'd been watching offstage and now maybe it was time for me to audition. 'Hey, babe,' he crooned in his haunting voice, 'don't you miss out on the fun, honey.' Angela looked up at me and said, 'Show him your tits, Ruthie.' So I pulled open my shirt and got my bra off. 'Come here, honey,' he said."

He felt her shiver and she laughed, something between embarrassment and remembered delight.

"Go on," he said.

"I can't believe I'm telling you this."

"She pimped for him and you were the deal."

"Anyone ever tell you, you have a cruel streak? Tim died of an overdose in 1980."

"Sorry."

"She showed me how. I was sick on the way back in the taxi. But hey, I blew Tim Hardin. I can see it on my tombstone: *Blew Tim Hardin at Seventeen.*"

They both laughed uneasily.

"What about the famous dance?"

She grabbed his arm. "Don't get me going on that. Anyway, Angela wasn't there. It was as if the general didn't show up for the big push and the troops were languishing in the trenches."

"And it was her birthday. Sandra's, too."

"Hey, that's right. Now I remember Angie told me later it was her birthday present to her sister, letting her go in her place."

"Quite a present: an eighteenth birthday that was really a nine-teenth."

Ruthie smiled. "No—you, an Irish hunk, wrapped in a ribbon."

"So who got the chaperone to come over and break in on us on the dance floor?"

"I was wondering if you remembered that."

"It was the spark—it got the whole thing going."

"If you want to know, I did. My date, Seth Higginson, was totally turned on by Sandra. She was just his type, soft-spoken, exquisitely featured, blue-eyes, blond-haired WASP. He couldn't take his eyes off her."

"You, huh?"

"I was pissed. He wasn't paying any attention to me. It even crossed my mind that Angela had let Sandra go in her place just to see if Seth would go after her. God knows, Angie had flirted with him enough, when he was with me. She could be cruel, pull your chain just to keep you on your toes. That's why I wanted Seth so bad. Later that night, we were caught going at it in a laundry hamper in the gym. The night watchman heard us, but he was decent, told us to get dressed and get the hell back to the dance."

"Another notch on your belt."

"No. I married Main Line Philadelphia, a nice guy, tournament direc-tor, but the schmuck had absolutely no sense of humor, and in the sack, he was even worse. Even Seth could laugh at stuff. Of course, the girls at Princeton just loved Seth—stinking rich and a great lover in the bargain. You train 'em and some other bitch gets the benefit." She laughed. "Why am I telling *you* this?"

"If you had to make a prediction about Angela's life, how would you see her ending up?"

She eyed him suspiciously.

"You're trying to get me to say something."

"No, I'm just wondering."

"You want me to say, like Janis Joplin, don't you? And *if* I thought that, it'd only be because nobody could have kept up that kind of a gig for a lifetime."

"And you miss her?"

"She was a beautiful WASP from a big house in the suburbs, had everything. And she hated her parents, especially her father. And yet she loved boys; she really knew about guys—what they liked, what they wanted. But she believed girls were as good, if not better. She wanted equality ... kind of like if we were on an equal footing sexually, we'd all be better people."

"Your remembrance of Sandra in the alumnae magazine ... well, it sounded more like regrets."

"Life is surviving regrets."

Ruthie suddenly stood and reached for his right hand and drew him up to her, assuming a ready stance, arm on his shoulder, her face tilted.

"What's it going to be, big boy, tango, rumba?"

"I don't know about the Judy Collins," he said, seeing the keen spark in her brown eyes, her lips poised and glistening.

"She's known sorrow, big time. Her son committed suicide."

"No."

"We should have been dates at the dance. You and me, two of a kind, scholarship kids. Michael ... Bill—whatever your name. We could've been made for each other."

He flinched when she'd said his name, Michael, but a moment later she danced him around the room in a gentle two-step to the Judy Collins, laying her head on his shoulder, as she sang along. "Who knows where the time goes...."

"Things might have turned out differently," he murmured as much to himself as to Ruthie.

"They always do." She sighed into his ear.

She led him back to the sofa and snuggled against his chest.

"Are you sure Angela never said anything to you about a baby brother who died, maybe the year before she and Sandra started at Alcott?"

She shook her head against his chest as if not to miss a beat of his heart.

"Not to me. Her family—they hardly existed."

"It must have been a terrible thing."

"You don't *still* have a thing for Sandra, do you?"

She pulled back from their half embrace to look into his eyes.

He wagged his eyebrows. "No more than you do for Angela."

She shivered and something akin to an expression of guilty chagrin passed across her face. "You know what they say—about the body never forgetting." Her dark eyebrows were pinched tight; she paused, as if a little perplexed. "You think it does, but it doesn't."

"There's something ... compelling about her family," he said.

She winced, her voice erupting with emotion. "Well, her mother was sure a bitch, and according to Angie, her dad just walked out on them."

"Yeah."

She squeezed his arm. "So, tell me, did she come?"

"What?"

She shoved him in the ribs. "When you made love to Sandra, did she come?"

"Christ."

"Well, did she or didn't she?"

"How the hell would I know? We were kids, idiots."

"Oh, you'd know ... you'd know."

"You think it really matters?"

"No, just kidding." She touched his cheek, his whiskers. "Just wondering how much of Angela she had in her."

"How much they shared?"

"The twin thing ... I mean, it's got to be a little spooky. Like I told you, there was this coolness between them; they barely spoke to each other ... like they knew, like they didn't have to say a word."

"Yeah, well, Angela had to be a tough act to follow."

Ruthie smiled uneasily and nodded.

"I'm not sure your beard really suits you."

"It's just for a laugh, while I complete my research on Thoreau."

She put a finger to the tip of his nose. "Michael Collins."

"Ruth Horowitz," he shot back.

Her teasing smile flickered out.

"Did I ever tell you I teach Thoreau to my twelfth-grade AP American literature class?"

"Yeah."

"They like his essay on civil disobedience and his abolitionist writings. The environmentalists think he's the greatest. But *Walden*, the transcendentalist stuff—they find it a little tame, a little obscure, maybe a bit behind the times."

"Oh, Henry's behind the times all right. That's kind of the point. You've got to find your way into his space. Then the world looks a little different, surprising even. Try your girls on the journals; that's where Henry really lets it all hang out."

"Maybe you should come teach a class or two when we get to Thoreau. You'd be perfect. You could make Thoreau live for them."

"I'd like that."

"I bet you're a great teacher," she said.

She sat up, held him at shoulder length, and took his injured hand, examining it, stroking the fingers, then turning over his hand to trace the lines in his palm. A puzzled look entered her dark eyes. "Funny thing, when I look back, I feel—well, sometimes—like all I ever really wanted was children."

"Children?"

"My parents retired to Tempe, Arizona, got a cute little mobile home. They drive all around the Southwest, play the slots in Vegas. They have a little sign by the front door: 'If the trailer is a-rockin', don't come a-knockin'.' I went out there once to see them, and once was enough. They're having a grand time with all the other suntanned, swinging old-timers, swigging their Viagra martinis. And you know what I figured out? They never really liked children."

The first thing the following morning, he went to the only florist on Main Street in Concord and made inquiries about a woman, a mutual friend of a friend, who'd been spotted the previous day coming out of the shop with a large bouquet of roses. Sure enough, the owner described a tall, well-dressed lady, good-looking, short blond hair, who had been in the day before, right as the shop opened in the morning, to buy a dozen long-stemmed roses.

William Channing touched his nose with a knowing air. "She had the most elegant nose, long and ... kind of aristocratic, I guess."

The owner, a man in his sixties with thinning hair, glanced up over his bifocals and pulled scissors out of a pocket to snip the stems of the bouquet he was making up.

William leaned forward on the counter, watching the preparation of his roses. He handed the owner Sandra Palmer's high school photograph and went on to explain how he'd lost track but had been hoping to catch up with her for some time. Palmer, old Concord family; they'd been in school together. The owner examined the photograph and nodded. The name didn't register. She'd paid with cash, not a credit card. She'd been driving a car and had parked right in front. Picked up the roses and drove off. And no, the owner said, he'd never seen her before, but she had the body language of someone who knew her way around, was familiar with Concord.

"Classy, too," the owner added, "with a kind of European flare." He handed back the photo. "But not so young."

William Channing had to bridle his expectations, but he was sure the woman at the florist had been Sandra. Angela, even if she had been able to identify the person who had sent her an E-mail using her sister's account, would have raised hell, would have swaggered into the inn demanding to know what was going on. Angela might even have alerted the police, filed a complaint. But Sandra would have known who it was; she would be quiet and circumspect—hopeful, but secretive and careful. My God, laying flowers on your own grave—imagine!

The thought made him smile, the way some of the stories about the uncertain fate of Michael Collins made him smile, as if his world was filling up with stories.

Sandra's resurrection began to take on a thrilling beauty. A picture began to develop in his mind about what had happened in her Cambridge apartment: a reunion, a birthday celebration, an unexpected argument leading to a fight between sisters. A terrible thing, perhaps going back to their childhood—and even before—prompted by the accident with the baby. A "coolness between them," as Ruthie had put it. The words *hate* and *resentment* in Sandra's letter. A past that had reemerged to strike down one of the twins.

Possibly an act of malice and jealousy: Angela killing herself and leaving everything to her tender and quiet sister, as if throwing her burned-out life in Sandra's face—that possibility began to take on wings.

Except for one thing. The woman in the flower shop had bought a dozen roses. Six roses were unaccounted for.

Often William Channing found himself staring at the twin sisters in the etching on his desk, wondering about those Venice days of long ago, and how those women with the same first names, Sandra and Angela Chillingworth, had inspired, inveigled, and confounded the artist Joseph Palmer, and perhaps his grandfather Giovanni Maronetti, as well.

It took some doing, but he finally tracked down Miranda, the assistant coroner who had processed the site of the suicide. Miranda had changed jobs, first moving to Nashua, New Hampshire, but then quitting her job as a paramedic, and moving to Tampa to start a degree program at the University of Florida in behavioral psychology. She was not happy with their phone conversation. And in truth, he was not crazy about getting the unhappy details of the suicide scene, except that the uncertain picture in his mind demanded those details.

"I know it's hard for you, but Sandra and I were real pals as kids, practically grew up next door to each other. And it's like, coming from the same neck of the woods—well, if there was something that could've made her so unhappy …"

"Mr. Channing, I'm sorry. I've already told you; I don't think I can help you—because that *is* the problem, don't you see. There *was* no reason."

"You were in there after the police…."

"Don't you get it? Nothing." There was a pause on the line. "Mr. Channing, I was good at my job, and it's a nasty job to be cleaning up after the dead and see that their lives are properly filed into the neat categories that society likes to hear about. We give order to chaos and the unthinkable. But I've seen a lot of death and more suicides than you or any normal person would care to know about. In the end, it's a job. But this was different. There was no chaos, nothing messy outside the state of the body and the area around it. Every death is different, but there is normally a pattern that establishes itself. The patterns comfort because they speak of something that can be understood. I am young, Mr. Channing, and not hardened. And sometimes I wept for my victims. You weep with the families when it's you that has to go see them, get an identification, turn over the personal effects. I'd even clean up stuff for the families, get rid of brain matter or blood, so that when I turned over a traffic victim's rings to her husband, he didn't have to be reminded what state they were in. But this was different."

"'Different'?"

"I've been in places where there was six inches of trash wall to wall, months of stale and rotted food, empty booze bottles packed like a recycle center—and don't get me going on the drug paraphernalia. This was the worst. Her place was clean, like she'd just swept and vacuumed and dusted. Food put away. And get this. Her computer was on; the cursor was blinking in the middle of a sentence she was writing in her thesis. Her papers were on her worktable, books open, pen uncapped. Photos of her family. I walked the scene a dozen times and I swear it was as if she had risen from her computer, walked to the kitchen and got that spanking new kitchen knife, and calmly went to the chair and slipped the knife into her uterus."

"Her uterus?"

"If she'd been a surgeon, she couldn't have done better."

"That's terrible."

"No, Mr. Channing, it's unimaginable. Do you get it now?"

"And no sign of a struggle—possibility of foul play?"

"Prints on the knife handle were as good as etched, much less the angle of the entry wound."

"You said she was naked, so how could she have just been sitting—"

"It was hot that week, hottest week in October in twenty years. There was no air conditioning. I think she'd been sitting there naked, maybe wearing a pair of panties—there were panties in the laundry hamper. Everything else was washed and folded in her drawers, hanging in her closet. The kitchen was spick-and-span."

"What did you say about a new knife?"

"Brand-new. A new set of three imported Henckel knives. She used the largest. The smaller ones were still in the gift box they came in. The box had a ribbon on it like it had been a birthday present; it also had an Italian price tag on it—in lira."

"Detective Murray said she'd cut her hair."

"Sometime before and carefully, meticulously, and she'd cleaned up after herself. Nothing to indicate she was rushed or mentally anguished or in a moment of despair. I swear she'd gotten up from her computer, maybe slipped off that pair of blue panties, and then gone ahead."

"Could someone have come in, maybe soon after, and cleaned up the place? Made it look better, more ordered, than it had really been?"

"Why in hell, Mr. Channing? Can you think of anybody who'd go in there, seeing how it was, and be able to do that?"

"And no doubt it was a suicide?"

"Like I said, there were no signs of a struggle, her hands were on the knife, her prints. No sex, no semen. Her boyfriend, if I recall, hadn't been with her in some weeks."

"Any possibility of HIV?"

"If so, it would be in the pathologist's report."

"Did you—"

"No, I did not process the body. A colleague and I brought her in, but we let the chief coroner do the autopsy. I'd had my fair share."

"Tell me something, Miranda. Forgive me if I'm overstepping the bounds here, but if she'd had a child at some point or maybe even an abortion, would that have come out in the coroner's report?"

"You mean did she have an episiotomy?"

"I guess."

"I don't know. The body was a little ripe, but yeah, maybe it could be in the report."

"And the family gets the coroner's report?"

"Normally, that's the case and pathology, later. But *her* father—I don't know."

"Joe Palmer—to a kid, he seemed a pretty remote kind of guy."

"I went out there to turn over her personal belongings. I mean, he was perfectly nice and well-spoken and everything. Sometimes they break down when you arrive—cry, want to hold you, talk ... like you're the last one to have seen their loved one alive, which isn't the case. But not him. He nodded and thanked me, took the stuff, and closed the door in my face."

"So you handed over all her stuff: wallet, credit cards, keys, jewelry—her passport, I suppose?"

"I don't remember a passport."

"You didn't find a passport in her possession?"

"Mr. Channing, you've got some funny questions for a childhood friend."

"Just curious, since she'd been living overseas for so many years."

"You know what, pal, I don't much like the sound of your voice anymore and I'm just going to hang up this receiver."

CHAPTER 14

The FedEx envelope containing the report from the investigator in San Francisco finally arrived. At first, William was gratified by what he read, seeing the telltale signs of a life that might well end in heartbreak and disaster, but then came more doubts.

Dear Mr. Channing:

As noted in our phone conversation, we have made much headway but have as yet been unable to locate Angela Palmer, aka Sandy Blue. Here is the preliminary report.

Angela arrived at Berkeley in the fall of 1970, in the thick of antiwar fervor, and seemed to fit right in with the radical temper of the times. She had two roommates, who described themselves as liberated and politically radical, out for a wild time. They were both "madly, crazily in love with Angie." They described her as off the radar screen, a party animal, very much into drugs, drinking, way out there sexually. Good-looking and knew it and liked to flirt, to use her body. Boasted of affairs with professors but made it clear she earned her marks. She was smart. People were in awe of her capacity to party and get her work done. Sometimes she went cold turkey, spent weeks in the library studying for exams. Her transcript shows a remarkable 3.9 average over two and a half years. Majored in art and anthropology, with numerous courses in archaeology. Friends describe her as broke half the time, which they found surprising, since it was assumed she came from a wealthy and prominent Boston family. Therefore, it was assumed she blew it on drugs and booze. In fact, her tuition went unpaid for long stretches. She seems to have spent money on dance classes, ballet and modern. Roommates commented on her energy and drive and a strangely compartmentalized life, as if there were things she refused to share with them. People would call her up in the middle of the night, people nobody there knew. She'd get stopped on the street by seeming strangers. By junior year, she was so broke, or so she claimed, that she began modeling for the life class at the San Francisco Academy of Arts for extra cash. Roommate's comment: "She got off on nude modeling."

Although all assumed her politically radical and antiwar, nobody ever remembers her actually participating in marches or protests. Once she was sitting in a bar with friends, stoned and drunk, when a TV news broadcast showed a violent antiwar sit-in. She is reported to have blurted out, "Those stupid sons of bitches, how would they like it if they were being shot at in the jungles and everybody back home was cheering the fuckers on?" This outburst was chalked up to a streak of bloody-minded perversity.

Spring of junior year, she dropped out; vanished, according to roommates. Dad, it seems, had even arrived to personally pay her back tuition, in cash, and then found her gone. The guy freaked, a former roommate said; she thought he was having a nervous breakdown.

In fact, she was continuing her ballet training in San Francisco and living under an assumed name, Sandy Summers, with an ex-marine flier in Redwood City. The man was partially disabled and, according to neighbors, was known to be violent. He was hooked on alcohol and painkillers; he died of lung cancer in 1988. At this time, she took theater classes and worked at a local VA hospital as a physical therapist. Her employee file shows a fine record of work, with only the highest ratings from doctors and nurses. Patients loved her; inspirational was a word used more than once. They were sorry to lose her after two years, when she went on the road with a small theater company.

The trail over the next few years is pretty thin. She traveled a lot; she changed her address often. She worked in regional theater. She modeled. She toured with an experimental dance company in the Southwest for eight months. She tried out for the San Francisco Ballet three times and failed the auditions. Dancers who remember her from that time speak of her with admiration; she was striking and talented, with a terrific stage presence, but hindered by her height and lack of early training. People spoke of her stage persona as proud and profoundly aristocratic, graceful, a class act. By all accounts, Angela Palmer had shed her radical lifestyle; she'd given up smoking, and nobody remembers her drinking or doing drugs—she was working too hard. She had various boyfriends, shared apartments with men and women, and took on modeling when she was hard up. People described her as private, very, very bright, a big reader. She seemed to wander in and out of people's lives. Most assumed she was bisexual.

After a series of injuries sidelined her dancing career, she turned up in Long Beach in the early eighties as a sexual therapist/surrogate at the famous Center for Marital and Sexual Studies headed by Drs. William Hartman and Marilyn Fithian, the so-called Masters and Johnson of the West Coast. No details of her employment were available, but an ex-patient (or client?) spoke of her in glowing terms as practiced and dedicated and tender in his therapy sessions. During this time, she was trying to make her way into the theater and film community.

It is unclear whether her transformation into Sandy Blue was a concerted career move or she just fell into the scene. She'd gotten into the burgeoning porn industry in mostly walk-on roles to make a buck, but her star quality as a sexual performer was quickly recognized and she was soon in demand and being paid relatively good money. Her early names were Leslie Deblue and Delia Delight and finally Sandy Blue. She'd gotten into the business at a propitious moment for female porn actresses. Not only was the industry booming with the explosion of the home video market for triple-X-rated films but also the "name" women, once exploited and poorly paid, were demanding higher salaries and getting more control of their product.

Within the industry, Sandy Blue was head and shoulders above the competition; not only were her acting skills of professional caliber but she was completely natural: relaxed, instinctive, sensuous, with a cool, aloof eroticism that sizzled on screen. She was in demand; she chose her partners and directors. Her name sold the product. By the late eighties, she'd formed her own production company, along with distribution and marketing, Sandy Blue Productions. The company began specializing in erotica for women, emphasizing the dominant role of the woman in sexual situations and catering to female fantasies. In the early Sandy Blue tapes, she always played the same character, the classy, aristocratic, distant femme fatale who is lusted after by men, the mysterious and unobtainable object of masculine desire. Later, as she took more control, finally directing her own productions, she went against trends and removed almost all explicit narrative elements from her films, going for more mood values, beautiful and expensive sets, top-notch jazz and classical scorings. Other porn stars wanted to work with her. They described Sandy Blue as totally on top of her sexuality, a natural-born fucktress, always with you in a scene, never faking it, always enjoying herself. Her cachet was authenticity. She insisted that the women have on-screen orgasms, prepping with vibrators if necessary. Her girl-on-girl tapes are especially prized in the lesbian community.

At the height of her popularity in the early nineties, Sandy Blue Productions was making a ton of money and had a wide cult following; overseas sales were booming. Many of the tapes are still best sellers. Offscreen, Sandy Blue was described as intensely private and a first-class businesswoman. She mixed little socially with other members of the industry. She spent a lot of her time in her home in Malibu, where she had a large library and a collection of Mayan artifacts. According to the few people who had seen her home, she was a demon collector of art, especially American prints from the forties and fifties, Bay Area abstract art of the fifties, and archaeological finds, Indian pottery, and textiles. There were the usual rumors about her sex life and marital status. Then she just dropped out of sight. With the exception of a single interview she gave to Playboy in September 1991, before her departure from the industry, there is little else about her private life or views. But she retains an almost-mythic stature in the industry, the best and sexiest chick of the golden age of porn, before the business was taken over by a new generation of Nautilus-trained bodies and bland bimbos with tit implants. Her tapes still sell well, but her new company, SandyBlue.com, which began as a mail-order business, quickly branched out into the booming E-commerce market. The company produces and markets a line of vibrators that are touted to be the best in the industry. In recent years, SandyBlue.com has become known for it holistic philosophy in terms of women's health and sexuality.

I have contacted the CEO of SandyBlue.com and the law firm that handles her business affairs. I am assured that she still runs the company but wishes to remain anonymous and out of the limelight. These explanations are reasonable, although slightly suspect. My sense is that no one has been in regular or even recent contact. If I had to guess, I'd bet she'd turned her back on the whole shebang. With the money she has, she's probably gone into something entirely different, possibly academia to follow up on earlier interests. I have contacted graduate departments in anthropology and archaeology on the West Coast and mailed off a lot of photographs. Presumably, she has changed her name again, and if she has the financial resources of SandyBlue.com at her disposal, she can probably cover her tracks pretty effectively. I have enclosed a copy of the interview she did for Playboy in 1991, along with a Sandy Blue's Greatest Hits tape and my invoice. Please advise how you would like us to proceed.

The Playboy interview began with a tasteful photograph of the subject clothed in blouse and jeans on a white sofa in the spacious living room of her Malibu home. Light off the ocean floods through the picture windows and across the white stucco walls.

PLAYBOY: You agreed to our conversation on the stipulation that you would not talk about your private life outside of the adult-entertainment industry. Is this strictly a "privacy issue" with you, or does it have to do with your on-screen persona: the mysterious and aloof femme fatale?

SANDY BLUE: Fundamentally, I believe an erotic actress should remain a blank to her public in terms of her personal biography, offscreen as well as on. The point of pornography, or erotic entertainment, is that it is body-focused, narrowed to the most pure and intimate physical acts. Artistically, that is the challenge: Your body, your very flesh, must take the full weight of meaning for your audience. It's not unlike the issues a dancer or choreographer faces. Actually, it is even closer to the challenges of a printmaker, say, an artist who restricts himself to ink on paper—that is, black and white, a negative and positive image to express the full gamut of form and color. The narrower the technical focus, the bigger the artistic challenge.

PLAYBOY: Are you saying that fully developed characters, plot and narrative and context in adult movies add nothing to the erotic associations?

S.B.: It is the difference between true erotica—great erotica—and run-of-the-mill porn. It's a question of balance, of course. Since some narrative context is required by the viewer, it will be imposed by the viewer. It's the body that matters, and the real trick for the performer is to be sexy by simply being sexy, being herself. As with the best literature, a great erotic actress and her director must give leeway to the viewer to add his or her associations to the sex happening on-screen, to engage their imagination, their fantasies. The visual experience is that of a voyeur; it is vicarious.

Women, like men, are stuck in the context of day-to-day life. That's why a purer, more abstract erotica is so appealing, because it is free from inhibiting associations and can focus body and soul on erotic fulfillment. All great art gravitates toward abstraction. Women like the real thing. They like genuine emotion; they like to see stuff that takes them to sensations and places they haven't been before. Great erotica, like great art, should open your life and take you to higher levels. A great painting is a great painting because every time you see it, you see something new.

PLAYBOY: To move from the sublime to the absurd, what would you say to your feminist critics who condemn pornography for degrading women and promoting male fantasies and power over women?

S.B.: Let's face it, good sex for a woman is about a healthy self-image and some technical proficiency in learning what gets her off. It is also about learning to separate sex from love and marriage and all those good things. Sex is a good in and of itself. Women are having more and better sex—having it their way. Sex is empowering them and making men happier, too, because it is a truly shared experience. A woman's body connected to her imagination and a modicum of know-how has potential for sexual gratification beyond the wildest dreams of our mothers. Probably beyond the capacity of most men, too. Men are discovering, to their chagrin, that women are, literally, designed for fantastic sex. A woman's body is a subtler instrument than a man's.

PLAYBOY: Do you enjoy doing what you do, or is it just a job? Are you as much a natural as you are made out to be?

S.B.: The body is like a beautiful and intimate landscape, a place we think we know well. But how often do we walk through a well-known place that we have taken for granted, only to have our senses awakened by a stray angle of sunlight through the trees, our own mind recalibrated—and we see something we missed all those times before ... and it is a revelation. This is what Thoreau understood. And for him, the landscape he knew so intimately, his native ground, was like an extension of his body, which he felt compelled to explore to the bottom of his soul. He embraced nature like a lover. But even he commented toward the end of his life that he had done so many surveying jobs around Concord that he couldn't go for walks anymore without thinking, That's so-and-so's woodlot, and that's so-and-so's … and so forth. And yes, anything can get stale.

PLAYBOY: You're not saying you're finding it hard to separate your work and private life?

S.B.: Remember, I have no private life.

PLAYBOY: What about a life after Sandy Blue?

S.B.: I always wanted to try my hand at gourmet cooking.

He flipped back to her photo at the beginning of the interview. How could he have missed it? Not that he read *Playboy* with any regularity, not since college days. And he'd seen his fair share of porn; he and Catherine had watched the occasional tape together … but never Sandy Blue. He found himself veering between exhilaration and sadness that such a dynamic personality might have ended up a suicide in that Cambridge apartment. The interview floored him: Everywhere there were echoes of her creative and talented forebears—not easily diverted to self-destruction. She even knew her Thoreau! How strange that the black sheep of the family could not resist the pull of home ground and its associated mythologies. Like what the investigator had said on the phone: "What's bred in the bone remains."

He clicked on to SandyBlue.com, to find her again enthroned on the Internet. His girl, his love, transmuted into electronic pixels radiating to the E-commerce universe.

Staring into her eyes, he could almost hear the bitchy voice of that freezing February day: *Come on, friend of Thoreau—whoever the hell you are—what's your secret? What's the bottom line here? What do you want? Look at my body. You'd still want it any which way, no? You still want to fuck her, don't you? Isn't that what it's really all about for a guy? Did you really love her? Who cares if it's Sandra or not? A body is a body, right?*

He shook his head at the portrait of Thoreau above the desk.

"Henry, what a terrible thing, to wish such a woman dead … so her sister might live."

He had to laugh to think how Henry, prudish Henry, would have been baffled and scandalized by modern women, especially an erotic actress.

And yet, if it was Angela who'd come back, who put those roses on the graves, she'd have swaggered into the inn and demanded to know who the hell was messing with her sister's E-mail address to harass her—surely she would. A woman like that might be capable of anything.

He shivered at the recurring thought: a ghastly crime, surely against human nature.

He'd done enough trial work to know how it happens: You build a case for the jury; you develop a scenario, expanding and refiguring where needed to accommodate the necessary facts, to build a picture that can leave little doubt.

Had he gotten it wrong? Could Angela have, in some way, contributed to the death of her sister?

He went back to the investigator's report, looking for the anomalies that might fit the case he wanted to make. "Those stupid sons of bitches, how would they like it if they were being shot at in the jungles and everybody back home was cheering the fuckers on?"

And then there was the business of shacking up with the disabled ex-marine flier and the job as physical therapist in a VA hospital. Loyalty … but loyalty to what, to whom?

It was as if some part of Angela was drawn to the afterlife of injury, the hurt and violence. Had she been a victim of abuse and thus prone to violence herself?

And what about those five roses on the baby's grave?

And the six missing roses?

His gaze drifted from the report to the etching of the twin sisters. Had history repeated itself? Sandra Chillingworth Palmer had died in childbirth and her sister, Angela Chillingworth, had gone on to take care of her child and find some success as a poet.

The play of headlights across the wall of his room distracted him. He went to the window and saw, to his intense displeasure, a police cruiser parked right in front of the inn. Hopefully, Slotnik was just downstairs flirting with Jennifer at the reception desk.

CHAPTER 15

"Heroes," said Jack the bartender. "That's the problem. There are no more heroes. No loyalty to anything."

The guy with the crew cut, Pete by name, nodded into his glass. "What ever happened to the Yastrzemskis?"

"Real heroes—fuck Yastrzemski—like you, Pete."

"I'm no hero," said Pete.

"Hear that, Bill." The bartender eyed William Channing and indicated his bar mate. "Pete here got blown up in Saudi. Dragged his sergeant down three floors; the man was cut to ribbons. Ain't that right, Pete?"

"Jesus, Jack, what else the fuck was I supposed to do?"

William noticed the tiny scars along Pete's forearm. He asked, "Get any kind of disability allowance?"

"Are you kidding? Hey man, we got counseling. We were supposed to cry our hearts out, not like you guys—that's what they always told us about you Vietnam guys, how you clammed it all up."

"You should talk to your congressman about a disability allowance."

Jack popped another Heineken. "Bet you were a hero, Bill?"

"Never fired a shot, never even got shot at."

"A likely story," said Jack, pouring the Heineken. "Pete, Billy, my bud here, will admit to nothing. Bet you didn't even notice his messed-up left paw. Amazing how he keeps it out of sight."

Pete looked over. "War wound?"

"Accident when I was a kid, messing with a lawn mower."

"Bullshit," said Jack. "Two years in med school says it's a gunshot wound at close range."

"You never told me you were in medical school, Jack," Pete said.

"I wasn't—just kidding." Jack raised an eyebrow and wiped around his glass and tapped the countertop. "Bill's a big listener, Pete. He thinks no one notices him behind his beard."

"You must have known lots of real heroes." Pete nodded at William. "Was it really like *Apocalypse Now*, the jungle and the gooks and all that shit?"

"I processed their papers." He took a long swallow of his Heineken.

"But you were *there*," said Pete.

"Come on, Mr. William Channing, professor, spit it out," said Jack, leaning forward over the bar. "From what I can make out, we're the only pals you got—except Ruthie, and I'm not sure she counts."

The two men watched him intently.

William Channing felt the voices connecting up inside him, his now only one of many. His mind was filling so fast with stories, he felt it only right that he should respond in kind, as if his story—all stories—had a life of its own.

"I was catching a ride on a Huey, loading up with staff and ARVN— South Vietnamese soldiers, three wounded guys on stretchers, a medic. Our base in the Central Highlands came under mortar attack near the end of the war. I was sitting there, scared shitless. The chopper was too full to take off. This American lieutenant climbs in and eyes the Vietnamese soldiers hunkered down in the cabin and points to two of them in the back and tells them to get out. They don't move. There was incoming all around. The lieutenant, Ranger, Arkansas drawl, makes eye contact with these two ARVN next to me—let them know he's not kidding—and tells them again. They shake their heads and won't move. He pulls out his thirty-eight and points it at them, one right next to me. I see the ARVN's hand move to the trigger on the M16 between his knees. Then—blam—just like that. The lieutenant blows his fuck-ing head off, brains all over creation, and as the guy keels over, his M16 goes off right next to my hand. The other ARVN scrambles out, screaming, and the Ranger lieutenant drags out the thing sprawled on the floor, apologizing to me for the mess the guy's M16 has made of my hand. End of story."

"Jesus fucking Christ," said Jack.

Pete shoved a hand through his crew cut. "None of our flyboys in the Gulf even took a casualty. They shitted their cockpits, but that was about it."

"I've got a hero for you, Jack," William said with a sudden rush of enthusiasm. It was as if the voices with which he spent his daylight hours, the books and journals and diaries, now clamored to join the company around the bar. He took his napkin and assiduously wiped at a damp spot, relishing the moment. "General Joseph Palmer—ever heard of him? Concord boy. His grave is in Sleepy Hollow. The man loses a leg at Antietam. Six months later, his regiment is supposed to make a frontal assault on Confederate lines north of Baton Rouge, through forest and underbrush and prepared obstacles against fortified positions. It will be suicide. The man has a wooden leg, can barely walk. But he's got to lead his men; he's an officer, see. So he rides to the attack on his horse. Sitting duck. He knows he's going to die, but it's the only way he can lead those Massachusetts boys. But get this, the Confederate officers see this guy riding on his horse, leading infantry, and they are so amazed at the display of bravery that they tell their men not to shoot this fellow officer. He still gets hit in the massacre that follows, but he survives—just—to become the youngest Union general in the war."

William Channing was a little soused and relishing his tale at the bar, and not a little amazed at himself for coming clean with his own Vietnam story. He'd never told a living soul the actual circumstances of his wounding before this night, including Catherine, who had always flinched when he mistakenly touched her with his left hand. Speaking his tale of a shameful wounding, given his present company and a bit too much to drink, allowed him to approach his quarry at a slightly different angle, a perspective that clarified a question in his mind.

As a boy and young man, General Joseph Palmer had known Thoreau. He had often accompanied Thoreau on his walks, sometimes in company with William Ellery Channing. By all accounts, Joseph Palmer was headed for a life as a scientist, perhaps an engineer or naturalist; he'd studied both subjects at Harvard. But when the Civil War came, he immediately volunteered and signed on as an officer in the Twentieth Massachusetts Infantry. His family attributed his precipitous decision to the influence of Thoreau, who by the late 1850s was a fervent abolitionist and supporter of John Brown. Thoreau had filled the young Palmer with a visceral hatred of slavery and urged him to action. There were hints in family diaries and letters that the Palmers never forgave Thoreau for encouraging young Joseph to go off to war. Later remembrances by Harvard classmates told of a most brilliant and promising man: a light to his generation, cut off by noble sacrifice.

Unburdening himself in this way, William Channing found himself vividly attuned to the voice of Joseph Palmer as he had found it in the volume of the general's correspondence in the library.

April 2, 1863

My dearest mother,

We had got two-thirds across the slaughter-field when, just as I was shouting to the men to keep closed on the color, pop I went off my horse like a rocket. As for me, God had been very good. I was spared life, and most probably another limb. The ball, a round one, luckily, struck in the joint of my wrist, shattering the bones. It was very painful. The other wound was slight. Buckshot struck the outside of my right ankle and glanced down, entering the flesh and passing through the sole of my foot. I was carried off the field and put in an ambulance to the river and then by steamboat to a near-destroyed railroad roundhouse on the outskirts of Baton Rouge, which had been converted into a hospital and where I remain after two weeks. The wound in my wrist has suppurated very freely and the constant discharge has weakened me. The heat is terrible—what it must be like in this place in July! The inflammation on the outside of my arm still continues and is quite painful. My great fear is that gangrene will set in, so that I shall lose my arm above the elbow, or my life even. We must pray not.

I have just received your letter of last May 13 and am much saddened to have the news of Henry Thoreau's death. Strangely, I was not surprised. After so much killing, what is another death? I have thought of Henry often; I remember back to my boyhood and rambles in the train of that great soul. In the eyes of the dead I have seen his face. I believe that Henry could not endure the slaughter of so many. I do not believe his sensitive soul could encompass the masses of men and munitions set on the move in the service of this bloody conflict to save the Union and end the abomination of slavery, a cause that stirred him to heights of indignation. But at what cost, dear Henry? The destruction of so many men's lives across some of the most beautiful farms and woodlands would find no place in his gentle surveying. The world as he came to know it, as he saw it and felt it be true, is no more. You wrote his was a gentle death, a serene passing; well, that is as it should be, for he was the gentlest and most serene of men. I am almost glad that he did not live to see this. Perhaps just knowing of the slaughter was too much. Did he have recourse to newspapers? Did he mention my name? If you could find out more about his last days, I would be glad to know of it.

As I lie on my cot in this burnt-out roundhouse, I often hear the sound of the approaching trains. This, too, reminds me of many a summer's day as a boy visiting the site of the building of the Fitchburg Railroad and finding Henry already there, from earliest morning, by the dew on his shoes, sitting very still by the side of the right-of-way but taking everything in. One would have thought the coming of the railroad would have been a perturbation for such a solitary.

And yet in later years, when interrupted in his surveying by the sound of the engine's whistle, he would look up and an enigmatic smile would come into his face, as if he saw all in his mind's eye: fresh news and fresh faces come from foreign parts, or perhaps in reverse, his mind moving outward along those unbroken rails to visit all the places and peoples that he read about in his books. I remember so well when he accompanied me to the station as we left for Boston and the war, how he gripped my arm with a show of such sadness and yet joy, telling me to see what there was to see and bring back to him reports of the world and all my successes. Ah, what successes, dear Henry. While he was alive I was never been able to write him. I could never tell him the truth. The railroad that he loved has been indispensable to our killing. It is the locomotive force to the organization of our vast numbers and the rapidity of deployment. The scale of our terrible business would be impossible otherwise. I am almost glad that Henry now sleeps well. Who of us in this generation will ever sleep so well again?

Sometimes at night, I wake to the moonlight through the broken roofing and I think back to my evening walks with Henry. We would often walk the tracks from Walden, feeling the heat of the day still held by the rails, and Henry would relate to me the names of some of the laborers who worked on the building of the railroad. He would stop at a place where once maybe a shack or shanty had been, where only he could remember what had once stood in that place, and recall to me some anecdote, speaking of a name, relaying to me snatches of a silent voice; and I am sure, wondering, as he always wondered, where they had gone and what had become of them, feeling that something of them remained, if only in his telling.

Dear Henry, may your peace now relieve you of the burden of recounting the voices withered on the vine over this last year.

Today, my dear friend from Harvard days, Edward Curtis, came by to visit. We talked of rides in the country, of cavalry skirmishes, of classmates living and gone. He has had enough of this war; he says when the war is done, he will have to live somewhere far away so as to remove himself from the memories.

Tonight, the surgeons come again to examine my wrist. Two bits of white bone came out this morning. I am determined to save my hand; my arm, surely one leg is enough of a sacrifice to the gods of war.

You write of hopes for excellent Concord strawberries this spring. I don't want all the strawberries to be gone before I get home. They have the meanest strawberries and the meanest tomatoes here that you can imagine. It's a mean place anyway, the whole state, and I wouldn't live here for it.

I long to get out on to salt water; that will set me up, I expect. Well, it won't be long now before I sail for Boston, I hope. I suppose you are all worrying yourselves at a great rate by this time. You ought to have got my last letters now. I dream of Concord and you, my family.

Love to all.

Your affectionate son, Joseph M.

As Joseph Palmer's voice wended through his mind, William Channing gazed at the bar's wall of faded black-and-white photographs—the martial subjects slightly blurred. These were of minutemen standing to arms, centenary reenactments of the famous battles, as old now to his eyes as the original battles to the town participants in the photographs. They gained a strange presence in his mind, ghosts reenacting the heroism of ghosts. And yet, like the voice of General Palmer, these black-and-white figures seemed transmitters of some brass-bottom reality: the terrible violence hovering on the periphery of all men's lives … phantoms dismissed, but nevertheless shaping the fate of the unborn … a fiery sword blocking retreat.

"Like I said," said Jack, an intent light in his blue eyes, "they don't make heroes like they used to."

William Channing's stare retreated from the photos on the wall and found the face of Jack illuminated by the glare of the television.

"We're all inheritors of violence, gentlemen. It's everywhere," he said.

Jack shot back, "Now that's one hell of a profundity, Bill—that the best you can do, professor?"

Pete had been pondering his glass for some time and suddenly piped up. "There was a guy from around here, up the Bedford Road. Real good family. Quarterback at Harvard—the girls used to fall over for this guy—everything was going well for him. He was a legend in these parts when I was a little kid. And the guy goes off and joins the army Seventh Calvary so he can fly helicopters."

William Channing smiled over his beer at Pete, as if had known it was coming, as if he'd known it would follow on from the voice of General Palmer: The circle of violence had penetrated even to gentle Concord.

"Hathaway," William exclaimed, as if to confirm this realization and prompt Pete to continue. "Robert Hathaway. His mother still lives up on the Bedford Road."

"You got it," said Pete. "There's a whole building at Hanscom Field named after him, Robert Hathaway—we knew him as Bobby in his football days. I went to his games as a kid. Now, he was something else. Flew choppers with the Seventh Calvary in Vietnam. Got a Purple Heart in the battle of the Ia Drang Valley. The citation for bravery is inscribed in bronze on the entrance. A year later, he was evacuating wounded through heavy enemy fire. Third time he went in, his chopper was already pretty shot up; he told the medics to load up the worst wounded and stay with the others on the ground. Vietcong were waiting for him, hosed his chopper down with automatic-weapon fire. Blew up in midair. That got him his second Purple Heart and Distinguished Service Cross."

"See—real heroes are dead heroes," said Jack.

Draining his beer with relish, William Channing indicated another with a tap of the bottle. "I see his mom almost every day on my jog out the Bedford Road."

He said this with such conviction that his drinking companion, Pete, looked at him a little funny, as though hearing an echo of his own thoughts.

Pete said. "Yeah, sure. My old man told me how Bobby Hathaway ran down a mailbox on Main Street—drunk he was, seventeen. His dad got him off. Judge sentenced him to sort mail after school for a month. Real hell-raiser—and the chicks, so I heard, couldn't get enough."

"Takes all kinds," says Jack.

"Trouble is, nobody believes in anything—no loyalty—except making money," said Pete.

"Loyalty." William Channing raised his glass to his circle of bar-stool philosophers.

"Pete here was quarterback of Concord High's undefeated team back in the early seventies," said Jack, raising an empty bottle in response to the salutation.

Pete winked. "Yeah right, and I can't even afford to live here anymore."

"Pete works at the penitentiary out on Route Two. Now, there's a rough and violent crew of motherfuckers for you. Pete, tell Bill about the new deal with the women guards."

"New women guards," said Pete. "They have them working with the worst inmates. Everybody loves them; the chicks flirt with the prisoners, prisoners with the chicks … *and do exactly* what they're requested to do without the usual threats and hassle."

"Ain't that something," said Jack. "Women doing a man's job. They're going to take over the world, see, before you know it." Jack put a hand on Pete's shoulder. "But you're always a hero in my playbook, Pete."

Pete downed his beer. "Hey, you know the worst part? You ask 'em out for a date on Saturday night, after hearing them sweet-talk those bastards all week—bitches won't even give you the time of day."

"Ain't that the truth," said Jack. "Woman like that, cut your balls off, William."

William Channing smiled. "Tell me, Jack, is that why you dropped out of med school—sight of blood?"

CHAPTER 16

———————

The side door of the roadside stand opened and the old man, carrying an armload of near-empty baskets, appeared out of the interior darkness into the failing dusk. A streetlamp down the road provided a thin veil of illumination as the two figures came together.

"Guess I'm too late," William Channing said, stopping, bending forward to catch his breath.

The old man squinted, peering in the direction of the voice.

"Never too late."

Joe Palmer rummaged in a basket, rejecting his first two choices, and then held up a misshapen ruddy green apple and handed it to the younger man.

"I got distracted by a stand of birches against the sunset on Brister's Hill," William said. He fingered the small fruit and then bit into it unreservedly. "Umm … good."

"Winter apple, Bourassa by name—exotic—you want to eat it near frozen. In another month, it will have more pluck and bite, a real stringent tartness." His voice was friendly, almost affectionate, smoothing the harder edges of a well-worn Yankee Brahman twang. "Here" —he took out another apple— "now try this on for size." He handed it over, then took one for himself and bit into it with relish, chewing, savoring, as if waiting for the full sensation to manifest itself. "Chinese Flowering, *Malus spectabilis*, texture like silk, warms in the mouth, a little lemony around the edges, nice bitter aftertaste."

William tried to follow the example, holding the two apples before him as if weighing them, while he chewed.

"Nice, really nice."

"You know what you are tasting, my friend?"

The tone of the older man's voice was familiar, almost paternal.

"A Chinese Flowering, wasn't it?"

"You are tasting time, a long, long time. A variety that flourished in the 1830s and 1840s and went into decline with the temperance movement against hard cider, and then was neglected for other table varieties—and forgotten. I found a tree nearly fifteen years ago near Stockbridge, made a graft, coaxed and coddled the thing along, and here you have a tiny but grand anachronism—extract of time itself, a crystallization of earth, sun, air, and water, that you can hold in one hand. In another month, you will cry with pleasure when you bite into this fruit."

Hearing the lovely grainy softness of the voice pronouncing this dirge-like appeal, the sound mixing with the rich flavor of the apple he chewed, he was lifted in a flood of good feeling. In the near distance, a fracture of welcome light in the farmhouse window. And beyond, a frieze of amethyst boughs against the pewter glow of the river. And there, as if translated out of the mix of voices that had absorbed him for weeks, a man standing before him in dungarees stained with splotches of paint. His frayed, unbuttoned collar showed a ragged neck of tendons; his frame was stooped and weathered—specter of a name incarnate. Intrepid captain, daring engineer, wounded veteran and friend to Thoreau, visionary artist ... father—the very manifestation of time and place in the guise of another human being. The miracle of endurance.

William mumbled, swallowing. "Strawberries, do you achieve the same magic with your strawberries?"

"Strawberries." Joe Palmer sighed slowly, as if picking over each syllable. "Now that you mention it, it was a lusty spring this year, good for strawberries. And, you know what? Once there was a summer apple called Early Strawberry, but it is gone, too, and I have yet to find it. But for the moment, there are some very fine Concord tomatoes. If you're partial, take some home with you."

"William Channing," he said, taking a step to shake hands. "I'm not sure the inn would take kindly to me showing up with my own tomatoes."

"Joe Palmer." The handshake was awkward as the old man balanced the baskets, a pressure lingering a moment more than required. "You've certainly been covering the country at a tidy clip."

"Getting back in shape from my rowing days, getting a feel for the place. I'm in town working on a book about Thoreau."

"Yes, I've heard your name mentioned. I thought old Henry had been pretty well written out, but I guess you've got the right name for it."

"Not many people remember poor old William Channing, but then again, he wasn't the greatest of poets."

"Ah, but a good friend to a better poet."

"Yes, a good friend. Actually, my subject is Thoreau and American landscape painting, his influence on turn-of-the-century artists."

"You know, my father was a painter."

"Not *the* Joseph Palmer?"

"That's the one."

"Funny, the connection had occurred to me, but I thought the family had lived somewhere up on the Bedford Road."

"We did, but as you see, no more."

There was no regret in the voice, no lingering sentiment for something past, just the plain fact.

William said with real enthusiasm, "But what a spread you've got here: a farm like this, in *this* day and age. Got to hand it to you."

"It's a way of life."

"Now, your father—interesting artist—his name keeps coming up in my research, but there doesn't seem to be much on him."

"Oh, you'd be surprised. There is a lot more than there used to be. There was a big retrospective of his work at the Boston Museum of Fine Art two years ago. He seems to be making a comeback, as they say, at least in some circles. I have a few small things of his you might like to see."

William felt a little faint as his heart surged.

"That would be great."

Joe Palmer turned toward the path to the house, paused, and turned back.

"My father read Thoreau avidly, so you might be able to draw your connection there. And his father, when he was a young man, was a friend of Thoreau."

"Careful now, you'll overstress my academic heart with such revelations."

Following Joe Palmer along the worn path to his front door, he thought of the tiny notice in the *Concord Journal* of October 16, 1966, recently ferreted out in the library archives.

Tragedy struck unexpectedly on Bedford Road yesterday morning when the infant son of Joseph and Abigail Palmer was found dead in his crib. Joey Palmer, age four months, was taken to Concord Hospital, where doctors examined the child and have, pending an autopsy, diagnosed a case of crib death complicated by an existing birth defect. A funeral service will be held next week. The family has asked that instead of flowers, contributions be sent to local charities supporting research into childhood diseases.

Four sentences circumscribing an act of fate or violence—the secret, the silence, the grief and guilt—had produced the world he was about to enter.

Joe Palmer ushered his guest into the well-lit interior of the house. The first floor was larger than he had expected. At some point, connecting walls had been opened out and the space enlarged by an addition on the back. Large unadorned windows offered a view toward the orchard and the river. The place was functional, bare-beamed, with halogen track lighting, and decorated with rustic wood furnishings, some antique, others beautiful handmade carpentry of recent vintage. A single wood-burning stove heated the area. There was a kitchen alcove, an office with two enormous architect's tables covered with invoices and a computer setup, a good-size library with wall-to-wall shelves packed to overflowing, a small dining area, and threadbare couches and easy chairs in the living room. Navajo scatter rugs showed off the original pine floorboards. A life reduced to essentials.

"Make yourself comfortable or—I know how researchers can be—have a look at the books." Joe Palmer set down his baskets in the kitchen. "I've got to make some quick calls to a few restaurants in Boston about deliveries tomorrow and then I'll get you up to speed with some real vintage cider."

It struck him, the thing about the house: It was the kind of place Thoreau wished for houses, an inside as open and manifest as a bird's nest, all the living spaces visible to the guest.

He consciously had to repress his eagerness to tear the place apart for any physical clue to the tantalizing bond he felt with this man—found in every glance: the nineteenth-century prints relating to apple cultivation, a mixture of Currier & Ives and botanicals plates with Latin inscriptions; an entire wall in the living room hung with paintings of early New England agricultural life.

He paused, his eye caught by an anomalous antique print of young women placing flowers on the graves of Union soldiers.

Only hours before, he had been waylaid by Marge Hathaway on his daily jog and asked if he'd like to accompany her to lay flowers on her son's grave. There, in a shaded out-of-the-way corner of Sleepy Hollow, was Bobby Hathaway's white marble stone with a dedication from his men in the First Battalion, 7th Cavalry Regiment. A tiny American flag waved in the breeze. Marge Hathaway, bouquet in hand, had sighed with pleasure and surprise to find six roses already on the grave, by then slightly wilted. A mother's grief, he thought: knowable only to itself.

Now he drew enormous comfort from that moment because it seemed to remove a terrible suspicion in his mind that Joe Palmer might have been the father of Baby Joey, who, he now figured, had probably been Angela's child by Bobby Hathaway. Marge Hathaway was either oblivious to the possibility or had no intention of letting on; her hostility toward Angela had all the hallmarks of a jealous mother. The child had been born sixteen years after the twins, a large gap, unless there had been an unplanned or unwanted pregnancy. He was certain that the death of the Palmer baby, the baby Sandra had told him had fallen from the changing table, had led to the estrangement of Sandra and Angela. If it were Angela's child, it would explain much.

Joe Palmer's voice droned on mechanically in the office as he took down orders.

William Channing moved on to the library, glad to give this question a rest, and began making a detailed examination of the hundreds of horticulture journals and scientific periodicals stacked on the shelves. And then, barely able to catch his breath, he saw it. A small early portrait of Sandra Chillingworth Palmer hanging in a shadowed corner behind a shelf: a neglected heirloom. He realized how attuned he was to the artist's style, the suggestive quality in the blurred edges of the forms, like the language of an intimate. He moved close to the painting, the face near alive to him, touching the Whistler frame. He withdrew a dusty fingerprint.

"You certainly don't waste any time getting to the point," said Joe Palmer with a smile as he came in and offered William a chilled glass of cider.

"She's lovely."

"Isn't she, and right over here are my father's volumes of Thoreau."

He went over and pulled out one of the books, a set of the 1898 Ticknor & Fields complete Thoreau in green morocco.

"Look at this," William exclaimed with genuine passion. "Underlining, notes in the margins."

"He was a very literate man, well read." Joe raised his glass. "What do you think of the cider?"

He tasted it. "Delicious. Nectar of the gods."

"It will get you well and drunk, should you care to do so. My own special reserve, to be found nowhere else. I've spent over twenty years refining the process. Next year, we'll begin commercially bottling the cider for sale by specialized suppliers throughout the Boston area."

"I feel like I've come to the source." He indicated the library.

Joe Palmer waved a hand. "The collections of a senile antiquarian to be sure. Discarded statistics and archives of a bygone age."

"Saving a gene pool. Preserving something ... good." He held up his glass in a congratulatory salute.

"It is a bracing and salutary thing to delve into the technical researches of our ancestors. One finds they were obsessed with the possibility of improvement, creating a more beautiful thing; in the case of the apple, by bringing together the most attractive characteristics in a hybrid. They were keen on simple improvements over time, subtle things that took much care and more patience. It is the art of patience we've largely lost."

"As was Thoreau, a connoisseur of apples, if I'm not mistaken."

"Of boiling it down to the essence, so as to miss nothing of importance."

"Always a tough order."

"Where did you say you were from, William?"

"Bill, please. From the Midwest. But I actually went to high school here, Emerson Academy. So I guess I qualify as a near New Englander."

"That explains your accent, around the edges."

William ran a hand through his whiskers, as if concerned for his appearance.

Joe Palmer patted his shoulder with a questioning look. "And the beard?"

"I thought a little sympathetic magic while I'm here doing the research."

He glanced away toward the painting, seeing the shapes of the spring blossoms behind the figure, clustered tufts of yellow-ivory, luffing sails upon an ocean of green.

"What happened to your hand?"

"Oh that." He slipped the hand back into the pocket of his sweatshirt, jolted by his carelessness. "A little accident in Vietnam. The surgeons did wonders. A little higher on the wrist and I would have lost the hand."

"Well, you are an odd man out for your generation. It must have put a crimp in your rowing career."

He nodded. "Not much of a grip."

"Perhaps I saw you row. I used to watch the boys row at Emerson from the gallery practically every Saturday afternoon in the spring … with my girls, if I could get away." He tipped back the rest of his glass and for a moment he seemed caught up in some pleasing vision. "Now, there's something that hasn't changed much—rowing. No fancy equipment, just good old sweat."

"Blood and sweat." William nodded and then gestured toward the corner and the small canvas. "I feel like I've known that face—funny."

"It's my mother, not more that seventeen or eighteen at the time. He painted her a lot. She was quite a paycheck for him as a model."

"Funny, she's so familiar."

"If you've seen anything by him, you've seen her before."

He came closer. "It's hard to know if she's the excuse for the landscape or the landscape's the excuse for her." He touched the frame reverently. "It kind of fits my thesis, turn-of-the-century Tonalism: the strong atmospheric quality, the intimate landscape setting, a known and loved place, dusk or dawn, the most dramatic features heightened to emphasize natural forms, moving toward the abstract, the symbolic even."

Joe Palmer watched the younger man intently, the lines in his face slackening.

"The language of the land."

"Language?" William asked.

"That's what Thoreau was after, when you come right down to it."

"Well, shall we put your dad to the test?" He smiled gamely and bent to the shelf of Thoreau, returning the volume in his hand and going down the row to the volumes of the journals, picking out one and flipping through the pages. "Hey, presto—look at this!" he exclaimed. He turned the page so Joe Palmer could see it, indicating the underlined portion with a finger. "All nature is classic and akin to art. The sumac and pine and hickory which surround my house remind me of the most graceful sculpture. Sometimes their tops, or a single limb or leaf, seems to have grown to a distinct expression as if it were a symbol for me to interpret." He raised his hand, glancing at his host. "Every natural form—palm leaves and acorns, oak leaves and sumac and dodder—are untranslatable aphorisms." His finger went to a note in dark pencil to the side. "And thus the frustrations and challenges of a lifetime's work."

The older man stood nodding, seemingly moved, perhaps surprised.

"Funny, I never really thought of my father as a follower of Thoreau, per se—or even much interested in speculations of that kind."

"Perhaps you were—you know how it is about fathers and sons—too close to him to notice."

Joe eyed the younger man with an expression hovering between regret and intrigue.

"My father—I barely knew the man."

"But here's the evidence," William said. "You'll have to let me borrow this."

He closed the book. His hand was shaking.

"To be sure." Joe contemplated the glass in his hand, at a loss. "My mother died giving birth to me. She was when I was growing up, a mystery, a presence—a kind of mythical ideal. It's hard to explain. She and my aunt were my father's models, his inspiration, the ideal on which he built his reputation, what he was. Well, the brouhaha anyway."

"Well ..." William paused, the thing percolating slowly to mind. "I mean ... the body is, in a way, just another extension of the landscape." He glanced away, a little embarrassed, going to the painting and then returning the book to the shelf. "You seem to be missing volume one, *Walden*."

"It's been missing as long as I can remember. Maybe in my rush," he said, throwing up a hand. "It's probably still at Sangamore—all his paintings and archives are there. That was his home in the Berkshires, after he left Concord." Joe Palmer gestured toward the living room.

"Let's get comfortable; my back ain't what it used to be. Here, let me get the bottle."

As Joe led him through the office on the way to the kitchen and back to the living room, he noticed a shard of marble used as a paperweight on a pile of invoices. The shock of recognition overcame any concern for safety. He picked up the broken piece of marble, examining the carving: a fragment of a woman's face.

Joe turned back to him from the kitchen with bottle in hand.

"That's a memento of my childhood summers at Sangamore. He had a sculptor working for him there, an Italian fella making things for the mill in Lowell. A real pal when I was a kid."

"A sculptor, huh?"

"Lovely man. You have to go there and see my father's paintings, for your research. May not be quite what you expect."

They sat together and drank. He could see that Joe was tired, so he offered that he should be getting back to the inn. But the old man encouraged him to stay, as if there was something on his mind, something the younger man's happy presence had crystallized but which he couldn't quite put a finger on. He began to cast around in a convivial tone.

"Speaking of Thoreau, Bill, you know, the most extraordinary thing about Henry David Thoreau, as well as Emerson and Alcott and his gang of windbag transcendentalists, is that they've turned out to be more right about human nature than even they, in their wildest imagination, could have suspected."

"Yes."

"Well, when you boil transcendentalism down, it's a belief that we are all individuals with our own talents and foibles, our strengths and weaknesses, upon which we must build in our own way. They believed man was endowed with certain instincts and capacities for moral judgment, things inborn and not necessarily due to upbringing and cultural circumstances. Well, all the recent work in genetics and evolutionary biology has proved them right. We are what we inherit, for better or worse, and it has come to us in a mixed bag of genes refined for our survival over tens of thousands of years of adaptation. We are truly rooted in the organic world, one and the same, just like Henry David Thoreau always suspected."

"So there's no escape."

"Only at our peril."

"So, we *are* who we are."

"Ah, but that's a tough one, take it from an expert. There's always natural variation—and chance, a bit of a crapshoot there."

"Joker in the deck."

"Love, desire, attraction: just nature's means of deception, assuring adaptation and survival. But I don't mean to bore you."

"Not at all."

"But tell me, when did you say you rowed at Emerson?"

"Late sixties."

"Hmm ... not great years for me. Divorced. Away from my family."

"And speaking of transcendentalists, you didn't have a daughter at Alcott Academy, by any chance? I seem to remember something ... the name at least."

Joe's face broke into a smile.

"Now there's a coincidence. I just heard from her the other day, first time in a very long time. She sent me an E-mail out of the blue. We're going to have lunch next week."

"What was her name?"

"Angela."

William's grip tightened on his glass as he felt blood rush to his face.

"Right, right, Angela Palmer. Didn't she go to Woodstock or something? Famous photo of her there in *Life* magazine."

Joe Palmer nodded pensively.

"I remember now, tall, with gorgeous blond hair. Whatever happened to her?"

"You should ask. Heaven knows." He sighed. "Your generation—about as crazy as they come."

"Some more than others."

"The truth is, Bill, I've been feeling pretty bad about Angela over the last year—a pretty awful year. Her sister died last year, Sandra."

"I'm sorry to hear that, Joe."

"I blame myself. The divorce and everything, I suppose I let the girls down. God knows, I tried to put it right, but their mother made everything very difficult. She was not a strong woman, strangely inbred and wound up like a knot."

William bent toward his host, swallowing hard, terrified to prompt him but unable to stop himself.

"Well, there's another problematic relationship: fathers and daughters. People say it's very complicated."

"Adolescent girls, late sixties—nothing in life, not even four years in the navy in the South Pacific, prepares you for that."

"They were strange times. I had a few bumps in the road myself," William replied.

"I tried to make it up between us. I was on my way out to San Francisco to see her when she was at Berkeley. It had been a rocky few years for me. I was sitting there in the airplane reading a strategic business plan for this new company I'd recently signed on with. I was a little down on my luck, near broke, to tell the truth. This business plan detailed a predatory marketing scheme, whereby we were going to cut prices on our product to below cost as a way of driving our regional competitors to the wall. Common as dishwater today, but then ... well, a brilliant plan, but I was revolted by it."

"Funny what ambition does when it gets you by the balls."

A knowing smile flickered on Joe Palmer's lips.

"Yes, so I suppose. An ambitious race we are. But funny thing, I remember how I just kept staring out the window, watching all those rivers and farms, mountains and deserts, then all the houses, that huge conurbation of our civilization. One had the feeling that the whole continent had been done over by the marketing men. So much lost along the way. I felt a deep sadness. I must have slept, because I remember waking and feeling that I'd been drifting over these vast landscapes. And when I looked out my window, there was this enormous swath of blue, as if the earth had suddenly ended. And I thought, Thank God—at last."

The old man rubbed at a paint stain on his pants.

"So Angela went to Berkeley. Did she keep up her dancing? Wasn't she doing a lot of ballet at Alcott Academy?"

"I don't know about her dancing, but when I got to Berkeley, I had the shock of finding that my daughter had dropped out months before. Not just dropped out but vanished. She'd been pretty crazy, but those were crazy times, so nobody seemed exactly surprised. They figured a commune maybe. I spent days looking for her. It was pretty depressing, imagining your daughter among those people. When I finally got back to the airport—I'd never even bothered with the business meeting—I found I'd missed my return flight to Boston. You might say I had lost my way and was a little turned around. I just stood there for the longest time staring up at the departure board, waiting for some place to register. It was like something from the dream I'd had on the incoming flight, of those vast unadulterated spaces of blue. Then I saw it: Sydney. A Quantas flight departing in ten minutes. I emptied my account for a one-way ticket and made it just as they were closing the door."

"Sydney, Australia?"

Joe Palmer held up his empty glass and turned it over like an hourglass.

"Bill, I had a wife who was a depressive alcoholic, a boy-crazy daughter who had disappeared, and her sister, who refused all entreaties to return from Europe, where my stupid wife had sent her."

"How long were you away?"

"Six, seven years … you might say. I lost track of time."

"What did you do?"

"I walked."

"Walked?"

"I lived with the aborigines in the bush. I wanted, I guess, to pare down life to the core. To see it at it most primitive level."

William leaned forward in his seat, as if suddenly intrigued by the deep-set eyes of the older man, the shamanlike intensity shining in the depths.

"Far out," he said, half in jest. "You … went back in time?"

"I sketched, I took notes, I wrote a lot of it up for a Ph.D. in anthropology at the University of Canberra."

William smiled, feeling the cider sizzle behind his eyes.

"A new life."

Joe Palmer frowned, concentrating on something.

"Bill, these people, these aborigines, lived in a broad, harsh landscape that had remained virtually unchanged for millennia—vast areas with relatively few prominent landmarks. Sometimes only a petrified tree, an unusual rock outcropping, an ancient streambed carved into the sandstone. I got pretty close to them, traveled with them, and learned some of their language, their stories, what they called their 'songlines.'"

"Their songlines?"

"Their songlines, Bill … this was how they related to their ancestral lands. They believed their ancestors were in the land and that their stories about their forebears connected them, literally, to the places where they had dwelled. They kept these songlines fresh in their heads, like a map to find their way around. Many of these places where their ancestors once dwelled had a story or event connected to some landmark. You see, they sang as they traveled, fragments of stories handed down by their ancestors, so that these places existed as a seamless songline, an enduring and recurrent present."

Joe refilled their glasses and sat back, his eyes filled with pleasure.

"Now, these places—we'd call them 'sacred' or 'holy'—filled their dreams. And from their perspective, the earth was dreaming, too; they were dreaming, the one and same dream, each vitalizing the other. As they walked the dreamlines of their ancestors, they became the journey, became their journeying ancestors. And when it came time for them to die, they would often return to the place of their conception, where they figured their life had sprung from the earth into their mother's womb, and there they would sing themselves back into the land and return from whence they had come."

Joe yawned, his eyes bleary.

William Channing raised his glass to his host.

"Joe, you've done Thoreau one better. Poor Henry, who failed to find himself an Indian who could tell much of their lost world. Henry, who never made it out west to see and study the Plains Indians. But you went all the way to Australia to immerse yourself in Paleolithic man. My hat's off to you, sir … that's quite something."

He returned to his room at the inn by way of the railway tracks behind Walden Pond, scouring the right-of-way for signs of the workmen's shanties that had, in Thoreau's day, populated that place. But he couldn't concentrate, his brain seething with doubts. Back in his room, he marched around, touching the stacks of books, going to the bay window and squinting into the lamplit night. Then he went into the bathroom to splash water on his face. Looking up from the sink, he was startled at the bearded stranger in the mirror. He toweled off and fumbled for his bottle of Tylenol and downed a couple of capsules in hopes of interdicting the usual headache, which increasingly plagued him in moments of agitation.

Joe Palmer was going to have lunch next week with Angela?

He could feel the joy in the old man's heart, a father's heart—after all, he was a father, too—father to a child he'd never known, who might never have been born. The equivocal joy at the possibility of being a father added to his consternation. Was it *his* E-mail that had brought her back? But of course she would have to use her sister's name, Angela; she'd have no choice ... until she actually met with Joe.

He left the aging face in the mirror and returned to his desk and Sandra's computer.

He opened her AOL account. No E-mails. He opened a reply with her address already in place and the cursor blinking in anticipation of his message. But what could he possibly write?

Can I join you and your father for lunch?

Even a single word might be misconstrued as a threat or a prevarication and send her running!

He thought back to the evening with Joe Palmer. It had him in knots, but he felt he'd handled it pretty well. He'd managed to restrain himself from asking more about Sandra or his grandfather Giovanni. Nothing about Sandra's pregnancy ... *refused to return from Europe.* Had she raised their child there?

Funny thing, after all the planning that had gone into his initial meeting with Joe, all his trepidation, it had been so easy. He liked the guy, felt drawn to him, as if they spoke the same language, were privy to the same voices. And Joe—he could barely admit it to himself—reminded him of Sandra: so genuine and such a fighter, clawing his way back into the world of Concord and his people. So desperate for companionship, and love—my God, the daughter you hadn't seen in years returns to your home ... to have touched her hand, looked into her eyes ... and then, suicide, the abyss!

And then out loud to himself, as if to hear it in his own voice, he said "Michael, my God ... the man is grandfather to your child."

That night, he slept fitfully. He dreamt of Sandra walking the streets of Concord in search of him. But in the dream, whenever he reached out to her, or screamed her name from his bay window, she'd seemed oblivious, fading at the sound of his call.

Often he awoke to the play of headlights cruising the walls of his room. He was terrified of another dream, of reaching to a tall blond woman and her turning to confront him, as Angela Palmer had turned to him on that freezing afternoon, vitriol and spite in her blue eyes, her voice a blade in his soul.

A few times, he got up and went to the bay window and stared out at the smudged hint of dawn behind the thinning trees on the square.

A police cruiser was parked on the square. Probably Slotnik was sound asleep; he couldn't decide if the policeman was hanging around the inn any more than usual, or just when Jennifer was on duty.

He went to Sandra's computer and laid his hand on the monitor, warm to the touch.

If he'd really summoned Sandra back ... returning home, to places filled with childhood memories, and yet fearful of being recognized, the thing would be like a living hell. Unless she'd returned for another purpose altogether. Unless she was utterly changed by whatever had happened in her Cambridge apartment.

Or was he slowly going out of his mind?

He tried to dismiss the most disturbing alternative: the possibility that an unimaginable crime had been committed.

He was a witness, of a kind. Had the police fucked up that badly? They had certainly missed Angela's E-mails in Sandra's computer.

Shaken at the thought of the capriciousness of human desire, he found himself moving to the door of his room and engaging the chain. Aghast, he crawled back into bed and pulled the covers over his head. The contradictions were beginning to overwhelm him. His headaches were more frequent, like a faint ringing residuum of his fall from the bridge. Often, he just wanted it to end, as if any kind of certainty was better than none.

Certainly the lunch with her father would do it ... and he would finally be free. Surely her father would know if this daughter was Sandra, wouldn't he?

CHAPTER 17

M idmorning, Ruthie knocked on his door.
"I had to see you." She careened about wearing a battered Princeton warm-up suit, first incredulous and then seeming to inventory the piles of books stacked around the desk, the scattering of index cards, the color reproductions of Joseph Palmer's paintings taped below the mantelpiece.

"Oh my God." She made a face. "What have you—it's like a mushroom cellar in here."

"Research."

"Your book—right, right." She was jumpy, grimacing as she rubbed at the small of her back. She touched the cover of the Palmer catalog on the reading table by his bed. "Guess who I saw this morning at team practice … I think?"

"I give up."

"Angela."

"You saw her? You talked to her?"

"Let me tell you, it was freaky. It's parents' weekend, and I was running the girls through a full court drill and happened to glance up. On the hillside behind the courts was a bunch of watching parents. There was a woman with a camcorder, taking videos of her daughter, I figured. Tall, short blond hair, classic features, and perfectly tailored skirt—well, I couldn't see that well. At first, I didn't think anything; then a few minutes later it hit me. Oh my God, it's Angie. I look up and she's still there, with her camcorder to her eye. I raised my hand and waved … like I was a screwball in someone's home movie. One of the other parents waved back, but nothing from her. Then I got distracted by a girl on court who'd sprained an ankle. And a minute later, I looked up again and she was gone. Then I thought, Am I going nuts?"

Trying to mask the relief in his voice, he asked, "Did you look for her?"

"Yeah. I mean, I wandered around campus, kept my eyes open. I wasn't exactly sure—you know."

"But she saw you?"

"Christ, I was wearing a cap. We've all gotten so fucking old anyway."

She stretched and groaned. "My back is killing me."

"She'd know *you*."

"How about a massage?"

"Short hair, chic clothes, you said?"

"The resemblance is incredible." She picked up a reproduction of *Dreaming Sisters* from the Boston Museum of Art. "Wow ... pretty kinky."

He twisted his mouth with impatience. "Would you know the difference?"

"Difference," she muttered, half with him. "You going to do the massage or not?"

"I mean, you haven't *seen* her since graduation."

She held up the reproduction, squinting—holding it at arm's length to read the caption.

"'*Dreaming Sisters*, 1924' ... amazing."

"If you didn't *know* it was Angela, what would you have thought?"

"Huh?" She made a face. "Anyone ever tell you you sound like a lawyer sometimes?" She spotted her reflection in the Federal-style mirror over the dresser and ran a hand through her frizzy hair. "Hey, maybe she *didn't* recognize me."

He met her eyes in the mirror for a second and then turned to the bay window. "So ..." he said in a calm and utterly disingenuous voice. "What do you suppose brings her back?"

She went to where he stood looking out the window and pressed herself into his shoulder and nuzzled his ear.

"Like you, maybe she just found out."

"Found out?"

"I don't know ... that Sandra had died."

He watched a woman in a blue parka walking across Monument Green.

She turned back to the desk and spotted an open bottle of Tylenol next to a bag from the drugstore. "Mind if I bum a couple?" she asked, shaking the bottle.

He turned to her with a vaguely distracted air.

"Help yourself."

"You don't do Prozac, by any chance? It does wonders for us older gals."

"Huh." He was staring out the window.

"Funny," she said, disappearing for a moment into the bathroom to get some water. "For a while there, I thought your scholarly thing wasn't quite on the level, like you were only going through the motions." She nodded at the piles of books and research materials. "It just shows ... Michael—can I call you Michael?—how age and disappointments with men can make one totally paranoid."

He rolled his eyes in a friendly way, trying not to panic. "Ever hear of Sandy Blue, SandyBlue.com?"

"Familiar." She tilted her head to examine the now-framed etching and photo of his mother in a silver frame on the desk. "I don't know, maybe I've heard my students talk about it—there's always the *latest thing.*"

He opened the drawer of his desk and pulled out a shrink-wrapped video and handed it to her: *Sandy Blue's Greatest Hits—The Greatest Couples' Tape of All Time!*

"What's this?" she asked.

"Take a look."

"Oh my God." Ruthie held the video at arm's length to better see the photo and read the label, then hugged the tape to her chest as her voice rose in childlike glee. "So this is what's happened to you, and you're still beautiful, Angie, so beautiful."

"So what do you think?" he asked.

"About what?"

"Was that the woman on the hillside by the tennis courts?"

"Are you kidding?" She laughed. "Where did you find this?"

"You can buy it on her site, SandyBlue.com."

"Well, good for her." She held it out again admiringly. "Sandy ... that's what Angie always called her." She glanced up, their eyes meeting in a look of almost wicked wonderment. "But you haven't even opened it."

"Don't have a VCR."

"Well, I sure do. Hey, Michael, it's almost Saturday night." She wriggled her hips. "We can go see if the trailer is a-rockin'."

He smiled and shrugged.

He collapsed in nervous exhaustion on his bed for a few minutes after Ruthie left; he was having a hard time reading her intentions. Now she was always teasing him with his real name.

Then he returned to the bay window. Was "Angie" in town for the lunch with her father? No, his sense from Joe Palmer was that it had been tentatively scheduled for the following week. She must be looking for him, checking things out, wondering, Who is William Channing? Should he just stay at the inn, or go out and try to intercept her? If it *was* Sandra, where was she staying, where would she go, and where would she look for him?

Actually, unlike thirty years before, there were at least three more inns in town, and another place out on route 2A.

He went to Sandra's computer and pulled up Angela's E-mail. Cookingwithfire@aol.com. He paused, scissoring his jaw.

"Go for it, Bill."

Waiting for you, Sandra, at the Concord Inn. William Channing.

He smacked the SEND icon. A minute later, the E-mail was returned.

She'd closed the account.

"Shit."

Identity theft. Sandra *had* taken on Angela's identity; he was sure of it. Sandy Blue, the whole nine yards. And she'd probably closed the account because it would leave her vulnerable to a fraud charge—impersonating the deceased, or was that just the warning Michael Collins might have offered to a client?

He knew from the report that Angela had been running her company at some remove. After the trauma of what had happened in her Cambridge apartment (perhaps Angela blamed Sandra for the death of her baby and her suicide was a sorry and perverse act of revenge), Sandra might well have felt compelled to make sense of her sister's unhappy life. Maybe she'd simply taken her sister's wallet and identification and gone to Angela's home, just to check it out (the image of that sunny Malibu beach house out of the pages of the *Playboy* interview came to mind). Maybe finding she had access to that parallel life brought on a strange thrill. And then, slowly, she had found herself drawn into her sister's exotic but sad existence, trying to understand how Angela's demons could leave her a suicide in that chair by the window. Maybe Sandra had liked what she found, a home on the beach somewhere and a big bank account, the frisson of pleasure in an erotic other life, perhaps intrigued by the ease with which she shed one existence for another.

Boy, did he understand that feeling.

So, when she'd been summoned back to Concord by his E-mail, it was not just William Channing, or even Michael Collins, she was looking for but the source of a potential threat, as well.

And, too, she'd want to discover how home ground felt to the black sheep of the family, her prodigal sister. She would visit Angela's old haunts, place flowers on the grave of her sister's young lover and father of her child, and attempt to grasp the chain of unhappiness—the violence, the tragic fate, the silence—that had led to her sister's suicide.

Not unlike what William Channing was doing with Michael Collins.

A thrilling breath caught in his chest and he glanced to his mentor above the desk. He raised up two fingers twisted together.

"Henry, we're like that. Only, she's doing me one better."

Dressed in khakis and a crew neck, not his usual running gear for his late-afternoon jog, he walked briskly toward his old school. The streets were seething with people in town for parents' weekend and the various Saturday sporting events at the schools. Good cover for reconnoitering. First, he made a quick tour of Alcott Academy, hoping he wouldn't bump into Ruthie, who was giving him apoplexy. She seemed strangely drawn to his younger self, that naïve Michael Collins, as if in a fit of nostalgia.

At the Emerson football game, he slipped into the cheering crowd of alumni and parents, teachers and students on the sidelines. With his preppy attire, he fit right in with the upscale crowd sporting the school colors of crimson and white. Were there teachers left who might remember him, who'd link him to the missing Michael Collins in the back pages of the *Globe*? The headmaster who had expelled him had retired over ten years before. But since he hadn't graduated, his name had not even been included with his class members' names carved into an oak panel in the assembly hall. He sought out faces in the crowd, especially the women, hoping that she would be drawn back by memories of him or her family. Of course, there was always the off chance that someone from his class, returning to watch a son playing football, a soccer-playing daughter, might recognize Michael Collins, even with the full beard.

Taking a seat in the back of the bleachers for a better vantage point, he surveyed the field, the fans, the ebb and flow of play. Everyone seemed so young.

He'd run into a few classmates over the years in Washington, and they'd always been perfectly friendly. Once a guy from his class had waltzed into his Capitol Hill office, a lobbyist for a major pharmaceutical company, and had apologized—just like that—saying, he felt the school had treated Michael badly. Hell, he could've been in the middle of a congressional campaign right now, friend of Jack Mahoney and a sure-thing winner. Between them, Michael Collins and Jack Mahoney could probably have squelched the grand jury probe. People would be coming up and shaking his hand, seeing him as a perfect example of the American way, proud that a kid from Lowell could make it to Congress and their school had been the ticket to make it all possible. In liberal Massachusetts, that kind of thing went over big-time. Hell, the school would probably have sought him out to make amends and return him to the graduate rolls.

Would Sandra have been pleased with such worldly success? Probably not, not someone devoted to a simple life and the preservation of the past and beautiful things. Unless she'd now had a taste of the celebrity life of Internet entrepreneur Sandy Blue.

Glancing off in the distance, across the playing fields, he noticed a tall woman walking with others toward the path to the boathouse and river. Her leggy, forthright stride looked familiar, but at such a distance she could be anyone. He was tempted to run after her, but some impulse to maintain dignified circumspection prevented him. If he started dashing off after every half-familiar female in sight, he'd end up making a fool of himself, or worse.

As he gazed off, an excerpt from Sandra's thesis (a new introduction she'd been working on, extracted from the bowels of her computer) drifted into his mind, the voice as clear as if she'd been sitting there with him.

It was not until I recently returned to visit my native Concord that an issue concerning Venetian building styles was finally resolved for me. I was reminded of my girlhood rambles, often with my father, when I would unexpectedly come upon an old fieldstone wall running through an abandoned meadow or wood and be possessed by a sudden pang of nostalgia, inexplicable, it would seem, in a young person. But I now realize that these old walls, beautiful as aesthetic objects, are more beautiful still because of the way the human imagination endows them with attachments both real and romantic. We respond to the craftsmanship and care that went into the arrangements of the stones; we feel the love and ultimately the loss that the first inhabitants must have experienced for their farms. The walls are all that remain. Their names are forgotten. How many times as a child did I come upon a tumbled stone from a wall and carefully return it to its place as one might a stone from a fallen altar? In these stones, we read our epitaph.

And likewise it occurred to me that the enormous amount of spolia that can be found everywhere in Venice had very much the same association for its citizens. These anomalous bits of stone carving from ancient Roman and Greek sites were incorporated into the very fabric of the city, embedded in walls, above doors and below windows, in places to be admired. These fragments of an older past were the psychic building blocks of a family's pedigree. In time, they became part of the very self-image of the family, in this most water-bound and rootless of cities.

The presence of these stones came to symbolize the continuity of human endurance, of the desire to be remembered, of the hope of prominent families to invent themselves in the shadow of older events. These surviving architectural fragments—family escutcheons and inscriptions, religious and mythic images, names of the dead—often tell us more of a family's desires and fears than any history. In the end, these artifacts come down to us as symbols of inescapable loss.

"Invention and reinvention …" He repeated this, like a private mantra, and looked around, as if surprised to find himself perched in the bleachers. He turned to the chapel bell tower against the cloudless blue … *as a stone from a fallen altar.* A shiver sliced through him at the thought of *the old kid's* fall from that tower: in the feeling of his own fall, Sandra's voice in the dingy pleading for his help.

Suddenly, he remembered the portrait of her artist grandfather in the dining hall!

He hurried from the stands and made his way across the familiar campus, past the music building and the practice rooms where he'd played the Chopin his mother had loved, his memory stirred by the familiar massive boughs of an ancient oak, and the remembered tone of an English teacher, Mark Blood, the first person he'd ever met who truly cared about poetry, cared about a scholarship kid from Lowell.

And the thought came to him that maybe he hadn't been as badly treated as he'd liked to believe—that he was less a victim of fate than of his own faithlessness.

When he found the portrait of Joseph Palmer in the deserted dining hall, it looked exactly as he remembered it from the night of the dance. Except now the ginger-haired artist with palette and brush stood with a critical stare directed at a new disciple, one William Channing. Perhaps this was how he'd scrutinized his model, with the characteristic squint Sandra Chillingworth Palmer would have known as he prepared to turn her body into an object of beauty and mystery.

That such sensuality lurked behind the straitlaced veneer of those times!

Nearby, he spotted a chair that had been removed from under a table and set back and angled in the direction of the portrait of Joseph Palmer. He walked over to the chair, touched the back, then sat and squinted. A blotch of glare now concealed the canvas.

He felt his pulse quicken, remembering the pressure of her hand on his at the dinner table before the dance, and in the pressure of that hand, the artist's voice in her voice later on the veranda, filling the gap of the empty years that still separated him from Sandra: *You're better than any one of them.*

Was that all Sandra had tapped into the night of the dance, nothing but his latent ambition, which in time would metastasize into rejection of his roots and his brother?

As if to sidestep an answer, he moved closer to the canvas, his eye caught by something in the shadowy recesses of the studio. There were two blue-and-white ginger jars, books stacked on the floor, figure sketches pinned to the wall, the sketch of the bridge in Venice with the Chillingworth twins. Peering into the deep background, he could just make out—the merest precipitate from the deepest shadows, a piano stool and hints of a ghostly keyboard.

Snatches from Palmer's Venetian diary as he'd found them in the catalog for the retrospective began to run through his mind: *I sketched rapidly to capture the bold expression in her eyes, the sharp articulation of her fingers—the rapture. I felt a similar power in my moving hand, but a power of expression I cannot as yet release. Ever since Angela's arrival, I cannot separate the twins. They are always off together, arm in arm, chatting away in conspiratorial voices. Sandra ... the wicked twinkle in my beloved's eye—she seeks to take Angela in, make a convert of her to her Venetian life, chez Manzoni and those wicked women. Sandra can be so seductive ... So now we are three, or are we more? Or less?*

"Can I help you, sir?"

It was a security watchman making his rounds.

"Oh ... I was supposed to meet my wife in the dining hall. She wanted to check out the paintings. She said something about a John Singer Sargent."

"The Sargent's over there." The security guard, an older man wearing a school baseball cap, pointed across the hall at the painting of the first headmaster and his wife.

"Right, beautiful thing." He recognized the watchman as the brother of the man who had collared Michael Collins as he stood on the bank of the river all those weeks before.

"But she was sitting right over there" —the security guard walked over and replaced a chair under the table— "oh, about an half an hour ago—give or take."

"She? Yeah, my wife." He fumbled in his pocket and got out a photograph. "She's got a mini reunion of her class at Alcott Academy this weekend." He showed the security man the photo. "They've all got their senior class photos."

"You're a lucky man, sir. Except for the short hair, I'd have recognized her immediately. She spent a good fifteen, twenty minutes with her camcorder and this painting." The security guard tipped his cap in the direction of Joseph Palmer's self-portrait.

"As well she might. It's her grandfather, you see—famous artist."

"Right. She said he was a big rower. If you want to catch up with her, she was on her way down to the river for the crew races."

As he made his way down the path to the river, he could feel her presence.

By the time he got to the boathouse, the crew races were just finishing up and the spectators were beginning to clear from the viewing gallery and dock. He inspected each passing face and then walked around the interior of the boathouse, as if to inventory those long-repaired 122 panes of glass. The viewing gallery and banister had been strengthened and buttressed.

He lingered by the dusty oak plaques listing the names of the crews by year. He found Joe Palmer's name on four consecutive teams in the years before the war. He found his name twice, his sophomore and junior year. His name was absent on the plaque of his senior year, when by all rights he should have been captain—by far the best rower in his year. As he studied his own name, Michael Collins, along with the names of his crewmates in his junior year, he realized that his lettering glittered just a fraction more than the others, as if someone had wet a finger and run it across his dusty name.

Something of that Michael Collins felt released from purgatory. He turned abruptly, aware of being watched, and saw a teenage girl and her mother staring down at him from the gallery railing. They smiled, embarrassed, maybe mistaking him for somebody else.

Mother and daughter hurried down the stairs; they were chatting about a boy in the Emerson first boat, perhaps a son and brother. He followed them out onto the dock. The Emerson boys and girls crews were just returning from upriver, their swaying torsos and dipping oars bannered by leafy boughs of russet and honey orange. His heart was beating so hard, he feared he might faint. He longed to yell out to them—some, to look at them, scholarship kids, blacks and Hispanics—to offer them tips about their technique. Go for it, guys. Don't be afraid. Clichés or no, his enthusiasm for these kids contained something of the pent-up faith he'd lost. It frustrated him that he couldn't step in and coach them, not really, that he couldn't take them by the hand—the way Ruthie did with her girls and did so well—and look into their fervent eyes and tell them the truth about life: to live as if there is no tomorrow, to love as truly as you can—fearlessly, investing yourself in the body of the world and outlasting the years.

CHAPTER 18

O n Saturday, on the way to the nursing home in Worcester, it rained all day, a good old-fashioned nor'easter, perhaps enough to break the semidraught conditions that had prevailed in New England since the spring. He drove slowly in his rented car, not exceeding the speed limit, and stayed in the right lane. The windshield wipers pumped furiously. It was good to be driving again, even if he felt a little vulnerable with his Michigan driver's license, bought from a graduate student who turned them out by the dozen. He wasn't eager to put the license to the test of a police computer check. But a bus or even a cab might attract more scrutiny. He was being cautious; he wanted to make sure he'd get back to Concord and the luncheon meeting in a few days of Joe Palmer and his daughter.

That glimpse of the woman—and he was almost sure it had been Sandra, where the path to the boathouse entered the woods—had lodged itself like a deep bruise in his breastbone.

Driving away from Concord filled him with low-level anxiety, as if his very being was now dependent on the town, succored by its name: an epicenter of habit, a crucible of personality; so that the act of leaving, the swish of tires on the pavement—a ripple from a timeless center into time—felt like the expiring sigh of an impostor.

Adding to his disquiet were the construction signs, at least three along Interstate 495 and 290: MAHONEY CONSTRUCTION CORP.—WE BUILD THE FUTURE INTO THE PAST. Hard to believe that once he had actually liked Jack Mahoney, liked his drive and ambition, and that they came from the same kind of background. "Michael, I'm the kind of Irish American who's going to show our pompous little Greek governor and his Harvard gang of Jews and blue bloods a thing or two: buildings that'll last the ages." That was how Jack had put it to him once. Jack, who had gone to MIT on scholarship. Jack, who liked to trot out his father for ribbon-cutting ceremonies, just to show his old man how he'd made good and rub his nose in the clean slate of a world he was creating. Once Jimmy—during the campaign in which he'd gotten his brother a job—had accused him of being in cahoots with Mahoney and bulldozing the old neighborhoods. Imagine that … he and Mahoney in cahoots. Except now every pickup truck and construction vehicle that passed him with its headlights flashing, sent spasms of fear and loathing up his spine.

Lines from the most recent newspaper stories passed through his mind: "According to a recently completed audit, Congressman Neeley's office reported $400,000.00 missing from a 1988 campaign account." "Sources in the congressman's office describe Collins as a one-man-show who rarely confided in others." Another source told of representative Neeley being depressed, baffled, and feeling betrayed by his top aide: "'I trusted Michael for everything, a man of meticulous integrity.'" "The FBI has sent a team of agents to Lowell to expedite the investigation into the disappearance of Michael Collins."

He fantasized how his father would have taken care of such outrageous calumny. His dad would have ambushed his enemies, would have waited in the shadows and clocked the sons of bitches.

He tried to picture the faces of his erstwhile Hill colleagues leaking their lies to the press, the businessmen and contractors with whom he'd worked on the contracts, getting them the rezoning bills, the local variances, the tax breaks so that the numbers worked, so that the political equations balanced out to everyone's benefit. Had he been so cynical that he'd kept his distance, figuring that the less he knew the better, and so had kept his own cards close to his chest—and thus remained invisible to himself?

The nursing home was a state-run semiprivate care facility on the outskirts of the old industrial quarter of Worcester. His heart sank at the sight. In the rain, the turn-of-the-century pseudo-Romanesque facade of red sandstone had turned a damp mud color. It might have been a handsome building once, probably financed by Worcester's early industrial fortunes, but was now neglected, the grounds turned into parking lots impinged on by chain-link fences and abandoned factories. He expected even worse upon entering, but had found, to his relief, that the interior had been recently renovated; new paint and lighting, carpets and bright, bold signs warmed up the place. Even the nursing staff seemed attentive and efficient. And—thank God—Abigail Palmer had a private room. He'd dreaded finding her warehoused in some impersonal ward.

The head nurse gave the numbered door a perfunctory knock and opened it. The room was a small oblong ending in a window and beige curtains. And seated in front of the window—six-over-six white sashes— was an old lady in a scroll-back chair with carved ball-and-claw feet. The chair seemed at odds with the other modern hospital furnishings.

"Abigail had a good week," said the nurse in a soft voice. She winked at him. She had red hair that was nicely set off by the light blue of her uniform. "I think her daughter's visit last week must have raised her spirits."

He stood staring a moment, speechless, the scene like something out of a Vermeer: old woman with a book in her lap, silvery hair perfectly groomed and swept back from a pale, wrinkled brow … and the silence, which was palpable. She didn't make a move or seem to notice the open door and the voices.

"Angela," he said softly, listening as if for the echo of his disembodied syllables.

"Lovely girl, just lovely."

He had to smile. "Yes, Angela and I were in school together in Concord. But, you know, I always had the sense she wasn't that close to her mother."

"Nice lady. Gave her mother a massage while she visited."

"As lovely as ever, you said?" He pulled at his beard. "She had the most beautiful long blond hair in high school."

"Shorter now, modern cut." The nurse thrust her head back. "Well-preserved—yes, lovely girl."

"She didn't leave a number or address, did she? I'd love to say hello."

"No. Didn't even bother with a phone call. Just showed up and signed the register. I think she was a little anxious about seeing her mother. I guess it had been awhile."

"Somebody told me she'd been living in Europe."

"Very fashionable. Her voice was …"

He said, very calmly, "A little singsongy, Italian maybe?"

"Yeah, something like that, I suppose."

He turned his head back to the room. "Does Mrs. Palmer's ex-husband ever come to visit?"

"Occasionally, but he makes her anxious. When she gets upset, that's when the problems start."

"Is it Alzheimer's?"

"Alzheimer's and loneliness. Her short-term memory has deteriorated significantly over the last year."

He was touched by the genuine concern he detected in her voice—not what he had expected.

"Sad to see her like this. I remember her with a big house and gardens."

"It's tough for older women. Their men die; their children go off." She ushered him into the room, reaching to adjust a needlepoint pillow on the bed, and gestured him forward.

He held back a moment, lowering his voice. "Does she know about her other daughter, Sandra?"

The nurse looked at him with a hint of pain in the compression of her kind eyes. She shrugged and touched his arm. "We thought it best not to mention it. And you know, when her daughter came to visit the other day, Abigail would only call her Sandra."

"No…."

"You see, a year back, it was Sandra who came to visit her—oh, two or three times, I believe. They seemed very attached."

"She called her Sandra?"

"Abigail is like that now—something gets her on a track and there's no getting her off it. Her daughter seemed to accept it pretty easy."

"Uprooted," he mumbled to himself, taking another step into the room. He could see beyond the old woman now, beyond the window, to the parking lot, a storm fence, and the delivery bays of a defunct furniture factory.

The nurse got a folding chair out of the corner, took it to the front of the room, and set it up next to where her patient sat.

"Abigail dear, you have a visitor." The nurse placed herself in easy line of sight and delicately swept fingers over the old lady's cheek, adjusting the collar of her blouse, giving her a pat on her shoulder. "It's Mr. Channing, an old friend of your family."

Strangely, mention of the name seemed to register. Abigail Palmer looked up a little mechanically, surveyed the view from her window, and thanked the nurse with gentile formality.

"So kind of you, Maureen. Nice to meet you, Mr. Channing."

She held out a trembling hand and he took it, finding it warm to the touch. Her milky gray eyes examined his face with barely a touch of discernible emotion and returned to their vigil. He followed her stare to the expanse of blacktop, a faint grid of yellow lines, a scattering of late-model cars, a single maple tree on the grass verge, now most of its orange leaves shed. He wasn't sure if he was disappointed or relieved not to see any of Sandra in her mother. She could be anybody, any old woman, a conduit of genetic inheritance, a vessel of conception and parturition, now discarded.

"I'll leave you two to chat," said the nurse. "When you're done, Mr. Channing, feel free to let yourself out; just be sure to sign the register again at the desk."

As the nurse closed the door, he was overcome with sudden panic at being left alone in this tiny room with the old lady. It wasn't the false pretenses as much as the feeling of compressed time inhabiting the four walls, something in the smells of talcum powder, damp wool, and wisps of faded perfume. He had thought through a number of approaches to take, but suddenly he felt unsure of what he was about, much less where it would lead. Finally, almost in desperation, he got out the one thing he had absolutely no intention of saying. What he often wished he'd admitted to her ex-husband, Joe.

"Mrs. Palmer, I was in love with Sandra."

Abigail Palmer's face remained neutral; then the thin lips gave way to a half smile, a tentative remembrance.

"You, too, poor thing, you and all the others." Her voice was sweet and clear, like a bell in calm air. "They were all in love with the great prodigy, the tragic Sandra Chillingworth."

"All of them?"

"If I had only known as much before I married."

He sat mute for a moment, watching the eyes of the old lady, the realization dawning on him. "Oh, I see, Sandra Chillingworth Palmer."

"Cold as their name, except for Sandra, a sun that never faded on the horizon of their little world up there in Manchester ... playing Symphony Hall at sixteen, Mozart piano concerto."

"She was beautiful. The paintings of her are breathtaking."

"When I married, she had been dead for thirty years, and yet it was as if it had only been the other day."

Her voice was hypnotic, her eyes distant. The seeming transformative effect of his presence—the family mythology already like well-worn cart tracks in his mind—emboldened him further, as if she'd been patiently waiting for him to jump-start her recollections.

"But your husband, surely ... she died when he was born."

"But you forget, there was always Aunt Angela." She raised a finger as if admonishing him. "Joe, of course, would tell you he was raised by Auntie."

He said precisely, as if addressing a silent jury with a brief prepared far in advance, "Angela Chillingworth ... she was something of a poet, if I'm not mistaken."

"But the truth is, he was raised by nannies mostly—although he'd never admit it. But the Chillingworths, the old grande dame herself, Martha—I never knew her, but she was as much a part of that house in Manchester as the stairs and banisters—the old witch had her claws into Joe. Martha wanted her daughters to be the next Clara Schumann. She married Chillingworth money. And they had money, you see, even after the crash; and nobody was going to go against them. All those summers we were summoned to their house in Manchester, having to endure Aunt Angie's ritual obeisance to her long-gone mother, her tales of Venice days past, of her poor sister's magnificent flowering—how the critics raved about her Mozart in Symphony Hall, and only sixteen—and her tragic death. One must be sensitive to these things—I scolded myself; Aunt Angie had been at her sister's side when she died in the maternity ward in Venice. Septicemia. Imagine, seeing your twin sister take two days to die in such awful pain."

He looked down into her lap and saw there a tan morocco-bound photograph album. There were other albums on a corner table, and even more on a small shelf against the wall, along with volumes on antiques and histories of Concord. The cover of the album was embossed in gold.

SUMMER
MANCHESTER-BY-THE-SEA
ANGELA CHILLINGWORTH

"You've been going through your photographs," he said.

"Rainy days always remind me of Manchester and the fog that would roll in off the ocean. Sent to me by her lawyers some years ago. Not a cent, just her damn photos and five volumes of her poetry—privately published, of course."

"Mind if I take a look?" He reached as if across some invisible divide of time; he would have it, snatch the album away and flee if need be.

She didn't answer, just removed a finger that had been marking a page. He lifted the album from her lap and shifted it to his. Her hands returned to her lap, gnarled and lined, hands that had endured lots of outdoor work.

He eagerly turned the pages.

The album began sometime in the early twenties, as near as he could figure. Black-and-white photos of a sprawling Shingle-style summer cottage topping a grassy bluff overlooking the sea, with wide lawns radiating from the wooden railing of the piazza, where an aging matriarch, a large, formidable figure, stood surveying her realm. A young boy with tennis racket lounged in a stripped canvas lawn chair next to his aunt, who, to look at her, could have just as well been the boy's mother, with her high, angular face and eyes set wide apart and sparkling clear, her gentle hand poised on the forehead of her young nephew. As he turned the pages, the gowns of the older ladies thinned over time to trim silk dresses, and the number of guests, especially by the mid-thirties, began a dramatic thinning-out, too. The young boy became a young man, tall and gangly and not afraid to show off his muscled torso—a refined beauty, not unlike his mother's. His arms and legs were corded tight and he stood proudly on the greensward, a gray sea awash behind, an oar planted at his side like a banner.

He paused at a page with a small photograph of a tea party on the wide veranda. Aunt Angela Chillingworth, seated, showing a hint of age in the lines around her eyes, and next to her the young athlete in open terry-cloth robe, and another man, in white suit and scruffy beard, his arm perched on the armrest of a wicker chair, holding a glass of iced tea in an enormous hand. The middle-aged man in the white suit stared out at the camera with a hint of unease, as if unused to his surroundings, fingering his beard; while Aunt Angela gazed toward her companion and nephew with an expression of measured joy, a relaxed confidence: perhaps, by then, queen of the roost. The young man had a sandwich in his hand and his mind on other things.

He lingered on this photo, unconsciously pulling at his own beard in imitation of the man in the white suit, his grandfather, Giovanni Maronetti.

Again turning pages, he had a sense of a hiatus, or it could have been the appearance of color photographs, the first very faded and only hinting at the true azure of the sea on the near horizon. Here was the young man, face now hardened and sun-burned—recognizable as Joe Palmer, dressed in his smart navy uniform, home from the war, on leave, perhaps on the verge of being mustered out, standing next to his proud aunt on the lawn, his arm wrapped affectionately around her still-thin waist, gladness sparking in her adoring eyes. Then, the flick of a finger, and pages of photographs in brilliant sharp color of the twins, Sandra and Angela, gamboling and running on the lawn in perfect matching hand-sewn smocks, on the way down to the beach in bathing suits, in the arms of their great-aunt on the veranda, sitting demurely in expansive wicker chairs, and there in the background the young wife, Abigail Palmer, channeling the flow of girlish energies, not entirely at ease, not really at home, but managing—at least enjoying the joy of her children.

He watched, near spellbound, as Sandra and Angela grew taller over the summers, their hair cascading down their backs, clothes changing to jeans and saddle shoes, to summer cotton dresses and finally to short skirts and shorter shorts: similarly dressed, but with distinctive different colors whenever photographed together. He couldn't help noticing the changing bodies, the nipples showing through the wet one-piece bathing suits, the jut of hips, the faces acquiring the mature lines he had known, the lips he had kissed, the image that haunted him in the paintings. And every now and then, particularly in the very last photographs, he sensed a similar response in the face of the old lady, their great-aunt Angela, that lost and dreamy look of remembrance. She had a cane by then, and then a walker—a moment caught off guard by the speeding shutter, seeing one of the girls as she turned or spoke, bathed in afternoon light on the veranda, the sparkle of reflected light off the blue sea filling her blond hair … memories of Venice days, of her sister, of her own careless youth in a big house by the sea.

"What a beautiful place," he got out finally.

Then Abigail's voice resumed, as if she'd returned from a long way off, caught in the midst of a thought.

"Aunt Angie spoiled the twins and filled their heads with nonsense. She would pay for the finest piano teachers at the New England Conservatory to give them piano lessons, but not a red cent for their schooling."

"Piano lessons?"

"Never took. They had the talent, but it never took them over."

"A tough profession, piano."

"Auntie would play for the twins, complaining how she lacked the genius of Sandra Chillingworth Palmer—'who threw it all away to model for your grandfather,' she'd tell them."

He murmured to himself, "One life for another."

"Days like this—she'd call them 'Corot days'—she would sit them down and go on about Venice and her sister and the great artist, their grandfather. Every April, she'd arrive in Concord and they'd make a big ceremony out of it. A grand procession for her sister's birthday—her birthday, too, of course. They'd gather roses from the back garden and march off together to Sleepy Hollow and lay the flowers at her monument and Aunt Angela would recite her poetry. Monstrous to put children through such an ordeal. Thank God, most of the paintings and things were left in Stockbridge, so the girls wouldn't have to see all that. It was bad enough when they came upon some of the old art journals."

"But it must have seemed, well, almost miraculous, twins again, and looking so much like their grandmother."

Abigail Palmer turned her face fully toward him for the first time, as if needing to quickly put him to rights.

"Who did you say you are?"

"William Channing, Mrs. Palmer. I'm an old friend of the family. I went to Emerson Academy. I knew your daughters."

Abigail raised a shaking hand as if to stop him, to interject.

"Not a miracle, Mr. Channing. Statistically, twins skipping a generation is not so rare. And it practically killed me. I was in the hospital for two weeks. Dear Aunt Angie never came once. It was always abstract for her, the poetry, the great artist, summers with the twins … Venice days."

He lifted the album and carefully replaced it in her lap, pointing out one of the photos.

"There's a man in this photo sitting with Angela Chillingworth and your husband when he was a young man. The man with the beard, the one in the white suit. Something about him is familiar."

She examined the photo and smiled, sarcasm in her reedy voice.

"Angela's Venetian lover. I never knew him—another mythic character in her pantheon. She carried a picture of him in a locket around her neck. He was a sculptor, I believe, the one who made the monument in Sleepy Hollow."

"They were lovers?"

Abigail Palmer tapped her lips with a forefinger.

"She was a big talker. Men terrified her, if you take my meaning, after what happened to her sister. But she liked to talk about his hands, his sculptors' hands." Her voice rose, as if reciting some well-worn family anecdote. "A Herculean grip, stained with sweat and marble dust, yet able to carve a line wafer-thin in the hardest stone."

"He was a fine artist."

"Artists can be very cruel, Mr. Channing … the wreckage they leave in their wake."

"Sandra, your daughter, was a fine artist."

He watched for the effect of his words and saw her hands close the album in her lap and come to rest with some finality upon the leather binding.

When he realized there would be no reply, he began again. "I guess it was hard for your husband to get away in the summers, to join you and the girls in Manchester."

"He … well, as long as he could treat them like tomboys …"

She failed to finish the sentence. Thinking she might be watching something beyond the rain-streaked window, he turned his gaze. He saw Abigail Palmer and himself reflected in the glass: an old woman in an antique chair, a desk lamp, a large bearded face bent toward her so as to miss nothing.

"I've heard it said that Joseph Palmer, the artist, is making something of a comeback."

"No better than a fancy pornographer."

"Well ..."

"Chillingworths got their own back—they broke him with legal bills."

He folded his face into his hands and then got it out as best he could.

"Mrs. Palmer, I need your help on something. You see, I knew Sandra quite well when she was at Alcott Academy ... and well ..."

A hand on his knee brought him up short.

The voice was that of a proud wife and mother. "I was once accused of being a prude, but I've always had a love of beautiful things, antiques. We shared that, you know, Joe and I. Hard work and honest craftsmanship. I always tell the twins how important it is to consider the feelings of others. Otherwise, we're no different from beasts in the fields. When we give ourselves over to the sensualist, the bonds of society unravel. 'Reciprocal propriety' was the way my mother always explained it to me."

"The nurse told me that your daughter Angela was in to see you last week. That must have been nice for you."

"Mr. Channing, you are mistaken. Only Sandra comes to visit. Angela would never bother, never care, as selfish and self-absorbed as her name-sake. Since she went off to college, she never once sent word of herself. I have to assume she is dead, Mr. Channing. It saddens but does not surprise me."

"I heard Sandra had a child when she was in Europe."

"Mr. Channing, children are a blessing and a curse."

"I guess twins ... well, there must be issues of competition and identity. It can't have been easy for you."

A change had come into her face, as if she had lost her way and was casting around for a landmark.

"What time is it?"

"Almost one."

"Almost one, well. I always picked up my girls in the afternoons, start-ing in kindergarten at one on the dot. I never drive. I believe in walking, that children should learn to walk, to feel the countryside beneath their feet, to look around and take in the world. There is always time to talk when you walk with children. My mother always said, 'If you're feeling poorly, go for a walk and set yourself right.'"

"Children are a blessing."

"People think children are for the consolation of old age, but it isn't true. Children are the way we return ourselves to the past."

"I was in love once, but I have no children."

He let out a breath and stared into the glass, seeing her face transposed upon the bleak stretches of blacktop. Her voice, when it revived, had a reedy lyricism.

"When I was a child, I used to walk by the river. There was an old meadow there, and an orchard, a rose garden. Of course, the house had been enlarged, as people with money tend to do. But it was still my great-great-grandfather's place, a Hosmer place. As a little girl, I promised myself I would live there one day."

He drew back, just enough to see her fully in profile, her hand resting on the worn armrest, and his gaze drifted lower, following the fluid antique lines of the chair to where a carved talon clutched at the floor.

"And so you did, Mrs. Palmer, and so you did." He thought he detected a faint smile flutter to her lips. "Mrs. Palmer, when Sandra went off to Europe her senior year—Geneva, I believe—she was expecting a child. Do you know what happened to that child?"

Outside, a gust of wind flung the rain against the window and they both turned to the sudden onslaught. Abigail Palmer blinked, as if something out there had interrupted her chain of thought.

"It is a great sadness to me that Sandra never married. Perhaps children might have brought her down to earth."

"She never had a child?"

She raised her hand to the side of her head as if to push back a strand of unruly hair, or to cup her ear to a distant sound.

"Did you know that the first settlers in Concord lived in caves in the hillside? In the earliest days, there was cold and Indians and near starvation. The sons of the first settlers became fierce Indian fighters, hardened killers and hunters. They had no education and were nearly illiterate. That early generation saw the look in their children's eyes; they glimpsed a world descending into barbarity ... no books, no history, no memory of who they were. We look back and glorify; they saw terror in the wilderness and the prospect of decline into darkness. That is why they taxed themselves and demanded two things: religion and education, a faith and a history ... all that stood between them and the abyss. You see, the town, Concord, was not just a hope but also their refuge. Teach your children well, Mr. Channing. Teach them to remember."

He remained a few minutes more, but she was tiring fast. He tried to take in her room, an entire life whittled down to a chair and a few books, photo albums, a bed and a window, and the faltering memory stored within. And beyond the window, through the rain: a distant yellow banner hanging off the derelict factory that had been on the edge of his vision the whole time. He squinted outward.

MAHONEY CONTRUCTION
—COMING SOON—
WORCESTER'S NEWEST OUTLET MALL.

CHAPTER 19

—————

He drove through the rain, needing to flesh out those photographs in the albums, as if to appropriate them for his own, before it was too late, as if the imminent failure of the old woman's memory would close one last window on a past he was desperate to possess for himself.

Clearly, Giovanni had been in love with Angela Chillingworth, or perhaps Sandra Chillingworth before that. As Abigail put it, they all had been in love with Sandra Chillingworth Palmer, piano prodigy. So much so that Giovanni had set his daughter on the path of a professional pianist; and from this, his own childhood filled with piano lessons at his mother's side; and Moira Maronetti Collins, forever frustrated at her unrecognized talent.

All emanations of that love.

"Sandra Chillingworth Palmer," he whispered to himself, trying to fathom the magnetism of the name and the woman behind the name.

Abigail's halting memories had caused a gravitational shift in him, as if his personal loss were coming under the sway of some larger loss: the power of love's attraction, which had redirected all their lives. Her frailty made everything seem that much more precarious, the time left to him that much more precious.

He drove on through the rain.

But at his destination, he found nothing. The grand Chillingworth house in Manchester, on the bluff overlooking Singing Beach, had been torn down over twenty years before and replaced with upscale saltbox condos, each with its own spectacular view of the Atlantic. He walked the dunes, walked the beach, glad for the wind and rain in his face, for the crashing waves and white-capped sea. If it had been a fine sunny day, any approximation of the summers held in Abigail's album, it might have been too much to bear. If the world contained in Abigail's photo album had to be gone, better it was obliterated, that there were no footholds left.

On a piece of paper in his pocket was the name of a doctor, the product of much research and gleaning of information on the Internet. It always seemed to come down to a name. It wasn't crucial that he know, but the best part of knowing was not having to wonder anymore. It was so much easier to lose himself in the sea and the sound of the waves and keep walking the firm shoulder of sand at high tide. But after a good hour, he summoned the necessary conviction and marched up the bluff to the tiny coast road. The time for certainty was at hand, until he'd definitively killed off one of Abigail and Joe Palmer's daughters.

A large condo on the bluff belonged to one Dr. Harvey R. Bartlett, retired head of OB-GYN at Massachusetts General, professor emeritus at Harvard Medical School. The way William figured it, the baby that had died and was buried in Sleepy Hollow had been Angela's. His confidence in this matter allowed him the brash role-playing that, in another scenario, could have made him a highly paid criminal defense lawyer.

Dr. Bartlett was expecting him, but not with any enthusiasm. The doctor's wife met him at the door of the condo and led him to the living room, with its large plate-glass windows and expansive views of the sea. The condo was all on a single floor, appointed with nautical and fishing decor, the perfect retirement home. Bartlett, pushing eighty, was in a wheelchair by the plate-glass window fronting the bluff. He had been tying flies on a worktable between his knees.

"You don't mind, Mr. Hathaway, if my wife sits down with us for this conversation." Dr. Bartlett waved to the sofa with the long-nosed pliers he'd been working with. "I think it's important that nothing be misinterpreted or possibly misrepresented."

"I agree," William said. "And please call me Bob."

"You look like you could use some tea; it's pretty fierce out there." The doctor turned from his interlocutor's matted hair and beard to the picture window and the windblown sea.

"I walked the beach some. I remember Angela telling me how much she liked it here as a girl. But awfully cold for swimming."

Dr. Bartlett ran a hand over his bald head and looked at the visitor over the tops of tortoiseshell glasses.

"You mentioned on the phone you were Angela's boyfriend when she was a girl—fifteen, junior high, wasn't it?" The doctor kept his poker face as he glanced across at his wife, who was bringing in the tea tray: a knowing look from her.

"This whole business is very awkward for me," William said. He took the cup of tea offered him, a little perplexed by the near-shamanlike certainty that allowed him to carry on in the way he was doing. "We were next-door neighbors to the Palmers in Concord. I knew the girls since they were kids. I was in the army, Seventh Cavalry. I was back home on leave. Angela was fifteen going on sixteen; she had a kid's crush on me. Something that should have been nothing turned into something. I'm not proud of this, you understand. Actually, I didn't know she was pregnant until I was back in Vietnam for my second tour. Given the circumstances, the ages, I was not eager to advertise the situation. A year later, when the child died, I was still overseas. I have to admit, I was relieved. Angela, I gather, went her own way. I went mine. It didn't prey on my mind much until recently, when I started to have problems at home. I was in Concord a few weeks back, visiting my mother. She told me that no one had seen Angela for years but that her twin sister, Sandra, died last year. It got me thinking. I found the grave of our child in Sleepy Hollow. Then I went and got the death certificate, and there was mention that you'd been consulted about the health of the baby before it died."

The doctor's wife clucked under her breath. "Terrible about Sandra. We saw it in the papers last year."

Dr. Bartlett turned from the picture window and took in the younger man. "Mr. Hathaway—Bob—I can't say I'm glad to be having this conversation. On the other hand, I'm somewhat relieved to know that *you* were the father, quite frankly."

The wife handed her husband a mug of steaming tea and he thanked her.

William eyed Dr. Bartlett as he bent to sip his tea: silver-haired eyebrows, perfectly manicured hands, a surgeon's hands, a little shaky, but still good enough to tie a first-rate fly. He said, "Doctor, I guess they did a pretty good job of covering it up."

"More than that, I'm afraid."

"The death certificate mentioned something about brain damage at birth."

"Bob, I, and my father before me, have known the Chillingworth family going back near three generations. My grandfather delivered the Chillingworth twins. It was Angela Chillingworth who recommended me to Abigail Palmer. I delivered her two girls. She had a hard time of it. And those old families, they tend to want boys, and Abigail was really in no shape to produce another child, boy or no boy. A delicate subject. It ate away at her for years. When Angela got pregnant, Abigail nearly had a breakdown right then. One went through the wringer with her on the subject when Angela was brought in for her checkups. The girl wouldn't say boo about the father. Frankly, I feared the worst. I didn't want to think it of Joe, but a doctor sees things he never wants to think possible. I knew Joe wanted a boy in the worst way—all Abigail would talk about. Then Abigail had the great idea. She pulled both twins from school before Christmas. Then she took them to Venice—Aunt Angela paid all expenses—to study piano at the music academy and learn Italian. Then she had them back here for the summer, for Angela's last trimester. They lost a whole year of school. The plan was for Angela to have the baby and the parents would adopt it as their own. Very neat, very discreet, nobody would have to know. I guess it only confirmed my worst suspicions—I never saw Joe that summer. Abigail was paranoid that they'd be found out, that somehow, somebody in Concord, would get wind of it. So when Angela went into labor—late July, I believe—instead of getting her right into the hospital in Boston as planned, Abigail delayed. Then she called me up all flustered and I drove like a bat out of hell to the Chillingworth place. The poor girl was well along in the delivery and so, better part of valor, I made the decision to complete the delivery right there. Which, of course, was just what Abigail had wanted, thinking, I'm sure, a home delivery would be more discreet."

The doctor looked over at his wife, who had been sitting silently, like a juror in court, watching her husband intently.

"I've delivered thousands of children. The real problems, I can count on one hand. And if we'd been in a proper delivery room, it wouldn't have happened, or at least we could have taken care of it. The baby got caught up, the umbilical cord around its neck. The delay, the lack of oxygen, resulted in severe brain damage. Frankly, the whole business was a disaster. I blamed myself. It was a judgment call: chances she'd deliver on the way to a local hospital versus ninety-nine times out of a hundred there wouldn't be complications with a home delivery. Probabilitywise, it was the right choice. But it weighs on me. Of course, what it did to the family—you can imagine." He took a sip of tea, glancing out the picture window at the jarring swoops of the feeding gulls.

"So when you got the call from the Concord Hospital, about the baby dying, you told them the facts."

"I never hid anything. You'll find the birth certificate in the Manchester town hall, I believe. Frankly, I looked on it as a blessing. I hoped the family might put it all behind them. A child like that, even if he lives, is like an albatross around your neck—your worst nightmare as a parent."

"You weren't surprised he died?"

"One hopes for the best, but unfortunately, one knows only too well."

The doctor's wife spoke, as if needing to get it out. "I'm sure it's what finally did in the girls' grandmother, old Angela Chillingworth."

"Oh Lord, yes," said Dr. Bartlett. "Poor old gal. She went to pieces; she was always nervous as a jackrabbit. But she doted on the twins; they were her lease on life ... the Chillingworths' last, best hope."

Dr. Bartlett finally put down the pliers in his work tray. He pulled off his glasses and rubbed at his eyes.

"Sally and I used to enjoy the Palmer twins when they were up for the summer. Old Angela Chillingworth would still trot out her lawn parties, like her mother before her, even if she had to have them catered. She'd have the girls pass the cucumber and salmon sandwiches so they'd be sure to pick up all the social graces. Delightful, those two. But you know what I remember, and it's etched into my mind as if were yesterday—the very last tea party. There couldn't have been more than ten people there. Most of the old Manchester crowd had passed away or gotten too old to stand out on a lawn in that July heat. Sally and I lingered on longer than we'd planned, as if we knew this might be the last roundup for Angela Chillingworth. She was already having trouble with her back, needed help with walking, and seemed to lose track of her thoughts. She doted on the twins—even if they never took to all the piano lessons, and young Angela looking fit to burst, pregnant in her white frock. You might think the old girl would want her grand-niece out of sight—but no. There she was, as serene and strong a beautiful girl as you could imagine. And her sister, Sandra, the talented one, the artistic one, she was there, standing next to her pregnant sister on the cusp of that great green lawn, looking out at the blue sea, in white, too, except she was as thin as a rail. That summer they were always chatting away with their great-aunt in broken Italian, about their time in Venice. I remember Sandra turning to her sister, a glance, a smile, a hint of wonder or envy, even fear—who can say what she must have felt with her twin like a billowing spinnaker, getting all the attention. And Abigail—aghast, in a total state that old Auntie Angela had insisted on another lawn party—under the circumstances. She slipped away, locked herself in her room."

The doctor paused, his chin eddying up and down, as if mesmerized by the gulls over the beach … or the vividness of his memories.

"Funny, the picture that stays with me is of old Angela Chillingworth suddenly pushing herself up from the tea table and walking with an exultant stride over to where young Angela was standing with her sister on the bluff. Without a moment of hesitation, she slipped her arms around the girl from behind and got her hands tucked under her belly, where she could feel the child—the 'Bambino,' they called him—and just stood with her like that, cheek against the back of her neck, maybe whispering a word of encouragement in her ear, all the while staring out at the sand and the blue sea, their two small shadows on that great lawn seeming to merge. Angela's sister stood just off to the side, watching the lingering embrace, a forlorn look in her eyes. Then she moved off, running toward the house, followed by her lengthening shadow. Funny, isn't it, what stays with you."

"Terrible," said Bartlett's wife. "To think of what happened to that poor girl."

"When I arrived for the delivery," said Bartlett, "Sandra was nowhere to be found. She had disappeared, run to the beach and disappeared."

"That's right," said his wife. "She had been asked to stand by the phone on the first floor. And when you first returned Abigail's call, you got no answer. It cost you half an hour."

"Yes, they always blamed her for that, poor girl."

"'Bambino,'" said his wife, shaking her head dismissively. "Immaculate conception—"

"Well, now we know," said Bartlett, nodding at their visitor.

"Angela Chillingworth—ridiculous business—was in Boston with her driver for the symphony board meeting when the girl went into labor."

"And old Angela—remember, Sally, right to the day before she died, she played that beat-up old Steinway in the front parlor."

"Forever complaining …" His wife patted at her perfectly coifed silver-blue hair, pulling her shoulders high, as if getting the posture right might better illicit the proper intonation. "'Oh, but my sister played it so very much better,'" she'd always say."

It continued to rain steadily on his return to Concord. He was beside himself, in near panic to get back to the inn. He was filled with the crazy expectation that Sandra would be right there in the Minuteman Lounge waiting for him. He kept seeing her as described by Dr. Bartlett, running across the sprawling greensward overlooking the sea, seeking safety. So much that he had anticipated had proved to be true. And like a skilled conjurer, he was falling in love with his prodigious sleight of hand.

There, in the Minuteman Lounge, he would take her hand and tell her, "Don't let them blame you; it wasn't your fault."

He hit the SEEK button on the radio, in search of a song on the oldies station from that fall of senior year that might further bolster his fantastic enterprise. Instead, he stumbled on the latest news bulletin.

"The Lowell police reported today that an FBI forensics team had located the personal effects of the missing congressional aide Michael Collins. The aide's wallet, identification, and pieces of clothing had been carefully buried, according to sources close to the case. The police are moving away from a theory of suicide to one of homicide or a well-conceived plan of disappearance and deception, possibly involving a change of identity. An all points bulletin for the arrest of Collins has been issued. More details at the top of the hour."

"Fuck."

He had to shout at himself. "Slow down, slow down … slow down." He switched the radio to a classical station. He flipped on cruise control and took his foot off the accelerator. He stared into the cascading curtains of rain across the highway and carefully reeled in the miles back to Concord.

Back at the inn, waiting for him—almost like a practical joke—was a manila envelope from Laura Ryder, curator of the recent Palmer retrospective and author of the catalog, and now the new director of the Palmer Gallery at the artist's historic home, Sangamore, in Stockbridge. She was reconfirming the arrangements for his visit to the archives two days hence and wanted him to know, per his inquiry, that she had found more material on the sculptor Giovanni Maronetti, who had lived at Sangamore with Joseph Palmer for seven years, between 1921 and 1928. She also included a transcript she had just unearthed from the 1926 libel trial, when Joseph Palmer had been forced to defend himself publicly. The excited tone of her letter, responding to his, was of a fellow fan-club member eager to share the drama of her discovery. Laura Ryder's letter ended with her noting a coincidence: Only the day before, Joseph Palmer's granddaughter had arrived at Sangamore and expressed a particular interest in the sculptures of Giovanni Maronetti housed in the studio barn. Also, she had made a copy of her grandfather's diary, which he kept while working in Venice.

"Granddaughter."

It was as if they were shadowing one another. And he and Concord were only one point on her agenda.

He was positively beside himself as the words of Joseph Palmer slid out of a manila envelope and into his waiting hands.

Transcript of general court of proceedings: *Chillingworth vs. Palmer*, May 12, 1926.

Q: What do you say to the critics who have condemned your painting over the last eight years, since your triumph with the Venice work, as gilded smut?

A: They are fools who fear to explore the truth of the human condition, who care nothing for the highest aims of art, and who project their morbid and sensualist fascination onto the work of others. They are the same petty critics who condemned MacMonnies's Bacchante, for the Boston Public Library, over thirty years ago. It is worse than staid old busybody Boston Puritanism; it is a complete lack of imagination.

Q: Do you champion modern art or modern women?

A: I champion myself. As Thoreau said, "Which is the richer, the sunset through the trees or I the beholder who am able to make it mine for having the eyes to see it right."

Q: Do you claim a moral dispensation as a transcendentalist?

A: No more so than any American. The eternal dwells within the common-place, behind the half-truths—if we only choose but to see it.

Q: But why the nude? Why not pure landscape?

A: Because we can only know what we love. My father was a general in the Civil War. As a boy, he was a friend of Thoreau. He died eight years after the war from complications he suffered from his many wounds. He died a haunted man because he loved how Thoreau had loved, had learned to see with the eye of a poet, and had suffered to know the full horror of human folly on the battlefields of the South.

Q: Do you mention this in reference to what has been described as a certain decadent morbidity in your works?

A: Thoreau said the earth is not a dead thing, but living poetry, like the leaves of a tree, which precede flowers and fruit. Thoreau was not a solitary; he did not seek to escape human affections. His solitude and silence were peopled to the rafters: in his books, in his dreams, his friendships. He cried at empty cellar holes, at tumbled-down walls and abandoned meadows. He heard the voices of the departed. He felt their heartache; he saw through the veil of human affections.

Q: Might not Thoreau have found your paintings disturbing?

A: Thoreau said, "The perception of beauty is a moral test." And he was above all things a lover. My paintings are full of love.

William Channing laid the transcript on his desk and nodded at the portrait on the wall.

Later, as he lay in bed listening to the nor'easter spew itself out against his bay window, he indulged himself with a spirited defense of his client, the artist versus the Chillingworths. He found himself drawn to the voice in the transcript. It was a voice of New England practicality, of no-nonsense certainty in a chosen life, defending the purpose of art: memorializing the soul's affections. And, too, a voice known to his grandfather for something close to seven years, a life at Sangamore before his move to Lowell, and yet never mentioned, at least not in Michael's hearing. The same voice as in Joseph Palmer's Venice diary, a few tantalizing excerpts of which he had found in the exhibition catalog. Clearly, Sandra, too, had found the diary compelling: the voice edging them both nearer the larger-than-life person of Sandra Chillingworth Palmer.

And all his weeks at the inn, where his mother had worked, where they had schemed like fellow conspirators over that long summer he had washed dishes ... and yet he could summon nothing in those conversations that elucidated his grandfather's past. How could he have remained so closed off to his own family for so many years, while the past of the Palmers took him over by the hour? What an indictment of his misplaced loyalties. Or was his perspective, that of the prosaic William Channing, just a tad off.

He glanced out his bay window as the rain rippled in curtains across the green, canting his chin left, then right, squinting.

And then he knew—what some part of him had known since seeing the name Palmer in the volume of Thoreau, the signature on the etching ... and even staring into the eyes of Sandra on the moonlit riverbank all those years before: The lives of Giovanni Maronetti and Joseph Palmer had been shaped by the tragic fate of the same women.

The inexorable law of compensation sealing that loss into all their lives.

Finally, the sound of the rain began to soothe his agitated mind. The rain and the wind lulled him into dreams where the byways of the past began to merge as one: the voice of Sandra eliding into her father's, translated into the artist's voice in the transcript and diary, and further back to the thoughts of a soldier recovering from his wounds in a burned-out railway shed, a far-off locomotive's whistle disturbing the conversation of a bearded man and a boy, their heads turning back to one another as the song of the rails faded through the woods.

And grafted onto this line of voices was another, a name, but as yet without a voice of her own: a radiant beauty, a prodigious talent, and a mysterious allure that had shaped lives unborn. The sensation of such enduring—undying—power thrilled him and he woke more than once with a throbbing erection, about which, he was loath to do anything.

CHAPTER 20

———

The morning dawned bright and cool and clean, the rain of the
day before like another world. He woke seized with panic.

The *Boston Globe* by his door had a front-page article
about the FBI investigation in Lowell. Sniffer dogs had located
Michael Collins's clothes, wallet, and keys, buried beneath the roots of a
tree. They had been unable to locate a body. Speculation was rampant.
A crime of some kind had been committed. Michael Collins was now on
the FBI's 'Most Wanted' list. Page six showed a photograph of a younger
Michael Collins bending over the desk of Congressman Neeley, pointing
out details in an architectural rendering to his boss.

"Fuck."

William Channing went to his window. A police cruiser was parked
on Monument Square, its flashers blinking. The cop—not Slotnik, who
would be off duty—had stopped someone in a blue Chevy Blazer and
was either writing out a ticket or taking down information.

He went to the desk and Sandra's computer and clicked on the E-mail
window. In a drawer he found the card of the *Globe* reporter he'd spoken
to in Boston, which included the guy's E-mail address. He didn't think much
of the reporter, but he figured that with the FBI now on his case, it was time
for Michael Collins to let his side of the story leak into cyberspace. Or at
least some of it, a few hints about the hit-and-run and why certain people
in the construction industry might want him out of the way, after trying
to buy his silence had failed. Enough to cover his ass. He chose his words
carefully, and very expertly laid a time line and a lifeline that he figured,
one day, he'd need when he testified before a grand jury. In this defense,
he realized with some chagrin, he was truly in his element.

Finally, clicking the SEND icon, he cast around for his next quarry. What day was Joe supposed to have lunch with Angela?

As far as he knew, the date hadn't been finalized. Should he call Joe? Maybe he should go over to Joe's farm and see if he could find this out. Or should he go and ransack the town again for signs of her? No, there could be nothing random, nothing to bring suspicion on himself. He had to resist the temptation to precipitous action and stick with his neat persona: consistency, predictability, habit—attributes of the otherworldly scholar. Besides, she was obviously making the rounds, feeling him out. Only a matter of time before their paths crossed.

Except time was running out. Police officer Slotnik was giving him the creeps, often sidling up to him in the pub and asking questions. "Gee, Bill, two hundred and eighty-five dollars a night on a professor's salary—guess I got into the wrong line of work." And Ruthie Cunningham was a real case: He liked her, even admired her, yet feared her all the same.

By late morning, he could resist no longer and was out early for his jog. He fairly flew along the roads, fueled by morning energy, feeling the postglacial undulations of the earth beneath the macadam, the trees overhead a fiery orange spangled with unshed rain drops, and in the distance the throaty, gesticulating paean of a park ranger on North Bridge, one of Jack the bartender's regulars, explaining to a gaggle of children and adults the bloody confrontation between the redcoats and minutemen. In the man's eyes, it was as if it had happened yesterday.

Something was different.

Had it to do with his trip, his time travel of the day before? That he'd missed a day? Or simply that he'd begun his daily jog a few hours early?

Something had changed, and not just the FBI. Something to do with the face, the name, the unheard voice pointing him elsewhere.

He was relieved to find Marge Hathaway in her accustomed place, clipping topiary in the front yard. The experience of his recent impersonation of her son now made her loss utterly real to him. No longer was she merely an old lady going about her habitual tasks, but the very image of endurance, of love lost. He felt a need to comfort her for her son, burned beyond recognition in a helicopter crash north of Da Nang, and her husband, a surgeon who had insisted on dying at home in his own bed, nursed by his wife of forty-seven years, struck down by a melanoma he, of all people, shouldn't have missed.

He turned as sudden laughter and screams impinged on his reverie: a blur of color as two little girls dashed across the front yard of the house next door, cutting across the shadows on the lawn in a fizz of giggles. Marge Hathaway heard the commotion, too, and as she lifted her face and turned, she caught sight of him standing across the road.

She waved and he jogged over.

"You're early, Bill. I was just thinking about you, on this glorious morning."

"I guess everybody needed the rain."

"Oh, the rain, yes. Bet you'll never guess whom I ran into this morning, I saw her walking in the orchard, filming the trees and the garden, and then she strolled right up to my kitchen door—big as life—like it had only been last week."

She jabbed a friendly elbow in his arm.

"Who might that be, Marge?"

"Sandra, your old pal. As lovely as the morning dew. My, she *has* held up well. Kept her figure, too. Only cut her honey blond hair, but I guess nobody wears it long anymore."

It was all he could do to resist embracing her, to shout to the skies, "Yes, yes, of course it's true." But he retained just enough of his poker face to coolly play the cards handed him.

He picked a leaf off her blue cardigan. "Hey, listen, some of us are just happy to keep what we've got."

He removed his Red Sox cap and ran a hand though his damp hair.

"Lovely woman. I think she was a little amazed an old bag like me was still kicking."

"You said something about filming?"

"Oh, you know, she had one of those little camcorders."

"I bet you must have surprised her, recognizing her so quickly."

"She had to laugh when I opened the kitchen door and greeted her the same as when she was a kid. 'Sandy,' I said, and she gave me the biggest smile and a terrific hug."

"Amazing you didn't get her mixed up—after so much time—with her sister."

"Oh, but you see, Angela wouldn't have just strolled on in like that. She got really sneaky as a teenager, very standoffish, almost as if she preferred to go unnoticed."

"Teenagers, it's a tough time."

"And I told her about you. Her old pal from Emerson."

"I'll bet that was a shockeroo."

"No, not at all. She seemed ... well, politely intrigued. I told her you were staying at the inn while you worked on your book about Thoreau."

"That was kind of you. Did she mention what brought her back to town?"

"Not in so many words, but I suppose it was obvious."

"Obvious?"

She spied a couple of offending leaves and clipped them.

"It always seemed to me, Bill, that there are two kinds of people in this world: those who stay put and those who are looking to stay put."

"She wasn't just passing through, then?"

"Oh, she was passing all right."

"Like last year—you told me, when you'd seen her in the orchard and she looked a little worse for wear."

"Oh, that's right—I'd forgotten. But she looked great this morning. She was wearing the most exquisite Italian skirt and blouse, and Ferragamo pumps—not the right shoes for walking around in an orchard. And just a touch of makeup. I told her Abigail would be proud to know her daughter had such fine taste."

He indicated with a jut of his chin the place next door. "She just came to see the old homestead."

"Actually, I don't believe she did go next door. The French are back, as you can see. The two little girls are like wild Indians."

"I guess it might be a little disconcerting with new people there. And your beautiful garden ..." He paused at the sound of little footsteps. "For hide-and-seek."

"I think it must be hard for women today. But then, it was always hard, getting married and leaving home."

"Did you ask her what she was doing?"

"I offered her coffee, but she seemed to get a little nervous, as if maybe she had appointments to keep. I suggested we get out the photo albums, but she politely declined. And then she saw the painting of her grandmother—my word, that got her attention. She took it down and held it in the sunlight by the window. Her voice got all excited and she was very animated. She said it needed cleaning, possibly relining, as if she knew quite a bit about such things. I thought she would at least ask me how I got it, or even offer to buy it back, but then she neatly replaced it and, without a word from me, went over to the piano, sat down, and played—Mozart rondo, the one the girls had always played for me as kids."

"Were they any good?"

"Oh, sure, but they couldn't handle all the lessons. Abigail even took them to Venice for a few months to study with a famous teacher. I think it exhausted them; they rarely played, at least for me, after that. And twins, competing in the same arena—they had to give it up, pressure like that, and go their own ways."

"I never heard her play; she never said boo."

"She even got a little teary-eyed, sitting there looking at the photos on the piano. She knew my son, you see; he was a big brother to the girls." Marge Hathaway seemed to catch herself, as if she'd detected something in her own voice that was unfamiliar. "They picked apples together."

She drew herself up, blinking hard.

"Marge, like I told you in the cemetery, we Vietnam vets appreciate what pilots like Bobby did. You should be proud of him. I will remember him for you, Marge; I will place flowers on his grave."

The old woman wiped at an eye, a stoic stiffening of the neck. "Would you, William? That would be kind of you."

"I'll make a point of it."

She reached to his arm for balance.

He patted her shoulder. "Did Sandra have a car?"

"No, no, same as you. She seemed to be walking. She was on her way back into town."

A shriek, giggles, a dash of denim and hair ribbons through the hedges. They both turned to the commotion. Repeated calls in French of a frenetic mother.

She snapped the clippers playfully in their direction. "A handful, those two."

He took a couple of steps back, as if trying to catch a glimpse of the children, seeing in the same moment the dormer windows in the upper story and the ungainly brick tower and gold cupola.

He nodded. "Tragedy, the business about the baby dying. Sandra told me about that once when we were rowing on the river. I got the sense from her that things, you know, were never quite the same afterward."

Marge Hathaway reached with the clippers and closed the blades with slow deliberation, watching as a leaf tumbled. "Of course, just between us, I never believed any of it—the adoption business. Abigail couldn't lie, and the poor child looked so much like Angela. Oh, it was uncanny." She nodded with a half grimace. "Bill, the most terrifying thing you discover when you get to be my age: all the subterfuge. How little you ever knew about anybody. And then, it's too late."

He turned from her honest eyes, almost embarrassed. "Maybe that explains Angela being so difficult, such a tough cookie."

"After the tragedy, she was even worse, moody and rebellious. For a year, she wouldn't speak to her sister, Sandra. Maybe I'm too hard, but I blame her for her parents' divorce. A man like Joe Palmer—take it from me—can't handle a thing like that."

"Teenage daughters?"

"My husband was a good friend of Joe's; they pruned the orchard every spring. A man has enough problems without having that lurking in the house."

"I'm sure teenage boys can be trouble, too."

"They take their trouble elsewhere. Oh, they might get into a scrape or two, but they are loyal to their family. Boys will always stand by you."

She turned to him with a self-mocking grin, straightening herself and resting the business end of the shears across her shoulder.

"That tower is so odd," he said, giving a nod in the direction of the cupola.

"And a nightmare to maintain. The French have petitioned the town council to tear the thing down. But the problem is, Thoreau climbed it, so it seems, so now it's considered a historical and architectural landmark."

"Thoreau, huh? It's amazing how Henry seems to turn up in the life of that family."

Marge laughed.

"Come on, I'll introduce you to Marie, and you can take a look at the old rattletrap. It'll give me a chance to put in a word about pruning and mulching the roses for the winter."

He had resisted the idea of asking to look around the old Palmer house, fearful of replacing what was ingrained in his imagination with what he knew would be the disappointing reality.

The French family was perfectly polite but couldn't have cared less about the history of the place. And too many antiquarians poking around. The wife was only interested in getting the girls bathed before Sunday lunch and making sure the lamb didn't burn in the oven. The husband waved him onward with an edge of condescending curtness. "Check it out, Monsieur Channing, but beware the tower—a death trap, for sure—*pour les enfants*, a death trap." The man, an executive with a French wine importer, made a show of a hand held to a furrowed brow for all the worry and annoyance of the stupid thing.

William Channing made his way through the many fine rooms on the first floor, trying to picture in his mind how the Palmers would have lived. He was saddened to find the slate swept so clean, what had once, in his earliest notions, been an impregnable fortress of immutable old Concord, glimpsed on that winter's day just after Christmas of his senior year through frosted windows. Now he found the grand high-ceilinged living room and library and sitting rooms filled with expensive modern Italian furnishing and splashy abstract paintings.

Not his taste. Certainly not Abigail Hosmer Palmer's.

And yet, even the Hosmers (Abigail Palmer's patrimony), who had sold the house to Capt. Samuel Palmer, had themselves taken it over from a previous family, who had faltered before the Revolution, and they, in turn, from a grandee landlord who had owned half the township, and all of it taken by subterfuge from the Indians, who had, never really claimed ownership in the first place.

The artist, Joseph Palmer, had left the place in the early twenties, fleeing its ghosts and a Chillingworth lawsuit, only returning to die a near ghost himself. While his son, Joe Palmer, by every reckoning, had struggled to keep the place afloat and then simply *walked* one day in 1967, turned his back and disappeared after having quit his job and finding himself in debt after losing some harebrained legal battles with his father's estate at Sangamore. William wondered if Joe Palmer, living only a fifteen-minute walk away, ever returned to gaze upon the old place. And Abigail, so broke that she immediately had to put the house on the market. According to Marge Hathaway, she had never set foot in the place again. A Hosmer who had failed to endure not once but twice! And Sandra. He could feel the muscle strain in his shoulders, her urging him on to row a little farther that night on the river. To get her back, to show him the orchard.

So, there it was: He *was* the family custodian.

He climbed the stairs to the second floor and walked the halls with a slow step, like an unwelcome accountant come to pore over ill-kept books, trying to conjure it in his mind, what had changed, what stories these bedrooms could tell. In one of them, the old captain had died, in another his grandchildren, a boy and girl, who had died of scarlet fever within hours of each other, whose graves he passed daily in Sleepy Hollow. And, of course, the Civil War captain and then general Joseph M. Palmer, had slowly died of his wounds and the dysentery that had almost killed him in a Confederate POW camp. Yet somehow he had managed to produce two children, the artist Joseph Palmer and his brother (one an artist and the other assuming the burden of running the mill in Lowell during the last decades of prosperity brought on by World War I), both born in a bedroom on the second floor, when people were conceived, born, and died in their own beds.

Going into the children's room at the end of the hall, up a tiny stairway, he found a large space strewn with dolls and paper cuttings and picture books, a lush leafy sunlight pouring in through gaily curtained windows. What a paradise! He went to the windows, trying each one, noting the slight variation of viewpoints west toward the river and the hay brown meadow beaded with stonewalls, as well as a good chunk of the craggy orchard next door. Wisteria clung in great knotted cords by the green shutters. Below, the rose garden set amid a checkerboard of redbrick pathways, where Marge Hathaway was quietly lecturing the new mistress of the house. And the *smells*, rising off the sunlit earth and pouring inward: redolent of roses and moss after rain and dried leafage. How perfect, even down to the carefully placed child guardrails installed across each window. If this had indeed been their childhood room—or had it been the nursery?—if a room could guarantee happiness, it would have to be this room. How could it not have been filled with love and happiness?

And yet ... A shiver went down his spine as he remembered Sandra's recounting the fall from the changing table: The death of a child in this room, or the nursery, had led to another death in her small apartment in Cambridge.

With a glance at his watch, spooked and panicked, he returned to the hallway and found a sturdy pull-down ladder that allowed access to the observation area by way of a trapdoor under the cupola. As he took the first step, he was aware of another voice in his head, the voice of Capt. Samuel Palmer as recorded in his memoirs. For a few minutes, memory of that stately voice proved a comfort as he found his way to the cupola, with its panoramic view of the Concord River ... the path from whence he'd come, and another hint at where he had yet to go.

It has been often asked by neighbors and family members why, at a rather advanced age, I bothered to construct the small observation tower in the midst of my country home. I plead the foolishness of whim about this matter. In fact, it was while researching my volume on my sea voyages and travels that the idea came to me. I was reminded of the pleasures I had had in the crow's nests of ships as a young man, when one could see the shape of the globe spread as a blue line from horizon to circling horizon. The illusion of one's centrality, especially at such a tender age, was compelling from that precarious vantage point. One had a grip on the passage of the day, the threat of inclement weather, and, most crucially, the shape of a vigilant man-of-war, the color of her flag, her speed and direction. From such a perch, I had called out mortal warnings and glimpsed the most sublime of nature's panoramas: the quenching sunset, the surfacing of a squadron of gray whales, the leap of multitudinous dolphins, each a dazzling diamond-backed apparition. Such a mixture of fear and awe is not easily forgot.

And, too, while plotting my reminiscences, I was brought to mind of travels in Europe, most particularly Venice, a city peopled with towers, some tipped like sundials and looking to topple at the first breath of wind, all, essentially, watchtowers to guard the city from surprise attack. Once, as a young man, I set myself the goal to climb every tower in that fabled city. I bribed and cajoled and sneaked my way up some dozen before I had utterly exhausted myself. To climb these towers, to that tiny place set in the wide blue of the Adriatic, was to understand the fragility of that fairest of cities, its vulnerability to that cradling sea, which could just as easily bring a hostile fleet to her gates as all the riches of the Orient.

And so with these reveries in mind, I thought to have my own watchtower. To be built with my own hands, and with no compelling purpose of any kind—only the joy in the building and the seeing. There was no Indian attack in the offing, no redcoats on the move to subdue rebellious Concord, and no debtors on my trail. Just our fair countryside spared of both contingency and calamity. Here was a geography of human habitation—about a ten-miles radius—to daily bless the weary eye of the marooned world traveler. From my angle, I saw the larger contours of the village anew, the way the river winds its way back toward the sea, the meadows so painstakingly cleared and drained by our ancestors, woodlots like shifting sandbars eroded by the axman's hungry eye, the roads weaving their dusty way to embrace the four corners of the globe. I found that my tower brought me new friends, one in particular, a local recluse and naturalist who was tempted to my perch more than once for an altered perspective on his domain.

At a certain age, one finds comfort in the faith that all things beat a path to your door; it is the hope of permanence when there is none. At night, the stars spread their glittering robes above me as I chart their unvarying courses in my longitudinal tables. I would think of friends in London contemplating dinner and fine port, perhaps dead, and I with no word of their passing; of loyal shipmates long abandoned to unmarked graves in the Solomon Islands; and the smiles of the native women of the Hawaiian Islands, those haunting naiads of the great blue. The sun rises and falls at my direction. The seasons display their finery and then reluctantly, with a dispirited bow, exit the stage. As the saying goes, I am captain of all I survey. And with this, the grandest illusion of all, the faint hope that we can know one place well above all others, to the marrow of our old bones, that across the wide globe there is one place which is forever ours, where we have our true dwelling this side of the River Styx.

He found Marge still in the rose garden by herself. The French family was starting their lunch.

"Did you find what you wanted?" she asked.

"I expect I'll only know once I've found it."

He followed her lead and bent to a rose to savor the smell.

She looked around and shook her head with a twist of irritation in her lips.

"Roses are indestructible; most everything else has gone to rack and ruin."

"And the house …"

"Abigail had to sell off most her furniture, all the old Hosmer pieces she found or thought she'd found over two decades in antique shops from here to Littleton." She returned her gaze from the far reaches of the garden and smiled at him. "You might still be able to catch Sandra; I think she said she was off to the inn for lunch with Joe."

CHAPTER 21

B y the time he made it back to the inn, panting and out of breath, she was long gone. The receptionist remembered her well: tall, elegant, short blond hair, gray pleated skirt, Armani scarf, mid-forties—a little nervous. She had inquired about him by name, William Channing, saying she'd been told by a mutual friend he was staying at the inn. Judy, the morning receptionist, had put a call through to his room, but, of course, he wasn't there. The woman had asked more about him, what he was doing at the inn, where he was living now. Judy told the woman he was a Thoreau scholar from a midwestern university, working on a book. The woman had seemed intrigued but a little unsure of herself. Then she had asked if, by any chance, there was a Michael Collins staying at the inn. Judy checked the computer and said no. By this time, she'd grown a little skeptical of the woman, who had taken a few minutes to videotape some of the downstairs period rooms, so she'd asked the lady if she wanted to leave her name and a message for William Channing. The woman had thought a moment, then said no, maybe she'd try back later. She had gone into the lounge, then gone to the front entrance and whipped out her cell phone to make a call. She had seemed in a hurry to leave, going out the back entrance into the parking lot.

He went upstairs and got a copy of Sandra's high school photo and showed it to Judy, who didn't even hesitate.

"Boy, don't some girls have all the luck. Except for the hair, that lady has taken good care of herself. Her shoes were a mess, though."

He ran. He made it to Joe Palmer's farm stand in record time, but exhausted, bent over, gasping for breath. A CLOSED sign hung on the signboard next to the road. The stand normally did gangbuster business on Sunday. He could detect no sign of life. He began walking toward the farmhouse, seeing it suddenly afresh in comparison with the old Palmer homestead: a thing reduced to the essentials of a life and held tight upon the earth. He knocked. Nothing. He walked the barnyard. The red barn was padlocked. Then he began along the road in the direction of the orchard and the river, passing one field after another.

He had little doubt now that the woman was Sandra. Only she could have put the clues together from his E-mails to realize that it might be Michael Collins calling her back. Fortunately, the receptionist hadn't seemed to register on the name: Michael Collins, onetime Washington political operative and accused influence peddler, now object of an FBI manhunt. William Channing's once-inviolate hermitage seemed more precarious than ever due to the utterance of his confederate's name in the lobby of the Concord Inn.

Adding to a sense of dislocation, everywhere he looked he found himself assaulted by a precarious ripeness and fecundity: bloated beefsteak tomatoes weighing down their vines, enormous yellow squash rising like cancer-ridden organs out of the damp black soil. The recent rain had left puddles in the road. Mud pulled at his shoes. He was brought up short by a smell and the sight of something horrible attached to the trunk of one of the oaks that lined the road. On inspection, he saw it was a raccoon carcass, a day or two old, splayed and stapled by the feet, crawling with flies and ants. Twenty feet farther on, past a field of tattered corn, another carcass, more decomposed than the first. He passed on quickly and fixed his gaze on the orchard ahead.

Out of the mass of green, color appeared in dots and bundles: red and russet and yellow-green; great gobs hanging from the branches. He felt a queer sense of oppression, of having stumbled upon some act of mass parturition. Apples underfoot, crushed, broken, nibbled, garnished with deer droppings. He found branches that had been recently cut, slashed, butchered. Fist-size ax wounds in many of the trunks. Graftings pulled apart and flung down.

"Get the fuck out of here."

The cry made him jump and he nearly fell, stepping on a bunch of fallen apples in the deep grass. He looked for the source. There, like a battered scarecrow tossed to earth, lay Joe Palmer against the trunk of one of his trees.

"It's me, Joe, Bill Channing."

He drew closer, seeing the disheveled hair, the mud caked on nicely pressed khakis, the hatchet flung to the side in the grass.

"Bill, ah Bill, my Thoreau friend." The old man raised a fragile hand in greeting. "How are you, Bill? Good sojourning—ha."

"Are you okay?"

"Of course I'm okay, if a little soused." He gave the younger man a thumbs-up. "Just pruning back a few of the old bastards. Let 'em know who's boss."

"Come on, let me help you up and get you back to the house."

"I'm fine, Bill, I'm fine." He pulled a hand over his reddened eyes and then wiped the hand on his blue oxford-cloth shirt. "Supposed to have lunch with my darling daughter today. And she fucking cancels on me—just like the little bitch."

The old man's breath, the curse, was like a mortar round going off in his brain. He bit at his lower lip and knelt in the grass nearby. The whiff of whiskey brought back the stubbled face of his own father.

"Sorry to hear it, Joe. Something came up, huh?"

"Jesus fucking Christ. She phones me from the inn. I could hear the goddamn piano playing in the cocktail lounge for Sunday brunch. Half an hour before we're supposed to meet and she says some business matter has come up and she needs to reschedule. Re—fucking—schedule. That's exactly the kind of shit—kind of lies—Angela was always coming up with."

"It happens. What is she, some kind of businesswoman now?"

"How the fuck should I know. Just like your generation, don't give a shit about common courtesy."

"Hey, that's the least of our sins. Come on, let me give you a hand here."

He grasped the old man's hand and gently helped to pull him to his feet. Joe grabbed an overhead branch and steadied himself.

"Whoring her way through school." The branch dipped and apples tumbled all around them. "Ever study genetics, Bill?"

"Can't say that I have."

"Fascinating stuff. Look at these old buggers around here. I've coddled them and grafted them and brought in bee colonies to pollenize them and then they do their thing. It is a very inexact science. There's always a degree of variation or chance or mutation; nature is never as scrupulous as many people think. It's fucking arbitrary. But maybe that won't last. Maybe before long, the biogeneticists will map all human genes down to the last twitch in your big toe. We'll all be open books, infinitely reproducible. That will be your brave new world, Bill, or maybe your kids'. Why the fuck don't you have any kids, Bill? You're not a faggot, are you?"

"Bad luck, Joe. Never met the right girl."

"But that's just it—you'll never know if she's the right one. I married a woman because … she'd lived in the same place all her life and her love seemed like the Rock of Gibraltar. But the roots were moribund; she couldn't fucking breathe."

"Sometimes—maybe it's just bad luck."

"Let me tell you what's scary about who we really are." The old man stuck a finger in the chest of the younger. "Each of us starts out as a single cell and ends up a vast collection of many different cells. And yet each of our cells still contains the same set of genes as the first. Every cell in our body knows all the shit the other cells know but each one only bothers to do its own thing. Doesn't that scare the shit out of you—boy? Does me."

"Guess I have to think about it."

"*That's* what I mean."

He saw the inflamed irises in the old man's eyes dilate, threaded with red.

"What … what we know?"

"Billy boy, I can't tell you how many times people come to me and tell me how much they liked something they bought at the stand. Next, they want a tip for their little veggie patch. They think I must have the secret because I grow fifteen different fucking kinds of potatoes. What they never understand is that there really isn't any secret. Oh sure, it's good to *know* a thing or two. But what they don't get is that it's a war out here. Nature is not some benign force that wants to cozy up with you. Nature doesn't give a shit. Nature just is. Some years, there's no rain, some years too much. Next week we get a freeze and it's a death sentence. Nature is aphids and beetles and a hundred kinds of fungi and viruses—don't get me talking about pigweed and foxtail—not to mention the goddamn deer and woodchucks. We had a raccoon raid the other night and the little motherfuckers did an entire quarter acre of our best Silver Queen corn. You should have seen it: lines knocked down, a bite, a nibble out of each cob, and onto something else. Nature's a vandal—a lie, a cheat; it doesn't care. You can't fight it; you can't placate it. You just deal with it. What people don't like to know is that for anything of quality, hecatombs must be slain to make room. We have to be ruthless, same as nature. We weed out, thin out, and trim back so that the best survives. People hate to trim a tree, but a tree is root and core; the limbs just sap nutrients. Cut 'em off, and what is left will thrive and do you proud. Life is fucking triage, Bill. Loss and deceit are just another path to survival. And love is nature's sleight of hand."

He took the old man's arm and began to lead him back toward the house.

"Just take it easy, Joe. She's probably been away a long time and needs to get her feet back on the ground. Why don't you send her an E-mail and tell her how much you miss her and want to see her."

"E-mail? How about an address. I haven't even had an address for her in thirty years."

"Have you got a phone number?"

"A cell phone—yes, yes, back in the office, I suppose."

"Okay, so invite her for dinner, Joe. Give her a chance."

Joe staggered and grabbed hold of the bough of a tree.

"Chance? How many chances does she want? I don't know about you, Bill, but I've about used up my chances. And I don't have the patience of your pal Thoreau, Bill. Hate to disillusion you, but Thoreau was an asshole. He left men like my grandfather to take their chances on the battlefield, do the dirty work for the abolitionist cause. And look where it got him."

"Let's invite her for dinner, Joe … you, me, and Henry Thoreau. Then, like you say, we'll cut to the roots of all that ails us."

Ruthie opened the door with a pair of wire clippers in one hand and a racket with the strings cut in the other.

"You okay?" he asked.

She put her arms awkwardly around him and hugged him. Her breath smelled of wine.

"I'm so depressed."

"What's the matter?"

"Didn't you see it in the *Concord News*?"

"In the *News*?"

"I'm fucked. Not only did they kick me off the board; they may even make me give up my investment in the club."

"Oh, the club."

"Yes, *my* tennis club."

"And they made you resign from the board of selectman?"

"No choice."

She shut the door with a smart click to dramatize her situation. She went into the kitchenette and opened another bottle of chilled Chablis, poured him a glass and topped up her own. He took the wineglass, his words automatic, as if his mind had slipped into a well-worn gear.

"Can they point to specific votes on the zoning change that applied to the tennis club, when your vote made a difference? Did you lobby on any bills?"

She stood before him like a shackled prisoner.

"No, not really, but you know how it is. You can always construe someone's motivations to fit the crime."

He said in all seriousness, "You resign without a fight and everyone assumes you're guilty."

"I didn't have a chance. I was … so the token female. The men on the board are old enough to be my father, just waiting for me to fuck up."

"Maybe you *should* get a lawyer."

"I hate lawyers, and it's such a lawyer thing." She tipped her glass back. "I got most of my savings in that project, my half of our house in the divorce settlement. I just wanted a piece of something—damn it—to call my own."

She tossed the racket onto a pile of them by the stringing machine and came around to him, Virginia Slims T-shirt down to her waist, blue Nike shorts, bare feet, and put her arm around him, bringing her face close.

"Kiss me," she demanded.

He kissed her and she clung tight, working her tongue over his lips.

"I know," she slurred, "I'm not as sexy as her videotape."

"You're just fine," he said, meaning it. "I envy you—really; I sometimes wish I'd become a high school teacher."

"Now, Angela, there's real balls for you."

"Don't be so sure; she may have ended up a very unhappy person."

"But she's a *star*." She went over to the television, pulling the videotape out of a drawer and bending to shove it into the VCR. "Come on, let's watch some more. You obviously need a jump start."

"You think that's such a good idea?" He indicated the connecting door to the dorm.

She glissaded over, slopping wine over her hand, and pushed a small bolt into place.

"Hell, the little darlings are probably holed up in chat rooms with their boyfriends, doing Internet sex or day trading." She waved him over to the couch in front of the television. "This is one of my favorite bits."

He turned to the television.

Brilliant sunshine, a walled garden thick with eucalyptus and palms and frangipani, the dazzle of a blue swimming pool trimmed in turquoise tile, the white back of a tall woman doing a steady butterfly.

"California sunshine." She raised her glass. "That's exactly how I always imagined her. Suppose it's *her* pool?"

"Could be anywhere."

The woman, dripping blond hair pasted like seaweed down the mobile bone structure of her back, walked out of the water on invisible stairs and over to a beach chair, where she dried herself with a white towel.

"Notice how her skin's so white?"

"She was a dancer."

"Smart girl, stay out of the sun … umm, and spread that oil."

The camera lingered as she spread the suntan lotion over her breasts and then got her fingers going between her legs.

He nodded. "That saxophone sound track is from Dizzy Gillespie at Newport. Suppose they had to pay for the rights?"

"She's finger-fucking herself and you're worried about legal niceties."

Her head rolled back in the chair, lips parting, eyes narrowing as the object of desire swam into view. A well-proportioned Adonis figure, tanned a golden brown, appeared from the pool.

"Get it? She's pulling this guy up from the depths of her libido. This is a California energy thing. She's visualizing her toy boy and he comes just watching her. See, see, and look at the veins in that thing."

He put his arm around Ruthie, hoping she might relax. She continued rubbing the crotch of his jeans.

"Yes," she cried. "Look at her hand on his head, directing the action; it's a total command and control operation."

"Do you have to deconstruct this thing?"

"How come you're not in the mood?"

"You know, she was in town today. She stood up her dad for lunch."

"Do you think she's faking it? I mean, look at the muscles in her thighs, the tendons; she's fucking giving birth."

"Here, here ..." He got his belt loosened.

"You'd rather fuck her."

"Actually, I'd just like to ask her a few questions—wouldn't you?"

"Come on baby, come on ..." She wiped at a tear in her eye. "She's there. Can't you feel it? Oh God, she's so young and beautiful."

"Ouch."

"Sorry."

The man stood and the woman reached for him, jerking him twice to produce an ejaculation of diaphanous semen over her breasts. She released her grip and redirected the rivulets upward, spreading the viscous wetness over her breasts, working it into her skin.

Ruthie screeched with pleasure. "Oh, Angie—yes. Do you get it? She's impregnable. She doesn't need his seed. She's no longer a repository, but she isn't afraid of his cum, either. God, can you remember when people weren't afraid, when semen wasn't poison?"

"Are you making this up as you go along?"

"Isn't she wonderful—evolution's darling?"

"What do you say we can it."

"Oh, Michael ..." She brought her face close to his, waiting to be kissed.

"Please." He kissed her gently. "Don't call me Michael."

"Michael, Michael ... what's in a name?"

"You're drunk."

"So take advantage of me."

She took off her T-shirt and cupped her breasts. "I know they're not as good as Angie's."

"You've got great tits. So, why don't you just turn it off?"

She bent toward the television.

A large spare bedroom with high stucco walls and huge French doors leading to a balcony or patio of terracotta tiles, blue beyond, a vastness of sea and sky. A bed, a brass railing, white sheets, Mediterranean light. Piano … Satie. A nude figure materializes on the bed, asleep but hands gripping the brass railing behind her head. Her skin is radiant with the light, white on white. The camera luxuriates in the texture of her body. Her eyes open finally to sunlight, waking to the day, feeling the light upon her skin, but her hands still seemingly shackled to the brass railing, her body twisting, opening itself to the light, yearning for the touch of the light. And from her body, a mirror image arises, wakes, a specter distilled from the damp morning flesh, kneeling between the raised thighs and staring into the eyes of her twin. The apparition reaches a hand to the upturned breasts, stroking, then bending forward, tossing her hair back, to kiss her waking self, tongues flicking like windblown flames: blue eyes—blue on blue, a dazzling blue—sparked with recognition.

"Don't you get it?" she purred. "Angie has mastered parthenogenesis."

He stared at the screen, his face bathed in emanations of light: light incorporeal and transient, light of light, illuminating the living past.

"Dreaming…. " he murmured. "Dreaming Sisters."

Ruthie cried out triumphantly, looking where she'd been stroking. "Hey, hey, hey … the trailer is a-rockin'!"

CHAPTER 22

———————

Introduction to Joseph Palmer: *Sunlight and Scandal,* by Laura Ryder

When I—an Italian Renaissance expert—was asked to do the retrospective on Joseph Palmer by the Boston Museum of Fine Arts, I had assumed that because the artist was in the permanent holdings of many major museums, Palmer must be a big name in American art circles. How wrong I was. There was little in the standard reference books besides dates and prizes won. Among scholars in the American field, he was considered a *retardataire* effusion of the Gilded Age, something clichéd, effete, starved of real life. His canvases eschewed bright Impressionism for a darker tonal brushwork; so he was well out of the mainstream. In the eyes of most experts, Palmer had been relegated to the status of a society painter, a footnote to more important artists like Whistler and Sargent. How could this be? This was an artist, I soon discovered, who had won practically every art prize going between 1890 and 1920, including a gold medal in Paris in 1898. He had studied with Carolus-Duran in Paris, as had Sargent. He was a friend and follower of Whistler in his last years. His contemporaries revered him. He was elected to the National Academy at the age of thirty-one. But Palmer, like other worthy American artists of the turn of the century, was overwhelmed by the onslaught of French Impressionism, then by European modernism after the Armory Show of 1913, then by the more vigorous and popular urban realism of the Ashcan School, and finally brought low by the Depression, which buried many fine fin de siècle reputations. The glittering society pieces and transcendentalist landscapes evocative of Emersonian idealism lost their public appeal.

When I began the project, I was startled to find that the BMFA had two works of Palmer, neither of which was on view, nor had they been exhibited in seventy-odd years. The first painting was a wonderful canvas from 1913 of his model Sandra Chillingworth standing in a meadow. The second could not even be found in the normal storerooms; it was locked away in the bowels of the museum in a special cage—lest it might escape! A young art handler and I carefully opened the wrapped picture and brought it out into the light. I was flabbergasted. The poor art handler could barely get a word out and had a hard time looking me in the eye. It was a double nude, *Dreaming Sisters*, 1924, the likes of which one couldn't imagine from that era, much less from the same hand who had painted such demure and refined women. It was one of the—I was soon to discover—infamous late figurative works. The models lie together in the meadow grasses, a careless yet highly erotic pose, knees spread, faces flushed, their exuberant flesh detailed with lush brush strokes of almost hallucinatory complexity. Here was the spontaneous eroticism of Schiele, the languor of Pearlstein, the subtle tonal formality of Whistler. To the modern eye: a masterpiece. I discovered that, late in life, Joseph Palmer had reinvented himself.

That painting stirred me to prodigious research. In the archives of the museum I found the files on the legal battle that had been instigated by the Chillingworth family when a trustee had donated the double nude in 1925. The painting had been exhibited for only a short time. In fact, it had been returned to the trustee, and it technically still belongs in his estate. Documents and newspapers from the period describe a concerted effort by the Chillingworths to block exhibition of this nude, and a number of others, mostly successful. Few of his late paintings were actually seen by the public in Palmer's lifetime, although they were reproduced in art journals. Many attributed the Chillingworth attacks to a vendetta stemming from the elopement of Sandra Chillingworth, Palmer's young model in the early paintings, to Venice in 1913 and her tragic death in 1914 after a botched delivery by a Venetian doctor. It was in Venice between 1913 and 1914 that Palmer completed his great Venice works, including the underappreciated etchings, and laid the groundwork for the leap to his innovative late work.

In the early twenties, after many skirmishes with the Chillingworth family, Joseph Palmer moved his home and studio, to a small farm in Stockbridge, where he virtually re-created his Concord homestead and added a large studio barn. Here he spent the remaining years of his life working in near seclusion on his figurative paintings; and it is in Stockbridge, at Sangamore, that most of the last work remains securely in storage, with an endowment put in place by the artist to preserve and maintain them. He sold few of the late figurative works, and when he did manage to exhibit them, the Chillingworth lawyers would pounce and a scandal-loving press would beat their way to his door.

I thought the key to Palmer's art lay in Concord with the artist's beloved orchards and meadows, his rose gardens outside the window of his carriage-house studio. But what I discovered in the mother lode of documentation at Sangamore—along with the "scandalous" nudes—was that Palmer's inspiration had as much to do with his wife's remarkable talent as a pianist, his erotic infatuation with her flesh—and mind—as with her tragic death. His late style is a celebration, body and soul, of this most extraordinary woman, Sandra Chillingworth Palmer.

At the bottom of the hill, William Channing pulled off to the side of the road where the gravel drive gave out on the grassy verge, stopped, and read the sign.

SANGAMORE –
HOME AND STUDIO OF AMERICAN ARTIST JOSEPH PALMER.
VISITORS FROM MAY TO SEPTEMBER: 10:00 A.M. TO DUSK.
AT OTHER TIMES BY APPOINTMENT ONLY.

He could just as easily have driven in, but for some reason he wanted to walk. The white farmhouse was about three hundred yards up the drive, on the crest of the shallow hill. He kept his eyes on the building as he walked, watching it take on definition. Then after a minute or two, he stopped and looked over the low-lying hills. He knew this place from the paintings. He knew it from old photographs of Concord before the woodlots had expanded and the meadows had filled with houses. And he knew from his correspondence with Laura Ryder that his grandfather Giovanni had lived here from 1921 to sometime in 1928.

The surrounding fields had been mowed and were dotted with hayricks. In the distance, cows grazed amidst fieldstone walls that had been lovingly preserved. Tufts of purple thistle and brown steeple grass and pallid Queen Anne's lace fringed the road before him. And in an abandoned meadow nearer the house, allowed to run riot with blue cornflowers, daisies, summer-shorn purple lupine, and basking wild sunflowers … the inspiration for *Dreaming Sisters* of 1924. The claustrophobic scent of the overgrown meadow brought him to a stop and he reached to the stone wall to steady himself. The rough rounded granite contour was warm and inviting to his touch.

He resumed walking. But now it was more like a dream of a walk. The land spoke to him as it had to the artist. Even the black locust trees that lined the last part of the drive seemed familiar. Rising out of a nearby hollow was a carefully preserved stand of first-growth white pine. The trees towered against the sky, reminding him of tall masts with shredded rigging, a strange sylvan graveyard. Perhaps this had reminded the artist of the grove of white pine sheltering the grave of his wife in Sleepy Hollow. In a patch of sunlight, the smells of cut hay came to him, mixed with the perfume of pine needles. And he understood.

How many times had his grandfather walked this road? How many times walking the Pawtucket Canal with his grandfather had he witnessed the old man reviewing this landscape in his tired eyes? And by gazing upon the walls of the Palmer Mill, those eyes were remembering not just this place—the calling and hopes pursued in this place—but other places, perhaps translated to scenes of his youth in Venice and apprenticeship in his father's and father's father's workshop, in the years before World War I when he'd met a beautiful American woman, wife of an artist and colleague ... whose death had changed everything.

Laura Ryder was waiting for him in her book-lined office in the brand-new museum and archive complex completed only months before. She was forty-something, of medium height, with wavy blond hair setting off a cheerful oval face.

"Hi, I've been so looking forward to meeting you." She shook his hand vigorously while examining his face with a gracious smile. "I must say your letter intrigued me."

"I was really taken with your catalog on Palmer at the BMFA."

She laughed, her voice throaty and warm.

"But your letter ... it was as if you knew all about the family."

"You know how it is—when you get into the research."

"Labor of love." She laughed again. "And look at me, I get the directorship at Sangamore. A whole new museum to run. I must have done something good in a previous life."

"But you'd be the natural choice, what with your rediscovery of Joseph Palmer."

"And Sandra Chillingworth Palmer."

"Of course."

"Funny, isn't it, where life leads you. But I'm not sure if you're what I expected. It's mostly women who wash up on my doorstep."

"Like yourself."

"Oh, no, weird academics who are into lesbian studies and deconstructing women's roles in art … and others." She played a little flirtatious vamp and tossed the end of her pale silk scarf behind her shoulder. "But you're about the right age. I don't know about the beard."

"Oh that, my Thoreau affectation, a little inside joke while I'm working on the book."

"Thoreau and American landscape painting," she mused. "Thing is, they end up mostly crazy in love with the model."

"The model?"

"Sandra Chillingworth Palmer: the tragic prodigy and heroine. The artist—don't you think?—is a mere translator of her outer beauty."

"Oh, I'd say you gave Joseph Palmer plenty of credit in your catalog and retrospective."

"But reading between the lines of your letter, I felt—what?—an infatuation with the creation as opposed to the creator."

"Well, that stands to reason, doesn't it?"

"Oh, yes, I suppose we all end up a little in bed with the artist … or his model."

She patted her unruly hair.

"He must have been a difficult man, by all accounts."

"Oh, the worst kind—a genius. Perfect foil for us masochists." She touched his elbow and gestured toward the door. "Come on, I'll show you around. Sorry for the blue jeans and grungy shirt, but we're still moving stuff around in the new building. We only got the paintings out of storage in the barn a few weeks ago."

He looked around at the charmingly detailed postmodern building as they passed through the storage and archive area.

"This place must have cost a fortune."

"Well, Palmer left a fortune, *in paintings*, and with no restrictions on deacquisitioning."

"You mean selling?"

"We sold one for over a quarter of a million last year, to help with construction costs on the new building."

"Yeah, I heard about that, Skinner's, wasn't it?"

"No more. Major institutions have standing offers to buy, especially the late work."

"The old boy must be chuckling in his grave, huh?"

"Success, the sweetest revenge of all. By next summer, Sangamore will be another Berkshire stop, after Norman Rockwell and Edith Wharton—a cut above, I hope." She opened the door to the gallery section of the building and flipped on a light switch. He noticed she seemed to walk with a limp. "We've tried to organize it into early, middle, and late periods. But we don't have that much early, since he sold a lot and the stuff remains scattered."

He went over to a small canvas of the young Sandra Chillingworth leaning against a stone wall.

"She's beautiful," he said with a beat of his eyebrows.

"My true love." She touched the frame and straightened the picture. "The spooky thing, how well Palmer timed the revived market for his work. He put practically everything the family had left into the initial endowment. Nothing was to be touched for three generations. The family would be excluded from interference in the trust until his great-grandson attainted his maturity, at which point, solely at the discretion of the board, the heir—a male heir, mind you—could take on Sangamore and promote the work of the artist."

"He excluded his own son?"

"The son, Joe Palmer, was brought up by the Chillingworths, or influenced by them—who knows. Father and son weren't very close. Actually, I gather from the records that the board of trustees allowed the son to join the board, sometime in the early sixties. But there was some brouhaha about him stealing books from the library in the main house. And then I think he even went to court to try to break the terms of the trust."

He turned to her, listening carefully. "Poor guy," he murmured, "it was *his* family after all. Like a wall gets built around your past."

"Father knows best," she rang out with an insouciant shrug, coming to a large canvas saturated in moody gray-greens, a woman in a long evening gown poised as if listening for something on the last tide of evening.

"Exquisite." He whistled.

"Now, you'll tell me all about the Thoreau influence, and you'll be right. But it wasn't until he hooked up with Sandra Chillingworth, when he was forty, that his reputation really took off."

"His muse."

"Oh, much, much more." She stood in front of the painting and assumed a lecturing air. "You can see his infatuation with those steely blue eyes and melancholy Brahman refinement. An instant hit with the public and the critics. He hit a nerve, caught the moment, and captured the yearning for a simpler bucolic world during the excesses of the Gilded Age. Boston and New York society couldn't get enough of his enamellike Vermeer jewels. Here she is: the American woman at her well-bred best, a triumph of evolution and pinnacle of Anglo-Saxon culture. She became a society star, a dazzling image; she was the Ivory soap girl of her time, ninety-nine-point-forty-four percent pure. What men liked to believe of their women and what women liked to believe of themselves. They rode to fame and fortune in tandem."

"First taste of celebrity culture."

"But the Chillingworths were scandalized to have their daughter so used, her every move recorded in the press. Distracted from her true calling."

"'Distracted'?"

"She was a child prodigy. At sixteen, she played a Mozart piano concerto with the Boston Symphony."

"She gave up the piano for Joseph Palmer?"

"O-o-oh no-o-o … she simply folded him in."

"Were they lovers, in the beginning?"

"Perish the thought." She imitated a Boston Brahman drawl. "She was just a teenager, and he a man of the world: student in Paris, confrere of Sanford White and Saint-Gaudens, who had a thing for sex with under-age women. A dangerous man! When she first went to Concord to pose, she was carefully chaperoned by her mother; then later, she was allowed to go with her twin sister and assiduously checked in every night at the inn. But she burned—look at her—she secretly burned."

They moved on to the next gallery, engulfed by a wave of aqueous colors as Laura Ryder switched on the overhead lights, the Venetian canvases ashimmer with turquoise and lapis lazuli and amber-gold: palaces and silver-beaked gondolas and bridges of russet brick.

"Triumph and tragedy," she intoned. "They eloped and sneaked off to Venice. Sandra Chillingworth married and got out from under the heavy hand of her parents. Joseph Palmer had new subject matter and a chance to stretch himself the way Whistler had a generation before—working out all these formal problems, intersections of mass and color, surface textures, raw sensual energy."

"He seduced her?"

She laughed. "No, no, *she* seduced him—blew him to smithereens; she confounded him, a man of experience."

He stopped before a painting—very formal, almost a portrait study—of Sandra Chillingworth Palmer in profile, seated at the piano in a grand rococo interior, surrounding walls, mirrors, paintings bathed in water-reflected light. She sat in perfect equipoise, hands dipping to the keys with a sure touch, a consummate professional. He was reminded of the black-and-white photo of his mother, and her admonitions: "Michael, back straight, shoulders relaxed, breathe through the phrasing."

In an awed voice, he muttered an echo from days before. "She must have been ... so very good."

"She spread her wings. What can I say? She met certain women, and possibly another man."

"Another man?"

"A little obscure, but it's all in his diary—at least Joseph Palmer's side of things. If only I could get my hands on her letters. *And then there are the drawings.* You will die; you will blush. I don't think we can ever exhibit the things."

He went around to the Venice paintings, moving close, the face of Sandra Chillingworth showing a new maturity, a raw, brooding quality—champing at the bit. He stopped before a large canvas of two women lying in half embrace in a drifting gondola.

"Then he begins to paint her double, these mirror images."

"Angela Chillingworth arrives in Venice to help with the pregnancy, with pleas from the parents for her sister to return to Boston. But dutiful Angela Chillingworth is pulled into sister's social whirl, and then by Palmer's inspiration to use them as interlocking and complementary elements in the paintings, the reflected images and metaphorical possibilities, very decadent, languorous fin de siècle stuff."

"A little kinky."

"A *little*?" She waved him on to the final galleries and the late nudes. "Hold your breath."

The Sangamore canvases, as Laura Ryder referred to them, were much larger than anything the artist had done before, many pure explosions of earth colors and skin tones, in which the women lay in the grass of the meadows, often asleep, dreaming, hands clutching at the earth, hair tangled with leaves, as if barely holding on to the edge of consciousness. In the last paintings, the figures seemed aged or perhaps worn-out, faces showing a deathly pallor, rib cages emaciated, limbs mere bone and sinew. The canvases were scumbled and scraped, the pigment swirled with palette knife as if to gain some approximation of the vital texture of the fall landscape.

He found the brooding darkness unsettling. "Not exactly sexy," he said.

"Expressionistic, a projection of inner states. You should see the sketches he did from 1915 to1916 of the wounded in the ambulances returning from the front, the exploded corpses in the mud of no-man's-land."

"Christ."

"What he saw in his father's eyes as a kid."

He looked at her, not a little chagrined to meet someone who had gone deeper into the artist than he. "Yeah?"

"But you want the Thoreau connection." She went to a medium-size canvas, sketchy, incomplete: a woman, a mother, seemingly moments after giving birth, squatting in the high grass, bloody thighs, holding something red and cheesy against her bosom. At the bottom of the canvas was a crisply painted epitaph: *How enduring are our bodies, after all! The forms of our brothers and sisters, our parents and children and wives lie still in the hills and fields round about us.*

He stared intently, trying to focus but distracted.

"Are you married, Bill?"

"Huh?"

"Married?"

"Me—no."

"No kids?"

"No."

"Well, that's about how it looks when you've given birth, and it feels worse, and you're glad to be alive, because you feel like your body has been turned inside out, and you've run up close to what's going to be your lot anyway."

"Except she didn't make it."

"A long haul from innocence." She took his arm in a friendly grip. "Come along, Thoreau," she said, laughing, "you need some fresh air. Wait till you see the main house."

Laura Ryder paused as she turned the key in the front door of the almost too perfect, too immaculately white clapboard farmhouse, indicating a new ramp that led to the added portico.

"The trustees had the state sue the board—sue themselves—to put in the wheelchair ramp and cover their asses on handicap access. That's how tight the trust agreement was written—no changes."

She opened the door, punched in a code on the security panel, and gave the thermostat a nudge. The pine floorboards squeaked despite the Persian runners along the hallway that led past the drawing room and library. Sunlight filtered through wooden venetian blinds. The rooms contained a tasteful mixture of federal and Hepplewhite furniture, everything polished to a milky iridescence; tabletops and sideboards were arranged with exquisite examples of blue-and-white Chinese Export porcelain. The chime of a grandfather clock sounded in the library, and he noticed the glint of the swinging brass pendulum. Library shelves were packed floor to ceiling with books. He could smell the brittle pages and beeswaxed morocco bindings. Books, novels, and art journals from the 1920s lay scattered in piles on the floor beside comfortable leather chairs, as if abandoned moments before, a few stacked on side tables, bookmarkers still in place. In every room, fresh-cut roses filled Lalique crystal vases adorned with sensuous Bacchantes.

All of this only just registered as his attention was drawn to the magnificent Steinway concert grand in the corner, stacked with piano music, a Chopin étude open above the keyboard. He walked over and examined the score, smiling in recognition. He played the first two phrases, the notes filling the room.

"Piano tuner comes twice a year, spring and fall. The roses are picked from the garden in the back on Mondays and Thursdays. The cleaners come on Tuesday. The grounds crew consists of a brother and sister team from down the road. This is how he set it up in 1921 and this is how he walked away from it in 1929, when he returned to Concord, to an empty house, where he died in the winter of 1933, virtually forgotten. Even the National Academy of Art failed to send the traditional wreath of mourning."

"Incredible."

She waved him on to the formal dining room, set with the best china and silverware. Family portraits covered the walls. French doors led out to the piazza and a view of the Berkshire Hills in the gray distance.

"I can show you his sketches for the rooms, every detail, every arrangement."

He went right to the family portraits, to the crude, almost childlike renditions of the early Puritan divines—each bearing harrowing and flinty stares of absolute purpose, clutching Bibles so that the itinerant artist could avoid the difficulty of depicting their hands; to the dashing Samuel Palmer with long blond hair over the collar of his captain's uniform; and then to the haunting emaciated face of the general in his fine brass-buttoned blue uniform, eyes sunken, one hand on the hilt of a dress sword, the other, tucked inside his jacket.

He turned to his host, sweeping the air with his arm. "Preserved in amber, but why?"

"Well, first I figured Palmer wanted to pass it on lock, stock, and barrel to posterity, a museum, an ego trip. Most artists care only about the paintings. Then I began to think it was a version of the Flaubert thing—live a bourgeois life but have a fantastic mind—as if maybe he wanted people to know that the guy who did the late weird erotic stuff was not some kind of nutcase, but had pulled it out of a stable tradition. Or maybe—"

"He did it for her." He turned and eyed Laura Ryder across the dining room table, her flushed cheeks nearly matching the ruby red in the Murano glass goblets. "He wanted it the way she remembered it from Concord days, how she loved it … and the best piano money could buy."

Laura Ryder reached to straighten a table setting.

"You see" —she looked up and held his gaze, smiling— "what I meant about your letter. It was as if you knew all about the effect Sandra Chillingworth Palmer had on him."

To himself, he murmured under his breath, "Jimmy—old brother, this man did you one better."

She led him through the formal gardens behind the house, a near-precise replication of the Concord garden, down to the brick paths among the roses.

The spacious red barn on its slight rise behind the apple orchard captivated him instantly, a thing anticipated, already deeply ingrained.

"We had to paint the barn this spring, and the engineer says we'll have to redo the foundations and some of the stone siding if we're going to have tourists wandering about." She pushed back the sliding door and they walked into the sunlit studio. "Palmer had it renovated and the skylights put in to give him the proper northern exposure. The new studio was the most practical reason for his move from Concord. He wanted to paint bigger, and his old studio in the carriage house was painfully small, certainly by today's standards."

They walked around through the muted shafts of dusty saffron filtering downward from the high skylights. He breathed in the lingering smells of linseed oil and turpentine, admiring the old raw beams, the hayloft, the flattened zinc tubes and cans of rotted brushes, enjoying the warmth that enfolded him, the rush of good—joyous—feelings.

"We had to get rid of a lot of the old rags and papers and bits of rolled canvas—fire hazard—when we moved the stored paintings. Still, it's pretty much how it was."

Her words had somehow detached themselves from his hearing. He was consumed with the warmth of the boarded-up air and in it another smell—more a sensation—rising like an electric current to his parched brain: marble dust. A wooden partition about eight feet high divided the ground floor of the barn; midway stood a single connecting door with a chipped porcelain handle. He turned the handle and went through into an adjacent studio. Blocks of uncut marble were stacked along the unfinished plank walls. And there in the center of the floor, as if lined up on parade and ready for his inspection, were five rows of finished figures, each about six feet in height. He went to them without hesitation but without rushing, noting the color and veining in the fine Verona marble, the high degree of finish, the detailing broad yet delicate, at once whimsical and dignified, each of the heads bespeaking a certain calm nobility.

"Mill workers," he said as she came over.

He began examining them more closely, caressing the faces: a young woman bent to a primitive loom like a musician to her harp; a man with handlebar mustache in apron and cap overseeing a carding machine; an aged woman, stooped and arthritic, attending ranks of bobbins; a machinist in overalls, his oil can poised to lubricate a camshaft; a matronly lady with wire-rimmed glasses bent to the inspection of finished cloth—a burler, like his grandmother. There were many more, thirty-three by his initial count, including squinty-eyed supervisors, floor sweepers, even a chief engineer in tie and bowler hat.

Finally, he stepped back, going to the far corner to see the group as a whole, to register the time and the labor and the love that had gone into the creation.

"It's a whole … era," he got out finally.

"So you see, I wasn't kidding about Giovanni Maronetti."

"When you said things, I thought you meant—I dunno—letters, documents."

"A couple of letters from Venice agreeing to come over in Palmer's employment." She went to one of the statues and blew at the dust covering the head. "In fact, I was told just the other day, 'firmly in the Venetian sculptural tradition, with perhaps just a touch of the Viennese Jugendstil.'"

He raised his eyebrows in a question, but she beat him to it.

"His granddaughter, last week, out of the blue—not like you, who wrote me such a nice detailed letter—shows up and wants to see the place and do some research." Laura Ryder bent to examine the marble face. "It was a little freaky; she was a dead ringer for her grandmother. But we got along like a house afire. Of course, she'd been here as a child with her father, visited quite a few times. I think she was a little awestruck to find it—you know—pretty much the same."

He had to struggle not to fall all over her with questions. He calmly went over and touched the face of the sculpture, mirroring her gesture.

"They all have a certain quality… ."

"Resemblance," she added. "And look" —she moved to the figure of the old woman setting the bobbins— "even as an old lady, she's got the Chillingworth forehead and the wide-set eyes."

"What were these for?"

"I can show you all the architects' plans in the archives. There was a whole sculptural program set for the mill building in Lowell, kind of like gargoyles, I suppose. A grand beautification project to honor the memory of his wife."

"So what happened?"

"Money ran low—or more likely, the Chillingworths pulled out of the project once the legal battles exploded over the late nudes. And then the Depression hit. The project was abandoned in the last years of the twenties."

"Could they have had a falling-out, Palmer and Maronetti?"

"It's hard to say. Maronetti carved the grave monument for Sandra Chillingworth in Venice, and Palmer was so pleased with his work, he brought him over to do something similar for her monument in Sleepy Hollow. I think he was here for about seven years. He had a room behind the studio back there. Maybe he'd had enough; no one ever accused Palmer of being an easy man to live with in his last years."

He walked over to the back of the studio, where a small bedroom had been added in the corner, a simple partition and door leading to a space big enough for a bed and bureau and washbasin. A window looked out into the orchard. He could see a side entrance and stairs, a tiny outhouse crumbling in the near distance.

"Not much of a life," he said, crossing a patch of light from the window and returning to the studio and the figures.

"Well, Palmer's granddaughter certainly seemed taken by the sculptures. I told her I could get them photographed for her, but she whipped out a camcorder and very systematically documented them. She was fascinated; she seemed to know her away around artworks, up close and personal, if you know what I mean."

He added, "To get the feel of them." Laura Ryder watched with a look of bemusement where his fingers explored one of the marble heads. "What did you say her name was—Sandra?" His voice caught and he had to force the last words out.

She laughed, "Actually, I called her that by mistake as we were working in the archives, and she practically jumped out of her skin. Seems she had a twin—talk about history repeating itself—Sandra, who, I gather, died very sadly last year, poor thing. No, this was Angela, named after the great-aunt."

"Angela," he said, for an instant deflated. "She knew her away around art, you said, chip off the old block."

"An artist? I don't know, but she sure knew her art history lingo—you can smell 'em a mile away." She laughed and made a gesture with her hands of something lacking a certain weight. "Like you, she seemed particularly interested in Palmer's Venetian work, with his diary and court transcripts. And, of course, Sandra Chillingworth Palmer. She latched onto the diary like a lost friend. Her eyes fairly lit up. 'His side of the story!' she exclaimed."

"You said something about letters—Sandra Chillingworth Palmer's letters."

"From Venice, to her twin sister back in Boston. In the diary, Palmer is always complaining about all the letters she writes to her twin, as if he's being left out. I asked Angela about those letters. And she smiled so sweetly, like the cat who had swallowed the canary."

"Did she have the letters?"

"She offered nothing. I couldn't blame her. If I got my hands on those letters, I sure wouldn't blab to anyone."

He sucked in his lower lip. "I would think it would be hard for her— know what I mean?—your family place, and you come back and it's as if you're just another tourist passing through."

"Oh, I don't think that bothered her. She was delighted to have the works so accessible, especially the archives. And I offered her the royal treatment, the guest room in the main house if she wanted to stay, but she turned me down. Buried herself in the Venetian material for half the day, photocopying like crazy, and then, just like that, disappeared into the night with a copy of Palmer's Venetian diary. Didn't even say good-bye."

"Families can be funny."

"Hey, tell me about it."

CHAPTER 23

Excerpt from a 1913 review by Charles Caffin of Joseph Palmer's paintings of Sandra Chillingworth:

The type has something of the character of a fine-blooded racehorse, long in its lines, clean-cut, spare of flesh, the bone and muscle felt beneath it, movement throughout accentuated—unmistakable signs of pedigree. Psychologically, as well, the type is a product of intensive breeding—a cross between the exacting narrowness of Puritanism and the spiritual sensuousness and freedom of Emerson; a transcendentalism of morals and imagination, blended with a little of the questioning and unrest of modern thought. It is, indeed, a new type; strenuous, with a sense of inherited responsibilities, but still having a certain air of self-compelling restraint, as if it held itself back a little in view of possibilities scarcely yet realized.

After a long afternoon in the archives and a candlelit dinner with Laura Ryder at the Red Lion Inn in Stockbridge, he decided to take up his host's invitation and make use of the master guest room in the main house. Not that it took much convincing. It had been Joseph Palmer's bedroom. The temptation had edged their conversation all through dinner. And then there were the etchings.

The Venice etchings hung on the tongue-and-groove paneling of the bedroom. Artist's proofs on seventeenth-century laid paper. Extremely rare and delicate, all in beautifully hand-carved curly-maple frames. She had shown him around, gotten him settled. And once in bed, he could see immediately how the etchings—"the artist's beloved etchings," Laura Ryder had called them—had been strategically placed: to the left of the mirror over the oak bureau, to the side of the Shaker rocker, next to the window, where they might be viewed by the sleeper.

But he was too exhausted, too keyed up to sleep. And on the wall opposite, the etching of the bridge with the two sisters, *his* etching, as if put there to properly welcome him to the life beckoning on the far horizon. With the exception of a few added lines, a slight variation in the wiping, the thing was a near-perfect match of the etching leaning against the back of his desk at the inn. The moonlight shone through the tangle of withered black locust leaves beyond the window and whitened the darkness of the room, bringing out the inky forms in the surrounding artifacts. There was a scent in the air he couldn't place: leather polish, wax, perhaps pine. He glanced out the window to the silhouetted white pine in the near distance. He could not rid himself of the notion that something of the physical presence of the artist remained in the room. Maybe it was the silence, so unlike the familiar buzz of the inn. As the coolness of the fall night penetrated deeper into the room, he was aware of the age that was beginning to eat away at his body, as it had for the artist on his return from Europe in 1917, just a year older than he was now, his twenty-one-year-old wife dead three years before. The loss, the grief, struck through him in a sudden shiver and he nestled further under his comforter, listening to the voice in the court transcript as if it were his own.

A: We are moral only insofar as we care deeply about the excellence of what we do. On the other hand, art is not about conventional morality; it is not about instruction or guidance, or religious uplift, but to give pleasure and open one to life's possibilities.

A: I paint the nude; I paint a body. Personality is completely immaterial to me. As I have already testified now, I no longer paint from the model, but from memory. In this regard, my work is entirely synthetic and a projection of feeling. I care little for detail as such. A woman is a woman is a woman ... a body a body. It is painted well or not; it exists or it does not. How it is interpreted is the business of the observer once the artist has done his job. If the artist has spoken truthfully in his work, he has done his job well.

A: If my colleagues criticize me, so be it. They believe their demure nudes are high art, as proper as their society portraits, graceful and pleasing and soothing in light and color effects. But they fear to probe or imply the latent power of the feminine. For them, beauty is only skin-deep. Their women are domesticated lambs; their bodies forever undefiled, in service to an idealization without the breath of life, certainly no inner life. They are mere ornament and make-believe. To pretend there is no sexual life, no birth and death, is the greatest travesty. To pretend that the nude is just a nude, a pure symbol of some exalted neoclassical state, is rubbish. It is total hypocrisy not to allow human nature her due.

"Yes ... yes." He found the urgent echo of his own voice a comfort, as if he was finally beginning to see with the artist's eyes.

The etchings were memory signatures of all that Palmer had loved and lost. Out of those long, silent, lonely nights at Sangamore would have to come canvas after canvas to fill the daylight hours. He could just make it out in the play of lines and shadow, the alchemist's true calling, of turning life into art, memory into the perennially human. The thing Laura Ryder had said of Joseph Palmer, paraphrasing Henry James: a man on whom nothing was lost. He'd glimpsed as much in the artist's diary and in those hundreds of sketches—as terrifying as they were beautiful. To have loved so hard, love not ethereal but of the body and through the body and utterly in the body—only to lose all. And then, somehow, to have found a way to go on, to remain in touch with the source.

He thought of sitting there with Laura Ryder at his elbow looking at those things, feeling in them the humid heat of the water-saturated city in the spring and summer of 1914—that most horrifying of years: all the most intimate secrets of the bedchamber.

The sketches, hundreds, sticking together in the portfolio, the paper ripped hurriedly from pads, smeared with lead and ink and pastel and sweat and wine and oily secretions and God knew what else: the knife-edged angle of light across distended nipples, blood-matted pubic hair, studies of splayed thighs and buttocks, semen bubbling from ragged, engorged labia, her sister's head cradled against her pregnant breasts, lips bent to kiss the great swollen belly. Studies of faces thrown back in such rapture that the underside of the top palate and teeth was visible—more a death's-head—a pool of sweat in the vee of tendons at the base of her neck.

And the Venice diary, two hundred-plus pages in the artist's precise handwriting, recounting the most intimate details of his struggles with his art and his idolatrous worship of the Chillingworth twins, who became his art. The pages offered glimpses of erotic fixation and tantalizing clues to the inner life—the illicit assignations—of Sandra Chillingworth Palmer, enough to captivate and haunt her granddaughters, even a born sensualist like Angela Palmer, aka Sandy Blue.

"Now you understand," Laura Ryder had told him, "why I could use only a few excerpts in the catalog—much less the sketches. My biography, well, I'll be lucky to get an R rating."

As he had anticipated, there had been pages on Giovanni Maronetti in the diary, the Venetian stonecutter who had been commissioned to make a monument for Sandra Chillingworth Palmer's grave in Venice on the burial island of San Michele. "Another man," Laura Ryder had said, among her many worshipers. Was Giovanni Maronetti the "other man"?

"San Michele," he murmured, giving it the Italian pronunciation in his grandfather's voice, wondrously … the Italian names and places beginning to take him over.

He closed his eyes, comforting himself that he'd drawn near his real quarry. And in his dreams and half dreams, he found himself making a plea to the jury: the artist and defendant, Joseph Palmer, versus the plaintiff, Chillingworth et al.

Ladies and gentlemen, this is what the great artists do best: capture those most genuine of moments—of love and arousal and ecstasy in their subject. Those instants experienced with such intensity that they live on in the mind, survive as rawest untrammeled emotion, stored up during a lifetime and rediscovered in the interlude between sleep and waking, before propriety and aging and disappointment dim them from our eyes. A little luck finds them translated onto canvas, the fine and beautiful and true, transforming as it is transformed into the better essence of ourselves. Ladies and gentlemen of the jury, the artist gives us the truth of ourselves.

Or was he just echoing the source of his quarry, the emanation of a voice passed in the blood and genes, light of light, glimpsed in the pages of a magazine?

And yes, erotica in its beauty and truth, its nuances and complexities of design does approach art; and for that matter, art is grounded in the erotic. Art is, fundamentally, how we imaginatively re-create life...and then hold on to it. The female body has been the nexus and centerpiece of art since the first Neolithic mother goddesses, right through Cycladic figurines, and the sculpture of Praxiteles and the Romans, which fixed and then preserved the female form as an iconic image, continuing on right through the Dark Ages and into the Renaissance and right through Victorian times. The nude has endured as the bearer of ultimate meaning, of beauty and form—and yes, the erotic; the shape and texture and rhythm and color of the human body—the human landscape—is how we best know the world. This, of course, is all hardwired genetics.

Perhaps it is about time the model was able to take control of her own image, make it her own, unencumbered by the preoccupations of intermediaries. In a sense, I guess, I become my own self-portrait. Like the greatest nudes, we exist outside time in another dimension; we become pure image, pure energy, a life force attracting life force—light of light, a testament of the purest gravitational field. In the eye of the beholder, we return life for life. If that is not art, I don't know what is.

When he arrived back at the inn the following day, ballasted with an armload of Xeroxes, he found himself feeling oddly distanced from the place, as if the night at Sangamore, the artist's voice in the diary (and Giovanni Maronetti's name—the very sound and rhythm of the Italian), was hastening him and Sandra on to other worlds. Even the friendly hello from the receptionist (did she ever wonder about Michael Collins, the name put to her by a strange woman only days before?) could not dispel his feeling of otherness. He stood becalmed for a minute in the reception area with his mail, staring at the telephone message from Joe Palmer—that name handed to him on a piece of pink paper having the feel of a reminder, a guilty tap on the shoulder, what with his copy of Joe's father's diary in his hand.

"Please come for dinner on Wednesday at 8:00. Angela will be there—have told her all about you. Ditch Henry," it read.

He walked slowly to his room, feeling as if he'd pushed out just far enough for that tether to snap, having slipped one gravitational field for another. In his room, he even found the piles of books and papers some-how odd, the blinking computer a disquieting presence, an opaque sea into which he had, perhaps, cast one too many stones.

Tomorrow night, less than thirty-six hours and he would know for sure. She couldn't fool her father, not in person. If it really *was* Angela, she would come, brash and bold, and tell William Channing to "go get a life." If it *was* Sandra—and he had little doubt—there was a good chance she'd stand up her dad again. She wouldn't have the nerve, wouldn't be able to handle attempting to play the part of her sister to her father's face. Nor would she be able to deal with his shock at the truth, the implica-tions of her deception, her crime. Unless … unless his presence might make it possible for her, if she knew Michael Collins would stand by her no matter what.

There was a bill from the San Francisco detective and a report summing up his most recent findings—or the lack of such. He and various colleagues in an assortment of guises had tried numerous times to break the security cordon around SandyBlue.com and find out the address or whereabouts of Sandy Blue, but even the communication of a message had been rejected. Bribery of low-level employees was tried twice, but to no avail. Either the staff was incredibly loyal to Sandy Blue or there was a tight cover-up and pretence about her continuing participation at the helm of the company. Further inquiries about Angela Palmer had produced only one match, a grad student in archaeology and anthropology at the University of New Mexico in the early 1990s. This Angela Palmer (the age was right, but the physical description was far from glamorous) had spent numerous summers in the Yucatán and Central America on archaeological digs, received her Ph.D., and then evaporated off the face of the earth after she came down with suspected malaria at a Yucatán dig and was taken to a local hospital in Mérida for treatment. She had been transferred to the Presbyterian Hospital in Albuquerque for follow-up care and treatment for secondary complications. Further inquiries would require substantial funds upfront to send an investigator to Albuquerque to run down potential leads.

He turned from the bay window, where he'd been surveying the square, and sat at the computer and clicked up the screen saver of Saint Augustine at his desk, his saintly face pensively turned toward a lighted window. William had finally found the painting in a book on Renaissance art. It was by the Venetian sixteenth-century artist Vittorio Carpaccio and was part of a cycle of paintings on the wall of a confraternity in Venice.

"Suspected malaria." He tried to factor this new tidbit of information into that confrontation in Sandra's apartment. Angela would have been overwrought, exhausted, disoriented—perhaps already sick, maybe from HIV, or malaria, or some obscure tropical disease (he still hadn't been able to finesse the issue of the pathologist's report with Joe Palmer). Or maybe she'd been losing her looks or was simply depressed and strung out. Maybe Sandra had gone to get a doctor, some medications; maybe Angela had forgotten or left behind her antidepressants or whatever medication one took for malaria. Or maybe they'd had a fight and an overwrought Sandra had fled her apartment to Concord for a day or two, only to find upon her return Angela's body. Instead of calling for help, phoning the police, Sandra had freaked out. Her home, her refuge, her new life after two decades of exile in Europe had been obliterated by the deranged—ruthless—act of her sister. She'd grabbed her wallet and passport—or maybe Angela's passport and credit cards and bank details, if that last sent E-mail message *was* from Angela—and headed for the hills. Would it be Beverly Hills, or Malibu, or Venice, California … or Venice, Italy?

That, at least, was how he'd prefer to present her case to a jury (fled the scene in panic and remained clueless to the mix-up).

And legally, she wouldn't even need a lawyer to tell her she was in deep shit. She could be accused of covering up a death, of leaving the scene of a death and possibly having some complicity in that death, or even worse. Murder? No, not even Angela would have been capable … unless she'd been sick and crazed, a manic-depressive. Then, Joe Palmer's violent breakdown the other afternoon had been pretty damn disturbing, galvanized by something more than disappointment at his daughter's cancellation.

But no, there was no history of violence in the Palmer family … victims, yes, but not perpetrators.

He was content with this version of events, to which his own experience made him privy … Sandra arriving in Concord, to find herself a living ghost amid scenes of her childhood.

Marge Hathaway—dependable Marge; he could rely on Marge's judgment. She had known Sandra instantly and welcomed her with open arms. And the woman Marge had embraced had been happy for the homecoming.

And tomorrow night, Sandra would join her father for dinner ... or probably falter on the doorstep. What was she thinking—Who the hell is William Channing? And Michael—had she read about the Michael Collins in the papers? What did she remember about him? Could she resolve the discrepancy between those names, between the Michael Collins she remembered and the accused?

On the other hand, who better to understand her problem—the dilemma of a parallel existence and the lies it necessitated—and ease her back, help her ... love her? And she had the diary, which told the truth about the family connections. Surely they were on the same path. The arc of the years was coming full circle.

Not to mention their child ... Michael Collins was father to her child.

He lowered his face to his hands, feeling the pounding in his brain coming on again, that part of him that resisted a life in the shadows, that wanted certainty, wanted it over one way or another.

A happy voice from the computer announced the arrival of E-mail. It was from the legal department of the *Boston Globe*.

Mr. Michael Collins: We have made the assumption from the material you sent via E-mail that you are the Michael Collins who was assistant to Congressman Neeley and whose car was found abandoned last month in Lowell. We want to thank you for your tips and countervailing evidence, if not outright repudiations, concerning the indictments that came out of the recent grand jury investigation into influence peddling surrounding the Lowell Plan in late 1980s and 1990s. We have also taken note of what you described as your precarious and dangerous situation. For these and other reasons, we have notified the appropriate authorities of our possession of this information. Under normal journalistic circumstances, we might have made use of this material in our reporting and certainly would not reveal our sources; but in this circumstance, given the highly charged political nature of the case, and coming in the midst of the current political season, this newspaper cannot be placed in a situation of potentially harboring unsolicited information that might benefit one side or another, possibly swaying a close election race. There is also the complicating factor that your chosen form of communication turns out to be the E-mail account of a deceased woman, an account that should be defunct, and so doubly contaminates the information provided. All these issues make communications problematic. On the other hand, we would be open to further thoughts from you regarding the current investigation. If you wished to provide a full account of your situation and your bona fides, including exculpatory evidence, we would be willing to consider printing the piece, but only under your name.

He read no further and immediately disconnected.

"That stupid son of a bitch."

It had been a calculated risk: an attempt to put a bee up Mahoney's ass.

What else should he have expected from that mealymouthed *Globe* reporter. That asshole could have had the story of lifetime, and instead he'd gone right up the corporate ladder and handed it over to the paper's legal department, and let the lawyers do their thing: protect everybody's ass.

And now he was in real jeopardy. Mahoney would get wind of the *Globe's* information; he'd either try to find Michael before the police or FBI did; or he'd make sure the files in Washington were expunged of documents that might bolster Michael Collins's innocence. How many memos had Michael written questioning cost overruns and padded accounting and missing funds? On the other hand, he hadn't exactly bothered to run down the irregularities, either.

Less than thirty-six hours until the diner with Joe.

Could they trace E-mail over a phone line from an unregistered source? Did the server automatically record the incoming number? He had no idea. Of course, if the police went to Sandra's landlady in Cambridge and discovered that William Channing had made off with Sandra's computer, they might be able to trace him back to the Concord Inn.

Jack Mahoney probably already knew of Michael Collins's resurrection. And now Michael had committed himself to refuting Mahoney's lies, or his cohort's lies, given under oath in the grand jury. But without documents, it would come down his word against the word of others. In the end, and it might take years, the money would talk, those who had taken and spent money—which would turn up: the bank accounts, the

Visa cards, the padded invoices—a nightmare for the accountants. The money trail would ultimately substantiate his testimony and refute the lies of his accusers, who had fingered Michael Collins under oath, thinking he would be out of the way.

It was almost as if his wily lawyerly self had laid the perfect trap from the get-go. Even if the statute of limitations had run out on the original crimes, they would be convicted of perjury. He smiled. The lies and cover-up, like a law of nature.

His heart sank at the thought of years of litigation and legal fees. There was his house in Washington, all his IRAs. His government pension would be safe, but he'd lose everything else. And he had already spent almost half the bribe money. The fake passport for Giovanni Maronetti, alone, had cost twenty thousand; it was good, disturbingly good, a lot better than the fake driver's license.

He switched off the computer, unplugged it, disconnected the modem and stuck it in a corner beneath a side table. His desk was returned to its near-original state, with the etching propped against the back, the green morocco *Walden*, the silver-framed photo of his mother, and the addition of Sandra's watercolor from her landlady. Items from a used-up life ready for departure. All would neatly fit in a small overnight bag, along with the artist's dairy.

He sat back, pondering.

But there would be no going back. After Joe's dinner, the future would lie elsewhere.

Then he remembered the bit of toy railroad track, which he'd banished to a drawer of the desk. He took out the curved piece of model railroad track going back to his father's childhood. What a pathetic residue of an even more pathetic life. Although Jimmy had obviously taken comfort in such heirlooms of his father. Jimmy had still loved the man. How was that possible after what he'd witnessed? How could two brothers be so different? How could twins like Sandra and Angela?

He fingered the bit of track. Maybe he owed Jimmy one last favor.

This, along with a few other things, still needed doing before William Channing could properly be given the heave-ho for another life.

CHAPTER 24

That afternoon, he went out for his farewell jog; he figured he'd have to spend the next afternoon, before the dinner with Joe, in final preparations for a move on short notice.

The afternoon was clear, with only a breath of low cirrus clouds against a pale blue sky. It was cool, almost cold, the first real hints of the winter to come, which would ravish the trees and spoil Joe's produce and transform the countryside into a stark, hard-edged approximation of itself.

He passed Emerson's house and scolded himself for never taking the time to tour the place with Annie Torcelli, with whom he'd spent a number of happy evenings sitting at Pete's bar. She was just closing the place for the night and he stopped and went over and said hello. Annie smiled and winked, kidding him about the beard and his scholarly affectations. Of course, Thoreau used to turn up on the Emerson's doorstep unannounced all the time, she told him; it was a disconcerting habit and there were many who thought Thoreau not a little in love with Emerson's wife.

"Well, perhaps, I'm a little in love with Annie," he told her, taking her hand and kissing it.

Annie Torcelli looked at her watch and pulled him inside.

"For you, gallant William, I'll give you the five-minute quickie tour."

The old house really was a marvel, everything of the scholar and writer's life preserved, perhaps the model for Joseph Palmer's conceit of a similar kind at Sangamore. He asked her on the way out what it was about Emerson that had so intrigued her as to spend her days giving tours to ditzy tourists. The man was after the truth, she said. He was unflinching. And she told him the story of how when Emerson's first wife, his beloved Ellen, died, he'd gone and opened her grave a year later, forcing himself to witness the horrid finality of death. And fifteen years after his five-year-old son, Waldo, had succumbed to scarlet fever, he made himself open the child's coffin to gaze upon its tiny remains. "Imagine the grief that dwelled within these walls," she said, ushering him out the door. "A man compelled to confront such things and yet continue to believe in the enduring glory and majesty of the physical world."

Annie's tale of grief fascinated and repelled him, tapping into an inner darkness. Yes, it had occurred to him to dig up Sandra's grave, if it could have resolved anything … but no, he could never have summoned the courage—or would it be madness?—to confront death in such a way.

"Are you okay, William?"

He banished such macabre thoughts and kissed Annie Torcelli on the cheek, then waited as she closed up and set the alarm system. A police car pulled up and officer Slotnik waved them over.

"You two see any kids on bicycles riding around, kids who don't look like they should be in Concord?"

"What do you mean by that, Don?" asked Annie, scowling.

"Kids, you know, not local."

"You mean, black," said Annie.

"I mean little thieves who have been breaking into cars at the Walden Pond parking lot, and stealing credit cards from tourists. How 'bout you, professor? You seem to get around about as much as anybody I know. Seen anything" —Slotnik eyed Ellen— "out of the ordinary?"

"Just the usual suspects."

"Will you be at the pub tonight, professor? You're not thinking of leaving us anytime soon, are you?"

"Wouldn't miss the company for the world."

"You all let me know now…."

Slotnik saluted and sped off.

He jogged out the Carlisle Road in the direction of the Old Manse, where he was struck by a profoundly odd and wonderful sight. On the grounds of the Old Manse was an encampment of Civil War soldiers in blue. Fires burned in front of pup tents. Rifles stacked. Soldiers stood and sat in groups, quietly contemplating the approaching dusk. The stillness of the scene was captivating, like something out of an old daguerreotype.

And there, to the side of the commander's tent, where an American flag fluttered, a tall figure sat on horseback, wearing the broad-brimmed hat of a cavalry officer. He walked closer to the mounted figure, whose face was in shadow beneath his hat. His hand was thrust into the front of his brass-buttoned tunic, and one stirruped leg was clearly a false one, a period leather prosthesis of some kind. The man sat upright, staring off toward the setting sun, as if intent on some inner vision. The resemblance to Civil War captain—by war's end, general—Joseph Manning Palmer was uncanny. William wanted to go over and speak to this soldier in blue, but he could not bring himself to do so, for fear of dissipating the illusion before he had properly absorbed it.

Then he spied another of the regulars from the pub, Dave Parker, the park ranger who did interpretive tours of the revolutionary battle sites. He made his way over to the stone wall, where Dave glowered out at the Civil War reenactment.

"You don't look very pleased, Dave," he said.

"I was against the permit, but I guess they have as much right to do their thing here as anybody."

"A little strange, I guess, so close to the Revolutionary battlefields."

"I wouldn't go as far as sacrilegious, maybe disrespectful, but actually, Captain Palmer's regiment was mustered on the grounds of the Old Manse before they marched off to the train station for Boston and points south."

"So the guy on the horse there, he's supposed to be Captain Palmer?"

"He's paying homage to the man. He lost a leg in Vietnam. He's researched his subject down to his underwear and hairstyle. These reenactors are fanatic about getting the details right. And there are no radios, no ice coolers, and no Coleman electric lanterns. Everything's authentic. He *is* Captain Palmer."

"It's like a dream out there."

"They're dreaming all right; they're stepping back and dancing in slow motion at the very edge of the dark woods."

"Men they never knew, whose blood they don't even carry."

"Yes, but they remember nonetheless. They celebrate the old Victorian virtues, a time when duty, honor, country meant something. There's none of the *me generation* out there."

There was the smell of wood smoke and coffee and pan-fried chicken.

William, a little dreamy himself, said "And then the trains will take these sleepers south."

"'To see the elephant,' as they called it."

"Without the railroad, hard to see how they could have fought the Civil War."

"And won it," Dave added. "If there had been railroads in 1776, the British would have suppressed the rebellion in a matter of months."

"And you, Dave, would be telling a very different story."

He jogged on, the purple dusk engulfing him. He did not bother with the Palmer Farm, since he already had his invitation for the following evening, nor the old Palmer homestead, because that was a thing now complete in itself, nor the family graves in Sleepy Hollow, whose stories were already well known to him—not after Annie Torcelli's ghastly tale about Emerson. Instead, he went straight out to Walden Pond and the site of Thoreau's cabin, where he would wait for the regular appearance of Tom Jandos, whose responsibility it was to make sure no stragglers got left behind when the park was closed.

He stood on the wooded shore and gazed out at the smooth face of the pond pricked with incipient starlight, in the gloaming, a thing of infinite extent. He held out his arms as if in embrace of a dancer, stepping side to side in a slow, awkward rhythm … the Johnny Rivers ballad, when he had first embraced her. He thought, too, of how Thoreau had fallen in love with a girl of seventeen, Ellen Sewall, pursuing her in his awkward way, only to have his marriage proposal rejected, a disappointment and loss that filled the remainder of his days. The loss was ultimately translated into Thoreau's humorous description of his pursuit of an elusive loon over the surface of Walden Pond: rowing over to one sighting and the next, only to have the loon disappear and then appear someplace else; all the while, the poet, listening to its plaintive call, had endeavored to divine the thoughts of his quarry. Not unlike the way he was trying to read Sandra's mind at a remove.

Had the hunter become the hunted, like the dance of the matador and the bull? In the dance, they were one and the same, all his means of pursuit and capture mirrored in his quarry, his instincts for evasion embodied in her fugitive soul. Both as necessary to each other as life itself.

He paused, his arms outstretched to the lovely illusion reflected in the quicksilver glass before him: watchful, waiting.

And there, coming along the shore path with plunging stride and beaked nose beneath the crisp brim of his ranger hat, was Tom Jandos, and like a muted wind chime, the bunch of keys to the parking lot gates were jingling at his belted waist.

"Hey, Tom, lovely sunset this evening."

"Missed most of it," grumbled Tom. "Had to report a car break-in. Lady had her credit cards stolen."

"Kind of spoils the atmosphere for you, I'll bet."

"Don Slotnik spoils it far more. Did you know he's been asking about you?"

"About me?"

"In the last few days, he's asked me twice if I thought you were legit, a real scholar."

"Well, I hope you didn't blow my cover."

"He said he checked with Wayne State and they never heard of you."

"That's because I'm a visiting professor *and* I'm on sabbatical."

"Don't explain it to me; I couldn't care less."

"Well, I hope Henry Thoreau will vouch for me."

"After fighting off the developers for twenty years, I've got more things to worry about than these little vandals."

"Was the pond really in that much danger?"

"Two hundred condos, rabbit warrens, just across the road, with the topmost units having views over the hill yonder and into the pond proper."

"That's awful."

"Builder named Mahoney—you see his crap all up and down One twenty-eight and Four ninety-five."

"Huh, no kidding. You stood up to the son of a bitch, then."

"Me and Robert Redford and every celebrity I could recruit."

"You got Redford?"

"And half a dozen more names. Amazing the effect of celebrated names in this day and age."

"You saved Walden, Tom; the world owes you thanks."

"I did it for me, not the world."

"You and Henry."

"Henry would have gotten bulldozed."

"So tell me, Tom. If you had to leave me with one thing, one thought about Henry, what would it be?"

Tom stood for a moment and pawed at the jut of his chin, lifting his great prehensile nose to the evening air.

"Henry believed in what he wrote down, that the poet is the preserver of the world, that his words are the elements—the atomic particles, if you will—of which Walden is made, which time can no longer alter, and thus is preserved for all who would prospect in his realm."

"He aspired to be God, then?"

"He aspired to contain the universe for just a moment or two before letting it go on—like a butterfly cupped in your palm, just long enough to conjure up the former and present inhabitants of these woods, including the likes of you and me."

"So, we exist at Henry's sufferance."

"And he at ours."

"Because he so loved the world."

"That he would suffer anything to get it between the pages of a book."

He took the ranger's arm and gave it a squeeze.

"Tom, it's been good to know you ... to know that Henry has so many devoted friends."

He made his way back to town by way of the railroad tracks, along the deep cutting that passed just behind Walden Pond.

And there for a moment as he made his way along the tracks, his father's voice came to him:

"Oh, Jimmy Collins ... a thousand mile a track he laid ... a thousand mile a sweat he poured ... his life a roadbed of constant sorrow ... except to those who knew his love or whiskey fist."

The little ditty kept passing through his mind, words passed on to him and his brother, Jimmy, from their father when they were children, with no more history or elaboration than that their great-great-grandfather had built—as if he had done it single-handedly—the Fitchburg Railway. An epigraph, a verse sung around a campfire … a life and heritage surviving in a few pitiful sentiments.

Or perhaps in Henry's words …

I had already bought the shanty of James Collins, an Irishman who worked on the Fitchburg Railroad, for boards. James Collins' shanty was considered an uncommonly fine one. When I called to see it he was not at home. I walked about the outside, at first unobserved from within, the window was so deep and high. It was of small dimensions, with a peaked cottage roof, and not much else to be seen, the dirt being raised five feet all around as if it were a compost heap. The roof was the soundest part, though a good deal warped and made brittle by the sun. Door-sill there was none, but a perennial passage for the hens under the door board. Mrs. C. came to the door and asked me to view it from the inside. The hens were driven in by my approach. It was dark, and had a dirt floor for the most part, dank, clammy, and aguish, only here a board and there a board which would not bear removal....

The tracks ahead gleamed in the slanting moonlight, the railroad embankment lifting from the surrounding right-of-way, thick with bush and bramble, only to dip once again into a stony trench as it approached the Route 2 overpass. He had rarely gone in this direction and certainly never at night. A solitary man walking off the beaten track at night might attract notice. Thoreau had relished his moonlight strolls, but everyone knew Henry, who took some pride in remaining all but invisible to the casual observer.

And so the son of Jimbo Collins walked the ties with a slow, deliberate gait, as if to count each and every one, carved notches in the earth, laid in the millions by the dirt-poor Irish laborers who had landed on Boston's docks. Thoreau referred to the ties as "sleepers," embodiments of the poor Irish who had invested themselves in the laying of track. But it was not these sleepers that attracted his gaze, but the old right-of-way, where he knew the shanties had been, the toolboxes of the laboring men, the laughable scraps of board and nail and the single window that had been the home of one James Collins.

Tracks laid by James Collins had carried Captain Joseph M. Palmer and his company to bloody southern battlefields, the same tracks that had secretly spirited off Joseph Palmer and Sandra Chillingworth to Boston and a liner to Glasgow and on to London and Paris and Venice.

His eye was caught by a dent in the forest floor, off to the side of the roadbed, where the embankment evened out and merged with the surrounding woods, there among some stunted silver birch and ash trees, almost invisible except for the peculiar texture of the pearly teal light and the cross-hatching of shadow on the leaf-layered earth. He walked the thirty feet to the rectangular depression, no more than a root cellar in dimensions, a nothing or next to nothing ... and yet, and yet; he circled it, skeptical, knowing he'd passed this point a dozen, maybe two dozen times in daylight or dusk and thought nothing of it. Couldn't even claim it a thing produced by human hands. He tested the sides, the center, but found no stones and no boards. He knelt and felt about in the cold, damp leaves, sensing a slight declivity in the surrounding area, a circumference ridge no more than an inch or two ... nothing. He thrust his hand deeper into the cold-layered earth, and like some furtive grave robber, the smell of sand and clay and rotted leaves filled his lungs. His fingers touched something hard with roughened, rusted edges. He took another breath and thrust his hand farther still into the deep, loamy, memory-starved earth.

He took his time with his last meal in the dining room, slowly finishing off the best bottle of wine the cellar had to offer—at $345 a bottle, a bargain, especially since Jack Mahoney was paying. Jack, who had failed to breech the Walden woods, thwarted by a laconic park ranger with celebrity backup.

The thought tempered the sadness he felt at how completely the memory of his mother had been extinguished from the inn. She had loved her seven years working in the place and the new life it had meant. Ridiculous, if walls had memories, that anyone should know or care. The inn was just a smooth-running engine of self-referential charm and hospitality, promoting a golden colonial past but having no more to do with that past then the guests who brought their ready-made expectations in the front door. New owners had taken it over just three years before. One was of Polish ancestry—she still spoke with an accent; she had run a B and B in Nahant. The dining room chef—a Cambodian refugee, had trained in New York and gone on to Paris to refine his culinary skills, and now he tantalized the town with his fusion dishes of Asian-French cuisine. The maids and housecleaning staff were mostly Hispanics from Central America. The waitresses were a mix of college women, pausing to make a few bucks before graduate school, and a few locals, like his mother had been, from blue-collar backgrounds in South Boston or Lawrence. The staff clocked in and out, the guests checked in and out, town citizens came and went ... and soon he, William Channing, aka Michael Collins, would be gone, too. And what of his transient life would remain within the walls of the inn?

There were only places and names surrounded by silence.

The after-dinner pianist was playing in the lounge, and for some reason he had forgone his usual repertoire of show tunes for a suite of Scarlatti sonatas: the classical stuff normally reserved for his final set, when the real aficionados lingered or showed up late. The pianist worked the harpsichord textures nicely, the rhythmic suspensions seeming to surround the last waitress in the dining room as she finished setting her tables for breakfast.

He knew that Scarlatti. In fact, he remembered sitting at the piano in the cocktail lounge with his mother as she took him through that very sonata. He'd gotten it—played it well; and she had sat back, relaxing her aching back, and smiled. And in the smile, in the music, the memory of her voice: "Oh, Giovanni, would've loved to hear you play it, Michael. He'd stand over me as a little girl and make sure I'd do my practice. Get home early, he would—can you believe it?—from his workshop to make sure I did my practice. He lived for that in me and I was so desperate to do him proud. Ah, it weighs on me still that I didn't do better with the piano. I remember your grandpa saying there's not a more beautiful thing on earth than a woman playing the piano."

The sudden recovery of memory was a shock to his system: the capriciousness of the past, even for an expert.

Through a haze, struggling for more recollections, he found himself staring at a pair of woman's hands hovering over a linen tablecloth. He'd been remembering his mother's large, agile hands, and these he saw now were far from beautiful or artistic; they were pudgy, reddened, arthritic. The hands slowed in their task and then came to rest by a collection of tiny Smucker's jam jars arranged on a plate. He lifted his dreaming eyes to the profiled face of the old woman, listening, too, to something contained in the Scarlatti—a lingering trill and then the promise of release in the closing cadence. The woman in the beige uniform with kelly green striping turned to him as if in silent assent. She nodded. Her face was heavy, jowly, a mop of auburn-gray hair. The instant of recognition caught them both off guard.

Cathy—her name was prominently displayed on her uniform—carefully flipped the last coffee cup and walked straight over and sat herself down at his table.

"Michael Collins. For a month now, I knew it was you, but I couldn't quite put the face right, and the beard. But it's your mother's nose; I see it clear as day now."

She'd never used the strong Southie accent with him before, now released from her large bosom like a sigh of relief. The sound of it was of the streets of Lowell as a boy; it was sweet and calmed his panic at hearing his name spoken out loud. The tone of her voice had not conjured the Michael Collins in the newspapers, but a vintage of some rarity … of childhood, and the comfort of maternal care.

"Cathy," he said, gauging the eyes, trying to see behind the folds and the crow's-feet and the pasty slack along the jaw. "Your hair was longer."

"I was younger, dear boy, and you were the demon dishwasher—your ma saw to that."

"You were her best friend."

"We were thick as thieves, your ma and me. She was the first to show me the ropes. I worshiped the ground she stood on, the way she worked her way up to the front desk and then the office."

"You giggled a lot. You got me hot chocolate. Once, you made me a banana split and I ate it in the corner of the kitchen while we separated cutlery from the dishwasher."

"You were such a handsome lad, a scholar, if I remember, the light of your ma's life. And I've been thinking about you, what with that fella Collins in the newspapers so much recently." She caught herself a moment. "Jesus, I thought that had to be you, coming from Lowell and everything—not that I believed what they said about you, not for a moment."

"Oh, not me Cathy. I changed my name years ago. I couldn't stand the name. It was my father's name."

"Ah, yes, I remember hearing about him. A hard man, was he?"

"He broke my mother's nose and ran out on her."

Cathy made a pained face.

"I'd forgotten that."

"She played that Scarlatti."

Cathy's brown eyes lingered on his, as she fingered an ivory crucifix at her throat.

"Ah, the music—yes, for a moment there I thought it was your mother; it came to me like that, Moira sitting in the lounge with her hair all tight back and practicing, with no one to hear except me and a few of the other girls setting up. Oh, such a talent she had, the poor darling. I loved that woman. She thought the world of you, Michael. It was such a comfort to her that you were in school with all those good Concord families, and her moving up, too. So proud she was."

In a motion of purest instinct he reached for her hand.

"It's William now, Cathy. Bill, if you like."

"William—yes, of course." She smiled. "Mr. Channing, I loved to hear her play."

"Bill."

"Bill."

"She played well, didn't she? She should have become a professional pianist. She could have been a music teacher."

His words came out almost as a pleading, recruiting of a fellow conspirator. As if in reply, she took his hand.

"Oh, it's a strange world. Someone like her comes along for the likes of me: so much talent and such a fine belief in herself. Sometimes people don't like those who are always pushing for promotions, but I never heard a word spoken against her."

He glanced a moment to the window, catching a glitter of headlights in the maples. Then, seeing her reflected face across from his, the subterfuge of luminous night erasing the decades, he smiled freely. The pianist had switched to a Bach prelude.

"Some of my happiest times were listening to her play the piano. I'd lie in bed at night and hear her play downstairs. It took me out of myself, Cathy; it took me far away."

"And when the cancer took her—oh, Jesus, Mary, and Joseph—it took something awful out of me, let me tell you. For a woman like her, who'd gotten so far. And to go so fast. It was something terrible to behold."

"I barely made it back for the funeral." He took the wine bottle and poured what was left into an extra glass and pushed it toward his fellow time traveler. "Join me. We'll toast her memory."

"Oh, I can't, against the rules." She touched the glass and smiled. "Moira was such a fighter, you know. Wouldn't admit she was sick, even to herself. I remember going to visit her in the hospital and she being all big smiles. She was planning to beat the thing. Your brother—Jimmy—wasn't it—wanted to have you come back from Vietnam, but your ma would have none of it. Didn't want you to see her that way. Not until she was good again."

"Is that right...."

"Oh my, she was a fighter. She'd be sitting there propped up in her hospital bed with a stack of travel brochures at her elbow. And she'd tell me, 'Cathy, I'm off to Italy. I've told the doctor I've bought my ticket and he's to have me on my feet in two weeks.'"

He touched her hand again. "My grandfather was from Italy, from Venice."

"Venice, that's the place. She said she was going there as soon as she was back on her feet."

He leaned forward across the table. "When did she change her name? When did she take back her father's name?"

"The name? Yes, what was that name she changed it to?"

"Maronetti." He picked up his glass and touched it to hers in a toast, pausing while she glanced around, then took up her glass and put it to her lips. "Cheers."

"Oh, sure, Maronetti, when she got the promotion to the front office, when she finished up the accounting course."

"You see, Cathy, Collins was always a bad-luck name."

"Ah, I hear you." She sipped again at the wine, gazing into his face. "I hear you, lad—you dear lad, your secret is forever safe with Cathy. And Maronetti ... what a lovely name it is, too."

Staring into Cathy's tearful eyes, hearing his grandfather's name from her lips, he knew that Michael Collins, like William Channing, was history, and where his new name might take him.

CHAPTER 25

———

Joe Palmer answered his knock almost immediately.

"It's you, William." He sighed, as if relieved.

"Bill, Joe, Bill."

"Come on in, boy; it's good to see you."

Joe wore threadbare tan corduroys, a blue button-down oxford-cloth shirt, frayed at the collar, and Teva sandals. His short gray hair was neatly combed. Even his cracked and hardened hands seemed softer in the lingering handshake, looking a little puffy and red, as if they had undergone a good scrubbing.

"I guess I'm a little early," William said, looking at his watch. The place, spruced up, smelled of wood polish, candles glittering in the dinning room, meat roasting in the oven.

"No, no, you're fine." Joe ushered him into the living room. A fire burned in the cast-iron stove. "Take a seat. I've just opened a bottle of Glenlivet—to ward off the chill, to celebrate."

He could see that the bottle already had a good two-inch deficit. "What are we celebrating?"

"Reunion."

"Just a smidgen, okay? I'm not much of scotch drinker. My father was an alcoholic, a bad one at that, and whiskey was his preferred weapon."

Joe eyed him kindly, as if appreciative of the revelatory intimacy, and poured him a touch.

"I've never known a *good* alcoholic, Bill."

While Joe went to the cast-iron stove and tossed another log on the fire, William sat back on the sofa and sipped the scotch, now glad to have it, anything to soothe his nerves, help the headache that had pressed like a splintered bone in back of his eyes all day.

"So, you actually talked her into coming, after she stood you up." He held up his glass in a show of support.

"She called back, just like she said she would. Wanted to come *here*." Joe raised a hand to indicate the farm. "I said fine, I'd cook her the freshest meal she'd ever had."

"Not roast raccoon, I hope."

"Venison."

"You're kidding me."

"Someone hit a big doe out on Route Two last night."

"Hey, roadkill."

"Are you okay, Bill?"

"Forgive me—long day. Busy, couldn't get out for my usual run. But this is good stuff." He drained his glass with a show of deliberation and poured himself a refill. "So ... you told her I'd be here?"

Joe looked intently at the younger man. "Yes. It's been such a long time since I've seen her, Bill, and after the mess before—well, I thought somebody of her generation—might be nice. She seemed quite taken with the idea."

He groaned inwardly. "Listen, I couldn't stand my father, either. I'm not sure I'd even want to be in the same room with the man—even *if* the bastard is still alive."

Joe looked judiciously into his glass, muscles flexing thoughtfully in his red-veined cheeks.

"Sorry, Joe, didn't mean that to sound the way it might have sounded."

"I was absolutely intent on being the best father possible to my two girls, after what I went through with my own father."

"Tell me about your daughters, Joe. You've said very little about them."

"Identical twins. Beautiful girls. For years, they were inseparable, lived in their own world, with their own language. Then puberty hit ... and they became different as the sun and moon."

"How so?"

"Sandra ... she was, well, she was the quiet one."

"Quiet! Quiet?"

"Relatively speaking."

"You said she'd died, Joe. Tell me what happened."

"If you don't mind, I'd rather not go into it."

"Sandra, huh, no doubt named after the famous Sandra Chillingworth Palmer." William slammed his empty glass on the table between them. "I got to tell you, Joe, Sangamore—those late paintings, something else. And that neat white clapboard farmhouse and the red barn ..." He waved his hand with a histrionic flourish. "Could have blown me over with a feather."

Joe watched him uneasily, his heavy gray-brown eyes seeming to register the near-manic facial rhythms in the younger man.

"Do you know, since you told me you were going to Sangamore for your research, I haven't been able to get it off my mind. I went into the office this morning and figured it out on my calculator, the days, roughly, when I saw my father. I was two when he came back from France. Three weeks in August, sometimes four at Sangamore. Christmas for a couple of days. He did make it for my graduation from Emerson. He was back in Concord by then, during the Depression. He never managed to make it to a single boat race. I came up with five hundred and twenty-five days total, give or take."

"But *quality time* with dad. And Sangamore, Joe, a paradise." He raised his glass in salute.

"Rules and routine. I could never bother him while he was working. I was never allowed in the studio, never. His lunch was brought to him in the studio by the housekeeper. Sometimes at dawn or dusk, he'd be out in the meadows doing sketches. I wasn't allowed within a hundred yards. In August, when I had my few weeks with my father, we had a formal dinner every evening. Aunt Angela was always there, chaperoning, so to speak. They talked about art and poetry and people they'd known in Venice. In their conversation, around the edges, they would reference my mother with a kind of awed rapture, but they would never utter her name. Odd, don't you think? After dinner, he'd sometimes take me for a walk, if the moon was up and the weather fine. Sometimes he read to me in the library: Henry Thoreau, as you might expect, what with the connection with his father. He never laid a hand on me to comfort me or discipline me. I revered him. I was terrified of him."

"Bet you were a great dad, Joe. Everything he wasn't, huh?"

"Raised by females. Nurses and nannies. Mother Chillingworth, the matriarch, forced me to take piano until I ran away from home. Then I was sent to boarding school. Manchester most summers and a dismal round of garden parties. There was sailing and rowing—thank God. And my aunt's friends, her artsy crowd of Boston hangers-on. She fancied herself a poet. If she hadn't had a crush on this sculptor who worked for my father at Sangamore, I don't know if I'd have gotten there the little I did."

William leaned forward, fingering his empty glass, like a fisherman aware of the sudden tension on the line. "The guy who did the figures of the mill workers—a boyfriend, huh?"

"Angela Chillingworth, my aunt Angie, refused to take the train. Always insisted on taking the Chillingworth Packard, riding high on those sweet-smelling leather seats, a lunch packed for the all-day trip to the Berkshires. By the time we'd get there, she'd be on the edge of her seat with anticipation. They were real pals, she and Giovanni. They laughed a lot together. You see, she had posed for him when he made the monument for my mother in Sleepy Hollow—and the one in Venice, too, I suppose. She never got over that."

"Ah, the monument—wonderful thing."

"Wonderful man. In some ways, I was closer to him than my own father. He had a heart, let me tell you. Took me swimming at the pond. Let me in his studio to see him work. But what I really loved was the little kitchen garden he had behind his room in the barn. He'd grow stuff for me. So when I got there in August, there'd be tomatoes and squash and corn ready to be tended and harvested. Christ, I'd almost forgotten about that. Take me blueberry picking, show me places that hadn't been picked out by the locals. He sang when he worked, gorgeous deep tenor voice. A demon for work. I always thought his things were so much more *real* than what my father did."

The younger man looked at his watch. "She's late," he snapped.

"Traffic. Here, have another drop."

"Did she say where she'd be coming from?"

"Manchester, I think, been staying at a motel in Manchester-by-the-Sea. The twins went there a lot as children."

"Tell me something, Joe. Why don't you have a single fucking photograph of your children around this place? I'm sorry, it's just a little weird."

Joe sat back, eyeing his guest, his leaden gaze then lifting to the walls and all the prints, the nineteenth-century children, apples in hands and pockets, more piled into their skirts.

"Bill, I grew up with pictures of my mother everywhere—on the walls, in photo albums and scrapbooks. She was a widely celebrated beauty. People look at you and wonder when you have a mother like that. They see your daughters and they wonder. Everyone thinks that genes are just handed down in neat little closed packages from one generation to the next, but, in fact, they are open books to be read by all. I was raised by women, and yet I knew nothing of them."

"Nothing, but you must've been surrounded by beauty."

"Beauty and breeding, as they used to say."

"The late paintings, Joe—such incredible things."

"Terrible things."

"Terrible?"

"Not until I was thirteen, did I have any hint. Rumors, of course, scandal, curiosity about the trial … but not the thing itself. I think I feared it, for I did not actively seek it out."

A log popped in the fireplace. They both jumped and leaned back from one another.

"Then it found me, at Sangamore. Hot summer … blueberries were scarce, water to be hauled to the tomato patch three times a day. I'd been down to the pond to cool off, and on the way back to the house I heard the sound of the chisel and that distinct snap of marble chips rattling on the floorboards of the barn. I couldn't imagine anyone working in that heat. I tried Giovanni's door, the room that connected with his studio, but it was locked; I'd never known it to be locked. There was music playing, a jazz saxophone, Aunt Angela's windup Victrola. I circled around to the front of the barn, and low and behold, the sliding door to my father's studio was open a crack. My father was away for a couple of days, called to a board meeting of the National Academy in New York. Maybe the housekeeper had been tidying up and had forgotten to lock it. I didn't think much about it; I just slipped in.

"My nostrils stung with fumes of spirits and turpentine, linseed oil and drying varnish. And in the hazy light pouring in from the skylights, I was suddenly made aware of all the paraphernalia of my father's work: easels and rolls of canvas, stretchers and old frames, and shelves of brushes and paints. And then there were the paintings, some finished and some not. I suppose one might say I discovered the other half of the human race. I wasn't that shocked, but I was faced with a distinct quandary. You see, I had never quite connected the person of my father with what he did. And suddenly, through the dust and smells of that place, I discovered what was true and beautiful in his eyes. What he loved. My mother—but *no* mother, and—well, a woman and a world that had nothing to do with me. I walked in a near trance, and found, to my chagrin, that my young body in my wet bathing suit had its own forthright response to his vision. It was my first lesson in what philosophers have called our 'higher nature': that our abstract notions of beauty, what the eye reveals and the body desires, are inextricably bound together."

Headlights flashed across the front window, grew in intensity, and then faded. They turned as one to the light and then back to the wood fire without exchanging looks.

"Throughout, I could hear the sound of the chisel and the world-weary music of the saxophone. There was a hayloft across an entire side of the barn, above the two studios. I climbed up the rickety ladder. The hayloft was full of rotting mattresses and bits of old leather harnesses and spider webs and the muck of barn swallows. I crawled on hands and knees, terrified of making a sound. I got over to Giovanni's side and pulled myself to the edge of the loft, where I had a good view of him from behind, where he was working on his marble. Aunt Angela was seated on the posing stand in an old muslin gown that hung off her shoulders, a fashion from before the war. The sculpture was of a woman at a hand loom. The face and neck and shoulders were nearly complete. Giovanni was sweating torrents in that close air; the red bandanna around his head was soaked. The silence between them was palpable. He would stop only to go over and wind up the Victrola. And the face of my aunt—well, I was transfixed. Her eyes were like lamps, her cheeks burning, sweat dripping, tendons in her long neck standing out ... and her blue eyes watched Giovanni with incendiary passion.

"That expression went though me like a knife. I couldn't move. Giovanni's hands were in a fever of motion, chipping and twisting and pulling at the marble as if desperate to free the image from the stone. And it was as if Angela felt those masterful hands against her skin, trying to control herself, to keep still when she seemed on the verge of fainting. She kept wetting her lips with her tongue, shifting her shoulders. Then, wordlessly, she reached to the top of the dress and pulled it lower on her shoulders so that more of her upper breasts would show; and as she produced more décolletage, the chisel would move faster. I had never imagined her like that. She was convulsed with her daring and pride—the freedom and exhilaration she was experiencing. And all the time, the blade of the chisel was working down lower and lower. I feared I might be sick. And then with a sigh of relief, as if finally freeing herself from the last vestiges of encumbering propriety, she pulled the gown to her waist. The song of the chisel never missed a beat. Her breasts rose with her every breath, shiny with perspiration. I couldn't help myself—I was a mess."

"So, they were lovers?"

"Lovers? I doubt it ever went much beyond that." Joe Palmer looked up with a weary grimace. "No, it had, looking back on it, more the quality of a set piece, of a well-rehearsed routine from a romanticized past. Perhaps I'm too hard on her."

"More likely, she was Boston society and he a poor stonecutter."

"No. Society women in her day were taking all kinds of people as their lovers, their voice coaches, their dance instructors. Art and sex and Freud were all the rage ... with discretion." He waved his glass. "Auntie was a bluff, a bad poetess and scared to death of sex. She died a 'virgin spinster' —that's what my wife called her in her more catty moments." Joe reached for the bottle. "Of course, that didn't stop my father from sending us back to Manchester two days later. Terrible row that night when he returned, after I'd gone to bed. Maybe because the door of his studio had been left unlocked. Maybe I moved something, touched something. Anyway, Giovanni was gone by first light. When I went back to his empty room and studio, I found the sculpture he'd been working on smashed to bits. Next day, the Chillingworth Packard arrived and picked up Auntie and me. My father remained in his studio, not even a good-bye. And then a year later, the Depression came and my father returned to Concord."

"Did you ever come across any correspondence from your mother or your aunt?"

"Like what—letters?"

"The curator at Sangamore mentioned to me that there might have been letters written by Sandra and Angela Chillingworth from Venice."

"First I've heard of it."

William looked at his watch. "She's pretty late."

"I know she'll come. I could hear it in her voice."

"So …" He contemplated the bottle a moment. "Did she, Aunt Angela, ever see this guy Maronetti again?"

"Maybe once or twice in Manchester before the war. Frankly, I think she preferred him a memory, a kind of mythic character—her Venetian lover. Filled the girls' heads with all kind of poppycock about him in later years—that and her sainted sister."

The phone rang in the office. Joe, whiskey sloshing from his glass, had trouble getting up and going to the phone. His guest sprang up and followed, stopping in the doorway, making no pretense about listening in.

"Hello, Angie, sweetheart. Yes, yes, I'm fine. I've just been waiting here with the young friend of mine I told you about; dinner's cooking as we speak…Oh, I see … at the airport—already. But couldn't you— … that busy. Well, but will you be through again soon? … Good, good … Well then, why not a phone number or address or something; we really should keep in touch. E-mail, yes, I see."

Listening to the old man, he felt flung into liars' limbo, somewhere between orgiastic exhilaration and bottomless despair. She was alive! He rushed up to the phone, just restraining himself from ripping the receiver from the old man's hand.

"Tell her I'll come right now and meet her at the airport."

"Angie …"

"Tell her to wait. I can be there in forty minutes."

Joe glanced up, flustered.

"Angie, the young man who is doing work on your grandfather—he seems very intent on meeting you. Can you just hold on a second?"

"Tell her I must see her; it's about her sister."

The receiver shook against Joe Palmer's ear.

"Angie, he says it's … about your sister. Angie?"

William grabbed the phone and shouted into it.

"Hello, this is Michael Collins, Sandra. It's me. Hello, hello …" A buzz and a sharp beeping. "Fuck, fuck," he shouted, and let the receiver drop.

Joe Palmer stood incredulous; he reached a hand to steady himself and knocked a pile of invoices off the side of the desk.

"What did you call her? What did you say your name was? What the hell's going on here?"

"Did she say where she was going?"

"Who are you? What do you want?"

"Did she say anything about a flight or airline?"

"She said she was at her gate." Joe braced himself on the desk. "What do you have to do with Sandra?" He tried pulling himself to his full height, struggling for control. "What's with you, buster?"

"Did she say where she was going?"

"Who are you? You're not another goddamn reporter, are you?"

William hung his head, desperation turning to resignation.

"Joe, I'm sorry. Too damn much of that good scotch. Come on, let's both go sit back down."

He took Joe's arm and guided him back to the living room and the sofa. Joe jerked his arm free, flopped onto the cushions, and threw his head back with a cry of frustration.

"What the fuck is going on here?"

"Nothing, fucking nothing."

"Don't scam me, boy. The truth, goddamn it."

"The truth?" William flinched and shook his head.

"Yes, the truth, or is that word no longer in your vocabulary?"

"Okay. I was in love with Sandra when I was eighteen, and she got pregnant. And I don't know what happened to her ... or the child."

Joe eyed him with wary curiosity. "So, you're the one."

"I'm the one." He raised his hand like a guilty schoolboy.

"My daughter is dead."

"So I've been told."

"And you came to me, thinking what?"

"I don't know what I think anymore."

"Collins ... Collins—that is your real name?"

"You will find the name in the Emerson boathouse, on the plaques of the crew teams, twice, along with yours and your father's."

"So you did row at Emerson?"

"I loved your daughter—Sandra."

"How sweet."

"Why the fuck wouldn't your daughter come to see you?"

"How should I know? I'm only her goddamn father."

"So tell me. Why'd Sandra fucking kill herself?"

Joe Palmer jerked to attention, his face rising to meet that of his accuser, but the light dimmed in his eyes.

"I ... don't know. And every goddamn day, I go over it a thousand times, and I still don't know."

The old man pulled a hand across his perspiring face.

The younger man reached for his glass, then, thinking better of it, pushed it aside.

"I'm sorry," he said. "I didn't come here for this. I only wanted to talk to your daughter. I wanted to find out if Sandra *had* our child." He hung his head. "I'm sorry."

Joe took the bottle and tipped it back to his lips.

"So it's the child. And you were the boy who got her pregnant?"

"I loved her."

"Let's do this right, son—here, a little Dutch courage."

Joe handed him the bottle.

"I'll puke if I have any more."

Joe opened his palm and tapped it: a baseline, a solid bottom.

"Sandra told me last year, when we had lunch in Cambridge, that she had a kid in Geneva. A boy. That whole business was arranged by my stupid, screwed-up, wife who never did have any goddamn common sense. I knew nothing about it, except coming up with the money." Joe shook his fist in a show of long-running exasperation. "She said something about the child's having been put up for adoption. A mess, she said, a horrible mistake."

"Oh." William stared at the bottle where it sloshed between the knees of his host. "Was she unhappy, do you think?"

"Sandra? She was lovely, on top of the world."

"So what, then?"

"I don't know." Joe leaned far forward as if to get his attention. "Don't you get it? I don't know."

"What's the story with Angela?"

"Angela—Jesus Christ, how long have you got? And by the way, what do I call you?"

"Stick with William. I've kinda gotten to like old William."

"Me, too, Bill, old boy. She was the one who—You are *still* a rowing man, right?"

"True blue."

"She'd cut every turn to the shore, push the stroke from the start line, risk everything to get what she wanted."

"And what was that?"

"Did I sleep with Angela? That's really what you and everybody is asking," Joe replied. "She was an incendiary. A flirt. An exhibitionist in love with herself."

"You fucked her!"

Joe's voice rose to a feeble shriek. "You think I'm a monster?"

"But you wanted to."

"You tell me, Bill. Think about it, to live around that, for any man, any father. Angela was my daughter and I loved her. She was my creation and I had to let her go or watch her burn. When she got herself pregnant, we did the very best we could to counsel her. We took her to the best doctors. First, we urged her to have an abortion. No, she was determined to have *her* baby. Then my wife seized on the situation. We'd adopt the baby—if it was a boy. We turned into a little den of conspirators. My wife, Abigail, insisted on this silly subterfuge about keeping the pregnancy secret. First, she pulled them both from school—as if Sandra should pay for her sister's sins; then they were off to Venice—of all places—to study piano and Italian; and then they were imprisoned up in Manchester for the last three months of Angela's pregnancy. Abigail was obsessed with the secrecy. It drove everybody crazy. She already had a drinking problem and not much judgment. The delivery was botched. I wasn't around, but my sense is that Abigail got it wrong, waited too long—and she, of all people, should have known better, hanging around gynecologists half her life. The boy, Joey, was born brain-damaged. Angela and her mother barely spoke a word to each other after that ... only to take care of the baby."

"Did you find out who the father was?"

"Take your pick. She was fifteen going on twenty and looked the part. She sneaked out at night. Police were picking her up at bars in Cambridge and dives around Hanscom Field. She had a standard reply to our inquiries about the father: 'It's *my* baby.'"

"Terrible thing for a fifteen-year-old."

"Almost sixteen at the birth." Joe's eyes sparked. "Let me tell you, she loved that little boy with every ounce of her being."

"Twenty-five years, Joe. What keeps a daughter away that long? And why the no-show again tonight?"

The old man lowered his gaze.

"I never laid a hand on her, if that's what you're getting at. But there was something between us—what can I say. She flirted with me for attention, competing with Sandra. Sandra began to be more withdrawn. I'd find Angela in the library with the art journals from the twenties, looking at the reproductions of the paintings, the nudes. Her mother and I had been trying for a boy for over a decade. Could we hide that? And then Angela pregnant, and the secrecy and silence … it was like a terrible retribution thrown in your face. I felt guilty, responsible for the whole mess."

"But twenty-five years, Joe? It's not right."

"She's a porn actress, or was. Friend of mine saw one of her things about ten years ago." Joe shrugged. "I couldn't care less, but maybe it weighs on her, who knows."

"And Sandra?"

"Believe it or not, before Angela got pregnant, we were a happy family. That's what makes it so hard."

"And Sandra, was she happy when she was going to Harvard?"

"Don't you get it, Bill? She was happy, happier than I'd ever known her. She had come back, come home. It's what she wanted. The long shadow of her sister was gone."

"Did you identify her body?"

"Christ, am I being cross-examined here? Have you been lying to me about your vocation, too?" Joe tipped the bottle high and awkwardly wiped at his chin. "Her landlady did, I guess, and under the circumstances, that was enough for me. What with that insouciant wiseass cop and the imbecilic reporter from the *Globe*."

"Did you get her passport?"

"What passport?"

"The coroner should've returned her passport to you."

"Just a few odds and ends. No passport."

"You're sure?"

"What the fuck do you want? Tears, scourging the soul? Don't you get it? She came back home. I held her again in my arms—damn you."

"What about a pathologist's report?"

Joe flung himself back on the sofa and covered his eyes.

"Can't remember what I even did with it."

William looked away, searching the walls to distract himself, collect his thoughts. There was a painting above the sofa of four young girls seated on an old sleigh under an apple bough. Each girl had an apple in hand, ready to bite into the succulent fruit. The girls wore lovely crinoline frocks, high-laced leather shoes, and colorful bows in their hair. Careless fall sunshine fell across their adorable faces.

Now he saw barricades against grief and loneliness.

"Joe, when I was with Sandra, senior year—we were rowing on the river, actually—she told me something that has haunted me to this day. It was a confession of sorts. Sandra told me how once she had been babysitting when you were out. And she had an accident with the baby. She said he fell off the changing table and was knocked unconscious, or maybe just stunned. She panicked, but then the baby seemed to recover and was okay. She put him back in the crib. But in the morning, he was dead. My memory is that she blamed herself for the child's death."

Joe wiped at his eyes and suddenly shot forward where he sat, his voice soft but firm.

"You ... made love to her?"

"I loved her, Joe."

"And she told you that?"

"Something *like* that. I don't remember her saying anything about brain damage ... or about her twin sister, for that matter."

Joe threw his head back and let out a repressed sigh, reaching for the bottle and holding it against his cheek for a moment. The golden liquid raced up one side of the bottle and then the other.

"Bill—I always liked the name Bill—there are really no such things as flaws in nature. And you see, Bill, a woman ... well, she is only nature's way of making another egg; and a flaw is only another way that nature spreads risk and looks for new avenues of opportunity. But for our family, well, up to Angela's pregnancy, we'd managed a pretty good life. I blame myself. I screwed up a job. I wasted an enormous sum fighting the board of trustees over Sangamore. Money problems. But I did try to regain some semblance of normalcy after the maelstrom of recriminations and subterfuge. Maybe that was my biggest mistake. Maybe I tried too hard. I should have just let nature take its course."

Joe offered the bottle to his younger companion, but it was refused with a curt offhand remark.

"Your aphids and beetles, wasn't it?"

Joe did not seem to hear or care.

"Abigail—after that child was born, it was booze on top of her anti-depressants, and more booze. She never left the house. I insisted we start over. I finally talked her into going to Boston with me. Dinner and the opera—we'd done it for years. It was October, lovely and warm. The girls could perfectly well take care of the baby—poor thing. Abigail even enjoyed the dinner, as if she was reclaiming happier bits of her earlier self. But maybe I let her have too much wine. She didn't make it past act two of *Tosca* before she got weepy and agitated. On the drive home, she became unglued. I was afraid for her safety. It was after twelve when we got back to the house. I hadn't even turned off the ignition before she was out of the car and racing for the front door. I just sat with the radio on, not wanting to go in, not wanting to deal with it.

"I must have dozed, I woke to a song on the radio, something by Perry Como from the fifties … a happier time—and we were happy back then. I got out and went into the garden to stretch my legs. There was a three-quarter moon … a distant bark nosing the waves of the distant hills. I walked through our old meadow to the river. I felt a surge of happiness. I'd come through the war; we had two lovely girls—a miracle of sorts. Even selling off the orchard and the land next door in the Depression had resulted in fine neighbors. In the early years, we'd go out antiquing, trying to fill up the old house after my father had left it an empty shell. You learn to live with the past; you make accommodations. Anyway, there I was, half-mesmerized by a rusty stain of light on the surface of the river, when something snapped back in my head. A terrible memory.

"I was on a destroyer in the South Pacific, escort duty. We'd had a report of a Jap cruiser being torpedoed in our area and were checking for confirmation, for survivors. It was dawn, the sun just coming up, and I was on lookout. I spotted this bloodred streak off the port bow. First, I thought it was the sunrise on the water, and then I realized it was a reflection off an oil slick. There was debris in the water. We slowed and got in as close as we dared. I and a couple of other officers got into a smaller craft for a closer inspection and maybe to get some identification on the vessel that had gone down. So we're out there, a thousand miles from nowhere, peering over the gunnels into this messy flotsam, wondering why we're not finding any survivors. And the sun is rising, you see, rising quickly, and suddenly the glare, the angle of refraction, changes, and the water—in an instant, matter of seconds—goes from opaque to crystal-clear. There, right there below us, just feet below the surface, a whole goddamn battle cruiser, all seven hundred feet of her. Not bottom-side up. Not on her side. Her top side just floating below the surface as gentle as you please, wheelhouse, smokestacks, antiaircraft emplacements … and everywhere, I mean everywhere, sharks, hundreds—mako, great white, tiger—swirling and chasing and speeding like demons out of hell, desperate, looking for anything they'd missed. It was like coming upon a sunken city and finding it pillaged and all its inhabitants carried off and butchered in dark corners. None of us had ever seen anything like that, a ship, right side up, not quite sunk—an underwater reef I suppose—to Davy Jones's locker."

Joe Palmer shot a glance at the younger man and tapped the bottle in his lap.

"You see, Bill, that is why we hug the earth and love our children."

William sat listening impassively, as if he was no longer even in the same room.

"That's when I turned back to the house. There was a cruel glint of gold in the cupola. I just had the worst feeling. I was coming back by the rose garden when I saw it. At first, I thought one of the girls had left her doll in the rose bed. But of course they were too old for that by then. Baby Joey was lying on his back in the soft dirt and mulch, unscratched. He was still warm to the touch, but definitely dead. It was right below the nursery window. He had been dropped. I panicked. In that pitiful sight, a return to normalcy, or worse to come. Like I said, I panicked and just scooped him up and ran with him into the kitchen. I bathed him in the sink, cleaned him up, and then carried him up the stairs to the nursery and put on a clean diaper and placed him back in the crib. I wanted to scream the place down, but the power of speech had deserted me. The windows of the nursery were wide open, the smell of the rose garden below wafting in on the night like a fragrant invitation from Morpheus himself. I blamed myself—on my watch. My worst fears had always been that some child would fall from that damn tower. And yet somehow, every fiber in me circled in frenzy around the idea of it being an accident … and I could put the clock back. I checked both girls' rooms. Angela was asleep. Sandra was under her covers. I went into our bedroom and found Abigail out cold; her sedatives and a near-empty bottle of gin were on the bedside table, enough to knock out a horse. I was terrified and yet comforted that all could sleep, as if nothing had happened. I got myself some of Abigail's sedatives and washed them back with half a bottle of gin. Then I just curled up in bed and waited for oblivion. All I could think about was that sunken cruiser and the sharks. In the morning, I was awakened by a shriek. It was Angela. She'd gone into the nursery for the morning feeding."

"And you never told anyone?"

"What was there to tell? The child was rushed to the hospital. The doctors knew all about his problems. They were almost relieved. Crib death was the neatest of explanations. Blessing in disguise. Get on with life. Except the silence—that never changed."

"But somebody—"

"We just stopped talking to one another—okay?"

William nodded, aware of his own voice, a hoarse whisper. "Silence."

"Perhaps," Joe said, "what you heard from Sandra's lips was one version of that silence."

William stood, a little shaky, going over to some of the nineteenth-century genre subjects, reviewing the charming scenes.

"It would be a terrible thing to have on your conscience."

"As terrible as it gets, you would think."

"You said, 'quiet,' Joe."

"Quiet?"

"You said Sandra was the quiet one. But I'll tell you something; I never knew anybody ..." He shook his head as his words came out in something of an invocation to his newfound gods. "Sandra saw and felt everything; nothing was lost on her, nothing.

"Tell me something, Joe," he continued. "Why didn't Angela come tonight? What would she have to hide?"

The old man had been avoiding his watchful eyes, but suddenly he shot him a piercing glance.

"Bill, old boy, I think it was *you* she didn't want to see."

"Me—hell, Joe, I barely exist." He fished in the pocket of his slacks and found what he was looking for, carefully placing it on the table next to the bottle, as if the two artifacts had something in common. "Wanna know where I come from, Joe? Take a look."

"What?" The old man raised his bleary eyes to take in the rusted bit of metal.

"That's right, a goddamn nail. I picked it by the railroad tracks. Old fucking iron nail rusted to shit, been in the ground a long time, too." He picked the thing up and closed his palm tight, squeezing until his knuckles turned white. "What a fucking pedigree, huh?"

CHAPTER 26

He walked back to the inn as quickly as he could manage, thinking he might be able to work off the scotch. When that didn't seem to help, he went to the side of the road and put two fingers down his throat and managed to bring up a good part of the Glenlivet. He felt a little better, and by the time he got to the parking lot of the inn, good enough to drive his rental car.

At a discount store in Weymouth, he bought two suitcases and a bunch of women's underwear and shoes. When he got to Logan Airport, he left the car in short-term parking and took the two suitcases with him. First, he checked the domestic terminal, then the international terminal. Most flights had already departed for the night. Then he gave roughly the same spiel to the customer service agents in both terminals.

"Hi, I was hoping you could help me. I just dropped off a fare about two hours ago, an attractive lady in her mid-forties. She forgot a bag in the trunk." He held up the Samsonite suitcase. "The last name, I believe, was Palmer. She told me a funny story about staying at the Palmer House in Chicago and people giving her a hard time about it. She was rushing to catch her flight. I don't know where she was going. But I really feel bad about the bag; she seemed like such a nice lady—big tipper, too."

The customer service agents couldn't have been more solicitous. He was promised a computer check of the passenger lists first thing in the morning. In each terminal, he got a receipt for the bag he left there and a telephone number he could call the next day.

When he got back to the inn, it was just past twelve. He found Slotnik in the lobby, talking to Jennifer, the receptionist.

"Ah, professor." said Slotnik. "There you are. We were worried about you when you didn't show at the pub."

"Sorry, I had a dinner engagement."

"Who with?"

"Gee, Don, I don't think it's any of your fucking business."

"Well, I just might make it my fucking business, professor."

William Channing turned to Jennifer, who seemed slightly amused.

"Do you let this guy be so rude to all your guests?"

"Don," said Jennifer, "lighten up."

"'Lighten up.' Is that all you can ever say to me?"

Jennifer raised an eyebrow, the color coming into her cheeks beginning to match her red hair. "I guess it just doesn't sink in."

She turned and handed William Channing his key and a pile of message slips.

"Another night, Don," he said, shuffling the message slips, "and maybe I'll take you through Thoreau's essay on civil disobedience."

Four phone messages from Ruthie.

When he went up to his room, he marveled: the clutter of a life so easily assumed and soon to be abandoned. He touched a finger to the cold glass of his bay window and located Slotnik's squad car. Why didn't Jennifer just blow him off for good? Over the weeks, the trees on the square had thinned and the streetlights shone even brighter against his window. Then he began a severe triage. The artist's diary, photocopies of a few drawings, the etching, and Sandra's undelivered letter to him—these he put aside. The green morocco *Walden*—it would have another owner now ... and he had the artist's diary. The bit of toy track he dropped in the wastebasket; he'd done his due diligence by Jimmy. The photograph of his mother he put with the etching. He hung Sandra's watercolor on the wall by the window.

He was interrupted by a soft knock on the door.

"It's me," Ruthie said. "I had a dream your room was empty, that you were gone."

She kissed him—a chaste kiss on the side of the lips—and handed him a folded copy of the *Globe*.

"Why would I be gone?"

She smiled uneasily. "All good things must come to an end."

"As you can see, I'm here."

He opened the newspaper.

She circled the room. "Your stuff is still here."

"Angela left without even seeing her dad."

"Yeah, well … just remember, I was in love with her first." She eyed him and then the newspaper in his hands.

"Well, you've always got the video."

"Right, the video. You'll let me keep it?"

"A memento."

"Enough … to bring *you* back, Michael?"

"Why don't you get out of your things."

The customer service desks were a little slow. He couldn't get an answer until midday. Domestic departures had nothing. International departures was another matter.

"Yeah, here it is, Palmer." He could hear the woman tapping away at her keyboard. "There was an S. Palmer on an eight-thirty Alitalia flight to Milan's Malpensa, Malpensa to Marcopolo, Venice. Could that be the one?"

"You said S. Palmer?"

"Ms. Sandra Palmer."

He turned to the brilliant morning light coming through his bay window.

"And her passport would have had to match the name on the ticket?"

"Absolutely."

He felt the blood drain from his head, as if the thing he had believed in most deeply, dismissed and revived a thousand times, had now risen from the shadows and spread its wings in the clear light of day.

"Hello, sir, are you still there?"

"Yeah, yeah, okay, that sounds right. Nice lady. So you've got an address for her in Venice or something—Sandra Palmer—so you can get her bag to her?"

"If she paid with a credit card. Let me see, round-trip ticket purchased in Venice two weeks ago at the airport, paid for in cash. She was supposed to fly back tonight but must have gone back a day early—in a rush, I'd guess."

"Cash, huh. Will that be a problem?"

"Alitalia can trace her. She's probably filed a lost-baggage claim. If she has a local address, she'd have left it going through Italian passport control. Just leave it to us. We'll put the bag on the same Alitalia flight tonight."

"Thanks. You guys are real pros. And, oh yeah, why don't you connect me to Alitalia ticketing, if you don't mind."

That afternoon, he attempted a halfhearted approximation of his habitual life, going out for an abbreviated version of his jog, more the motions of the thing than the thing itself. Enough to convince Don Slotnik. His mind was wonderfully clear. Not even a whiff of a headache. He noted a pile of cigarette butts by the curb, right where Slotnik's police cruiser had been parked the previous night. He could still feel the pulse of the town as succinctly as the beat of his own heart, but he knew it would never be a part of him. It was different, too, now that he knew she had come and gone, and where she had gone and where he was going. And certainly no one would miss him. His absence might be remarked on for a day or two by the staff in the inn. Perhaps the story of his more infamous self, the fugitive, if it came to that, might have legs in the local papers. Jack might add him to the list of characters he'd like to tell about in the bar. And surely Ruthie would remember the good times!—and, hopefully, her promise to keep her mouth shut until he had a chance to clear his name, now that he'd explained it all to her. Someday, she'd corroborate his testimony in a grand jury hearing. In another life, he could have fallen in love with Ruthie. And what would happen to his books? Maybe they could become part of the Thoreau Room, decorative accessories to welcome future guests.

He paid his final respects at the family graves, leaving a bit of Queen Anne's lace on Sandra's, saying a hopeful prayer over the child's tiny marker. He saluted the general. And finally, standing before the memorial carved by his grandfather, staring into that serene face—grace incarnate—he felt again, more surely than ever, the love of the artist invested in that stone, realizing that his eyes would perhaps be the last to ever know or care. And it came to him with sudden lucidity—a similar realization must have come to Emerson when he opened the graves of his wife and son—that whatever vital spark remained of the Palmer family, "the root and core," in Joe's words, had long since been translated into the invisible fabric of human affection: the finest part preserved in the artifacts of silence and slow time.

They alive in him only as he was alive.

On leaving his room for the last time, he turned to Thoreau's portrait above the empty desk.

"Henry, I guess this is it. Maybe you're the lucky one; you'll always have visitors at your door."

He straightened the frame and went downstairs.

He had dinner in the pub, a sandwich and a Heineken, listening to Jack, wondering when Slotnik would show up.

"Billy, let me tell you, people spend their whole lives around here trying to stop the clock. They want to stop somebody tearing down a nineteenth-century eyesore tenement on the Texas Road, or a cell phone tower by the Mobil station on Route Two, or a new soccer field for Emerson Academy, which'll mean cutting down a few trees near the Silver Brook Sanctuary. They want the place to stay the same, their place to stay the same, as if somehow it will save their lives. Nobody can save their lives; it can't be done. You can't get there from here."

He left his sandwich half-eaten and his glass half-empty while he excused himself to take a pee. When he slipped out back into the parking lot with his overnight bag, he noted Slotnik's police cruiser parked across from the exit of the parking lot on the Carlisle Road. He went to his rental car, opened the door, placed the keys in plain view on the driver's seat, and closed the door.

"Hi, Joe. I just wanted you to have this."

He handed the green morocco *Walden* to the slightly stooped man in the doorway. Joe Palmer looked a little ragged around the gills, unshaven, still wearing his muddy work clothes.

"I thought you already returned the ones you borrowed." Joe drew back to examine the cover in the interior light.

"There was one that got misplaced along the way."

"*Walden*? But where did this come from?"

"Let's just say it's been in good keeping."

"Bill, won't you come in? ..."

"Michael, actually, but we can stick with Bill, if you like."

"Have a drink, one for the road."

"I've got to be going."

"Yes, I suppose you must."

"Thanks, Joe."

"You'll let me know, when you find her."

"You may have to find out from her."

Joe stepped forward, framed in the light, stooped, past tired.

"Remember, the road ... well, it's not as long as you think."

Joe held out his hand and he grasped it.

"And you, you've got a harvest to get in."

"My songlines."

He backed out of the light.

"Yes, yes, yes...."

He stood by the lip of Walden Pond for only a few minutes, turning occasionally to the shallows, where the patchy moonlight picked up the undulant form of an oak leaf beneath the surface, a tiny cramped hand twisting and scrapping at the sandy bottom. Thoreau, like Ovid and even Darwin, had seen metamorphosis everywhere: the human instinct to identification, the transmigration of all forms, the endless cycle of growth and decay and loss; that the land is only as sacred as the love invested by the lover; that the gods have never truly died out, but only been transformed with new names; that all perception of truth is in the direction of analogue; that a life well lived epitomizes the best in all things. This much he would try to carry with him, especially now, with the artist's diary—a faith and ambition to last the ages.

It was late and he was finally alone.

He looked up at the banners of white pine unfurled upon the star-encrusted night and let fly with the bit of old iron he'd been fingering, pausing only long enough to register the thin splash, the invisible ripples dashing outward in a failed race with an ever-expanding universe. He then took the trail around the pond from the old house site and climbed the far hill to the railroad cutting and followed the tracks back to Concord station.

Tracks laid by one James Collins, tracks that had taken Captain Joseph M. Palmer and his company of Union infantry off to war, tracks that had spirited away the eloping artist, Joseph Palmer, and his model, the young Sandra Chillingworth, to Boston and Glasgow … and another life.

He slipped on board the last commuter train of the night, heading east.

I left the woods for as good a reason as I went there.
Perhaps it seemed to me that I had several more lives to live,
and could not spare any more time for that one.

PART TWO

CHAPTER 27

FROM THE DIARY OF JOSEPH PALMER

Venice, September 7, 1913

Finally, there is respite from our mad dash to Europe. We are firmly ensconced in our lovely, if somewhat dowdy, room overlooking the Rio San Vio and the Zattere. It is early morning and the gulls hover past our windows, mingling their cries with the shouts of the boatmen as if to call us out to the day. For me, it is as if we yet linger in a dream. I look up from my writing table to my sleeping angel across the room and feel as if we have stolen into this fabled city like thieves in the night, fearful of what we will find but ready to steal all. We will live; we will re-create the world anew. For a week, we restrained ourselves on shipboard and on the Venice-bound train, vowing to hold back until our marriage vows, but last night we resigned ourselves to love's attraction. My happiness is unbounded! I am continually astonished at how little, it seems, I knew her and how much still remains to be known.

She insists that we must be careful, and so we are very careful. No prospect of motherhood enters our plans.

On shipboard, her nose was never out of a book; she devoured Byron, Ruskin, James, the poet Rilke! I have no idea what the man writes. Already she is steeped in the history and literature of this city, as if she is compelled to some intellectual mastery to match her prodigies with the keyboard. Strange, too, how after complaining to me in my Concord rose garden, as we made our lovers' vows, that she was sick to death of the piano, she could not resist practicing in the salon of the ship. She pretended it was nothing.

Last evening in the darkened compartment of our train, my darling Sandra fell asleep with a book open in her lap, lulled by the sound of the tracks, while there on the horizon, as the train slowed its precipitous plunge, the glittering eyelets of light strewn upon the watery abyss, our destination and new home—at last. I thought to wake her, to shout that marvelous name—Venezia, Serenissima—but found myself so entranced by the reflection of my beloved's sleeping face in the window that I could barely utter a sigh of rapture. In her nocturnal double I could detect neither shame nor abandon, nor any fear of the condemnation that is sure to follow on our heels from Concord and Boston. How brave, how intrepid, how sure she is of her heart's longings. And so young—what will my friends and colleagues think?

And when I spoke her name and pointed to the onrush of lights across the lagoon, she only smiled and said, "It will be nice to disappear, Joseph—away from the Boston papers. I so look forward to becoming invisible." Invisible! Poor girl, if she thinks she can hide in her books ... No eyes can resist such a face, such a figure.

As for me, I dwell constantly on Jimmy Whistler, my friend and mentor from student days, come to this same city some thirty-five years ago, bankrupt, an exile from a waspish press, come to renew his inspiration and set himself upon the path to true greatness: the Venice of the nocturnes, the pastels and etchings that would reveal Venice as no one had known it before, and place his name with the immortals. How often in my student years I was tempted to do Venice, but then thought better, deciding to wait until I was ready, until I had something more to offer than clichéd butter on canvas. Already, I struggle to see—to feel—through the master's eyes and make the city my own. With my beloved at my side as inspiration and helpmeet, I hope to produce work to last for more than a winter-season sensation at the NA annual. From the bully bear of ambition, may the gods yet preserve me.

In this regard, I am pleased with our choice of humble pensione, reminiscent of student days in Paris and ambitions to outdo Velázquez. Such a step down from Chillingworth standards, but which will allow us a frugal existence off the beaten path of the tourist trade, where we can dwell close to the real life of the city. Last night upon entrance to our room, Sandra laughed wickedly and held up a dusty white-gloved fingertip. "What would mother say?"

As I sit in reverie, planning my assault, my senses burn: the lapping water, dance of reflected light in the smoky green Murano chandelier, leaping dolphins in the rosewood headboard, a burst of bronze sienna in my beloved's hair upon the white of her pillow, the line of her collarbone into the bare shoulder, and the lingering perfume of her body—everywhere. I am reminded of her prescient comment just weeks ago as we schemed: "Joseph, we'll make it our Walden; we'll leap into the dark." Her bravery and wisdom is beyond her years—and she has the energy of youth! Here I am past forty and I feel as if I must learn to see all over again, such beauty and sadness mixed in her dreaming eyes. What does she dream? Last night—I was astonished! Do they see different, more intensely? I find myself seeking a deeper extension of myself in her, through her reflected eyes, and this translated to paint.

Ah, how my ambition bridles. I long to be off and put a dagger to the bland and facile Impressionism that is so much the rage and glut of public taste in Boston.

Wake, wake, my love! Here is the new life I promised.

Venice, September 12

We are married! What a joy. I had no idea that such an official sanction could mean such bliss. We are one, two steeds in tandem. It makes us brave, makes us free. Even the pompous Englishman, the Reverend Charles Darlington, turned out to be a pretty good sport, inviting a few members of the British community—no Americans being available, he said—to stand witness at the ceremony. An opinionated and lively lot, interested in the arts, dropping names of Lord this and Lady that. Of course, none could take their eyes off Sandra in her splendid white gown of Burano lace, the women more smitten than the men. With the exception of the Scotsman, Horatio Brown, the author and old Venice hand, who immediately took up Sandra—one minute and they were disagreeing on Ruskin—and offered to show us around Venice. He has promised to find her a piano, a dozen if she wishes. He seems to know everyone and all the secrets of the place. He even knew Jimmy when he was in Venice, has lunched with James at Rye, and has a nodding acquaintance with Sargent and Edward Curtis, a college friend of my father, who has a magnificent palazzo on the Grand Canal. The past seems to gush in his veins. I would like to paint his portrait; his fissured and mottled tusk of a face and deep-set eyes touch on the very physiognomy of memory.

Venice, October 7

I have been busy. The work goes well, but the challenges overwhelm. Color, everywhere color, but like nowhere else on earth: muted and refined and transparent, every crumbling wall and waterway a different nuance and texture to be interpreted. Every rio, every campo, every turning bring new discoveries, tantalizing prospects. There are so many perspectives to analyze, so many shadings of purpose, veils to be lifted. Thankfully, I have my etching going now, which allows respite from color and a chance to concentrate on line and form. It was Whistler's secret, to secure the critical detail as focal point and work outward, leaving much to the imagination. At every turning, Jimmy Whistler seems to grab my arm and I hear his sharp voice: "Another Whister, Joe. Ah, but it's already been done and done better, my boy." I must lay my own claim, as did Thoreau—step outside myself and see beyond the habitual and routine, perhaps with the perspective of a field mouse.

Sandra—and books, guides, maps!—accompanies me everywhere as model. We are inseparable morning and night; she disappears in the afternoon to her piano—"just to keep my fingers limber," she says. When she poses for me here by the side of the canal or in a gondola, her beauty seems to absorb the dazzle of the city, the play of light in her hair, the soft shimmering green lights across her face, and her eyes take on the colors of sea and sky. These will all be great sellers back in Boston and New York, but somehow I ache for more, to show her off more, to capture her inner being and active mind. I have begun drawing her in our room, when she is asleep, or in her bath. At first, she was shy and ashamed of these nudes, but now she seems to accept them more and more; I dare say she even begins to enjoy them, seeing her bodily beauty transposed to paper. She preens with new confidence. I long to have her so in the outdoors, with the full affect of light playing off her skin. Only in the late afternoon, when she returns, does the light off our balcony offer any chance of such modeling. Nothing quite like this has been attempted in Venice—Giverny, yes, but not here with Venetian light. Is it ambition or love that dares me in these things?

Of late, Sandra has accepted invitations to tea from some of Horatio Brown's lady friends. There is the princesse—somebody de Polignac, American father and Singer fortune, at the Palazzo Manzoni, where there is a sophisticated but strangely neurotic group of artistic women who are drawn to Sandra. Big on music, she tells me. There is a piano. A young Russian composer—genius. She flushes when she relates their gossip. They seem to have taken to her—a potential convert! I'm sure she's a young spark in their jaded lives. It is all Fauré and Satie and somebody called Stravinsky. But it's good she has some female company, because I know how much she misses her sister, Angela. Each evening on her return to the pensione, she eagerly checks for mail, in hopes of a letter from Angela or her mother for "official" reaction to our wedding and reconciliation to our new state. Barely a day goes by that she does not write to her sister. I in my diary and she to Angela, as if she must banish her real thoughts, less I intercept them. How I long to know what confidences are exchanged.

She insists we must find a piano for her to practice on daily—to try out some of this Stravinsky. It is odd, for less than a month ago, when we made our plans for escape, she vowed never to touch the piano again. I would not have dared such an elopement if she had not pleaded her need for a break and a fresh start—"a slave to your art, dearest Joseph" being her exact words. And now she seems more intent on the damn piano than ever. Venice has its way with her.

Venice, October 15

Spent a strange and fascinating evening with Edward Curtis and his wife in the Casa Alvisi, thanks to Horatio Brown, who mentioned us to them. Of course, the moment Sandra laid her eyes on their concert grand, she became strangely quiet, as if overcome by her heart's desire. Later, she gripped my arm as if in a swoon, "It's a Bechstein, the best in the world." In truth, I was dreading the invitation, since they know both our families; but of course I was intrigued because of their distinguished friends and already-legendary—nay, mythic—soirees. Whistler, James, Sargent—all habitués of the Alvisi and its veteran exiles in Venice. Their drawing room overlooking the Grand Canal is an Ali Baba's cave of treasures.

Old Curtis welcomed us with open arms. Not a word, not a hint of disapproval. Over a splendid dinner and the best wines from the Abruzzi region, candlelight twinkling in Sandra's wide eyes, we talked of the art world— he deplores Boston's recent infatuation with Cézanne and Matisse, preferring Renoir and particularly Degas, whom he considers a paragon of true artistic value—and reminisced about Venice past and the America of his youth.

The old man kept staring at me, making me feel not a little uncomfortable, especially when I realized it was my father he saw in me. They had known each other at Harvard and then as cavalry officers in northern Virginia. With wine, he became quite melancholy and reflective, returning again to my father and the war. He spoke of once having stayed up the whole night with my wounded father at an army hospital in Baton Rouge. Curtis had come through unscathed, unlike my father, who suffered so terribly. I was soon under the spell of Curtis's stories. Whereas I remembered my father a near invalid with failing constitution, he remembered a man of vigor—a grand example of what he described as moral courage. In the flicker of candlelight, I felt privy to conversations around campfires, of battlefields burdened with the bodies of the dead and dying—terrible things that men of our generation will never know. How Curtis went on about him—how even after the war he had campaigned for reconciliation between North and South. I had the sense that he saw in my father the shattered hopes of his generation, the best gone and the rest lost to the scramble of ambition and moneymaking by the war profiteers.

I felt diminished. I still hear the old man pontificating on his balcony over the Grand Canal—Sandra's piano playing drifting outward—going on about the decline of Boston and the strikes in the Lowell mills. And I, I who have left all that tedious business to my brother while I pursue the life of an artist. Perhaps my Venetian idyll is just another escape for the guilty and careless. In my dreams, I hear my father's voice as if translated back to me by a younger Curtis: "Ah, Joe, his ambition was to leave the world a better place; a poet or naturalist, he should have been. If only you had heard how he spoke to his men in the cause of freedom."

Such words take me back to my boyhood, when I sat by father's invalid bed and heard his stories about his rambles with Thoreau as a young man. "Go," he would finally gasp, exhausted by his telling. "Go and find that pine on Brister Hill or that landing along the river and the ruined dock where the heron fish. Tell me if it is still as I remember it. Tell me of the purple veils of light at dusk. Go."

Life is indeed strange. How in a city far away, I should catch a glimpse of the life my father never had.

Venice, October 18

Etching going very well, though the process is slow. I find it concentrates the mind and leads to ideas for larger works, and also encourages emphasis on surface texture and not just spendthrift color. Whistler's secret: Stick to the thing itself, the artwork; let it be the meaning and not the illusion of the world reflected in the viewer's eye. This from the Greeks. Thoreau knew it, too: the force embodied in natural objects, their symbolic power. Sargent lost this in his later works, not to mention wasting his time on portraits; his early work had such lovely surface and brooding, evocative tones; his paving stones were alive. I fear to fall into the trap of the Venice potboiler. I must cut to gristle and bone.

Sandra is very changed; I can't put my finger on it. On our outings, she is bored while posing, impatient to get back to her books, her piano—a new repertoire to be mastered. Only in the morning light after her bath is she truly alive to my pencil and paper. She eagerly dispenses with her towel or gown and situates herself in the sunlight to show herself off to best effect. She is proud. She examines my drawings, as if seeking ways of improving them by being more responsive. The issue is electric between us. When I set pencil to paper, it is as if I caress her, her body as expressive as her face. Often we cannot control ourselves. She is suddenly quite demanding of her own pleasure, guiding my hands, ministering to herself. It thrills me to heaven—her hands, her exquisite, skillful fingering of her sex. How? The ecstasy in her face stirs me to the passion of a young man—and to paint her so! Still, we are careful, lest we are swept away. I am delighted but astonished. I, a man of the world—yet I seem to know nothing of feminine desire. Could it be the women at the Manzoni?

The Curtises have kindly given her carte blanche to practice on their grand piano whenever she wants. She is like a demon in her practice—the prodigy returns! I have never seen her happier, especially now that she is again in correspondence with her sister, Angela. The Chillingworths seem resigned to our fait accompli, even to the point of setting up a monthly allowance for their dear daughter at Cook's. As if I am not capable of providing comfortably for her.

Now she has her own money to go along with her own joys.

Venice, November 1

The weather has grown colder, but the sun shines bright and all the colors sharpen with a new intensity, penetrating the lagoon waters and reflecting back crystalline tinctures that cry out for a rearrangement of the palette, for hard, steely Prussian blue and gray-azures and an enormous squeeze of lemon yellow. I try to visit the Bellini in the Frari daily, to feast on that palpable atmosphere; the sfumato is miraculous. In the Virgin's eyes, the terrible premonition of a tragic fate.

My one-man racing shell arrived from Henley yesterday—a splendid craft and a chance to see the city as never before. I row and it takes me right back to my youth on the Concord River. From such a vantage point, I will make Venice mine. I will become the water rat of the art world.

Our lives have settled into a pleasant rhythm, an almost-unvaried routine that so facilitates concentration for the work at hand. Body and soul find a certain synchronous regulation that allows them to pull a single oar. We are out early and work fiercely together until lunch. Then I go off for etching and exploration, on the lookout for exotic locales and new subject matter. Sandra is off—I am resigned—to piano practice and tea with those horrible women. We meet back at the pensione for bath and rest, then on to evening rendezvous with Sandra's friends—Horatio Brown, as ever a sparkling companion—often a concert at the Scuola Grande di San Rocco after dinner with the Curtises, and of course Florians to mingle with the local society. With the winter months settling in, the tourist hordes have left and only the firmly planted expatriates remain. I couldn't help but laugh when an older English woman, a widow and intimate of the coterie chez Manzoni bemoaned to me how her children, having grown up abroad, have lost all feeling for their home and country, none of the pride or honor that home feeling gives. No wonder these people live on the curl of the next wave, the latest art enthusiasm or call to revolution. God knows with what they fill Sandra's head. She can be elusive, sly, lost to herself at times—surprising. She hums strange music, her fingers keeping time, distracting me like the devil.

On the way home last night, she wanted to take a gondola instead of our usual quiet walk by way of the Giglio and San Stefano. Behind San Marco, she found a gondola with canopy and instructed the gondolier in near flawless Italian—dialect no less—to choose a circuitous route. She put a handful of notes in his hand. I was aghast. Nestled down in the darkness beneath the canopy, among the rugs and cushions, she kissed me and whispered that she has been longing to make love outdoors—and now this moment! I was tempted at her eagerness and impetuous indiscretion. The air was strangely warm so close to the water, but I protested the near presence of our gondolier. She laughed—oh how wickedly—and explained to me, as if I were some college boy, that the man expected no less. But the difficulty? She took my hand in hers, laid her fingers on mine, playing them like notes. Then she slipped one of my fingers in her mouth and bit me. "My water rat," she hissed as she nibbled my ear. And so the city weaves its spell, we resigning ourselves to its tidal oblivion, which seems to conjure the most carnal desire. We burn—we live. We threw care to the wind!

She was up the following morning, writing rapidly to her sister, as if to get it down before the feeling was lost—letters that she will not let me read.

I suppose they must have their secrets, her twin confidante, from whom she has been separated for longer than ever before. She is like an eagle fledgling yearning to push its sibling from the soft-feathered aerie.

Venice, November 27

Spent an hour with the Bellini Madonna in the Frari this morning. The early sunlight streaming into the sacristy made the atmosphere in the thing of ravishing beauty; it is palpable, as if alive to the inner life of the subject—a mother's reverie, the terrible fate acknowledged in her eyes. I must work up my glazes to try to achieve a similar effect.

I have had strangely troubling dreams, perhaps due to old man Curtis leaving for the winter and his house in Palm Beach. He insisted on buying a painting and some etchings to take with him—mementos, he said. I hear voices again, my father's, or I think it is my father, but more likely Curtis relating something my father said in his wine-softened growl. I have dreams of being lost in woods or among unfamiliar meadows—my father's repeated "Go" echoing in my ears—and coming upon terrible sights of carnage described to me by Curtis. I see so vividly, it is as if I had been there—clumps of Confederate bodies, a gray-and-tan litter, bloated and blackened, hived with lumps of green heads. Is it possible something of me had been there, something of my father's memory come down to me, something of his thwarted hopes and ambitions? Or do I glimpse the unseen future?

The wonder of it—to have traveled so far, to hear my father's true voice for the first time. Only now do I begin to see the full extent of our relations.

Sandra failed to meet at our rendezvous for work this morning and then missed lunch, leaving a note that she suffered a headache and needed extra time for practice. This piano business is beginning to infuriate me.

Venice, December 11

The weather has turned much colder and the most amazing fogs and sensuous mists float up from the canals, veiling and muting colors, adding to the mystery of where space and form intersect. This is Whistler's season. No wonder he found such inspiration for his delicate pastels, which offer the merest hints, while leaving the rest to the imagination. I am trying more colored papers with my pastels and darkening the underpainting on my canvases. But Jimmy Whistler haunts me. I keep stumbling on places already found by him, depicted in pastels and etching on the walls of the Fine Arts Society on Bond Street, found by me as a young art student. Do his pastels and etchings have a life separate from the artist in my memory? Does the art live in us, or we in the art? Does beauty exist without the beholder? I sometimes fear I would bury dear Jimmy with my own ambition given half the talent.

Rowing the canals has changed so many of my perceptions of the city, especially the bridges. At water level, the bridges take on new dimensions, something in the angle and the refraction of light, the way one passes into the surface reflection. In this season of mist, they float and materialize, evaporate and go nowhere. The white Istrian stone and worn brick and silvered wrought iron spin fantastic webs above waterborne reflections. I pose Sandra—champing at the bit—endlessly on bridges and work my fingers to the bone with etching needle in the cold. The arches are like fantastic eyelets opening onto a world of metamorphosis. Oh, to be a camera eye! What chance do I have to freeze time when all I freeze are my fingers? And so goes my water rat life.

Venice, December 25

It is early on Christmas morning and I sit writing while Sandra sleeps. I cannot contain my joy. After celebrations at Florians last night, Sandra astonished me again by insisting that we go to midnight Mass at the Frari. I have been reluctant, since I seem to retain some old Puritan aversion to the hoary pomp and abominable Catholic imagery that festoons the interior of these churches. To me, they reek of an ancient, murderous, Clothonian-inspired magic, the dark cells from which the hounds of the Inquisition crawled forth in persecution of science and reason. Yet I could not help but be moved by the spacious brick vaulting of the Frari and the lovely old wooden beams picked out by a thousand candle flames and, of course, Titian's crimson pyre of a Madonna winging skyward above all the priestly hokum. A child's choir sang quite beautifully and the congregation, though smothered in incense, displayed a wonderful sense of community solidarity, which one had to admire. If only such social harmony could be had in Lowell or Boston, instead of the constant turmoil of the immigrant masses.

Sandra had her reasons for bringing me—as she does everything else—and as soon as the service ended, she took me by the hand and led me into the sacristy to visit that miracle of a painting, Giovanni Bellini's triptych of the Madonna and Child Flanked by Saints. We stood before it together, her hand tightening on mine, and then Sandra whispered the news in my ear: She is expecting a child! I turned to her, her eyes, desperate to fathom her feelings. Happy? Terrified? Dumbfounded? What of our precautions! But then we embraced with pure bliss. A child ... I tremble. Fatherhood for the likes of me, careless old rue? My model!

She puts a good face on it, but I sense she is crestfallen. All her unspoken plans for her new repertoire. Horatio Brown has been filling her head with thoughts of a London debut.

The gondola—it must have been the gondola. A frivolous moment and the world is irrevocably altered. I think back in my mind; I go over it endlessly. By God, it had to be what she wanted! How perverse women can be.

Little did she know that the Christmas gift I have for her is a small marble statue carved by a local artisan, Giovanni Maronetti, with whom I have struck up a marvelous friendship. The statue is of one of the tiny angels playing the lute at the bottom of the same Bellini painting.

Life is strange. Even when Sandra and I follow divergent paths, they intersect in unexpected ways. Life will have its way with us.

A child, fatherhood—surely I am the luckiest water rat in the world. One must believe in luck.

Venice, January 22, 1914

The cold has made work outside for long spells difficult. I have found an old press and working area for the etchings in a printing shop near the Frari and spend much time with acid and printer's ink to get the things to come out right. Some success with my bridges. Sandra spends more and more time practicing at Casa Alvisi. She seems near obsessed with her playing, as if her new state brings on greater compunctions. I find her at the pensione, soaking her aching hands in warm water. Away from her mother's domineering demands, her music has taken her over as when she was sixteen. Perhaps she wants to take up her neglected career as concert pianist—and leave me without a model!? She denies all: "You have me, Joseph. Isn't that enough?" I quake at the thought of losing her—but then there is the child. I tell myself I should be happy; the child will bond us.

Curtis's servants are solicitous of her every whim, as if she has been crowned queen of their ancient kingdom by the sea; they set up coal braziers by the piano to warm the room when her hands get too cold. I miss old Curtis—can't say why exactly.

Mornings, we spend a lot of time in our room at the pensione while I draw Sandra. I thought her incipient motherhood might dim her passions, but instead it seems to have heightened her awareness of her body and time's passing. I fear not being able to keep apace with her demands and long for the fever of passion of student days past. Her breasts have enlarged somewhat, the nipples slightly distended—beautiful, gorgeous things with the most distinctive fructifying contours. She flaunts herself to me and wonders out loud if I will still want her when she is big with child. I draw madly, as if I must draw sustenance for a lifetime. I begin to see how it was that Giorgione and Titian painted so many nudes, how there is something about this city, the light, the very atmosphere, even the rhythms of the waves, that is conducive to the rendering of feminine flesh. Or perhaps I am entirely naïve in these matters and cannot admit to the role of the erotic and sensual in the eye of the artist. Can anyone really believe that Giorgione and Titian did not feel sexual allure for their models? It is their natural beauty—indeed, the shameless eroticism that eschews the ideal and classical—that makes their women live. They are human and transient and thus enduring. It is the bracing role of the sexual—dare we call it love?—that is at the core of the creative power of this city.

Sometimes I feel Sandra sees this deeper than I—the music, the physical playing, seems to direct her to states of existence to which I remain deaf and dumb. Yesterday, she demanded I go to watch her play the piano at Casa Alvisi. "Paint me like this, why not," she cried. Damned difficult. I sketched rapidly to capture the bold expression in her eyes, the sharp articulation of her fingers—the rapture. I felt a similar power in my moving hand, but a power of expression I cannot as yet release. Her devilish hands! I am too careful, too aware of myself. I hate and love her hands in equal measure.

At Florians this evening, she kept rereading a letter from Angela, finally released by her parents to come and join us in the spring. The prospect of Angela's company makes her giddy with expectation. Florians, with its constant hubbub—the Manzoni crowd flitting like hummingbirds to every flower—seems to bring out an anxious nervousness in Sandra. She fears to miss a minute. She flaunts the new fullness of her décolletage. She gabs with the musicians in the orchestra. Steals my cigarettes. She gestures wildly with her hands in joking imitation of the Italians. I will go buy a paper or cigar, and when I return, I often find one of her Manzoni Salomes whispering in her ear—something wicked and cutting, no doubt. Often she will not leave, preferring to remain with her friends and to send me home alone to the pensione, returning only hours later. Then she sleeps late and our work schedule is further abbreviated.

Venice, March 21

Sandra is ecstatic. She and Angela simply fell upon one another with hugs and tears and laughter, standing for minutes there on the Zattere landing, staring at each other as if into a mirror to evaluate the minutest changes over the course of their separation. I must admit it is a bit of a shock to have developed such intimacies with Sandra and suddenly have her exact twin appear by her side. Of course, I had known Angela before and they are quite different, especially now that Sandra has escaped the provincial enthusiasms of the Chillingworth clan. The intellectual and emotional gap has widened. Angela was never one to show herself off—God knows, she had the chance, with her sister's success. I believe Sandra is similarly disconcerted—though she dare not admit as much to me—to have her sister here, when she has so willingly exchanged her old life for the new. But ever since Angela's arrival, I cannot separate them. They are always off together, arm in arm, chatting away in conspiratorial voices. Sandra, of course, wants all the news from home, but, in turn, I suspect—the wicked twinkle in my beloved's eye—she seeks to take Angela in, make a convert of her to Venetian life, chez Manzoni and those wicked women. Sandra can be very seductive in that way when her enthusiasms are up. They do make a pretty picture together. So now we are three, or are we more? Or less?

Sadly, too, I am reminded of my near-estrangement from my brother, William, who toils ceaselessly in the difficult business of the Lowell mill. Even the London papers report the labor troubles.

Venice, May 2

The brilliant weather continues, but I am deeply saddened by the news that old Curtis died of pneumonia in Palm Beach a couple of weeks ago. I gather it was quick and relatively painless. I feel an emptiness I can't quite explain.

I can't imagine him not returning to his gracious jewel of a palazzo. It is as if a world has flickered out with him. Whistler a decade gone; James, so they say, never leaves his flat in London; and Sargent is forever waylaid by society portraits. The brilliance of their art will live on; one has to believe that. And I feel old, surrounded as I am by these young fillies.

Distressing news from my brother also. More strikes in the Lowell mills and more labor unrest expected. They are under pressure to raise wages, but profits remain dismally low. Brother William writes that negotiations are hard—so many immigrant groups, few even speak the language. Greeks, Poles, Italians; half the time, they are at one another's throats. Radical social doctrines are preached in the streets. Anarchists abound. How can a coherent culture be woven from such disparate elements? William doesn't complain, but I know the doctors are still concerned about his heart after his breakdown last year. All this while I idle away in Venice.

But the work does go well, from strength to strength. My winter drudgery can now be poured into larger canvases. I refine my color and dig for the marrow. And lo and behold, I have not one model, but two. It was uncanny, almost from the moment of Angela's arrival Sandra's remarkable constitution began to wane. Sandra tires from her pregnancy by late morning. At her prompting—no, bold-faced, bullying insistence—she has recruited Angela to spell her. And then, pure inspiration, while I was working on my bridge pictures, they would often stand together and chat—and voilà, the composition was perfect. The two posed together at the apogee of the arc create a mysterious resonance, the mirrored images an additional abstract element complimenting the reflected span in the canal below. Here is a subject not entertained by Jimmy Whistler—a subject to make the city mine. That my name might live with that of Whistler.

Of course, posed on the bridge, they exchange endless confidences and giggles—surely at my expense—during the tedious business of waiting for the light. It is like a secret language they use to exclude me. What do they whisper to one another? I try to read their faces. If only I can get the look onto paper and canvas. I have become their cat's-paw.

Often they simply drift off and leave me fuming while they scamper to the working-class neighborhood for a drink or to hunt bargains in the shops of the craftsmen. Sandra was so taken with my Christmas present of the cherub that she has gotten my stonecutter, Giovanni, to work up a couple of things for her parents' garden at their summer house in Manchester. I overheard Sandra's comment to Angela: "Oh, his hands, Angie, like a god's, like a Michelangelo."

I, too, find myself fascinated with Giovanni Maronetti. His tradition of stone-cutting has been passed down for at least five generations. When we walk, he can point out to me work by the family on buildings all over the city, as if his daily life, the very paths he follows, are hallowed by memories of the family concern. Imagine such a thing in America, a nation so new and so transformed by cheap machined reproductions.

Venice, May 30

We are all exhausted with the work and heat and the rush to complete as much as we can before our early departure for Boston. Angela helps me in the afternoon, when Sandra is napping or at piano practice. The mosquitoes in the afternoon are sometimes too much and we retreat to the trattorias for ice creams. Sandra is early to bed and so leaves Florians to Angela and me. In the night's humidity, Sandra lies naked beside me, staring at the ceiling, asking about Florians, if Angela enjoyed herself. She is hot and plagued by dreams. Her belly is swollen to a lovely roundness. I love to feel our child inside, to draw her like that, but she seems now almost embarrassed. She is anxious. She says I will not love her fat and with children. I assure her often. I should draw Angela, she says with moody conviction. It seems she has shown her sister my portfolio of drawings. I am aghast. "It would be good for her," she says. "It will bring her out." Even now, Sandra wants her loving, though not as energetic as before. She is determined that I have my full satisfactions and she throws herself into these with enthusiasm, inventing new ways of erotic pleasure. And during her ministrations, her hair thrown back, she goes on again about her sister, half joking, half serious, saying that she will teach her all she needs to know to take care of me—"like this, and this," and she kisses me wonderfully—"and you, dearest Joseph, like this and this." She does it to tease and stimulate new visions in my mind, but it excites her as much as it does me. "Angela," she whispers, catching up her hair and making a sad, bereft face and indicating the adjoining wall of our rooms, "all alone and unable to join our play." Instead of one soul grafted to mine, now it is the power of two—the dynamo of these wild alternating currents harnessed to my imagination. How we dare one another to disaster—our water-rat deceptions?

Or am I the one deceived? After a concert at the Fenice, Sandra waxes nostalgic for her prodigy days, touring New York, Washington, Chicago, and San

Francisco, playing her Mozart piano concerto. Horatio Brown has promised an introduction to the top London impresario. How she decried all that—and her mother's whip hand—to me in the first year of her modeling, as I sold out exhibitions in New York and Boston. Then I was useful to her, and she to me.

Music haunts her mind. In the middle of the night, she will be awake, her fingers playing invisible notes on the bedcovers. She yearns for the concert audience again. She speaks of Angela as nursemaid. There is something yet of her mother's calculating ambition in her blood!

Venice, June 8

The days are sultry and sublime. I rush the work at white heat, knowing we have less than a month. I feel a new energy in the brushstroke, a freedom of expression that hovers before my eyes—still ungrasped. None of us can bear the thought of departure. My surfaces shimmer and tantalize; all is on a higher plane—and my new model—what can I say? She blooms.

Sandra has been told by the local doctor to stay out of the heat of the day and so remains behind, reading and seemingly content. She practices only an hour or two. Angela, in turn, genuinely seems to relish her opportunity; she improves day to day. Sandra has instructed her about everything! Sends Angela out to take over much of her social life with the women of the Manzoni, including piano practice at Casa Alvisi. Angela suffered, I think, in Sandra's shadow: a fine pianist, but their mother had early on settled on Sandra as "the talented one." Angela rushes home to share all with Sandra. Not a jot of jealousy seems to enter between them, as if they cannot bear to keep secrets from each other, or that they nourish each other on would-be secrets. It is a little disconcerting, how Angela anticipates my needs so well, will answer a question or respond to some subject in almost precisely the same tone, the very words her sister might use, not to mention the tilt of the head, the play of the eyes—dare I say more? My pen trembles. Angela is something of a poet, recording her thoughts in spare moments or writing letters home. She is shier certainly—more is hidden—but one senses the same powers beneath the surface.

She is like an added circuit to our ambition. Or is it more a closing circle feeding upon itself?

Venice, June 14

I have bought our steamship tickets home. What a row it caused. Sandra is irrational on the subject. Now she talks about having the baby here! She goes on and on about staying and renting the Casa Alvisi—even buying the place with her father's help! "A music school," she says. "Why not turn it into a music academy where the greatest musicians can train and composers write music for them." Crazy things.

I have it on good authority that medical practices here are not up to the standard of London, much less Boston. I tell her it is out of the question. We have already delayed beyond prudence. We can always return, I tell her, but there is something desperate in her demeanor. The other day, we found her gone from the pensione—without note or word—upon our return in the afternoon; it transpires she has gotten the key to the Curtises' garden on the Giudecca. She had been taking the afternoon sun. There is a lovely orchard there, she tells me, a delightful place. All her emotions are heightened. She laughs, she cries, and then, like a summer squall, a blackness comes over her and for hours she is silent and withdrawn. Perhaps it is her delicate condition. But Angela says her mother is also prone to black moods—no Chillingworth will admit to such physical shortcomings. "'Walking, girls'" says Angela, imitating her mother's commanding voice, "'or practicing scales for two hours, is the best cure for what ails the feminine breast.'"

These women are beyond me—demons and angels.

Only at night, or in my sketchbook, do I feel I possess my love fully. How I love the look of her, to hold her great swelling breasts and ripening belly. At night, she takes my hand and presses it against her womb, as if seeking some kind of reassurance. I lie upon her breast and, I swear, I can hear both their hearts. Or is it the drumming of her fingers on my spine playing Scriabin? I think, too, of dear Angela next door, reading, writing—we hear her restless footsteps sometimes late at night. We never say it in so many words, but in the secret darkness we miss her and would have her come to us.

Venice, June 20

I am haunted. I am set reeling backward. Last night, Angela and I strolled to Florians after dinner. Sandra was exhausted and fairly pushed us out the door, as if she would have some part of her carry on and drink to the dregs. At Florians, we were nearly assaulted by Sandra's women friends, some having just returned after the hiatus of the winter months. They fell all over Angela, exchanging risqué confidences in stage whispers, eyeing me brazenly, admiring her clothes; and Angela was all the part. Some, I would swear, did not recognize the difference, did not know of Sandra's present state. Angela said nothing and I watched, I observed, numb with a rising thrill, brandy taking me over.

On the way home, we were passing Casa Alvisi and Angela suddenly took my hand, as if on impulse—but I think not—and pulled me to the land entrance. She had the key now, Sandra's key, and opened the door and sang out to the old caretaker that she had come to play the piano. The old wizened fellow, bent almost double with age, harkened to her call, a desperate gladness in his rheumy eyes upon seeing her. He began an agitated ramble as he led us to the second floor and the grand drawing room and began lighting the candles. As the splendid drawing room came alive around me—marvelous canvas by canvas, gilded furnishings, glittering chandeliers, shutters thrown open to the plashing voice of the Grand Canal—I found myself transported to when Sargent, James, and Zorn reigned like gods in Parnassus. Angela began to play the piano, beautifully, too beautifully, and our little majordomo slowly bowed his way from our presence, all toothless smiles. "Ah, signorina, bellesimo," he said, making fawning gestures with his hands.

An Austrian count has made an offer for Casa Alvisi and Sandra has let the old man believe that the Chillingworths will make a counteroffer. And what is my role in this Chillingworth charade; they who could buy up half of Boston?

I turned and turned on brandy wings, enchanted as if by Velázquez strokes of cadmium blue as she played, Chopin—not Stravinsky. Making my way to the balcony, I found there the swath of city and lagoon in breathless moonlit suspension. I had to close my eyes, as if to regain my bearings. For a moment, I thought I heard old Curtis's baritone, and in this an even more distant voice, and thought of my youthful rambles along the Concord River. I opened my eyes, perplexed, and as I did, Angela stopped playing and the last cords echoed over the pearl white waters below. I turned, suddenly frightened, and found her at the piano in that place of Elysian splendor, candlelight bathing her bowed head, her white shoulders; and it was as it had been, as it had ever been—and would be evermore, as if time were halted. I felt such hope! And she stood, hesitantly, I think, and took a few steps in my direction. Standing outside the frame of the French doors, I looked up then. Our eyes met. She was no longer afraid, but proud as Diana. She turned her face from one side to the other for my inspection, the unspoken question hovering amid the intervening space. Then something startled her, perhaps seeing herself reflected in that remarkable mosaic floor, eyes sharpening to points of gold as she shifted her shoulders and lowered her décolletage a fraction more. The silence there like an eternity—and with it the ambition to move beyond our allotted lives into the eternal life of the city. But who will remember our passing?

These women—I am taken over; I am lost.

Venice, June 28

I cannot write, I cannot write its name. Does death have a name? My soul sinks to nothing.

Venice, June 29

Angela, how like her name, a ministering angel to the dead and dying and the just born. She thrusts my son into my arms and tells me to look, just look. But I cannot bear it, the tiny murderer. I have become a beast, a loveless monster. I rage at the doctor. They say he has left town.

Venice, June 30

Today, we buried her. I cannot write her name. What is in a name? I can still write it—Angela. But what does that conjure? A young mother with babe in arms: the image of one's grief embracing the thing that killed her. But she is the bravest of us, for she bore witness to the suffering and not I, not until the end, when the suffering had done its cruel work. She takes care of the child as if were her own, keeping it in her room, hiring a wet nurse—she with the living and me with the dead.

Venice, July 2

Thinking back on the funeral at San Michele, I find myself confused, as if I had dreamt the thing and it will not come clear in my mind. There was some comfort in the beauty of that place, the brick-walled enclosure and the swaying cedars and summer flowers. I give thanks for the many kind souls who attended. How many in such a short time she had touched with her beauty and intelligence. Horatio Brown, a man of the old school, shed copious tears, telling me she had the finest mind of any woman he had ever known. Of course, Giovanni—poor Giovanni—I knew well; he could not get a word out, but sat in silence, his face buried in his great palms. The Manzoni women were dignified, their black-veiled faces quite stricken with grief. But there was another, a young foreign-looking man, a total stranger, who haunts me. He stood among the mourners in great agitation. At the end of the service, he finally came and shook my hand. He spoke Russian-accented English. It seems he was once a famous piano and composition teacher at the music conservatory in Saint Petersburg, until the czar's police arrested him for revolutionary activity. His dark-circled eyes were streaming tears. It seems Sandra had been studying with him since our second week in Venice, every afternoon, and she had told me nothing. "A genius," he got out in broken English, "she was a musical genius." He said this to me as if I were a fool who had failed to grasp her gifts—an imbecile without art! Then he turned and strode away, muttering curses under his breath.

Today, wandering among the graves in that enclosure, I found myself struggling to place the face of that young Russian, familiar and not. Then it came to me—how many nights at Florians had he been there with the Manzoni crowd, their darling, another of their prodigies?

Purveyor of Stravinsky!

I manage to find some consolation in my beloved's final resting place, a strangely appropriate spot, there among the victims of shipwreck and cholera, the misbegotten deaths of the traveler and the exiled—whose ambitions outran their reach.

The baby did not cry once at the burial. The baby does not seem to know how to cry.

I row. Truly a water rat at the last.

Venice, July 3

We drift like shipwrecks. I inhabit an empty room. She is next door with the child. We fear to walk where people will see us. We fear to speak her name. We fear to learn to live without her. We hold on and inertia takes over. We fear what we should find back in Boston. The Chillingworths cable daily, terrible things. Their lawyers threaten me with legal action. Angela's father demands she return with the child. So we drift and the world drifts with us.

Venice, July 6

Last night, we walked. We avoided the old places, Florians, Casa Alvisi, Palazzo Manzoni. We walked down the Zattere, where the ships come in, huge and looming in the night, small cities of light. We drank among the transient sailors, fellow exiles. And still the faces turned to hers. We lingered along the sturgeon sweep of the Giudecca, she on the edge of the quay, I hanging back in the shadows between the purple lamps. It was as if my life had gone into eclipse, gone to distant, irrecoverable memory, as if one had crossed a ridgeline and now descended the far side, suddenly in shadow, but fearing to look back at the companion lingering behind, her face still in light. And then she turned to me, her features a sudden fire of amethyst agitation, and she whispered, her voice rising, "You must do it for her; you must finish the paintings so that she will live. I will help. Tell me what you need. Tell me—so that my sister will live."

I confronted her with the young Russian pianist. "Tell me," I demanded. She shrieked with dismissive laughter. "A charlatan, a socialist—a nobody." She kissed me, smothering my agony. She took my arm to direct my footsteps.

Later, she came to my room. No lamp was lit—but we burned. She knew exactly—everything. And I gave myself to everything. My heart was stopped.

Venice, July 20

I am determined to finish, to complete what can be completed. We separate early now, before breakfast. She is off to Giovanni to pose for Sandra's monument. I stay behind to paint. I paint out of duty, for her, that not all is lost. In the afternoon, I stroll down the Zattere and weave my way into the labyrinth of the city to the stonecutter's shop and check on the progress. He is a fine craftsman—no, better, an artist. I give guidelines, but I want the rendering to be in the style and tradition of the city where she died. I want the hand in the stone to praise not just her beauty but her love and wisdom. Giovanni takes me aside and speaks in a hoarse whisper. "The hands," he says, and makes the motions of a pianist. He fears he cannot do justice to her hands. I gesture to his patient model and assure him that I have complete confidence in his skills.

And such skills, passed down through the generations. I feel as if the very spirit of the city is embodied in Giovanni. Would it be the same back home: that art might rule our lives so. My mind is made up: When the monument is complete, I go.

Angela has her own plans for Giovanni. She wants to take him to America, another artist for the Chillingworths to invest in. I tell her he will be lost once removed from the traditions and comforts of his native city. At times, she is more hardheaded than her sister—these Chillingworths will be my ruin.

Venice, July 25

Rumors of war everywhere. Every café sprouts an aviary of rustling papers. Since the shooting of the archduke and the mobilization of Austria, all is frenzied. Patriotic hearts beat quickly; the hotels empty, as if a tidal wave looms on the horizon. People speak of mysterious ship movements in the Adriatic. I work up the last of the paintings, and I pore over my humble etchings, mere wisps of paper and ink renderings of a world crumbling before my eyes. But my drawings, my precious drawings—I go over them at night; I dream of them. What to destroy, what to keep. The drawings contain the true life; they open possibilities of renewal. I sometimes feel as I have rowed hard into the current, fighting all the way, and now that I have seen the far shore, I am swept backward. My goal is no longer ahead of me, but behind. I have exhausted this life.

We must flee each other before it is too late.

Venice, August 2

War, war, war—the streets ring with the cry; the newspapers fling their inky headlines in the face of countless readers. This is ambition gone mad. Rumors of British fleet movements. The place empties. Even old Horatio Brown fears he must leave. Like a child, I am intrigued, to witness the conflagration on the horizon, perhaps to cauterize memory. I think about my father. I think about Curtis and all he told me. All that they saw and endured—now, like a premonition of what is to come.

The monument—completed in the last days of peace—is done and it is good. The hands—by Jove, a triumph. And so I must leave her, too.

I sold the shell to an Italian at the local rowing club for next to nothing.

Venice, August 8

The packers have spent two days in my room. All canvases crated. The drawings and prints I keep with me. Already there are first reports of battles and naval engagements. I have booked Angela and child out of Naples for New York.

Yesterday we had the monument placed on her grave in San Michele. It is magnificent, the likeness, the loveliness of her body radiating peace and gentleness of spirit—especially now, against the backdrop of war. The hands—dear Giovanni, yes—I could have done no better. Angela cried, but the child in the nurse's arm made not a peep. Giovanni comforted her. No sign of the Russian.

Angela and Giovanni have become pals; she has been his model and he has seen to the tender core of her. We walk together now at night, the three of us, and it is good; he saves us from ourselves. She speaks to him of America; she has plans for a memorial. Giovanni is quite the socialist, as are most of the artisans. He thinks the war a bad thing and designed by the capitalists to crush the workers. Perhaps he is right. As we sat at Florians for a farewell drink, I noticed Giovanni's hands as if for the first time. I should have drawn his battered and dirty hands, such honest working hands. I will miss him.

All is finished. My train for Paris leaves tomorrow. I sit at my desk and listen to the voices of the water against the stones of the Rio San Vio—voices at peace with memory, or reminders of a shameful past?

CHAPTER 28

It got to the point where time past and present began merging in his mind, Joseph Palmer's diary his indispensable guide to his search. There were moments when he wasn't sure if it was Sandra Palmer he was after or Sandra Chillingworth—so ardent was his desire to hear her voice, her side of the story.

After checking with the Venetian authorities—the police, post office, even the alien-registration office—in his search for Sandra, he spent days and then weeks showing her photo at hotels and pensiones, at restaurants and museums, and came up with nothing but shrugs of mild amusement and smug disinterest. Once, maybe twice, he'd seen someone at a distance who had looked like her, but then lost them. And so he'd find himself returning to the diary, weaving paths to the Casa Alvisi and the Palazzo Manzoni and Florians, searching for the bridge near the Frari on which Joseph Palmer had posed the sisters.

Hadn't Sandra left Sangamore with a copy of the diary? Surely she would be drawn to the places frequented by her forebears. Places, wonder of wonders, virtually unchanged since her grandparents' day.

He might have been more concerned about the probabilities of the whole business if he hadn't immediately found the painting.

He had gone to the modest pensione mentioned in the diary (now a first-class pensione and more expensive than his room at the Concord Inn) and asked for a second-floor room overlooking the Rio San Vio. The painting, a study of a bridge over a canal, was the first thing glimpsed when the double doors to the room were opened: the canvas in a cheap frame, bracketed on the wall by the French doors to the balcony and an ornate floral mirror of Murano glass above the sink. The tiny span was similar to the bridge in the etching, but without figures, and the composition was horizontal.

The thing sealed his expectations. It was Joseph and Sandra Chillingworth Palmer's room, confirmed by the copies he'd brought with him of the artist's drawings.

The painting had been placed there—waiting for him to discover.

Whereas the etching had a feel of the private and permanent, of time frozen, the painting, with its translucent color masses, seemed more alive to the moment. A presence haunting and mercurial, responding as much to his moods as the play of sunlight and the passage of the hours.

Studying the back of the stretcher, which was caked in dust and cobwebs, he could just make out Joseph Palmer's penciled scribble: *number eleven, version three, half past six in the evening, April 18, 1914 – better than version one.* He turned it in his hands, feeling the contour and weight of this talismanic object, as much a physical fragment of a human soul as his mind could conceive. Had it been given as a memento, forgotten, or simply discarded in the final rush of leaving?

Certainly worth serious money in the revived market for Palmer's work!

The painting would be first thing he'd look for upon waking, when the sunlight through the French doors brought out the thick pigments of peach and ocher and Delft blue, floating the color masses before his eyes, as if the reflected light off the Rio San Vio had seeped under the dirt and faded varnish into the very paint and glazes, until the thing burned.

It made the voice of Joseph Palmer in the diary absolutely real to him.

The old lady who owned the pensione (past ninety and spending her days in a back room watching television) knew nothing about the painting or the artist. To her, the thing was simply an odd bit of furnishing that had been on that wall between the French doors and the mirror since she could remember. When pressed on the subject of an American artist and his wife who had stayed in the pensione from 1913 to 1914, the old lady shook her mop of white curls, a world-weary smile appearing on her face at the very thought of such a length of time; but then, carving the features of a lovely face in hand gestures upon her aged jowls, she mentioned an enduring image from her childhood, when her grandfather still ran the pensione, of a tall, elegant lady with long blond hair, an American lady and her husband strolling down the Zattere. "Beautiful," she repeated, "but so sad ... *una donna bellissima, ma triste*." Alas, even the guest register from those days before the Great Patriotic War was no more. And with that, she'd gone back to her TV show.

The painting became another window onto that most illusive quarry, the stream of living memory.

When he returned to his room, often in despair, at the end of a long day of walking, the painting would sustain him. He would situate himself at the writing table and review the diary once again for clues, the etching and the photo of his mother at his elbow, the painting an upward glance—all lending credence to his new life.

Who would have believed what William Channing had managed in Concord? Even the accounts in the *International Herald Tribune* of the FBI raid on the Concord Inn for the missing Michael Collins had expressed amazement at the meticulous planning of his disappearance, how well the fugitive had concealed himself, how completely he had blended in with his surroundings. The police were still baffled by it all, not to mention where the suspect had fled.

And now with a new name and the passport of one Giovanni Maronetti in hand, a very pricey gift of the Internet, he was prepared to repeat his Concord performance and track down his illusive quarry. But without a computer or E-mail. Only ambition and a water rat's eyes.

The diary tantalized him. The circumstances of Sandra Chillingworth Palmer's pregnancy, despite all the "precautions." How she had manipulated her husband and sister to provide herself space and time for a return to her piano career. Her sister as model, then lover and nursemaid! And what of that offstage personage, the young Russian, professor of piano and composition, with whom Sandra Chillingworth had studied every day, and not a word to her clueless husband? Or Horatio Brown, or even Giovanni Maronetti?

As if the city itself was complicit in their deceits.

Like the artist, he longed to read those letters Sandra Chillingworth Palmer had written her sister. He wanted to believe the best about that brilliant woman, as he did about Sandra, even though she had lied to him—about her age, having a twin sister, baby Joey's birth defect, even the time she'd spent in Venice studying piano with her sister—and used him as part of her deceit. She was hardly blameless, as if the selfish usage of others was hardwired in the Chillingworth genes.

About Sandra's child given up for adoption—his child, he wondered endlessly.

At night, the slippery caress of the starched linen sheets allowed the further mingling of his dreams with those of the artist and his model. The carved rosewood headboard with rising dolphins, tails entwined above lunging waves, beckoned his touch. Renditions of the dolphins had appeared many times in the artist's sketches: the nude Sandra Chillingworth Palmer lying sprawled in postcoital bliss, a draped arm across her swollen belly, hand over her pubic mound to stem a drool of semen. He'd even managed to photocopy a few of the drawings, the copies slipped between the pages of the diary as visual reminders of the artist's cuckolded ambition.

Not a sketch remained of those prodigious hands—and only a single painting at Sangamore of Sandra Chillingworth playing the piano. He began to wonder if Palmer's late work was less about love and more an obsessive cover-up, even an indictment of love.

Often he found himself absentmindedly fingering the carving of entwined dolphins, as if talismanic of the thing he sought: the attraction of bodies, which had given birth to the world as he knew it: a bond conceived in love but forever in thrall to deceit and ambition. The law of compensation like a force of gravity.

Not that his vestigial lawyerly self didn't manage a few meager protests over such philosophic flights, much less his modus operandi: all the difficulties of finding a fugitive in a foreign city, much less going by clues in a ninety-year-old diary! If she'd flown to Boston from Venice and then returned, what was to say she hadn't simply moved on, perhaps changed her name, especially if she'd realized what had happened back in the States, if she'd suspected someone was onto her fraudulent ways? Would she have gone into hiding, or had she reassumed her previous life as a restorer or artist, an art historian or teacher? Perhaps monitoring Angela's business affairs from afar. Or maybe Angela's money allowed her some fabulous lifestyle—on the French Riviera, say, someplace he could barely imagine.

Even weighed down with these doubts, he headed out each morning with Sandra's photograph in his pocket. Whenever he found an ongoing restoration project (and they were everywhere), he would stop to make inquiries, showing the experts and craftsmen her photograph. To no avail. He inspected countless passing women's faces, and if a likely figure in the distance required a sprint to catch up, he did it, despite making a complete fool of himself on a regular basis as he startled some female tourist with his mad dash.

Returning in the evening, tired and disappointed, remembering all the shaking heads and queer looks he'd elicited, he'd turn again to the elegantly scripted pages of the diary for something he had overlooked

Could the diary be believed? There had been no revisions or additions, no pages removed, and the meticulous chronology had been sustained throughout. It contained unflinching appraisals of the artist's motivations and faults. And with clear purpose, Palmer had left the diary and the drawings in his archive with his paintings, preserving it—his version of the truth—for posterity, the way he'd preserved Sangamore. To cover his tracks—that his version should outlast that of any competitors.

And what to think about Joseph Palmer's coldness toward his son, not to mention excluding him in his will from the estate? Lest the son, tainted by the Chillingworths, tamper with the father's legacy.

There were nights he could barely sleep, shuttled between erotic dreams and chary skepticism and aroused insomnia. Going to the antique mirror above the sink at 3:00 AM, he was reminded of the voyeur's face in the mirror in Palmer's painting of Florians in the Boston Museum of Fine Arts: the artist, or the young Russian pianist, or, just possibly, one Giovanni Maronetti? And of his night of lovemaking with Sandra by the Concord River, her face thrown back in the moonlight beneath his gaze—that face was now the face of Sandra Chillingworth in the artist's sketches. While Joseph Palmer's failure to take precautions with his seductive bride in the gondola echoed Michael's own failure ... and his besotted naïveté.

As the fall days grew shorter and the nights cooled and the ripe odors of the side canals elided to scents of crisp brine and burning sulfur coal,

the Venice of the diary coalesced with his own quotidian life. He noted
the same pastel gray mists the artist had noted, not to mention the mottled
porphyry and butter-amethyst and lucent cranberry-green in the weathered facades along the Grand Canal. Light, light, light, the artist had
forever cried to his gods … a light filtered and distilled, tinctured and
refracted from surface to surface. Or was Venice a swindle, a thousand
and one masks? All that really mattered was the artist's ambition, his
angle of vision, and that near-obsessive search—genetic marker found
in all the Palmers—for the symbolic armature that suffuses and supports
the material world.

Then he found it.

The bridge was two hundred yards south of the Frari—just where
it should have been. He'd seen it innumerable times without recognizing it, because Joseph Palmer had been on the canal in his rowing shell
and low to the water—a water rat's eye view. He knelt on the pavement of the fondamenta with his cheek pressed to the iron railing. He
squinted into the sheen of dusty olive-blue obscuring the face of the
canal, trying to match the sinuous arch of the bridge with its painted
and etched twin.

Clearly, the artist had adjusted the architecture behind and to the
sides like props on a stage; he'd shifted the ambient tones and raised and
lowered the span to suit the composition. All Palmer cared about were the
relationships of color and mass and the soft-edged contours where forms
intersected. And the matching—tantalizing—gaze of the sisters.

Twice, he was almost sure he'd caught sight of her. His first sighting
had been of a tall, lithesome figure with cropped hair on a vaporetti landing along the Riva degli Schiavoni. She disappeared with a large crowd
of passengers into a number 5 water bus before he could get on board.
Another time, near the same vaporetti stop, it was a tall woman in blue
jeans and sweater taking a corner off the *riva* toward San Zaccaria. But
again he failed to catch up before she, too, disappeared at some indeter-
minate turning or doorway. Always beguiling, the city seemed to drop just
enough crumbs to keep his hopes from utterly flagging. He was counting
on Venice emptying itself of tourists and so elucidating his search. But, of
course, with the cold, people would increasingly remain indoors.

Early on, he'd tried the Protestant cemetery on the burial island of San Michele and the grave monument his grandfather had carved for Sandra Chillingworth Palmer.

This tiny patch of consecrated earth was chock-a-block with lichen-scared graves and statuary, most of nineteenth-century vintage; the place smelled of sere grass and aromatic cypresses—a complete remove from the damp confines of the city across the lagoon.

The standing white marble figure marking Sandra Chillingworth Palmer's grave was in a cramped corner, pressed in by older monuments on all sides. The sculpture was pure Venetian, an evocation of the Bellini Madonna in the sacristy of the Frari—especially the eyes, the tear-verging, knowing eyes. The face, the unmistakable high brow and tapering nose, had obviously been done from life. A modern woman in near-diaphanous robes, standing straight-backed, proud of her New England pedigree. There was almost nothing of the veiled erotic energy of the Concord monument. Something almost chaste, even virginal about the girlish body and small breasts showing beneath the robes, as if giving lie to her hideous end. Only her large hands, though hanging loosely at her sides, displayed a distinctive strength and vigor, every vein and tendon delineated, as if Giovanni had wanted to preserve something of her reputation as a great musician.

Staring at his grandfather's creation, he couldn't help feeling that memory of her physical artistry, much less her compelling intellect, had elapsed over time, to be replaced by images both meditative and sexual—barely touching on her inner life. And perhaps Angela, her granddaughter, had felt the need to redeploy that image and recover something of the integrity of the original—a voice all her own: *The turned-on and turned-out woman ... your ass no longer back of the class.*

He smiled at the memory of Sandy Blue's voice ... a world of female accomplishment and pleasure without hassle or fear, men just one of the possible accessories. Her tapes were in all the video shops. Italians were big-time fans.

But what of Sandra Chillingworth, the child prodigy who had played Mozart in Symphony Hall at sixteen? What of that Russian pianist and composer? What of the Chillingworth letters?

He quickly gave up on the monument, fearing a growing morbid fascination: that he might yet settle for the romanticized dead and forgo the living.

By the third week of December, fog shrouded the city most mornings, sometimes giving way to sunshine by midday, at others thickening to a cool, misty rain. He spent more and more time indoors, nursing drinks at trattorias, watching the passing stream of pedestrians, with occasional glances at his *International Herald Tribune* for any news out of Boston or Washington.

Sometimes he had to laugh at the ineptitude, and the laughing kept him sane.

A *Newsweek* exclusive told how William Channing had left a note for the receptionist at the inn, spelling out a family emergency that had made it necessary for him to leave suddenly for his home in Michigan. In the note, William Channing had bequeathed the receptionist the books left behind in his room; what she didn't want could be donated to the inn. Days later, long after Channing had fled, the FBI had raided the Concord Inn. They'd broken into the Thoreau Room and arrested the current inhabitant, a local dealer in rare books, who had gone to the inn for his weekly tryst with his lover. On that particular day, the book dealer had lingered in the Thoreau Room at the conclusion of his assignation, intrigued by some of the old books left by a previous occupant, books that the custodial staff had taken upon themselves to deploy as decorative accessories about the room. The poor man had not only gotten his name in the paper but was facing divorce proceeding from his wife. There had been enormous confusion surrounding the former inhabitant of the Thoreau Room, William Channing. Even in the face of police and FBI inquiries and photos of Michael Collins, the staff of the inn attested to this Thoreau scholar's probity and bona fides, maintaining a touching loyalty to the Bill Channing they remembered.

He had to laugh.

Just as well he'd disposed of her computer in the Dumpster in the parking lot before he'd left.

And notwithstanding their disclaimers to the contrary, after the failed FBI raid, the *Globe* had followed up on his E-mail tips and launched an investigation of its own into campaign financing by the construction industry and contracts on the Lowell Plan, handing Jack Mahoney one hell of a bellyache. Then in late November, the whole story had dropped off the face of a cliff and, if the papers were to be believed, Michael Collins and William Channing had returned to limbo.

His resolve began to weaken. He was drinking more, tempting his father's demons.

Even if he found her, what future would be left to him? Years of trials and legal fees. Even a successful defense would mean personal bankruptcy. His cash—once having seemed inexhaustible—was running low. The pensione was three hundred dollars a day. And as his cash disappeared into currency exchanges throughout the city, so the legitimacy of his defense: that his abrupt disappearance and hiding fueled by the cash had been a reasonable action, given that his life had been threatened. But the longer he hid out, the tougher it would be to reclaim anything worth having of his previous life. What jury would believe a man who had taken the money and run, who had traded on not just one alias but two, and who had skipped the country?

He began to wonder if he'd argued himself down a blind alley and was too damn stupid to realize it. Like his sculptor grandfather, Giovanni Maronetti, cheated and badly used, who had ended up in dead-end Lowell—cat's paw of Chillingworths and Palmers alike.

Even his grandfather proved elusive. He'd made the rounds of the small artisan shops and the stonecutters south of the church of the Frari, asking after the Maronetti family. Only one old man who oversaw the work of his sons, who produced headstones for the funeral trade, remembered anything at all. The man had mumbled that, yes, yes, there had been such a family when he was a boy, but—and his undulant hands described dispersing smoke—they, or perhaps just the son, had gone away, perhaps to America; he couldn't be sure.

He found himself haunted by the old man's gesture of lives going up in smoke.

Nevertheless, he continued to wander the streets around the great Franciscan church of the Frari, going into the sacristy to visit the Bellini

Madonna as Joseph Palmer and his wife had done, crossing and re-crossing the tiny bridge that had inspired the artist's etchings. He kept in mind Thoreau's admonition that the only way to truly see, to capture the essence of change amidst changelessness, was to know one small circuit of the landscape like your own heartbeat. And that's how he noticed them, a group of drawings and watercolors hung with paperclips on a red ribbon in the display window of an art supply shop on the Campo dei Frari. The window had been rehung for Christmas and the drawings and watercolors were for sale. He stared though the window at the lovely sketches of sinuous poplars with an ancient bell tower in the distance. Most were of the tower itself seen from different angles and perspectives, especially the four-columned logia and rustic brickwork. None were signed.

Something was familiar in the vibrancy of the line and the luxuriant tone of the crosshatching and blue-gray washes to create depth and subtle shadow. The woman behind the counter of the shop was wearing a denim painter's smock emblazoned with a cartoon Santa Claus. Yes, she said, they are very fine and cheap, perfect Christmas presents. He bought two of the watercolors of the bell tower and began a casual conversation as the saleswoman prepared to wrap them between pieces of cardboard.

He pointed to the bell tower in the watercolor and asked where it was.

"Santa Maria Assunta."

"Santa Maria … dove, where did you say?"

The woman smiled sweetly at his faltering Italian and replied in near perfect English. "On the island of Torcello. The American lady works there."

"The artist?"

"A restorer, I think. But yes, an artist. She brings me things to sell when she needs more supplies."

"Of course, I knew it; she's an old friend of mine." He pushed the high school graduation photo of Sandra across the counter.

The woman scissored her chin. "Perhaps, but not so young."

He laughed in spite of himself and touched her arm with a gesture of thanks and not a little relief. "Sandra Palmer, always so hard on herself … she never wanted to sign her work."

This drew a curious look but also a look confirming an existing suspicion.

"Ah, yes ... so that is her name. Good artists, they are never happy with the result."

CHAPTER 29

As soon as the number 18 vaporetto left the burial island of San Michele in its wake, heading for the outer islands and Torcello, he felt an odd sense of release, as if this voyage was the thing neglected from the get-go. Somewhere out there—he leaned forward over the bow railing, peering over the gray plane of water to a smudge of russet-green bobbing on the horizon—had to be a place where one could plant one's feet on true terra firma, in earth so hallowed with extraordinary age that further metamorphosis was impossible. No more compass corrections, no more calculations. He'd read up enough on the history of Venice to know that Torcello was the seedbed of Venetian civilization, the first inhabited island of the lagoon, going back to the fourth century A.D. Refugees from the ravages of Attila had first settled there. Eventually, the island had been abandoned after plague and economic decline, its inhabitants heading for thriving Riva Alto—Rialto, the nucleus of modern Venice. Torcello had slipped into uninhabited obscurity.

Nearing the island, he could make out a lone campanile of tan brick with an observation area consisting of three white columns fretting four arched windows. It seemed to rise out of an overgrown obscurity. Sight of the tower brought on a fever of latent anxieties. Leaning far over the bow rail, as if tempting catastrophe, he indulged his sense of fear and pleasure that the prospect of falling gave him, some residuum of his fall from the Andover Street bridge, of a plunge without surcease ... just the gentle buoying of waters. The certainty crept in upon him that it was this tower, of the many towers he had known (how many he passed every day in Venice), that presided over what had been eluding him all along, a near-deserted island where the lost part of himself might come to light, the rest only a distraction.

Disembarking, he found himself alone on the quay. He was so emotionally drained that he was initially unable to bring himself to do what he'd come for. Instead of taking the cinder path to the cathedral, he let himself wander, keeping the campanile of the cathedral in sight, as if a beacon for his circulating footsteps along the tiny footpaths. He passed fallow vineyards and stark olive groves. Small shuttered buildings, a dovecote, weathered cypresses, an overgrown garden with fragments of ancient marble—fluted columns and Corinthian capitals—scattered in the grass. He found himself overwhelmed by it all ... the vastness of time's moving shadow, of how effortlessly the earth reclaimed the pitiful artifacts of what had once been a thriving city. Only the old cathedral, whose ancient campanile accompanied him on every horizon, remained as testament to what had been. The autumnal feel of the landscape allowed him a sloughing of expectation and acknowledgment of the ultimate insignificance of all that he was about. Amid the obliterated remnants of an entire civilization, what did his loss—his family's extinction—count for, his but one in a universe of perennial loss. Loss was the commonest ailment of the human race. Deception ... endemic. He breathed deeply of the earth-scented air and tried to gather his resolve.

By the time he finally entered the near-deserted *campo* of Santa Maria Assunta, letting his gaze indulge the ancient brickwork of the cathedral and nearby baptistery and campanile, he was prepared to give her up, resigned to the inevitability of failure.

Above all, he yearned for peace of mind.

He entered the cathedral. The interior was cool, almost cold. He zipped up his fleece pullover. Silver-blue light filtered down from the high windows. His footsteps echoed. He found himself infatuated with the uncluttered spaces, the purity of the rounded arches, the lack of accumulated life and busy worship. The main apse was covered in scaffolding and screened with green plastic mesh. Sunlit mosaics covered the entire west wall. The scenes were of doomsday, of bowed sinners led off to damnation. The mosaics sparkled in the sunlight, looking as if they had been recently cleaned and restored—completed yesterday and not eight centuries before. He stood staring: a glimpse of the end of time—for the deceivers and deceived alike.

Then he turned away with a slight shiver and walked down the center aisle toward the main apse, drifting under the spell of the luminous tones of magenta-blue. This was what life and architecture should aspire to—so it struck him: a kind of stately simplicity, some platonic ideal—a perfect room and perfect place, endowed with a woman's name. As the sweet breath of the stone came over him, he remembered the painting of the daydreaming Saint Augustine emblazoned on Sandra's computer screen, the face of the saint turned to the otherworldly light.

The place was as he might have dreamed it.

He went to a cordoned-off work area by the marble iconostasis at the front of the apse. Carved there were exotic Byzantine peacocks. He stood very still, aware of a slight tapping punctuated by a thin scraping noise and the creaking of the scaffolding. Somewhere above, screened by the green webbing, a restorer was busy. He stepped into the cordoned-off area, staring up at chinks of brilliant gold mosaics behind the scaffolding. Footsteps above, glimpses of a figure moving down a ladder, a blue beret and blue work apron, yellow rubber gloves, bucket in hand.

He waited in dead stillness, as if some animate part of him had fled and left a mere shadow.

He recognized the thin Chillingworth nose the moment she reached the bottom of the ladder. She turned to deposit the bucket in a corner of her work area. She was unaware of his presence and began searching among the bottles on one of the trolleys.

His felt invisible, drained of substance and sensation. He couldn't remember his name. He couldn't even put her name to his lips, much less open his mouth. And then a feeling of claustrophobia, as if the great space of the apse was shrinking to an area no bigger than a studio packed with artist's tools and brushes. He wanted to make some motion, but he could not. Terror filled him: that he really was invisible, that he'd crossed some permeable membrane, to find himself trapped outside himself.

She sighed and shook her head with irritation at something lacking or misplaced on the trolley. She pulled off her yellow gloves and laid them over the handles of the trolley and then pulled off her beret, freeing her short brassy hair.

He extended a hand but could not be sure it was reaching out.

She started back, seeing him there.

"Sandra," he got out, his extended hand going to his whiskerless chin as if needful of making sure of his own flesh and blood.

She reacted to his voice with a startled grunt and caught herself on the trolley, fear tightening her blue eyes.

"Sandra," he said again, taking a step, feeling the stone floor beneath his feet.

"I'm sorry," she shot back with sudden equilibrium, her face steady with a wary squint. "Do I know you?"

"Sandra, it's me, Michael Collins—remember? From Emerson Academy … Concord."

Her expression softened at the mention of names. She shook her hair back, pursing her lips, eyes withdrawn in an instant of thoughtful deliberation.

Her voice had a soft chiming cadence. "She … Sandra was my sister, my twin sister."

"Oh, I see." He took another step, aware of penetrating through to some more intimate space, as if experiencing a sudden change in atmospheric pressure, blood rising to his face, his lips. Blinking, he saw now the age lines, the reddened hands that she seemed to be hiding by keeping them folded in front of her. "Once, I was really in love with her." The echo of his voice rebounded, as if from somewhere else. "Then, somehow, we lost contact. She kind of disappeared."

"Yeah, she got shipped off to Switzerland."

"Switzerland?"

"What did you say your name was?"

"Michael, Michael Collins." He looked around a bit sheepishly, currents of joy and fear and disbelief running riot in his veins. "Amazing, finding you here."

Her blue eyes narrowed, a play of quickening emotions in their corners.

"Right. Now I remember … *something* about you."

"I loved her." It came out more agonized than he wanted, an instinct to candor he feared the moment the words were gone.

She shook her head. "I'm sorry to have to tell you this, but she died last year."

"Oh … God." He closed his eyes, reaching to a marble column to ground himself in some reality more substantial than what he was facing.

"It was *really* horrible," she enunciated with a staccato rhythm, heart-felt but laced with warning. "I don't like to talk about it—if you know what I mean."

He took a deep breath. "I didn't know—"

"What brings you here?"

He had to think the words out. "Travel, sabbatical—you know, Venice."

"Business or pleasure?"

She stood with shoulders forward, taking control.

"Tell me what happened."

"Like I said, I'd rather not talk about it, okay?"

"Why did she go to Switzerland?"

"She got herself pregnant."

"I see. You don't know—"

"The baby, you mean. Put up for adoption. To tell you the truth, we really didn't keep in touch much."

"For adoption?"

"So," she said with a quick turn to attend to a matter of housekeeping and draw a line under the previous subject. "Something special about Venice?"

He barely registered her question, so intent was he on her movement. She was rummaging behind some bags of lime and pulled out her back-pack, as if possibly concerned for its safety.

Her words had echoed in the high vaulting and he looked up. "Venice," he got out. "My grandfather came from Venice."

"No kidding." She cocked her head, pulling a tube of hand cream from her bag.

He said very precisely. "Giovanni Maronetti was his name, a stone carver."

"Giovanni Maronetti," she repeated, giving the name a perfect Ital-ian singsong, an incredulous smile lengthening her lips. "No wonder there's something familiar about you. My great-aunt knew a Giovanni Maronetti. She'd show us photos of him in her albums in Manchester. Of course" —she paused to cap the tube and begin rubbing the cream into her hands— "Aunt Angie was ... well, eccentric. He was her *Venetian* lover."

He came closer, watching her hands twist in greasy struggle.

"What a coincidence." He was taken aback at the cynical defensiveness that had edged his voice. "I think he went to America in 1921 or thereabouts, to work for the artist Joseph Palmer."

"Absolutely right. Worked for my grandfather for a while and then … I don't know." She smiled, slipping the tube into the bag and fixing him with raised eyebrows. "But I guess *you* do."

"He moved to Lowell; he spent the rest of his life carving grave monuments."

"Is that right…." Her voice faded, as if the subject had been too banal for words. Then after a pensive examination of his face, her eyes met his full on. "How extraordinary."

He said. "Kids do crazy things."

It was as if she was right with him. "So, you were the guy with Sandra at the dance."

"We make things up, hide behind half-truths—even lie, lose the path and find ourselves someplace we never expected to be."

"Like Venice, huh?"

"Like Concord: Main Street, a freezing winter's day. You were wearing a long gray coat and black leather boots … and we were about to have a hot chocolate at the inn."

Her eyes wavered, deepening with consternation. Then a swift glance at her watch. "Listen, I'm afraid I really must get back to work. It's been nice meeting you."

He took a step toward her and she stepped back.

He raised an empty palm. "There hasn't been a day I haven't thought about her."

"I'm sorry you had to find out like this, from me."

He was close enough to grab her, embrace her, to feel the heat of her.

"Can we at least have a meal? I'd like to talk to you about Sandra."

"I'm not sure that's a great idea … for either of us." She stepped back again, under cover of surrounding shadow.

"Just to talk."

"I'm not sure it's really possible. My schedule is pretty tight right now."

"A drink?" He focused on her intently. "That way, I don't have to come all the way out here and keep bugging you."

Her gaze narrowed in the half-light, taking his full measure. She gestured, a flippant fling of an open palm. "Sure, why not." She reached for her yellow gloves. "Tell you what, why don't we meet at Florians—tonight, say eight-thirty."

"Great…. What did you say your name was?"

"I didn't, at least for now." She held up a gloved hand with the flattened palm toward him. "Ciao, Michael."

CHAPTER 30

He left Santa Maria Assunta in a near-daze of contradictions, at once both giddily happy and confused, resigned and relieved and a little aghast at how easily they had both settled into the most convenient and painless lies. Walking the path back to the vaporetti stop, oblivious of the landscape that had so captivated him an hour before, he sensed a mutuality of instinct, the possibility of a distillation of personality to the barest root elements and a fresh start. Her face and still-young body had taken him over.

All the way back to Venice, and that evening soaking in his tub, he felt the joy of sloughing off one life for another, one mask after another. He thought back to her face, aged but retaining much of the beauty and grace of her youth, of her progenitors: a throwback, and yet so modern in her work clothes with short hair and dirty hands. And those eyes, the blues filling and deepening to purple azure in that diaphanous shadow-filled place … eyes that, at the very least, must have looked upon the suicide of her sister. His lawyerly self, his rational twin, kept insinuating cautionary admonitions to his client to ease forth the necessary confession and gain her acquittal: the implications of perceived complicity, a plea bargain for failure to report a death, for impersonating the deceased. Stress, temporary insanity, nervous breakdown, a decision in the heat of a traumatic incident that had then taken on a momentum of its own? He saw the jury's nodding heads.

He marveled at how easily one's life became another, as effortlessly as Sandy Blue had risen from her sensual dream self, only to then embrace her double. Going back into his room to dry off from his bath, he glanced from the painting and caught sight of himself in the Murano mirror: a younger Giovanni Maronetti from the old man he'd known as a boy, but the same ruggedly handsome Italian features—absent the beard, the Roman nose, an exacting stare under pinched, dark eyebrows. And behind that face in the mirror, lay the bed with its entwined rosewood dolphins. The hoot of a boat horn sounded as a vessel passed in the Rio San Vio. He turned. Reflected in the dull glass of the French doors was a ghostly figure with a full erection tenting the linen towel around his waist.

Once he was outside on the lamplit Zattere on the way to Florians, his provisional future fell away again and he was back in the arms of Joseph Palmer's diary, the artist passing his favorite haunts: the Accademia bridge and the chandelier-lit interior of Casa Alvisi, the Palazzo Manzoni, the church of the Giglio with the angels on its rooftop blowing their trumpets of gold, the fashionable shops where the young bride had bought her wedding dress and trousseau, the lace underwear glimpsed in disarray in the drawings, and finally the Piazza San Marco, bathed in a halcyon glow.

What did age—any age—matter?

He took an inside table at Florians, next to the glass partitions, where he could immerse himself in the passing life of the square, bathe himself in the treacly melodies poured forth by the white-jacketed orchestra: Lehár and Strauss and—yes, Chopin, the later gaily waltzed up, as if it had only been yesterday, that fin de siècle world brought striding back to him, swirling out of the fog on the piazza in the guise of an elegant woman wearing a full-length loden coat and fur-trimmed collar. Her blond hair was swept back in dramatic moussed creases, face tastefully made up, only enough to emphasize the undiminished beauty of the eyes and the perfection of the cheekbones. She was stunning, regal, her artisan self transformed. She barged through the phalanx of waiters by the door to slip into the seat across from his like the most insouciant of habitués.

"So, Michael, tell me what you're up to." She signaled the waiter, who seemed to know her; she'd have what her companion was having, she told him.

"I'm on sabbatical."

She began easing off her black leather gloves, finger by finger.

"Research on your grandfather?"

"Not exactly. I'm a Thoreau scholar."

"In Venice?"

"Thoreau and American landscape painting. I've been researching the life of Joseph Palmer, *your* grandfather. You see, I found his Venetian diary—it's quite something."

She laid her gloves neatly on the linen tablecloth and, spotting the waiter again, made a rolling motion with her fingers toward her mouth, indicating the *dolci* plate.

"And Giovanni Maronetti?"

"Yes, Giovanni, too, seems to play a part in Joseph Palmer's and his model's life. And it sure would be nice to know what Sandra Chillingworth Palmer wrote in her letters from Venice."

Seeing his eyes go to her hands, she playfully stuck them beneath the table.

"Don't look at them; they're awful. The plaster and resins don't come off and I can't keep washing them. The nails are a disaster."

"Honest dirt."

"Old dirt—the oldest."

"Pianist's hands?"

She glanced around. "Hasn't changed much." She sighed.

He followed her eyes to the garlanded frescoes, the Murano-glass chandeliers, and the well-heeled patrons in fluid Armani grays. Turning back to her, he was startled to find his face in the mirror directly above where she sat, as if her presence at the table had completed a composition lacking an essential element. It came to him with suddenness: the painting, *Florians*, in the Boston Museum of Fine Arts ... the watching face in the mirror behind the two sisters, the iconology of infidelity and deception.

"Oh," he spouted giddily, "give or take a hundred years."

"But a little the worse for wear." She directed his attention to where she stamped her foot. "See what the '66 flood did to the inlaid floor. And there's the high-water mark on the frescoes, almost impossible to get the salt crystals out of plaster." She paused at the arrival of the waiter. "You okay?"

The waiter dropped off her brandy and the dessert plate. Michael held his glass up to hers, trying to keep his hand from shaking.

"Sounds like the city has taken quite a beating."

She took a sip, letting the warm liquid linger in her mouth. "Moisture, rising damp, salt, atmospheric pollutants, chemical runoff, time—all take their toll."

He rolled his brandy snifter. "You've come through well. Haven't changed much—you look great."

She held her drink up in mocking salute and took another sip.

"I have to tell you, I was seriously contemplating a no-show this evening. An old boyfriend of my sister—who needs it? But I must admit, I was a little intrigued by the Maronetti connection. And then the name, Michael Collins, that had a familiar ring."

"Common as dishwater."

"And then there it was again in a month-old copy of the *International Herald Tribune* back at my place: grand jury investigation into congressional influence peddling, a mysterious figure who skipped town with a lot of cash and dropped off the face of the earth. And I thought, Hey, far-out, this dude washes up on *my* shore."

"I guess Venice can be a pretty useful backwater for all kinds of sins."

She got a napoleon off the plate and took a big bite, mumbling. "So hungry ... umm," then licked her finger. "But you know what fascinates me: how we were going to change the world—remember? Put our own seal on the modus operandi. And then everybody comes along twenty years later, cutting the same old corners."

"You grow up, try things out, find what works, what doesn't."

She finished the napoleon, eyes narrowing with pleasure, folding the little green doily and licking her fingers again.

"Know what matters? That it's genuine, the real thing, the authentic you. The rest doesn't matter."

"How I felt at that dance."

She sat bolt upright, surprised but intrigued.

"That stupid dance," she said softly, as if struggling to refrain from the facetious.

"Kids do stupid things. It doesn't mean it wasn't real." He looked away and then right at her. "I was in love with you."

Her eyes snapped to attention.

"Whoa ... take it easy, okay?"

"It's okay. I can imagine you've been through hell."

She cocked her head, curiosity spilling into irritation.

"Listen, you get laid, get my sister pregnant at a prep school mixer, a *long* time ago. What makes you the expert? What the fuck do you know about anything?"

He fished in his coat pocket and brought out some yellowed pages torn from a spiral notebook and handed them across the table. "The truth when I read it. Do you remember? It was confiscated and only recently returned to me."

She opened the pages of Sandra's letter to him after the night of the dance and carefully spread them on the tablecloth, smoothing them down, leaning back to read them. He could see the skin at the intersection of her brows tightening, crinkling, a hint of trembling. By the second page, her eyes were tearing up and she had to wipe at them with the back of her hand. Finally, she closed her eyes and sat back, pushing at the sheets of paper as if to hurry them away.

"How dare you show me this? Stupid little idiot." She grabbed her napkin and dabbed at her cheeks.

"Genuine enough for you to feel like that?"

"She was a damn fool. She had no idea what she was doing."

"Guess it runs in the family. Her grandmother running off with an artist to marry in Venice … and maybe worse."

Her head snapped forward. "Just what the fuck *are* you up to?"

"Listen …" He bent forward to pronounce her name and then restrained himself. "I can help. We can explain things."

She laughed. "'We'? Oh, explain away. I forgot you're a lawyer. I'll bet you're good at making just about any case the situation or client requires. Or do you just make it up as you go along?"

He leaned across the table. "I found you."

"Is that it, a trip down memory lane? Your last romantic illusion from school days?"

"Christ, never did I imagine you'd end up so cynical, so bitter."

His words seem to break something in her. Her shoulders lost their lift, her stare drifting inward. She began to shake her head.

"Until a few hours ago, I was just fine." She got up suddenly and grabbed her bag and gloves and headed for the door. "I'm sorry I couldn't be more help to you."

He called after her, but seeing she wasn't going to wait, he hastily fumbled in his pocket for some money and left it on the table. He followed at a safe distance, where he wouldn't lose her. She walked slowly, clearly not intent on escaping him, her gaze lowered to the damp pavement as if careful of her steps or lost in thought. He was a little high from the drinks, veering between panic when he lost her for a moment around a sharp turn and anger when she hovered ahead of him, not even bothering with a backward glance.

Then she lost momentum, slowed and stopped, facing a late-night trattoria where locals had gathered for drinks and dancing. She went inside and took a seat at a small table. He followed and sat across from her. She avoided his eyes and ordered a cappuccino from a young waiter who gave her shoulder a familiar pat. Michael had the same. The music was loud, the cigarette smoke thick. He assumed a casual air and inspected the soccer posters hanging behind the bar. On the small dance floor, couples eddied in lethargic embrace to insipid Euro pop. She sipped her coffee and stared at the dancers. Then, as if some calculation of cause and effect had clicked in her mind—or maybe because the music finally got to her—she downed her coffee, shed her coat, and went over to the jukebox and began a careful examination of the playlist. She fed a coin into the machine and punched in her selections, then stood waiting in her short black dress. Her legs were long and shapely. When her song began, she came over and took him by the hand.

On the dance floor, she assumed a determinedly proper stance. The song was Crosby, Stills, Nash & Young: "Teach Your Children Well." It was not much to dance to, but it took him back, which seemed the point. In the half-light and shadow and wretched smoke, her face lost twenty years. But the exercise felt awkward and self-conscious. The touch of her was odd, her perfume nice, her hair a little hard-edged for his taste. He wanted to give himself to the moment. As if supremely conscious of this need in him, she put both her arms around his waist to draw him close. The feel of her was thrilling in a drowning sort of way, the curve of her lower back, the softness of her breasts … at last a bodily reality.

"Is this more like it?" he heard her whisper.

He didn't have a chance to reply before her mouth had found his, her tongue rippling aggressively, probing his lips. Then she slipped the kiss as the song ended and nuzzled his ear for a moment, nipping at the lobe.

"My place, come on."

Their destination turned out to be practically around the corner, not the humble apartment he had expected, but the entire *piano nobile* of a monstrous palazzo overlooking the Rio dei Greci. For the first time, he detected nervousness as she fumbled with her keys, then barged through the front door with a kind of desperate swagger, as if to get it over with. She switched on lights as she marched through one glorious room after another. The place was a dazzling display: everywhere, museum-quality works of art. The ceilings soared into frescoed lands populated with mythic creatures. Baroque chandeliers of Murano glass fountained above their heads. There were threadbare tapestries and Chinese export porcelain, rococo furniture inlaid with mother-of-pearl, cabinets of Renaissance silver and Roman gems and Macedonian seals. Persian rugs softened their footsteps as she led him on, pointing out the highlights: the Caneletto over the carved marble fireplace by Pietro Lombardo, the Guardis and Longhis in the sitting room, the Modigliani nude over the double bed in the master bedroom, and the Morandi still life in the library. Her voice was mechanical, as if simply reviewing the evidence. He was brought up short by the Bechstein grand piano and began to inspect the photos in silver frames. Her voice didn't miss a beat.

"I've been living with him for the last year. It's his Venetian pied-à-terre. He's a banker in Milan. His family, his bank, they've given generously to restoration projects all over the city.

"You're his" —he picked up one of the silver-framed photos— "live-in conservator."

"He likes me here, especially when he's away for long stretches."

"Security' sake." He examined the photo of the distinguished gray-haired man in tweed jacket and riding boots.

"Yes, we're lovers."

He replaced the photo next to one of an al fresco luncheon party, the entire extended family. He went to the ivory keys, reaching with his right hand to play a few bars of Chopin, while keeping his eyes fixed on her with an accusatory squint.

"You're his mistress."

She reached to close the cover over the keyboard. "Whatever you like."

"What happens when the family descends en masse?"

"They go mostly to their mountain place in Cortina."

"He's funding the restoration of the mosaics?"

"His bank."

"Lock, stock, and barrel."

"I'm on salary and it's not very much."

"His place." He jutted an angry jaw at the four walls.

"I enjoy my time with him. He's handsome, engaging, smart, a connoisseur of the very first rank, and, yes, he's a great lover."

"Christ, he could be your father."

"Ah, low blow." She reached to adjust one of the silver frames. "Please don't get your fingerprints all over."

"Fuck this. This is pure convenience."

He walked away and crossed the room to the great swath of windows and French doors leading to the carved Gothic balcony and scintillating view of San Zaccaria in the near distance.

She followed, cornering him. "What did you come for? What did you expect *exactly*? Married, a few kids?"

"And look at this," he cried, spreading his arms. "A room with a view—a big fat fucking glorious view. I'd kill for a view like this."

"Ah, the real you," she said with icy snideness.

He turned with a histrionic flourish. "So, what about *his* family?"

"He's a terrific father. His second bunch of kids, after his first wife died. His wife is happy, in her way."

"Does he love you?"

"I think you better go now."

"This is a fucking museum. There's no love here."

"What would you know about love?" She made an obscene pumping gesture with her hand.

He jerked a hand across his face, as if shocked by a blow.

"I'm sorry. Please, Sandra—"

"Don't ever call me that," she shrieked. "Don't do it."

"What does he call you?"

"Just leave now, please." She turned and walked to the door of the room and began switching off lights.

He followed, glancing around, shaking his head.

"How could I compete with this … the past incarnate."

She had the front door open and waited with head bowed, hand gripped on the brass security chain. He stopped on the threshold, staring into the darkness of the stairway.

"This isn't a game," she rasped out with a sigh. "The alternative to survival isn't worth discussing."

"Just tell me one thing." He took a step into the stairwell and turned to where she stood. "Why didn't you go to your father's for dinner?"

She looked straight through him, her head beginning to nod.

"You ... it *was* you."

He waved a disgusted hand and was gone.

CHAPTER 31

He slept for almost three days. He hoped to slip back to some bedrock of unconsciousness, free of memory and empty of sensation: a canvas scraped clean. Sometimes he wondered if he had refrained from touching her, refused the dance ... kept it abstract, whether the absurdity of the whole business would have become clear. Better being the total idiot than having this leaden lump of despair in his chest. He thought back to the hour wandering on Torcello before he found her, when he'd almost gotten outside himself enough to gain some approximation of happiness. He dreamed of those places, the wan veneer of sunlight in the olive groves and vineyards battened down for the winter, the dovecote, the marbles—all overseen by that lovely campanile.

The memory of the island, of the light in the cathedral, these solidified his resolve. He had to get beyond desire or despair and playing games of cat and mouse. She was simply responding to the threat he posed, no matter what names they used, no matter his benign intentions. He knew too much. He walked his room, realizing how stupid he'd been not to go to the superintendent of monuments first thing and inquire after her. Why hadn't he thought to do that? Had some part of him been afraid to bring the business to a conclusion, for fear of what he'd find?

He went to his worktable and got out an excerpt from her Ph.D. thesis, a new introduction she'd been working up just a week before Angela arrived in Cambridge. She'd eschewed technical jargon and let her enthusiasm for her subject come through. As he reread the introduction, he tried to match the printed voice to the woman's he'd sat with at Florians.

Working as a restorer in Venice is an experience unlike that anywhere else. Of course, the city is like nowhere else. It seduces lavishly. The seduction is visual and the spell that is woven is one of a confluence of sensation, not disparity. It is the triumph of light and color over detail, of the spirit inherent in form. But what most dazzles and often baffles the veteran restorer is the delicate valence, the synergistic bond, between the various arts in this elusive city.

One can say, as many do, that it is simply Venice. Artists love the texture of Venetian light; they love the refracted color that softens shapes and makes for pleasing pattern. The same light and color can be found in all the building crafts, the mosaic floors of San Donato or San Marco, in the filigree of the Ca'd'Oro and the brickwork of the Doge's Palace. But when one gets close to the artwork, close enough to get your hands dirty, to feel the grain, the shape of a chiseled contour, the flourish of the brush stroke, one feels something different: that among the craftsmen and artists there exists an affinity of emotion that goes beyond form and color to man's deepest needs: his abiding love, a love for the striking power of illumination that fixes transient beauty—the moment of inspiration—in memory. Art is memory. For the artist, this memory of light and color is more real than the reality. It is joy made manifest. And nowhere is this more true than in Venice.

This atmosphere of love—for want of a better expression—is, strangely, more apparent when one is separated from it by time and distance. As I sit at my computer in Cambridge, staring into a garden of sky-blue hydrangeas, I am more aware than ever of the overpowering presence of light and color— the rarest tonalities—in the Venice I remember. One senses more completely how—walking the city, moving through space—the line between art and nature has been blurred, how the way we see reflects our way of being, how our awareness of love is only as good as our capacity to love, that without an authenticity of spirit, the genuine remains beyond our grasp.

The triumph of Venice in the aesthetic sphere was to find an alliance between material value and beauty and thus elucidate a spiritual power. At a distance it reaches us like an afterglow, which, in turn, can reilluminate beauty neglected elsewhere, those bits of gold in the slurry of our life. It helps us believe in the possibility of a community of spirit—a family—that endures through time, of a whole greater than the sum of its parts. The artist is our better self—if only we are wise enough to see and never give up seeing. And in this, one is reminded, too, of Thoreau, who wrote that the true lover exists in a certain fragrance of the spirit.

One phrase stood out: "Without an authenticity of spirit." Not unlike what she'd said to him at Florians: "Know what matters? That's it's genuine, the real thing, the authentic you."

No wonder she'd blown him off.

He was a total fake. No better than a stalker, a parasite on the lives of others. Even his alter ego, William Channing, had indulged in self-serving lies and lame excuses, behaving without a shred of dignity. No wonder she'd never mentioned William Channing or Concord. How could she have?

His only hope was to jettison everything or give her up. Somehow he needed to get himself regrounded in an abiding instinctual life, free of ambition, calculation and deceit—something along the lines of what he'd felt wandering on Torcello.

But where to start?

He went to the municipal center and the office of the superintendent of monuments. He strode in and told the secretary that Sandra Palmer had asked him to meet her there in the office at five, after she got off work. The young lady, sporting a retro bouffant hairdo, didn't bat a fake eyelash; she smiled and turned to the clock on the wall and noted the time of the Torcello vaporetto: the 3:48 that would get Sandra back in time for her appointment. He sat in the waiting area and pretended to read a local newspaper. The receptionist kept glancing at his face and finally asked if he was from nearby. No, he said, came from the States, he told her. She gestured to indicate his face, his Italian features. Yes, he said, his grandfather. They chatted on amicably in his halting Italian mixed with English. It wasn't the first time he been mistaken for a local. The secretary told him that Sandra had been working in Venice off and on for at least seven years, except when she'd returned two years before to do some graduate work in America. She'd come back sooner than expected. A two-week holiday this October. The talented American woman was highly respected in the restoration community and much sought after. They chatted a bit more, but when five o'clock had come and gone, he got up with a shrug and they agreed she must have missed the 3:48 vaporetto. No problem, he'd go wait for her at the Fondamenta Nouove and the 4:52 vaporetto from Torcello, which got in a little before 6:00. The receptionist noted that Sandra often stayed at her place on Torcello during the week, returning to Venice on the weekends. A flat, she indicated with a thrust of her lips, a magnificent place—or so she had been told.

He thanked the receptionist and walked out into the night, infused with a peculiar happiness. He walked all over the city as if he belonged. He walked past her darkened flat near San Zaccaria. The woman he'd glimpsed twice getting on and off the number 5 vaporetto on the Riva degli Schiavoni walking toward San Zaccaria had been Sandra. If he'd been a little faster on his feet, or staked out the *riva*, he would have found her within weeks of his arrival.

He'd gotten it right. He'd never stopped believing that it was Sandra who had survived—not for a moment. How could she condemn him for that?

But how could he begrudge her a life and love of her own? How could he fault her for rejecting him? He'd taken money, he was on the run from the FBI, and, as William Channing, he had insinuated himself into the life of her father, mother, her family. How insidious could you get? The moment he showed her Sandra's letter—her letter—she must have realized everything. Really, he was no better than a stalker.

William Channing and Michael Collins were equally distasteful to him. He yearned to do away with those names and free himself. Again his thoughts drifted back to Torcello: the leafless trees, the bare trellises in the vineyards, the comfort of ruins.

On Christmas Eve, he bought himself a colorful silk tie and a new Armani jacket. A few hours later, so attired, he left his room to have a bang-up dinner, as if blowing off the last of his money might force some conclusion to the whole affair. He was sick of the competing lives that vied in his brain. He wanted someone or something to take him over, put him out of his misery, so he could stop thinking about it and just be himself.

On the Zattere, he breathed the cool mist rolling in off the Giudecca Canal, gulping the sea air as he tried to retrieve the contemplative remove of that Torcello afternoon, when he'd been an outrider on the edges of civilization. As he walked, his immediate surroundings returned him to the diary and those distant evenings on the Zattere when Angela Chillingworth and Joseph Palmer had held one another for dear life, marooned in the guilty irresolution that would take a world war to finally send them packing.

He saw them walking with his grandfather Giovanni, the three bound to one another by the loss. Perhaps Giovanni's gentle presence had been a saving grace, preventing further temptation on the part of Joseph Palmer and his sister-in-law, Angela Chillingworth. In Michael's dreams, the three linked hands and danced a stately pavanne, turning, nodding to one another in acknowledgment of the phantom presence, the radiant beauty at their elbows, perhaps listening for snatches of her voice, her laughter, her Scriabin. The rhythm of their steps, like his, shadowed by her unlived life.

How he yearned for something of her voice.

He walked on, listening, watching the wavelets sweep the quay. In the distance, moored ocean liners like miniature cities festooned with seasonal lights. He found a trattoria in the working-class neighborhood near San Sebastiano and sat down for a Christmas Eve dinner. It delighted him that the waiters in Venice always addressed him in Italian, assuming as much by his face, his Italian just good enough to pull it off while ordering a meal. The place was crammed with a festive crowd, and after a bottle of wine and much pasta, he found himself buoyed by the animated conversations on all sides, the simple joys. It occurred to him that the fathers or grandfathers of the boatmen and artisans at the surrounding tables might well have known his grandfather, might even have laid eyes on that beautiful American lady in mourning black—or her sister when she was alive.

It saddened him to think that there was probably no one left who had actually seen Sandra Chillingworth Palmer alive, except maybe the old lady proprietor of the pensione, who had remembered only at his prompting. No one after Joe Palmer to be touched by her sad fate, a life extinguished on the verge of great things. Of course, there was Sandra; she had copied Joseph Palmer's diary, and even intimated knowledge of letters written by the Chillingworth twins. Just the thought of reading those letters—what they might offer about Giovanni, not to mention Sandra Chillingworth's infidelity—thrilled him. Maybe that was the role left to him now: an empty vessel to be filled with the histories of others. The last standard-bearer after the chain of living memory had been snapped. He should have been a teacher like Ruthie Cunningham, nurturing a love and respect for literature in the young, perhaps a quiet academic life—a voyeur parasite of more talented lives than his own—in a tiny college town ... something approximating the quiet of Torcello.

When he finally staggered out into the fog-saturated streets, the weight of his personal failings seemed less. He felt a simple gladness at the Christmas lights in the windows, the doors hung with beribboned wreaths. From all over the city, a gentle, insistent tolling broke out, bell after bell taking up the call. He walked and walked, as if under the spell of a single ravenous love, feeling almost at home, listening, repeating the names of *campi* and *calli* through which he passed, the names of saints and apostles, patriarchs and doges, captains and generals hurrying him onward.

At a turning, the great door of the church of the Frari opened before him, haloed candlelight spilling out like embers from a great bonfire. He felt transported to some scene of ancient ritual, when even Venice was young, when men still had to light their way with flame in the darkness. From every pathway and bridge, worshipers appeared in their best clothes, shepherding children, carrying swaddled infants, gravitating to that luminous portal. And music, music everywhere. The organ an uplifting sigh on the night. Voices of the choir soaring upward. And there, rising above all in robes of flaming crimson, the ascendant Madonna, goddesslike, lifted on angels' wings. He let himself be drawn in with the others, one among the multitude—one story among many—joining that vast constellation of worshipers, and like them, giving himself over to the strangest story of all: the mystery of the soul's defiance in face of death, and thus impelled to embrace the dark waters in the guise of a virgin mother—so the names and places might endure. All in the name of love ... in the wild deceitful hope.

Later, returning to the pensione, he walked slowly up the Zattere, finding himself mesmerized by the swollen sphere of the moon riding low upon the far shoreline. It was big-bellied and the color of tarnished silver. He was captivated, marveling like a child at an enormous balloon descending from the sky. As he walked, his eyes turned to the water, the moon began unraveling in a cascade of milky petals upon the waves, only to be impaled on the dome of Il Redentore, and finally drawn down and downward, until extinguished on the toothy blade of the Lido. He sat on the quay by the bridge nearest the pensione, listening to the incoming tide. Gray mists stirred against the stars and the soft lament of a church bell announced the dawn of another Christmas.

CHAPTER 32

"Aren't you freezing?"

He hadn't heard her footsteps. Her words barely registered; he had to pull himself back.

"You okay?" she asked, touching his shoulder.

He turned, seeing her standing in the dim lamplight: sneakers, jeans, sweater and parka vest, baseball cap. He eased himself up, stiff and damp. She handed him a bottle of champagne tied with a red ribbon. Her breath floated in a mist.

"I thought you might need help celebrating," she said. Her eyes watched him, an intent pewter blue, not a stitch of makeup.

"How did you find me?"

She looked to the left and right along the Zattere. "Where else would *you* be?" She blew on her hands. "Why don't you open the bottle?"

He fumbled with the wire and struggled with the cork, his fingers nearly numb. The cork popped and arced into the canal. They laughed.

He offered her the bottle and she drank long and deep and then passed it back to him.

"You'd be amazed," she said, watching as he tipped the bottle back, "how many women I know spent half their adult life trying not to get pregnant and the other half trying to do the opposite. I guess I fail on both counts."

He watched her close her eyes and draw her breath in and hold it.

She blew out her cheeks as if to finally get the thing off her chest. "But I loved that child. I held him in my arms after he was born and nursed him for three whole days—that wasn't part of the deal. The adoption had been all agreed to ahead of time. The Geneva agency was very precise about how it was to be done. And they were a really nice childless couple. They promised to love him. I was supposed to be able to see him once a week for the first few months. Then they did this disappearing act. Suddenly, the agency didn't seem to have a proper address—as if I'd done something wrong. I kept waiting. I hung around finishing school, hoping they'd get back in touch. I just wanted to see him. Never a word, not a single goddamn word. I kept hoping—for years. Every child I saw in the street, I'd wonder. Every new town, I'd see somebody's kid and calculate the age. He'd be in his late twenties by now, and I guess I wouldn't even recognize him."

"Did he have a name?"

"They called him Andre."

He put his arm around her and they stood for a few minutes in silence. Then she looked at him, waiting. He felt her shiver and he ushered her inside and upstairs to his room.

She went right to the French doors to check the view. She inspected everything: the diary on the desk, the etching, the photocopied drawings, the photo of his mother.

She picked up the photo and smiled. "I remember her from the dining room of the inn."

Then she went to the carved entwined dolphins on the headboard, fingering them as if spellbound.

She said with a hint of chagrin, "You *actually* got their room. I came by, not a week after I got back, and asked to see the room but I was told it was occupied. Oh my God." Her gaze fell on the painting. She steadied herself a moment, shaken that she'd missed it, passed within inches when she'd gone to the French doors. Then, like that, she was turning it over in her hands. "Unbelievable—*here*? It's dirty, but the fluidity of the brushstrokes, the tonal rhythms … Did anybody know?"

He shook his head. "The owner, the old lady, she has only the vaguest memory from childhood of the artist and the beautiful lady."

Reverently, she replaced the painting. "It's filthy. Suppose they'd let me clean it? It's worth something, too." She went to the dolphins again, her fingers lingering on the carving. "It's like a part of me was conceived in this place." She seemed to shiver and went again to the etching, touching the glass, looking up at him. "Yours?"

"It's dedicated by the artist: 'To my friend and fellow artist, Giovanni Maronetti.'"

"So it *is* yours. I checked with the reception desk downstairs: the name you're using now." She laughed at the awkward pursing of his lips. "Don't worry, I'm just as bad as you—no, probably worse."

She indicated the pages of Joseph Palmer's diary on his worktable. "As a child, I was oblivious of this, of so much, not like my sister, who used to sneak into Dad's study and go through the old art magazines, thrilled, I guess, at the glamour of old scandal. I suppose it was Angela's ambition to be different, to stand out, to be remembered. I'd come upon her sitting in silence, staring at a portrait of our grandmother in the dining room, mesmerized by that beautiful woman. The power of that image, that goddess, it was like a kind of dark magic. It seemed to take her over. When she changed, when her body changed, she seemed to gain some of that magic power over people. I felt like a tiny moon trying to resist her gravity. And yet now, after reading his diary and my grandmother's letters—Aunt Angie's, too—I feel it all flow back into me and … well, it begins to make sense—what was once only bewilderment and a need to escape."

"While you became an artist, a creator—not just the creation."

"I did a terrible thing."

"Maybe you became the thing your namesake would have, if she had lived."

"A concert pianist?" She shook her head. "I was just okay."

"A career, an artist in her own right."

"Did you hear me? I told you I did a terrible thing."

"It doesn't matter, not right now."

"Don't you want the truth—my secret, isn't that what you came for?"

"It can wait."

She winced and pulled off her cap, unsnapping the down vest. She seemed nonplussed by his passive demeanor, casting around for another tack to take.

"Angela wouldn't even let me in the nursery, wouldn't let me change her baby. As if she saw me as a threat. Just because I missed a phone call."

He blinked back tears, sensing her struggle. "You told me, that night on the river. You don't have to go through it again."

She turned to him with an expression of wonder and curiosity.

"I did, didn't I. I'd almost forgotten."

"The baby … falling—you know."

She lowered her eyes. "Yes …"

"Just now, you said something about letters?"

She smiled as if relieved to change the subject.

"Ah, it was your bizarre E-mail that did it—from my address."

"I located your computer."

"Ah …"

"You must have gone to Angela's place; I guess she left you all her details."

"Oh yes, Angela left me everything. It was quite extraordinary what I found. I found I couldn't let a day go by without checking her E-mail: her fan mail, customer suggestions, her staff keeping her abreast while they shamelessly raised their salaries and benefits. But your E-mail—that was a shock." She blew out her lips in a gesture of exhaustion. "A little weird, don't you think? But it was enough, your little missive, to get me back for a couple of weeks, to get me thinking about—well, loose ends. Among other things, the letters Sandra Chillingworth Palmer sent to her sister from Venice, and Angela Chillingworth's letters to her mother. They'd been sitting in the law office files for over thirty years because nobody in the family had bothered to claim them." She tapped the diary. "And, of course, there's this, his side of things.

"If you've been around enough artwork, you begin to understand. Artists are lucky in that respect; they destroy failed efforts, scrape it away, paint it over, and change their minds. Only later, up close, do their mistakes, the *pentimenti*, reappear."

"We all make mistakes, and life is full of deceit."

"Yes, but there are mistakes, *and then* there are *mistakes*."

He pulled himself to full height, biting his lip.

He said, "You mean Angela's suicide wasn't a mistake."

She squinted in the half-light to better read his face.

"So, you *do* need to know."

"We don't need to talk about it … not now."

"At some point we do."

"Listen …" He paused and went to the shelf above the sink and got two glasses. "You have to figure with such a crazy life, in the limelight, age and then emotional burnout."

"The aging porn star, you mean." She watched as he poured what was left of the champagne. "You know, *she* was the reason I decided to go back to Harvard for graduate work. My boyfriend here, his ex-wife gave him one of her tapes. Sandy Blue has quite the following over here, big-time. Italians are really into porn. Let's just say, he was a little blown away. And I had to explain. But then he totally got into it. Bought more of her videos and his friends … well, I felt like I couldn't show my face. I'd get looks in the street, still do. Suddenly, Harvard seemed to be the perfect idea."

Her brow furrowed with the effort of recounting all this.

With dizzy exuberance, he raised the glass he had poured for her. "Well, here's to Angela, to Sandy Blue, may her tapes live forever."

She cried, "Sex and drugs and rock and roll." Then she rolled her eyes and gave a despairing wave. "Sometimes, to hear it, you'd think that's *all* we were about."

"But she left you with everything, right?"

"Actually, I haven't quite gone there yet—her bank accounts, I mean. I can't see myself doing that."

"Just as well," he said, as if offering professional advice.

He handed her the glass and she drank and went to the French doors, a violet wash veiling her face as she ran a hand through her hair and angled her head to see the lights on the Giudecca.

"Snow," she said. "The radio said there could be snow."

She turned back to him, lips compressed in thought, took a couple of deep breaths, and then let fly, as if she'd finally gotten herself psyched.

"Angela, you know, just arrived on my doorstep without warning, long ratty hair. She'd been on a long flight. It was my birthday."

"Her birthday."

She eyed him sharply and then smiled.

"That's right. You see, I'd complained to SandyBlue.com and the message had been relayed to her—that's how we got back in touch after all the years. But I didn't expect her to show up in Cambridge. She was almost belligerent at first, then very subdued. I thought she was medicated or something. She went on and on about needing to see me, needing to see Concord—Dad—for the last time. That's how she put it, 'the last time.' It scared me. She was not the cocky, assertive Angela I remembered. She told me she'd gotten a Ph.D. in archaeology. She'd opened a restaurant in Santa Fe—casting around for a new gig—but the cooking and management just left her exhausted. She said something about testing positive for HIV."

"Oh God, not HIV. I thought it was malaria or something."

"Malaria?" She cocked her head. "Oh, well, that seemed to be the least of her problems. I just hugged her. It kind of floored me. And Michael, she was so bitter, like the world—even with her successes—had stomped all over her. She blamed my mother for her baby being retarded; she blamed me for little Joey dying, and she blamed my father for saying nothing and walking away. That's how she saw it: that we hated her and abandoned her. Later, I left her soaking in the bathtub. She'd arrived with only the clothes on her back, so I took them to the Laundromat. I stopped at the Harvard Coop for some fresh clothes. Then I went to the grocery store to get stuff for dinner, some good wine. A real home-cooked meal to cheer her up—fat chance."

She shrugged with a helpless shudder.

"An argument," he said, "old scores to settle."

"Worse, the same old scores about missing the phone call from the doctor and the delay during her delivery. A bottle of wine under her belt and she was right back to the spiteful teenager who had been the bane of my existence. She got so steamed up she finally walked out on me at two in the morning. Disappeared into the night."

"You emailed her."

She glanced at him, a flicker of annoyance.

"And the next day I went to look for her. First Cambridge, the Common, where her gang of druggies hung out in the late sixties, and then to Concord, her old haunts … Bobby's grave—and Joey. I exhausted myself and just grabbed a room at the inn and passed out. Next day, when I finally made it back to my apartment, I found her, like that, staring out the window into the garden. I was violently sick. And … in the toilet—she'd tried to flush all the hair she'd cut. She'd used my makeup. Maybe it was her way of revenge, a frenzy of revenge and bitterness, I don't know."

He waited a moment and then spoke a little above a whisper. "For the missed phone call from the doctor, for your accident with the changing table."

"Accident?"

Watching her closely, he said, "The baby … falling from the changing table."

An involuntary shiver seemed to convulse her. She tipped back the last of her champagne and turned from his intent stare toward the French doors, her long neck bent forward.

"I guess you can't blame her, that she'd never gotten over it. I mean, you don't, not the death of a child."

"So you panicked," he said, rushing now. "You grabbed your passport and a few things and got the hell out of there."

She nodded quickly. "Yeah, I freaked. It was a nightmare. No, worse. She'd left a will—can you believe it—a scribbled will, making everything over to me: her company, her financial assets, her access codes. I couldn't bring myself to do it—make a claim. I just wanted to get away."

"Get back to the simple life." He came up behind her and put a hand on her shoulder. "You probably didn't even realize that people would get it wrong."

"It was weeks before I found out. I just happened to stumble upon a copy of the *Boston Globe*. It was the wildest thing."

"To find you'd died."

"Yeah, but a kind of rush, to be on my own like that, free, seeing the world from the outside."

He prompted. "Without you." He waited a beat, feeling every syllable. "What they said about you."

"Even when we were kids, Angela was incapable of forgiveness. She lived only for herself. She couldn't stand a world where she wasn't the center of attention, when she could turn every head in a room—and Daddy, Jesus." She smiled. "And of course, I was with her all the time. I wanted it, too—sort of—but I refused her the satisfaction of competing, going along with her craziness."

He saw her vague image in the glass of the French doors. Her eyes had a peculiar luster, as if they'd penetrated far beyond, left him and that place. He squeezed her tighter, as if to encourage her eyes to return, to withdraw from the distance.

"So she tried to stick you with her life ..."

"We like to think," she said, her tone ruminative, "like children think, that we are pure in our desire and there are no consequences."

He added, "To suffer love's attraction ... even with all the deceit."

He watched for her reaction as she moved from his embrace and reached to the doors of the balcony. She fingered the inside edge of one of the panes.

"We make a little frame around our life and think we are inviolable."

"If only for a little while."

She suddenly seemed to be aware of his continued prompting. She was watching him now in the window glass. He took a step and squeezed her arms, and she turned and kissed him, holding him, a tropical current washing over him: the merest hint of perfume, the taste of her lips like wine, the heat of her body. He pulled back a moment to see her eyes properly.

"How strange for you, in limbo, with two lives."

Her eyes brightened with a febrile intensity.

"*You* should know."

"And Mr. Sugar Daddy?" he asked.

"He didn't even bother with a Christmas card. New Year's is out, too. Already a meter of snow in Cortina and the skiing is great. And you were right: There *is* no love."

They kissed tenderly. She took his glass and finished it off then placed it on the sink and raised her eyes to his.

"Do you think we can manage this?" She made a fountaining motion with her hands that might have included the room, or perhaps everything beyond the room. "No plans, no agonies, nothing about what happened or didn't, or what happened over the last year. I just couldn't take any of that. I know it's a tall order."

"Our little frame," he said, and paused. "Our little silence."

"But we're the experts, you and me, on secrets," she said, her voice throaty and soft now. She shivered. "I'm frozen through. I was waiting for hours."

"I went to midnight Mass at the Frari."

"Of course ... my dearest dear, of course you did ... and how was the Bellini?" Her imitation of Victorian endearments was wickedly, hysterically accurate.

"You will let me see her letters, won't you?"

"Tomorrow, tomorrow ..."

She squeezed his hand once and disappeared into the bathroom. He stood for a moment, trying to regain his bearings. He scrounged in the drawer of the desk and found two old candle ends and carefully lit them, then secured them in the bottom of two glasses, placing one on each of the bedside tables. He undressed and got under the comforter and closed his eyes. He heard the water running into the tub and then silence. His body began to warm under the comforter and he could smell the starched linen sheets and beeswax polish. Heralded in the sound of the lapping, the tolling of a bell: the coming of voices.

His eyes opened at the sound of the turned handle of the bathroom door and he saw the two flames reflected in the Murrano Glass chandelier leap from the disturbance. Crystal shadows flickered in the molded acanthus leaves on the ceiling. He saw her cross to the French doors, stopping an instant to lay a hand on the pages of the artist's diary. Her long, lithe body in the candlelight retained much of the form of her youth, the milky skin along the back of her thighs and shoulders materializing out of the near darkness by the doors like a figure in a nocturne. Her pale demeanor offered no clue to what it was she saw beyond the windows, or if she felt any particular reticence or enthusiasm for what was to be, only a desire, perhaps, to let the moment deepen in her, to regain some inner repose that came by exposing herself to the night, the fate that hovered over all such meetings of body and soul. When she did finally turn back to him, a flush of amber light in her eyes, he felt in her a kind of peace, a concerted resignation that she had crossed the invisible boundary between one life and another and was now free to return to his.

She got into bed beside him. For minutes, they lay wordless; then he turned to her. He felt a great happiness simply by gazing upon her face, his desire like a flame feeding upon itself, as if drawn from an infinity of desires, of voices above the waves. There was the distant tolling of a bell and then the groan of the bedsprings as he reached a hand to her. The sharp point of her hip, the plane of her belly warming to his touch as his palm moved to the undersloping curve of her breasts and the rigid outcroppings of her nipples. Then downward to the freshet of hair on her pubic mound and into her thighs. Her legs parted for his hand as they would for that of a familiar lover. He began to kiss her very tenderly, not wanting to waken her fully or in any way force her to reveal herself to him, at least no more than she wished. First body ... then soul. He sensed, too, in her repose a mutuality of interest, that it was for him to make of her what he would and lead her someplace outside herself, and she him. New stories for old. He molded her mouth with his, using his tongue as if to impart a new language now that the old was given up, a voice that would not betray her. Beneath his kisses and the rhythm of his fingers, her kisses began to welcome him.

And beyond, the voice of the waves like the voice of silence moving over the fields of first creation, urging him on.

He moved downward with the instincts of a convert for the source of his new faith—was it joy, or ambition to banish the inexperienced lover of years before? Perhaps new innocence for old. Her knees tented the darkness for him. She was smooth and soap-scented and his lips again found her lips, his tongue ardent and joyful. He was determined to incinerate any last pretense of purity. In her slow yielding, in the sweet, pungent outpourings of her body, he felt poured back into himself, as if healing the deficit of a near century of loss.

In the sensation of her body beneath his roving hands the inspiration to a thousand paintings and countless sculptures. In her throaty cries, other cries swelled upward on the deepest currents. In her voice, another voice. "Now, Michael, now." He couldn't leave off, not until swept back by her tugging hands, birthing him upward, gently urging his return to her flickering girlish eyes. She touched his face, fingering the ridges of his cheeks, the declivity at his chin, the juttings of his dark brows, as if remaking him in her own mind and exchanging past joy—or was it loss?—for similar coin.

She licked his lips, his chin, cleansing and kissing him. Then she gently but firmly maneuvered him onto his side at an angle to her, pulling up her right leg against his shoulder and bracing her left upraised on his hip, placing his hand on her breast, instructing his motion across the nipple. For a moment, he was near-mesmerized at her stage directions, then captivated, taking her with brute force, as if every known ambition was translated to where his flesh entered hers, where her fingers moved in a blur. Only to find she had already passed him by. Her deceit confirmed in her sibilant cries and the flurried articulation of her moving fingers, slowing, slowing ... slowing. He raced onward like a petulant boy, struggling in the flickering candlelight to catch a glimpse of the wonder and hope that had filled her cries, to fuse his release from desire with hers, mirrored in her watching eyes. Except her flame-lit eyes were sealed shut, her face fallen back on the pillow, as if to dissuade him from any such hope: that in love's release part of us might live forever. It crushed something in him.

Then, as if aware of his consternation, she propped herself on an elbow, holding his burning gaze in hers as she squeezed; then she reached down and circled him with her fingers, tightening and relaxing her grip with rhythmic virtuosity, until wringing him empty inside her.

They woke late on Christmas morning to the shouts of children on the Zattere. The city outside their window was covered in nearly two inches of snow. The scene was so fantastic, so unexpected, they were struck dumb. They rushed into their clothes and headed for the Zattere to be part of this confectionery dream of gingerbread palaces, of doorjambs ankle-deep in powdered sugar and marzipan churches lush with frosted icing. Even the denizens wandered around awestruck, taking in this once-in-a-decade phenomenon. Every turning was a joy. Children shrieked and skidded and threw snowballs. It was strangely warm and humid and the snow would be gone by afternoon.

They had to see every inch of the transformed city before it was too late: the lagoon translated to a New England fishing village. They were ecstatic, unreflectively happy. They held hands, often stopped to kiss, to embrace, groping like teenagers. They flew on wings of cappuccino and day-old *dolci*, oblivious to their soaked feet. They threaded well-trodden paths, careful to fit their steps into those imprinted before them. Again and again, scenes of childhood stopped them as they dodged careening bikes with ribbons still attached, ducked slushy snowballs. Even the great bells above tolled with muffled, knitted-wool charm. By afternoon, the *campi* had turned to gray gruel and everything dripped as if the entire town were shedding tears of gladness.

By early evening, they retired to Florians for more coffee and stale sandwiches. The place had lost its magic. Maybe it was their frozen feet, or, more likely, the delicate task that still needed to be accomplished. She didn't say a word as they tramped to her palatial flat. The small overnight bag was already packed and waiting in the foyer. She slung it casually over her shoulder and closed the door without so much as a backward glance, then dropped the keys through the mail slot. Another door, another life—snap of the fingers.

She had the week off between Christmas and New Year's. They barely left his room except for meals and to stretch their legs. Their sex, at first confined to the rickety old bed, was like a voyage on a tiny craft across uncharted seas: frenzied lovemaking, becalmed stretches of tender touching, pools of crystal sunlight reflected from the sea green Murano chandelier, sudden squalls of fractioning limbs, ebbing tides of sweat-matted hair, and the dead calm of sleep, until waking to probe again for a windward passage, testing for what the years had denied them, until exhausted, released again by sleep—blessed sleep. The bedclothes like shredded rigging strewn across the floor.

Often he felt like a pulped fruit from which she still yearned to extract the penultimate drop. A few days before New Year's, she declared the bed out of bounds: "Enough is enough, old boy." But it was never enough. He was never deep enough, never hard enough or big enough, never enough to fill her fully or reach those hidden veins of sensation that remained untapped. Her robe fell conveniently open, always when she was scrunched up in the leather easy chair devouring her complete Jane

Austen. Her labia peeked at him. She'd absentmindedly rub an exposed nipple. He'd go down on her and she'd continue reading and pretend he had no effect on her, primly declaiming Jane Austen in choking cries and half whispers. His damaged hand fascinated her: symbol of a faraway war and time that he instinctively sought to conceal. The two good fingers and thumb tapped something in her and she devised new scenarios. She was ovulating and creamy and she instructed him, one knee balanced on the armrest, to insert two fingers and massage her on the outside with his thumb, while she took him in her mouth, moving in tandem, coordinating their rhythms until their bodies short-circuited almost to the second. She was triumphant at their achievement.

Then she discovered the possibilities of the enormous claw-footed bathtub, the porcelain worn to piebald patches, an antique by any measure. A bath used by Joseph Palmer and Sandra Chillingworth Palmer, and the sketches of the nude bather to prove it. "Do you suppose," she asked, "they ever bathed together?" She got their routine down, as if routine and discipline were how she managed life. She'd lather his face and he'd lather her pubic mound; then she'd shave him with head back on the side of the tub and he her as she straddled the tub, legs dangling over either side. The ritual was creepy and erotic, like playing doctor or hammering a nail though a plastic doll, playing at corrupted innocence. She was perverse and funny and yet strangely pure when it came to sex. She laughed off condoms like a poor joke. She had no diaphragm or birth-control pills as far as he could detect. He figured IUDs had gone out with the dinosaurs, but he knew enough not to ask. And, of course, nothing about Concord or William Channing. Not a peep about young Steve Ballard, her Harvard student and lover—no wonder the poor kid was so infatuated.

Often, early in the morning, he would wake after a night of lovemaking and find her sitting in a chair nearby the bed, sketchpad on her knees, drawing his sleeping face, or where she had drawn back the blankets to uncover his torso. It was a little unnerving. Even frightening, because he could detect an incendiary anger and frustration in her blue eyes. Sometimes tears. Until one morning, woken by her scream, he saw her fling the sketchpad and pencil across the room.

"What a fucking waste of my life."

It was the last time he saw her put pencil to paper.

They had a blowout on New Year's, going to the Cipriani—her treat—on the Giudecca to celebrate. At midnight, she pulled him out of the festivities and they walked the expansive grounds of the grand hotel hand in hand. The night was chilly. They passed the empty Olympic-size swimming pool, the tarpaulin cover an iridescent blue under the half-moon. The bare winter garden was like a fading snapshot of a stay at an elegant summer villa; the rigid poplars and shapely topiary seemed like marble copies of themselves.

"They came here," she said, fingering the leaves of a clipped shrub.

"Who?"

"Sandra and Angela Chillingworth."

"To the Cipriani?"

"No, silly." She kissed him long and tenderly. "This was once the Curtises' private garden ... scene of the crime."

"Crime?"

"Their garden of earthly delights ..."

By the time the holiday break was over, he had less than a thousand dollars left. But she had a couple of surprises for him. She had a place on Torcello, a small rented farmhouse until June (she'd used the banker's apartment in Venice only on weekends), when the restoration job was scheduled for completion. And she'd gotten him a job as a laborer on the restoration project; she'd put in the application on the morning before Christmas Eve, using the name Giovanni Maronetti. Somehow, she had finessed his lack of a work permit, or papers, not to mention his passport. That gave him pause—but for barely a moment. Nothing about her surprised him anymore, not even that she could read him better than he himself. When he'd first walked the tiny paths of Torcello, he'd gone right by her cottage, stopping at the gate and looking into the garden with the dovecote and marble fragments littering the grass. It was as if she was guiding him into the simple life of instinct, in lee of time, he'd glimpsed that first day on Torcello. The old routines of their first ten days together were jettisoned for a new set of routines, as if she was used to shedding lives like last season's fashions.

"You've got the hands—hand—for restoration work, Michael," she said with a wonderful quirky smile as she showed him around the tiny cottage, taking his good hand and holding it to her breast. "An artist's hands, the hands of a Venetian lover."

He couldn't help but detect a certain mocking tone in her voice. And a moment later, she handed him, as promised, the packet of Chillingworth letters.

CHAPTER 33

Venice, December 25, 1913

Dearest Angie,

Merry, Merry Christmas. Oh how I miss you, Angie, and everyone—even if Joseph and I are never to be forgiven. I didn't even have a Christmas tree this morning to rush down to and worry about getting your presents confused with mine. What wicked and spoiled children we were, tallying it all up with fierce eyes all around. But, of course, we are beyond all that nonsense now.

This has been a wonderful, even magical Christmas for Joseph and me, with just ourselves to worship and spoil and pamper. Now with the winter season fully upon us, extended forays in the out-of-doors are limited, we spend more time in our cozy room and studio. Demon work still prevails, but he has shifted his ground, fixing his steely gaze upon me as never before: I am ravished at pencil point, stroked with pastel crayon, scrubbed with charcoal, and suitably threatened with etching needle so that I dare not stray too far!

Forgive me, dearest Angela, if I am still a bit giddy. Please do not pass on any of these confidences to Mother, who would certainly take them amiss. But I live. I celebrate. My darling husband has surely gotten to the quick of me. It is not like our early Concord days: those pretty poppies of paintings that sold so well at Vose Gallery, with all my pouting pride for the world to admire. No more. We embark on a more challenging journey, of the flesh, to be sure, but in the soul's carriage, with vistas expanding inward as much as out. I watch his vision grow, as he does mine. We crave each other body and soul. Girlish dreams are banished. I grow bold under his exacting eye, creating in myself as he creates in me. I dare not put it down on paper, even for you, my oldest friend and confidante, though I long to do so, for you to feel and see—yes, see—as I do. How different the world can seem, uncorsetted, abandoned to the life we really are.

Oh Angie, you must meet my new friends at the palazzo Manzoni, poets and dancers and duchesses, and—dare I say it?—courtesans of the first rank. They would turn your ear on the possibilities of our sex. They preach not just equality with the male sex but our innate superiority. I blush even to think on their proofs. And yet I feel it in my bones when Joseph's hands fly over his sketch pad—the hunted has become the huntress. I see things in him never seen before—good things, but troubling to the once innocent. How can I put it? Men are so vulnerable, so tied to the mast of their ambition, while we are forced to navigate by subterfuge, by giving in and yet finding our own way. And yet our power of soul and intellect is the equal or better.

That is why I came with Joseph, to get away and allow myself the chance to embrace that power fully. I've begun practicing the piano again, challenging myself to move beyond the staid repertoire of my Boston Conservatory days to some new music by Igor Stravinsky and Scriabin, who are all the rage among the Manzoni set. I met a professor of piano and composition at the Manzoni, a young Russian with godlike talent and eyes that pierce quite through one. Dimitri has taken me on as a pupil. He pushes me, startles me at every turn. He knows all the young composers and has promised to write music for me. It is dizzying stuff—crazy jazz rhythms and atonalities—but it begins to grow on one; it stretches the technique and takes me out of my-self. If I can master the difficulties, I might be the first to perform these pieces in America. Now that the Curtises have gone for the winter, I have been given carte blanche to play their Bechstein grand in the drawing room of the Casa Alvisi. It is an extraordinary instrument. I play, and I stare out at another grand, the Grand Canal—oh the light, and the acoustics, Angela, the light and the music!

I don't think Joseph can appreciate my music. He is a bit old and set in his ways. Often he is tired in the evening; he is all morning work and no play. He is jealous of my women friends and disapproves. I dare not mention Dimitri, nor broach the subject of my future. But I can't see myself going on as just a pretty face and figure to sell Joseph's painting. Don't breathe a word to mother; she will only gloat.

Joseph doesn't know it, but the Curtises' caretaker gave me the key to their private garden on the island of the Giudecca. Sometimes I go there to be alone and escape the demands of husband and teacher. I love to walk among the trees, the gnarled cedars and crooked cypresses, tiny apricot and cherry orchards. Everywhere are scattered ancient bits of stone, ruined statues and fragments of classical temples. How strange in this waterland to enter a tiny gate and find oneself in a garden hermitage.

As I walk or read poetry in the waning afternoon sunlight, I find myself contemplating stories told me by my friend Horatio Brown, the scholar and memoirist I mentioned to you in my last letter. We argue Ruskin like cat and dog. I am sometimes haunted by Brown's voice, his stories about the old Venetians—"pack rats"—he calls them, who traveled the world for the spoils of the ancients in order to "bed," as he puts it, themselves with the illustrious dead. But the thing is, I do see; I begin to see. When I walk in the Curtises' garden alone, I feel moments of deepest reverie, when that continuum of past and present presses hard at one's back. It is like the way Joseph always goes on about Concord; he seems to find history at every turning. At such time, I will open up my Ovid, Metamorphoses—do you know the place, dear sister?—and read the lines there: "nam quod fuit ante, relictum est, fitque, quod haut fuerat, momentaque cuncta novantur.": "For that which once existed is no more, and that which was not has come to be; and so the whole round of motion is gone through again."

When studying Ovid in school, this passage meant nothing to me, as if I lived in a daydream.

Funny, how this city wakens one's dreaming self. One simply must travel, Angela; one must move beyond oneself and see. I had to leave Boston and Concord—and Mother—the newspapers and gossip, to find myself again. Music really does put us in touch with the great souls. And Dimitri is a genius. Forgive me if I begin to sound like Mother. How is your practice? Do you keep it up?

How I yearn for your dear company. Do press our case to Father and Mother. Use what stratagem you think best. Tell Mother I am practicing piano again and am contemplating a return to the concert stage. If they think your coming might hasten my return, then use it. Nothing here will be truly complete without you a part of it—something of me will always be missing. I am raised high on the wings of love but require a disciple to complete the journey. Come with the spring and life will dazzle you. Your loving sister, Sandra

Venice, January 24, 1914

My dearest Angie,

I am thrilled that my glorious news will be bringing you here, almost as if our little "surprise" was the necessary fillip to reunite us. Suddenly, time is finite; the clock ticks. Joseph is all afever with new ideas and no time to waste. My teacher at the conservatory, Dimitri, pushes me harder. He loves my Scriabin. It is as if a glittering treasure hovers at my aching fingertips and I must learn to reach into some as yet-untapped vein of myself. Dimitri is composing for me, strange, scary music—like the end of the world. He says at my rate of progress, I will be ready to play concerts by summer, perhaps in the festival in Verona, and later Milan and Turin. I have said nothing to him about the child.

I treasure this new life growing within me that compliments the life growing beyond. But I have terrible fears as well, as if one is standing alone on an undiscovered shore and casting stones, watching the ripples spread to the invisible future, for the help that may never come. Maybe it is Dimitri's music. He is a socialist, as are many at the Manzoni. He thinks the revolution is imminent and a new world will soon sweep away the past. He says I and his music will be the herald of the new age. Men and their ambitions!

Joseph is desolate at the news that Curtis is ill. The old man somehow rekindled memories of his father. Sometimes, Joseph wakes at night and cannot get back to sleep, and I ask him what troubles him. He says he sees his father's eyes, not just his eyes as he knew them as a boy when his father was ailing, but what those eyes saw. I suppose terrible things of war as told him by Curtis. I do not really like Curtis, he reminds me too much of you know who. Of course, Father sat out the war and made his millions.

Do you suppose Father would like a palazzo of his own? Might it not be the perfect thing? Think of the soirees and private concerts. Perhaps a school of music. Perhaps you might whisper in his ear, tell him how much his friends and business partners might admire a man with a palazzo in Venice. And think what fun we would have!

Joseph can act a bit old at times, so preoccupied with his work and his thoughts. Sometimes when he cannot sleep, he will light the lamp and take up his volume of Thoreau. He will read to me and suddenly something will strike him and he will pause and say, "Yes, yes, my father said as much," or, "My father showed me that place." He drifts out of himself and leaves me. Then wicked, wicked me rises at his side and I lift my nightgown—dare I write such thing to you, my innocent darling?—and bring him back. I fear one can get all too used to this wickedness.

And you, my poetess sister, must experience Venice in a gondola by night. Byron did not become Byron by keeping himself chastely locked away.

Do alert Dr. Townsend to my condition and get from him any advice or reading matter relevant to my state. I suppose it would make sense to have a nursery set up at home—just in case—and a nurse hired, but I'm sure Mother will take care of all that. How strange my feelings. I have read that motherhood heighens our emotions and plays on our fears. I long for your face, your laughter, to shock your Puritan soul. I have people for you to meet. When I smell the sea, I remember the beach at Manchester and our endless summer days—two naughty little girls. Let us kick down a few more sand castles. Love, Sandra

CHAPTER 34

The cottage on Torcello was rustic, simple, barely two rooms, with an outhouse in the garden behind. The owner lived on the island of Burano and used the cottage only seasonally to tend his vineyard and vegetable garden. In July and August, he rented it out as a vacation cottage. It was not really meant for winter use. The terra-cotta roof kept the rain out, but the rust-colored stucco walls and the green shutters over the windows seemed to let in every freezing draft. They wore coats and sweaters indoors and moved their one electric heater from the bedroom to the kitchen-living area for warmth. The furnishings were cheap and worn, as if scavenged from a garbage dump. The only hot water came from the small heating cylinder above the kitchen sink. A cracked bathtub with a cold-water faucet took up one corner of the kitchen. It was certainly cozy, quite removed from the few other houses on the island.

Gardens surrounded the cottage on three sides and on the fourth was a vineyard, and beyond this, through a line of scrawny winter poplars, a glimpse on fair days of the distant Alps. The single bedroom window was angled toward the vegetable garden and the vineyard; the January garden was a starved hoary green, the vineyard patterned with the stark ligaments of vine trellises. He found the garden somewhat haunted by the departed: the empty dovecote, the two patchy cypresses by the gate, and the discarded marble fragments embedded in the earth. In the moonlight, these ancient fragments glowed like terminus stones, boundary markers between the spirit world and the summer gone and the spring to come. Beyond the front gate, a narrow cinder path led a circuitous route to the tiny *campo* in front of Santa Maria Assunta. There was something of the specter of hibernation about the place, of dreams, a harboring of emotional resources that even the occasional jet slipping past overhead into Marco Polo Airport did little to disturb.

And on the near horizon stood the bell tower of the cathedral with its four watching windows. A comfort. A tease.

At first, he was sure they were going to freeze to death, but after the first two cold weeks of January, the weather became milder and only occasionally did the cold winds from the Alps make things really uncomfortable. It was a life in miniature circumscribed by bare walls, a total of five windows and the warped green door that didn't close properly.

And then there was the painting of the bridge on the wall of the bedroom.

Sandra had talked the old lady, owner of the pensione, into selling the Palmer painting. He had watched a little amazed as she pulled this off, employing charm and chutzpah to make the buy: a memento of Venice, she'd exclaimed, waving around a wad of lire notes like a ditzy American tourist—without once mentioning that the artist had been her grandfather, much less that the canvas might be worth a small fortune. Then she'd cleaned the painting and varnished it and found a period Whistler frame in an antique shop. She was very pleased with herself.

"See, see … how it sings, how alive it is!"

She'd hung it on the wall across from the bedroom window, where the dawn light would flood the picture.

"What do you think—shrine to the ancestors?"

The rhythm of their days was nearly unvarying. She'd be the first up and would switch on the electric heater. Then she might spend a few minutes reading at the rickety wooden table, where she kept her copy of the diary and the letters of her grandmother and great-aunt. She happily shared the letters with him, a hint of sly triumph in her smile at all her confederates had concealed from Joseph Palmer. Occasionally, she'd read week-old copies of the *International Herald Tribune*. There was an ongoing trial in Boston over kickbacks on the Lowell Plan. They barely mentioned it to each other or let it intrude on their singular world. Mostly, she read Italian cookbooks and her ubiquitous complete Jane Austen, a battered Everyman edition from a used-books store in Cambridge, Classics-Hurrah, the purple price sticker still on the cover: $5.95.

Then she'd go into the kitchen, fire up the hot-water cylinder, put the kettle on, and switch on a battered cassette player to do her morning exercises: Pilates stretching, working with some weights, a general strengthening. Then she'd wash herself, make breakfast for both of them—normally, oatmeal with bananas and a pot of strong coffee—and then they were off to Santa Maria Assunta for the day. He worked with the laborers, moving materials in and out of the restoration site, assisting the restoration experts on particular jobs. When she could, she'd have him work at her side and teach him restoration skills. She was very good at what she did.

By the time they got home, it would be dark and they'd be physically exhausted. She liked to cook, though frustrated at the lack of ingredients at hand. On Saturdays, they'd take the vaporetto to Burano for groceries. While dinner was under way, she'd attach a garden hose to the hot-water tap over the sink and fill the bathtub with hot water from the heating cylinder, adding a kettle or two of boiling water from the stove. They'd use the same water or simply share the bath, cramped as it was. After dinner and lots of wine, they'd read (sometimes to each other) and listen to classical music on the radio or her CD player—sometimes funky things like Scriabin's piano sonatas and the like, of which she had a small collection of CDs. The piano music stirred something in him, a latent yearning, to the point he could almost feel the missing fingers on his left hand in the bass passages.

She would help him with his Italian, which was improving quickly from conversations with his fellow workmen—dialect, no less. It was as if he was reclaiming the lost tongue of his grandfather, the voice of a life he might have known better if only he'd known enough of the language to ask the right questions. At night, the wind often sounded a constant purr over the roof tiles. In bed, they fell asleep in each other's arms, huddled together for warmth. Their lovemaking was mostly on weekends, and even then, the cold kept things at a tepid pace, the two of them often confined to their clothes like some absurdly modest Victorian couple. The logistics made it hard to climax together; often, they would come solo, staring intently into each other's eyes.

He was a little surprised how quickly she had folded him into her island life, as if he were some wanderer stumbled upon Calypso's lair. Yet he was the most willing of victims. She was a master at diversion, but then, so was he. They fed off each other. She lived on the cusp of the moment, if often under the spell of the past's genius. They talked often about the artist Joseph Palmer, and Sandra and Angela Chillingworth, discussed how Giovanni Maronetti had been drawn into their guilty embraces.

Exchanging thoughts, reflections on the letters and the diary. But of her immediate family, her childhood, she would give away almost nothing. She spoke of her early years in Europe—and her pain about her lost child, but nothing more. The sad end of Angela was no longer broached. He, in turn, never brought up William Channing—persona non grata—and Concord, and she never inquired. That was their deal.

And among her possessions there was not even a photograph or stray snapshot anywhere. It was as if one world ended with the diary and the letters and another began with them now.

Occasionally, around the edges, when high on a morning espresso or with a little too much wine after dinner, she would pepper him with questions, challenge his way of thinking, how he reacted to aspects of the diary and the letters (as if emphasizing the two sides to the story, guys versus girls). She jabbed like a shadow boxer, half kidding but not: "Is that you or Giovanni?" "Where's that courtroom swagger ... Michael, that big swinging dick I've been reading so much about?" "Whose child do you think Sandra Chillingworth had, anyway?"

He was unfazed by her banter. It was as if they'd stepped back so far, the past was only a tantalizing abstraction.

He did have one special and private joy, which she had no interest in sharing. One of his fellow workmen was teaching him to row the Venetian *sandolo*, a smaller version of the gondola used as a working skiff. The beauty of it, the wonder, was that standing and using both hands on a single oar, his handicap was almost entirely erased. It thrilled him to the core.

"How do you know that you've got it back at the right angle?" he asked.

He watched as she tapped the bit of gold tessera into place and leaned back to examine her work.

"The context," she said, "how it works with the others—photographs if I screw up, if I need to check."

"Almost like being the artist yourself, as if you can feel what they felt."

"No. It was original with them; it was their whole world, everything they believed in."

He gazed up at the glittering expanse above their heads sheathed in scaffolding and green plastic mesh.

"They were inspired."

"Look closely," she said. "See how the gold tesserae for the background are arranged in horizontal rows, until they reach the contour of the figure; then the artist shifted the two rows around the contour—just a fraction, just enough that when viewed from the floor of the nave, the figure stands out against the gold field."

"The artist had to be this close," he said, "and yet know how it needed to look from far away." He shook his head. "Talk about faith in yourself."

"Faith ... to really believe in *something*."

It was there again, the tone beginning to creep into her voice, the inflection at the corner of her eyes. He asked, "You think we don't believe in anything ... anymore?"

"What did you believe—all those years you were in Washington?"

"Let's not go over that again."

"Doesn't it make you angry, what's in the papers about the trial—what they say about you?"

"Politics. Washington: Old scandal or new, something to yak about."

"But you act as if nothing of what you did mattered. I mean, you people got entire parts of Lowell renovated, old mills preserved, museums built, jobs created ... and the whole thing seems to come down to whether some people along the way took a little money to tide them over."

"You're saying that doesn't matter?"

"You're the lawyer."

"It's illegal, and, yes, corruption tends to breed corruption."

"Wait till you've worked a few years in Italy."

"What are you saying?"

"What do you think it cost to create this?" She spread her arms across the wall. "How many corners were cut in the building of Venice?"

"So you're saying it doesn't matter?"

"I'm saying everything comes with a cost, the good and the bad. But I don't think the good should be lost sight of, either."

"That sounds ... well, like a pretty good sixties accounting style."

"So what have you got against the sixties?"

"Nothing. After all, Angela certainly came through it with flying colors."

She snapped the lid of the plastic bottle with a hint of irritation. "What does that mean?"

"Of course, some of us ended up in Vietnam."

"Poor you. You got yourself into Vietnam."

"I got drafted."

"That's what you say, but just because you lost that Harvard scholarship doesn't mean you couldn't have gotten in somewhere else, somewhere less exalted maybe, and gotten your student deferment."

"The hell."

"Hey, you were mad at me, at all of us, for that sniveling, self-satisfied preppy bullshit. You wanted to prove something; you wanted to be better."

"Believe me, after I was in Vietnam awhile, I just wanted not to get shot."

"Anyway, Angela would've been more your type."

He cocked his head in mock horror. "And what's that supposed to mean? Because she fell in love with a marine flier?"

"Army, Seventh Calvary."

"Right, Seventh Calvary."

"At least she had the power of her convictions."

"Yeah, and look where it got her."

"That's a shitty thing to say."

"Damn right."

"So, why *did* you go to Washington?"

"I thought—hell, I figured I'd make the world a better place."

"Bullshit. You went to law school, keys to the system, pretty Establishment stuff."

"It didn't really feel that way."

She smiled icily. "Maybe it never does."

"Greasing the wheels, doing deals behind the scenes" —he glanced at his hands caked in dust— "it can become addictive, the invisibility."

"I think my father was into that for a while, until his world came apart."

"You mean when Angela started fucking with his mind."

She sounded every syllable. "I never said she did anything wrong."

"But she knew what she was doing to him."

"She was a stupid kid."

He said in a flat academic tone, "She was fifteen going on twenty."

"She loved Bobby Hathaway. She loved that baby when all the rest of us wanted it not to be. She was pretty gutsy, when you come right down to it."

Her rising voice echoed. He pushed back from where they sat on the scaffolding to get a better look at her; she'd never quite opened up like this before, and he was intrigued.

He said quietly, as if to give her one more gentle push. "Like her grandmother, Sandra Chillingworth, able to manipulate the hell out of the men in her life."

"Ah, so that's how you see it: Sandra Chillingworth gave into temptation and got burned."

"In the gondola, she hedged her bets … in case she got found out with Dimitri."

"Maybe she was already pregnant with Dimitri's baby and just wanted to cover her tracks."

He smiled, not a little dumbfounded.

"Angela, from what I've heard, embraced temptation like the Holy Grail."

"And what about you? How have you handled temptation?"

"I coached from the sidelines. I brought the players together. I knew about the infractions, but I hid my eyes because I was an officer of the court and could not know about such things."

She eyed him intently. "You enjoyed being better than they were, above it all."

He bit down on his lower lip. "Hey, I took the money."

"And ran. Because you believed in something."

"Would it make you happy to believe that's the case?"

"To believe what?"

"My faith that the woman I loved, the woman I remembered, could never have killed herself."

"It would, I guess, be nice to think so."

She nodded as if in acknowledgement of her own internal accounting and then stood up, extending her hands upward, letting the tips of her fingers move lightly over the tessellated surface like grasses in a running stream.

She said, almost as if reading it from somewhere inside herself, "I believe in the power of what we create, that the scattered fragments of the firmament can be brought together in us and become something stronger still—better." She reached a hand to his. "That *how* we love matters more than *who* we are."

CHAPTER 35

Venice, March 24, 1914

Dear Mama and Papa,

Even after Sandra's letters, I was not prepared for the wonders that met me coming out of the train station, when I gazed for the first time upon the Grand Canal. What enchantment! Sandra had me quickly packed in a gondola and off for sight seeing on the way to the pensione. She seems positively re-born, brighter and keener and full of gaiety. Between exchanges of news of home and her time in Venice, she rattled off the history of every palace we glided past, filling me in on anecdotes about her new friends and perilous adventures.

I must admit I was first shocked at the humble lodging presented me after our tour of the more fashionable parts of town. But I quickly grasped the charm and the necessity of such a place for Joseph's work. He likes to be near the more humble neighborhoods, where the real life of the city is lived, "a little grit between the teeth," as he puts it. Ever the hard charger and solid opinions for my dear brother-in-law. I found their room had been transformed into a studio; paintings and easels and boxes of colors fill the place, along with the smell of turpentine and oils. There is barely space to pass. And yet they are oblivious to the clutter, so intent are they on their lives and work compressed into that tiny space. They can barely take their eyes off each other. Joseph is busier than a ship's steward in a storm, and to my untutored eye, his work of the last year is a distinct cut above what he produced before. He was so kind upon my arrival, solicitous of my every need as I was stored away in the room next to theirs. He is quite the gentleman, though I know you find this hard to believe, but easily distracted by his artistic enthusiasms. One minute, he is hanging on one's every word, the next, he's out the door for a canted ray of afternoon light to be captured in some distant corner of the city, then returns hours later in a flurry of canvases and sketch pads, copper plates filling the pockets of his jacket. Then he is off for an evening row on the lagoon. But have no doubt he loves our Sandra and has made a true goddess of her, so much so that I often find myself blushing to my toes.

Sandra claims that her condition is slowing her down, but I find it hard to believe, given the pace she maintains. You will be happy to know she practices many hours every day, more than when we were children. She has introduced me to her new piano teacher, Dimitri. He is Russian and has thinning blond hair, tempestuous eyes, and long, tapering fingers that spill over the keyboard. His playing is perfectly transparent; the high notes sing and glitter like stars in a night sky. I don't know how he does it. I've agreed to study with him, too. Sandra insisted. But of course it is a waste of his time. I think he can use the money. He wears the same rumpled gray suit and smokes endless cigarettes. He composes, too, but his music, strange modern atonalities, gives me headaches. Sandra made me promise not to let on about her condition to Dimitri; she thinks his music, along with that of other moderns like Scriabin and Stravinsky, will change the way we hear music. I beg to differ but keep my thoughts to myself.

Sandra is very charged with her enthusiasms and seems madly intent on making me a convert. Where once she seemed to keep me at arm's length from her modeling and life with Joseph, now she positively pulls me in, sharing confidences, bringing me along on modeling expeditions and insisting that I spell her or that we pose together. Joseph has taken to the idea with alacrity, seeming intrigued with the new possibilities, with the "counterpoint," as he calls it. We love the chance to gossip, laugh, and make fun of Joe, like naughty children again. Sandra can be dismissive of his work in private moments. Frankly, I think this modeling business is quite overblown. In the past, she made it out to be hard, exacting work, but now she makes light of the "outdoor work," as she calls it, implying with a sly smile that the real artistic challenge happens under different circumstances. She is positively mysterious at times. Often, I have the sensation of having stumbled in upon them after a great hurricane of passion, while they are a little amazed to have survived, to have come through the storm, glad to have me about so that they can step back for a breather. Perhaps the prospect of a child has sobered them.

Sandra's women friends are a lot to take for any length of time: socialists and suffragettes, man-haters and seductresses, a wicked crew as they cackle over tea and try to shock us Boston girls. Sandra can be a tad bizarre at these times, playing to this crowd of duchesses and dowagers, altering stories of our girlhood to fit the audience's preconceptions about identical twins. Like an artist scrubbing out a first effort, she enjoys reinventing herself, often at my expense, a naughty joke that makes me squirm as her unwitting accomplice. I am relieved when she goes to her piano practice at Casa Alvisi and I can have time to myself to walk the city and see it through my own eyes. I practice my Italian with the young stonecutter, Giovanni, who made your Christmas present. I teach him English in return. He has the most scandalous repertoire of jokes about priests. Isn't it strange, in such a Catholic country, that some elements of the population hate the church with such venom?

By the by, Sandra is absolutely intent on the Casa Alvisi; she tells me she has written to you with the purchase price. She says she cannot bear the thought of losing the place to another party and will not come away until it is secured. The poor old servants are convinced of her intentions. Can you find the funds? It really is a most magnificent palace. If you could see it, Father, you would have it. It comes with pictures!

All is well. The date of return is not yet broached, at least not in my presence, but time—even here—will have its say. Love to you both, your daughter, Angela

He woke beside her, seeing lines of peach-streaked clouds beyond the window. March had been unusually warm. There were days when they didn't even bother with the heater. He pulled back the down comforter and eased his sweaty body out and over to the window, opening it all the way. Luminous moonlight saturated the garden, leaving etched masses of darkness in the thinned myrtle hedge, tram lines of silverpoint in the vineyard beyond. He liked best the silhouetted poplars past the vineyard, something of Monet gone south for the winter. Along the grassy bottom of the hedge were some bits of carved marble, a glossy white in the slanted light, pilfered God knew when or where. He could smell the earth and it brought back longings for places remembered and not ... perhaps a Concord spring.

He turned to the bed and saw her lying there, one breast uncovered. The whiteness of her face and shoulders was startling, as if finding something of the outside—some essence of transfigured light—translated into skin and bone. Her body seemed strangely reborn and lushly young, and he realized it had been ages since he'd seen her entirely naked and not shivering. It made him question his desire, how much was grounded in the particular flesh of the beloved and how much always existed as an instinct of memory, a lust impressed into the flesh by a genetic disposition to move beyond the self and survive. He ran his tongue over his lips, still flavored with her cunt, as if ever needful of making sure of her inimitable self. He marveled at the light that invested her with such beauty, as if, for the first time, understanding the full measure of the flesh to inspire love. Love in the abstract was such a pitiful illusion. If love was real and true, it was a thing of flesh: of flesh born, flesh moving through flesh, and, too, dying in the flesh. Unless …

Her eyes opened as if willed by his gaze.

"What are you doing?" she asked.

He bent and kissed her waking eyes.

"Wishing I was an artist, so I could keep this moment."

"Oh …" She yawned. "A poet, you were going to be a poet."

"And you'd be my Beatrice."

"Beatrice," she echoed, giving it a lovely Italian lilt. "Well, hardly."

"I'd ravish you at pencil point."

"Or compose a suite of piano études."

"Hmm … to live forever."

She sat up. "Oh, the smells, the garden. I was dreaming about the garden … or was it the Curtises' garden on the Guidecca—funny."

"It's like … Do you remember the moonlight on the river, the night of the dance?"

"Scene of the crime." She smiled, as if coming out of the ether. "Tell me what it was like for you. Was it really the first time?"

"I was petrified. But you were too beautiful … nineteen and beautiful."

"You were swept away, or did I really seduce you?"

He went over to her and sat down.

"You tell me."

"It was a beautiful moonlit night and it was Indian summer."

"Was it an accident that you got pregnant?"

"You could've taken precautions."

"You told me not to worry."

"Then I got swept off my feet."

"You make it sound like a joke."

"Maybe" —she turned her head from his gaze— "I'd been a good girl just too long."

"Why'd you lie to me about your age?"

"Don't you get it? There was a year of my life—none of us wanted to remember."

"Here, in Venice, with your mother and sister, studying piano."

"With my pregnant fifteen-year-old twin—think about it. And then four months isolated with auntie in Manchester."

"Did you want a baby because of what happened?"

"Don't start with the pop psychology."

"You're pregnant, aren't you?"

"Why do you say that?"

"You haven't had your period since we've been together."

"I'm an old lady past my prime."

He took her hand.

"I love you," he said, looking away toward the window, as if embarrassed or even afraid.

She squeezed his hand, feeling for the new calluses. "As much as that night by the river?"

"I think it's different when you get older."

"You mean we know each other better ... now."

"Well, we've jettisoned a lot of bad stuff, huh?"

"Have we?" she said.

"Remember, in the dinghy—all the bad stuff?"

"I guess it can never be the same."

"But we're the same. Getting pregnant."

She said in a dream-softened voice, "Funny, when you put it that way."

"But it's what you wanted."

"It's a little amazing, believe me."

"Getting what you wanted?"

She squeezed his hand again and placed it on her belly. "I don't think we'd be here if it wasn't."

"So ... that's your pebble?"

"We, you just said, wasn't it ... about getting pregnant?" She brought his hand to her lips and kissed the palm. "You smell of me; that's nice."

"Go on," he said, holding the back of his hand to her lips.

But she only kissed him again and sighed. "It's sad, don't you think, living in the shadow of genius and not being able to strike out on your own? Sometimes I feel like such a failure."

CHAPTER 36

By late April the weather had turned wonderfully warm and sunny, and by May it was positively hot. The island swarmed with brilliant blossoms, while the garden around the house thickened with cornflowers and forsythia and honeysuckle. Songbirds flocked into the surrounding thickets and trees. They threw open every shutter and window, leaving the door wide open, as if needing to eliminate all demarcation between indoors and out. It was increasingly hard to spend so much of the day in the cool, musty confines of the cathedral. When he could get away early, he would take out his *sandolo*, which he'd bought secondhand on Burano with his first paycheck, and row around the island and through the abandoned canals. He was addicted with the rhythm of the movement, the exact reversal of what he'd been used to: sitting, pulling, with one's back toward the direction of the movement. It was like seeing the world being born in every forward stroke, especially on clear afternoons when the white-capped Alps breached the blue edge of the universe. On weekends, he'd row her to Burano, where they'd do their shopping at the local grocery store.

His torso and arms became fully muscled, and she touched him in ways that let him know how she enjoyed his new body.

Then the owner of the cottage began showing up to work in the garden and vineyard, turning over the soil and planting vegetables during the afternoons, when they were away at Santa Maria Assunta. They'd run into him on the way home as he was finishing up his work. For some reason, the owner's presence seemed to annoy her. At first, she tried to pretend otherwise, but he could tell she was on edge. Finally, one afternoon, she left work early and cornered the owner in the garden. She offered to do the work for him: weeding and pruning and generally keeping the place up, in exchange for him taking something off the rent and letting them have some of the harvest. She was very businesslike about this, friendly but firm, making sure it came across as a quid pro quo and not a favor. The owner didn't take much convincing. He was a busy man and soon assented to the plan. He left them to it.

From then on, she could barely wait to finish up in the cathedral and get back to the garden. Most of the major work on the mosaics was done, just tedious details to complete. She threw herself into gardening with real flare. He was surprised at her enthusiasm, her energy, finding himself quickly drawn into the work, too, especially the heavier tasks, following her lead, as in so much else. It cut into his rowing time, but that was okay. He loved watching her, down on her knees, scraping away with a trowel, pruning, digging, getting herself covered in dirt. It tapped some need in her: her father's daughter. He found an old wood-handled scythe and sharpened it and spent a lot of time cutting the grass in the garden and along the paths surrounding the house. Handling the scythe was a little awkward with his bad hand, but the rhythm of the mowing, the sound of the blade, and the smell of cut grass were deeply satisfying.

By evening, with the sun low behind terra firma and the shadows deep and long, they would quit, dirty and sweaty, then strip and hose each other off. He loved spraying the water over her body, watching it course over her enlarged breasts and distended nipples and drip onto her rounded belly and into the shock of ash-blond hair below. Her flesh in the waning light was very white and lovely, especially against the backdrop of luxurious greens. It stirred him, not so much erotically as spiritually, filling him with sensations of well-being, of richness, of a lush and habitual rootedness.

The thing summoning visions of *Dreaming Sisters* in the Boston Museum of Fine Arts, the nude figures in a summer meadow burning behind his eyeballs: the ambiguous embrace, the tangled limbs and disheveled hair, the swooning half-parted lips … and the molten strokes of pigment—writhing on the canvas.

He liked to touch her, dry her off, feel the power and endurance of her ripening body, which seemed to take strength from its closeness to the soil. Some unspoken spirit came over her in that enclosed garden on the cusp of night. She would walk about, bend to the bits of old marble in the grass by the hedge, musing. The silence and the light and the peace of twilight heralded a completion. Their time on Torcello was coming to an end. The scaffolding would be coming down in a week. The dedication ceremony was scheduled for the end of May and they would only be able to keep the cottage through the second week of June, after which it would be rented to vacationers for ten times what they were paying.

"So, where are you—where are we—going to have the baby?" he asked again.

She did not look up from where she knelt among the rows of potatoes.

"There's a restoration job scheduled for the Visitazione on the Zattere, two blocks from your old pensione, if you can believe it. A two-year job, beginning in September. There's something in Verona, a church, about eighteen months."

"You can't keep doing this, not with the baby coming. You'll have to take some time off, at least from the hard physical labor."

"Hell—what's a month, give or take? You take care of the kid. The job will support the two of us, three of us, although maybe not in style."

He knelt besides her and began rubbing her shoulders. "You don't have to pull my chain about taking care of the baby. That's not what's at issue and you know it."

"I think we're doing okay as is."

"I want to marry you."

"We can do that, too, I suppose."

He stopped rubbing her shoulders for a few seconds, took a deep breath, and began again. "When does your passport expire?" he asked.

"I don't know."

"Where is it, by the way?"

"Why, have you been looking for it?"

"No. I mean, at some point, it's sure to be canceled. And let me tell you, my passport won't exactly bear much scrutiny."

"You can fudge almost anything over here, my dear Giovanni, if you pay people."

She smiled when she called him Giovanni, now like a pet name, a term of endearment between them.

He grimaced and tried to smile. "How much more fudging can we take?"

"Whatever it takes to stay together."

"Maybe it's time to go back."

"To the States?"

"You don't think we can have a real life back there?"

"Here we can be … who we want to be."

"But it's still living a lie. Would you want to start off with a child like that?"

"Tell me something, if you'd never met me—the dance, the river—what would have happened to you?"

"Ah, the theory of a parallel universe." He bent his face to her sweaty neck and took her breasts in his hands. "Of course, my mother wanted me to be a pianist at first, but then she realized it was an impossibly difficult career—what with her disappointments. So, it was going to be a Harvard Ph.D. in English, teaching, world's expert on Thoreau and Emerson."

"So you gave up teaching for law?"

"Listen, I have a confession to make. The only thing I wanted was you … and, well, maybe the rest would have followed."

She seemed to stiffen under his hands.

"Michael, don't freak out or anything, but I've been doing some checking. There's a job teaching English at the Dominican school on the Rio Terrà Foscarini for the fall. Next year, there's going to be an opening at the university for a teacher of American literature."

"You're a little scary when do you this stuff."

"I told you: I want us to be together."

"Don't you think a university job will require a background check?"

"It can be handled."

"But what are we running away from? If we turn ourselves in, what with the extenuating circumstances … there's nothing that can't be explained."

She turned her face up to his, examining his eyes. "You told me it would be years of trials, not to mention the cost."

"I've lost everything, one way or the other."

"So, maybe we could—you know, the easiest thing: go back and leave things just the way they are."

"Oh my God." He groaned. "And take on Angela's life, all that baggage? What about the people running her business? They must suspect something, not having heard from her in over a year and a half."

She sat up on her haunches with a guilty grin. "Oh, they've heard."

"So, you still stay in touch?"

"An E-mail occasionally, to keep them on their toes."

"What the hell do you tell them?"

She giggled. "'Keep up the good work, guys.'"

"Maybe they're just as happy, probably lining their pockets."

"Probably. Sales are skyrocketing."

"How do you do E-mails?"

"When I go for my checkups with the doctor, at the superintendent's office."

She reached up to him, squeezing his hand. "Haven't you been happy?" she asked.

"Incredibly."

"Well, isn't that enough?"

"Not if it's a lie … forever."

She got up and dusted her knees and turned to him.

"What do you think I feel in the morning when I look in the mirror? I still see it, you know; I see her face, in that chair, looking out the window. It horrifies me. That's all that's waiting for *me* back there."

She turned and began walking for the gate.

"Wait, where are you going?"

"Just going to take a walk."

"I'll go with you."

"No, go and do your rowing." She waved a reassuring hand. "Don't worry, I'm not going to do anything stupid."

CHAPTER 37

Venice, May 29, 1914

Dearest Mama:

Please don't show this letter to Papa. I despair of my sister. She is showing with the child, she tires, but she does nothing to plan for departure. She simply dismisses my entreaties and throws me into her life. "I'm sick to death of modeling," she hisses. She withdraws from us with her piano or disappears off to her garden to conspire with Dimitri. She practices to exhaustion at Casa Alvisi. She is under the spell of Dimitri, and he under hers. For all his talent, he is a rogue, a madman. He whispers in my ear, "The child is mine and I love her—I will immortalize her in my music." He threatens to tell Joseph. And Joseph knows nothing. Sandra keeps so much from him. Has Father really agreed to buy the Casa Alvisi for a music academy as she says? I fear it is another of her subterfuges; it is her way to keep Dimitri. But she won't come away without the Casa Alvisi; I am convinced. Perhaps Papa should at least agree to the purchase, enough to get her to return.

I tremble with apprehension. I am put in a false position with Joseph, making excuses for my sister and sustaining her lies. I spend more and more time with him; he is truly a fine man. This can't be good, can't be right. Often I can't sleep for worry. It is as if they both conspire to throw me into the tempestuous sea and I must develop new strategies to survive. I find myself emboldened, surprised at my impetuosity. I never knew Sandra could be so wicked. I'm glad the nursery is all ready. I do my best. I will feel much better when Sandra is on shipboard and back in steady hands.

Tell Father to go ahead with the purchase and I will do the rest.

All my love, Angela

Venice, July 1, 1914

Dearest Mama:

Forgive me for not having been able to write to you for the past few days; I simply had not the strength. I know the telegram must have come as a terrible shock. Rest assured that Sandra's child is large and well formed and doing fine, as healthy a boy as might be hoped. I have arranged for a nursemaid and my room has now been set up as a nursery. How cruel God is: my woman's hopes of motherhood delivered me in such a cruel manner.

Joseph is devastated. We exist in a daze. We can barely talk; we cling to each other like shipwrecked waifs on a raft. Yesterday, we buried dear Sandra in the Protestant cemetery on the island of San Michele. It was a lovely warm day with a fresh breeze, the very sort of day she loved. The small brick-walled enclosure smelled of the summer and the small cedars that grow in that place. What astonished me was how many mourners attended the service, people who had known her for less than a year, many who had met her perhaps only once. All were similarly touched by her and felt a deep need to pay their respects. People have been so kind. But I cannot bear to look in their faces, feel their gaze in mine.

I told Sandra's teacher, Dimitri, not to attend the funeral, but he refused. He made a fool of himself. The man is crazy. He follows me; he hangs about, lurking in the shadows. I sent him a large sum of money to go away.

I have enough on my hands with Joseph and the baby. Joseph was almost mad with grief. He blames himself for everything, for the delay in returning to Boston, for the incompetent doctor. But I must tell you, that the baby was full size and my sister tarried, and she knew she tarried. Did you know that she was negotiating with Curtis's lawyers to buy Casa Alvisi? Did father offer her the money? Joseph can barely bring himself to look at the child, seeing as he does the instrument of his beloved's death. Oh, what a handsome child and a fitting tribute to Sandra. Without the immediate responsibilities thrust upon me for his welfare, I am not sure I could have withstood the horror and sorrow.

Forgive me for sharing the truth with you, Mama, but you are the only one I can speak to of this. I lie to Joseph. The truth is, her death was terrible. She was in agony for the better part of two days. I remained by her side throughout, trying the best I could to comfort her, to distract and encourage, to witness her screams. She was so brave, but in my worst nightmares, I could never have conceived the suffering that is the lot of our sex. It beggars one's faith in a benevolent deity. I felt so helpless in the face of her torments. The doctors and nurses spoke no English, and my Italian is only rudimentary. Much of the time, they seemed utterly resigned to her fate, especially near the end of her agonies, when the doctor performed the most unspeakable butchery on my poor sister. I am convinced that they were determined only to save the child and that she was sacrificed to that end.

She was so brave; she willed that the child should live, even if that meant the destruction of her body. During those awful hours, she refused to let Joseph see her in such a state. She would grab my hand and shake her head like a madwoman: "No, don't let him see me like this; he must never see me like this." I had to promise her and then lie to him to keep him away, pretend that it was not as bad as it was. And so when the child was finally born and she was cleaned up, Joseph found her ravished by the ordeal, weak, exhausted, barely able to speak, yet with an expression of such joy in her eyes as she held the infant to her breast. But it was too late. She seemed to fade before our eyes. Her body was so weakened that when the sepsis set in, she had no strength left to fight.

Her last thoughts whispered to me and Joseph were to take care of the child and to remember her to you and Papa, whose affection she never forgot or neglected, even with the many misunderstandings of the previous year. Thank God for the child and the future. And so we go on. We live enshrouded by her memory, which seems to haunt every corner of this city. Joseph cannot work or make plans. But we are determined to have a fitting memorial for her grave and so have commissioned an Italian sculptor, Giovanni, whom I have mentioned in my previous letters. He is practically one of us by now, as much moved by Sandra's death as we, and so the ideal choice. I am called on to model. I play the piano for Giovanni, as Sandra did, so he can get the hands. In the studio, I stand and close my eyes to the sound of the hammer and chisel and am haunted by my own face, by the hospital bed, my own flesh and blood dying before my eyes.

Dearest Mother, Sandra died in pursuit of all you wished for her. She was practicing the piano right up until the end. She was going to surprise you. She wanted to return one day and take Boston and New York by storm. Sandra loved you and her thoughts were with you—and Papa—and her native ground at the end. Your loving daughter, Angela

CHAPTER 38

The work of getting the scaffolding down nearly exhausted him. He had never done such hard physical labor in his life. For the first time, even being in good shape, he recognized the reality of his age, the limits of his strength and endurance. The younger men did most of the heavy lifting and were very nice about it, given his handicap, but the decline in his powers made him feel oddly vulnerable.

Sometimes in the night, he'd wake with a little frisson of fear, his body misted in a cold sweat. He'd check her sleeping face and creep down to the tiny wharf on the abandoned canal where he kept his *sandolo*, his one real possession. He'd row out onto the lagoon dressed in shorts and T-shirt, give himself over to the moonlight—the finest mother-of-pearl lace stretched across the obsidian sky—and the rhythm of his body and the sound of the dipping oar. Sometimes he was tempted never to stop. Sometimes he felt as if he were dancing on the edge of the earth.

Once her work was done, she lost all interest in the project and left the cleanup and removal of the scaffolding to the workmen. With the scaffolding removed, she and a couple of guys from the superintendent's office spent a few days making videos of the restored mosaics, shooting them from various angles, working with both natural light and the artificial lights being installed to illuminate the apse. This done, she began to spend her time in the garden or working at new recipes in the kitchen, or she would simply disappear for the day, taking the vaporetto to Venice. She told him it was to see her doctor or to talk with her boss, the superintendent of monuments, about job possibilities. Perhaps send an E-mail to SandyBlue.com, toying with the possibilities. She was perfectly open about these things and wasn't secretive in the slightest, but he found it disconcerting to come home to the cottage bone-weary and not find her there. At such times, her few belongings—clothes hanging on hooks against the wall, her stacks of books and tapes on the floor, the table with the diary and letters—seemed a pathetic residue, less than one might find in an overnight hotel room, as if her life might simply blow away in the next gust of wind.

Feeling lonely, he'd start preparing dinner. He did it precisely as she'd done it. He knew exactly which pots and utensils she used and the order in which she used them. He began slicing and chopping the vegetables, realizing how good and quick she was with the knives, how effortlessly she worked. He got the water boiling for the pasta, washed the salad, and set the table and opened the wine. Once this was done, he might sit at the table and flip through the diary, or reread the letters, the voices as immediate as the sound of the birds flitting about in the oncoming twilight. Neither of them bothered much anymore with the week-old *International Herald Tribunes*. Or sometimes, he would just walk to the vaporetto stop and sit on the quay, staring out over the sunset-streaked waters of the lagoon, waiting for her return on the last boat of the day.

In these moments, he often thought about his grandfather Giovanni, whose name he had appropriated, whose features he bore, as if some part of Giovanni had returned home and might explain himself. He thought back to Giovanni's walks along the Pawtucket Canal, when he must have remembered back to his youth in Venice, or wondered about his days at Sangamore, working in the studio barn with Joseph Palmer. Had he been embittered, sad, resentful? His employer had cruelly dismissed him—betrayed him and his fine work. Angela Chillingworth may have strung him along, perhaps for years. Yet he'd never mentioned a word to his family about those lost years when he had first come to America. At least Michael had never heard as much from his mother. Perhaps Giovanni had felt a fool to believe his love could be returned by the likes of Angela Chillingworth, and so had invested those failed ambitions in his art, or piano lessons for his daughter … a concert career thwarted by the Depression. Perhaps it had been enough; perhaps Giovanni *had* found peace, peace in the work of his hands, the work in which he found the best of himself. What more could a man want? And this the very thing that had so incensed his father, Jimbo Collins, that Giovanni seemed to live such a contented life, carving symbols to link the generations, that something of love's bonds might endure. Such things being to Jimbo Collins a constant reminder of his family's ever-fading fortunes and frustrated aspirations.

Occasionally, upon reflection, he wondered if Giovanni's experience should serve as a warning. Had Michael Collins embraced Sandra and this island existence too completely? Had he lost something of himself in the bargain, a dynamic of the soul—ambition? Yet he had never been happier. He reconciled himself to his lot with the thought that they, Palmers and Maronettis alike, were all fools to a love beyond their reach … prey to the law of compensation like all mortals, genius or not. And if he was heading for a fall, better a fall from grace than from blind ambition.

CHAPTER 39

Venice, August 3, 1914

Dearest Mama,

I suppose you have heard the news of the war. It is on everyone's lips. My friend, the talented sculptor Giovanni, who has just finished Sandra's monument, scoffs at the war news; he says it will bring only bad things. He is such a fine fellow and I enjoy his humble company. He knows the city in ways we cannot. We walk and he can point out carving done by his father and grandfather, even his great-grandfather, the very fabric of the city marked with his family's skill and love. It is as if a little part of the city—the city she loved—is translated in his hands to the monument for your daughter. I have great plans for him and I will tell you more when we return.

Joseph packs with a heavy heart as the war presses on every front. He is distracted, aloof, crushed. I try without success to get him to spend more time with his son. I make my final pilgrimages around the city, a place that seems to empty by the hour. Passing Casa Alvisi the other evening, I was hailed by Curtis's old manservant and majordomo, who ushered me into the palazzo with a flurry of entreaties. I was a little nonplussed, distracted with fond memories, and before I knew it, I found myself at the Bechstein grand playing Chopin, staring out at the moonlit waters of the Canale Grande. I played and played, my music from childhood practice coming back to me as if by magic, letting my soul simply float upon the music. I felt strangely buoyed on the night, as if the last in a long line of gentle spirits who had found delight in that place. And then seeing the old man in the corner with tears in his eyes, I realized, and it went through me like a knife, that he thought I was Sandra, that he, poor man, had no idea what had happened to her. Unbeknownst, I had taken on her mantle in his heart and I knew to the bottom of my soul that I was playing for her, that in a sense I was her, living through her and in him, and that this final image would remain with him to his dying day. I careened between wicked enchantment and horror at my role, finding myself taken over and taken out of myself. When finally I managed to get away, it was not before the old man had slipped into my hand a large rusty key he insisted upon parting with before I melted into the night.

Only the next morning did I realize that the key was not for the Casa Alvisi, which, as you know, Sandra had designs upon, but for the garden on the Giudecca. As if some buried instinct took me over, I gathered up the child, hailed a gondola, and within minutes was across the water and fitting the key to the tiny gate. Beyond the high brick wall was the most splendid little garden laid out with gravel paths, winding between arbors and small orchards and flower beds. Strategically placed in the garden were fragments of marble with a patina of age about them that simply drew one's touch, as if to the very heart of burnished time. I found myself a sunny corner and sat with the child, singing to him, letting him breathe deeply of the earth and trees and flowers, so unlike that terrible room where he had first drawn breath. And I knew what Sandra had felt there, why she had loved so much; and, of course, it was true; I was holding part of her to my breast—God forgive me, to the bottom of my heart.

As I sat with baby Joe, I heard a noise and turned. There behind me near the gate, which I had failed to lock, was Dimitri. I told him to leave, but he would not. I could not raise my voice or be any more forceful in my protests because of the baby. He came nearer and began walking about as if he knew the place well, caressing the ancient statuary with his repulsively stringy fingers. He was trying to be kind in his mongrel fashion, finally coming and sitting nearby to smoke his cigarettes. He cooed at the child. He began to talk excitedly about news of the war, which was on the front page of every newspaper. "The war will change everything," he said. "The child will grow up in a new world, where the gardens and palaces of the rich will belong to the people and great art will flourish as never before." He was planning to return to Saint Petersburg and compose hymns to the revolution.

He fell silent and fastened his eyes on me. Then he began wiping away tears. He told me, glancing around at the garden, how much he loved Sandra. I told him to be off. Between tears, he told me again that the child was his. He offered to take me on as a student. "Surely you have the genius of your sister," he told me. I could barely control myself and I was terrified he would go to Joseph with his lies.

I bribed him again with money, money enough for his train ticket. I told him to meet me at Florians that evening and I would give him the money. And finally we were left alone.

I will return home soon bearing with me your grandchild.

Date of my sailing will follow by telegram. Love, Angela

On the evening before the dedication ceremony for the restoration of the mosaics, Sandra returned to the cottage from a last inspection of the apse, seeming a little lost. She had a video camera and spent a few minutes shooting the cottage and the gardens. Later, he couldn't quite get an answer from her about whether she was pleased with the job, if she was glad it was over, or perhaps a little sad that a year's labor was at an end. As they sat in the bath together before dinner, her back to his chest, he massaging her shoulders, he sensed again how deeply she lived within herself, somewhere so self-contained and possibly fragile that if he pushed too hard, she might be harmed. It occurred to him that her opacity, his failure to read her, might have something to do with the fact that she was leading the very life he might have imagined her leading, perhaps an overly idealized version of a simple unaffected existence close to the land. Or was she simply, for his benefit or hers, indulging some atavistic return to the life of her New England forebears? An approximation of what she'd glimpsed of her father's life on his Concord farm? He sensed she was trying to prove something, as if he'd questioned her bona fides and she was providing him with answers. And yet as he sat in the bath, his fingers pressed to her soapy breasts, she felt more real and true to him than anything on God's green earth.

Then, like that, she was out of the tub and going overboard on dinner. He lingered in the tub, watching the blur of the knife as she chopped. A new recipe. She'd pored over her cookbooks. There was fresh cibatta, courtesy of a fellow restorer who came every day from Murano, and gossamer-thin Parma ham and extra virgin olive oil, and, to top it off, a superb bottle of '86 Amorone, nectar of the gods. After the meal, she took his hand and kissed his fingers and asked him to do her a favor. Still holding his right hand, she pressed a key into his palm and closed his fist with her hand.

"I've left a front-row seat for you. I'd like you to go to the cathedral and spend some time with *our* work and then let me know what you *really* think. Okay?"

It seemed odd, this request, but he went obediently, glad for the dinner and the upbeat mood, enjoying the evening walk along the grassy paths, the island now so empty of the tourists, who usually came in droves during the daylight hours. The place, for a little while longer, especially at night, still felt like theirs. He breathed deeply and stared up into the sky, the sheerest aquamarine silk, with vague threads of starlight woven in. The greens—infinite shades of green—of the foliage in the surrounding pastures and vineyards seemed to hover in suspension before his eyes. Birds nesting in the hedgerows sang out at his unexpected approach and twittered at his retreat.

He suddenly realized that the key to the work entrance of the cathedral was still gripped tightly in his hand, and the feel of it caused him to stop and look up. Ahead, the brick campanile of the cathedral reared up tall and straight in the moonlight, an ever-welcoming presence, its four Byzantine windows set off by three marble columns that shone like silver ingots on dark velvet. A metal weather vane or lightning rod on the roof glinted against the stars. It took him back to the first moment he'd stepped ashore from the rowboat and looked up at the observation tower at the Palmer homestead … the sense that someone had been waiting and watching for him there. It struck him that the way she'd pressed the key into his hand had the feel of conscious imitation, almost a ritual act, as if putting part of herself into his safekeeping, making over her disturbed dreams. Not unlike how the old servant in the Casa Alvisi had pressed a key into the hands of Sandra and Angela Chillingworth, a key to the Curtises' walled garden on the Giudecca full of ancient *spolia*, wreckage of civilizations among the apricot and cherry trees, reminders of catastrophic loss. The price of metamorphoses, as Sandra Chillingworth Palmer had noted to her sister: where that which once existed is no more, and yet that which was not has come to be.

At the small side entrance to the cathedral, he let himself in. The silence and the absolute dark had a numbing effect, as if he'd dropped into sheer space, but without falling, only drifting on invisible currents. He wavered for seconds, stumbling like a drunk as he groped in the darkness of the side aisle. He found the switch to light the mosaics. The apse blossomed with an unearthly gold radiance. He staggered back. Not what he expected, not at all. To have spent months inches away from that dirt-encrusted wall, then to have the whole thing come alive, an infinitude of tiny suns, bee-swarming suns run riot, a painful silent buzz behind his eyes.

He bowed his head for a moment, blinking away the searing afterimages so that his eyes might adjust to the spectacle.

Looking again, he saw that the golden apse was no longer such a shock to the system. He examined the serene face of the Madonna. He was pleased to think how their work had released her from a shadow existence to reclaim her rightful place in the firmament, even if all she really had been was a mere conduit for human genetic material, as Joe Palmer had put it to him that day in the orchard. Walking down the nave toward the apse with his eyes upraised, he became aware of the majestic innocence of the greatest art, reining in the imagination beyond time and contingency (with a little helpful restoration along the way).

The chairs for the dedication ceremony had been set up in lines at the front of the nave. One chair had been placed a little forward of the first line and there was an envelope on it with his name printed in blue ink. He recognized her handwriting and opened it and sat in the chair to read her letter. He'd been half-expecting something of the sort.

Dear Michael,

There are things I need to tell you that I simply have not been able to tell you in person and that I don't think I was capable of telling you before this. As you must have guessed, the girl at that dance, the girl you were with that night on the river, lied to you, and more importantly, lied to herself. I think she was in denial and trying to deal with a wound that would not heal. The sad thing is that I find it hard to connect myself with her anymore, as if she were another person. But since you have come along, I have been desperate to try to get her back and let her live again—at least for you. It has been such an odd process, on the one hand to try to dig back into oneself, on the other, to relive the lives of my grandmother and grandfather and great-aunt, as if their lives might offer some clue to our own lives. And then there is you, who watches us all from the outside, who knows our history, our foundering enterprise. I see it in your eyes when you make love to me; I sometimes feel that my body belongs somewhere else. And, oh yes, there are moments when I feel your hands on my body and I yearn for a man I have never known. What an intricate labyrinth of cause and effect and deceit we have constructed for ourselves, and even trying to find our way back along our path of twine, we find it branching in unknown directions.

Often I fear that I sift it all only to make more excuses for myself. But my sins are my own and there are no excuses. One likes to believe that one can point to the day, the hour, and say, This is what happened and it led to this. But I'm not sure it works that way. Sometimes I lie awake at night in your arms, feeling your heartbeat, the sweat of your body, the taste of your semen, and I remember back to all the rooms I have passed through to see where the past intersected my future and changed things forever.

My mother seems to fade, as good and kind and foolish as she was. Is that because we are too alike? I suppose as girls it is our fathers who take us out of ourselves. He was the one who insisted our room be kept tidy—shipshape, like everything else in his neatly ordered world. He was the one who would mysteriously disappear and reappear, who put us in boats to row us away from our home and gardens and the pastures we loved, who took us up into that crazy, dangerous tower and held us high above the land so that it became miniature patterns and something apart from ourselves. I suppose that's what fathers—men—in fact, all do: They take us away.

Only now do I see the spell cast over him by those bewitching portraits of his mother. Of course, there was the undeniably romantic image of his artist father, who treated his son like one of the unpleasant complications in a life dedicated to rare beauty. I realize now that when he took us to Sangamore, despite the sturdy eyebrows and steady voice, he longed for something that he could never, ever explain to the likes of us as little girls. He knew the late paintings well; he would spend hours with them while we played in the gardens. He knew they were fine things, and he must have known that someday they would be valuable and that the true genius of his father would be recognized. And certainly, for it would only be natural, he must have yearned for a spark of that talent, looked into his soul for the inspiration that caused such things to be created. And what did he find there? Was it love or desire, do you suppose, that he saw in those paintings, or the cover-up of a cuckold's disappointments and the depredations of a talented but feckless woman. What must he have felt as we matured, as my sister, Angela, started with the provocative clothes and makeup? Angela had radar for these things. She saw everything from the outside in; she only saw herself through the eyes of others. She was a force of gravity, and the more she attracted others into her orbit, the more brightly her sun shone—and the further I sheared away from her dangerous path. The woods and pastures became my haunts.

I suppose what Angela discovered—maybe she glimpsed it first in those paintings of her grandmother, was the latent power that must lie at the synapse point of the generations. I don't know if it's a sexual thing as much as a way out, a means of escape into life. All I know is that the more she wanted out, the more I wanted things to stay the same. I didn't mind her flirting with Dad or sneaking around with Bobby Hathaway, but she had no right to get herself pregnant. And I have to think she did it on purpose, as her way of escaping, putting her finger in the eye of the world. It tore my mother apart: the son she could never produce. My father, that tower of probity and order, cowered in terror at the mere implication of his complicity, perhaps at the seeming revelation of his most hidden lusts. As for me, it was as if my whole world was being torn apart.

My mother practically had a nervous breakdown, what with all the deceit and hiding that summer of Angela's pregnancy in Manchester. Venice had been bad enough, with Angela skipping her music classes, moping, flirting, hanging out with older students. While poor old Auntie Angela, propriety's queen bee, nearly freaked out at having her pregnant niece around, looking so much like her pregnant sister of all those years before in Venice. Then she embraced the whole stupid charade like a new lease on life, only to be conveniently away in Boston at one of her board meetings on the day when Angela went into labor. And then when Mom botched the arrangements for the delivery with her criminal delay in calling the doctor, she blamed me. Yes, I ran away; I was terrified. Nobody said anything about staying by the phone. When Aunt Angie finally returned, she had a near breakdown. Nobody thought to change her bloodstained bedsheets. I'm sure it brought on her precipitous decline and death less than two years later. So the Palmers had their beautiful baby boy, only he nearly suffocated due to his umbilical cord getting caught around his neck—damaged goods for careless, spendthrift lives.

Nothing was ever the same after that. Mom was a nervous guilty wreck; Dad never even came up to Manchester that summer. He was already in flight. I hated that summer. When that baby was born brain-damaged I secretly exalted. I felt vindicated, that Angela had gotten what she deserved. Forgive me: I hoped he'd die in the delivery. What a mess, Michael. You should have stayed away; you should have run a million miles. The only one who came out of that hellish business with any integrity was Angela. To think what she went through. And then with all the tests showing the extent of the damage, she stuck by her child with a love and dedication that to this day rocks me. She wore herself out emotionally and physically trying to nurture that baby into some kind of life, never giving up. While I soured away in a purgatory of hate. Biding my time, I suppose.

Even so, the night it happened seems so unreal to me that I still see myself as an alien presence masquerading as myself. What I remember was the baby crying. And instead of the thump of Angela's feet on the squeaking floorboards of the hallway, the crying continued. Mom and Dad had gone to Boston for the opera, Dad dragging my weepy, hysterical mother out into the night, as if he could force the clock back to the early days of their marriage. Normally, the slightest sound woke Angela. She must have been worn out. The baby kept crying, a weak, choking cry. Still nothing from Angela. I got up and tiptoed out of my room and across the hall. Angela's door was closed. Probably a draft had closed it. It was so hot for October and all the windows upstairs were open. I thought about knocking and waking her. But she'd been so bitchy—she'd bought into Mom's lie about me and the phone—that the thought of confronting her in the middle of the night frightened me. So I walked down the hall to the nursery. Another taboo.

I had been told never to go into the nursery, never to touch the baby. She simply didn't trust me. Can you imagine that? My own sister! Baby Joey was lying there crying, his poor distorted face even more distressed than normal. For a moment, I felt such love for the poor thing. I picked him up and tried to comfort him. He stopped crying for a few seconds, as if startled, examining me in the moonlit darkness to see if his mother had come. I cuddled him, spoke soothingly to him, checked his dry diaper. He seemed to calm, and when I took a breath, I could smell that wonderful baby. For that minute, I loved that little baby as if he were mine. Then he started to bawl again and twist in my arms, as if he'd found me out for an imposter. I'd show him. I went to the white wicker rocking chair where Angela sat to feed him and sat down myself, rocking in hopes of calming him. It didn't work. Then, I don't know quite what possessed me, but I pulled up my T-shirt and placed him at my breast. He actually took the nipple and sucked, but whether it was because there was no milk or because he recognized it wasn't Angela, he pulled back with a piercing whine, as if he were in agony. It shocked me, hurt me, and out of that seeming rejection came a black despair and rage.

I got up, wanting to leave him in the crib and run away, but I smelled the outside, the fall smells drifting in, and I went to the open window and looked out at the pale night and the river in the distance. I think the air calmed him, as if I was giving him a last glimpse of the world he would never inherit. I remember the roving clouds and the shapes of the thinning trees. I don't remember dropping him. Whether he slipped from my arms or I simply let him go, I cannot truthfully say. All I know is that I wanted him gone, because he was an interloper, a changeling, a destitute spirit who had brought chaos into our near-perfect world and split me forever from my sister—my father.

We were madly in love with Dad.

Do you understand now my silence, my lie to you on the river?

I remember cowering in my bed, crying myself to sleep, being terrified in the morning, as if there was no waking up from this nightmare. I heard noises outside, voices, people on the stairs, and then a long spell of silence. But no one came into my room. At some point, I ventured out and went downstairs. My mother was sitting in the living room with a drink in her hand, already drunk. She told me matter-of-factly that little Joey had been found dead in the crib that morning by Angela. She held the drink up to me as if in mock salute. Just as well, she told me, poor boy was doomed to a vegetable existence, according to all the doctors. Dad was at the hospital with Angela. They didn't return till much later. The doctors, the coroner, everybody just assumed it was crib death or complications from the brain damage. Everybody nodded sympathetically and mumbled things like "All for the best," as if everybody was a little guilty that all our worst hopes had actually come true. Angela barely talked to me for almost a year, but then, she didn't talk much to anybody, not until my parents divorced and we went away to Alcott Academy. Then she really came into her own.

For a long time, I viewed myself as an almost unwitting instrument in the hands of blind fate. My fate was just to be an impulse in that network of desire and repose, perhaps a neuron receptor gone faulty for a moment, but in fundamental harmony with unforgiving nature, which discards the unwanted, the defective, the unloved. We can talk ourselves into almost anything. But of course, what I did, must have done, is unforgivable.

Bad enough—and that before I even met you.

Then, I took your son and lost him. In this, I am guilty of something possibly even worse—a lack of faith. It bothered me that I never heard from you.

It never even occurred to me that your letters would be intercepted. Then people began bad-mouthing you, and, worse, I started to believe them. Angela rolled her sarcastic eyes, as if to let me know what a fool I was even to think about elbowing her territory. When my mother insisted on Geneva and the private school, it was a little like that summer at Manchester all over again, but at least out of sight of my family. I didn't protest, kick and scream, go find you like I should have—like any normal person would have. I went like a pig to slaughter. And yes, to answer your question: I guess I did get pregnant on purpose. It was over a week after my period. Somewhere in my fucked up head, I must have seen pregnancy as a way of escape from everything.

So, I used you. No better than my namesake, who used her husband and then her sister, to have her way, to have her creepy piano teacher and Casa Alvisi.

If there is any truth in me it is that I loved our child. When I held him and then, against the agreement I'd signed, starting breast-feeding him, I knew I couldn't go along. I'd keep him, even after signing all the papers. I should have been cannier, just skipped town with him. But I blew that, too.

What can I say? You brought me a renewed faith, and in return I showed an empty hand. In fact, I did try to get in touch with you. I wrote to Harvard and found you weren't there. I called the inn from Geneva. I got your mother on the line. I told her about the baby. I asked about you. I could hear it in her voice, how much she hated me. She told me you were in Vietnam. She blamed me.

And so, to answer your question—how many questions you have—yes, I do owe the world a life, maybe two. For that there is no forgiveness. A life without faith. And so maybe it is for the best that your "first" love, Sandra, died. To the world, she walked tall, but always, always on such thin ice.

I love you, but I am glad she is dead. When I got your weird E-mail—to Angela, of all people—and returned to Concord and found the reality of "Sandra's" death, the nothingness of her death, I was actually thrilled. Because the girl you remember from the dance, whom you unduly idealize, died a long while back, choked on her faithlessness. I am tougher for it. Haven't you noticed?

There is no going back to what we were, believe me. And believe me when I tell you how much I love you.

He was puzzled but also faintly relieved that there was no catastrophic deception coming out of her confession. Also, pleased at how near he'd gotten it right, that he'd hung in there—his faith in her absolute—against all odds. Surely, in the eyes of her family—the captain and general and artist—certainly in Joe Palmer's eyes—a worthy son-in-law. She had thrown down a gauntlet, a template for their continuing together. He found no reason he couldn't agree to her terms: a life in exile. Weren't they all a little older, a little wiser, a little tougher?

And though she never asked for his forgiveness, he could forgive her anything, even dropping that brain-damaged child out the window—just as Joe had described it. And he a guy who had neglected his brother for over twenty years, barely speaking to him except to end up in some stupid argument, who was he to judge?

As he made his way back to Sandra, he thought about his brother's little girl in the yellow dress, flitting among the graves; of Sandra as a young girl, fleeing from her pregnant sister and great-aunt across the green lawn at Manchester-by-the-Sea; of her pleas to him on the river to row just a little farther. How vulnerable yet invincible women were.

When he got back to the cottage, he found her sitting out in the garden, staring up at the stars, her face wet with tears. He went to her and kissed her, comforting her as best he could. He spoke her name over and over, as if needing to give it back to her—so she might accept herself again. He still loved that name. He told her he loved her more than ever, yet he sensed his words were of little help to her. She refused any more discussion, as if to seal their bargain at face value—the words she had set down and left for him in the cathedral would be the end of it.

And so it was agreed: No more need be said.

CHAPTER 40

The dedication ceremony went off without a hitch. Sandra and the members of the team were personally thanked by the mayor and city officials. Her old lover was there with his wife, representing the family bank: very distinguished, very dapper, in his late sixties at least, old enough to be her father. They exchanged greetings and he congratulated her without so much as a hint of a previous relationship.

Then the work was truly over. They'd have two final weeks in the cottage before they'd have to move on.

She seemed to recover her spirits quickly, as if the cathartic effect of her confession in the cathedral had taken hold. She was spending most of her time gardening, comparing recipes in cookbooks and preparing meals. She was hungry all the time. Clearly, she was drawing strength from the pregnancy, confident that all was going well. The doctor was pleased, she said, patting the nice bulge in her belly. Her blood was up, her cheeks blooming with color under the slight tan from all the outdoor work. She had been careful always to wear a broad-brimmed straw hat while working in the garden. The weather just got warmer and more humid, with only the occasional thundershower to cool things off. The early evening and night became their favorite times, especially when all the tourists were gone and they had the island pretty much to themselves again. They would take walks along the narrow paths and gaze out over the lagoon toward the distant spires of Venice or to the north and the mainland and the great Alpine peaks, a looming, distant presence against the night sky. Or he might row her out in the *sandolo* and they would lie back on cushions and drift under the stars.

It was so hot in the first part of night that they would often strip in the garden and hose each other off. He loved her waxing belly and liked to kneel in the grass when she was dripping wet to feel it, kiss it, bring his ear close to listen for the stirring of life within. He felt truly happy, almost beyond memory or worry. And she was so proud, like some archaic fertility goddess with her bulging belly and swollen breasts. She liked making love in the garden at night. He felt the need to be careful, but in some ways she was more sexual than ever, as if she'd been freed from the want of her own gratification and could indulge in his body, take him over. She liked best simply to stroke him off or take him in her mouth and massage his prostate. It sent him over the sky. She seemed to relish the taste of his supercharged ejaculate, lying back on the grass and spreading his semen over her breasts and belly, rubbing it deep into her skin, as if indulging some sympathetic magic. They laughed about this little ritual, but then, she always did seem to like a few ritual moments in her day.

Because they napped so much during daylight hours, they were often wide-awake until well past midnight. They would talk while staring up at the sky. She had him nearly won over to a life in exile, but he still wrestled with a nagging uncertainty, which he tried to banish by playing devil's advocate. She called it his one bad habit.

"Of course, there's another way we could do things," he said, staring upward, searching the Cygnus constellation for the starry cross.

"'Do things'?"

"Go back."

"I thought we'd agreed that really wasn't much of an option anymore."

"I know, but some part of me feels like it's giving up."

"What's to give up?"

"We could go back; you could go back and just, like you said, leave things be."

"So that's your plan B—leave Sandra dead?"

"Less complicated for everybody concerned, certainly less of a shock, especially for your dad. You could pull it off, with him, I mean, couldn't you? You'd just have to use her name."

"Angela?"

"How hard would that be?"

"Christ. She was a porn star. She has a whole world, a company, a fan club, for Christ sake—zillions of people who know her."

"Well, no one seems to be exactly missing her, and you've been staying in touch, so to speak."

"Yeah, but I've never actually gone and met any of her people, her managers."

"You never went to her restaurant in Sante Fe?"

"I talked to the manager on the phone. I've spoken to people in the company; they seem just as happy not to have Angela around. I think she was a tough boss."

"You're pretty tough. It couldn't be that hard, not for you."

"Thanks a lot." She laughed, as if relishing the new role he was proposing. "Hell, they've got her tapes. What else do they need?"

"Well, you could meet them briefly and then retire, sell the company. Then you could do anything you want. You could go back to being an artist, or go back to school, and teach. Or we could go off to live on a farm somewhere. I could teach high school."

"Hey, we could use her money; we could hire the best lawyers and get you off. If money was no problem, would that make a difference in terms of your case?"

"It would definitely help. And if it went to trial, I could certainly post bond."

"Well, there you are."

"And I'd be a good teacher. Hell, you'd be a great teacher."

"An ex-porn star?"

"Well, there's plenty of restoration work in the States. I know the perfect guy you could work for, name's Maloney, construction firm specializing in restoring old mill buildings—ever hear of him?"

She laughed.

"But, my dear Giovanni, you've *got* your interview at the Dominican school on Friday."

"I know, but it's not the same. How long can we go on pretending before something catches up with us?"

"Who's pretending?" She reached for his hand and squeezed it. "She's got quite a following, you know. Her tapes are in all the stores, right here in Venice. I mean, even now I get funny looks from people who can't quite place me."

"So, she'd just be a body, an image, a brand name: Sandy Blue. People will forget or stop caring about the person."

"Really?"

"Like Sandra Chillingworth Palmer."

"Until some wiseass comes along and ferrets her out."

"Ah, so that's it."

"So, is that the woman you want to marry? You want to go back to the States and have your child grow up with a mother like that? Those tapes will be around for fucking ever."

"I don't know, kids today ... they'd hardly raise an eyebrow."

"Not if it's your mother!"

He reached a finger skyward, as if tracing something out there.

"Does it ever bother you," he said, "that what we're seeing, the starlight, is millions of years of time all in the same moment, and worlds before our world was even born, and much of it probably dead—burned out tens of thousands of years ago?"

"I only care about this moment." Her hand went to the bulge of her belly.

"It's spooky, though: Time really is relative."

"Like Sandy Blue."

"Huh?"

"She told me, 'In my business, you do something—a crazy year or two out of your whole life—and it's there forever.'"

"She regretted what she'd done?"

"Proud, more likely. She'll have the last laugh."

"Because ... like the stars ... dead and gone, but the light remains."

"Something like that."

"Stardust reigniting stardust."

"Hmm."

"Give the devil her due—Angela was a pretty amazing gal," he said.

"Yeah, right—just your type."

"Well, there's always plan A: the truth option."

"I thought we'd exhausted plan A. Besides, that would be another mess. Just imagine: 'Porn Queen commits suicide.' The tabloids would have a field day; interest in her would revive. They'd market her as the suicide sex siren. Worst of all, they'd probably turn it into a disgusting morality play. They'd reexamine our childhood, the sixties, extrapolate the tragic consequences of the free-love generation, how she was exploited and degraded and ended up some depressive, diseased suicide in her sister's apartment. The Christian Right would see it as God's justice, the radical feminists would make her out as a victim of male oppression, and the mainstream press would indulge in a lot of delicate soul-searching about sixties values having come home to roost."

He turned on his side to see her face in the pale moonlight, bemused to realize how much thought she'd obviously given the idea.

"You sound almost protective of our *dear Angela*. And, you've got quite an imagination."

"Hey, like you told me, I'd be in legal hot water. And we wouldn't have her money to bail us out over legal fees."

"Point taken, counselor."

He reached to her belly and rested his palm on the underside, waiting.

He asked after a time, "Do you really want to have the baby here?"

"Come to the hospital with me and meet my gynecologist. Believe me, it's all very up-to-date. I've got us set for birth classes, and you're slated to cut the umbilical cord."

"I keep forgetting, you've been through this before."

"Not to worry. Women are having babies in their forties all the time now."

"Still, I'd feel better in the States."

"I bet you'd get off on being married to an aging porno star."

"I never thought about it ... much."

"Bullshit. It even kind of turns me on—those tapes were something. At least, I'd feel like I did something with my life."

"Mozzarella turns you on."

She laughed. "How would you handle your deal?"

"Well, I'd probably get my fifteen minutes of fame and have to do a lot of explaining before a grand jury, but then I'd have quite a bit of leverage, too. Those assholes have lied themselves out onto at least a dozen limbs. At the very least, a plea bargain."

"And we'd have Angela's money; she must have made millions."

"And I can sell my house on Capitol Hill; the equity would probably be enough to pay back the four hundred grand."

"What are the chances you could get off?"

He smiled. "If my celebrity wife were willing to pay for the best legal help in the land, well ..."

She gripped his arm.

"Would you be in any danger?"

"Not now, not after all the indictments and the trials."

"So, whatever I did, you'd have to face the music. Humph ... well, plan B might prove interesting." She ran her hands over her enlarged breasts.

He moved over her, a shadow against the stars, running his lips over the taunt skin of her womb, kissing her bulging belly button, and then moving down to her pudendum.

"Umm ..." She sighed. "Listen, if you don't like the Dominican school, we'll bag it and go back to the States: plan B, leave things as they are. It might be simpler. Like you said, with Angela's money, we could do whatever we wanted. We're good at winging it, you and I."

He paused a moment, looking up past the swell of her womb. "When you're like this, I think I prefer staying, like this ... here ... kissing you forever."

"Oh, you'd tire of me."

"Never."

"Do I taste any different?"

"Yummier than ever."

She pulled herself up onto her elbows to watch him and saw her enlarged breasts moon-shadowed across her belly.

"Aren't my tits something?" In reply, he moved up to nuzzle them, taking a nipple in his mouth and sucking gently. "I wish I could keep these tits forever." She stroked his hair and mooed. "A breeder, a big fat cow for you." She laughed wickedly, rubbing her other breast against his cheek. "Oh yes, baby ... a little harder. Use your teeth. Ugh ... it never felt so good."

He leaned back on his haunches, amused by her Sandy Blue trash talk. Or was she indulging a burlesque of *Dreaming Sisters*, the painting's delicious hints of subterfuge and shape-shifting ... and ruthless deceptions?

She reached to his erection and began to stroke him. "Come on my tits."

"I miss coming inside you."

"What, you don't like the mess?"

"Mess?"

"You and Joseph Palmer. Why do you think Sandra Chillingworth had him make love to her in a gondola?"

"He ..."

"He wouldn't—precautions to the wind—have known what else to do."

"Do you really think Sandra Chillingworth was using her sister?"

"She was pimping her sister. She was planning to take on Casa Alvisi and Dimitri, and have Joseph Palmer take Angela home with him."

"Jesus."

"Believe me, I know exactly how she was thinking."

On Friday morning, he had to be up early to get the vaporetto for his interview for the teaching job at the Dominican school near the Zattere. She had breakfast all ready and some strong coffee brewed. They were both quiet and a little tentative around each other as they ate. They would have to give up the cottage—a whole life—on Tuesday morning. She had a small apartment lined up for them in the working-class section near Santa Marta, not far from the railway station. It was the neighborhood where his grandfather's family had lived. She had opted for the job at the Visitazione on the Zattere and passed on the job in Verona. So it was now up to him. If he wanted to take the teaching job, they would stay; if not, they'd go back, put plan B into play.

He had a sense she was bending over backward to make it his choice and be a good trouper. He kidded her about not leading the witness. He even suspected she had made up her mind about the possibility of returning to the States, tempted, in some way, to take on Angela's life and see if she could pull it off, sell off SandyBlue.com, pay his legal expenses, and grubstake them to a new life. The prospect even tempted him, he admitted to himself, to prove he could take on Angela Palmer, even as her reputation and alter ego faded into history—and settle a few scores of his own.

She walked him to the landing and waited with him until the vaporetto arrived. There was a lot to do in the garden and the cottage to have it all ready to turn over to the owner by Tuesday. He laughed and accused her of planning to harvest everything in the vegetable garden before they left. She laughed and slapped his wrist, kissed him good-bye and wished him good luck. Then she kissed him again, really laying it on. It was like a thunderbolt of sexual energy, a teenager's first kiss. He stood alone at the stern railing, reeling from the kiss, and waved. She stood on the quay, waving back.

A deliveryman wheeling a large cardboard box off the vaporetto stopped to ask her a question. She glanced at the box, its top emblazoned with a brand name in blue letters, Siemens, and replied to the deliveryman, pointing toward the tiny path leading to the house. Then she turned back to the vaporetto and waved again.

She was wearing a loose-fitting sundress with a flowery pattern, an Italian Laura Ashley knockoff. As the vaporetto pulled back from the quay and turned for the channel, she put on her straw hat to shield her face from the glare of the sun. Bathed in this intense light, she seemed almost a mirage, the light playing tricks as he tried to read her face. She kept waving, almost girlish in her exuberance. He waved in reply. Then she gave a little jutted vamp of her hips, patted her belly, and jerked down the top of her dress for an instant, flashing her breasts. He laughed and waved until she disappeared as the vaporetto turned for the Burano channel.

The whole way to Venice, he felt a world of possibilities, as if life was really full of choices. The trip seemed over in minutes, and instead of taking the number 5 vaporetto from the Fondamenta Nuove around the outside of the city to the Zattere, he decided to walk it—try out his land legs. He'd walk across the city, get the measure of the place and settle his mind. After six months, he was a little shocked at the numbers of tourists in high season, the hustle and bustle and fevered commerce. Around a corner near San Marco, he passed a video store. On impulse, he went in. An entire section in the rear of the shop was devoted to adult X-rated tapes. The Italians—denizens of a Catholic country—were amazingly blasé about porn. And sure enough, there was a whole series of Sandy Blue tapes and DVDs, shrink-wrapped and bearing tasteful graphics and gorgeous color photos from her videos. He picked out a copy, *For Couples Only,* "produced and directed by Sandy

Blue," and examined the familiar face and body, the setting: Malibu beach house, swimming pool and blue sky, California early eighties chic. Already dated. He stood staring at the little time capsule in his hand. The previous fall in Concord, when he saw that tape of her greatest hits, she'd seemed so much older. Now, she seemed so young. It all flashed through his mind again: plan B, the idea of returning to the States with Angela Palmer, aka Sandy Blue. It kind of turned him on. He smiled. Michael and Angela Palmer Collins might just kick a few asses. The frisson of excitement at such a prospect remained with him as he left the shop and turned the corner into the expanse of the Piazza San Marco.

The job interview at the Dominican school on the Rio Foscarini went well. The headmaster, a tall, balding man with piercing hazel eyes, wearing the dun-colored robes of the order, bent eagerly over his desk, intently discussing English literature with the new prospect. When Michael mentioned the family connection, the Maronetti family of stonecutters, the headmaster laughed with pleasure—the grandson of a son of the city returning after almost a century. "A circle," said the headmaster, making 180-degree arcs with two pointed fingers, "a poetic completion." And he praised Giovanni Maronetti's spoken Italian, even the vernacular—it was almost perfect. "Not bad for a second-generation American returning to the old country." It was Michael's turn to smile at that.

Pulling a pack of cigarettes from the open sleeve of his brown robe, so deftly done as to seem a conjurer's trick, the headmaster tumbled on in accented English. They needed a real American, someone hip, who could relate to fifteen- and sixteen-year-olds mesmerized by all the worst in American culture—the music and television, the violent movies and video games, the loveless sex—and turn them toward the great names: Hemingway and Fitzgerald and Steinbeck. "Have you read *The Grapes of Wrath*?" He had, but he admitted that his expertise was a bit earlier, more late nineteenth century. "Good, good," came the increasingly eager reply. "Henry James and Stephen Crane." With a raised palm, as if presenting an elaborate concoction, he replied, "Thoreau and Emerson and, of course, Mark Twain and Melville."

"*Tom Sawyer—perfecto.*"

The headmaster lighted up and with a raised hand noted the required hours, the pay, even a housing allowance. He motioned the younger man to the window of his office overlooking the large courtyard, which had been converted into a blacktop soccer pitch with basketball nets along the sides. The air was filled with the shouts of the boys as a soccer ball careened off a wall painted with the mouth of a goal. Touching a nicotine-stained fingertip to his temple, the headmaster squinted. "They live like so," he said, holding his undulating palm over the space between them, indicating a vast hollow below. "Of the past, they suspect nothing; they care nothing. Only for the moment do they live. This saddens me greatly."

Michael wandered the city for hours in a half daze, feeling the ballast settle, the solidity of the stones beneath his feet, the friendly prospect. And later as he watched the campanili and terra-cotta rooftops of the city fade across the wake of the vaporetto, he wondered where the fulcrum point had been. When did the gravity of the past gain a critical mass and become the place where you dwelled most completely, when the greater part of your life was done.

Giovanni Maronetti loved the feel of the water and the translucent plain of the lagoon. He couldn't wait to get back to his *sandolo* and scud along, roofed under those opal-and-orange clouds, open himself body and soul to the smell of the sea and the wide spaces of blue beyond the Lido.

The journey home ended all too quickly.

The cottage was empty. In the middle of the kitchen floor was a large cardboard box. A new Siemens television set. Something the owner must have ordered for the summer tenants.

He was about to go out and look for her, when his mobile phone rang. He smiled at the sound of her voice. She'd forgotten about her checkup in the city, she told him. The doctor had been running late and she'd missed the last boat. She'd stay the night with a friend and come out first thing tomorrow. "How did it go?" she asked. He was enthusiastic, going on and on about how much he liked the headmaster. His voice was mellow with relief. She didn't seem surprised. "I fixed a pasta salad for dinner; it's in the refrigerator. I took a bag full of stuff with me to save the hassle on Tuesday morning." "What's with the television?" he asked. "For the owner," she said. She told him she loved him. He told her the same. He told her to call in the morning and let him know what vaporetto she'd be taking so he could meet her boat. "How about a blowout dinner at the Locanda Cipriani to celebrate?"

"Ciao, Giovanni."

"Ciao, Sandra."

Funny, she never used the name Giovanni except when kidding him about something.

He found the presence of the cardboard box containing the television somehow unsettling—a modern upgrade to draw a line under their island existence.

That evening, he ate quickly and went out to walk the island paths by himself, missing her terribly, but glad in a way to be alone to say his good-byes. He wondered momentarily if he was more in love with this island life—his romantic streak, as she often called it—than he was with Sandra. Or was it love that so anchored the soul? Could love exist entirely absent the home ground where it had first taken root: the first memories that enfold the beloved? Was it love that tied names inextricably to places? A vague sense of gnawing doubt brought him up short by the grassy bank of a disused canal, as if he'd wandered into some numbed state of suspended disbelief ... the comfort he felt under her direction.

"So, I used you," she had written. "No better than my namesake."

There were things in that letter she'd left for him in Santa Maria Assunta that still gave him pause. Had she really called his mother at the inn to ask about him and tell her about the child? Surely if he'd gotten back in time, she'd have told him then about Sandra and the baby. Unless she'd known something of Giovanni's early life and how he'd come to grief at the hands of the Palmers and Chillingworths. Did she die with that secret, that belief that history cruelly repeats itself? At least, she'd be proud of her son as a teacher of literature ... a life devoted to higher things, a mere conduit of genius perhaps, but a not ignoble fate.

How bizarre that a single unturned fact or distortion of the truth could realign entire lifetimes. He held out his hands, as if balancing love's joys and deceits, one hand fine and strong, the other ugly and awkward, both marked by new calluses from rowing the *sandolo*. Before him on the still waters of the old canal, his moon-shadowed companion.

"Giovanni Maronetti," he said, repeating the name like an incantation to re-anchor his drifting presence, sounding the syllables with a full Italian inflection, so unlike the way he'd heard it in the Lowell of his childhood. And in the name, the realization that his grandfather's walks along the Pawtucket Canal had not been about dreams of his youth in Venice, rather Giovanni had been imagining the rundown Palmer Mill as it should have been: how his sculptures would have looked, and how Sandra and, later, Angela Chillingworth's decorative scheme might still be realized. That was all any artist cared about: that his work might live. Love be damned.

He smiled to himself. Who knows, maybe Jack Mahoney would go for such a scheme?

He began walking along the bank of the old canal, staring ahead to where it let out onto the silver expanse of the lagoon. He was tempted to get out the *sandolo*. Then he stopped again, feeling for an unsettling moment as if he'd been left bobbing in Sandra's wake. It wasn't like her to forget an appointment, miss a boat. Women were strange in a way, one moment demanding, the next fiercely protective, and yielding ... drawing you in until you had given yourself over to their life. The way Sandra Chillingworth Palmer had woven her spell, at the last, deceiving her husband and sister. The way Sandra *had* created an entire life for him, a beautiful and simple frame of a life, just like she'd implied on that first night at the pensione. She'd given him exactly what he'd desired ... something disingenuous, even insidious? For a moment, this realization detonated a pang of rising uncertainty. Had he missed her signals, the thing she really wanted from him: a firm decision? Even Thoreau understood that Walden was only a stopping place: to gather strength and go on. Henry, who had written—was it in the journals?—"Most men can be easily transplanted from here to there, for they have so little root—no tap root—or their roots penetrate so little way, that you can thrust a shovel quite under them and take them up, roots and all."

He looked up to where the bell tower of the campanile was saturated in moonlight, the four windows dark cavities between fiery white columns. His knees buckled and he shivered with apprehension and reached to a tree branch to steady himself.

And there had been other clues in her letter, if only he'd had the heart to recognize them ... a plea to shift his allegiance to a more hardened and ambitious version of herself, true heir to those captains and generals, almost as if she'd been prompting him to give up on Sandra and go for plan B. Maybe she really did hate herself, always complaining about her failures as an artist, a mother ... a woman.

And there were things, too, that didn't quite match up in her confession. She hadn't mentioned anything about Angela arriving at her apartment in Cambridge and then leaving and presumably returning, responding to Sandra's frenzied E-mail plea.

If Angela had been HIV-positive, surely that would've made it into the newspapers. At the very least, it would have been in the pathologist's report; Joe would have mentioned it to him. Or had he been too ashamed?

He continued walking, these questions and others slipping away into the night sky as he turned his mind to the happy prospect of teaching youngsters American literature, and thoughts of having children of his own. He felt good about such a life and the hope of making the best of the past live again for those yet unborn.

And, he thought, too, about Sandra's fine breasts and big belly and soon found himself in love with her all over again, and the ground firming beneath his steps.

The stars shone brilliant and pure in the garden upon his return. He inventoried the bits of ancient marble guarding the perimeter of the grounds, the poplars like dark flames behind the low tapestry of the vineyard, the dovecote by the gate full of silent watchers. Then he lay down in the grass and stared upward into the vast spaces of time and memory. He was a little in awe of all those universes born and dying millions of years before, and of the few geniuses who managed a grubstake against such a backdrop. And what had he managed ... the *he* who was all that remained of his family, Collins and Maronetti? The *he* about to be subsumed in another's life. For a few minutes more, he found a peculiar pleasure in thinking about Angela Chillingworth walking in the Curtises' walled garden on the Giudecca—now the grounds of the Cipriani—with her sister's child, knowing to the bottom of her soul that her sister had seen her own death in that place: *et in Arcadia ergo.* There among the fruit trees and antique marbles, holding the baby aloft so that he might see the wonder of it, smell the earth and feel the breeze and so be freed of his mother's fears ... her sins?

Or was it there, hidden behind the walls of the garden, where Sandra Chillingworth Palmer and that rogue Dimitri, her piano master, had had their assignations ... *scene of the crime?*

Conception and gestation, birth and death...*and so the whole round of motion is gone through again. Aphids and beetles ... and viruses ... pigweed ... and goddamn deer and woodchucks ... Nature's a vandal—a lie, a cheat ... Life is a fucking triage, Bill. Loss and deceit are just another path to survival. And love is nature's sleight of hand.*

When he started awake in the grass and finally dragged himself inside to bed, he realized she had taken the painting. Drawing on the wisdom of her ancestors, her first instinct had been to move the household gods.

CHAPTER 41

A little after 8:00 AM, he woke from a restless sleep and called her on his cell phone. Her phone was either switched off or she was out of range, so he left a message.

He decided to go wait for her on the quay, feeling the need to get away from the house and garden, and the damn box in the middle of the kitchen. But before he could even get the coffee brewed, there was a knock on the door. He smiled with relief and went to open it.

The FedEx man was waiting with a package in hand. It was surreal, as if the wide world had tracked him down to his hiding place, laughing at his pretensions of escape. He signed for the delivery.

He was very frightened. For a minute, he stared at the unopened package on the kitchen table. He could tell her handwriting on the shipping label, from a drop-off point near San Marco. Finally he opened it, memories of another FedEx package spilling through his mind.

There was a videocassette, her cell phone, and a bunch of documents—some legal papers in Italian, copies of articles from a French, language newspaper, copies of letters, and CDs of a Russian composer. For a moment, he held the unlabeled videocassette in his hand, and then he understood he was meant to view it, right away, that the television/VCR was for him.

It took a few minutes to unpack it and get it set up on the kitchen table and plugged in. He pushed the cassette into the player and waited.

She appeared sitting on a slab of marble with the lower half of a carved female figure behind. Her head was bowed. She was wearing the same sundress she'd worn when he'd last seen her on the quay. As she raised her face, the camera panned back a bit so that Sandra Chillingworth Palmer's monument in the Protestant cemetery came fully into the frame. She threw back her head with just a hint of a theatrical flourish, then adjusted a wireless microphone clipped to the front of her dress.

"Michael, I don't quite know where to begin." She looked straight into the camera, and he sensed a sudden confidence come into her voice, as if the presence of the camera gave her strength. "I'm sorry to have to do it like this. But I simply couldn't summon up the courage to tell you face-to-face, not after everything that has happened. That is my fault ... perhaps as much as yours. Besides, I wanted you to have it whole, to be able to hold the truth in your hand, so to speak, for the record."

She smiled knowingly, cupping her hands and then gesturing as if to the frame of the shot and toward the cameraman.

He pulled a plastic lawn chair over to the kitchen table and dropped into the seat as if every ounce of strength had suddenly exited his body.

"Besides, you might say this is more my milieu, where I've had some experience at getting at the truth—of a kind. And because, as you'll see, the truth I'm trying to get at goes beyond words. I'm going to do my best, Michael, so bear with me. And don't worry about the cameraman; actually, it's a woman, a film student at the university, and her English is terrible ... so this *really* is just between us. You should know that I've been working on this off and on for a couple of weeks." She paused, shaking her head and blinking into the soft sunlight, then wiping quickly at tears.

"Actually, this is the moment I've dreaded since I went to find you on the Zattere on Christmas Eve—I still shiver—when I gave my sister back her life ... for you, for me, for a time. I feel awful, not having the courage to do this in person, but I couldn't bear to see your beautiful sad eyes, which I have come to love so well. Michael, I must let her go; I must leave her bleeding and dead in her chair by the window. I must let her finally die for both our sakes."

She swiped at her cheeks, her brassy hair shimmering.

"Oh God, I can just see your face, the disappointment in your eyes, still resisting to the core of your being. It's what I love in you—maybe fear in you? But I must do it." Her face lifted and firmed. "Sandra is dead, Michael. Please let her go. You must have suspected. Or did you manage to lead the witness so well? What a splendid lie we learned to live. We are such good gamblers, you and I. We up the ante; we bluff fearlessly. We change masks like drunken revelers at Carnival."

She raised a hand as if to fend off some unseen reply, then stood and turned toward the monument of Sandra Chillingworth Palmer, then looked back to the camera with a look of near incredulity.

"Isn't it funny we never came here together, to make a little pilgrimage to her altar—my alter ego. Why is that, do you suppose, Michael? Just the smell of the dry grass, the heated marble, the scent of the cypresses—cedars actually … it's like I can feel your presence with me here. It reminds me of home, of Concord, in a strange way. Do you suppose that's why we never came, because of Concord—where you loved her, which we could never really discuss without blowing our cover?"

She blew out her cheeks with frustration.

"Did you ever feel like you were going crazy? I sure did. That's the scary thing: We're so much alike in many ways. I can feel your anger, hear your voice tremble as you tell me to go to hell, or would it be another million questions? But this is a shared duplicity. Dupes of love, don't your think?"

She paused, it struck him, like a veteran actress upon the stage, giving it a few beats, perhaps a little too enamored of her own performance. Then she nodded, making up her mind about what she was going to say next.

"When you first found me, I was blown away. I knew that some-body—first a William Channing—remember him?—was on my trail. Marge Hathaway thought Bill the nicest boy she'd ever met; my father saw him as the kind of guy he'd always wanted for a son, or a son-in-law. Was that you, Michael? No, I don't want to know." She pulled a hand across her eyes, a pause to get back on track. "What I saw in your amazed and love-struck eyes … I … I recognized your need to find Sandra as if it was my own. You see, I had come to Venice to find her, too, now almost two years ago. But as it turned out, it was you who found her—you, who, as always, seemed to have most of the answers, but the wrong questions."

She smiled icily and squinted into the sunlight.

"Had you forgotten to tell me about charming William Channing? Or were you just too fucking embarrassed to admit to him?"

She held up her hand again, as if anticipating his reply.

"I'm sorry, maybe that's why I can't do this face-to-face—I can't handle William Channing right now. But I know what Michael Collins would say. You'd plead to me about the dance and your sad fate. Fate is bullshit. We make our own life, mistakes and all. Know what, Michael? Sandra should never have been at the dance that night. I should have been. She came to me and pleaded to take my place: my sister, whom I hated—yes, then I really did—who I knew was in some way complicit in the death of my baby. And yes, she had been firmly instructed to stay by the phone and wait for the doctor's call but she ran out on me. And when she came to me before the dance, I was intrigued, fascinated by her tears. 'It's my birthday, too,' she pleaded. She'd never had the slightest interest in boys. What had gotten into her? And no small sacrifice. My whole gang was banking on the time of their lives. And you see, I *was* there; my eyes and ears were everywhere. Can you blame me for making sure she got caught, or at least for not covering up for her? It would have been an easy thing. I wanted her to pay for her presumption. God, who knows what we feel at that age. Then to find out she was pregnant—I didn't know whether to laugh or cry. Some brainy scholarship boy from Lowell! I wanted her to burn."

She raised her hands in a gesture of wringing despair. She turned her back to the camera, hung her head for a few seconds, and turned again with renewed resolve.

He sat back, pawing slowly at his chin, glancing around at the kitchen as if needing to place himself in time and space.

"There, I've given you a reason to hate me. Maybe it will be easier for you now."

She lowered her gaze and stood silent for half a minute. Then she took a few steps and went and sat again on the slab of Sandra Chillingworth Palmer's grave.

"And what's really amazing, Michael, is how much I'd actually managed to forget—until you showed me Sandra's letter at Florians. Did you learn that little trick in law school—break down the witness with the introduction of a surprising bit of evidence? Or was that the slick William Channing doing his damnedest ... *your secret*. I almost died of grief that night after you left me at the palazzo, because her nineteen-year-old's feelings echoed exactly how I'd felt about Bobby Hathaway as a teenager. And you know, that's another weird thing; I don't think I ever talked to you about Bobby Hathaway. How could I? Yet I feel as if you know about him. How *is* that? As soon as I read her words, they felt like my words, the starstruck teenager I once was a long time ago. Dumb little girls to love so freely, so absolutely. Well, I lost Bobby and his baby, too. But that letter of Sandra's broke something in me, made me realize how awful I'd been, how callous. Give me credit, Michael. I felt awful. But we shared that, too, you and I—that loss and the bitterness."

She blinked back what seemed to be tears and reached to the base of the marble, where she sat and pulled up a yellow flower, cupping it to her nose, breathing deeply.

"Did you know that over the seven or so years that Sandra worked in Venice, she often came here to maintain the grave? Yeah, she told me that. I guess that's why it looks so good. After Florians, after you left the palazzo, I was so down. For days I could barely get out of bed. Who the hell was this guy who claimed to be my sister's old boyfriend? I knew about William Channing, friend of Thoreau, the guy who sent me an E-mail on my sister's *stolen* computer; he was one hell of a cagey operator. Then there was the Michael Collins all over the Boston papers. Standing in the lobby of the Concord Inn that day, making inquiries about this mysterious William Channing, it hit me like a bolt out of the blue, the connection between the name in the newspapers and Sandra's boyfriend at Emerson—wow, what to make of that? Sandra and I had talked about you in Cambridge. So, you see, it was like I *knew* who you were, although not really. Then before Christmas, when I called your pensione on a hunch, William Channing wasn't there, just like Michael Collins wasn't there when I stopped by the inn. But there was an American with an Italian name, Giovanni Maronetti. That's when I told myself, Angie, you've met your match."

She dropped the flower and nodded knowingly.

"On Christmas Eve, when I waited for you in the cold on the Zattere, I thought a lot about that freezing afternoon on the street in Concord." She looked hard into the camera, which seemed to respond by panning in for a close-up. "Don't make that face, that inscrutable twist of the mouth you do. How could we fucking talk about it ... right?"

Her voice became more controlled, an icy anger to get her through.

"You want the truth? All those years ago back on Main Street, I was on the verge of telling you to go find Sandra and love her. But you turned down my suggestion to go to the inn for hot chocolate, like you were frightened of me. And you were right to be frightened. I would probably have taken you back to the inn for that hot chocolate and played along with you ... and then, who knows, I might have gotten us a room and seduced you right then and there, just to get back at Sandra ... to spoil it for both of you. But of course there was the off chance—how you love parallel universes—that I'd have done the right thing and told you the truth about Sandra being sent off to Geneva, and you two could have dropped out, saddled with a child at such a young age, and probably come to hate each other. You'd have tired of her, Michael; she'd have bored the likes of you, in the end."

She held up a halting hand and then made a fist, pounding at her forehead.

"I can't believe I just told you that, gave you another reason to hate me. But I'm not doing any retakes here; I'm not going to edit out my fumbled attempts at the truth. Just give me the benefit of the doubt. Maybe it was good you got it wrong; maybe you should thank me. I gave you the edge, the bitterness and cynicism that got you so far. A little ambition and bile in the soul does one good, take it from an expert. You needed more than a poetic sensibility to rebuild half of Lowell, as much as you like to trash what you accomplished."

She stood in half profile, wincing and then bowing her head as if needing to compose herself for going on, or to make a display of her swollen belly in the sundress.

"And all these months, I kept waiting for you to ask me: Why, when you returned to the States, didn't you look me up? Weren't you curious about the father of your child? Well, it was one of the first things I asked Sandra in her Cambridge apartment. And she went to her file and pulled out some clippings from the *Boston Globe*, about Michael Collins the Washington insider, the power broker, the political fixer extraordinaire. Sandra just looked at me with a helpless grimace: 'A smooth operator like him would hate the likes of me.' And so there you have it, Michael, from Sandra's own lips, her judgment on the odds of you two ever making it work."

She bowed her head as if not a little ashamed.

"But at some point, you seem to have lost your edge. Why?"

She looked into the camera, then began to nod slowly, as if something was coming clear.

"You don't even need to be here, Michael. I can feel your anger, and I prefer you angry to sad. We'd sit together in our little kitchen, and I'd hold you and you'd pull free and toss your shoulders the way you do when you're upset. Would you slap me? I wouldn't mind a little anger; we're such control freaks. But don't hate me. I lost, too. That's what binds us; that's what we truly see in each other: the loss. *You,* my darling—yes, *you*—don't know what it is to hold on to ghosts."

The frame drew back from her face, the monument behind reentering the frame, as if she needed a prop, the company of ghosts to continue.

"Don't believe what people told you about me as a teenager, okay?" She wrapped her arms under her breasts as if suddenly cold. "God, I wish I could touch your face. Feel your hands rubbing my back or stroking my breasts the way you like to do. You understand, don't you, how hard it is to do this ... to pretend, to really believe you're here with me?"

"Maybe my teenage reputation as a firebrand was well earned. But the reputation was my shield; my sword, my ambition, was my love for Bobby Hathaway ... the losses and hurt that came of that love. Nobody will ever know how much I loved him and what I went through when he died. Talk about what might have been—*your* favorite subject."

She looked straight into the lens, and as she did, the picture before him segued from the brick enclosure to scenes of an orchard in fall. The shift was an added shock to his reeling mind. He reached to the PAUSE button, freezing the line of apple trees bowed with their fruit, the shimmer of the Concord River behind. He was wiping at his tears but as disoriented as he felt, it was worse to be aware of the television on the kitchen table, to be alone in their kitchen with the television. He reached to the PLAY button and dropped back into his chair.

The scenes along the river and in the orchard and pasture were unsteady, a handheld camcorder being walked through a remembered place, dwelling for moments on sections of the fieldstone wall, the grass in the orchard patterned with fallen apples … the thing beautiful, like a dream of remembered places. And then her words continued, but in the soft, almost scripted rhythms of a voice-over.

"Sandra and I knew Bobby from the time we were little girls. He was older by eight years, kind of like the older brother we never had, crew cut-handsome and tough as nails. He was a big-time football star at Emerson when we were growing up, then played at Harvard. But instead of going into the corporate world, he joined the army Seventh Calvary. He had a warrior's soul. Christ, we envied him all the older-guy stuff he could do when we were kids, the stuff he got away with. Sandra and I both had a crush on him. A soldier. He was in Vietnam before it was Vietnam. Before we all lost our taste for patriotism.

"I'd hear the rumble of his Chevy Impala as he made the turn into the driveway next door and my heart would leap. In a flash, I'd be at the window, searching through the thinning fall leaves for a glimpse as he staggered out with his six-pack and made his way down to the river. I was a precocious fifteen. He was on leave after his first tour in Vietnam. I'd climb out the window and down the wisteria vine, with Sandra calling me softly back.

"Bobby kept a boat by the river. He loved to fish at night, to row. Sometimes he'd be getting his gear together; sometimes he'd already be out and I'd wait in the long grass under the apple trees for his return. He discouraged me, scolded me at first, but then he kind of got used to the idea. He was like an older brother. We talked. He was drunk a lot of the time. He'd row me out for a little fishing. I'd sip his beers, help bait his hooks just like Dad had taught me. He told me stories about Saigon and Manila. He loved machines, loved flying helicopters. He'd had close calls, seen terrible things; I could always tell by the change in his voice, the look in his eyes. But he believed deeply in what he was doing, saving those poor people from communism. I suppose he was an anachronism, even then, a throwback to some crude natural piety, the righteous few. But I was crazy in love.

"I seduced him—okay. There is no other word for it. I wanted him and I wanted him to want me. I wore T-shirts without a bra. I was a show-off. The irony is that if he'd been a typical guy of that age and time, he'd have walloped me or raped me and I'd have probably hated every second and become a real frigid monster. But he was a fantastic lover. I suppose he must've had girlfriends or prostitutes in the bars of Manila who'd shown him the ropes. He held out for the longest time, but finally I managed to get him kissing me, touching me in the long grass under the trees, having to push the apples out of our way to get comfortable. He loved my breasts. He had large calloused hands and a beautiful body, muscled and long-limbed. He'd always stop me when I got to my jeans, insisting I keep them on. He had self-control like no man I've ever known. And when I did finally get them off, he did something I had no idea about—he went down on me in the grass. I was shocked, grossed out. But he knew what he was doing. He peeled me open with his tongue, gently, gently, gently; and that's how I had my first orgasm, lying back under the stars with Bobby, and it was the best thing I'd ever known. I was in love with my body, my orgasm, and Bobby Hathaway, who loved my cunt, and who seemed an indispensable part of that lovely world of dried grass perfumed with rotting apples. Bobby *was* my home. Can you understand that?

"For years, I wished that we had fucked like demons in that warm Indian summer under the apple trees, but he was a military man, a highly trained pilot trusted with expensive machinery and other people's lives and he wasn't going to take chances with the fifteen-year-old girl next door and get her banged up and his career ruined. I like to believe he was in love with me, certainly with my body. Every night during the last ten days of his leave, he did his thing, our thing, like it was the only thing in God's green universe. He'd keep at it for an hour or more, drink a little beer, eat an apple, and we'd talk and he'd begin again. In school, I'd be half-asleep, dreaming about those orgasms and just counting the minutes until I'd get back. I wanted him, too. I was fascinated by the bulge in his jeans ... but it took some doing. Discipline. His Saigon girlfriends must have known a thing or two on that score, because when he finally gave in and guided my hand and then my mouth—well, I've never been able to improve upon it. He laughed and sighed so deeply. He said I was a natural, and it was true. From the get-go, I loved it. The taste of semen is the taste of Bobby and the long grass and the heat and the moonlight and the fragrance of apples. I knew he was going to die."

The camera panned across the overgrown pasture below the white picket fence of a formal garden … and in the distance the Palmer homestead and the brick tower with the gold cupola. The shot segued to the brick enclosure of the Protestant cemetery, where a woman sat with head bowed. The sunlight seemed to have thinned; the shadows on the wall behind had lengthened, as if a breach in the time continuum had occurred. She raised her face, lips compressed with emotion, eyes imploring his.

"Do you remember those smells, Michael, along the river—meadow grass and the sweet fern? How I love the smell of sweet fern in the late summer." Her eyes hardened straight into the camera lens. "You were there, weren't you? And don't think you have any right to be jealous of Bobby—Christ, I've had to endure you loving Sandra for months."

She suddenly stood, as if impatient with the whole business, and went to the tall, stately figure of Sandra Chillingworth Palmer, reaching to the marble, where the robe fell in folds from the shoulder.

"Don't you think I haven't wondered about you and her by the river—your moonlight? Pregnant—was it fate? Forget it. I got myself pregnant just like she did. After years as a physical therapist, a dancer, an actress, I am still amazed how the body shapes its own destiny and finds its way. Sure, it's discipline, but it's also love—love's ambition claiming its own. Some part of me just knew. I wanted Bobby inside me just like I wanted you, to become a part of me before it was too late."

She turned to the camera with a look of riveting determination that he'd never seen before. And as if to hide this side of her, the scene again segued back to the orchard and the rose garden behind the Palmer homestead, the place he'd known from Joseph Palmer's paintings, from Sandra's paintings … which he thought of as exclusively his own, until presented with yet another vision of these places, her home.

"It was our last night before he was off to Fort Benning for advanced training in the new generation of Huey gunships. He was joining the First Battalion, Seventh Cavalry, and headed back to Vietnam. By then, I knew his body better than my own. I moved over him and kissed him and squatted and must've gotten it in right on the money. I felt him coming, the heat, the liquid power, and I just kissed him and kissed him and told him I was only kissing him, promising I was only kissing him. He had tears in his eyes—to be taken over like that by a nice little girl.

"Then he was gone. I was like an addict—gone cold turkey. The skies turned gray and I began to panic. And there was Sandra watching me, jealous like the devil. I wrote to Bobby at Fort Benning, then to an APO number in Saigon. Not a single letter. How could he write me? He called me once from Hue, a few days before mother dragged us off to Venice. He said he'd been trying, but of course I had to be the one who picked up the phone. He told me he always thought of me in the worst times. He told me he loved me. I didn't tell him about the baby. I hold on to the crackle of static on that overseas line and those words … words that got me through everything. I wrote him postcards from Venice, every day. After music class, I'd go lose myself in the streets and sit by a canal and smoke and write him a postcard. Christ, every time I see a stupid post-card of Venice, I remember. A guy in his unit told me it had been kind of a joke, how he flew with all these postcards—for luck—stuffed into his pockets. The postcards burned up with the helicopter."

Scenes of the Concord he remembered faded again to the brick enclo-sure where the narrator of the voice-over stood staring up at the image of her grandmother.

"Words, Michael, the way we remake our world." She smiled gamely. "Okay, so now you know—or did you already, know? Don't look shocked, because I can tell exactly what you're thinking: was it Bobby I've been making love to over all the last months? So *whom* were you thinking about? I can hear you now as you turn my argument back on itself. You object, a leading question to the witness—you had no idea? Or did checking with the office of the superintendent of monuments convince you of my bona fides? The receptionist told me the next day how you charmed the pants off her: I knew then I had to do something. Come on, Michael, some part of you must've had an inkling—how else did you know so much about me, my company? How did you manage to know so much about Angela—or was William Channing a secret fan of SandyBlue.com, too?"

She stood with hands on hips like a mother scolding a child. When she spoke, it was just short of a shriek.

"Know what really gets me, Michael? How could you still love Sandra—

once you knew she killed my baby and then abandoned yours? How she used you like Sandra Chillingworth used everybody. I remember how she gloated when Mom yanked her from school: 'I'm off to Europe, and this time without you,' she told me."

She waved in the air as if to rid herself of the heated tone in her voice, then spoke in a more calm and controlled tone.

"Of course, my pregnancy was no surprise to Sandra. We used to get our periods practically to the minute. Can you believe—she missed her period, just like me! I freaked. I was stupid enough to get checked out by the family doctor and he blabbed to my mother. It was like a neutron bomb had gone off in the family: shock, moral recriminations and denial, lurid advice on abortion and threats and then, presto, the weird master plan—almost embracing my fall—the child to be adopted by my parents and raised as one of us, one of the family. Even my father signed on, hopes for the strapping son he never had, I suppose.

"And then, after we got back from Venice—at least, I could drink and smoke—the dreariest summer of my life in dowdy Manchester-by-the-Sea with my great-aunt and namesake, Angela Chillingworth. But I've got to hand it to her—after her initial shock, she took me in, loved me, never mind all her eccentricities. She was the only one who really loved me—me and Venice and her long-dead twin sister. Mother with her gin and tonics. Dad a no-show. Sandra always eyeing me, jealous that I'd had Bobby, veering around like she was on speed, lost between hate and envy. I just wanted to be by myself. I used to walk on the beach to get away from everybody.

"In late July, two days after I'd gotten word that Bobby had been killed in combat—a casual comment of my mother's after a conversation with good old Marge Hathaway, her DAR buddy, next door—I had the baby. I've gone over it a million times. Did my mother really do it on purpose, leave the call to the doctor until I was too far along to make it to the hospital delivery room? There *was* a missed call from the doctor. Mother had told Sandra to wait by the downstairs phone, the only one in the house. But Sandra freaked; she just freaked and ran away. So there I was, spread-eagle on my aunt's bed on the top floor in ninety-eight-degree heat with the best gynecologist in Boston screwing around with my insides, panicking without a squad of nurses at his elbow and the equipment he needed—and me not being able to give birth fast enough to save Bobby's child.

"I was in free fall. The only time in my life I felt out of control. Mom was incoherent, Auntie in Boston, and Sandra—where was she? Walking off her cramps on the beach. I thought I was dead—past dead and way beyond the pain—because I saw it in my mind even before my fate found me. I think I was ready to die. It was five minutes before the doctor got Joey breathing. I'll give Dr. Bartlett that much. He never quit on my son.

"Then it was like, Let the great charade begin. Baby Joey was officially adopted. We went back to school. Mom took care of Joey. But I became more and more attached, especially after everyone began losing their enthusiasm for the deal once the full extent of the brain damage became fully known. The doctors said that even if he survived, he'd be in an institution all his life. But that wasn't how I saw it. Little Joey was my chance to keep something of Bobby alive."

He'd been spellbound by her voice, by the eye of the camera plodding along the beach, occasionally swooping upward to catch the flight of a gull, the sea beyond: a vast gray anonymity. And then an abrupt jump cut to the narrator seated again with an arm propping her chin, something of Rodin's *Thinker*.

"Who am I to tell you this—now? You think Vietnam was a bad joke played on you. Well, Bobby died for your little joke. And you don't give a fuck about Angela? How could you ever love such a bitch? Maybe you don't have the balls for plan B—can I blame you for that?" She glanced up at the figure behind her. "You know, I can't stand that she has my face. How's that for an ego." She laughed. "And I'm not going to plead for your love, Michael. I'm not going to make a case for Angela. What the hell can I tell you that you don't already know?

"I can see that look coming into your face, all that boyish innocence, like the world has been out to deceive you, take something from you. Dry your tears, Michael; don't feel so fucking sorry for yourself. Get mad at me. You're a survivor, like me. It's your faithless Sandra who lied to you, not me. I'd never have let you down."

She got up and began pacing, gesturing with exaggeration. He couldn't help thinking she looked like a public defender making a case to the jury.

"The night Joey died, I had heard him crying. I was so exhausted—by everything. I waited longer than usual before getting up, hoping he might quiet. Mom and Dad had gone to the opera in Boston. Just Sandra and I were home. The crying stopped. Had I heard footsteps? Sandra? I scrambled out of bed and tiptoed down the hall to the nursery, what had been our childhood room. I peeked in and saw Sandra standing over the changing table. She was comforting him, cooing to him. Instead of storming in at her, I was actually touched, that she cared, that maybe she even loved him. After all, once upon a time, we had shared everything. Let her be, I told myself. I gave in to my better self. Maybe we can start over again—just us twins against the world. I went back to bed happy.

"I woke up suddenly in the morning after the worst nightmare about falling and not being able to catch myself. I ran into the nursery and found Joey dead in his crib. I knew it was Sandra. She had been in my nightmare. And I still have that nightmare about falling, my baby falling from my arms and my not being able to break his fall. I make myself climb the scaffold every day; I have to make myself do it."

She stopped in her pacing, wiping at her tears.

"I couldn't stop screaming. And then there was the ambulance and the hospital and frantic doctors and nurses pulling little Joey from my arms. Somebody hit me with a sedative and I woke hours later. I woke up to silent faces everywhere. Not the silence of regret, but the silence of relief. My father ever the stoic, my mother in such a drunken stupor when I got home that she fell going up the stairs and hit her head and had to go to the emergency room to get it stitched up. But the worst—I could see straight through Sandra's silence. She hid herself, not a word of consolation. We stopped talking. But I could match them silence for silence and then some. What I had, nobody was going to take from me again.

"For years, I used to keep my stash of dope near Bobby's grave in Sleepy Hollow, and I'd go there at night and stare up at those white pines and smoke dope and masturbate and remember. They like to tell us nice little girls that sex and love are two different things—bullshit. I was weaned on a love that was wholly physical, an eroticism rooted in the body, and that's all I know."

She closed her eyes, letting the tears stream down her cheeks.

"So, there you are, Michael. Do you have what you want? Was that the secret you were after? Have I made my case? But I don't begrudge you your truth; you earned it. I'm not a great believer in fate, but I believe in you. Of all people, you're the only one who could understand … you, who'd rather know people through the distance of the past, between the lines. It takes a cynical romantic to believe and then deal with the consequences."

She forced a smile and wiped at her face with the sleeves of her dress. A shadow had appeared in the foreground; he couldn't help wondering at the time lapse, how many takes had been required, how much editing, or if she really got it out on the first try.

"Or don't you believe me, Michael?"

Her look, her accusation froze him.

"What, do you suppose, will be left of us when there are no more letters, no more diaries, when some computer virus eliminates our E-mail memories?"

She shook her head a little despairingly and ran her fingers through her hair.

"But I guess what I really want to do is to thank you for giving me a chance to explain Sandra to myself, to kick in the door of her heart as much as I dare, to see how she could have done the terrible things she did. Through you, I found a window into her soul. Do you think I had it about right in Sandra's confession to you at Santa Maria Assunta?"

She tilted her head.

"Oh, yes, did I fail to mention—little Joey had dirt between his toes when I found him dead in his crib? You see, Michael, over all the years, I never stopped wondering about Sandra, envying her life in some ways, my hate dimming to curiosity and then a vague love of what we had in early childhood. Isn't that right—time the great healer?

"When I decided to deep-six Sandy Blue, when I no longer wanted to compete with the silicone airheads and Nautilus babes getting into the business, I went for a complete break. My mail-order company, before SandyBlue.com, was making tons of money, but I wanted to try on something where I could prove to myself—maybe to my father, too—that I could use my brains, not just my body, something out of the limelight. I took my old name back—Angela Palmer, no more Sandy Blue—and checked into the University of New Mexico to study art and archaeology. I got a M.A. and then a Ph.D. I spent three years working on digs in the Yucatán and Peru, years, literally, in the wilderness. Then I got a bad case of malaria and spent over two months in the hospital. That was enough to convince me to switch fields to classical archaeology. I spent a year and a half in Rome—and I discovered food!—studying classical architecture and working on some Etruscan sites, much of which required restoration skills. Then I spent a year at the University of Bologna in a post-doc archaeology program—talk about incredible food—and began getting interested in Italian cuisine. I thought about opening a restaurant in the States, maybe San Francisco.

"Then almost two years ago now, I got this E-mail from Sandra passed on from the front office of SandyBlue.com. She complained about the Italian boyfriend and the Sandy Blue tapes and said she'd left Venice and gone back to Harvard to get her doctorate—away from the restoration biz and her banker boyfriend. I was surprised to find out she'd been living in Italy, too. It intrigued me, as if some force field was narrowing our orbits. We sent E-mails back and forth and I thought, What the hell, a birthday reunion. I'd played out the archaeology gig and was about to move back to the States and start my restaurant. I took a flight to Boston.

"I had a room at the Treadway Inn on Harvard Square. I went grocery shopping, checking out the availability and quality of ingredients in the local supermarket. I was going to cook her this great Bolognese meal—wine, too. I took a taxi to her place and lugged in the groceries and wine. I think it threw her a little, me arriving like that to cook dinner. She wasn't much of a cook, even after all her years abroad. I gave her a housewarming present, a very expensive set of Henckel kitchen knives. We talked for a couple of hours while I prepared the meal. I showed her all the tricks of the trade, how they do it in Bologna. We drank lots of wine. She had barely changed, still the long hair and quiet, determined ways. Her accent was a little refined and expressive in that Italian way from all the years over here, but then, so was mine. That was a tad weird. All these years, and yet we still had this special language all our own. She seemed a little fragile, a little uptight, but smart, talented like the devil. A boyfriend at Harvard she didn't really want to talk about. She even admitted that it really wasn't my porno tapes that had sent her fleeing from Venice—that was an excuse to get away from her creepy banker boyfriend, who was abusing her—but news of the planned retrospective of Joseph Palmer at the Boston Museum of Fine Arts. She'd been contacted for information by this wildly enthusiastic woman, Laura Ryder, who was doing the catalog.

"In those first hours we were together, I think we were both relieved. A lot of time had passed after all. I was kind of proud of her, like none of the crap from before really mattered. God knows what her expectations were of me after seeing my tapes—which had given her old man, the banker, a new lease on life!

"We ate dinner and had more wine. The meal reminded her of Italy and she got a little weepy and nostalgic. Maybe we'd had too much wine. Maybe I was a little full of myself, proud of the meal I'd cooked her, as if to show her up. The mood began to shift. I got the feeling that Sandra was almost disappointed that Sandy Blue was history, that I showed up with short mousy hair, no makeup, grunge clothes—not the glamorous star. I was deep into the anonymity of my life as the unworldly scholar. Actually, what she didn't like was that I had, in an uncanny way, moved onto her turf—twins are the worst on that score. She kept hinting that I'd done it on purpose. I loved my new life, moving in the shadows of an obscure scholarly existence while my other self, my video self, was getting people turned on all over the world. It was so cool. People, strangers, look at you in the street and can't place you. I stayed in touch with the business by E-mail, suggesting new product lines, getting great ideas from women in Europe. Italian women know a thing or two, let me tell you. There was something deeply satisfying about this kind of hermetic bifurcation, the exacting discipline of living one life out of the quiet center of another."

She looked up with a pensive calm, lips open and poised, as if aware of another presence.

"But I don't need to tell *you*, Michael, do I? So after dinner, cleaning up, we were getting a little testy with each other. It was amazing how much her world matched mine. Eerie: the simple apartment with just her books and research. She lived for her work and was totally engrossed in her thesis and the world of the past—you two share that much, Michael, you'll be glad to know. She'd lived a peripatetic existence—just one damn

place after another, never quite marrying. The Italian boyfriend, I know
from personal experience, was a close call. In fact, I totally identified with
her. We even talked shop, technical stuff about restoration. So much of
my archaeological training had included restoration issues, including the
maintenance and documentation of ancient sites."

She paused and pursed her lips.

"I can feel the lawyer in you, Michael: Out with it, Angela, spell it
out. But you wouldn't be so cruel—would you, Michael? Did you really
bite on my story about Angela arriving on Sandra's doorstep, a deadbeat
and HIV-positive? Is that how you'd have liked me to end up? That was
your plan A, wasn't it—to let Angela die."

He cringed at the hard cynicism in her voice, the narrowed eyes.

"Think what you like, but believe me, there isn't a day goes by I don't
go over that last evening with Sandra. You're such a mind reader—didn't
it show? Maybe it was the old rivalry thing fueled by the wine. Something
got us going, maybe me using her childhood nickname, Sandy—Sandy
Blue. She was pissed about that. But then we got onto the subject of our
father. She had visited him a couple of times on the farm in Concord.
Maybe I made some disparaging remark—the old green-eyed monster:
jealousy. She defended him. Then she was on my case about fucking with
his head as an adolescent—the flirting thing. Christ, what daughter *doesn't*
flirt with her father? She accused me of emotional blackmail about Joey.
Bullshit, the adoption business wasn't my idea at all; it was all Mom's
doing. Next moment, she was blaming me for Mom's alcoholism and
the divorce. I lost it."

Angela Palmer threw up her hands. Her voice faltered and she glanced
at her camerawoman as if suddenly panicked.

"Maybe—I don't know—I can't do this." The camera lost focus for
a moment. She took a deep breath. "It's okay. I know you're going to
hate me. But don't forget, Michael, I defended you when she and I talked.
So I guess I laid into her by telling her how she'd never had the guts to
see anything through, always cringing in the shadows, fawning around
for attention as a teenager. Then I told her about you, how I'd run into
you on the street that winter in Concord, how crazy in love you'd been
and how'd she'd fucked up by walking away from you and then from
her baby, too. Those moments when you confronted me in the freezing

cold on Main Street came back to me in a flash. I told her exactly how stricken you'd looked, the tears in your eyes, your purple lips quivering with hurt. God, I laid it on. But it was true, damn it. You still do it, that hurt, righteousness thing. Oh God."

She gestured desperately at the camerawoman and for an instant the screen went blank. A moment later, she was back, still overwrought, but getting out her story with a brittle, quivering voice.

"I could tell that really flattened her. She *saw* you. I could see it in her eyes. I told her how stupid she'd been to believe the stories about you. How dumb to let the adoption people swipe her baby—shit, she had no excuse to let that happen. She mumbled something about the baby and Geneva and calling your mother. But that just brought it all up in spiteful torrents of brimstone. I backed toward the door as if wanting to escape before I went too far. What did she know about disappointments and loss? It spewed out of me. I pointed my finger and called her a fucking murderer. First, she'd fucked up the phone call from the doctor; then she'd waited for another chance. I told her I'd always known she'd killed my baby. Gone into the nursery that night and dropped him. The fact that she didn't even try to defend herself only made it worse. I shouted it: 'Fucking murderer.' And for the first time, I absolutely believed that to be the reality—as if everything had followed from her crime. I was fucking crazy. And then before I ran, I told her that she might just as well have killed her own child, abandoning it like that. Oh God, I ran. I ran as if terrified of my own reflection. I feared I might strangle her."

She hung her head, sobbing, and made a motion and the camera panned away and then made an uneven jump cut to scenes of Concord and Sleepy Hollow and the Palmer graves.

"And then I walked all night to get rid of the anger, and as I walked, I went over it in my mind: Had I told the truth? Had I said the unsayable? I had shattered the silence. That night was like a flood on my shoulders; I felt drowned by my own words. By morning, I was at Sleepy Hollow and I found my way to Bobby's grave and curled up on the grass besides it and slept. All those years, and it still felt like yesterday. I must have slept until late afternoon. I got up in a daze and tried to get my head together. I went to Joey's grave and I cried again and I felt the flood receding. I was weak, light-headed.

"I felt like a ghost drifting through the old haunts of childhood. I walked everywhere, out to our old house and down to the orchard next door. And who should I run into there but Bobby's mother, Marge Hathaway, who had never liked me for beans. Except she assumed I was Sandra, nice lovable Sandra. That dropped me another few notches. I got a room at the inn, had dinner, and went to bed. I slept fitfully for two days.

"When I got back to the Treadway Inn in Cambridge, I found a stack of phone messages from Sandra. For three days, she'd been calling. It was almost midnight. I called but she didn't answer. I walked over there in a kind of daze. The heat was awful. I rang the doorbell. Then I turned the handle. It was open. Inside, it looked just as I'd left it. Two empty wine bottles and glasses on the small kitchen table, some sheets of paper with writing, a letter, newspaper clippings. Her computer was on, her AOL account, waiting for E-mail. I called her name. I was afraid I'd startle her out of sleep. I tried the bedroom, then, coming back into the living room, I saw her reflection in the glass of the bay window, the high-backed chair, then the pool of blood expanding on the floor beneath. I was only a few minutes late.

"I have seen bad things in my time—a woman who'd overdosed and drowned in her own vomit, a slit-throat suicide at a VA hospital. It wasn't just because she was my sister; it was her expression. Her face was serene, staring, dull eyes shining with love, as if holding memories of a better time. But to have used that knife—my gift to her—and slipped it in like it was sexy butter—shit, oh shit. And maybe if she hadn't cut her hair like that, perhaps I wouldn't have done what I did."

The scenes of Sleepy Hollow, Sandra's grave, the face in the monument of Sandra Chillingworth Palmer faded and segued to the same face in the funeral sculpture in the Protestant enclosure. Then the camera retreated to include a woman sitting in half shadow, the daylight failing. Angela Palmer looked up; her face was drawn, her eyes shimmering dully in the half-light.

"Don't you get it, Michael? She did it to get back at me—and you—for abandoning her. I'm sorry, but it was selfish what she did. She had no right. Don't agonize about it—not now, not ever. She had it her way."

Angela picked up some papers from beside her on the monument and held them up … the evidence.

"Then I found the letter on the table that had been sent to her by the adoption agency in Geneva. It had arrived the day before. The letter was from the Swiss family who had adopted her son twenty-eight years ago. The family was writing almost two months after the fact to let her know that her son had been killed in an automobile accident. He had been studying architecture. A tall, handsome golden-haired young man with a happy-go-lucky attitude. He'd been drinking and he missed a hairpin turn at three AM and the car plunged two hundred feet and ended up in a ravine. Luckily, no one else was hurt. It had obviously taken the family some time to come to terms with his death and to summon the courage to write to the birth mother to let her know the fate of her son. They apologized for running off with her son in the first place, afraid she'd change her mind. But they'd cared for him well—Andre. They had loved him and he'd made their life a joy.

"I devoured their letter, like I could have been reading about the life my child never had. A bit of a problem in his teenage years, rebellious, not quite fitting the mold of Swiss propriety. A champion downhill skier until he tore ligaments. Something of a loner, feeling a lack somewhere in himself. They admitted it—they'd never told him he was adopted. They had deceived him. It was God's judgment on their selfishness, they said."

She looked at the documents in her hand.

"Michael, I've left you copies of their letter and the newspaper clippings about his skiing medals." She wiped at tears. "I cried then, too, Michael, sitting at Sandra's kitchen table reading their letter. I can cry and mourn and let her go, because I've been there … and because you loved her enough to believe the best about her. Can you leave it at that?

"Carrying your child, our son—I had the test for Down's and he is a boy—I feel your loss and my sister's as if it were my own. And yeah, as you always kept probing: Sandra admitted she was trying to get pregnant by some Harvard undergrad she'd been hanging out with—and couldn't manage it. Anyway … this moment as I sit with this monument carved by your grandfather to the memory of my grandmother … well, I can understand, finally, the despair that allowed Sandra to inflict that terrible wound upon herself. Her judgment on herself—her barren self. As Sandra Chillingworth must have faced her death and seen it as a judgment on her infidelity. And I also begin to see how grief and pain are passed on through the generations in ways that we may never fathom. How many times we figure it out, only to find it is already too late ... that the lies have become the reality. That is what I discovered in my grandfather's diary ... and the Chillingworth letters.

"Yes, it was premeditated what I did. The Swiss family had made it clear that they wanted to meet Sandra and personally embrace her and seek forgiveness and tell her more about her son. What truly brave people they are! Old-style Calvinists. I figured it was the least I could do for them, and for Sandra. I took their letter. I took her passport and some relevant correspondence from her previous employers. I even cleaned up the place; she left the bathroom a mess with her hair cuttings.

"So I headed out. I closed her door behind me and was on a flight the next day for Geneva. And once I began—met that Swiss couple, who practically took me in as one of their own, drove me around for a week to Andre's favorite places, prayed at his grave, showed me his skiing medals, told me how much he looked like me, cried on my shoulder—I couldn't give her up.

"That's when I went to live in Venice. I used her name, her passport, her credentials; it was as if she'd never left. People fell all over themselves to welcome me back, telling me how much they liked my new hairstyle and kidding me about how my Italian was a little rusty—a Roman accent, or was it Bolognese. I had to wing it on the work front at first, but I've always been a quick study. It was as if I'd spent all those years preparing myself for the role. It was effortless. And when Giorgio, the banker, caught up with me, I moved right in with him—waiting for my chance to get even with the bastard. For a while, I was into it. We watched my old videos together—top that if you can, Michael."

She laughed hysterically.

"I thought with Giorgio, maybe I could get to parts of my character I'd missed. But he was all surface and glitter and good times. She'd left nothing with him. I was so pissed by his cavalier attitude that I turned the tables on him. I threatened to blackmail him if he didn't sell me the flat. That or I'd rat to his wife and let the world know about his kinky sex life. When I handed him a cashier's check for the flat for six million dollars, he almost passed out. Didn't you like the Modigliani in the bedroom?

"You see, that was it, I had drawn so close to her and yet I felt a void.

Something I had overlooked … and then, out of the blue, I get this E-mail to Sandra from a friend of Thoreau with my dead sister's E-mail address: 'Your secret is safe.' What the hell did you think you were doing? Talk about scary and weird. Christ, Michael—and all this time not a goddamn peep about William Channing out of you. You had your chances. Were you too embarrassed to admit it? You had to have stolen her computer, lied your head off. Your E-mail almost drove me crazy, like her revenging spirit was after me.

"'Your secret is safe.' What the hell was I supposed to think? How insidious of you. I thought I was being accused—if not of murder, then of pushing her to kill herself. And Concord—first, I thought my father had her computer and was accusing me of something unthinkable. I was overwhelmed with guilt. And then it hit me, after living her life for almost a year: I'd gone to see her in Cambridge, practically bragging about my new life, cooking that dinner, proud of my Ph.D., crowing about my work in Rome and Bologna. Like I'd done her one better and was rubbing her nose in it. I hadn't meant to, but it must have seemed that way to her, that I'd stolen her life, too. And what I'd said to her was unforgivable. Don't you see? Your fucked-up E-mail and my guilt brought me back, to find if it had really been my fault … if just possibly I'd falsely accused her of killing my baby. Did this William Channing know something I didn't? Her secret? Hell, Michael, you never condemned her dropping my baby—not ever."

Swiping at her tears, her hair, Angela waved at the camera to cut. But it rolled on. The scene returned to Concord.

He stood, one hand on the back of the kitchen chair, eyes glassy as the downstairs period rooms at the inn filled the screen, the camera slowly, lovingly, exploring the colonial décor.

"Was that the effect you hoped for, Michael? So I sent you an E-mail in reply but I got nothing but that cryptic: 'Your secret is safe.' And William Channing—was that on purpose? It freaked me. I took a couple of weeks off work and flew to Boston. I was terrified what I might find. Spending that year in Venice had made me curious about Joseph Palmer and Sandra Chillingworth Palmer—I hadn't given them a thought since childhood. I contacted the Boston law firm and found out about the Chillingworth letters—that began to ease me into the past. Then I began making forays into Concord. I paid my respects at Sandra's grave, at

Joey's, and Bobby's. I walked about town. I kept waiting for someone to recognize me, to stop me in my tracks and break the spell—this William Channing, or possibly the infamous Michael Collins. I wanted this phantom E-mailer to show himself, to wake me up and tell me it was okay, that I hadn't falsely accused her, that I wasn't to blame for what happened. But I found no one.

"I kept wondering about Sandra; she always was such a homebody ... but even returning hadn't been enough to save her. Had Concord changed? Had she been utterly forgotten? Did it matter? It was as if something of me had died with her and it didn't matter. We are born and live and die and disappear as if we'd never been. The more I returned to Concord, the more depressed and lonely I felt.

"Except, I ran into Marge Hathaway again and she thought I was Sandra. How I wanted to hold her and stroke her old face and tell her how much I loved Bobby ... even knowing how she'd always detested me. And as if that weren't enough, she told me about a William Channing staying at the inn, a guy who was a friend of mine, no less, in high school. And not only that but I was supposed to meet my father for lunch at the inn within the hour. I went to the inn and asked at reception, and sure enough, there really was a William Channing staying in the Thoreau Room. The receptionist tried your room and then said you were probably out jogging. I tried to get more out of the receptionist about you, but she started to get a little leery of me. Of course, she knew nothing about Michael Collins. It blew my mind. I canceled on my dad and left."

The camera eye lingered on the fireplace in the Minuteman Lounge, afternoon light filtering through a white-sash window, a quick glimpse of the empty Queen Anne chair where he'd sat evenings reading the diaries and memoirs of the Palmer family.

"You can be a little insidious, Michael. I finally looked up William Ellery Channing in an encyclopedia. Friend of Thoreau, a horrible poet, moody and morose, and a bad husband and worse father. Why did you choose William Channing? Is that the real you? His wife and children left him—did you know that? What could have possessed you? You like hiding, don't you, Michael? Pretending—maybe that is the real you. Maybe that's why I can't do this face-to-face. You do that business with your left hand, hiding it in your pocket, standing in profile to everybody to keep it out of sight. It drives me fucking nuts."

Again the scenes behind the voice shifted. Sangamore now, and the drive of black locust trees leading to the farmhouse and red barn behind, and then the lines of marble sculptures in the studio. Shots of the faces, the mill workers, the more than two dozen figures that had never found their niche in the grand plans for renovating and beautifying the Palmer Mill.

"From then on, I shied away from Concord. Visiting my mother was the worst—you would have thought Angela never existed. Then there was Sangamore and that matronly curator who couldn't stop gushing about my grandfather and looking at me like she'd seen the Second Coming. But the paintings, as well as the diary and drawings, made it all worthwhile. And yes, Michael, those lovely sculptures—they took my breath away. I had always loved Sangamore as a kid and I knew how much it had meant to my father, the only place where he'd really had any kind of life with his own father. So I summoned the courage and gave my father one more try. And then what happens? An invitation to dinner at his place and—'Oh, by the way, there's somebody I'd like you to meet, a friend of mine who knew you from high school: William Channing, charming young man.'

"Christ, Michael, can you blame me for freaking out, for being a no-show and taking the next flight back? My father alone would have been tough enough, but to have this creepy guy as part of the mix—no way.

"At least I had the diary and the letters—my heritage—to give me courage, and with that a new faith that my wildness, and, yes, my deceit, had a history ... in the cause of creation. There's some comfort there, don't you think? Sandra Chillingworth had inspired me as a girl—her fantastic power to inspire others—but the diary and letters offered not just the solace of continuity but a renewed conviction that my path had brought me full circle: as creator and model. They endure in *me*, Michael—lies and all; they are *mine*, not yours."

She shook her head, took a swig of water, sighed deeply, and went on.

"But of Sandra, her guilt or innocence, and my role as judge and executioner, I had found nothing; she remained a cipher—until you came along and found me in Santa Maria Assunta. You were the missing link—thank

God, not William Channing—the lover I had missed, my sister's beloved. Funny word, that—so Victorian; but you're a literary antediluvian, right? When I saw your eyes, when I heard your voice break, when I read her letter, I realized you were the key. Through you, I could get to places in her I could never get to on my own—her crime, her secret. All of that has been true. You have opened her soul and released me. For that alone, I can never thank you enough.

 "And don't you dare accuse me of manipulating you with the letter I left at Santa Maria Assunta. What you read was how she really was. It was my way of forgiving her and moving on. But all you did was come crawling back to me with her name on your lips like a goddamn litany. Did you ever have one nice thing to say about Angela?

"So now you have all your evidence—or do you? Will you ever have enough—if you don't know yourself?"

She pulled herself to her full height, the waning light falling across her head and shoulders.

"The light's going, Michael; we're losing the light here."

He saw her make a despairing gesture and the screen once again fill with scenes of Concord, a kind of refrain of what had gone before.

As he stood back, wiping at his own tears, he felt an odd pulling in his gut—the happy memories the scenes invoked—then a sharp tightening in his chest as her voice began to filter through the familiar views.

"Concord, Michael … remember? This is the one part that still perplexes me, the part of you I can't quite picture. Did you go to Concord to escape Michael Collins or to find Sandra … and found you'd lost both? I wanted you to see these videos I did of my hometown, because I want you to understand that I know it well, and I really *was* there looking for you … and I never found you, which is perhaps just as well. Do you know why, Michael? Because you were *never* there. Oh, something of you perhaps, but I don't want to think about him anymore—let's flush this William Channing. If he existed, he was more like a specter suffering under the illusion that Sandra was alive; perhaps he had some kind of ambitious dream, or perhaps he was a little mad—but it was false. She was dead, and Michael, *you* were never *really* there … because your reason for being there never existed. Because there's never any escaping who we are, nor bringing the dead back to life. And creepy William Channing was the biggest sham of all."

The scenes of Concord fell away to the shadow-streaked brick enclosure and a lone figure. Angela Palmer was gesturing, trying to grapple with her thoughts, as if they were things of the air surrounding her.

"Believe me, I *was* there and it was my home and my family. Is this the truth you can handle, or do you need a different spin? You can be so fucking protean, Michael. You blame your father for so much, yet there is more of him in you than you dare imagine. There's a rich streak of Irish romantic fatalism in you, a raw anger at life's bum deals. And don't forget, it was my great-aunt Angela whom your grandfather Giovanni loved—and she him. Isn't that where this all began—her Venetian lover—at least in your head?

"But I love that in you, but Sandra would have scoffed at it. I've always been a romantic fatalist and I've made millions—if money is to be the scorecard for our success as human beings in the E-commerce future. Throw yourself to the wolves, Michael, feel the bite—it stirs the soul strings. It's not just what's in our genes but what we do with them. I'm proud of Sandy Blue—when I am moldering in my grave, she will continue to get women in touch with their bodies, and young men to masturbate and fantasize and keep her forever young and beautiful. You can't beat that, Michael? Think about it."

She took a couple steps toward the camera, her face going into deeper shadow.

"Don't let the technology fool you, Michael. This is the real me." She pulled up her dress to show her bulging stomach, the distended belly button. "We are surrounded by death and dreams, but this is real" —she patted her bulge— "the only you and me that will ever matter." She dropped the dress. "Funny, the feeling creeping over me all this time: I've felt like you've been right here at my shoulder, with me for the whole ride. But now it's as if you're slipping away, your protective camouflage changing, Michael—William, Bill—Giovanni? Who did you say you were? Well, the light's going, so it's time to wrap it up."

She looked at her watch and the camera panned to deep focus, moving in on the marble figure, the other graves, the cedars and the wall surrounding her, crowding her on all sides, as if she had undergone some diminishment.

"But there is one last stop for us, Michael. Just in case you think you have a corner on the truth, that you're the only expert. Come with me and see how close, how far."

Angela waved the camera eye to follow her, weaving past the jumbled graves, out the door of the enclosure, a sharp right turn, and a matter of only a dozen steps farther, another right turn into the neighboring enclosure. The camera paused a moment to record the marble sign for the Christian Orthodox cemetery.

"There." She pointed and the camera lingered on a tiny stone marker with a small intaglio plaque and profiled head, held with steel clamps against the brick wall.

"Dimitri Miaskovsky, composer, pianist, and teacher. He may be my grandfather. And he did make it back to Saint Petersburg, where he fell in with the Bolsheviks and became a bit player in the Revolution. For thirty years, he composed music for the Communist Party, marches and overtures and dedications. One of his marches was played endlessly on the radio during World War Two. Most of his stuff is awful, forgettable. Many of his contemporaries in the union of musicians and composers were executed by Stalin. He escaped by the skin of his teeth in the late forties and returned to Venice, where he'd been an exile once before, from the czar's police. He died here in obscurity. He asked only that his ashes be scattered here, and a plaque of remembrance be erected. Recently, some of his early piano pieces have come to light, his Venetian elegies: jazzy, dark, atonal—haunting and lovely. Worthy enough to be recorded by some serious pianists. You listened to his work many evenings with me, Michael. It wasn't all Scriabin. Didn't you feel it? The lovelorn yearning in his music will make you weep when you think about Sandra Chillingworth Palmer. Music inspired by love ... or deceit? Or does ambition always carry a measure of deceit? Or does love care?

"You tell me, Michael."

The figure of a woman, now in such deep shadow as to be almost invisible, seemed to be shaking her head as if perplexed.

"As you see this, I will be on a flight back to San Francisco. I did not deceive you, or, if I did, I think you will admit, it was a shared deceit. I have found a way home. My child will help me steer clear of the dead hand of the past. Come visit the lovely figure your grandfather carved,

Michael, on the far side of this wall. The image endures, but she is gone and Sandra is gone. Death is everywhere. Doesn't it make you sad, Michael, as if all that will remain of any of us are a few inked markings on a page? But you know this—your Thoreau was all about loss."

She walked forward to a patch of last sunlight, hints of soft peach and mauve emphasizing her most striking features.

"So where do we make a stand? I love you. But Sandra is dead except for those who loved her. I am a fighter. I need brash, tough, creative people. To be in the thick of it. I love sex and I loved the sex we had. I love the child I carry—your son—joy incarnate. But I want him to be free of the past. And I can't take any more of our little Walden life. My sojourn is over. I don't want a life pining away over the past. I want to live big-time, while there is time. I will be going public with SandyBlue.com on the stock exchange next year, an IPO, and I guarantee you it will be the biggest and best company of its kind. New products and services for women—their turn, finally. Then I'm cashing out and I'm going to do a whole chain of restaurants emphasizing wonderful healthy food at reasonable prices, Italian with a hint of Mexican, and a line of cookbooks.

"So go back and clear your name. Go in the face of those who have wronged you and get justice. And Michael—come on, you must have known about the bribes, if not the details. So what. Be proud of your work. Don't forget, people who build something worth building, like the artist who creates something worth creating, are always stepping on toes and cutting corners. How do you think Venice got built? Hey, we'll cut a deal with Mahoney: do the Palmer Mill our way, with your grandfather's sculptures. Be strong and your son will be proud of you. And Michael, William Channing was a cheat and a manipulator, the very sort of charges brought against Michael Collins. Go figure."

She bowed her head and surveyed the graves and then, with a shrug, looked toward the camera as if for help.

"Sandra would have loved William Channing, but he was a loser, a second rater playing second fiddle to better minds like Thoreau. You aspire to be an artist; well, I guess you did it. You resurrected the dead; you re-created Sandra—with my help. Now leave her be. And if what I know about my genetically minded father is true, he would understand—my baby, your baby, is as good as Sandra's baby. Sandra will live in our child.

Isn't that enough? Our child is the true miracle.

"Are you still with me, Michael? In this lovely place, this walled garden on an island in the lagoon—or with me in that 'City by the Bay'? Come back to me. First, go to Switzerland and see the people who raised your son. Talk to them and share their grief. See the world if you must. Row your heart out. I have opened my heart for you to see... ."

She began to walk out of the frame, then paused and turned as if for a last volley.

"Know what, Michael? You need me—I'm the only one who knows who you really are. And I love you, okay?"

She looked away, as if almost embarrassed.

"Oh, and listen, among the papers I sent with the video is a deed to the house on Torcello. I bought it from Antonio. I mean, shit, we did so much work in the garden, I couldn't stand giving the place back to him. It's in my name and you can stay as long as you want. There are a few more letters from Angela Chillingworth's estate that I didn't show you. And so that's it. And you're welcome to use Giorgio's old flat in Venice. I left the keys in an envelope with your name on it with the guy in the video store around the corner. Just be careful—the art thieves in Italy are merciless. Ciao, Michael. You know where you can reach me by E-mail. Ciao. Okay, okay ... I know: what a smooth operator."

She walked out of the frame, an empty hiss of blank tape all that remained.

He got up slowly and pushed the STOP and REWIND buttons. He then went to the documents and began to go through them.

Eventually, he sat back and tentatively smiled to himself, a departed spirit suddenly finding himself in limbo, unhappy to find himself there, but aware that the alternative might be far worse. He began laughing and laughing, until he was tired of laughing.

Getting up, he pushed the EJECT button on the VCR, removed the tape, unplugged the television, and lifted it onto his shoulder. Marching out with it, he walked down the path to the old canal and heaved the thing into the water. It sank out of sight immediately. Twenty paces farther on was his moored *sandolo*. He got his oar from where it hung on a pair of nails on a tree trunk, untied the painter, and then stepped in and began rowing himself toward the lagoon. Once out of the canal, he leaned hard into his oar and in seconds was headed into the vast blue beyond the Lido.

Of course, he told himself, he'd known the truth from the moment he'd set foot on Torcello all those months before, in the chilly December sunshine. He'd played along, if only to give Sandra a chance to explain herself and find their forgiveness, to allow her to live again for a time, to love and find respite, and break the silence of the years. The seven months on the island was Sandra's gift, the very life that had been in safekeeping for them over all the lost years. And that would remain, as the island would remain, as much his story as hers, perhaps a story to be passed on to his children and grandchildren. More a mythic sojourn than reality. She would always be with them: in the dappled light of fall leafage, in a smudge of ink or pigment, in words on a page, the flicker of a video image (performance art, as he would one day come to think of it) ... flowing into the stream of living memory. As are all those who return in others to reinvest the names and places of this earth with their love ... who suffered the attraction.

CHAPTER 42

Calais, October 22, 1916

Dearest Angela,

I have had enough; I am coming home. If I never see France or Europe again, it will suit me just fine. At least I have done my duty with the ambulance corps. I see no end to this terrible war and no good coming from it. Victor and vanquished will be equally maimed. The unspeakable horrors of the dressing stations and hospitals will never leave my memory. The bucolic landscapes of Picardy I knew as a young art student have been turned into muddy cesspools of shredded flesh. I was hoping the experience might cauterize memory, but instead it has sharpened it. I have seen the worst man can do. I know what my poor father knew and I can forgive him and love him and honor his sacrifice, in a cause surely with more nobility of purpose than this wretched waste. I wonder if there is a fit subject left to my hand. I have made studies and sketches, but I am tempted to burn them. I long for home and gentle Concord and yet fear what I may find there. I long to see you and the child. I am glad he is well. I think often on how I may find a way to keep his mother's memory alive and the urgent passion that was her legacy to us. Do put in a good word for me to your grieving parents. Your loving brother-in-law, Joseph

Sangamore, Stockbridge November, 17, 1929

Dear Angela:

My apologies for stampeding you and young Joe off the farm last August. The housekeeper was aghast. And I really can't have you and Giovanni going on like that under my son's nose. What could you have been thinking, and leaving the door to the studio unlocked? What possessed you? Don't you think I had enough to endure of such damn nonsense with your sister and foreigners? Can't you see how Giovanni has pined away for you all these years? It's really unfair of you to keep your little charade going. The man must learn to make his own life; he's still young and so talented.

You have left me no choice but to let Giovanni go. Besides, given my present economic state, there's no money for anything, much less the renovations to the mill, which will never happen—not now, not if your mother has her way. I gave Giovanni a thousand dollars, which stretched me considerably at this moment with all my legal bills. I have not been able to sell a major painting in over a year—the art market has gone to hell with the stock market. I fear I have gone out of fashion. I will miss Giovanni. Joe Junior will miss him, but hopefully Giovanni will find his way to a proper life. But I have to tell you, that before he left, he smashed the marble figure he was working on and stole a book from the library. So much for loyalty. After all our years together, I'd never have thought it.

I'm delighted young Joe has started at Emerson. Maybe now I'll have a chance to see more of him. Give him my love, Joseph

Lowell, June 21, 1931

Dear Miss Angela,

Since I leave Mr. Palmer, I travel very much in America. There is no work. I go to Chicago for some time, where there live many Italians. I go to San Francisco and work there for many months, but not the work of my hands. I find I love America more and more. A man can become lost in a big place, but also he can build a good life. But I think so many things move fast here, people do not have time for the simple things, for the things made with the hands. There is much land in California but not so many things made by the hands of the artist.

For some time, I think maybe I will return to Venice. But there is no work in that place. My brother died in the war and my father last year also. My mother lives with her sister, but I think she is a very sad lady. She is old. My aunt writes to me not to come back to Venice. She say there is no work.

Those times with you and Mr. Palmer and your sister in Venice were the best for me. I had much happiness in those times. I remember the smiles and the laughter of your sister. So many jokes she made. Do you remember when she learns to speak the Italian? She make the signs with her hands more than the Italians and we laugh until there come to our eyes many tears. I never had so much a heavy heart when she died. Never did I work so hard to make something beautiful for her. Do you remember how you helped me so much—yes. I see your face and I make it the face of your sister. She has your hands, too. I think my best work come from the memory of those days, of the face like an angel of Mrs. Sandra. I miss the time to make the work with you and to play with the boy, young Joe, at Sangamore. He is a good boy. I believe he has the heart of his mother. It is in his eyes. He grows, I am sure, to honor his mother.

Maybe you can speak to Mr. Palmer for me and let him know that I have come to live in this city where is his factory. It is not so far from Concord, where I made the monument for Mrs. Sandra. I see the Palmer Mill every day and I remember all the good work I made with the marbles. I write to Mr. Palmer at Sangamore and there come no answer. Has he moved? Tell him I am ready to work. Tell him I have a book to give back to him.

There are no jobs here. The mills are closing and men are out of work. But I am lucky. There are many Italians and others who need the monuments in the graveyard. This is not work for a rich man, but there is always work. This Lowell city is a strange place. So many different people. Italians I can understand but not so good the Greek, the Polish, the Jewish, and the French from Canada. There are so many languages. Sometimes there is fighting. But all people must work and all must die and in the end it is the same for everybody. It is a good place for my work, so that the families can remember who give them life. The people come and walk on Sundays and look at my stones. The children play among the stones. It is peaceful here in my shop near the river. I think of you many times. I hope you are well. I am here if it is possible for you to find me. Your loving friend, Giovanni

SISTERS BY THE SEA

Oh Sister, sister by the sea,
Sing to me of white-capped days of blue,
Of time's gold-hazed departures and returns—as in all things.
Turning, turning, turning away ...
A schooner's bell atolling ... .
Fallen runners aslant the green-swarded shore,
Where sandy dunes whisper and fade away.

As do blooded skies a pinched brow soothe,
Staccato clouds, Scriabin-like beneath your leaping hands,
Stilled now behind garden walls ... rotted brick embraced by tidal choirs.
Passing, passing, sisters by the sea,
Strolling by delicate palaces ... ungainly rowers on eternity.
Sforzando—girls! ... so tipsy towers at lovers' partings,
Toll changes over the changeless sea.

Angela Chillingworth
Meditations on Metamorphosis
Beacon Hill Press, 1937

Concord, April 8, 2001

Dear Michael,

I was glad to hear from you and that the plea bargain is shaping up well. I wish I could take up your offer on Venice, but it's been kind of a rough winter. My back has gone out and I've had to get in extra help. My ex-wife, Abigail, died last month in the nursing home, a heart attack, very quick. The funeral took a lot out of me because it brought back so much. It was a sad affair. Only one of her old friends made it, Marge Hathaway, our neighbor for many years. Her son died in Vietnam. Her husband, George, a surgeon, nicest guy I ever knew. When we were young men after the war, he'd come to me every spring and ask if I thought anything needed doing about the apple orchard. I knew next to nothing in those days. But because he kept mentioning it—as if the orchard still belonged to us—I started paying attention, reading up on the subject. Funny how things come to be.

Something I've been meaning to write you about. Going through Abigail's things, I came across a bunch of her old letters, things she must have been meaning to send to the girls but, for whatever reason, failed to mail them. In her roundabout way, she kept encouraging them not to blame themselves for what happened to the baby, between the lines, trying to shift the burden of guilt to herself. I keep going over it in my mind, that terrible night of which I once spoke to you; and the more I go over it in light of those unsent letters, the more convinced I am that when she dashed out of the car that night upon our return from Boston, she may well have gone to her room, downed her medications, drunk herself into a stupor and—who knows—gone into the nursery and done a terrible thing. She was certainly manic enough. The rest of her life was a tailspin of guilt and alcoholism, medication and collapse. I sent copies of the letters to Angela, but I haven't heard from her yet.

Do you know how she's doing?

On the Palmer Farm Trust: I've had the lawyers draw up the papers and all we have to do is put in the names. I've already had groups of schoolchildren visit for the day and do a little work around the farm, learn how it all operates, with talks about how their forebears worked and lived on the land. Good stuff. Like you, I've gotten to like teaching. Do let me know your decision as soon as you can. You're a perfect match for the director's job. And, of course, I'm sure you could find a way to fit Thoreau into your teaching programs.

By the way, it's stipulated in the trust my father set up for Sangamore and his estate that when his great-grandson—a male heir, no less—reached the age of twenty-one, he would be legally entitled to inherit Sangamore and run the foundation—with the board of directors' guidance. I contested this part of the trust in the late sixties, failed and saddled myself with ruinous legal costs. Do you suppose Angela knows?

You wrote asking about the pathologist's report on Sandra's suicide. I managed to dig it out of my files the other day. I guess I was so distraught that I'd stuck it away unread when it first arrived. It wasn't pretty: she was HIV positive. A death sentence I suppose. Her blood work also showed traces of artemisinin, an antimalarial drug. Hard to figure where she'd picked up malaria since it had been eradicated in Italy decades ago. The report did note she'd had a hysterectomy at some point—poor dear. Not what I would have expected—no, not at all.

Take care of yourself, my boy, and good luck. Fondest regards, Joe Palmer

Subj: Angela Palmer Whereabouts
Date: April 15, 2001
From: pratner@youcanthide.com
To: Gmaronetti@libero.it

Bill, we can't restart our investigation without upfront payment. Besides, your subject, your old flame—whatever, has resurfaced big as life, and with a new baby son in arms. Angela Palmer, aka Sandy Blue just sold her Malibu house last month and is planning to take SandyBlue.com public. It's been all over the financial press—you must be more than a little out of touch not to have seen it. She's been interviewed by Bloomberg and the WSJ. All kinds of plans to expand her business and start a chain of Italian health food restaurants.

FYI: A few tidbits from the original investigation have trickled in. Angela Palmer's treatment records at the hospital in Mérida, Mexico and the Presbyterian Hospital in Albuquerque, where she was an outpatient for years, have disappeared.

What's with your email address?—no, don't tell me.

Subj: Angela Palmer Outstanding Student Tuition
Date: April 21, 2001
From: internationaldesk@unibo.it
To: Gmaronetti@libero.it

Dear Mr. Maronetti: I checked with the registrar of international students and there is no record of an American student, Angela Palmer, being enrolled in the archaeology program of the University of Bologna in the years 1998 to

1999. So there are, of course, no outstanding debts. Perhaps your cousin was enrolled at another Italian university.

Subj: Angela Palmer lost camcorder
Date: April 29, 2001
From: concierge@treadwayinn.com
To: Gmaronetti@libero.it

Checked with registration and lost-and-found, no record of Angela Palmer being a guest in Oct. 1999 and no lost camcorders. Week of Oct. 12, 1999 we were booked up with a Harvard Medical School dermatologists convention—just a lot of lifted faces.

Subj: Sandra Palmer Suicide
Date: May 3, 2001
From: murray.sean@cambridgepd.gov
To: Gmaronetti@libero.it

Mr. Channing:

Sorry to hear you're still chewing over your old flame's suicide. I guess even a sabbatical in Italy can't get you far enough away. Me and missus went to Rome on our honeymoon. I think I gained 20 lbs. To answer your question about the knife wound and whether it could have been inflicted by another party: anything is possible, but as I must have mentioned when we met, there were no signs of a violent struggle, the wound was surgically clean, and the dead woman's prints were all over the knife.

Move on Bill. Bad things happen to good people.

Detective Lieutenant, Sean Murray

May 22, 2001

Dear Ruthie:

Just a note to let you know that I may return to the vicinity of Concord, probably sometime in the fall, although I don't have any firm dates. I've been teaching school for the last year and wouldn't mind continuing teaching back in the
States. Could you keep an eye out for me for any English teaching jobs in the
local schools? Public or private, doesn't matter. Thanks very much. I look forward to seeing you again.

    Best,
    Michael Collins

May 23, 2001

Dear Michelle:

I met you at my brother, Jimmy's funeral almost two years ago. Forgive me
for breaking a confidence, but Father Murphy did let it out that Jimmy was
your daughter's father. As you probably know, Jimmy and I were never close
and that was almost entirely my fault. I wish it had been otherwise. I may be
returning to the States in a few months and might be settling not far from
Lowell. I was hoping I might see you and your daughter at that time. Perhaps
there is something I can do for your daughter. I would like to do something. If
you would like me to get to know her as an uncle or friend of the family, that
would be fine. If not, I would be happy to help provide for her financial support and educational expenses as the years go by. Her grandmother was a
pianist of concert caliber. I would be delighted to pay for her to study piano. I
look forward to hearing from you.

    My best wishes,
    Michael Collins

Subj: A deal!
Date: July 23, 2001
From: cookingwithfire@cookingwithfire.com
To: Gmaronetti@libero.it

Lawyers have cut a deal with federal prosecutor—expensive but doable. Pick your date and point of entry (that's me!) and all will be arranged. Love and mozzarella. Did you read about the IPO? It's front-page news in the Financial Times.

CHAPTER 43

He stared out the window of the Alitalia 747 headed for Boston's Logan Airport, following the coastline as it unfolded all the way south from Newfoundland to the vast bent elbow of Cape Cod embracing the blue. And then the dent in the coast that he knew was the mouth of a river and the town of Newburyport. As the wing dipped in preparation for the landing approach, he was allowed a view of the river, a broad green ribbon, as the plane headed inland and then made a precipitous turn, revealing a distant conurbation of buildings, streets, and bridges. Squinting, he thought he could just make out another silver capillary meeting up at that junction point, near where a falls had given rise to a city. "*Merrimack*," he said to himself, and then, "*Concord*." The names of two rivers. The names brought to mind the boyhood face of his brother reflected in the river, and he said the names again, feeling the hairs on the back of his neck rise with the pleasure of homecoming. And in the name *Concord*, memories of another face, and the voice of a young woman.

Not change ... but changelessness ... being reborn—with a purpose.

He nodded to himself, and his lips pressed together in a quivering smile, and for a few minutes more he closed his teary eyes.

The inspector took his passport, looked at the name and photo, glanced at his face, and slid the inside cover through the bar-code reader.

"Welcome back to the States, Mr. Maronetti."

"It's good to be back," he said, and took his passport.

There were three men, a woman, and a small boy less than two years old waiting for him just beyond immigration control. He held out his passport to the one who was clearly an FBI agent, the buzz cut and boring suit giving him away. The agent took the passport, glanced at the photo, and handed it to the man beside him, who wore a U.S. marshal's badge. The marshal was massive with biceps that barely fitted the arms of his jacket.

"Mr. Collins, welcome to Boston; you are under arrest." The agent pulled out a laminated card from his suit pocket and began to read from it.

A third man, impeccably dressed in an expensive suit, his silver gray hair perfectly combed, immediately came forward and objected.

"Mr. Buell, spare us the Miranda drill. I'm his lawyer, and Mr. Collins is well aware of his rights. Let's finesse the formalities, please." The lawyer reached out and shook his new client's hand. "Mr. Collins, Gordon Davenport. Everything is arranged at the courthouse. With any luck, this should take only a few hours of your time."

The lawyer stepped aside so the woman with the boy could come forward. Her short blond hair, even under the fluorescent lighting, shimmered with honey highlights; she was stylishly dressed in an Armani suit of grayish blue pastel, a classy fluid cut that still managed to show off her splendid figure. She hesitated for only a moment to review his face, the graying of his dark hair at the temples, his healthy suntanned face and Roman nose. He kept his left hand in his pocket, but when she embraced him, he encircled her with both arms. Her hands were long and soft and the fingers beautifully manicured where they surrounded his neck. Then, almost in a single motion, she released him and picked up the little boy standing at her knee. The boy had long ginger-colored hair and blue eyes and seemed a little lost amid the to-ing and fro-ing in the arrival area.

"Joseph, this is Daddy."

The miniature blue-eyed face seemed a little dumbfounded and the boy looked at the other expectant faces as if not quite sure what was going on. She handed him to his father, who took him in his arms and held him so he could get a good look at the boy and the boy could get a good look at him.

"Hi there, Joseph, big guy. *Come stai?* And what a fine lad you are, too."

The boy smiled.

"Daddy," the boy said, peering around.

The FBI agent checked his watch. The U.S. marshal stared at the woman, barely able to take his eyes off her familiar face, perhaps a little annoyed that he couldn't quite place her. The lawyer felt in his inside pocket for the $1.5 million check to post bail. The woman shouldered a large leather purse containing diapers and six manila files on six locations for a new restaurant chain, then put her arm around the ex-fugitive as they began to move off.

"How's the Modigliani?" she asked.

"The leak wasn't so bad; it's all fixed," he said, shifting the boy to one arm and giving him a squeeze.

"Daddy," said the little boy suddenly, leaning back, his blue eyes sparked with light, as if it had all come clear in his mind.

The sounding of the name, or the child's tone of discovery seemed to stagger the woman for a moment. Michael felt her arm around his waist freeze up and then suddenly release. She reached for his free hand, his good callused right hand and lifted it to her face, her lips, her hurried kiss translated an instant later into an act that seared his heart. She bit deep into the knuckle of his ring finger as if to brand him forever.

ACKNOWLEDGMENTS

To my agent Susan Schulman, one of the keenest minds in publishing, whose wisdom and unflinching advice helped navigate *Love's Attraction* to a safe harbor. Sally Arteseros, a master editor of her generation, who did so much to make *Love's Attraction* a better novel. Carol Edwards, simply one of the best copy editors in the business, whose exacting eye caught the errors before they became errors: a stickler for prose of the highest order. Fiona Hallowell, my editor at Winsted Press, a consummate professional, whose advice and sure-handed guidance is reflected in every page of *Love's Attraction*. Cover designer Jason Boherer, a rising star among book designers, who actually read the novel and designed a sumptuous cover to reflect the story within. And Liz Driesbach, our fantastic page designer, who worked tirelessly to integrate the text with the artwork and so create a visual feast for the reader.

For my great grandfather, Captain Charles Manning USN (1844–1913), chief engineer at the Amoskeag Mills in Manchester, New Hampshire during the last decades of the nineteenth century, who inspired parts of the character of Captain Samuel Palmer. And his brother-in-law, General William Francis Bartlett (1840–1876), my great uncle, wounded four times in the Civil War, hero of many engagements and loyal son of Massachusetts, who inspired some of the words and deeds of General Joseph Palmer herein. And last but far from least, my wonderful mother, Mary Manning Cleveland, who kept these lives alive to me through all her ninety-two years, so that I, in turn, might let parts of them live again.

Artwork Credits
Photography by Becket Logan

End Papers: James McNeill Whistler, *The Riva No. 2*, 1880–81. Etching, 8½ x 12 in. Private Collection.

Chapter 1: Ernest David Roth, *Gondola and Doorway*, 1905. Etching, 9 x 4½ in. Private collection.

Chapter 23: Clifford Addams, *A Venetian Waterway*, c. 1920. Etching, 10 x 15¾ in. Private collection.

Chapter 27: James McNeill Whistler, *The Two Doorways*, 1880. Etching, 7⅞ x 11⅜ in. Private Collection.

Chapter 28: James McNeill Whistler, *The Riva No. 2*, 1880–81. Etching, 8½ x 12 in. Private collection.

Chapter 29: John Marin, *Bridge, Venezia*, 1907. Etching, 5 x 7 in. Private collection.

Chapter 30: Clifford Addams, *Ma Porte à Venise*, 1914. Etching, 8 x 5 in. Private collection.

Chapter 31: James McNeill Whistler, *The Little Mast*, 1879–80. Etching, 10½ x 7¼ in. Private Collection.

Chapter 32: Clifford Addams, *Venetian Fête Scene (San Giorgio: Nocturne, Venice)*, 1914. Etching, 6½ x 14 in. Private collection.

Chapter 33: Joseph Pennell, *The Rialto*, 1883. Etching, 10 x 12 in., Private collection.

Chapter 34: Frank Duveneck, *The Bridge of Sighs*, 1883. Etching, 11 x 8½ in. Private collection.

Chapter 35: Donald Shaw MacLaughlan, *Canal, Venice*, 1908. Etching, 10½ x 14¼ in. Private collection.

Chapter 36: Frank Duveneck, *San Pietro in Castello*, c. 1883. Etching, 11 x 15 in. Private collection.

Chapter 37: Frank Duveneck, *Riva Degli Schiavoni, No. 2*, 1880. Etching, 13 x 8½ in. Private collection.

Chapter 38: Ernest David Roth, *Campo Santa Margherita*, 1906. Etching, 8 x 10¾ in. Private collection.

Chapter 39: John Marin, *Palazzo Dario*, 1907. Etching, 7½ x 5½ in. Private collection.

Chapter 40: Otto Bacher, *Two Boats, Venice*, 1880. Etching, 3½ x 9 in. Private collection.

Chapter 41: Joseph Pennell, *On the Riva, From Pennell's Window*, 1883. Etching, 8 x 10 in. Private collection.

Chapter 42: Joseph Pennell, *Café Orientale*, 1911. Etching, 9 x 12¼ in. Private collection.

Chapter 43: Robert Swain Gifford, *Near the Coast*, 1887. Etching, 2½ x 4½ in. Private collection.

Also by David Adams Cleveland

With a Gemlike Flame (novel)

A History of American Tonalism: 1880–1920

*Intimate Landscapes: Charles Warren Eaton and the
Tonalist Movement in American Art, 1880–1920*

Ross Braught: A Visual Diary

JOSHUA NEFSKY

DAVID ADAMS CLEVELAND is a novelist and
art historian. His first novel, *With a Gemlike Flame*,
drew wide praise for its evocation of Venice and the
hunt for a lost masterpiece by Raphael. His most recent
art history book, *A History of American Tonalism*,
won the Silver Medal in Art History in the Book of
the Year Awards, 2010; and Outstanding Academic
Title 2011 from the American Library Association;
it was the best-selling American art history book in
2011 and 2012. He and his wife live in New York
where he works as an art advisor with his son, Carter
Cleveland, founder of Artsy.net, the new internet site
making all the world's art accessible to anyone with
an internet connection.